afraid to walk the road of thorny brush. . . . The major thing is that Thomas Sanchez has dared to put the dream to paper."
—San Francisco Chronicle

"The most disturbing thing about this novel is that you must constantly remind yourself that it is fiction, but fiction so real that you know that it all really happened. Thomas Sanchez has written with rare sensitivity and empathy . . . rare craftsmanship for which so many authors strive and never achieve. Rabbit Boss will bother the conscience of many readers."
—Columbus Dispatch

"If Rabbit Boss were concerned principally with exploitation of the American Indian it would stand with other recent books on the subject. Its missions and message go beyond the grievances of the past to embrace the ethos of a people in the timeless, raceless search of men to transcend themselves."
—Indianapolis Star

Rabbit Boss is a magnificent literary achievement, a towering five year labor of love by a profound young California author. In this book we are present at the death of a people and a dream. This could very well be the definitive novel of the American Indian nightmare. Rabbit Boss is a masterpiece of extraordinary strength and poetry and beauty."
—The El Paso Sandpaper

"While the white man has done an energetic job of opening up the tragic history, he rarely has been able to write from inside the Indian psyche. One of the remarkable things about Sanchez' book is that his disappearing little Washo tribe is as there as a next door neighbor, being and expressing instead of being observed."
—Phoenix Gazette

"Marvelously styled, image-rich, poetic and powerful prose. His words reach inside and touch hidden emotional places. This is possibly the finest tribute to the Indian dream and its death yet written. This is the kind of book about what has happened to the Indians that is long overdue."
—Sacramento Bee

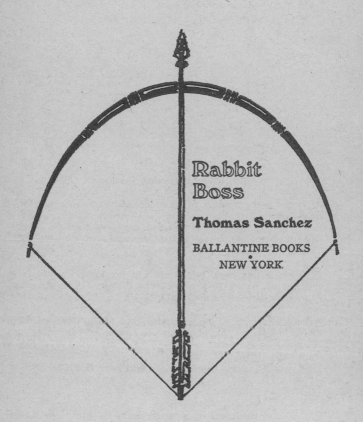

Rabbit Boss

Thomas Sanchez

BALLANTINE BOOKS
·
NEW YORK

Portions of this book have appeared previously in *Works in Progress, Oui* magazine, and *Cutting Edges: Young American Fiction for the '70s,* edited by Jack Hicks.

Acknowledgement is made to Maryland Music Corporation, a division of Muzak, for permission to reprint lines from the song "Butterfly."

Library of Congress Catalog Card Number: 72-11028

ISBN 0-345-23847-8-195

This edition published by arrangement with Alfred A. Knopf, Inc.

Manufactured in the United States of America

First Ballantine Books Edition: March 1974
Fourth Printing: August 1976

Cover art by Carl Swanson

This One
in the beginning is for the lady
Stephanie Dante,
Mother of Dante Paloma,
who laid five years from the heart
of her youth in the ground
so the words of this novel
could rise up
and sing.

The Washo is a small tribe of about 500 Indians, living in the extreme Western part of Nevada, and Eastern California. They are usually a harmless people, with much less physical and mental development than the Paiutes, and more degraded morally. They are indolent, improvident, and much addicted to the vices and evil practices common in savage life. They manifest an almost uncontrollable appetite for intoxicating drinks. They are sensual and filthy, and are annually diminishing in numbers from the diseases contracted through their indulgences. A few have learned the English language and will do light work for a reasonable compensation. They spend the winter months about the villages and habitations of white men, from whom they obtain tolerable supplies of food and clothing. The spring, summer, and autumn months are spent in fishing about Washo and Tahoe lakes and the streams which flow through their country. They also gather grass seed and pine nuts, hunt rabbits, hares, and ducks. There is no suitable place for a reservation in the bounds of their territory, and, in view of their rapidly diminishing numbers and the diseases to which they are subjected, none is required.

28th ANNUAL REPORT OF THE COMMISSIONER
OF INDIAN AFFAIRS TO
THE SECRETARY OF THE INTERIOR
(SUPERINTENDENT PARKER, 1866)

Book
One

Tikoi

(My Father)

THE WASHO watched. The Washo watched through the trees. The Washo watched through the trees as *they* ate themselves. His chin lifted, head cocked rigid to one side as he watched through the leaves, the branches, the bark. The waiting winter light fell flat on the trees, on him, on *them*. The light hung in the branches, caught, glistening in the dead weight of snow that bent them down. The Washo watched between these trees pierced through the snow like spears being driven back, back into the snow that was as high as two men, one standing on the other, back into the frozen Earth. In this silence he heard a sound, a sound which did not come from *them*, a sound that was familiar to him, a sound that rushed over him watching down the slight slope of the mountain, a sound that crashed the silence of the trees, the silence of *them* on the higher snow packed in the lowness of the valley along the shore of the lake, a sound that was indifferent to what he was watching, a sound indifferent to all except the pure energy of its own existence, the sound of Geese. He looked up from *them* who were on the lake to the power in the Sky, the power of *Musege*, his brothers in nature who had secret medicine, strong medicine that many times was superior to his own, medicine which he had tried to capture, imitate, kill. He watched the *Power*, he watched it move in the Sky, the strength of the slick feathered wings digging

into the coldness of the air in a seemingly effortless attempt of moving the Birds across the tops of trees, over
the scene below. He watched the Birds as they moved off,
long out of imaginary bow range. They seemed to be
drifting slowly as if in a dream, but this was no dream, although it seemed like one for the air was sharp like the
stoneknife at his side, it was a cold which he could not remember for any other winters, although he had heard his
grandfather speak of one winter so cold that the frozen
trees splintered like two boulders smashed into each other.
Yet it was not only this cold; something seemed to suck
him down, make it difficult to breathe, to move, the only
thing easy was to watch, to wait. It was much like the
feeling he had once before as a younger man, as if that
feeling was a preparation for this. The feeling came upon
him one night as he lay asleep under his new Rabbit blanket with his two daughters and their mother that his
Power had gone to another place; even the strength running deep in his bones fled. He awoke, tried to lift the
softness of the blanket from his body, but could not,
could not even raise his hands. He spoke loudly so that his
two daughters and their mother would awake. Help me
lift this blanket from us. All four tried to push together, it
was of no use, they all lay back in their weakness, felt the
heavy burden closing on their skin, weighting them down.
In the morning when they awoke he asked if they remembered what had passed during the night. They did, but
none could agree if it was true in the way of having taken
place or true in the way of the dream. They did never
again sleep in that *gadu*, even one more night. One thing
he did know to be true as he watched down through the
trees to the high snow by the lake shore, this was no
dream. The body sprawled on the snow, split open, one of
them standing over it with a hatchet hanging limp in his
hand, the thickness of blood dripping slowly from the
blade to the snow, each drop silently splashing red into
the coldness, lightening into pink as it sought to touch all
flakes with its warmth, its color. A boot smashed into the
pinkish splotch of soiled snow, one of *them* bent over the
body. Above the gash from the hatchet he plunged a thick

knife, cut in along the heart, slashed the skin away over the ribs, leaving them exposed for an instant before he brought the butt of the knife down, breaking through. He yanked the broken bones away, once more cut in around the heart, this time freeing it, grabbing hold, the beat lingering in its firm flesh, pulsing weakly in his fist. He tugged it from its place, leaving a sucking hole, looked up around him, no one moved, their eyes tight on the meat clutched in the man's hand, sweat and saliva dripped onto the hair growing out from the bottom of his face, crystallizing into sharp chinks of ice. His head jerked looking from one to the other. Slowly he lifted the heart to his lips, the red slipping between his white cold fingers, moving down his wrists, splashed on the cracked leather boots. He opened his mouth, the smoke of his breath spurting in the air, the teeth clamped down on the warm meat. The one with the hatchet raised it high above his head, brought it down on the sprawled, heartless body, the blade sliced cleanly through the neck as if it were a slender log, sinking deep in the snow. He picked up the head, his fingers locked in the hair of the dripping globe, and tossed it away. Released, it spun toward the lake. The others watched it float in the quiet cold of morning air, then drop, landing softly on the open whiteness; it did not roll, the eyes turned down in the coldness, buried away from *them*. The people fell, as if the head had severed the strings that held their bodies rigid, the claws of their hands tearing the clothes from the body beneath them, ripping into flesh. A sound exploded, seeming to shake the snow from the trees, crashing up the roll of slope where the Washo stood, stripping everything of meaning in its path, driving into him like the jagged flint of an arrowtip. He did not move, did not move as he watched, as he heard the last whimper from the jagged, shouted cry of pain from the one of *them* who was falling on the torn body. It was as if *he* were falling, falling from a cloud, his body felt hollow as it plunged, the rising Earth beating up, straight, into his face, into the face of the woman as she fell on the wet, ravaged body, her arms spread out stiff as the hands beat into the snow, digging, trying to hang onto the very coldness itself. One of *them* moved toward her, his entire body straining against its own weight as he forced the three long steps to come up to her, the big jacket splitting open down the middle as he reached to pull a knife tucked under his belt, its blade sparkling between the clear winter light and the whiteness of the snow, caught, glinting blindingly like the splashing rays of Sun in the water of the lake. With one hand he yanked the woman up by the hair, pulling her bloodstreaked face off the exposed body. He put the knife to her throat; the arm stiffened as if to slit open the neck of a wounded Deer. The man with the hatchet moved, one leg came up, the boot hooking with a crack under the jaw of the one with the knife, throwing him backwards into the snow, almost pitching the long knife from his hand. He raised his arm and brought the hatchet down with a rush of air. The other one rolled over, the hatchet slicing next to him, burying itself in the snow up to the handle, he jabbed with the knife a single hard stroke. The blade disappeared into the chest. The man dropped, his hand still locked around the wooden handle of the hatchet as the dead weight of his body hit the snow. The one with the knife stood up, hot breath flaring from his wide nostrils. He did notice a young boy move past him to the body, lift an ax his own height and chop fiercely at the leg.

The Washo watched *them* moving slowly on the snow, clumsy, like Bears in water. He had been watching silently all morning, had seen, had seen them hunched, away from each other, mouths tearing at knots of flesh, faces smeared the color of a dying Sun. He had seen through the trees. He felt a hand on his shoulder, he turned and saw his brother. For a moment he felt ashamed, ashamed that he did not hear him approach, but then, he had been watching. He looked into his face, they did not speak, he too had seen, he too knew. They left, slowly, through the snow, they made their way up the slope of the mountain to the ridge and walked in silence away from the Sun.

On the top of the ridge it was easier to walk. He felt as his Deerhide wrapped feet pulled lightly out of the deep snow with each step that this winter must surely end; and

when the waters ran once more it would wash away all of
what he had seen, and when the Earth around the lake
had again turned up black, free of its white burden, *they*
would be gone. These things he thought as he walked
ahead of his brother, away from the Sun, towards his people, towards his home on the Big Lake in the Sky, Tahoe.
As they turned off the ridge and headed down into the
first valley, soft bits of snow began to fall. The Indians
pulled their Rabbit blankets closer about them and walked
on. They had moved steadily from where they had come,
never looking back. When the snow cleared the Sun had
left the Sky; they followed the Stars, they knew from the
night they could continue until the next afternoon. Then
they would be home.

She sat naked from the waist up on the thick mat of
branches. Her bent legs settled softly into the skins. She
watched out the opening of the strong *galisdangal* her husband had built from cut limbs of trees, stacked close and
tall, lashed with strips of Beaverhide to form a circle of
protection against the mountain winds. Her brown eyes
sunk deep in her blunt round face appeared aware of
nothing, but she was watching. She was watching out
across the small bay of the Big Lake, and behind it at the
white wall of mountain. She had been watching this direction many days now. First she watched for her husband,
and when finally he did not come his brother was sent.
Now she watched for both. It was silent this day, as had
been all the days of this winter; even the trees bent in silence under the winds. The only sound she could hear was
the sucking of her baby. She held the weight of its body to
her breast with one crooked arm, and watched. She gazed
at the mountain waiting for only one thing, its white wall
a backdrop for movements in her mind. Sitting, waiting
for the small black shape of her husband on the white
wall, she thought of him and how when the baby had finally come out and the old lady, her mother's cousin, had cut
the cord from her body with a sharp wooden knife, his
thin, hardset face cracked into smile, he placed an arrow

in his bow, and shot it at the dull winter Sun. It sailed
high, then fell, sticking up straight in the snow at his
younger brother's feet. He looked at the arrow, turned
and walked to the Lake Tahoe. Out a short distance on
the ice the men followed him, each with a half hidden
grin on his face, for he had to take the ritual bath after
birth in icecold water. He brought out his knife, jabbed a
circle in the white hard crust, finally breaking an opening
large enough for his body. He turned towards the men, but
his eyes did not meet theirs; he was looking over their
heads, back at the *galisdangal.* He knew that his young
wife was watching as he loosened the rawhide string of his
leather breechcloth and let it fall, then jumped into the
hole, the water splashing up above his waist. The men's
laughter came like a cloudburst; laughing so hard they
forgot themselves, toppled to the snow and rolled around
in howling fits. His teeth began to chatter and he clenched
them as he sank to his knees, his head going under water,
his whole body submerged in freezing slush. As he
climbed out from the hole the men found the strength to
stand up and brush the snow from their almost naked
bodies. He used the Deerskin breechcloth to wipe himself,
then looped it back around his waist. He gently stooped,
placed his knife at the rim of the hole, its thin stone blade
facing inward in testimony as the traditional gift of birth
for one of the men to take, then walked off. Some days
later the piece of cord from the baby's belly fell to the
ground. She told her husband he must go and hunt meat,
for until now he had been forbidden to eat it. When he returned there would be the happiness of the babyfeast, and
all but she would fill themselves on his killings. She must
fast longer, to bring the power of endurance upon the
child. Before he left she touched her hand to his face and
spoke of how she was sorry in her heart that the baby was
in the winter and it was expected of him to hunt in the
snow, how she had wished it had come like most others,
when the pinenuts were being gathered. It was bad for
him as husband to have to fast from meat and salt and
not be allowed to sleep at night until the cord fell. She
could bear it, she was a woman, but it was bad for a man

to do without strength during the white days. She must have done something to bring the baby in the winter, she must have called down some evil upon herself. The waterfall, she thought, that must have been the evil power. But she did not tell him, she only touched his face and spoke of her grief. How it made her weep to bend his shoulders with her burdens. Before he left he tied the newly fallen umbilical cord around a stick and placed it at the right side of the child's winnowing basket so that he would grow quickly and have a powerful right hand. Since then, every day she had gone to the place where he had buried the afterbirth of the child. She stared at the frozen Earth, could see beneath it to that part of her wrapped moistly in bark, waiting to grow again within her stomach, to become heavy with flesh, to suck at her breast, to walk the mountains and taste the spring berries between its lips. She would gaze at the spot where she knew it to be. She knew it was buried upright, and wondered if in the spring he would return to dig it up and rebury it facing down so that it would grow deep in the black Earth and bring her the power to once more give him a child.

She saw what she had been waiting for. The men outside were shouting, their voices booming out across the flatness of the Big Lake in celebration. Celebration was in her heart; she hugged the child closer to her skin and waited for the two distant figures that had appeared on the white wall to make their way down to camp.

The man with the two Eagle feathers held tightly against his head by a leather band stood watching in silence, his bare feet planted firmly in the ankle deep snow. He watched as his two youngest sons walked toward him through the forest along the shore of the Big Lake. He knew this was not right. Something was not as it should be. It was not just the fact that his son with the new boychild had been gone for more than fourteen nights' passing; it was greater than that. He hated the power of the feelings he had, he hated them because they were mostly right, like the time the sagebrush laughed when he was

young, he had been right then too. He could not understand this power he had, he did not try to, he had been
deceived for many years in believing that he could unrav-
el this. Now he only hated it. He hated this winter. Not
the cold, he could suffer that, he hated its silence, its
length. Each day it challenged him, and each day he grew
more bitter. It was the bitterness which allowed him to
meet the challenge each day, the bitterness which allowed
him to survive, and it was just that which he hated, for he
knew it was the winter which gave him the strength to live
through each day, only so it could challenge him again the
next. But he did not fight. He had learned long ago that
you cannot fight, you cannot fight for you are the only
one that can be killed. You must wait and watch to survive. Only in this manner advantage can be taken of the
situation, by surprising it and adopting its terms. Like the
winter it is not something to be killed, it is impossible to
capture its power, but it can be, in a miserable way, imi-
tated. You can learn how to make your body grow cold
with the winter, how to fill your mind with the warm image of spring Sun, a woman's flesh moving in the strong
smell of a Rabbit blanket. Deceit is survival. You must
look like the tree in the snow, dead and buried, but deep
within the roots remain warm in hope, for spring always
does come, winter always must pass, things do get better.
But the old man could no longer take warmth from these
thoughts. The cold had penetrated his roots, and now he
met each day like the stone. The winter washed over him,
it was only the fact that the winter did wash over him
which held him together in bitterness.

As the Indian approached, his father loomed larger, he
seemed a gray stone growing from the snow. He walked
steadily toward him, his brother following in his footsteps. The men that had set up the cheer, which reached
his ears from the surface of the Big Lake as he and his
brother started down the last steep white mountainside,
had fallen silent and stood behind the father, waiting for
him to speak. He stopped at the edge of the camp and
faced his father across the snow.

"Gayabuc," the old man's lips spoke the word after

staring for some time into the face of his son. "You bring no killings for the babyfeast." The son did not speak. Both men were silent, facing each other with feet rooted in the snow. "Do you not remember why you left the camp? Do you not remember the boychild?"

"There will be no babyfeast for Gayabuc, for anyone," the Indian's words fell flat in the clearing.

"It is not the way," the old man stated.

"I have seen the way before me and followed it as I was taught, but my eyes have now seen new things, things for which I have no teaching, no power."

"For what new things are you without power?" the old man asked in a low voice, knowing that once again his feeling was right.

"*Them.*"

The father looked at the son but the fear did not show in his eyes. For many years now his people had heard that others, others with skin like the snow, had come into the high mountains from the desert, but he had not seen *them,* none of his people had seen *them.* But there had been many stories among other people. He himself had come upon a Paiute not more than three summers past that made much talk about seeing *them* and following *them* up into the mountains, but never getting close enough to look *them* in the face. *They* were tall men, tall as the men that came long ago in his father's father's time and stole the children. *Their* bodies were heavy. The women too, the animals, wild stone-eyed beasts, were larger than both together. In this he knew that the Paiute was not lying. For all the stories spoke of *their* great size and strength, of how *they* did not carry bows, but sticks, sticks from which fire would burst and animals would fall. There was one story which came from the desert that told of how the sticks had made an Indian fall, an Indian, it was spoken true, that got too close to *their* power, and who had looked in *their* faces. This he had heard. He had no proof, but this he believed. He believed all, because not having seen *them,* he had seen *their* tracks some winters ago. They were tracks like no animal would make; they were great in size, and deep. He knew *they* must be heavy and he had no desire to follow *them,* for he could sense that *their* path was evil. All of this he spoke not to those of his camp, for he knew their way was to be frightened and the stories which did reach their ears had placed sorrow on their days. He spoke only to his middle son; the oldest was dead. And when he was alive he was not one to believe his father, so he spoke only to Gayabuc of *them.*

"Go to the mother of your son," he pointed to the *galisdangal* where she sat. "Go, Gayabuc."

The Indian did not move, his brother behind him did not move.

"Go, Gayabuc." The old man's voice came at his son again.

"I have seen *them* eat . . ."

The old man said nothing, he waited as his son fell silent, he waited, watching his face. He waited for what his son had no teaching, no power.

"I have seen *them* eat of *themselves.*"

"Go to your *galisdangal,* Gayabuc."

"I have seen *them* eat the flesh from *their* own bodies."

"Go!"

He went. The Indian who would have no joyous babyfeast for his first boychild went. He turned from his father towards his wife, each foot leaving its soft black imprint in the snow as he walked up the rise to where she waited.

2

WITH EACH step his boots smacked hard on the packed snow. A horse. A horse, if only it hadn't rained last night he could have brought her. If it had been any other horse he would have, but not her. Too many times he had seen horses slip on slick crusted rainpacked snow, one horseshoe going out from underneath, then the knee slamming to the ice with the weight of the body behind. No, he would not take the chance of her fracturing any bones; she was so fragile. In the spring he could use her. When the snow was gone, she could gallop free; she would like that. He stopped, for all the time he was walking his eyes were searching the flat bush covered land in front of him. In front of him, way in front, was a dark form, which to anyone else would have looked like part of the patch of bush it was next to, but it wasn't, and he knew it. He knew what to do now that he had spotted it. He raised the long rifle in front of him, the butt of the worn wood stock firmly pressed against his shoulder in a comfortable position. The barrel level, pointed straight out at the form. The sound of the shot was quick. It cracked sharply in the cold open air and was gone. The form in the distance grew smaller, did not move from where it was, it simply grew smaller, slumped dead under the dark weight of its body. He released his finger from the trigger; it clicked back into place. He slung the rifle over his shoulder and

moved forward. When he reached the rabbit he did not
have to kick it with his boot to make certain it was dead,
the bullet had ripped open the side of the head, blood
moved slowly to the snow from the opening. He picked it
up, could feel the warmth of the body beneath the fur on
his fingers. He spread the back legs and slowly shook his
head. A male. For six days he had shot nothing but males,
the whole winter he had only killed twenty females. He
didn't understand it. The winter before he had shot that
many females in just two days. With one of the strips of
leather tied to his wide belt he wrapped the rabbit's hind
legs securely and let it hang down. He moved forward
again, each step ringing a loud hollow sound on the snow.
He looked down at the stiffening body slapping at his leg,
it had been warned. Doesn't he make so much noise
stomping around on this snow that they know two weeks
in advance he's coming? But do you think they would
hide? No. They're all so simple. He gives them a sporting
chance. Still, they can't keep themselves alive a day longer. They know that if they don't hide he's going to get
them; even if they do hide he'll still get them. He gives
them warning he's coming, but do they slip into hiding?
No. They're all so dumb. It is difficult to understand why
they insist on being, but they do. If only they would hide.
Maybe they could live a week longer, maybe a month,
even to spring. Everything, no matter how stupid, at least
deserves to live till spring. Even one day, one day longer
to live, it would seem to mean a lot. Maybe they get cold,
cold and tired of hunting food that just isn't there when
more than three feet of snow has buried everything worth
eating. Maybe they just get tired of gnawing cold sagebrush, get tired and quit, quit and wait for him. He gives
them a chance, he plays the game fair, fairer than anyone
plays with him. He stopped. Before him was a dead rabbit, its gray legs sticking stiff in front of it against the
white. Stretched out in a neat line between the legs were
the sausage bodies of twelve newborn rabbits. He put a
shell in the rifle, cocked it, aimed the barrel at the dead
mother's head and pulled the trigger. He tied the rabbit on
his belt and squatted; looked at the imprint left by the

body. The bullet had gone through her skull, a black hole about the width of his little finger penetrated the snow, the babies in the neat row along the line left by her belly. He touched one. It was dead. He rolled each cold body over. The last one, the last one was warm, not much, but at least warmer than his finger. He scooped it up, cupped it to his mouth, took a deep breath. Slow, very slow, he let the warm air exhale between his lips onto the bit of fur covered flesh. Standing in the cattle field he breathed the heat from his body, the snow sweeping out flat beneath his feet, reaching in all directions to the mountains that ringed him, mountains so high it took the Sun half a day's climb before its stretching light rolled down the steep slopes filling the valley, touching all parts of its hard floor. He opened his jacket, tucked the small animal under the shirt next to his skin, and moved on. His boots smacking out with each step, the two rabbits flopping at his side.

"Three is all you got Joe?"

He looked at the tall boy as he shut the gate of the fence which formed a perfect box around the three storied house jutting up sharply from the snow and was the exact same color. "Uh-huh, three's about it I guess."

"What do you mean, Joe, you guess three?" The boy walked forward, a brown dog with its head up following right behind.

"Could be three, could be it ain't."

"Could be it ain't, why?" The boy stopped in front of him, the dog sniffing at the hanging rabbits.

"Could be what you see here is three, but what if it was the President's truth that each ate three apiece before I got to them? That would make three and six and nine. Could be it ain't three, but nine. So your old man could owe for nine."

"Rabbits can't eat one another, Joe," the boy glanced up with a look of pride on his face for knowing just what the truth was.

"You ever seen it? You ever been hungry enough to eat somebody?" He placed a hand on the boy's head and felt him shake it. "Then how do you know it ain't so?"

The boy did not answer, he looked away, then at the dog, its tail swinging back and forth in the early evening air, sniffing at the rabbits.

"Sam," the boy turned his eyes toward the broadfaced front porch of the house. "Sam," the voice called again, it was a woman's voice and it came from the front door that was held open a few inches. "Get in here for your dinner," the words shot from the crack across the snow covered yard. The boy looked at the man with the rabbits, lowered his head and went in the house, the brown dog settling at the side of the door where he disappeared. The man walked around the house to the back, pulled open the screen door and knocked, then waited.

"Birdsong," the door opened. He could feel the warm air from the kitchen on his face, and for a moment, see the children at the long table, the woman seated with a baby on her lap; her hair he could see, not her face. "Birdsong," the man stood in front of him, the door closing behind, "How many?"

"Three."

"Three hell, it's hardly worth it, is it, three?"

He looked at the man in front of the closed door, the face was smooth and easy. After thirty years it was still unmarked. "Three, Mr. Dixel."

"Males again?"

"Males."

"That's two-bits a head. Here's six-bits," he reached into the starched front pocket of his slacks and brought out a handful of change.

"And one female."

"Twelve-bits then, altogether," he held the coins out to the Indian.

"Wait," Birdsong put his hand up, then reached into his jacket under his shirt and brought out the tiny rabbit, holding the bit of warmth in his open palm.

"What the hell is that," the man looked at the rabbit, then at the Indian.

"A rabbit."

"You don't think I'm going to pay you for it?"

"Why not?"

"Because . . . because it isn't even grown."

"It would be by spring."

"But this isn't spring."

"Course not, but if it were it would be six-bits worth of rabbit 'cause it's a female."

"How in the hell do you know that when it isn't any bigger than your thumb. Besides, it looks dead."

"Touch it."

"So it's warm," the man looked him in the face. "But it isn't six-bits worth warm."

"What difference is it if it is warm, you're paying for it dead."

"Two cents I'll give you, my dinner's getting cold."

"A nickel."

"Two cents."

"I'll keep it."

"Suit yourself. Here's your twelve-bits," he handed the money over and turned back into the house, the door closing tight behind him.

At night he had the dream. The dream was exploding now. Blasting with ever increasing regularity. Two, three nights a week it came to him. During the day he tried to move away from it, defend himself, fight it. During the day he would not think of it, and when it would come to him, when he would least expect it, he would turn his face to the sun, his eyes open, and the brilliance of the mountain light would drive the memory of the dream back, pushing it deep in his mind, flooding it with light, drowning it in whiteness. In the evenings, when he was tired and it would slip up on him, forcing its pictures into reality, then he would hit his eyes with closed fists, and he would keep hitting them, forcing the blackness into his head where the dream had found its way to flare up in streaks of white and pounding flashing stars, boldly destroying the place of the dream. But at night, asleep, he was defenseless. The dream would come. Slowly at first, seeping into the darkness, taking shape, catching him, soothing, it came like a song hung deep in black. Softly it sang, until it knew it was safe, then louder, louder it grew, breaking into a hard chant, slashing back and forth in the dark, racing into a dance, a dance of lizards, slipping and wrapping themselves about a pine tree, the trunk swirling with slick, stone-gray bodies, the chant droning like the sound of a far off chainsaw coming louder, hideously buzzing, the bark spraying away from the trunk beneath the brittle scales of slithering bellies, exposing the white meat of the tree, the bodies moving on its open moistness, cutting deeper, the tails lashing fiercely as they grow closer to the place where the sap flows, the air filled with ripping as the trunk cracks, splits, crashing away from where it stood in two separate parts. The silence, the silence of where the tree stood, takes shape, hardens, thickens, rounds into a boulder in the summer sun. Clinging to its side, immovable, is one lizard, its body still, making only a slight movement of delicate blue gills, as they softly, noiselessly suck at the air. And when he was young, with his brother, they would come upon a lizard caught in the sun, thinking it couldn't be seen, thinking it was part of the rock, invisible, but they had searched for it. They had spent the hot day and all the ones before it walking through the forests, finding open spaces in the trees, spaces where there would be only the warmth of the sun, warmth falling on rocks, boulders, perhaps a lizard, and they hunted with an air-rifle, a gun that had been given by their father to both of them on one of their birthdays; of all the things to shoot the sting of a round copper bee-bee into, and maybe kill, none held their attention like the lizard, for the lizard was a soundless creature, a creature that looked like it should be destroyed, a creature that once the bee-bee had penetrated its cold blooded body did not move, did not make a sound, a creature that looked as if it begged to be killed, that if it were large enough so the stroke of its scaled tail could crush a man it would desire spears hurled at it, penetrating the armor of its scales, driving home to its heart, releasing it from being what it was not. And when he and his brother came to the boulder they saw it. First he shot, the bee-bee tearing a perfectly round hole into the back, then ricocheting straight out, and it was as if nothing had happened, he had to keep his eyes on the lizard to realize something had, he kept his eyes on the hole in the back, and his brother shot, the bee-bee going through the arm-less body making a soft ping on the rock beneath, then bouncing straight out. They would gaze at the two holes, one next to the other, and wonder why the lizard would not, did not, *move*. They would wait for blood, but it nev-er came, they knew it wouldn't, and they would stay, each taking a shot; slowly the holes began to merge into one, the lizard's feet still rigidly hooked in the boulder, most of its back blown out, the stone showing beneath. Finally they would tire, move to the large rock in the sun and pick the reptile up by the tail, its body would slip away from the tail to the ground and they would pick it up again, one of them putting the tail in his pocket to later place with the others. They would hold the body up and look through the hole in the back and see the sunlight on the other side.

In the morning the rabbit was alive. He did not expect it to be. He warmed some milk over the still glowing coals in the fireplace, then twisted a bit of cloth and dipped it in the milk. As the rabbit sucked at the rag he watched and knew it would live to be full-grown, for it seemed not right that it had survived this long, so it must live. When he finished with the rabbit he placed it back on the old handkerchief folded near the fire and went outside to feed his horse. The air was quiet with the smell of pine, the sky was clear, except for some slivers of white clouds he no-ticed spread out over the bank of mountains to the west. He knew it would snow by dark. He had built a shed off one side of his one room house, this was the stable for the horse. He pushed open the wooden doors of the front. His horse rose from the hay where she was sleeping and walked to him, nuzzling her white nose against his shoul-der. "Shasta," he spoke softly, rubbing the palm of his hand against her neck. He touched his lips to the soft hide of her face; she smelled of hay and salt. He fed her, put the bridle he had braided last spring over her head, and led her through the door. Around and around they moved in a wide circle on the snow in front of the house, the man and the horse, the man making certain to step in his own footprints as he retraced the circle, his head down, eyes to the ground, following his own trail, and that of the horse.

"Why don't you come up and eat?"

His eyes came off the track in front of him and saw the woman who stood with her hands resting on the top strand of barbedwire fence that stretched in front of his house dividing it from the road. The darkness of her face held no expression; it was shaped like the moon with a wisp of hair in front obscuring eyes deep in shadows.

"It's noon."

The sun was over his head, the slivers of clouds had grown thick, pushing halfway out across the valley, almost touching the pale disc of winter light. His horse let out a snort and nudged his back, trying to make him move once more around the footdeep circle their feet had beaten darkly into the snow. He led her back in the shed, slipped the bridle off and hung it on the peg over the silver inlaid saddle, then joined the woman waiting on the other side of the fence. Together they walked down the slit of wire bordered road that pierced straight through the emptiness of the cattle fields.

"I brought him," the woman announced, shutting the door behind them.

"Joe," the man sitting deep in a gray chair pulled close in front of the flames wrapping around the logs stacked neatly in the fireplace greeted him without getting up. "Sit down, sit down," he slapped a chair beside him and pulled it in closer to the fire, his face stretched in a smile. "Good you come, Joe, awful good."

"Good you come, Joe, good," the small girl sitting at the man's feet repeated, her face flushed from the warmth of fire.

Birdsong stood by the door looking at his brother-in-law and his young niece. He moved over in front of the fire, his hands held stiffly at his sides, then sat in the chair offered. "Felix," he nodded his head in a short jerk.

"We was expectin' you earlier, Joe, Sunday dinner just like always," the man turned in his chair, a note of hurt in his voice. "We been waitin' on you, but you never showed. So finally I told Sarah Dick, Sarah, you better get yourself on down the road and find out what's holdin' up that brother of yours."

"*She* was," the woman's voice came in sharply from the kitchen.

"Sarah Dick," the man moved his body in the chair towards the door from where the crackling of frying chicken came. "Why don't you just leave Joe be about that horse."

"He was with her as usual, walkin' round and round in their own rut, lookin' down at his feet, just circlin'."

The man turned his back to the voice as if the action refuted her existence and gave Birdsong a look of one just caught with five deuces in his hand. "Joe, I'm glad you could make it on over today for dinner." He settled deeper in his chair, waiting to hear his hospitality given thanks. It did not come. He stared into the fire waiting for it, but it still did not come. "Joe," he spoke again as if it were the first time since the man arrived. "I want to thank you for tightnin up that stretch of fence for me back last week. It's hard to keep a piece of ranch going and runnin a gas station at the same time, but I'm sure you know that, maybe you don't, I don't know anyway, but I appreciate what you did for me just the same."

"I can count to six, Joe."

"Not now, Sue Dick," the man touched the girl's shoulder. "Me an your uncle is talkin."

"I don't believe it," Birdsong pushed his legs out, resting his boots on the stone hearth.

"That we was talkin," the man almost shouted.

"No, that the girl can count to eight."

"Six, I said six."

"That's right," the man confirmed. "It was six she said."

"Don't believe it even so."

"I could do it."

"Six ain't no good, you got two numbers after six, and that's just to make eight."

"Well I can go all the way up to six anyways."

"Joe believes you," the man touched the girl again. "It's just that he thinks eight is more important than six."

"No I don't, how can *eight* be more important than six if she can't *go* all the way up to six."

"Yes I could, to six anyways."

"Easy thing to say, different to prove."

"Well I could. I could do it the way you showed me."

"Ain't nothin wrong with that, long as you can do it, that's the main thing, doesn't make any difference how you get there."

"Just you listen then," the girl stood up, one side of her body glowing yellow from the fire. "One little, two little, three little Indians, fi . . . , no, I mean four, four little, five little, six little, six little Indian girls."

"Never would of believed you had it in you. You come around tomorrow about dark and I'll boost you up on Shasta."

"Tomorrow!"

"That's what I said, didn't I."

The girl sat down, faced toward the fire's warm glow.

"It's hard work, Joe," the man spoke again as if he had never been interrupted. "It's hard runnin a gas station and a piece of ranch at the same time."

"Chicken."

"Chicken, what do you mean chicken? I didn't say anythin about chickens."

"Chicken is what I smell."

"Sure you do, Sarah Dick makes it every . . ."

"Chicken, now let me figure this, the last time I ever had any chicken was, yes, that was it, why just the Sunday past, last time I was here."

"And I ate four pieces," the girl announced.

"Like I was explainin, Joe . . ."

"No you didn't eat four pieces, you only ate two."

"It was four, I counted them, I could count to four then."

"Must of made a mistake somewhere."

"Four. Three wings and a leg."

"Don't seem right, chicken's only got two wings."

The girl stopped, her gaze caught on her uncle's face, the face the color of blowing dust on a summer day, the face like her mother's, expressionless. "Maybe that's so," she finally answered. "Maybe a chicken's only got two wings, but I had four pieces anyways. You just watch me this time, I'll show you I can. Just you be watching."

"I will be."

"As I was saying, Joe, it's rough for a man to . . ."

"It's on the table if you're for eatin it."

"Thanks, Sarah Dick," the man turned in his chair and gave her his stretched smile. "Me an' Joe'll be there in a minute or two."

"Sue," Birdsong stood up and looked down at the small girl. "Let's see if you can find three wings on this chicken."

They ate the chicken in silence. Felix took an almost empty pack of cigarettes from his shirt pocket, put one in his mouth and lit it, then threw the pack to the other end of the table.

"Don't smoke, Felix," Birdsong pushed the paper package that landed next to his plate away with a thick finger.

"Sorry, Joe, keep forgettin."

"Felix maybe gonna buy us a TV, Joe. What do you think of that?"

He looked in his sister's face and said nothing.

"Not a new one, of course," Felix informed, puffs of smoke escaping from his mouth with each word. "Not too old either, of course."

"Course," Sarah Dick added. "We won't be able to get as many channels as folks in Reno or Sacramento. But we can get one real good one, and the other about half as good."

"Jonny and Minnie Scisson's got it. You know them Joe, live over 'cross the valley in Loyalton. Jonny's been going to the meetin's with me over to Truckee. Thirty people they had there last month, be bigger next time, gettin bigger all the time. All tribes comin, Washo, Paiute,

Mono, Maidu, why even four Shoshone come in all the way from Utah."

"He doesn't want to hear about it."

"Sure he does, don't you Joe."

"He doesn't."

"Four, I ate four," the girl dropped the bones in her uncle's plate.

"Joe likes to hear what us Indians are doin for ourselves."

"No he doesn't."

"Count 'em, that's four."

"Don't you, Joe."

"That's only three and a half."

"What, three and a half what?" Felix questioned his brother-in-law, the smile on his face stretching out in all directions.

"Three and a half chicken bones."

"So what has that got to do with what we was talkin about?"

"Everything, one's a neck. She said she ate four and everybody knows there ain't hardly no meat on a neck. It only counts for half."

"That was a fat chicken," the girl insisted.

"What's this got to do with what I was talkin about," Felix repeated, his smile stretched so far it was about to snap.

"Everything, Indians only count for half, half man, they ain't white."

"I don't think that's fair, Joe. Every time we talk you find some way to bring the conversation around to the fact that I'm only half Paiute."

"I wasn't talkin about you, Felix, I was talkin about chicken necks and Indians."

"Well, I'm an Indian."

"Then you're only half. Best you can ever be is half."

"That's just why we have meetin's. That's just the reason."

"You won't find the other half there."

"How do you know, you never been to none. Why don't you come and find out."

"Don't have to, I already know."

"How do you already know?"

"Because every Sunday I come over here you start in talkin about those meetin's for the Indian to better himself and you ask me to go."

"So how do you know they don't do any good?"

"Cause you're still only half."

Felix pressed his cigarette butt in the slime of gravy on his plate, it made a small hiss and he spoke, "What do you think you are, whole, one hundred percent?"

"Didn't say that."

"You can't, that's why. You don't have the nerve. You don't do anything for yourself. You hire on for a day or two whenever some rancher in the valley needs fencin or buckin hay or an extra hand with the cattle."

"I am the Rabbit Boss."

"But you're not a Washo Rabbit Boss, you're a strawhat, a *hired* whiteman Rabbit Boss."

"Ain't no difference as I see it, Rabbit Boss is Rabbit Boss no matter what time he's living in, any end you look through it's all the same."

"The same," Felix leaned across his plate, his smile stretched so tight it was twitching. "How can you sit at my table, in my house, and tell me it means the same where I know it don't. How can you abuse your own people who were real Rabbit Bosses, respected men that were needed for all to survive. How can you compare yourself to them that did something, something noble. You! You're nothing but a strawhat, a hired Indian with a rifle, hired by a whiteman to keep the rabbits from chomping up all his range grass or his stupid cattle from fallin into their holes and breakin a leg that holds up all those pounds of money meat. You're a hired game warden, you ain't even that, you're just an exterminator. That's it, an exterminator, like one of them guys you get when the termites is eatin your house and you get him quick so's he can exterminate before the house comes fallin down round your ears."

"Ain't no termites in this valley, too cold."

"That's not what I meant."

"Well that's what you said."

"Example, Joe," Felix let out a sigh and sat back in his chair, lighting another cigarette. "Just an example. Can't you understand what an example is?"

"No, it ain't got nothin to do with me."

"Why do you do what you do Joe?"

"It's the only thing for an Indian to do."

"It isn't, that's just the point," Felix was leaning over his plate again. "There ain't too many Indians left in this valley anymore, and those that are all have some kind of job."

"So do I."

"But it's not a respectful job."

"Is to me."

"But it isn't to *them*."

"It's not *their* job, it's mine."

"Your job is outdated, Joe. They have no need for you. You're just cheaper than poison."

"It would kill the cattle, they tried it once."

"The whole idea of what you're doin is out of time. You're the last livin Rabbit Boss there is, I haven't heard of any others in the complete State of California, and there's certainly none over the hill in Nevada. When you die it's over. No one will care, let alone notice."

"What's that got to do with me?"

"It's got everything to do with you, you're an Indian."

"But you're talkin about a dead Indian, makes no difference to a dead Indian if it's over when he dies."

"You're not dead yet."

"So what are you going on about Felix?"

"Joe, I'm talkin about you, your past and your future. Before *they* came a little over a hundred years ago there were over three thousand of your people, now you're lucky if you can scare up three hundred Washo. The Washo, the Paiute, all the Indians got to get together and join with the whiteman before we don't have anything to join with. They made a mess of this country of ours and this is the Indian's last chance to straighten them out. If we get organized and join them as an organization of people then we can point to a nobler way of life through example. Examples of art and nature and brotherhood and . . ."

"Felix," Birdsong interrupted. "Why is it every Sunday you go on about how Indians are the last hope. You tell me the same thing week after week, year after year, you never even bother to change the words around a little, and you go over to Truckee and tell it to those people at the meetin's and then they tell it back to you again and back and forth it goes, you all tellin each other how if *they* don't recognize you as an organization *they* will come to ruin just like that place in history called Rome, because you're the last hope. You keep pumping yourselves up about bein the last hope and all the while *they* keep going on like they always been, without you, and all the time no closer to that Rome place than when *they* was tearin the mountains down for gold and silver or rippin the trees from everywhere to put up houses. *They* didn't need you then and *they* don't need you now, and if *they* do reach that place like Rome there won't be no redman alive to see it."

"Joe, you're an ignorant man and a twice as ignorant Indian."

"Goodbye," Birdsong stood up quickly, the chair falling to the floor behind him.

"Joe!" The word sprung in the room and before its sound died out Felix had been around the table, righted the chair, and pushed his brother-in-law back down. "Joe," he returned to the spot where he had spoken the word the first time. "How would you like to better yourself real good? What do you say, real good?" He watched the dark eyes, the eyes that sat the same way in his wife's face. He tried to search in them, get around behind them, finally, knowing it was impossible, he spoke in a low voice, but swiftly, trying to catch the eyes by surprise. "How would you like to sell your place down the road," he threw the words at the eyes like a bucket of cold water. "How would you like to sell that twenty acres of nowhere land to me and make yourself a load of real good money? He waited to see what damage the words would do to the eyes, they did none.

Birdsong got out of his chair and opened the door, then turned to the man seated at the head of the table. "Felix, you're more crazy than I ever thought of you bein." The door shut behind him, leaving the man alone in his house, with his daughter and wife.

The knock came again but he did not answer. He squatted on the stone hearth in front of the fire, holding the rabbit in one large hand, listening to the whining sound it made as it sucked at the twisted milk soaked rag in its mouth. When he finished he laid the animal back in its place and opened the door.

"Birdsong," the man who was walking back to his parked jeep turned in the snow and greeted.

"Come in."

"Damn if this ain't the coldest winter I can remember since I come up to the Sierra," he declared from beneath the broad rim of a beige felt hat as he hunched before the fire, rubbing gloved hands together with quick hard jerks.

"It could be colder."

"Well if it could," he gave a short laugh and began massaging his shoulders beneath the green jacket. "You'd be damn sure I wouldn't stick around to freeze in it. Your kind can stand it, you've got cold blood. But us California Fish and Game people, now, we're about the warmest blooded creatures that God ever had hike around the High Sierra."

"What is it you want, Ralph?"

"By God Birdsong, what on God's earth do you have there on that rag, is it alive?"

"It's alive."

"It can't be a rabbit, can it?"

"You can see it is."

"Good Holy Mother, how can a tiny thing like that live in the winter, let alone without its mother? Birdsong, you must have some extra talents you been hiding on everyone, you're a sly one you are. Damn, I wonder how that thing lives?"

"It lives because I . . ."

"Never mind, I understand all about rabbits. You

know, Birdsong," his voice was loud over the thumping sound his clapped gloved hands made. "Instead of taking in stray rabbits you ought to get yourself some furniture. My God, this place is a shambles." He let his eyes roam around the room in silent testimony to his statement. It didn't take long, he cast a disapproving gaze at the brass bed, pot belly stove and one highback chair, the middle of its seat knocked out; balanced over the remaining wood sides as if it were growing out of the hole like some strange flower was a black leather accordion, the cracked pearl on the keys a worn glimmer of the sparkle they once held.

"Got all the extras I need," Birdsong spoke, stopping the eyes before they got to the guns racked above the mantel.

"Maybe so, maybe so," the man slapped both gloved hands against his knees and stood up. "I have a job for you."

"What?"

"Snakes."

"Bit too early."

"Not according to the data in Sacramento."

"Data in Sacramento's got nothin to do with snakes in the Sierra."

"The State's got machines in Sacramento, smarter than you and me put together will ever be, those machines are a million dollars right and if the card comes up punched now for snakes, then it's *now* for snakes. You want the job or not? It makes no difference to me who's right or wrong." He moved to the door and put his hand on the knob.

"Where?"

"Horsetail Falls."

"Who else is going?"

"Ben Dora."

"He goes I stay."

"You then, so let's move it. I haven't the whole morning to stand around and discuss it. I want to be home before dark, promised my wife I'd take her over to Greyeagle for dinner. You had your breakfast?"

"Yes."

"Good, no time to waste, we've a long way to go."

They got in the jeep and drove on the flat road out of the valley that was sunk into the sky itself, they climbed into the mountains, the black pavement worming its way through the snow that had been thrown up on both sides by the snowplows in high banks like white waves. When they reached the ridge of the first mountain Birdsong wiped the moisture from the plastic of the back window, through the clear swipes his hand made in the wet blur he could see below to the valley. He could see far in the distance, but not to the other side. He could see its silence, its flatness, the few houses that were scattered and remote as if they had been tossed haphazardly into the bowl like black dice. In Truckee Ralph bought two cases of dynamite. Birdsong strapped them with rope against the bed of the jeep. They drove on, following the road along the shore of Donner Lake and up another mountain, over a bridge shaped like a concrete rainbow, spanning a granite split in the mountain that was aimed like a giant rifle sight at the lake below. The snow began to fall, slightly, slowly, in its own time. Birdsong kept wiping his side window to look out, so if there was one along the road he would see it, and seize it in his mind, the fragile snowplant, growing straight and delicate from the whiteness, its color splashing in bold contrast, as if the glorious ceremony of its intricate existence etched in the very cold that buried most other living things in four and a half months of death each year but breathed life into this only plant, sustained it, nurtured it, this beautiful bastard celebrated as proof of its own beauty; and when it died, when the snow would give way to sun and sink from sight into the black earth, it would kill that which it celebrated, gave birth to, would destroy its own flower of existence, the blazing snowplant. Birdsong searched in the falling snow as the jeep moved along, looking for that blaze of color that his people called *Honowah*, and for him it was special, singular. It was the color of his dreams. He saw one. He heard the wipers of the jeep slapping back and forth and he saw one, only for an instant, in passing, he saw the burst of crimson against the whiteness, and it was gone, fled, but he held its image in his mind, clinging to it until they would pass by another, and once more the color would grow, brighter. The jeep whined through the mountains, jerking at almost regular intervals as Ralph shifted gears, but always moving.

"I sure as you can see don't like driving all over God's mountain roads in the falling snow with a load of dynamite in the back. Don't like it at all, you can mark that down. I just don't like it."

Birdsong heard Ralph's words spoken loud and tight in the smallness of the cab, over the slapping whir of the wipers which had formed a drone deep in his mind, their monotonous rhythm continuously backing his thought, his thought of crimson, shattered by Ralph's words, drained of meaning drained by a simple act of intrusion, of speech. He broke from his gaze out the window into the snow and turned in his seat. "What'd you say?"

"You don't care about dying, do you Birdsong." Ralph put his gloved hand on the gearshift knob and pushed it forward. "Makes no difference to you one way or the other," he spoke even louder over the increased whine from the engine. "That's the trouble with people today, Indians in particular, don't care whether they live or die. Like Ben Dora for instance, now there's a man wants to die, and is honest about it, I got nothing against a man not wanting to live, as long as he is honest about it, as a matter of fact I can't help but have a certain respect for a man like that, only trouble with Ben is that he figures the only way to go and get himself killed is to kill someone else, then let the State go to the trouble of killing him, that's a bad way to get yourself killed, killing someone else."

"Dora's no Indian."

"Of course he isn't, I know that, I said most people, most people don't care much one way or the other whether they live or die. I just happened to be mentioning Dora. The way he terrorizes most people in that valley is a death wish."

"Dora makes no wishes."

"Hell man, that's not what I meant by 'wish.' "

"It's what you said."

"It's not what I mean, not in the way you mean it. What I was saying was that a man learns a lot in my profession, dealing day in and day out like I do with pure nature, seeing life and death, not like some guy with a tie that sits behind a desk all day staring at four pissgreen walls, that's not for me. We must not destroy nature, and we won't, not so long as we have science to protect it." He placed his hand on the shift and pulled it toward him. "You're not listening to a word I'm saying, are you?"

"No."

"You could care less whether you live or die, whether nature lives or dies."

"Right."

"You know Birdsong, I don't see one damn thing noble in your situation."

"Neither do I."

"Hell, is that the only way you can communicate, with one word grunts. You've worked for me countless times and I've never heard you say one thing worthwhile. You never try to talk, to get to know me as a man."

"I didn't ask you to hire me."

"That's right, you didn't, but did it ever occur to you, just once maybe, that I'm trying to help you out."

"No."

"I don't understand your bitterness, you have property, health, that's one hell of a lot more than most people ever have."

Birdsong said nothing. He turned and wiped another clear space on the gray moisture of the plastic window and looked out into the implacable whiteness, no longer seeking the flash of crimson, just watching.

"It's a godsend I have fourwheel drive in this jeep," Ralph spoke to himself. He shifted into another gear and kept silent as they drove higher into the mountains. Finally, he pulled over to the side of the road, turned off the engine, reached under the seat and pulled out two empty backpacks, handing one to Birdsong, and they got out.

Birdsong stood on the road, stamping his boots on the snowcoated pavement. He watched as Ralph untied one of the small wooden boxes, pried it open with a screwdriver. The lid came up, exposed the dry neatly packed sticks of dynamite, pieces of fallen snow melted quickly on the tight red wrappings. Ralph passed sticks to Birdsong who placed them gently in the back of a pack; when the box was half empty he loaded his own pack.

"Why the extra box?"

Ralph gave a smile like a little boy's, hitching up his loaded pack and pulling the shoulder straps down securely over his green jacket. "Birdsong, whenever the State gives you money to buy something always buy twice as much as you need because you never know if they'll give you money for the same thing again, Gimbel's law."

A Greyhound bus came around the blind corner above them. They stepped off the pavement and watched it come forward, the powerful headlights piercing the fallen snow directly in front, the massive eight wheels swishing a dull sound on the pavement as it passed, exposing the sign above the wideglass front declaring: TAHOE EXPRESS, the passengers in the rolling gunmetal gray box turning their heads together as one to the sight of two men standing patiently in the ever increasing whiteness, their faces shapeless blurs behind foggy tinted glass.

"Those jockeys," Ralph shouted over the din of the engine, the tailwind blowing soiled snow in his face, "would drive those rigs over the ocean in a hurricane if a casino was waiting on the other side."

They remained until the large object turned out of sight behind some trees, the last of its sound gone from the air. All was quiet again, the quiet of falling snow. They stood in the silence, the two men, then Birdsong walked across the road into the trees. Ralph followed. Birdsong stepped over a stream that ran narrow and noisy through the trees that grew closer together and taller.

"That was stupid."

"What," Birdsong looked at Ralph who was unhitching his pack.

"I forgot the snowshoes. We won't get halfway up this mountain without them." He handed his pack over and walked back through the trees.

Birdsong stood alone, holding the dynamite in the center of the stillness, listening back into its deepness as the wind cut it in sharp parts through the trees heavy with snow. This side of the mountain was sheltered from the main force of wind and the snow was light. The snakes hibernated here in the rocks, the rocks made it dangerous for men, the snow piled in between them, filling the open spaces level to the height of the boulders so if great care were not taken, or snowshoes not worn, a man could be walking on a hardpack that felt secure and solid beneath his feet; the next step might be into a soft pocket, the weight of his body would cut into the snow, slicing down, ten, forty, eighty feet of suffocating drop. But the snakes were up there, it was the only way, the only time to get them all together. The silence was breaking up, being pulled apart as the heavy sound of Ralph making his way through the trees reached him.

"Thanks," Ralph took his pack, put his arms through the shoulder straps and hitched it up. "Hope this clears out of here in a while," he cocked his head back and looked into the gray sky from beneath the protective brim of his hat. "Make it a lot easier on us if it would." He shifted uneasily under the weight on his back, moving back and forth, watching Birdsong lace the last snowshoe onto his boots, waiting for him to lead the way.

They started. Birdsong in front, leading up the mountain, slowly, higher, towards the rocks, the snakes. He kept his eyes on the snow in front of him, it was dangerous here, the rocks were always shifting beneath the sinking weight of snow, then being covered over again. The trees began to thin and they picked up the stream they had crossed by the road. It was wider, running hard through the slot it cut in the ice. He followed alongside, there was another motion in the air, not just the sound of wind, it was a sound of leaves being crushed in a hand, but far away so that it did not come with a splintering in the air, but steady, and low, murmuring. There were few trees left, the ones that did manage to grow were short and squat, hunched close against the cold. Soon even these trees were gone. Still he followed the stream. The other sound came stronger, pulling even with that of the wind, challenging it. He could see up the mountain, there was nothing to stop his gaze. He could not see to the top, the swirling bits of snow thickened and grew into a gray wall that stopped his vision. He continued toward the wall, always pushing it back, dissolving it. The sound of the wind had been lost, buried beneath the other sound which had grown into a rumble, a belching roar sucking everything out of the air, drawing it down to earth, forcing it to the source, the stream, water. The stream in front of him was driving furiously with the force of six lakes behind it. The air opened up and he could see the energy swirling; the currents from the falling water cleared the snow above, he could see up the mountain along the watery path to where the falls began, dropping in sections, one long suspended tumble onto another, a crushing ladder. The mist sprayed into the open, then disappeared, its substance invisible, driving into the air, giving way once more to the snow, and he knew soon to turn west. He made his way to the next fall of water, the ground rising steeply, the snow as high as the boulders, smoothed over them. The weight on his back tugged at his shoulders, not much, but as he continued he knew it was there, and this made it a burden, pulling him closer to the ground. Ahead, a piece of mountain pierced through the snow, exposed, a sheer crag of granite, tall as a mature redwood, a cliff of gray. He walked away from the falls, no longer toward the top of the mountain but toward the cliff, the crash of water staying with him. Stone domes rose from the whiteness, boulders, dominated by the darkness of the cliff. He was close to the place he wanted to be. Each step came down heavy as he moved through the domes, the web of snowshoe pressing firmly into the cold, supporting the clumsiness of his body, each step smaller than the last, one following another, one striking the snow, not stopping, breaking through, its tearing sound joining with the roar of falls filling his ears. His body drops, he bends one knee to catch at the break in the snow. It holds. For a moment his weight is suspended, then slips, making the hole in the snow the size of his body. He falls with the knee bent, slamming against the wet surface of a boulder; twisiting him, knocking against the side of another rock, his body stopping, wedged between two stones.

His head rested against stone, facing up through the gaping hole torn in the snow above, snow that had packed in between the two boulders, melted out beneath, trickling down the slick sides until the area was hollow, leaving a slice of ice spanning the boulders like a glass bridge. The sky swirled, snowflakes drifted through the hole, their coolness melting on his face. The sheet of ice that was not broken from his fall was puckered underneath from gathered droplets of water dripping down in the dampness. He saw a hat through the hole, then a face beneath it, red and shiny from the cold, the mouth opening and closing, "You know you almost blew us sky high! We're damn lucky to be alive you and me! That was close, very close, they don't get one hair closer than that. Boom! And it's all over. A fall like that could set that dynamite off quick as an owl can wink. Don't you make any sudden moves now, you still got some pretty tricky stuff strapped on your back. Are you hurt?"

"You better stop talkin and get off that ice or you're goin to be down here sittin next to me."

"The way you fell through that snow I thought you probably wouldn't come up until China, or India maybe. Damn lucky you fell in between two boulders that come together nice and convenient like and not in some chasm. Can you stand?"

"I can stand. You just get off there so you don't make it harder for me to get out." He placed his palms flat against the wet rocks and pressed, his legs coming up straight, one knee bent out with quick spears of pain. He stood, keeping balance with his hands, his head just beneath the hole, the one knee throbbing. He could see Ralph through the opening, standing off to the side.

"Hand out the pack first." Ralph moved closer.

He unstrapped the pack and passed it out, then hit around the hole with his hand, knocking the thinner ice away, bits of the cold falling on his face. He put his arms up through the hole, reaching his hands to the solid surface above, spread his feet, placing one snowshoe on each rock for balance and hoisted the weight of his body from the hole.

"Here's your pack," Ralph presented it as if it was a reward for his getting out. "Very close that. Too close, really, you never know when Boom! It's all over except the insurance."

Birdsong headed once more for the cliff, the steps coming even shorter, his knee opening in new pain with each movement. When he reached the cliff he walked on beneath it, almost brushing against the sheer wall.

"That's a bad leg you got there. Yes, it's pretty bad. Maybe you shouldn't go on. You could fall again, walking on a wobbly leg like that. Maybe we should head back."

Birdsong swung around and faced Ralph, the snow swirling between them. His breathing slowed, was softer, the sound of the falls thick in the air. "I'm not going back," the words sank into the muted roar of the falls, lost their shape, became obscure.

"Now look, if it's the pay you're worried about don't. I hired you for the day and I'll pay fair for it. No use killing yourself just because you might think I won't pay if we don't finish. I don't know what ever gave you that idea. I've always been square."

"I don't give a goddam."

"Let's not get hasty, Birdsong. I think we're both worn down. We've been knocking ourselves out on this climb. What the hell do machines in Sacramento know about whether or not it's going to snow on the day they punched for snakes? Why don't we go on back down? It may be dark by the time we get back and I don't want to walk out of here playing hopscotch in the dark."

Birdsong was already moving, continuing along the base of the cliff, the steps coming quicker for the pain had spured out, filling his leg, jabbing at his entire body; he moved with it, went into it, it was fast, soon he was beyond the cliff, out from under it, onto the far side, the side sheltered by the monolithic intrusion on the landscape. The deflected winds from the cliff drove the snow over this section, the ground a translucent cover of white, leaving bare the jagged rocks and in their paths the short rugged bushes. Slicing through this, cutting in diagonal lines across the mountain until lost on the far side, diminishing in the snow, were separations in the earth, cracks, narrow enough for a man to step over, wide enough for him to fall in. On this side of the cliff, filling continuously into the void, rushing into this last gap of silence, the tumbling, echoing drone of the falls funneled into a blare. He walked up the far side of the cliff, across to the cracks. At the first one he stopped, his eyes roving over the rocks at its edge, over the gray surfaces. He moved on, stepping over the chasm, heading further up the mountain. At the second split in the earth he did not stop but stepped over, toward the next. When he came to its edge he halted, his eyes again studying the rocks. There was no change in the eyes as he slipped the pack from his back and took out a long red stick.

"This is the place, huh? You can tell by the markings on the rocks?"

He did not look up, he did not expect the voice, but it made no difference.

Ralph came closer to him, his breath hard, short puffs of moisture shooting from his nose and mouth. "Those are five minute fuses on these little babies, slow burners, so we have plenty of time for running. They'll give about the same blast as the ones we used a couple of years back. Not enough to rip this mountain open and start a big slide below, just enough to blow to bits all those cozy rattlers coiled around one another, their bellies popping with eggs jammed full of more little snakes and . . ."

Birdsong lit the fuse. It fizzled slowly, the bright smouldering head giving off traces of black smoke.

"Don't wait around to find a birthday cake to stick it in," Ralph shouted, stepping back from the lit explosive.

Birdsong held the red stick over the open chasm, let it slip through his fingers. The lit fuse illuminated the darkness as it plunged, its wan light flickering, reflected off the close stone walls, then gone, deep into the darkness, plummeting, twirling and flashing into the center of the mountain.

He leaped over the chasm, going away from it, around behind a boulder, sat down with his back flat against it, rigid, the sound from the falls rushing into the void about him, singing in his ears, pressing him even more tightly against the stone, giving way only for a moment as the new sound of the blast mounted it, terse, fleeting, and was gone, thundering up the short distance to the top of the mountain, into the snowy air. He waited, his back still and close as if it grew from the stone. He closed his eyes to the mountain, to the sound that had just passed him, then opened them, stood up and went back to the split earth. Ralph was standing at the edge, wisps of smoke rising at his feet, drifting into the wind in front of him, distorting his figure behind the ethereal haze.

"No good," Birdsong stood over the narrow chasm, straddling it, looking down.

"No warm little babies in there, but we'll get them, that's a fact of sight," Ralph shook his head slowly, the brim of his hat slicing at the air.

Birdsong moved up to the next chasm. He got down on his hands and knees, looked closely at the rocks smooth and flat, jerked up and took three sticks of dynamite from the pack, struck a match, the wind blew it out, he struck another, lighting all three charges and dropping them, one, two, three into the earth, watching them descend, watching for the last light. A hand was on his arm, the fingers pressing through the jacket, clamped down, digging into the bone, shaking him. "Don't you know!" The shiny red face screwed up in pain. "Damn man! Don't you realize there's a road down there! You want to slide this whole mountain down, and us with it!" The face was close to his; Birdsong could feel the heat from it on his own, the hot breath on his skin. He stared into the tight blue eyes, said nothing, heard nothing, except the falls.

"Let's get the hell out of here!"

He listened to the crushing sound of water, could see the flame tumbling in the darkness between the damp rocks. The hand pulled at his arm, yanking, moving him a few steps away from the chasm, tugging fiercely as if it were going to rip the arm from its socket. Then it was released, the hand was gone, he stood alone in the sound, moved a few more steps down the steep incline, the bulky snowshoes catching on jags of rock, twisting him, tumbling him to the ground, his knee striking the snow, a trigger of pain setting off the blast deep in the earth, the ground beneath giving only a slight tremble as the power slashed up through damp, deep rocks, pushing the blood of a hundred blasted bodies between them, a wash of crimson spewing out of the crack into air, bits of reptile flesh raining down the swirling sky, touching his body, falling lightly on his face.

3

CAPTAIN REX stood riding the flatbed car of the Train singing the songs Birds sang long ago that he had learned in
dreams. He liked to sing. He liked to open his mouth
wide, his lips wet, letting the music come from deep within, to hear its ancestry in his ears, to hear it get up into
the air rushing past, whistling about his head, through his
blowing black hair, out into the open spaces between the
mountains. He liked to stamp his boots hard against the
split oaken planks beneath his feet, he liked to stomp
them with a rhythm, the same slick, pumping rhythm the
iron wheels made storming over the tracks. He liked those
boots, he got them off a dead miner, they were almost a
perfect fit, almost new when he pulled them from the
dead body; the miner must have bought them in Folsom
Town, maybe Placerville, couldn't have walked long on
them, barely a scuff mark, must have been green, one of
the ones pouring into and all over the Sierras, searching,
no 'timer would be caught dead in a pair of boots like
that, and wasn't. Now the boots were worn down,
cracked, split, but comfortable. He liked their feel as he
pounded them down. He hopped on them, worked into a
bounce, then a skip, finally he held his own dance, hopping, skipping, jumping in wide arched lengths on the bed
of the car, moving up and down its length, its width, sucking the air that smacked his face into his lungs, screaming

41

out his feathered song against the metallic roar of the slicing wheels on the slot of track, his lungs aching, bursting,
burning his tight throat in a flame of pain. His head
thrown back, he tried to best the sound of the screeching
steam whistle blowing up front of the bulky, slamming
cars, he tried to push his music above it, shatter it, leaving
only his song implanted in the mountains, the trace of its
memory, but it was a worthy opponent, a true opponent,
and as always, it beat him down, triumphed, he held the
last note against it as long as he could, then let it go, in
defeat. He beat his boots down in such crashing violent
thuds of anger that he lost his balance, tripped into the
motion of the Train itself, his body tossed flat on the
coarse wood, scraping the skin of his chin away from the
face, stopping his head at the edge of the thick wooden
platform. He stared straight down. The hot air from the
friction of churning wheels blowing hard into his face as
he watched the rocky ground flashing by with such gray
speed it seemed to merge into the smoothed intricate surface of the baskets his mother used to weave in the winter. In spring all his people would gather up the pinenuts
and drop them into the baskets, heaping them into tall
hard brownshelled mounds. He could see beyond the tight
strip of ground running next to the track, over and down
the side of the canyon split perfectly open like a redwood,
at the bottom a bright blue streak shot in a straight fierce
line, the blade that split the Earth. He watched the river
speeding in the opposite direction of the Train, but always
running even with it, the river that *they* call Truckee; hah,
his laugh came back in his ears, Truckee, an old quick-
eyed slow handed Paiute who was shot at Sutter's Fort by
a bartender from the place called New Orleans the year
the big Railroad machines first crossed the mountains,
they named it for him because he showed it to *them*, led
them to it first and *they* thought *they* discovered it from
him, when everyone knew it was in this part of the Sierra
a Washo river, always had been, always would be. He
laughed again, it made him feel the pain of his chin, he
lifted his head and could see a smear of crimson on the
rough wood. He touched the wound gently with his fin-

gers, the sudden sting made his head flinch. He pushed himself up, reached into the frayed pocket of his checked jacket that was given to him the night he got beat up in the town of Reno and pulled out his pocket-pistol, raised the thin glass bottle to his lips, sucked thickly at the warm whiskey until it was gone, then threw the bottle across the car into the cliff of mountain that banked closely on the opposite side. The Train lurched, he swore and spit some brown juice in front of his boots. The Train was slowing, braking down to take the sharp curve of track in front of it, the mass of steel and wood straining, swaying as it made the curve. He waited, watched until his car rounded the curve and he could see where the mountains opened up, set deep within them, the cold heart of a lake, flashing bluer, closer and deeper than the Sky above, the lake *they* called Donner, the lake he called *Winiaho*, the lake that caused the ghost of his father to walk the hard land of his dreams, for it was there that Gayabuc saw *them* eat of *their* own flesh and taught of *their* ways to his son so that he would always beware. He gave a great laugh as he watched smoke rising from the cabins through the trees on the clear lakeshore below in the sharp distance, the laugh boiled in him, brought out the strange melancholy of the ancient Birds, their sweet, tonguebeaked voices bubbling up through his lips, leaping into the virgin air in joyous direct attempt of a simple triumph. The sound was strong now, again the iron challenge of the Train had been taken up and the implacable rhythm of its natural opposite sought its equal in a place now foreign. The battle raged as the Train continued rambling on along the cut of track etched high up on the edge of the plunging mountainside, the man's eyes sunk in the water off to the side far down in front of him, then both funneled into darkness, taking their sounds with them as the Train moved forward into the snowsheds, the planks of timbers boxed over the tracks for protection, anchored against the mountain, a forest of cut and constructed wood built by countless men, stretching for miles where the snow is piled fiercely, driven in crushing slides during winter, shutting out almost all trace of day, of Sky. The cold air in the

confined horizontal shaft thundered with the sound of the
train, the man's song stabbing in bursts of echoes against
the boarded walls, each successive wave becoming weaker,
ebbing through the chinks in the towering ceiling where
slices of light broke through, dissolved in the obscure interior. When the Train broke from the tunnel into the sudden flare of Sunlight it pointed down the mountain toward
the lake and the man did not notice that he was once
more in the open. He sat, his large body hunched in the
middle of the exposed platform, the song gone from his
lips.

The yellowmen were everywhere. All along the track in
straight lines as far as his eyes could see were the yellowmen, their bare backs bent in silence, building in the glare
of mountain Sun. They did not look up as the Train rolled
slowly between them, they paid no attention to the Indian
sat hunched in the middle of one flatbed car, watching
their every move through squinted eyes deep in his face,
they noticed nothing as the Train moved along the shore of
the lake, through the open rolling meadow, into the tall pine,
then where the pines had been cut to build the town, passing the boarding houses, hotels, saloons, and shacks
clumped together in the sheltered canyon of the river, the
town that fed the men to the Railroad yards. The Train
slowed to a stop, was switched to another track, the air
was thick with shouts, the heavy metal sound of machin-
ery, boxcars stood, square and bulky, men moving to and
away from them, the noise from the town drove into and
above all other sounds, roaring completely over the rush
of water in the river on the far side of the tracks. The Indian sat, he had not moved in the motion around him, he
waited, he waited in the Sun until a man made his way
along the Train, a blue-billed cap on his bald head, a gold
badge on the collar of his blue shirt, at each car he
paused, studied it, then wrote hurriedly in a notebook,
when he came to the Indian he slapped the back of his
neck and spat a thick brown syrup into the weeds sprouting from under the iron rail of track and grinned.

"How's bout it Cap'n, your lil pic-a-nic about over and
done?"

The Indian stood up. "Mr. Dolay, you got a drink for the Cappin. That's one long dry, dirty, dusty haul clear to up here from Dutchflats."

"Shore is now Cap'n, a man would have to be three parts dead in the head or have the brains of a muleass to be goin about workin in it with a heavy jacket like that on his back."

"It's the only one I got."

"Why don't you leave it up to the hotel?"

"Somebodied steal it from the Cappin."

"Hah!" The man's laugh flew into the air with wet bits of tobacco, "That there is your one big downfall Cap'n, no trust, you ain't got no trust in your fellow man, noblest creature that's ever sat down to a bar and you got no more trust in 'em than your own self. You'll never make it along in this world with that there idea, I'm tellin you the straight side of it Cap'n, you got to change your ways if you aim a whole lot to get along with civilized men."

"You got that drink for me Mr. Dolay?"

"Like I was continuin fore you broke me off Cap'n, rudeness is another bad trait you got, men has to know polite conversation, give and take, I was sayin when you took instead of give that it's just about break-time for me. I been goin pretty hard at it all day about and I was just sayin to myself fore I spotted you siesta'in up there in the sun, 'Arthur, Arthur Dolay,' I was sayin to myself. 'Why don't you take it easy and quit drivin yourself, have a sit-down in the shade of the next car and take a little refresh-mint.' How's that idea peal to you Cap'n?" he stared up, one eye closed to the sun, the other fixed on the Indian.

"Peals to me 'bout the same way it peals to you. You got your pocket pistol?"

"Have you ever knowed me not to pack it?"

The Indian leaped down, "No I ain't never Mr. Dolay. Let's get at it."

"Hold on there," the man took a step backwards, the other eye popping open. "Nother thing you got to learn is politeness, can't you never get that fixed in your mind right? You ain't never goin to be fit for the society of this here town of Truckee, let alone nowhere else."

"But I ain't goin nowhere else."

"Shore you're goin somewheres else, every man goes somewheres else, even Indians, it's natural, you're young, you just don't know it yet. You're goin somewheres else."

"The only place I want to go right now is in the shade to have a drink."

"Dammit, ain't you ever to learn, that's just like an Indian, invitin hisself right into your own house for Sunday dinner."

"Forget it then Mr. Dolay," the Indian shoved his hands in his pockets and turned. "I'll go get my own pay and drink it."

"Hold on now Cap'n," the man spit loudly, the juice hitting into the dry weeds, clinging. "I didn't say I wasn't goin to invite you, I just wanted to point out some education missin out of your background, it's that an Indian's got so much educatin to be done on him that sometimes it takes a whole long while before things get done. Here," he pulled a bottle from beneath his belt, took a long slow drink and held it out, wiping his mouth.

The Indian took the bottle and tipped it to his lips. "Thanks Mr. Dolay." He handed it back.

"Why don't we sit down in the shade of that car over there, it's a bit out of the way, maybe none of the boys'll spot us and come a bummer."

They sat down, resting their shoulders against the cool thick iron wheel. The man took a steady, hard drink, the Indian watched the flesh of the adam's apple bob up and down in a throb as the liquid passed through the throat, then he took the bottle and gulped at the clear whiskey.

"Mormon women," the man spat in front of him, leaving a brown stain on the earth. "Mormon women," he spoke the words louder and spat twice as hard.

"What about Mormon women?" the Indian asked, passing the bottle back.

"Mormon women," the man took another swig as if to wash the words down. "Mormon women stink."

"I wouldn't know, Mr. Dolay," the Indian took the bottle back. "I ain't never snuck up close enough to one to get in a good smell, but if you say it's so I'll take your word for it."

"Word on it hell, I'm a thority on it."

"You know a lot of things alright."

"But I know Mormon women best of all."

The Indian drank again, shook his head in agreement, decided to ask why but didn't.

"Because I married one Mormon woman, that's why."

"And she stinks?"

"Don't you offend my wife, Indian," the man grabbed the bottle back and hugged it to his chest.

"I ain't Mr. Dolay, I was just askin a question," the Indian dropped his hands in his lap with a moan.

"Oh, questions is different, education is a fine thing, specially for an Indian. How old are you anyways?"

"How old?" the Indian's face went blank.

"Yah, how many years you been alive?"

"I don't know, I never thought about it."

"Well when was you born? You remember that much do you?"

"No, I don't remember it."

"Indian, what do you remember?"

"I don't know, I never thought a whole lot on it. What I done I done, I guess."

"How old do you think you are? Here, gimme that bottle back fore you hog it all down."

"You mean in years?"

"I shore don't mean in coon's age."

"Twenty-five, thirty maybe."

"Twenty-five or thirty, you can't never be too young to learn boy, never too young. I'm not such an old man myself you know, fifty-two this winter past. I seen a bit in my time though, went through alotta country, some places civilized man never even seen before. This here country is the worst I ever been in, desert on one side, big ocean on the other, so a man ends up stuck in the middle on mountains so steep you almost fall on your face soon as you take a step. Lotta money in this country though, big money. I come here with the first, in '48 believe it was, headed this way before that but got sidetracked over in Salt Lake town, you ever been there Cap'n? No, I wouldn't think so. Terrible place, nothin but salt and muck and Mormons. Mormons say they developed that place, hah, developed, I think they grew right up out of the sea that dried up there years back in time. They've developed that place so well a man can't find a drink even if he was to hock his hide, and no gamblin, no money either, not one penny to be made, people all live like Diggers, scroungin and pokin around in that dry dirt praying for a miracle of somethin to grow, and when it finally do they got to eat it up quick as you like and say another mouthful of prayers just to keep alive so's they can scrounge around some more. I come into that town from Dakota country, just passin through as quick as I could, big storm was blowin up, blizzards whoppin everythin for a hundred miles around, I barely come through the Rockies with my skin in one piece, couldn't see the town when I come to it, snow was so thick, if I had I would a kept on goin blizzard or no, but anyways I put up in a hotel there, hah," he slapped his knee and spit. "Hotel! Some folks' house; had put up a sign in the front window, Rooms To Let By Night Or Day. So I went on in to dry my bones and gives em my cash for the night. Weren't no other boys puttin up there cept one of these kind we're gettin from I-talie, can't hardly speak no more than a half word of English like most Indians up around here. Well, when I get in there the whole family is sittin down to dinner, the I-talie boy with em, and the father is prayin, they're all there with their heads bowed for the longest time, the father goin on about this and that thing, thankin for the meal, and it weren't nothin to be prayin up that much about I'm here to tell you, about two seconds worth of prayer would have covered that meal for thanks and for shore the next twenty to come, but the father kept on mumblin, wantin to make shore there were no one last thing left on that table that would be hot, and me I'm gettin cramps in my legs and my neck got a big crook in it from being humble and still he goes right on ahead as if God hisself were sittin right across the table from him; it weren't, it were the I-talie, and when the father finishes up he shouts out AMEN and starts makin

funny signs all over his face and chest like he was salutin
his Pope and the father shouts out even louder than the
I-talie boy had, Ain't no Cath-O-Lick prayers lowed at
Mormin table, this here's Mormin food, got from a Mormin God and growed by Mormin hands and Cath-O-Licks
ain't got nothin to do with it, his whole head done burned
brighter than the coals in the fireplace and he was jabbin
his fork in the air as if he were gonna stab and run every
Cath-O-Lick ghost outta the room that the I-talie boy
brought in with him, and his wife come over and begun
talkin in such a low voice that I had to strain my ears to
hear and if what she said made any sense atall it would
never be heard noways, finally she got him sat down, his
chest heavin in and out like a bellows and he begun shou-
tin that he may be poor and have to take in lodgers but he
don't have to stand for no Romans sayin foreign words
over Mormin food, and the food were ruint for him and
he weren't going to touch it long as the I-talie boy was in
the room, then it was the I-talie got up and says he is
shore sorry bout being a bother and causin the trouble he
had, but nobody understood him anyways and the mother
was pushin him back where he begun, her mouth movin
fast but the words comin slow so he couldn't hear even if
it would make sense, and the whole time I'm lookin at
them and down at my Mormon dinner that's been prayed
at and fought over and if you ever ain't looked at a Mormon dinner you ain't missed one apple fallin. Potatoes,
cold potatoes, mashed, sliced, peeled, unpeeled, cut, twisted, baked and fried. I was lookin at those potatoes knowin
that if I didn't get to them soon I would be dead of star-
vin, and when I took my eyes offn them I sees the Mormon mother is shovin whole forkfuls of potatoes into the
I-talie's mouth, and every time he finishes swallowin a
mouthful and begins gulpin air she shoves another heap
full into him. So I just figure out it's time we could all eat
now and it don't take me more than thirty seconds of a
horsetail swish to swoop up those potatoes and pack em in
my stomach for later use, and I'm done for the rest hardly
begun so's when I looked up again the mother's still pum-
pin the I-talie boy up, and the father's just a-sittin there,

breathin hard but with his hands folded up on his lap and the cold heap of untouched potatoes heaped in front of him. I had the first time to look about me and see who else I was eatin dinner with. Damn!" He slapped at the air in front of him, "They grow bigger hossflies in these mountains than those Egyps grow elephants. Girls, that's all there was, this Mormon had five daughters, no wonder they got run outta so many places, all they can rear is females, then they got to marry four apiece just to keep em happy. And have you ever seen a Mormon woman? No, course not. Hah! Let me tell you Cap'n, sittin around me at that table was the most ugliest creatures that ever had a dress tied on it, uglier even than a lot of your squaw-women you bucks keep hidden up around here. A Mormon woman has the body of a potato fed ox and the face of a seagull. Mormon women bulged right up out of the salt in that Utah land like a blight rollin round like a loose barrel of molasses. And slow. Slow! It takes them a half an hour to blink. So having finished my dinner and all, I just sat around gazin at em, givin em the up and down and across, my eyes searchin all over em, tryin to find some woman beneath all that bulk, some life, but my gaze sunk like a stone in all that mud. There was this one there, probably the oldest, thirty maybe, the youngest bein about fifteen, she had all this hair piled right on top of her head like straw in wet mortar slapped on a brick, she was sittin there like she growed right up out of the chair and was about to collapse it, had the look of her father in the face, her lips were movin, just slight you know, no sound, as if she were talkin to herself what she was thinkin and didn't think nobodied noticed, or care even. I thought that was pretty funny so I was about to give out a big laugh and all that came up was a potato burp, the mother dropped the fork right out of the I-talie's face, it clanged down on the plate like a bell and everyone just gaped at me with their faces hangin out, cept the father and this one girl with the lips movin. Finally, I got so tired of nobody sayin nothin or doin nothin that I thought I'd just get things started. Scuse me, folks, I says, then once again the mother was spoonin into the I-talie and a couple of the girls had finished up on their potatoes and were talkin back and forth in slow voices that even they couldn't hear. Me, I was watchin those lips movin and it got to botherin me, like somethin was agoin on that I wasn't being let in on so I decided to see what would happen if I kicked her under the table, nothin did so I kicked her again a little harder and she still didn't flinch, so I really cocked one and shot it out, figgered it'd register through all that hanging flesh, but it didn't, instead the father turned to me and says nice and polite as you please, If you kick me once more I'm going to toss you out in the snow, Christians are not kickers. And once again the room got real still and they left it up to me to get the conversation rollin so I says, Scuse me folks. They then all turned away and took up where they left off. I was tired of speech makin so I settled back in my chair and studied real hard on what the movin lips were sayin, figgered if I had the answer to that I'd learn a whole lot bout Mormon women and their workin insides, but I couldn't and everybody was gettin up, the women clearin off the table, cept the father's plate, and me and the I-talie was just standin around, there weren't bein but the one room, all the others had been made into bedrooms. I saw the movin lips had got up too, takin up a big portion of the room, towerin over all the other girls, her hair almost touchin the ceilin and spendin ten minutes to pick up a knife and carry it away, so I decided I'd go over and give her a pinch and see if she would budge or give out a sound, so I mosied in her direction and when I come up on her with her back to me I says, Scuse me folks, but do you have one of them checkerboard games or is that against Mormon thinkin? At the same time I had a hunk of her behind between my thumb and finger and squeezin with all I had like one of them oranges. No human bein makes a sound like the one that blasted out of them lungs, it just knocked the whole sound of the blizzard outside back up where it came from, almost tore the roof right off the rafters and throwed me and the I-talie boy flat up agin the wall. When the blast was gone and me and the I-talie couldn't hear nothin but ringin like church bells there came four words that even

drove that sound out of our heads. *Daddy! I been spoiled!*
Well I don't have to tell you Cap'n that I was a bit out of
line being how the situation was, but I hadn't ever ruint
any girls before and I was to be shore I wasn't about to
begin then, a little bruised flesh maybe, but that ain't never spoilt the fruit. So when everything quieted on down,
cept movin lips, she was set down at the table with her
face in her hands blubberin on so it sounded like waves
slappin up agin a ship. I said nice and loud so ever one
could hear good, even her, Scuse me folks, I musta
slipped. Stranger, the father stood up slow, his hands still
folded and hangin in front of him like a net. Stranger, he
says, like the word was stokin up the red in his face, I
don't have no notion where you hail from, nor who your
folks are, or what your religious ways are about, but I do
know where you are now. Mormin country stranger, and
case you ain't heard the word yet we treat our women
with Christian respect, respect for their feminine ways an
sex, an the act you just done violated upon the Godgiven
right of purity bestowed for every woman in His Kingdom an is a sin of the highest degree agin His very own.
His fingers was turnin white he was pullin that net so
tight, an because we're Christian practicing folk we believe in just punishment for wrong doings. Stranger, you
better come along with me peaceful like to the town jail
so's you can await trial for the ugly deed you performed
in my house, this is a wholesome community and wild animals like yourself are usually locked up for fifteen years
of hard labor to the benefit of all mankind. Well Cap'n,
what you think I said to that, it was a tight fit all right.
Scuse me, I says, beggin your humble pardon Mister, but
I'm a Christian boy myself, not like this I-talie boy here,
but A-mer-i-can Sunday school kind, an I see your ways
clear as the Light Itself, but Mister, you raised a batch o
the most pretty gals this wanderin boy has ever had the
privilege of feastin his eyes on, an when I sees your older
daughter my heart bout jumped right up through my
mouth and I was so lightheaded with what I seen I just
lost all natural control of decent behavior! So Cap'n, I
stayed around in that Salt Lake town for five years with

my new wife, each year she's a ploppin out another girl for me, you cain't beat down that Mormon blood, Cap'n, it's too thick, sucks the life right out of your hide. What happin then was in '48 ol movin lips hears bout John Marshall an she says, Arthur, lets us pull up stakes and move on over to California an get some that gold lying around over there, we got a head start on most folks. You bet I tore outta that Mormon town in two days, thought I'd be pullin potatoes out of that country for the rest of my life. I pretty near galloped our wagon clear cross the desert tryin to get to where I was going to begin with. Thing is when I finally got out to this country I realized it weren't no prize neither. I never seen so many people runnin round bumpin into one nother, shootin one nother, cheatin. I got out, let me tell you Cap'n, I got right out of that game, didn't have a penny, hiked roun all these Sierras for two years waitin to catch a big one by the tail, but I got out, moved the family down to Placerville and worked in the new Im-porium store they put up there, then they started up this here big railroad, Trans-Continental they said it was going to be and I hired on as a whipjack over the coolies they was sailin in here from China country, did that for many years, makin shore ol John would work his tail, then they decided I was a promotion an give me this official number job with a badge, one of the highest up I am Cap'n, give the boys around here somethin to shoot for, even so it ain't enough to feed eight women on. Ah, that's a shame, now there's a cryin sight," he held the bottle out top down, staring through the murky brown glass. "That's all there is for a hard workin man, our vacation time is up." He threw the bottle, watched it smash into the track across from him, the glass shattering on the iron rail. "Cap'n, let's you and me get on with our work," he stretched his arms quickly in the air as if he was ready to flap off. "Still on the Comp'ny's time y'know. Got to watch out for the Comp'ny Cap'n, always watch out for your better interests. Where's your people?"

"Back by the caboose."

"Let's mosie down there."

They walked the long line of idle squared cars, the man pausing to write in his notebook at each, the Indian, hands in his pockets, kicking at the oil blackened rocks.

"This the one," the man asked, closing his notebook with a slap at the last car.

"Looks like it," the Indian nodded.

"Open her up then.".

The Indian pulled the heavy holding board out of its slot, then shoved at one of the two high doors, pushing it back along the creaking rollers; the hot air from inside the car rushed out through the black opening. The Indian stepped back, wiped the sweat off his forehead and waved the hot air away from his face.

"Well Cap'n, are they in there or ain't they in there," the man thumped the notebook against his leg as he strained to see into the black opening, not taking one step closer to it.

"It's the one I put em in Mr. Dolay. I don't see how they would of got out."

"I can see em now Cap'n, somethin is movin in there anyways."

Out of the black came a form, a woman, her face wet, her twisted, matted hair hanging over the forehead, to the sides, falling on the shoulders like strips of black knotted rags. She spoke. The words came up lightly from her throat, shaped and held in the air like cuts of crystal, she moved no further, as if afraid to destroy the words.

"What did she say Cap'n," the man turned away from the woman, looked only at the Indian in front of him.

"She says they're very happy the journey is over, it is long, it is hot, it is dry."

"Ain't that nice," the man knocked a finger against the blue cap and grinned. "You speak to them and tell them that the Railroad is pleased they enjoyed the trip and that they have a friend in the Railroad and any time we can give em a ride to a place where the pigweed grows thick along the tracks and they can pick it we shore will."

The Indian spoke to the woman and she disappeared back into the darkness; a man came out where the woman disappeared, he had a fur headpiece pulled over the top of

his cropped black hair and only one arm, he slipped down
out of the doorway and moved off through the cars, saying nothing to the other Indian. The woman reappeared, a
child strapped to her back on a board crossed with leather, a basket in one arm, packed thick with weeds. Behind
her, others came, all carrying the large baskets, little children with fat brown faces and frail old bright haired men.
The Indian watched this silent procession from the black
hole until the slowest had slid into the Sunlight and
moved away.

"That about all of em Cap'n?" the man asked, staring
at the hole as he impatiently rapped his fingers against the
notebook.

"Should be, I'll take a look." The Indian jumped up
through the black hole, the man could hear his footsteps,
wooden, hollow, coming from within. "That's it," the Indian jumped back out into the light. "They're all gone."

"Shut er up."

He slid the door back even with the other and lifted the
board into place behind its slots.

"Make shore they all go home. The Comp'ny don't like
strange Indians hanging round the yard." The man walked
toward the caboose, then turned, the pages of the notebook fluttering under his thumb, "Come round tomorrow
for a couple a bits and some whiskey for your trouble."

The Indian watched the man move off, put his hands in
his pockets and made his way across the rows of tracks,
between and around the cars, heading from the town toward the river running at the bottom of the slope that an-
gled away from the tracks. He passed the dump, saw the
brownskinned women picking their way nimbly over the
discarded trash of the town, he saw his mother, standing
on one of the cluttered piles, a rag of bandanna tied on
her face across the nose, digging in the waste. She did not
notice him and he did not call, he moved noiselessly past,
the sound from the Trains and town above was dying
quickly as he neared the river, going through a stand of
pines which hadn't all been cut. There were houses about
him now, strips of frayed canvas which had been begged
or painstakingly saved from the dump, stretched over

sturdy stick frames open to the Sky. He went beyond
these, closer to the river where there was one shack built
up out of broken crate boards from the railroad yard. He
brushed back the flour sack covering the small opening on
one side and entered his house. It was dark, there were no
windows, he could see his brother sitting crosslegged on
the dirt floor in the shadows of a corner, his shirt off, the
stub of his arm sticking out from the shoulder, deep
brown and twisted, like half a broken Bird's wing. His
brother said nothing. He could feel the eyes on him,
searching around his face. He moved in the cool shadows,
felt under the Rabbit blanket, the *dayoliti*, piled softly on
the hard dirt, the blanket made by the hands of his grandfather, a Rabbit Boss, passed to his father. Gayabuc, who
did not have it when they found him, his body frozen in
the snow, a naked brown outline. Now it was his, the first
born. He reached beneath its softness, felt the smoothed
glass surface of a bottle, brought it out, yanked the cork
from the neck with his teeth and took a drink that burned
at his throat. Ahhhh, he let the sigh into the close room
and rested against the rough boarded wall.

"*Musege.*"

The word floated in the air, seeking a way out of the
tightness, hugging at the earthen floor, growing to fill the
space.

"*Musege!*"

He could see the top half of his brother's body move,
jerk forward in its shadow, slinging the word out from between his lips like a stone.

"*Musege,* white beast, mad white beast, wild man!"

The words slashed up against him, against the wall behind; he took another drink.

"I spit on you *Musege,*" his brother's head whipped, the
wet white ball hissing across the room, striking the earth
in front of his boots.

"Do you want a drink," he stretched the bottle out in
front of him.

"I do not drink *Musege,*" the brother leaned back, his
hand pressed hard against the dirt floor.

"Might do you some good."

"I have been done all the good I ever want from you and your kind, madman."

"*They* stole away most of what we had when *they* came, at least *they* brought something along to make us forget."

"Hah! Listen to the *Musege*. Forget, hah! He thinks he's Washo, thinks he has something to forget. Remember this, *Musege*, remember this always, you are white, your heart pumps white, not Washo."

"I am a Washo son," he spoke the words calmly through wet lips. "I am born Washo. I die Washo."

"You are already a dead Washo."

"I am respected by the people."

"Hah! Listen to the wild Bear. You are not respected, you are feared."

"The people do not have to stay around me, they can move away, such is the path of our fathers."

"The people do not stay because of you, they stay because of the dump."

"Many others still gather and hunt on the land, the mountains are many and large, there is room for all who want."

"Many others die in the mountains, are run away, you know this, you do not fool me, sly, mad Bear. *They* call you Captain, Captain Rex, because you get the people to do what *they* want. You can keep the people away from *them*."

"I keep *them* away from the people."

"Yes! That is true. You keep *them* away from the people so you are the only one *they* go to when *they* need favors. Many favors you have to give of the people's land."

"I give, not take favors, only money."

"You take only money. Only money while they take the land! Rip open its skin, plunge huge wooden holes into its heart, slaughter its trees!"

"You are the fool, Brother," he took another drink, sloshing the warm liquid around his mouth, swallowing it with a gulp. "Foolish because you sit and hate me and talk about what *they* do; if you are so brave you should join the Shoshone, take what you think was taken from you."

"With one arm!"

He could see his brother lean sharply forward in the shadow.

"One arm I have! What is a man with one arm! You— you chopped my arm off!"

"You went of your own choosing."

"I was a fool. I did not know *their* ways. You knew! You knew from the beginning. You could have stopped me!"

"I knew no more than you."

"Liar! Lying Bear. You are the one that took the paper and money from the man with the shiny hat. You are the one who put your sign on the paper. Then you gave me the paper and half the money and told me to go with *them*, that I would learn *their* ways. That I could come back and teach the people much. And *they* sent me across the desert and over the mountains of rock to a strange land where men were killing. *They* tried to kill me. But I fooled *them*. I fooled you. *They* only got my arm. My arm! Do you hear. I am still alive!" His body rose, the head bumping the ceiling. "Hah! Only my arm!" The words rushed before him as he sliced across the room, slapping the bottle from his brother's hand, the glass slamming against the wood wall, the liquid oozing out, sinking into the earth. "You chopped it off! Blew it off with a cannon!" He grabbed his brother with his one hand, pulling him up by the jacket and throwing him against the wall, the back of his hand whipping through the shadows, slapping into the face. "Coward! *Musege!*" He spat the words. "White killer!" The words followed behind the others, crashing into them as his brother grabbed the hard stump, twisted and spun him around in the shadows, knocking him flat on his back and stomping in two steps from the room.

"Oh, Cappin, we have been waiting for you. We don't like to intrude on family get togethers. We just been waitin here for you to finish."

He looked up at the Paiute sitting on the spotted horse,

the leather of the saddle creaking as his light body swayed gently.

"What do you want?" He asked the question of the other two Indians, one holding a rope to a horse behind his own.

"Biz-niz, Cappin, only biz-niz," the first answered, adjusting the three long feathers under his headband.

"I don't want any business with you. The last time we went out I nearly got shot. What kind of business is this?"

"John. Same as last," the first gave a short chuckle. "Only this time we been watchin long enough to determine just how many there be."

"Twenty," one of the others added.

"Twenty, Max Squirrel. I knew Paiutes was slow thinkin, but not two weeks slow."

"They got no gun, Cappin."

"None that you can see you mean."

"None."

"How long you been watchin?"

"Almost a week."

"An they ain't seen you in a week of days?"

"Nope, we stayed low on our bellies."

"Where?"

"Bout four hours in from Emigrant Gap."

"That's a day and a half."

"At least."

"Do they got anything?"

"We seen it."

"John sure knows where to hunt it, any place there ain't no Whites."

"Not too many Whites looking after it for miles in any direction, gave up on it long ago."

"You think we can pull it up on twenty, Squirrel?"

Squirrel snorted through his flat broad nose, making a sound like a beaver slapping his tail on the water. "John ain't nothin but a squaw, don't have nothin in him but rice. Don't have to worry none about twenty Johns, they never kill an Indian like a White would."

"I know that." Captain Rex jammed his hands in his

pockets. "But is the camp laid out so that four of us can take it?"

"Just as if we planned it," he leaned over in his saddle. "You cashin in Cappin?"

Captain Rex took a step forward, put a finger on the throat of the spotted horse, "Where did you steal these?"

"Carson Meadows."

"How long?"

"Three days. We figured we'd maybe leave them for John if we weren't in too much of a hurry, make him a trade."

"Better trade fast," Captain Rex grabbed a handful of mane on the spare horse and swung himself up, "or we're going to be four dead Indians."

They rode out of the camp along the river, up and across the tracks, out of the canyon, keeping to the ridge, dropping into a valley, heading northwest along a small stream. They went straight through the night, working the horses in between the trees from the light of the moon, stopping only when the horses demanded. As morning broke they crossed the dirt road that cut between the high mountains into the place called Emigrant Gap. It was late afternoon when they came into the Chinese camp, jumped from their horses, Captain Rex and Squirrel moving forward, the two Paiutes behind with drawn bows.

"John!" Squirrel shouted out in the clearing of the trees at the six Chinese who froze in their bent positions.

"Ah, welcome, welcome Indian mans," one of the Chinese stood, his face opening in a smile, holding the pick with which he had been hacking the rock. "Welcome to our camp Indian mans," he bowed, two, three, six times, almost touching his forehead to the stony ground, his waistlength braided hair swinging in front of him, swishing back and forth. "You want Melican coffee? We got plenty Melican coffee." He stood up again, his thin shoulders folded in like paper, the tiny hands knotted together in a pale ball.

"Hey John! What you doin on Paiute land? This all Paiute land and I'm the one Paiute Cappin Chief!"

"Me workin. Workin hard. Have deed to claim this

land now belong to us who workin hard on it. Who you say you are? Show-shone? This no Show-shone land, they land far away," he pointed a bony finger behind him. "Far, far away, Show-shone land," he jabbed the finger at the air to show just how great a distance it was. "Far away."

"Paiute Cappin Chief, John, I said I was the one Paiute Cappin. How you file claim over this land if you got no ears, John? No ears, no man. This my land," he made a large circle with his hand. "All of it, John."

"Melican Cappin come by one, two day ago. He say, John, this my land, me collect tax from you. Twenty dollah, John give twenty dollah for one thirty days."

"Damn Merican man," Squirrel stamped the heel of his moccasined foot at the ground. "Damn, damn, damn," he kicked at a stone. "Me the Cappin John, the one Paiute Cappin. Merican man trick you. Me kill Merican man, me kill plenty Merican man in only one day. Me want tax from you. It ain't Cappin's fault if you stupid and pay out to the wrong one."

The Chinese bowed his head, rubbed hard at his chin, closed his eyes tight as if he were concentrating on the birds singing in the trees. "How much you want?" He quickly looked up, the hands disappearing into the sides of his tattered silk smock.

"Fifty-five dollars for one fifteen days."

"You got wrong Chinaman, Cappin. Me no got fifty-five. Me poor, make no dollah chippin all day at rock Sorry alot Cappin, poor Chinaman, Melican man he catch him and tax all his dollah, no leave none. Chinaman no got fifty-five," he bowed slow and deep.

"John!" Squirrel screamed, the word jerking the bowed Chinese up as if he were on a string. "You pay to me the one Paiute Cappin, fifty-five dollars or me study on killing all you right now on my land. Sabe!"

"No got tax money, Cappin, so sad," he bowed again, moving backwards as he bobbed up and down. The two Paiutes stepped forward, bows pulled, an extra arrow clenched tight between their teeth. "So sad, Cappin, feel so sad," he kept bobbing, backed into the other Chinese clumped together like cloth covered sticks. He scattered them apart, they raised their picks and shovels high overhead, furious sounds leaping from their throats, then charged the intruders behind a shield of sound, the bombardment of shouts released more Chinese slipping from behind rocks and trees, beating gongs, clanking stones against kettles, some with faces puffed up full of air like yellow balloons as they shrieked one note of battle on wooden flutes, others setting their faces in fearful attitudes, howling like wounded dogs, throwing their bodies about as if an invisible foe was punching their bodies about like bags of straw. Darting red tongues in and out between their thin lips like snakes, hunching on the ground like whistling skinny frogs, waddling like ducks, arms stretched out and flapping, turning somersaults, their braided hair slashing about like tails, attacking, circling, revealing to the attackers their front line of defense, they pushed the enemy into a tight knot, surrounded by hideous howls, drawing menacingly close, close enough for Squirrel to reach out and punch a twirling shrieking figure behind the neck, sprawling him across the clearing. Ending all cry of battle the warriors dropped their implements of terror, retreated into a cowering mass, balled up with hands behind their heads.

"Hah!" Squirrel's laugh ripped out at the whimpering pile of bodies. H . . . h . . hey John," he tried to catch his breath. "You shore make one scary killer—Hah! John!" His face turned hard, the sharp black eyes growing tight and mean, "Paiute Cappin wants one fifty-five dollars, pronto!" He moved forward.

"Not so fast Captain," the voice came from a boulder, a tall Chinese stepped around the side, a black cap pulled hard on his head, a red silk robe flowing to the ground, a rifle pointed at the Indians. "Don't try to jump this gun, Captain. It's got enough to drive a six inch hole through all four of you," he raised the rifle higher, a finger on the trigger. "We've had enough of your kind, tax collectors, red or white, it makes no difference, you think you can just walk in and take from the Chinaman Squaw anytime you get the taste for it but—"

The arrow stuck in his heart, the snap of the Paiute's bow string vibrating in the silence of the clearing, the Chinese man falling like a red tower. The Indians watched the body. The sun had leveled with the trees, the clearing streaked with rays of gold.

"Time's up now John," Captain Rex strode over to the whimpering men. "You," he poked a finger into the quivering back of the one who talked in the beginning. "One fifty-five dollars, Merican, no tricks." The man did not move. "Now!" He jabbed the back harder, it did not straighten. He pulled the smock up, unstrapping the money belt wrapped around the tiny exposed waist and slung it over his shoulder.

"Mister Indian Man," the Chinese turned his head up, tears rolling from the slits of his eyes down the smooth face. "He no have bullet, he no shoot Indian Man."

Captain Rex went back to the horses; the others were mounted. "You shoot straight," he said to one of the Paiutes, and they rode off.

. . .

"It's five gold dollars to drink at this here stablishment for Injuns."

"We got five times ten a that and then some," Squirrel leaned over the polished oak counter and stared into the face that had half an unlit cigar clamped between its teeth.

"Put it up then," the bartender's words came around the cigar in a blurred lump.

The two Indians laid their money down, got their drinks and made their way through the crowded room, straining their eyes in the smoke blue air searching for some spare space. The tables jammed with men, elbows cocking and uncocking as they drained the glasses clutched tight in blistered fists. Not all were blistered, one pair was gloved, raising the glass daintily to pursed lips, taking the liquid in, meditatively, the man pushed back in the chair, eyes drifting in and out through the thick redwood raftered ceiling, wandering over the elk head that grew from the main wall, monstrous, glaring down through lucid amberglass eyes. The man fastened on the eyes, raised a finger to his thin nose and stroked it, let the finger run off the smooth bridge, touch the moustache, lips, caress the trim lines of the beard. He turned, looked straight at the two Indians, the one light on his feet, cased in stained leather shirt and pants, beaded sash around the waist, tight mean eyes. The other dressed heavier, large body, not quite fat, but you can't tell with an Indian, scar on the left cheek, eyes shot full of red. "You boys," the man raised a gloved finger in the air. "You boys," he shouted into the thick roar over the piano that pounded out songs by itself.

Captain Rex saw the gloved hand, the white broadcloth coat, just slightly frayed at the cuff. It was a Bummer. He nudged Squirrel, they shouldered their way through the pack of men separating them from the table.

"Ahhh," the Bummer stood, his back straight as a board, his checkered pants showing over the tabletop, tipping his high shiny black hat a fraction above the hairline. "Glad you boys could make it through that gang. Truckee is no place for a soul to be by himself to enjoy the quiet of his own good company with a decanter of excellent Cuban Rum. Cuban, that reminds me," his hand slipped inside the coat and came out with three thin cigars, "sit down boys, have a Cuban smoke." He handed them cigars as they sat, sliced off the tip of his own with a slender silver pocketknife, placed it between his lips, struck a match, held it a half inch in front of the tip and sucked the flame into the tobacco. "Hard to come by a good roll like this," the words glided from his mouth on slivers of smoke. "Light up boys, don't be bashful. That's right, smoke them right up, get some of that tropical jungle air in your lungs. What tribe you boys from?" He turned the cigar in his teeth, pointing it toward Captain Rex.

"Paiute," Squirrel answered. "I'm a redblooded Paiute."

"Is that so," the Bummer's eyes opened wide, the thick lashes beating into one another. "I didn't know there were any left. I thought we nabbed every little squaw between here and Sante Fe."

"I was born before you came," Squirrel lowered his eyes to the liquid in his glass.

"And you Injun, what tribe you from?"

"I ain't."

"You ain't, Ho, you're the funniest looking Swede I ever laid my eyes on. You got to hail from some tribe boy, all you Injuns do, that's your way."

"Washo. I'm Washo. We have no tribe."

"No tribe hell, that's the damndest thing I ever heard, no tribe, all you Injuns got tribes, that's the way you live. You must take me for green boy. Why an Injun without a tribe is like a bull with brass nipples."

"We go now Mister," Captain Rex pushed his chair out and stood.

"Hold on one minute boy," the Bummer reached down beside him, brought up a gold handled cane and stretched it across the table, pushing the tip lightly against the Indian's neck. "Just hold all your ponies down," he smiled, the lips pulled back exposing the two front teeth capped with the same metal as the cane handle. "Sit yourself down Injun boy and behave like a Whiteman. You Injuns get more uppity everyday. Think you can come and go as you please. Don't have a stone's idea of how much you owe us. Sit down I said," he poked the cane harder.

Captain Rex looked at the man with the gold metal shining in his gaping mouth and sat.

"That's right, now there's a good fellow. I see your drink's up. Tender!" He shouted without taking his eyes off the Indian. "You boys prospectors?"

"No we ain't, we just—"

"Shut up, boy. I was talking to this Injun here. You just keep your trap shut and finish on up your drink. Here comes the tender now." He settled back as the glasses were refilled, picked up his, holding it in front of Captain Rex. "Here's to a pleasant friendship Injun." He drank, watching over the rim of the glass to make certain the Indians followed his example. "Now then, what was it we was discussing? Yes, you was going to tell me if you was a prospector or not."

"I aint."

"You mean you aint now. All you Injuns are, you just aint saying, just waiting while we run around for years making a fool out of ourselves then you're going to walk on over and pick it all up, now that we give you something to buy with it and it's worth it to bend your back just once or twice stooping over to get it."

"I aint."

The Bummer put the cigar to his mouth again and drew deep, blowing a pile of smoke out, "That's a pity, you could make a fortune. I bet you know where that Gold Lake is up Downieville way."

"Never heard of it."

"I didn't ask you if you heard of it, I said I bet you know where it is."

"I never been there."

"Sure you have, all you Injuns have, you been all over this country. You know that lake's up there someplace by the Yuba, you know men been digging around that country for a long time now, trying to find that lake with gold glowing up from its bottom."

"I never been there."

"That's too bad for you Injun," the Bummer ground his cigar in the can in front of him. "You know Injun, I seen sights like that in my day. I was down in Trinidad country in '52 when old Mama Ocean herself was tossing up cartloads of golden nuggets on the sand. I seen it once and I aim to see it again. Everyone is shouting silver now, but that gold had just barely begun to be touched. It's still there where it always was and I'm cashing in. What do you think Injun? You think I'm going to cash in?"

"I wouldn't know."

"No," the Bummer looked at Captain Rex, his eyes riveted on the scar that slashed his cheek. "I guess you wouldn't. Then again," he winked, "maybe you would. What was it you said you did?"

"Nothin," Squirrel answered, setting his glass down. "We don't do nothin but lie round in the sun all day."

"I told you to shut up," the Bummer smiled his lips in a tight curve. "So shut up! You going to answer my question or not Injun?" He turned back to Captain Rex.

"Odd jobs."

"Is that a natural fact, odd jobs. Most Injuns can't even speak let alone learn how to do an odd job."

"We learned."

"I bet you did. What kind of odd jobs is it you do?"

"The odder the better," Squirrel laughed.

"I told you to shut up!" The Bummer jerked around. "If you make one more sound," he placed his hand lightly on the glistening handle of the cane, "I'm going to ram this right through one of your beady eyes, then you can have a glass one put in like that elk hanging up there on the wall; you'll see real good then."

Squirrel gulped the rest of his drink, his eyes rising to the elk.

"What kind of job is it you do Injun? You trying to play funny games with me? Make me repeat everything twice?"

"For the Iron Road I work," Captain Rex looked straight at the Bummer.

"What could you ever do for the Railroad?"

"Odd jobs."

"Don't get smart with me Injun boy, this little stick here can go through your eye as quick as it can through your sidekick's, it's not too choosy."

"I take the people on the Iron Road so that they can pick pigweed along the iron tracks."

"Pick pigweed, what the hell would someone want with a weed that only grows out from rocks and railroad tracks? What the hell could somebody do with it, let alone an Injun?"

"Eat it."

"You sure you're not playing games with me Injun boy?" The Bummer laid his gloved hand on the cane.

"You asked. I told."

"Now I'm going to ask again. What is it you do?"

"Odd jobs."

"Lookit you lying Injun," the Bummer leaned across the table. "You don't come in this barroom where they don't give a redman a drink for less than three dollars American. You don't come in this bar with gold jingling in your pockets an expect me to believe you just saved it up doing odd jobs. I ain't green Injun, so just you suppose you tell me where you and your sidekick come running into all those coins? If what you say the first time out don't set right with me I'm going to put this stick right through your head, sabe?"

"John."

"Where?"

"Back in behind the place called Emigrant Gap."

"That's true," the Bummer nodded. "John has been up in that part of the country. I done a little tax collecting myself, but you don't have the right to tax John, Injun boy. What you did was an illegal act. John has a claim on that land and he doesn't have to pay out one cent to you. You and your partner here could be hung up by your necks right outside in just a matter of minutes if I was to announce to these honest gents in this room that you tax collected off a legally deeded mine. You're in a pack of trouble Redman. You're in more trouble than you ever thought you could get in outside of your T-pee. Let's just examine your case. One, I could declare right now what a lawbreaker you are and you would be put to quick justice in short time, and the fairest I might add. Two, I could go for the district marshal who just happens to be in these parts right this moment over at Donner Lake and turn you over to him to atone for your sins against our mountain society. Three, you could ease your conscience and relieve yourselves of that burden of packing all that money about and simply transfer it to me to make certain it is transported back to the lawfully wronged owners. At last, number four, being a sportive man, I could invite you two boys outside and down the street for a little gambling. What do you say Injun boy, pick a number, anyone a winner."

"What kind of gamblin is your number four?"

"Ah my good fellow," his trim eyebrows raised high up into his forehead. "I should have known you were after my own heart itself, fair as I tried to lay it out, a true sport you are. *Badger*," his eyebrows came down, the smirk on his face melted by a scowl, *"Badger baiting."*

"In a box or barrel?"

"Barrel."

"What's the stakes?"

"Ten to one, on the dogs of course, dear boy."

"Do we get to throw our own bet?"

"Now don't be silly Injun boy, sport is sport, and you good fellow, have the badger. If you don't think it's right choose number one, two, or three. Hang or get yourself a chance at earning five hundred dollars American."

Captain Rex took a drink of whiskey, swishing the liquid around in his mouth with his tongue, the taste of alcohol rising in his nose.

"Make up your mind quick Injun boy."

Captain Rex swallowed, looked between the Bummer's eyes, at the delicate bridge of the nose. "Mister," he spoke slowly without moving his eyes, "your bet is on."

They made their way from the bar into the dust of the street, the man with the goldhandled cane walking jauntily in front, his stovepipe black hat tilted top his head at a truculent angle, the two Indians trotting behind. The man strode regally through the mob of noisy men flowing in hard dirty currents along the high boardwalk, streaming into others, islands of bodies back to back, with faces in newspapers, noses almost touching the printed words. He picked his way nimbly through the forces, adroitly darting in and out at a moment's opening, riding with this wave and that; a sleek racing boat, the two Indians in tow. He steamed down an alley, simply navigated through a squall of galloping horsedrawn wagons, drifted onto another boardwalk, a calm one, and proceeded down to the end where the town ceased, suddenly broke off, the mountains towering up in all directions. The gambling party made its way up a short rise to a small box of corral with men sitting around on the rooting planks like bears on a branch, dogs leashed beneath them, tugging at the sagging boards.

"John C. Luther!" One of the men dropped from his perch with a thump, the club of hand held out in greeting. "Where you been? We been sittin round here since before noon seein who could collect the most slivers in his behind."

"Very good, very good," the Bummer shook the offered club warmly. "I was fortunately detained up at the Silver Elk, couple of boys begged me to be let in on the proceedings. You know me Elliot, what a puddle of pudding I am beneath it all, never one to refuse a couple of boys some fun."

Elliot looked at the two Indians, his gaze going right between them. "One body is good as nother I spose, make for higher stakes." He turned back to the Bummer. "Why don't you come over with the men and have a snort. The badger ain't here yet."

"It's not!" The Bummer slammed the butt of his cane against the ground. "What's hold up Ike!"

"Caint find a barrel big enough to get the badger in," Elliot grinned. "He's a big un."

"Well then," the Bummer took the neatly folded silk handkerchief from his vest pocket, swirled it over the metal cane handle and replaced it. "We do have time for a bit of refreshment before the festivities. Boys," he nodded to the Indians. "Would you care to join us gents?"

"It would honor us," Squirrel accepted politely.

"He has a voice," the Bummer looked at Elliot in surprise. "He's been silent so long I was beginning to wonder if someone had slit his vocal cords, poor boy."

"I'm surprised he speaks English at all," Elliot's face grew into a sour mask of disapproval.

"Now you shouldn't go judging every creature by the color of its skin and the way it smells Elliot," the Bummer touched the end of his cane to the man's chin. "Don't be too hard on our boys here. They're educated, no longer simple heathens, coming up in the world."

"How bout that drink John C.?" Elliot shifted impatiently.

"That we must Elliot, first why don't you collect ten dollars apiece from these two boys for the privilege of refreshing themselves with us and for the advancement of their education."

Captain Rex reached in his pocket, put his hand around some coins and closed his fist, they felt hot, heavy like stones, he could feel the sweat on his face, beneath his arms, trickling cool down his sides, the sun burning through the trees on the back of his neck.

"Are you or are you not going to pay this gent for a privilege Injun boy," the Bummer asked loudly, looking down as he swirled the handkerchief on the metal again.

Captain Rex kept one of the coins in his palm and held it out. The man took it.

"I said ten dollars apiece," the Bummer glared at Squirrel. "You pay too. I thought you boys were smart, now it turns out you're proving me wrong, that's something I don't like."

Squirrel handed over his money.

The Indians walked up to the corral, the barking dogs tugging at their ropes, yanking their necks as they lunged at the intruders.

"Curious," the Bummer smiled. "Canines are not partial to Injun scents." He mounted the corral and sat rigidly, the two Indians getting up at his side. "Nice little gathering of spectators," he beamed, scanning the men sitting on every available space around the wooden box, their mouths opening only to jam in another bottle neck. Elliot handed him a filled brown bottle. "Pardon me," he held the bottle in front of the Indian next to him. "Would you be so kind as to free the opening of this decanter." Captain Rex yanked the cork with his teeth and spit it out. "Thanks very much," he took the bottle back, wiping the opening with his handkerchief then taking two swift gulps, he emptied half the contents. "Your turn, I believe," he offered the whiskey to the Indian who tipped it and drained it, tossing the empty glass to the dirt.

"What bout mine," Squirrel jabbed Captain Rex in the arm. "That was for the two of us."

"Nobody said nothin bout two. I just drank my share."

"Who do you think you are? Just what do you think you are?" Squirrel's tight eyes faded in his face, he grabbed the front of Captain Rex's jacket and tumbled him from the fence.

The laughter around the corral whirred through his head, pressuring, closing like a vise as he stood up. He could feel the sun, could feel it burn as his fist shot out,

knocking Squirrel in the chest, toppling him over backwards. He watched Squirrel fall, it was as if he himself
were falling, spinning, smashing into the dirt, the blood
pounding in his head, the Birds singing their songs, primi-
tive, antique sounds smouldering in his chest, welling up
through his throat, tearing from his mouth in ancestral
fury, the air of the corral conquered in the winging beat
of feathered relics, his head swung back and he sang in
the Sun.

"It's the badger!" The words split the sound in the corral, piercing the man who sang from dreams, submerging
the echo of time, the sound escaping into trees.

The buckboard slammed in by the man, the horses'
hooves throwing up dirt digging into the ground and
stopped. Two men struggled the large barrel off the back
of the wagon, working it to the ground, then turning the
team of horses around and riding out of the corral. The
men cheered, waving their hats in the air. The Bummer
strode to the middle of the clearing, put one gloved hand
on the barrel lid and held up the other for silence.

"Gents! If you please," he coughed into his gloved hand
and continued. "The game will now begin." The men fell
silent. "The rules are, as you know, that the game is divided evenly into three sections. You may bet on all sections,
or just the one of your personal choice. The first section is
that of drawing the beast out of the barrel, you bet on
whether the hounds will or won't. The second section begins when the beast is out, if the dogs can't bring him out
we'll kick the barrel over; this section will be individual
fights only, if you think you have the dog to beat him then
go it with him. The last section, if the beast survives, will
be against all dogs left. The odds in all sections are three
to one on the dogs. Mister Franks is going around pres-
ently to collect and record all wagers before the match; no
verbal bets will be taken while the game is progressing.
Remember you are at your honor in all occurring debts."

"What's your bet Injun?" the little man demanded, his
swollen eyes staring at Captain Rex behind thick glasses.

"I'm going with the dogs."

"House odds?"

"House odds."

"What's the name?"

"Rex, Cappin Rex."

"Last name?"

"Don't have none."

"What do you mean, don't have none," the little man's eyes jerked from his scribbling, his pencil poised over the black book. "You got to have one, ain't legal if you don't."

"Mister Franks," the Bummer appeared behind the little man. "I think I can speak for our friend here, he is with my party."

"Oh Mister John C., I didn't know," the little man apologized, his gaze dropping from the Indian. "I wouldn't have bothered him if I had known he was with you."

"You did right Mister Franks, all men here bet, now what's the problem with the Injun boy?"

"I was just recording his bet but he don't have a last name to go by, you told me to put down first and last names, no exceptions."

"That's right, I most assuredly did, a man must have two names, first and last, it's only Christian."

"Yes sir, it's certainly natural, even for an Injun."

"Most certainly so Mister Franks," the Bummer patted him on the shoulder. "Now then Injun boy, tell the man your name so he can put it down."

"Cappin Rex."

"Rex what?" the Bummer leaned against his cane.

"Rex nothin, that's all of it, that's all *they* gave me, that's all *they've* ever called me."

"They must of given you a full Christian name."

"I'm not Christian."

"We're all Christians here bud," the little man poked a finger in the Indian's face. "Injuns or not."

"Just put it down as it is, Mister Franks, the men are anxious for the game, we'll attend to it later."

"But Mister John C., I think we should get his full name," the little man licked the lead of his pencil nervously.

"I don't give a damn what you—"

"Birdsong. Call him Birdsong," Squirrel leaned over the corral fence, pointing his finger at Captain Rex. "Birdsong his name should be. Hah. He's always singing like some wild bird beast, like some crazy loco Injun!"

"Like some drunk Injun you mean," the Bummer smiled. "Put it down that way Mister Franks, Rex Birdsong. What's his bet?"

"House odds on the dogs."

"You lying cheating Injun," the Bummer's face filled with red, as he aimed his cane at the Indian's throat. "Ten to one Mister Franks, that's what this filthy Injun's bet is! Ten to one on the badger! Mark that down, and this one too," he poked the cane at Squirrel. "The same odds. Get their money." He swung the cane again at Captain Rex, "And I'll settle with you later." He turned his back and moved to the barrel, holding his hands up, "Gents, all opening bets have been covered! Mister Elliot, would you please commence!"

Elliot came to the center, "Get all those dogs in here pronto!" He shouted at the men standing by the tied dogs straining at their ropes. "They smell that cute lil badger," he laughed.

The men brought the dogs in, unleashed them and stepped back. Elliot flipped the lid off the barrel and leaped away as the dogs lunged at the large wood tub, surrounded it, pressing their noses against the wood and barking, their tails slicing through the air behind them like flags. A long red dog leaned up on his hind legs against the barrel and stuck his head over the opening. A claw swished up, slashing for an instant, ripping the dog's nose, sending it flying back and yelping off. The other dogs circled faster, their barks blurring into one fierce threat, building to a point. They charged, hurling their bodies against the barrel, trying to break through the barrier, knocking it over, rolling it to its side and scrambling for a position at the opening. "Go em dogs," one of the men on the fence yelled. "Go em all the way!"

"Get them damn dogs out of here!" Elliot jumped off the fence, waving the men to hurry up as they ran to their dogs, grabbing them behind the neck, dropping nooses over the heads and pulling them away.

"Who wants to go first!" Elliot shouted.

"My dog'll take it on," a man in a red flannel shirt rolled to the elbows stepped forward, his dog tugging at the leash in front of him.

"He's all yours," Elliot jumped on the fence.

The man slipped the noose from the dog's neck, it sprung across the ground, disappearing into the barrel. The only sound the men heard was the gnashing of teeth and a long hiss, then a howl blasted the dog from the mouth of the barrel, the badger's teeth clamped on a front leg. The dog ran, spinning his body, but the badger held onto the dog twice its size. The man in the red shirt rushed forward and kicked the badger in the head, knocking him from the dog. He picked up his losing entry and hurried out of the corral.

"Who's next, you men?" Elliot hopped down again.

"I got a dog's half wolf," a man walked out to the center. "Timber wolf is what he is," the man grinned and pushed the sweatstained hat further back on his head.

Elliot looked at the dog standing calmly at its master's side, the razor slice of nose, the powerful legs pushing up from the ground. "No," he shook his head. "That dog'll kill em off to fast. This here badger's got some more fight left in him fore we cut em off so quick."

"That's right," a man shouted from the fence. "Let some other hounds have a go first."

"Yah," cried another. "Hold your wolf on back. We got lots of time. Don't want to settle that beast's hash too easy."

"We'll go er," a fat man fingering a moustache lumbered out next to the man with the wolf dog, a yellow mongrel with half a tail trotting behind.

"Your show pardner," Elliot waved him on.

The men spoke lowly making individual bets as the yellow dog cautiously approached the badger who was plopped down in the thick dust, coiled in a steel gray ball. The yellow dog stopped, sniffed at the air and scratched the dry earth. The fat man waddled up, kicking his boot

into the dog's rear, "Get on up there you lazy coyote."
The dog jumped to one side of the badger, then hopped to
the other side. The badger did not move, its belly flat to
the ground like a snake, its wary eye fixed on the dog's every action. The dog growled with his nose pointed at the
badger and circled, poking tentatively at the coiled tail.
"Come on you lousy cur!" A shout came from the square
of spectators, "Fight em! Fight em you yellow dog coward!" The dog moved to the badger's front, sniffing closer,
almost touching the furry head with the slash of white
above the eyes, the badge. He stamped his paw in front of
the animal; the badger's head darted up, the flash of teeth
exposed for a moment in the sun. The mouth clamped beneath the chin, sinking into the throat with one hard twist.
The yellow dog gave a short whine, staggered to its knees
and fell on its side, his throat gashed open.

"That's it! That's it!" A man screamed. "Bring on out
that there gent with the wild wolf dog! Give us a show for
the money!"

The man with the wolf dog released it. Straight across
the clearing it advanced to the badger. The prey sprung
up, its back hunched high, lips snarled over the gums, two
rows of needleteeth ready. The dog came on fast, the massive jaws wide, saliva dripping from the corners of the
mouth, the tail up rigid, a sharp spoke of rudder; smooth
white scars from previous battles crossed the ribstretched
hide. He headed into the badger, feinted with his head as
if to strike, then moving quickly, seeking the opening
where the needleteeth would not be. One paw whipped,
catching the badger on the side of the head, flipping him.
The attacker dashed in for the kill, but the badger was
ready, waiting for the strike and hit with his own paw, a
quick fierce bite sinking into one side of the dog's mouth,
ripping into the lip. Both animals locked together. The
battlers rolled over, thrashing in the dust. The men
jumped from the fence, closing together on the fight, eyes
burning as they stared into the dirty pulsating cloud and
heard the gnash of teeth against bone, the tear of flesh.

"Waahoo! There he goes!"

A form leaped from the dust.

"It ain't the badger. It's the wolf dog!"

The dust thinned. The men huddled silent, hoping, until the dust cleared. The badger was reared back, swiping the air around him at the men, his panting mouth full of hair, tongue bleeding, his small face caked with dust and blood, a gash down his side.

"That damn beast ain't never goin to die!"

"Bring in all them dogs! Let em go it again, all of em!"

"No! Make it fair! Stand back and give him breathing space first!"

"I'm for bashin his brains out with a club!"

"Give it a drink! It's thirsty!"

"Kill him is what I say. Kill him now!"

"Gents!" the Bummer held up his gloved hand as he poked his cane playfully at the badger, the animal slashing futilely at the gold tip. "Rules is rules. We abide by the law. Let all the dogs have at him at once in even match. Then, if they don't whip him," he raised his gloved hand in front of thin lips, "then gents, then you can kill him."

The men backed up, spreading out their arena. Those with dogs ran and got them, holding them tight on their leashes in a circle about the badger.

"Release them!" the Bummer called out.

The dogs broke from their ropes as they smashed in against the animal, the men laughing, shouting into the rising dust, clapping their hands together until the last dog trotted off from the humped rag of a body.

4

I CAN smell the Antelope in the Sky.
                    Treading on soft tongues of snow
plant. Moving many times through the trees. Always the
trees. It is the way of my people. Close to their animal
skin, the hide tight on their bodies; I can smell. Can smell
wet wood. Underneath a cut pile, after snows are melted,
rains are gone, the bottom pieces with faces pressed in
damp Earth. Faces covered with mildew. That is their
smell. The smell of gray fibres growing softly. Thickly
into a mask. Masks moving in the Sky. Brown bodies
turning. Watching peacefully as I stalk. I am sly. I am
swift. I am the one to apprehend them. Waiting to allow
me passage. Slipping my knife into their Spirits. Cutting
the meat from their sides. I am the boss of them that allow me to feast, to grow. I am strong boss of my people.
Not a leader. A boss of Antelope hunts. I am the Antelope Boss. The one to point the way. To direct a finger at
the Sky. Announce—there, that is where I smelled them,
tasted their scent, heard their hooves beat beneath my
eyes, that is the place they moved through my dreams the
night before this one, now it is time, we must go, go before fifteen days have passed, you must follow me who
will follow them, lead you to where they await us, where
they are still, where the wind caresses the shortness of
their fur, holds the thin legs straight to Earth, that is

where I shall lead, North, over five mountains, to the spot where hunger ends. Hunger does not end. I know it is not true. It is true that the Antelope wait us there. Only a few. Numbers as small as our people. People who would laugh to me if I were to tell them of the dreams. Tell them where to hunt. The people who would say—we can no longer hunt, *they* forbid it, forbid us to stalk our own meat, what good are your dreams now, as good as dust, we no longer need the Antelope Boss, you dream in the wrong time. They would laugh saying this to me. For I can see into them. Hear the plant of sadness growing within. Roots filling all space of the body. I know they still have dreams come to them in the black water of night. So I do not go and speak of the Antelope. I must leave the Antelope to rot in the Sky. Grow rancid stiff and soft with worms. This is what does not allow for me to quit my dreams. This scent of death breathing steady as a spear through my thoughts. These masks that stalk me into days. All of this pierces the time of trees I move through. Pulses in the air that touches me. Can be seen escaping from my eyes. From the eyes of us. It is the scent of walking on a dead land. A land sunk to the heart. Guarded over only by memory. Defended in battle of dreams. So I do not go now and speak of Antelope. The meat is rotten. Fouled from falling years of disuse. It is the stench in the circle of my people. A reminder. I must forget. Lie my dreams. Seek into another dream. Slip unnoticed through the years falling quickly upon my body. Avoid detection on the land crushed flat from waste. I must never raise my head. To crawl is to survive. In the end it is I who shall stand straight. Covered in a new blanket woven from fresh dreams. Dreams that shape hard and sharp in the virgin Sky. Cutting away the dead skin of a wasted land. Along the lakes I shall walk in my new robes. Released. Sparkling my image on the quiet waters. Again the forests shall grow thick and free. The Birds return. The fences fall. And in their shadow the openness will find its home once more. These things shall pass in my time. For I have cut the face of *their* time with my father's stone knife. I have dreamed. It is true. I have seen

time rush like a strong river into the hole of a Mouse.
Disappear. Disappear on watery wings into the bowels of
the Earth. Beating furiously to meet with the dead. The
place where fires have grown cold. Where the graves
shudder in the echo of dead songs and dances have failed.
I have cut with my knife into that place where everything
is gone. Vanished. I am young now. My hair grows long
and gray like a baby's. I have nothing to eat. I am preparing for my journey. I wait beneath the waiting Sky. Patient. I am dying of thirst. For I am close to the source of
all water. I have been to the place where dances fail. I live
my days in that land. I know that land. Know it like the
creases scarred in my hand. Creases my eyes have journeyed over, back and through many times. Like the long
slender valleys of the high mountains where in twilight the
Birds blaze in the bursting glory of falling Sun. Sparkle in
the dying day. The Sun I have traveled under on the hot
lands. Thick and choking on sagebrush that rides the swell
of blurred hills beaten down from the face of the Sun.
Smothered in heat. I have kept up my journey into the
snow that burns on my face. Relentless. The white that
cannot be stopped. That stops all things. Freezes time. But
from under grows a new birth which finds me still moving
on the flat lands. Like a Bug in search of a Bird. In no
outward hurry to reach the place where both shall meet.
But boiling inside the dream of how the meeting shall be.
I was not lost on the sage plain. I was a man growing
young in my search. This gave me warmth. Made me
move. I no longer needed my feet. They had turned to ice
like the ground itself. So it was not they who moved me. I
needed no feet to take me where I was going. In the night.
In the distance. Large clumps of sagebrush covered with
snow grew up from the desert floor. They looked like winter houses in which lived people. A fire around which they
gathered. And maybe *him*. I continued. Making my way
to each sagebrush clump. Stopping, and asking—Yao, are
you in there? Maybe they were. Maybe it was not sagebrush heaped over high with a white cone of snow. Maybe
people were sleeping. I waited. Asked once more. Then
never again. Moved on in the spread of distance. Came to

another piled high mound of snow and asked—Yao, are you in there? No voices. No sound. Again I gathered my search about me, pulling the Rabbit blanket close under my chin. All into the white night I asked. My voice blowing in the silence. The words scattering in the white drift falling lightly out of the Sky. Then the Sky herself was empty. The Moon jumped in the heavens. A brilliant young bull. Sucking all stars out of black. Prancing. It had become almost like the day. Now my eyes saw. Sparks splashing in the air. My search closed me in its fist. As I drew closer flames raced up. Around them sat three men. Hunched over. Bent into the fire. Their faces aflame with the light. They made no move as I approached. But they knew of my existence. It was if they had been watching me forever in the search. Had been staring into the fire twelve days and watching my every move. Charted my course. When I came behind them I stood and waited. I began to feel my feet again, now that I stopped moving. The flesh within the boots planted near the fiire on the solid splotch of ground bare of snow growing warm. Coming alive. One of the men stood. Moved around me. Came back with a fresh pile of cut sagebrush and threw it in the fire. The cold sticks hissing in the blaze as new sparks cracked and danced from their bark. "You are the Antelope Walker?" The words came from the man in front of me. They came from his body. Through the heavy back bent powerfully into the fire. Through the black coat that fit thickly on his back. "You are the Washo?" "Yao." My answer went into the back. Was lost there. For no one knew of my coming. My being lost on the plain for twelve days and one more night. I was far from my people high in the mountains. I stopped the once at the village of his home. To seek him. But he himself was not there. It was told he himself was on the hotlands now grown cold. Far off. Had been gone since even the snows began. Without food. Some said he was never to return. Others spoke of his going to the place where trees of thorn grow higher than the man. "Yao, I am the Washo." "Sit with us then, Washo, you the one the Whites call Hallelujah Bob." I moved to the open space on the other side

of the fire. To the place across from the man with the
black coat. I sat. I could not see into the face. The head
was hooked down by a black hat. A hat such as never before I've seen. The brim wide. Cut sharply round. A flat
circle. Flat stillness of a desert lake. The crown mounted
taller than two heads. A bold mountain cone of dead fire
that pushes up from the desert floor and through the seasons is whipped and lashed and caressed by the fingers of
the wind, until it is narrow and smooth, like the slender
pinenut baskets the women weave. A tight hammered
band of silver spun around the broad base of the crown,
anchored to the flaring brim. The high crown seems to
have toppled the head forward in a landslide and buried it
beneath the brim. The image of the flames caught on the
black felt, flickering violently. The hat and man himself a
blaze. Even though his eyes are buried deep I know he
watches me through the flames. Now he sees the hulking
Rabbit blanket hung heavy on my shoulders, draped over
my body in a tent of fur. Now he traces my face. Can feel
the gaze move over my skin worn like the stone itself.
Can feel the gaze penetrate the slashes of scar that have
long since closed the deep wounds running down my
cheeks. Can feel it blow through the hair that grows from
my upper lip, thinly, but each piece sharp and brittle, the
gaze blows through the hair a careful wind moving in
trees. I sat as his gaze clouded around me and the Sky
opened into gold, the prancing Moon quiet and dim in the
new light, slipping back into hiding, ignoring the gold
light as he passes away and disappears. Behind his gaze
was the flat of the land. Flaring out farther than the distance of the eye. His figure blocked a hole on the horizon,
the silhouette cut its dark space at the place where the
rolling snow met the gold Sky. In front of him the flames
were sleeping. Puffs of white smoke streaming from the
shallow charred pit that had been scooped out in the
night's heat. "Stand up Washo." I stood. "Take the Rabbit
blanket from your body." The fur slipped silently from
my flesh, falling in a soft heap on the bare ground behind
me. His hat tilted back, the face swelling up beneath. The
skin hung heavy in the shadow beneath the brim. The

gray eyes held wide apart and sunk in large holes tied with sharp wrinkles caught in laughter or frozen in the final squint of pain. The deep eyes moved over all skin of my body. Patiently seeking out each rip in the brown hide. Easing into the string of swellings whipped about my legs. "Turn Washo." The gaze burned hot on my flesh. Stinging the scabs that cake over my shoulders and shower jagged-ly down the slope of my back. With the thick of each moment I can feel the eyes lift a scab. Linger in the jagged tear. Then move on. "Cover your body and sit Washo." With my legs crossed beneath me I stare into the place where the flames once were. The three men in front of me a hard wall against the mounting dawn. All is darkness on this side of the wall. I am with him. "When the Sun died." He speaks to me in my darkness. The words falling quiet dust on the soft hide of my trembling. "He fell from the heart of the Sky herself. A lance through his golden body. He dropped away from Earth and gave up to the night. There was the stillness of sleep. Sleep before birth. I was taken up through sleep. The journey was long and without direction. I existed in the fear between two worlds. Belonging to none. My face the face of a cloud. When I once more touched the Earth it was not Earth. Waters were running beneath my feet. I was afraid. I would sink. Sink like a stone to the heart of death. But I could walk. And I walked not alone. All about me bodies were moving. Bodies of the dead. Bodies of Birds and Animals I had hunted. All were alive. All were covered with flesh. All greeted me. All gave of me the flesh of Ghost. I feast-ed. One day was all days. All days were one day. I cried with the happiness of the child. All the People and Animals were together. All were one. Living one in the other. The waters had washed clean the Earth forever. All Whites were drowned. All White things dead. Only Indians. Indians way up high. Indians in high places everywhere. Indians on water. Game growing thick in the air. Indians in their young flesh across the lands. My pockets were filled with wild mountain plums. My lips stained purple from a thousand kisses. The Ghost Pony was sent. Its hooves beating across water.

Behind as it came the water disappeared. The land
was given up to us a baby once more. Mountains grew.
The people sang. The mountains grew higher. The people
sang up all the trees. The Ghost Pony turned paler the
closer it came. Each hoof print left behind filled with a
lake. The people sang the Fish up. The tears of all new
things washed down their faces. The people danced their
birth. Danced the Pony into their midst. The pale flanks
glistening with the strain of giving all new things. The
broad forehead slashed with the red pattern of sacred
paint. The people all touched this holy sign where the
Pony had nudged the shoulder of the Big Man himself.
They touched their fingertips to the firm flesh of their own
bodies. Tracing the blazing crimson across their faces.
Anointing their chest and legs. Anointing with the blood
of all things. Of the Spirit. Their dance erupted anew.
They danced their joy. Joy of being touched by the Spirit.
And I was lifted high. Onto the heaving back of the Ghost
Pony. We plunged from the newborn Earth into darkness.
The Ghost Pony ate into the belly of night. For a thousand falls the eternal dark tried to wrestle the life from
the Ghost Pony. The pounding of the hoofbeats shouted
the killer down. The Sun himself was back in the Sky.
The lance wound through his body grown over golden and
solid. The Sun lived. I felt myself grow out of the heaving
stillness of sleep. I awoke on the dark side of the mountain . . ." His words stopped. The shadow of his face was
hung in silence. I was saddened the flow was broken. The
echo of his words all covered with wings. Beating into the
vanishing air. One of the men at his side moved to his
feet. His arms spread out. Caught in the light behind
them. "Christ," he whispered into the space before him.
"Could I ask to know if now I should return to my family
and give to them the food that hasn't been there since I have
been gone with you?" The Christ raised a hand. His body
sinking deeper in his black clothes. The one standing
moved quietly away. Walking into the Sun. We sat alone.
The three. The Christ not speaking as the day marched
over us. In the pit scooped out by the fire a yellowbacked
Spider moved simply and swiftly over the bones of dead

wood. I could feel the eyes of the Christ on the yellowback as it bore its burden of casting out a web in the place
now charred barren. Sending up a great sail of fibers from
its body. The wind moving trembling fingers through the
glassy sheet arched in preparation. The spider clung to its
essence. Lacing its net with one-eyed determination. The
determination of the woman weaving the globe of basket.
Thin willows trembling in her darting fingers. Anchored
for once in their place in the shape. The hard yellowstone
of her ring flashing the trace of pattern. I had asked her
where such a stone would come from. She told me how
she was young and still living on the shores of the Big
Lake in the Sky. How she would always clean her body in
the stream running small into the lake. One morning a
White from the camp on the opposite shore came to her
and smiled. He said he would like to make his new camp
where she stood, and he would be no harm to her. He
took the yellowstone ring from his end finger and placed
it in her hand. Forever they would be friends he said. He
thanked her for allowing him the use of the small stream.
When she next returned to the stream she saw the man with
many others. Already they had made many trees fall. She
watched them across the fence that had been built. She
watched them along the stream that ran small into the Big
Lake. She felt the ring on her finger. Looked at the gray
speckles dancing in the yellow stone as the sun touched it.
As she talked the wind poked tiny mouths of cold air
through the chinks in the branches bowed above our
heads protecting us from the snows that had been falling
for nineteen days. She had almost completed the basket. It
was large. Like her. And sat rooted in her lap. Waiting the
completion that would come. Six others sat on the hard
earth of the floor. I had watched them all come from the
neat stacks of stripped willows at her side. I was silent
with her. Listening to the movement of her fingers. The
rustle and scrape of willows as they moulded beneath her
light flesh. Each movement was mine. I sat like her. With
my thin boy shoulders high like a rider on a Horse. My
head intently bent down to the task before me. Sometimes
my hands would move. The willow weightless between my

fingers as I would stab it through the binding and lock it in its place. And I would catch myself. Catch myself weaving baskets in the air. She herself would say nothing. Her eyes only looking on her work. But I knew she saw those hands of mine building. I was embarrassed. And I would hold them still. Keep them steady and slip them beneath my skinbone legs out of sight. But the blood kept moving. Waiting to guide the gliding willow. Kept building the basket with her warm brown hands and calloused fingertips. So I would talk to her and ask her still again where such a yellow stone like that could come from. And always she would tell me. Tell me through to her watching the gray speckles dancing in the stone as the Sun touched it. And I watched closely again to see if the speckles were still dancing as the stone on her finger flashed from the light of the fire. But the fire was low. Few coals were glowing. Soon it would go out. I brought to it a new stick which I placed in the black bowl of earth that gave us our warmth. I got down on my knees and leaned my face close to the coals which glowed bright from the breath of my mouth and soon the new stick was blazing. I liked to feed the fire. It gave me something to do with my hands. The blood forgot the building of the basket and they were calm. And whenever I started a new stick she would look up to me with the broad lips spreading across her face as the acorn color of her eyes brightened a quick smile. I kept the sticks going for her and I was always sad as she lowered her head again to the building. I could hear her building as I slept and often in the dark hours I would wake to the music of her fingers to feed the fire and never could I stop hearing her as she guided the design. Once when I woke the dark hours were gone, the sticks were cold and she was dead. Her large body was folded over her work, the willows still ready in her fingers. The yellowstone ring was like a bright Bird against her pale flesh and I slipped it onto my own hand, then pulled the basket gently from the hollow fold of her body. My fingers continued to weave the willows, filling the pattern that her own fingers had shaped. When the basket was complete in its perfection I ran my hands over the

tight smoothness and up the slick sides. I traced the hard
rounded rim that locked all the single pieces into one,
then again slipped my hands down the deep bowl that
grew into exact flatness at the bottom, feeling the hardness
of knots that secured all strands into one. I untied the
knots I had tied for her. The tension of the pattern
snapped. The firm bowl loosening as the willows flared
away from each other, seeking their original shape, released from the mold. Then I would begin again the building. Until once more the shape would be as intended before I would undo the completeness. The sticks stopped
burning when the snow stopped and I no longer fed the
fire. I kept at my work. Sometimes I would put down the
basket and take from the folded leaves a piece of seed
mush. This would taste good and I would chew slowly.
When I was finished and again took up my basket I
sucked at the seeds stuck in my teeth. Sometimes I could
not get all the seeds and they would stay between my
teeth while I slept in the dark hours and there was a great
noise all around, hard feet struck the ground again, and
harder again. The blanket that kept the dark outside
moved and from its place two white men towered into the
shelter, bright red handkerchiefs held tight over their noses and mouth. I could see them clearly, the whites of their
eyes twisting as they searched in the dark, trying to see
what the black shapes were. One of them put out a hand
and it touched my face, the stiff fingers moving over my
flesh. The hand went around my neck and closed. It
yanked me up off the mat. My whole weight went into the
air and came down on a wide back. The man turned, his
one arm strapping me against his body as he moved
through the blanket, I heard the other man shout and
jump toward us. I twisted my head and could see in the
corner my father's mother, bent over, the basket at her
side, and I was out in the night, stars showering over my
head, streaking like rivers of fresh milk in the clean Sky. I
was thrown up behind a man on a Horse. I held onto his
coat. All around silent men on Horses waited in the night.
Then it was bright, brighter than the stars, I could see all
the flat white faces watching from beneath the hats, long

shooting sticks resting across the saddles of Horses flaming from the quick fire of the shelter. The blazing dome of the branches grew smaller and the hard crack of burning wood became more distant as the Horses rode across the land and into the night. When the Horses stopped rolling over the land and became still I was lowered and pulled across the ground and pushed through the open small door of a wood board shelter. The door was closed and I could hear the clang of metal as the bolt was thrown into its lock. In the morning I opened my eyes. Slivers of wood stuck in the skin of my back where I had slept on the wood floor. Tongues of Sun sliced through the long cracks between the boards of the wall, making the little space of the room hot, hotter than I had been since the long days of the pinenut harvest in the fall, long before my mother and her husband had sent me into the flat of the big valley's heart to feed my father's mother fire with sticks during the short white days. I could feel the small seeds of grain beneath my bare feet. Scattered across the floor were tiny golden seeds and in the corner was a brown sack, its top open and I ran my hands into the cool seeds that bulged the sack out at its bottom. I pulled out fistfuls of seed and stuffed them into my mouth. They were hard and sweet. I feasted. Soon the sack was empty and my belly puffed smooth and firm. I rested from my eating, sitting in front of a chink in the wood and looking out. The white was gone from the ground. The Earth was bare and turned up a thick mud where Horses and men had been in front of the house taller than a pine tree and the color of snow. A wire fence went in a square around the house. A Whiteman was walking along the fence. His steps beat the ground like a hammer and I could hear them in my shack. I watched as he walked, moving my head to see him better through the crack. He came to a gate and opened it, walking toward me, growing bigger and closer. Then he stopped. His head turned and I could see the eyes beneath the hat. He started again. Coming toward me. His black boots slapping in the mud. Behind him the door of the house opened and through it came a woman, the bottom of her long gray dress almost touching the mud as she followed across the yard in the man's footsteps. They were very close and I could feel their power. I moved away from the crack and hid my body in the dark of the corner. My body shook through the bones and it grew cold, the hard pins of bumps crawled over my flesh. I wanted to cry out in the room. To shout my voice for a weapon to beat off these Whites coming for me. Coming to eat me. To tear my young boy flesh from its bones and chew it between their teeth. That is what all Whites want. To eat the flesh of others. That is true. It is told to me by my uncle, the Captain, and he knows of everything, has seen of everything, through his own eyes and the eyes of others. I could hear the sound coming from my mouth. The moan slipping between my lips. I pressed them together and the sound in the air ended. But in me the sound grew like a wind and blew through my bones and I looked across the room and my grandmother was not there, no baskets at her side, no one could hear my cry for help, my grandmother was burned to the ground in her winter house that sat in the heart of the snowcovered valley. I heard the bolt in the lock slip loose and the door was open. Sun poured in and washed over my huddled body, its brightness laid over my shivering skin like a bright blanket. Then it was gone, torn off. The door banged into the opening. I was again alone, hung in the dark corner. Outside the heavy sucking sound of boots pulling out of mud moved off. Slowly my hands moved away from my eyes and I could see I was again alone and safe. The Whites had gone and in front of the door were two thick rounded potatoes. I crawled across the floor and put my face close to the brown lumps. The skins were dry and split. I scooped them up in my hands and they were warm, like stones that have baked in the day's Sun. I raised one to my mouth and felt its heat close to my face. But my lips would not part to receive the food. The potato grew heavy in my hand and its stone weight sank to the floor and rolled from my grasp. It was filled with evil. Both were filled with evil. They were the food from the stomach of death. The Whites had tried to trick me. Had tried to put the food of death in my stomach. So that they

could come and take my lifeless body and tear from it the
flesh. I moved away from the evil and hid in the dark of
my corner. I did not take my eyes from the power that sat
lumped in front of the door. The Sun shot through the
cracks of the shed and slashed across the two brown split
skins. As I watched the power I knew that I must die.
That was the only escape from the boards that squared in
a prison around my small body. The Whites would get the
body but not the Ghost. My Ghost would go free. It
would not have the poison from their food of death in its
Spirit. I closed my eyes in the darkness of the corner and
prepared to die. My hands rested on the empty grain sack
beneath me, I could feel the coarseness of the burred material pricking into my palms, each prick like each seed
that I had swallowed. My hands closed into fists. I beat at
the rumpled sack beneath me. Beating and beating and
beating the skin from my knuckles. The blood of my
hands blotting into the grain dusty burlap. They had won.
Their triumph was complete. Like the Captain had always
told it to be. The brown lumps of potatoes in front of the
door in the knifelight Sun meant nothing. That they had
the poison of death in them meant nothing. I had already
made meal of the food from the stomach of the dead.
They had tricked me. I felt the puffed flesh of my belly.
Beneath my fingers were the seeds I had swallowed that
morning. Seeds of evil sprouting roots in my blood. The
plant of death growing in my Spirit. The Whites had used
their power on me. Like the Captain had always told it to
be. The Whites had trapped me into one room with one
sack of poison grain. And I ate of it. Now they would
capture the flesh of my body and the flesh of my Spirit.
Now I would die without honor. Without escape. They
would take me in excess. The darkness of the corner folded me in its blackness. I was solid with the wood my bare
back pressed against. I waited for the life to run from me
like water. To spill out on the rough planked floor like a
lake on the sands in the desert Sun. A lake that exists only
in the eye. A mirage that is clearer and deeper than the
blue high mountain waters. I watched as the life flowed
from me into the lake on the planked floor that ran fur-

ther into the distance than the eye can see. My life existed
outside of my small boy body huddled in the corner. My
life existed outside of the coarse flesh and bones the
Whites had stolen from the winter valley floor and
trapped in this small room. My life existed only as mirage,
clearer and deeper than the blue high mountain waters.
Outside my body, in the dark, I sought no more than the
moment. All the moments since my beginning through
eight bright seasons of Sun past pulled like a string and
knotted into this one hollow time that grew about my
young flesh a hard shell. "He's alive." The words cracked
the surface of the mirage. "The poor red devil is alive."
The boot raised against my skin nudged into my ribs tumbling my body out of the corner swimming with the Sun
pouring through the open door. "I can see for myself he's
alive, Johnny Doc, but does he got the Injun fever?" The
voice fell down on my face like rain splashing in a barrel.
I could see the gray eyes beneath the brim of the hat staring down as if they were watching a river at the bottom of
a canyon. His black boots next to my face were the same
I had seen slapping through the mud. It was the one who
brought to me the food from the stomach of the dead, the
potatoes. "It appears he ain't got no fever, 'cepting of
course he's two and a half times starved. Damned if this
little Injun boy don't look like a skinned rabbit that's been
rotting in the sun for a month of Sundays, smells like it
too. Why hell Frank, why didn't you at least give the red
devil something to put in his miserable belly?" "Now here
Johnny Doc, don't you go a throwing them kinda words
on me, you yourself know as fact what I done up at Elephant Head. I risked my own hide burning that town to
the ground to kill all that Injun fever. Sides, far as this
one is concerned we coulda left him to fry with the old
dead squaw we found him with out in the valley. But you
know like I know we didn't haul him all the way in here
and risk fever ourselves just to starve what life was left in
him out. Rachael herself has been putting two hot potatoes a day in here for him to eat. Look to there, look for
yourself." The one called Johnny Doc looked at the six
brown lumps caught in the Sun streaming through the

open door. He looked for a long time, scratching at the
skin of his face, listening to the steady hum of flies moving slow and sure through the brittle sharp air as they
dropped softly onto the dried skins, hooking their hard
bodies into the open softness of the white splits running
yellow with pus. He scratched some more at the side of
his face, the sharp sound of his nails raking across the
short hard hair that poked from his chin buried the drone
of the flies. "Frank," the word grew from his lips and
filled the room as he took two quick steps and kicked the
potatoes out the door into the day with one solid movement of his boot. "You better get Rachael scrub that Injun boy down and get somethin in his stomach. If you
don't it look like you went to a hatful of trouble for nothing." "But do he have the Injun plague? Do he have the
T-burkulur?" The Johnny Doc was already out in the day,
but his words came back through the open door and I
could hear them mixed with the angry hiss of the flies. "It
ain't no T.B. bugs he's got to worry about. You just un-
lock him from that shed." I listened as the hard hooves of
a Horse beat off into the silence of the valley and through
the door came a woman, her long gray dress almost scraping the bare boards of the floor. She put her hand in my
hair and pulled me from the room into the day. I could
see the house taller than a pine tree and the color snow as
I tried to make my legs beneath me move, but my feet
slipped like Fish in the thick mud as I was drug around
the house and dumped in a barrel of rainwater, the woman's strong hands holding my head down, then yanking it
up, then pushing it down, the water slapping white under
my chin and coming quickly into my mouth, filling me up
until my throat burned from trying to choke it all out. She
let me stand on my own legs in the barrel while her hands
worked steady and complete over my body with the hard
cold soap, her breathing heavy in my face as she grunted
from the strain of rubbing my chest and between my legs.
She pushed me back under, my knees banging against the
rock sides of the barrel. Her fingers dug into the scalp as
the soapy water flooded into my open mouth crying out
from the pain of her nails tearing into my head. The man

with the black boots held a Horse blanket out before him. The woman pulled me dripping from the barrel and the blanket folded coarse and stiff about my body closing off the day. When the blanket was taken from me the clothes of the Whiteman dressed my nakedness and I stood alone in front of the black iron of the stove with the wood burning deep within its stomach. "Do he talk?" I turned my head. A boy the size of me was standing next to the black boots, blond hair growing all over his head. "I don't think he do," the black boots answered without taking his eyes from me. "What we goin do with him then?" "I can't really say." The black boots took the gray hat from his head and sank into the chair behind him, the air rushing a soft stream between his lips in a slight whistle that could almost not be heard in the hollow warmth of the big room. "I can't really say what it is we goin do with him. All I know is he's here. That's all. He's just here."

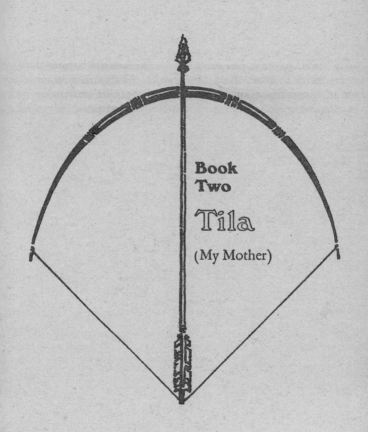

Book Two

Tila

(My Mother)

1

THE Fox of the Earth was released. The Washo moved the stick in the dirt. His eyes tracing the dusty face of the Fox his stick had scratched out. The wind blowing between his bent knees tickled the drawing, blurring the face staring up at him. The Fox is sly and swift and he wondered deep within him why *they* were the Fox. All he had seen of *them* was slow and clumsy. He threw the stick, it landed by a pale rock and he was angry, angry that *they* filled his thoughts, stalking him through the days and into his dream. He knew that if he could not think of *them* through one day *they* would be gone, but that was impossible. He had seen the bones. He had returned to the place of *their* camp by the lake with his father to watch. The journey was effortless, the Earth had turned up black, the snows gone, but when they reached the place on the mountain where he watched *them* during the winter *they* were gone, the shore of the lake was untouched. His father wanted to turn back, saying his son had offended the Ghosts and they gave him the dream of the ones with white skins during the winter, it was only a dream, this was his suffering for some grave offense he committed against his Ancestors' memory. But he himself could see the shore of the lake was not as it should be. Many of the tall trees were cut. About two bodylengths up, the bare trunks poking steep, they were chopped harshly in the

middle of their growth and the rest of the tree's body was
gone. Flesh from the trees' bodies had become winter
shelters such as never before had been built in the mountains. He knew this was the work of those with the White
skin. He knew the trees were cut at the snowline where
the Whites had camped during winter. He walked in front
of his father as they approached the cut trees in silence.
The wind blew straight out in front of them across the
lake. He squatted beneath one of the bare trunks. "Those
are not the bones of Animals," his father's words came
over his shoulder with the blowing wind. "We must go.
We have come too far already." He could feel the hand
on his shoulder, but it weighted him down like a stone, he
could not move, the bones beneath the trunk held his
eyes. He could not leave the bones and soon his father
was gone. He watched until the Sky grew black. He spent
the night by the cut tree. There were no stars and he
could not see the bones so he did not sleep. In the morning the bones were there as they had been the day before,
and the days before that back into the winter, the rock-
hard white surfaces charred black and split sharp down
the long middles where the bone marrow had been dug
out. "*They* have eaten all there is to eat," he spoke his
words out to the cut trunk. "If *they* had teeth of stone not
even the bones would be left to rot in the ground. *They*
would eat all." He moved from the cut tree and away
from the bones, but he found others, burnt, split, like the
flesh of warrior Ghosts that had been rained on the Earth
in silence. He read the bones for the sign they were. He
knew they were left to grow. Soon their bodies would return in many numbers. He could feel their presence as he
moved through the cut trees. The bones scattered on the
shore of the lake was the eye keeping watch on him, the
eye of the Fox, the eye of the Fox that sinks like a cave in
front of his questions. As he walked he moved further
into the darkness, having only the cut trees and burnt
bones as his guide, he was alone, he was alone with *them*.
Would he walk forever in the eye of the Fox, would all
the trees be cut, the forests slashed at their waists, would
only bones mark his path, would *they* feed on all flesh. He

wondered this deep within him as he watched the wind erase almost all trace of the Fox he had etched in the dust.

With the morning he awoke. From the side of the mother of his children he moved out beneath the Sky. Smoke was blowing white from a fire glowing in front of his brother's *gadu*, already some of the men were there, being part of the morning. He came to the fire like the other men, not because he sought warmth, for the coolness of the morning was natural on his naked skin, but for the reason that the fire was the beginning of the day, and he sat in front of it between the other men and ate the scoop of pinenut mush still hot from the basket until he felt it heavy in his stomach. Basa stood, his brother stood, and laughed into the air, the Birds jumped in the trees, back in the forest a Bear rolled in the water; coming quickly through the camp, his Rabbit robe hung high from his shoulders signaling the hunt that would fill the day, was the Rabbit Boss. He stopped at the point of the fire in the middle of Basa's laughter, across his face was frozen the smile from the years of squinting into the Sun. "Basa, my son," he spoke into the laughter. "Why is it on the morning of the Rabbit hunt you laugh? You take the pleasure of what is to come like the child takes a new toy to its breast. The one who should laugh like the brook is your brother. It is on this day he will take for his first son a Rabbit robe that will protect and warm him through the young seasons of his life. Gayabuc, my son," he looked down at the man who had only eyes for the fire. "What say you, this morning of the hunt?" The old man who stood with the strength of a rock waited, but in the space where his oldest son's answer should be there was nothing. To the old man this was answer enough. "Gayabuc has time only for the Fox." He let his breath out heavy in the air. "His body is with us but his heart is with the Ghost on yonder lake." Now he knew his son would speak. "I say on this morning of the hunt," Gayabuc pulled to his feet, "it is not the time of Gumsaba, of the Big Time. It is still the time of the first season. The Rabbits was the only creatures in the forest with less flesh on their bones than

us. The white days have been many and hard beyond
what most of us have memory of. The Rabbits will be
weak, the meat tough and sharp in the mouth. I say why
do we go into the forest and hunt Rabbit before his time.
Fish is in the lake and he waits for us to eat him." "Yes,
Fish is in the lake," the old man turned his eyes away
from his son. Out across the morning flatness of the lake a
silver arch split the surface and hung one still moment
like a Bird before slapping once more into obscurity.
"Fish is in the lake," he repeated, for it was so, it could
not be denied, his son was right, the Rabbits would be
weak and without much flesh. It would not be their time,
and this son, this Gayabuc, knew what he himself had forbidden to be spoken of, that when the time of the Gumsaba was come, when the berries weighted the green bushes
to the ground and the Rabbit was heavy with flesh, it
would not be the time of his people, for he had the dream
hung in his head like a string of trout Fish in the sun.
Those that his son had seen during the white days would
return, the bodies that owned the bones would return to
claim them, for he too had the dream and could look nowhere without seeing their Ghosts. The Rabbit must be
taken in this first season. "Our bellies are small like the
Bird," he looked to all men around the fire. "And you
Gayabuc, can make the baby robe for your first son. Rabbit's fur is thick and warm from the white days, it will be
good. The time of Rabbit is here. It is the time of *Pelleu*."

They went away from the Big Lake in the Sky, from
Tahoe. The winter home was left behind. The Rabbit Boss
led the way into the forest. Behind him came the two sons
and the other men in silence while the women, burdened
with baskets and children, followed far back in the path
of the men, their voices distant like startled Birds in the
rain. Painted Stick walked slowly, her small steps matching those of the other women. Her son was light in the
willow cradle strapped to her back. She took pleasure in
the weight her son's body offered her. She hoped for him
to grow heavier with each step and bend her to the Earth.
She wanted him to bend her back like the strong bow. He

was her man now. The father of this child-man, Gayabuc, had escaped her. His Spirit was no longer with her through the night. There was the touch of flesh beneath the Rabbit blanket, but his hands no longer locked on the warm stone of her breast as he moved like a dark cloud into the heart of her body. He had not moved into the heart of her body since he disappeared into the white for the hunt that would return with meat strapped heavy on the back, meat for the babyfeast of his first son. He returned with no meat weighing down his shoulders but only talk of the White Ghosts of the lake yonder. Soon his talk of the White Ghosts was slower and finally it was gone, and with it his Spirit went, to the yonder lake, where he told of the White Ghosts that ate of *themselves*, his eyes spoke only of that now, emptied his body of all else. His eyes saw away from her, from the first son, from his father, and this was her doing, it was her offense, for the sign read she had wronged him, the baby was brought out of her body in winter, not in soft gold days of the Big Time, not in Gumsaba. The waterfall roared in her memory. This was the terrible offense. Now she paid its heavy cost, the Spirit of her child's father lost. The waterfall in her memory crashed over her body, the cold water rushing through her hair, slapping it the length of her brown back, flowing over her swinging breasts, washing down her stomach into the soft tangled darkness between her legs where the hardness of his body was thrust cold and sunk in the deepness. The water swirled around her legs, around his legs bent to her, it boiled a cold foam beneath them, supporting the tight slant of her calves. Then he was gone. She stood alone between the rocks where the waters were quiet. Beneath the silent surface her brown legs glowed in the blue. She leaned against the log jammed between the rocks and watched the needle points of the high trees jab a long row across the open Sky as the blood ran out of her body into the perfect blue. It spread in the blue a large pink cloud, moving out from her, swelling. When she looked from the trees to the water she dipped her hand in the pink cloud growing from her, it slipped through her fingers, splintering into the calm pool.

She leaned her face to the disturbed waters that stirred the color of fire from the movement of her hand, her lips almost touching the cold surface as the moan rose. It came slowly from her throat at the sight of the cloud reforming, spreading thicker in the water. He had broken the life from her beneath the waterfall. Her face sank into the pool filling with blood. She scooped at the cloud grown large and red, her hands thrashing through the crimson slivers of her life, trying to gather it to her. She moaned as her hands clamped between her legs, pressing hard into the mound of hair erupting blood, holding back her life. It stopped. The cloud grew no larger, it hung suspended in the blue, dying around her. She was still, waiting its return. But it came no more. She was alone in the blue of the pool, the brown roots of her legs melting into the blue itself where she saw the silver flash of fish, felt it move against her skin, felt its sharp dart brush against her knee, cutting her body from the water and sending her blind flesh into the forest, heaving between silent brittle bark of tall trees, her naked feet slapping against the golden crust of dried pine needles that cracked beneath each running footprint. The Sun caught high in the still branches overhead and spilled down in brilliant shafts slicing the long green shadowed path with bright doors of light that her body raced through, breaking in and out of the gold and green and into the full day filling the great place in the forest where trees did not grow and the people lived on the gentle grass where she stopped, damp hair flung around her shoulders and the cry from her lips burning across the grass to the huddled women splitting the white bellies of silver Trout with long graysharp stones, "Mother!" The stones stopped in the white bellies as twelve eyes the color of damp earth flung wide with the single terror of a Fawn that has just had an arrow pass through the narrow of its neck. The eyes held the girl at the edge of the trees where the only movement was the heaving flesh of breasts. "Mother!" The cry came again, carrying up the slight slope of grass. "The life was broken within me and flowed into the quiet pool by the fall!" The women did not move. The girl could not feel their eyes on her face puffed with pain, and she felt them not on her heaving flesh, but lower, down the roll of stomach to the dark tangle between her legs dripping a steady crimson fall to the grass, and behind her, in the forest, was the trail splattered with the blood that had spilt thick down her trembling thighs. At first there was one laugh from the women with the sharp stones, it was short and caught the girl staring at the wet space centered between her dust covered feet, then it was joined by another and the grass was covered with the happy sound bubbling from the lips of the women with the stones, filling the clearing in the forest up to the tree points stuck in the Sky, bubbling like a hot soup overflowing the edges of a bowl. The flow of laughter raised the girl's head, the eyes in the dark puffed face showed the tears that raged for the blind moment that held her in the ignorance of her own body. "Girl," one of the women spoke, laying her knife into the grass and coming with her whole body full off the ground and her feet solid beneath her up to the girl at the edge of the forest whose dark face flashed with the shame and hatred of her youth. "Girl, you fear for nothing. It is your first Season. It is the Season of the Woman." These words came to the girl through the sound of laughter from the women on the grass, and further within her to her mind, deeper still, to her heart, was the sound of the waterfall.

She did not eat for four days. It was a hard time. The berries thick with juice dropped from the bushes and she stooped to gather them but could not suck at their sweetness. She gathered the berries into her basket and walked with its weight, her fingertips stained with the fragrance that flared in her nostrils and was forbidden her. During the day others would come and scoop the sweetness from her basket and laugh as the juice ran from their mouths. Once he came, but he took only one berry and crushed its fatness with his thumb and streaked the sweet print of fruit across the thick lips and bent to her breast and sucked at her swollen nipple until she pushed him back in the leaves and he too laughed, the white of his teeth sharp in the Sun as she rubbed the red circle from her breast.

All that she had, she gave away. The berries, the nuts picked one by one, the Fish cleaned and split, the sap balls she plucked from the bark of the high pines, all was given up, for in this first Season of the Woman she need be generous, a generosity that would stay with her and keep alive the others the long time of the Woman and into her death. She slept little, for the four days without food for the stomach were fed with examples that would shape her from a girl to a Woman and she did not want to be weak and lazy in spirit. On the morning of the second day without food the sister of her father gave her to drink of the warm water that was scented with the sugar of pine, she raised the basket cup to her lips and the sister said, "Young girl, I will guide you into the time of Woman, from this moment you will not leave me. I will assist you to stand like the tree. Do not be afraid. I will keep you from all the wrong ways. It was said Gayabuc came into you before the beginning of your time. You must hide your face from him. He must not come to you. He must not touch of your skin before your Dance of the Woman or all the Antelope and Deer will run from him, he will be a poor hunter, he will not be a full man." She took the cup from the girl and met her dark eyes almost lost in the falling black hair, "Have you acted with a good heart in all things during the days before the start of your first Season?" The girl did not answer, outside the bark of a Dog cut the early morning, and within her roared the waterfall and the heat. "If you have not," the sister put her hand in the girl's tangled hair, "the signs will speak, the ground beneath your feet will turn to water and Coyote will eat the heart from the children that crawl from you. AHHH," she let her old shoulders sag with the weight of her breasts. "Such talk is not good. You have acted wisely, you have eaten of nothing since the beginning and for that you will live to the age of the Bear herself and never will you ache for food, for you will have all the food you have eaten as you pass from the girl to the Woman. You will not," she leaned her whole body forward, the smell of nuts coming from her brown teeth, "ever go hungry. You are young, your flesh is hard, you are pretty like the laugh," she tugged the girl's hair. "You say nothing, but it is good you do not comb this hair, it is forbidden to you, it will turn to the color of ashes if you comb it, it is forbidden to you even wash the dirt from the skin of your body in the cold streams, not even your face may be washed gently, to do so would wrinkle it like the dead leaf, and you must not drink of the pure water, to do so means the sickness to death. AHHH, but you have been instructed in all these ways of the first season and all the seasons since you were the small girl, and the year last you were with my daughter's girl in her first season, you carried the barren stick and you learned much. You have prepared yourself for this time, of that I am sure, you know it is forbidden to make your body for the men during this first Season, during all Seasons until you die, you must not make the men approach." She tugged at the girl's hair. "I will cut this hair, that is the way, and if we cut it now it will grow quickly and thick for all your life and glow like the Moon." She laughed and clapped her hands and cut the girl's hair in swift, sharp strokes and wrapped it firmly in green leaves. Together they went to the stream and the sister tossed half of the loose thick hair into the air, it fell scattered on the clear water and floated, slowly, blindly, over the gleaming rocks beneath and out of sight. "Goodbye hair," the sister called, and she laughed with the gurgling of the water rushing over the rocks in front of her feet. "You will be safe hair, and grow as long as the stream and return to this girl when she is old and without much hair, like me, hah, and you will keep her warm during cold white nights." She fell to her knees and scooped the soft Earth next to the stream with her hands and buried the remaining hair deep, packing it hard with mud. "It will come back to you in life," the sister stood, the heavy flesh of her body trembling with anticipation. "It will grow rich and dark like the Earth it is planted in and cover your days, but that, of course, is only if you be good and stay back from the men during your Season, you must not look above the ground at your feet for fear your eyes will fall upon hunters going out for food into the forest with their weapons, and look

not you into the face of those who gather the Rabbit, for
you are unclean in your Season, and if you gaze only the
once onto the man the animals will run from him in the
forest and the fish will sink from him in the waters and
the babies in you will rot like the Worm in the cocoon
and the people will grow with Dog sickness and die in
their beds. Hah!" She laughed, clapped her hands and
looked suddenly to the stream. "But you are the good girl,
you are the one who has been instructed in all these ways
of the first Season and all the Seasons since you were the
small girl, you know you must keep your head bowed to
the Earth and your body straight and strong so the dead
blood flows quickly away to the ground. Come, come
come come!" She took the girl's hand and pulled her from
the stream. They moved back up the slope, the people
now were out in the day and the children saw the old
woman and the young girl being pulled behind and came
running between the huts, following the shouts and laughter that broke unexpectedly from their young throats like
icicles from a tree, their small hands linking together as
they whipped out in a winding chain behind the young
girl, who saw them not, never lifting her bowed head
once. He saw her. Saw the hair that once grew a fine thick
mane down her back was chopped off. He was sad at this
and he followed the girl far back, behind the children,
watching the proud, strong slope of her bent neck as her
eyes saw nothing but the path before her. It was in her
walk something that pulled him to her, he had seen her
that first time, come into the camp with her father and his
family, her father had the Deer vest with solid blue feathers from the winter Bird, his name was Blue Breast, he
was brother to the woman that was mother to him and
had come from the hot valley over the mountain where he
had lived with others beside the shallow lake, but there
had been another woman come to him in the same hut
and she was followed after some days by her man and
there had been words and a fishingknife cut to the heart
of the man, so Blue Breast came with his two women and
family to the camp of Gayabuc's father by the Lake in the
Sky, it was the girl come into the camp for the first time

walking through the late afternoon with the full basket braced on her jutted hip that he watched and felt his blood move with each of her small steps, he wanted her there, in front of everyone, in front of the Sun, on the hard straw grass, but she looked to him not, she walked effortlessly behind her father, the Owl glides through the trees of the Moonless forest, he watched this same walk now over the heads of the small children, and when the old woman pulled the girl into her hut and slapped the blanket down in the openness behind her scattering the laughing children he stood silent, his blood still moving in the trace of her tiny steps, watching. The old sister sat in the center of her hut on the Rabbit blanket worn of dense fur and showing splotches of its cracked yellow skin like angry scars, the air came quickly through her lips and the girl standing with her head bowed sensed the strong smell of nuts swelling around her. "Run girl," the old sister mixed her words with the loud sound of her breath. "Run hard during your Season and when you feel your body getting slow run some more and you will not grow soft like me and have a spinning head every time you walk around yourself. Work and run so you will not be lazy and short of life air, gather firewood for your mother so your arms will be strong to carry the children, HaH, and hold the men down when they try to sneak away. Run hard, work hard, walk straight, keep your fast for the four days, do these things and you will not die young and the strength of the flesh shall not desert you." The old sister came to her feet in the hut and tipped the young girl's chin until the clear earthen eyes gazed into her own. "But you are the good girl, you are the one who has been instructed in all these ways of the first Season and of all the Seasons since you were the small girl, and in the coming days you will grow weak without the food in your belly and from the hard work you will keep doing for your mother and all of the people. You will need the strong stick to support the weight of your body, you will need the strong stick to keep you straight and the dead blood flowing to the ground. Will not you need this stick to guide you into the Season of the Woman?" the old sister asked. "Will you not need this support?" "This guide I need," the young girl spoke full into the hut. "This support I need." "Ahhhh," the old sister let the mass of her flesh rest on the bones, "it is good you are in need of this support, of this guide, for I have been at work this night past on just such a stick, a strong, straight, hard stick that is light to the touch but will bear all your burden, a fine stick cut from the elderberry tree by my own hands, a stick that has been stripped of all brittle bark, peeled of its thick skin to its white meat, a painted stick." She slipped away from the young girl into the early morning shadows that filled the hut and emerged with a long thinly rolled blanket cradled in her arms, she unwrapped the blanket slowly, rolling each curve out smooth, the loose skin around her mouth pulled tight with the solemnity of her movements. The girl watched as the blanket unfurled and gathered on the floor, leaving exposed in the old sister's hands a painted stick longer and straighter than the length of her young body. "Stick," the old sister spoke completely to the object in her grasp. "Oh my stick, stand you straight. Help this young girl through her first Season of the Woman, through all Seasons of the Woman, for all her time. Don't fall down my stick. Stand you straight," her fist hardened at the top of the wood and she pushed the shaft upright, planting it firmly in the Earth beneath her. "Support the burden! Don't fail. Stick, don't fail!" She thrust the object further from her until it pushed against the girl's body, snapping her erect. "Take it," she commanded. The girl took it to her. "Lean your face against it." The girl pressed her face to the shaft, the green smell of wood filled her nostrils; beneath her clenched hands flared the painted red ocher band coiling around the stick to its bottom securely anchored between her dusty feet. "Now you are ready to meet the Season," the old sister spoke without taking her eyes from the stick. "Keep the painted stick with you as you would your own arm, as you would your own leg, move with it. If it falls to the Earth you will not grow straight. If it falls your days will grow crooked into life. You will die young." When the girl emerged from the hut the waiting children sent up a shout that tore the tranquil rhythm from the morning Sky, but when they saw the painted stick they fell silent. On the fourth day of her first Season the girl was so weak from the food she had not eaten that she could not stand without the stick.

At dusk the flame went up from the upheaved peak of the mountain that kept constant vigil on the camp below. The fire roared into the Sky, its illumination declaring on the dark faces below the beginning of the feast into the time of the Woman. The dark faces waited with eyes to the peak, as they had waited since the Sun cut the day in half and the girl and old sister left for the journey up the mountain's spine. They knew the girl was weak from the stomach with no food and was burdened with a basket of coals to start her fire in the Sky, but her painted stick contained much power and the old woman's legs were not so loose in the muscles and would guide the young girl to the peak where the four piles of cut fir branches would receive the coals and burn into night, cleansing the four days of the girl's first Season, signaling her time as a Woman; this flame growing from the dead wood piles of the first Season the dark faces saw tower above them, and they watched in silence for the smoke. On the peak the smoke was slow in coming, the girl leaned her hollow body against the strength of her painted stick and waited for the sign from the fire she had created, the old sister sat with the rolls of her immense body piled against a tree and cried out at the fire in front of the girl. "Oh flame, burn away all dirt that falls from the girl's first Season. Oh flame, burn burn burn. But we wait here flame. We wait at the door to the Sky for your wise sign. Give us your sign oh flame. Give us your smoke. Give us your sign. Spit your smoke into the Sky so all people below can see the girl has acted good and according to the ways gathered from all the examples taught her since she was the small girl. Oh smoke, send forward your white tongue into the Sky to the stars, give the girl the path to walk the long life. Give the girl a straight long life. Ahhh," the old sister moved the whole weight of her body from the ground, keeping her back supported by the trunk of the tree. "Ahhh, I see you coming, oh smoke, I see you coming. Come out you, come out. Up you! Go up! Hug you not to the Earth a child hugging its mother's breast. Up you! Go up! Go up smoke! Hug you not to the Earth a white blanket. Get you into the Sky! Cling you not to the Earth, giving the girl no long path to follow, no long life, let that not be your sign!" The girl heard the force of the old sister's words behind her, she heard the words whistle through the air and sink in the doom of the white cloud's sign spreading out at her feet, thickening up to her knees; she heard the words through the roar of the waterfall deep in her head. "Get you into the Sky!" The words came again, not with a whistle, not with a simple force, but with the full fury of a body flying at the crawling smoke, the feet kicking at the white blanket that refused to be sucked up in the roaring flame. If it were not for the strength of the painted stick the girl's body would have fallen out beneath her, for the old sister remained part of the tree, she had not moved, she was not the powerful body racing around the base of the fire which showed its glistening broad brown back as it stooped to match its strength with the mist that refused to flower in the Sky, the feet stomping its demand, its hand slicing through white, knifing into the implacable cloud. The head turned with its challenge, "Get you into the Sky!" The command forced the girl to brace the stick deep in the Earth between her legs for it pulled the branches of the tall trees down and let them loose with a rush of wind that crashed over the peak, violently hooking the skirts of the flat smoke and hurling it upward, towering the white shaft deep in the night Sky. The rising smoke left the brown body hanging motionless, exposed in the moment of ill-defined light from the heat of the fire before it was gone, slipped into the trees, the darkness of the forest shutting its green eye behind. The girl spun around in the absence, the suddenness disturbing the balance of her body, the stick loosening from her grasp as the lightness of her feet gave way to her voice calling after the brown back that disappeared into the moving trees. The old sister caught

her body and closed a hand over the open mouth. "Do not
call girl. Do not call to him. He is gone now. Do not let
your voice touch his ears, you will kill his days, you will
make the Animals flee his bow. He has fought the power
of the smoke and forced it give you the sign of long life. I
know not if it is good, but it is done. It is over. Do not
dampen your feet with tears. He is all gone now. Gayabuc
is gone."

Blue Breast was the first to see the sign. The smoke had
spoken its truth. He turned his face on the people gathered. It was close now, close to the time the daughter of
his wife would come to full Woman. His face spoke of the
pride his daughter's passing into the new time brought
into him, the shape of her behavior in the four long days
past declared her the owner of a complete life, the sign of
the white smoke in the black Sky rising its ladder to the
stars gave its proof of this fact to all who had eyes to see,
the girl would live long, she behaved well, this joy pushed
from the heart of Blue Breast and through his lips, "The
girl has acted true to the ways. I invite all the friends who
have seen her fire in the Sky and come to share the first
happiness of her time to feast and dance with us this
night, all the night, to the new day of her time. I ask you
to wait with us until the daughter of my wife comes down
from the mountaintop to begin the Dance of the Woman.
I ask of you to go to her with your hearts and offer her
the strength to win the race to us, to win the race from
the mountaintop, as it must be, as she has acted true to
the ways." As the words of Blue Breast flowed from his
heart the women sat together on the ground, facing the
place where the Sun is born into every day, facing the fire
of the camp, and beyond it, high to the girl's fire on the
mountain peak. They sat with the thick fingers of their
hands laced tightly together and laid firmly on the leather
aprons banded securely around their waists. Together
memories of their own first Season buried beneath the days
of the full Woman unearthed and it was their time, it was
their race down the mountain weak from the stomach
with no food, with only the stick to support and the old
sister's winter hardened hands to guide, to guide directly

like the stream guides the Fish. These memories strung
through them each one and beaded together with a chant
sharply poking into the air from the unthinking movement
of their lips. The pattern of sound cut over the heads of
men in the camp, up the mountain to the girl who had begun the race after the smoke spoke its sign, and a girl
from the camp arrived, a girl with a tall stick, but barren,
the bark stripped clean and the green wood left to itself,
without the pattern of red earthen paint swirling up at its
base and snaking solid at the top, without the power. This
girl with the barren stick must be defeated according to
the ways, for if she stepped first foot in the camp all the
girl had worked for, been guided to, would disgrace her,
for the young one with the barren stick who had not approached her first Season would prove strength greater
than the girl passing into the Woman and this would be a
strong sign, the sign would decree she was not prepared,
had acted wrongly and was distant from taking her place
with the full women that knew the bodies of men and the
ways of growth deep in their bellies, and it was this that
gave the girl strength to make her way down the dark side
of the mountain with all the speed her body sucked from
the power of the painted stick, it was this that made the
girl feel not the blade of the rocks cutting through the
leather bindings wrapped tightly about her feet, split and
sliced from the downward path of flight, soaked red from
the blind wounds opening the flesh as she fled to meet herself at the door to the Woman. "Hold up girl!" the old sister caught her around the waist as the full laughter
jumped from her lips to the damp night air. "Hahhh, girl,
slow you down. You ahead in the race to your time. You
are strong and swift. Slow you down or you will lose your
guide. You will leave me behind. Slow you. Hahhh. You
are swift." The girl continued, the old sister tied like a
stone about her waist, the light from the camp was close
in the trees, it was almost done, she lifted her eyes from
the ground and let her hurrying feet carry her toward the
end, but her body stopped, the feet ceased to step one in
front of the other, for the eyes saw, moving quietly, steadily ahead, across the faint path the leader, the girl with

the barren stick. "Aiyeeee!" The old sister peered around the girl's waist, her cry catching the girl with the barren stick in front on the path and spinning her around. She turned, her young face looking back, the brown flesh immobile, her eyes spread wide to the woman on the other side of her body, ignorant to the consequences that if she won the race she defeated herself, and she was gone, her barren stick striking out its own trail. The girl could not move, she rested against her painted stick, all was lost, her mind asked no questions. "It is not over!" The old sister shouted at the girl's immovable shape. "It is not defeat!" There was only the empty path ahead and the girl saw no further than her painted stick, the loss was clear, no questions were in her mind. "You must make your time!" The sister screamed, coming from behind the girl. "You must meet yourself at the door!" She seized the stick, the suddenness left the girl standing straight. "You will go into your time," the sister announced, and her body became a sudden grace, the old bones guiding the hulking flesh down the path into the open night with effortless speed.

When the girl came into the camp she had already won the race. The old sister stood in the center of the people holding the painted stick high above all heads, the house of the Woman the girl had built in the past four days was not lost, it was just begun. "Painted Stick. Painted Stick. Painted Stick," the children surrounded the girl in her triumph, locking their hands together in a happy circle which guided her to the ground pounded flat with stones for the dancing. The old sister passed the painted stick to the girl. "Painted Stick. Painted Stick. Painted Stick," the children beat the sound out with their lips. The girl's heart turned proud, for the sound was just not a name for the power she held in her hands, it was the power of her brown, erect body standing secure on the dance ground, it was the name of a Woman, it was her name. She stabbed the stick deep into the Earth and let it stand strong with its own power. The girl with the barren stick came forward and stopped a shadow's length in front of the painted stick and with the full force of her youth plunged the barren stick into the ground and let it stand. The women closed in a wall around the girls, their chants corded together, weaving an ancient female curtain that isolated the men who stood clear of this alien island, the glow of the fire washing its muted light over their searching faces. The two girls were alone in the eye of the women surrounding them like a ship of darkness guided only by the slow chant that moved through their blood and linking them one to the other in an endless chain, the two girls held steady to the mast of their sticks rising above all heads, they hooked their left arms together and stood shoulder to shoulder as their eyes turned east, over the heads of the women to the further darkness, each held silent until her right leg lifted slowly from the ground along her calf, then crossed in front and came to rest in front of the left foot, the women around them swayed with the movement, then back as the motion was completed in the opposite direction, the chanting grew thick in the air as the two girls holding together swung like a pendulum, gravitating first to the force of the barren stick, then being pulled back to the painted stick. In the movement between the two sticks the girl's journey of the past four days crystallized, this was the charted course of her dying youth; ahead, through the immense round body of water, was the time of the Woman. The struggle between the two times fed the blood of the girl with no food. The swinging motion in the distance from one stick to the other gathered full momentum as she quickened her pace, leaning the weight of her body into her companion with each faster step between the two points until she reached a full hop and the space between the two sticks was blurred into one time. "Hop. Hop. Hop." The old sister moved between the two sticks and followed the existing rhythm which flowed naturally from her. "Hop. Hop. Hop.—Hop like rain from a cloud." The girl felt the solid Earth beneath the soles of her feet and into it ran the dead blood that broke from the clash of her body. "Hop. Hop. Hop." The girl's mother joined with the rhythm behind the old sister. "Hop. Hop. Hop." Pieces from the chanting wall of women fell away into the natural movement at the core, forming behind the old sister and mother a line which arched and completed itself as it fused at its beginning with the girl, forming an inner circle at the heart of the ceaseless time. The girl felt the full power of those joined with her in the unbroken line she was part of. She felt it shake loose all the dead blood. She felt it break away the time of her youth. She felt her young days flowing into the Earth at her feet. She yanked the painted stick from its place and held it high above the waves of long hair. She was empty. The life running slick down her legs ceased, the dampness between the rise of her thighs died. The painted stick tipped in the air above all women, releasing them from the burden of the girl's first season and launching all commonly in the same generous flesh. From the outside the men saw the sign of the painted stick over the heads of the swaying women and set afire piles of cut wood circling the camp, freezing the night stars, bursting the oblique shapes of the women with strong light. They came toward the wall of chanting women separating them from the core and the painted stick, finding their way into the outer circle which, before the sign of the stick, excluded them from the core. The presence of their bodies swelled the outer circle of women, widening the area in the center. Blue Breast stood with the other men in their part of the circle, a song came to his lips, it sang from his heart to the painted stick hung in the air by his daughter's hand. All those along the circle heard the song and joined it with their hearts. With the song the men grew in numbers until they became half the circle. They raised their left feet and moved in the direction the Sun travels the day, dragging their right feet slowly behind them, leaving a straight line in the Earth. Some of the older women separated themselves from the circle and moved toward the leaping bodies at the core, where they stood closely together watching the outside dancers. Gayabuc remained beyond the circle of dancers, stalking around its outer boundaries feeding fresh wood into the fires. It was when there was one star left to itself in the graying Sky that the first man penetrated the inner circle. He came slowly, a short time after the women had brought the small boys to the core, he sang the song of men, and danced with halted motions among the leaping women, holding his body away from their flesh, his actions remaining independent. In the length it took for the last star to die in the Sky the women's pattern at the core of the circle was broken by the men dancing in their own time, one of them broke from his dance and pulled the painted stick down from the height the girl had kept it through the night, she let it slip from her cramped hands, thankful to be released of its burden, she gave it up to her father who ran with it held strongly above his head up the mountain where he tied it straight to the cold side of a young tree so his daughter would be able to endure the cold of the long white days that would meet her many times in her Season of the Woman, he planted the base of the staff with the weight of large stones to protect it from falling or bending in the strong winds, he took his full time to secure the painted stick's position for it must stand firm to aid his daughter through her journey of the Woman, if it snapped in the wind she would break her back and be bent for life. As he came down from the mountain he was certain of the staff's strength to withstand the complete force of the coming days, it would support the burden of the girl's journey, giving the muscles of her legs the strength and lightness of the Deer, making her travels through the mountains effortless, he knew her legs would not weaken for the time the stick held tall, and it would hold. When Blue Breast reached the camp it was more day than night. He watched over the smoking pits of dying fire as one of the men made his way around the outside circle of dancers, seeking an opening, when he reached the gap in the circle between the last man and the first woman he slipped cautiously into the center ring and began his own, slow dance, his eyes to the ground and his feet directing him to the core where his rhythm fell into time with the girl, who moved the weight of her body carefully with the full pain of the night she had given up to in final dance, the man matched her every step without raising his eyes from the soft puffs of dust the soles of his feet clouded into the air, he held the flesh of his body back from hers, not once did their skin touch, for the beat of the dance locked them together, bound them one to the other in their separation, bound them forever. Blue Breast smiled, this man wanted his daughter, he wanted to release her babies, he wanted her body to be beneath his, to separate him from the earth, and this daughter has accepted, she has moved with his time, she is truly the Woman, she shall go to him. Blue Breast thought, she shall meet his flesh, it will be arranged, it will come to pass. He looked to the Sky. It was now a new day. Soon the Sun would show his face over the mountain.

The girl stopped dancing. She turned her body to the first strong rays of the morning light and stood silent. The old sister pulled the string on the leather apron and let it fall to the girl's feet, leaving her body naked and complete in the center of the people. The large basket of fine flat weeds woven through the long white days past in preparation for the girl's time was carried into the center of the ring and set at the girl's feet. She placed one foot in its wide straw bowl, then the other foot, she stood within its round shape of boundary, only she, with all the women before her, knew the secret sign of the weave banded darkly around the rim. The old sister slashed a finger dipped in the bright, blood colored earthen paint down from the center skin of the girl's head to the point of her chin, "Head. Head. Keep out the wind. Head. Head. Keep thee quiet. Head. Head. Keep out the rain. Head. Head. Keep out the pain. Serve this woman well." She streaked the red down the sides of the girl's neck, the length of her arms to her fingertips, "Arms. Arms. Bear the burden. Arms. Arms. Bear the wood. Arms. Arms. Bear the babies. Arms. Arms. Hold the husband tight." Her fingers worked quickly, spiraling the paint around the bulge of breast and down the curve of stomach. "Breasts. Breasts. Hang heavy with the milk. Feed all babies full with your juice. Be warm for the man. Stomach. Stomach. Have no cramps. Hold tight. Be strong. Grow big. Don't let the babies go too soon." The paint flashed down the girl's legs and covered her feet, "Legs. Legs. Be light. Be swift. Walk far. Carry the woman to her end. Feet. Feet. Don't split. Run uphill. Don't die in the cold. Carry the woman far." The old sister dried her hands of the paint on the girl's back until it blazed like the rising Sun. "You will take this," she held a flat basket to the girl's mouth. The girl dipped her head, touching her lips to the mixture on the straw plate, the fragrance rose in her nostrils flared wide inhaling what she had denied herself during the four days past, she felt her whole body awaken, ache with the hunger she had learned to live in harmony with, she sucked up the mixture of tough Deermeat and pinenut soaked tender in sagbrush water, the saliva ran freely from the corners of her mouth and she threw her head back, full with the first heavy taste of food, her teeth ground at the chunks of meat, her throat working, sucking at something solid for the first time in four days, then it tightened, burned at the back of the girl's mouth, pained with its own dryness as the girl spun her head down and spit the food to the ground. "Ahhhh," the old sister smiled in her patient eyes. "You are wise. You are strong. You denied yourself. You have the power to deny yourself. You have the power. You are the Woman." She brushed the girl with the warm ashes of the night's fire, stroking her face gray, then down her shoulders and over her body. "The girl dies out of you, you are not lazy, you endure the pain, of the stomach with no food, of heavy burdens, of hard travel, you are swift, you stand straight when you are weak, you give up all you have, you are a Woman. Go Woman, go and bathe, wash the selfish girl from you and be clean. Woman, go into your time, go Woman." For the first time in four days the girl lifted her eyes and looked at all the people, her eyes filled with the sight of men and women equally, and over their heads the Sun broke full in the Sky. It was a new day. She saw it for the first time. The small girls gathered to her person, they laughed with the Birds, anxious, as she stepped from the bowl of her basket and threw it into them. She watched their young bodies struggle together until one girl emerged with the prize, she held it high at the ends of her arms, beyond reach of all the outstretched hands, she did not want to part with her good fortune, she alone held the sign woven into the basket, and this would bring her easy from the girl into the Woman when it was her time. Blue Breast raised his hands and pronounced his joy, "My friends, those that have gathered to the sign of the daughter of my wife's fire on the mountaintop and come here to follow her through the night into her time of the Woman in the new day, I ask you who are weak from giving your bodies to the Dance of the Woman to fold your legs that have carried you well through the night and sit with us on the blankets to feast the new Woman who walks among us, to fill your stomachs on the sweet meat of the running Antelope, to suck the sugar eggs of the Bees and drink the black juice of the Sunberry." The food was brought heavy in the baskets and laid open on the ground as the husband of her mother spoke from the heart and the girl fled. She fled to the river to wash the youth from her body. When she reached the river's edge she sank into the coolness of the flowing waters and let it strip the paint and ashes from her skin. She waited patiently until the last traces of red and gray smeared from her brownness and clouded in the current to be carried downstream. She felt the new lightness of her body and the shortness of her chopped hair and it left her unfamiliar to herself. She searched in the blue ripping surface for the image of the Woman she now was. The reflection she saw caught in the quick movement of the water was that of a man. His image loomed over her, splashing across the wet surface to the far bank. She turned slowly until she met his body as it slipped from its image into the water with her. His hands came to her and stroked the wetness of her short hair. She felt the strength of the fingers smooth the hair straight against her face. His body swelled and her legs moved beneath her to meet his weight pushing her down against the bank. She sank deeply as he came into the heart of her body, the mud growing up full around her back.

Gayabuc did not hear the sound of the women far behind. In his head there were no women. The face of his mother did not live in his thoughts and it had been many days since the young face of the mother of his own son

lost its color, then its flesh, then ceased to exist in his
thoughts even as an obscure skeleton. In the head of Gayabuc there was only space for the Fox to live. His feet
carried him blindly behind his father through the forest to
the place of the Rabbit while he sat within his own memory of the white days past, matching his eyes with those of
the unblinking Fox; from this height he looked down to
where *they* ate the flesh from *their* bodies. "Gayabuc." He
heard the name, it floated into him, seeking to attach itself
to his person, to move him back to his place. "Gayabuc."
It came again, a stone dropped in the quiet water, a boulder rolled in his vision, separating him from the Fox, for
the moment it was gone, slipped from sight in the blink of
an eye. "Gayabuc," his father put a hand to his shoulder
and stopped him. "What say you? The Sun is heavy in the
Sky, soon it will drop. Ahead is *Pelleu*. Ahead is the Rabbit. We have walked the day. The Rabbit will wait. We
will camp. Make ready, and prepare the nets. What say
you? Tell this to those that follow." Gayabuc turned and
told the people that in this place at the edge of the tall
trees where the land broke out in front of them flat and
newly green for the distance of a valley a camp they
would make. With evening the people prepared their nets,
they had been woven and pulled together strong during
the long white days past, the plant fiber was tough and
had been dried thoroughly before being meshed securely
in squares no larger than four fists that would stop the
thrust of an Animal the weight of a man's arm. When
light turned to dark the net of each family was lashed to
that of another until the final net rolled out in one long
piece the length of three hundred men standing shoulder
to shoulder. The people slept deeply the first night in the
new camp, each knowing the net of his family served as a
link in the barrier that would stop the run of the Rabbit.
In the first light of the morning the men took the net and
walked along the far side of the flat, green hard land until
for a long time they were out of sight of the women.
When the women had finished eating the pinenut mush
left in the bottom of the baskets from the early breakfast
of the men a boy came quickly in among them. He stood,

his thin chest heaving and running sweat in the morning light. The women waited for his words. After he was certain that all had gathered around him and given up their eating he used his power wisely, he did not speak. The women said nothing, waiting only for his word, one of them left and hurried back to the boy with a straw cup rolling spring water over its brim. The boy swept the cup from the woman's hand, tipped it to the Sky and drained the water into his panting chest. "EieeeYah," he flung the empty cup to the ground and sat on a rock. "The men . . ." he let his breath out slow, directing the words to the patient eyes surrounding him. "The men have set the net." With the end of his words the boy was left sitting alone on the rock in the middle of camp, the women were gone, flung far across the green field in a noisy line, slashing with sticks the soft wet grass, kicking the freshswirled holes in the Earth, clacking a sharp sound out in the morning air as they beat two stones together in their hands, on they marched, beating the air with their tongues, running one between the other, their loud shouts female, urgent, hysterical, *"Pelleu,* run run! Rabbit, run run! Flee your home! Flee your home or we will eat you! Rabbit, run run! *Pelleu! Pelleu!"* Before them the grass moved, swayed with the rushing brown bodies. "Rabbit! Rabbit!" The grass swelled, trembled with an immense movement. "Rabbit! Rabbit!" The field was alive, frantic with fierce waves of brown. "Rabbit! Rabbit!" The grass ended and the ground rolled out flat and barren. *"Pelleu! Pelleu!"* The brown bodies broke from their cover and hurled themselves through the air, the desperate flight carrying them great lengths over the hard, bare land. "Rabbit! Rabbit!" The women stormed from the grass onto the bare ground, directing the flood of frantic movement before them, the dust from the blind race obscuring their shouting faces. The men could see them coming. They stood waiting behind the long net as high as their thighs arched out across the bare ground, anchored at each of its two far ends by an old man and a small boy. They could see it coming now like a great brown wind. They waited behind the barrier, each guarding his family's

section of the net, waiting to take what would come into
it, what was his. They watched as the great crest of the
brown wind drew closer, seeing in its dusty wake the
blurred, dirtstreaked faces of the women. They waited
with clubs clenched firmly and the sharp stones poised
over their heads, some just held the strength of their
hands at ready. "Rabbit! Rabbit! Rabbit! Rabbit!" The
sound clawed at their ears, cried out through the wave,
pierced the pounding bodies as the ground shook loose,
boiled up and the first rabbit struck the tense net. A club
swung and cut through the air with the full force of a
blade, separating the head from the thumping body
wedged fiercely in the barrier. *"Pelleu! Pelleu!"* All along
the net the rabbits hit, the lunge of their brown bodies
slamming out of the air against the armed wall, their
weight sagging the woven strength with a full and final
thrust. While the Sun rose and sat at the top of the Sky
the men beat back the brown waves, their clubs thudding
into soft Animal's skulls, crushing the temples in the slush
of blind instants, tearing the struggling bodies from the
trap of the net and slamming them silent to the ground.
"Rabbit! Rabbit! Rabbit!" The furious force of the wom-
en drove from behind, their sticks cracking into bones of
the swirling movement at their feet, the warm blood
splashed on their dusty bodies. The children descended
from the sides in screaming spears, the sudden swing of
their blunt sticks ending the crippled flight from the lay-
ered mass of broken bodies. The net sagged with its burden, the stakes driven into the Earth to support it all
along the line snapped and sank with the weight.
"Aeyieee! Aeyieee!" The Rabbit Boss threw his hands to
the sky, the robe of his rabbit blanket hung loosely about
his shoulders and swayed over the ground. "We have our
want today," his voice rose large over the sudden silence.
"It is today we have our need." His eyes moved quickly
up and down the distance of the line, a thick gray blanket
of bodies piled high, forming a soft fence between the
people. "We have today our need. Today there is no hurry. Let us stop. Let us return to our home. It is today we
have our need."

"THAT RABBIT'S got big all of a sudden Joe. What do you call it?"

"Don't need to call it nothing. Don't never ask nothing of it."

The boy leaned forward, his nose stuck up like a dog pointing at the stiff ears of the soft gray animal, "How do it know what to do then if you don't ask nothing of it?"

"Rabbits know what to do. They ain't like people. They don't have to be told. You just leave them be and they'll go on and do just what they always have."

"Well it could be," the boy settled his back against the stiffness of the chair, "but I can't see a whole lot what it is they done. This one though, sure has got big all of a sudden."

"It's all of a sudden if you consider winter to spring all of a sudden. I don't. A man could die. A man could get born. All of that time there is a lot of coming and going, no matter which side you look at it from. It's a hard time. It ain't all of a sudden."

"What are you going to do with that there rabbit Joe? You going to throw it in the pot and boil it?"

"Haven't figured it yet."

"Me myself, I don't like stewed rabbit. It don't taste healthy. Whenever I eat it I make sure to hold my nose.

My mother says that's not polite. She says it's the same as all other meat. I don't think so though."

"You just keep a hold of your dog's collar there. He don't seem so choosy what's served up on his plate."

"Maybe I should get him on outside," the boy stood up, jerking the dog's head back.

"Maybe you should," Birdsong opened the door and let the sun into the room.

"You know if you don't want to eat it," the boy stepped out into the open and turned his back on the sun, "my paw will give you two bits for it."

"Your paw had a chance to buy this rabbit back last winter but he passed it up. It won't never be for sale again. Besides, it ain't no two-bit male, it's a six-bit female."

"Could I let my dog go now Joe?"

"Sure, don't bother me none."

The boy let the collar slip from his grasp and the dog ran out from the house and into the ditch along the road, his nose tunneling in the thick green blades of grass.

"That dog of yours is going to get hisself a rabbit dinner before noon, boy. One way or the other."

"Joe, Paw says if your banged-up leg is a lot better to come up to the house and give the others a hand with the fencin' over to the Johnson field. He wants all the barbwire torn out so he can run horses on that field while it's green."

"Who's he got working for him now?"

"Ben Dora, Jandy, and I think Jimmy from Loyalton, too."

"Sam, you get home and tell Mister Dixel I don't work with Ben Dora. Mister Dixel knows that but you tell him anyway so next time he don't forget and send you over here to fetch me." He watched as the boy moved off down the road into the heart of the valley, the dog sniffing behind until they were both out of sight, and beyond where they had disappeared, he could see the high roof of the white house, floating on the spread of the flat land like a cloud. It was spring and his leg felt good. He stamped it on the ground, the tight puffs of pain around the knee encour-

aged him, for weeks after he had blasted the snakes with
Ralph he could feel nothing in the leg, it was like a piece
of lumber somehow attached to his body that he had to
drag around after him. It had been easier to crawl and let
the leg pull blindly behind. He waited until the early dark
of each day before he crawled from the house to the barn.
It was easier going in the snow, he learned to let his body
glide on the cold, the fins of his elbows striking against
the white crust, guiding him into the barn where he fed
the horse until her belly was fat and she settled herself
into the musk of hay to sleep out the night. Sometimes he
felt the feeling go out of his whole body until it was all
part of the numb leg and he couldn't move himself to the
house so he slept with his back pressed against the spine
of the horse. But this he tried to avoid, for the warmth of
her flesh and the full sweet smell of her breath made him
sleep past the time the sun came up and he had to crawl
back to the house in daylight when someone passing on
the road might see him. He took enough chance as it was
to crawl in darkness. Once he was almost to the barn
when a car pulled off the road and someone got out, the
two lights slashed across the glistening snow, cutting
through the deep trail his crawling body had forged. He
couldn't see who it was. He kept his face down in the
snow, hoping the headlights would not penetrate the shadow his body was lumped in. Whoever it was came back
out to the car and shut the bright lights, then went in the
house to wait for him. He laughed softly as the time
passed, his lips brushing the ice beneath his face, his bad
leg was under him so if it froze he would never feel it. As
winter lost its grip on the days the feeling in his leg began
to come back, and by the time the snow left the ground
he could stand. He used the leg carefully at first, walking
about the small room of his house holding tightly to a
staff he had carved out of the short days. The rabbit
sensed what this new movement meant. As the feeling
came back in his leg the rabbit grew and followed behind
him as he hobbled about the room. The first day he trusted himself to walk outside the rabbit came with him. He
thought it would run off in its first freedom. He had not

wanted the day to come, for he had promised himself every time the rabbit sat hunched on his lap, as he stroked the strong gray ears, that the first day he was able to walk out of the house the rabbit could go with him and it would be free to choose its own direction. But it stayed with him, always on the side of his bad leg, as if he knew it was needed there, to support that part of him not yet healed. He knew on his first day out standing on his own two feet that the rabbit was never going to leave him and so he never thought to build a cage. "What do you call it," the boy had said. What do you call it? What do you call something you fed by hand, letting it suck on a milk-soaked rag until it could lap up milk on its own like a cat, something that rubbed itself against that part of your body which had lost all feeling, as if it was trying to rub its own life into you. What do you call something whose dead mother you put a bullet through the head so you could collect the six-bits that was being offered. The rabbit didn't have a name, as the fish you hook in the stream doesn't have a name. The leg felt good and he didn't limp as he walked down the road. By the time he passed his sister's house the pain in his knee was almost a comfort, and a mile beyond that when he heard the wail of children coming from the stand of pines in front of Ben Dora's place he couldn't distinguish the bad leg from the good one, so when Ed Jesen pulled his pickup off the road and offered him a ride up front in the cab the rest of the way into Satley he felt he would have no trouble making it in and back alone. But when he finally walked into Felix's gasstation, got an Orange Crush from the machine and gulped it down he didn't know if the leg would hold out to take him back.

"How's the leg holding up, Joe?" Felix appeared from the back, setting the red grease rag he wiped his hands clean with square on the top of the glossy red Coke machine, then jangled through his bunch of keys on the end of a retractable silver band tied to a belt loop. "Got so many keys here I can't keep 'em all straight," he counted through the five keys three or four times, stopping in between each count to hold one up to the sun and let the light play off the bright copper. He did this with each key, squinting one eye and popping the other like a jeweler or a fruit picker who is trying to decide just which one of the pears should be dropped in the bucket, which is the most perfect, the most pleasing to eye and need. "Got a key here for every damn thing, so many keys can't keep count. Look here," he held a skinny one with sharp bits of teeth darting along its metal spine to the sun. "This one's for the pump, no gas goes in or out without this special little baby. And this one," he offered up a stubby, blunt-nosed piece of metal at arm's length and turned it swiftly in his fingers to admire it from the many angles of its two flat sides, "opens up the cash register. It's my favorite. And this here one is to both the men's and ladies' comfort stations, lot more convenient that way, some service stations have two but I feel that's one too many, it's hard enough keeping together all that I need as it is, and of course if you only have one you cut down the possible vandalism that is likely to occur in your average comfort stations by fifty percent. I never leave my comfort stations unlocked so anyone in the general public can walk in just as easy as you please like he was in his own house. No sir, nobody walks through those doors unless he does business here, unless he's a legitimate customer, and I've got the only key to make sure they don't. Any customer has need of my comfort station all's he got to do is ask me and I'll open it up for him right now, if I'm pumping gas he'll just have to wait until I'm through so's I can open up, that way too you cut down on the overcrowding, one in and one out at a time, it's the way your better service stations over to Reno and Truckee do it, and people ain't coming out here thinking they can take advantage, this is the only Standard Station on Highway Eighty-Nine for forty miles or more and it's the best one, first class, A-One-Hundred-Per-Cent." He slipped one of the keys into the lock of the machine and his body jerked with surprise as the door flew open. He let the retractable silver band slap the keys back into their holder and pulled a bottle of Coke from the exposed slot with as much studied determination as a man pulling on his socks. "Whew," he flicked the running foam from the neck of the bottle and took a short swig, "it shore has been a busy one today." He leaned back on his hightopped black maintenance shoes with the doublethick guaranteed-not-to-slip-in-grease-or-water-corrugated-rubber-soles and surveyed the empty road in both directions; the only movement for miles along the straight, silent blacktop was an occasional steer scratching his bony rump against the taut barbwire, sending a subtle vibration up and down the stretch of deserted road. "You should have seen it this morning, Joe. I almost burnt the nozzles off the hoses I was pumping so quick. I could have used two, three attendants. Did they come in, one right after the other. It's good to have a rest." He sucked out from the foam on the bottom and set his bottle in the center of the empty rack molded onto the side of the machine. "I get a good return on this pop. I pay nothing for the machine. They install it and service it once a month right on the day. I get three cents back on every bottle sold. Three cents! Imagine. I get three cents back on every bottle sold and I do nothing. They just set the machine there, the people put their money in and I get three cents. In goes their dime, out comes my three cents. You know what I've been negotiating on for the past two months?" His lips pursed in a simple, secret smile as his hand brushed at the bold red cloth badge sewn on his chest that was the one island of color on the starched purity of his white shirt and pants and declared: FELIX-ITS A PLEASURE. "I knew it. I knew you wouldn't guess it. It's so simple to figure too. Think of it, Satley only has two buildings to its name, my service station and the Post-Office, because we have the Post-Office they have to call us a town, you've got to have a town to have a Post-Office, the Government can't just up and put a Post-Office building just anywhere that doesn't have a name. So there's me and the Post-Office, that's the whole town, of course there's Odus' place across the road there so that makes three buildings, course Odus' place and the Post-Office ain't much more than deserted shacks, but anyway me and the Post-Office is the only commercial buildings, if you want to get groceries or a drink you've got to go up the road to Sierraville or four

miles over to Art's place, there ain't nothing of that sort
here in Satley, except Mary and her daughter Laura sell
eggs and bread and candy bars and a few other little
things out of the Post-Office, which I think, I'm even
shore of it, is breaking one or two or maybe more U.S.
Federal Statutes, but that's not what I'm thinking. I'm
thinking here we are, the only commerce on this end of
the valley, setting right on top of California Interstate
U.S. Highway Number Eighty-Nine, the road that goes
clear across the top of the Sierra Nevada Mountains and
gets its even shake of tourist during the hot weather and a
lot of them got to pull in here for gas because I'm the
only Standard Station for forty miles or more, and when
they get out and stretch they generally will have a thirst
and drop a dime into this here machine so's I'll get my
three cents, but it's something more they want, it's something will make their trip a pleasure, it's a snack. How
about that, Joe. It's a snack they want. So I've been negotiating the past two months with a big firm over to Reno
called SNACKETTE, they'll put in free of charge to me a
brand new machine on the wall right next to the cash register where I can keep my eye on it full of peanuts, lifesavers, and candy bars, all behind little glass windows so
they can see what they're paying their nickel for, each and
every item will be one nickel and I get back two cents on
the nickel. Can you beat that. Two cents on the nickel is
better than what the pop machines gives me back. Now
you tell me, who's going to walk on across the street there
into that broken down, dark Post-Office and buy a candy
bar from Mary and Laura when they can put their nickel
in my shiny new SNACKETTE, turn the knob and out
comes the same thing, fresher too."

Birdsong slipped his empty Orange Crush bottle into
the rack next to Felix's, walked across the street and let
the screen door of the Post-Office slam against its worn
hinges behind him, loosening the conspiracy of a few idle
cobwebs hung at deceptive, awkward angles from the low
ceiling. "Laura." The girl behind the counter, her body
propped up on a stool and laid back into the corner like a
discarded sack, flipped the page of her comic book over.

"Laura, give me one of those candy bars out of the box there."

"Which kind," the girl flicked the edge of the page without looking up. "We got three kinds, TOOTSIE-ROLL, LOOK, and HERSHEY WITH NUTS."

"Give me one of those with the red wrapper."

"LOOK. That's LOOK. Cost a nickel."

"Just what I want. Give it to me."

The girl rolled the comic book up like a club and pulled her body from the corner, the bare wood of the floor creaking under the unexpected weight. "Why Mister Joe," her face floated up before him, pale as a lemon brought up from the bottom of a bucket, her gray eyes blinking blindly like the gills of a fish, trying to adjust themselves to the dull light filtering unevenly through the rusted screen of the door. "I never knew it was you," she spoke not to his face but to one of the buttons on his shirt, the last one before the shirt entirely disappeared beneath his belt.

"Well it was me from the beginning. Just like today is Monday, March number twenty, the first day of spring."

"That's true Mister Joe," she nodded at the button above the belt as her voice snagged on the beginning of a giggle and she turned her face to the rounded hump of bare shoulder sticking out of the sagging material of her dress, her mouth open as if she were going to bit it off or yawn. "It's a funny thing you come in Mister Joe because there's a letter here for you." She slid open a drawer and watched as her fingers fumbled through a stack of mail. She felt the weight of each letter, her thumbs scraping against the grain of the clean white envelopes. "I think this should be the one," she held it out in front of her like a pet squirrel with a nut. "Joe Birdsong, General Delivery, Satley, California. That's all the right things to say if it's for you," she let the letter drop on the counter and her mouth turned up in a half smile because it didn't break like an egg.

"What about my LOOK," Birdsong picked up the letter.

"You don't get no magazines," the girl focused her attention again on the button.

"I mean the candy bar."

"What candy bar?"

"The candy bar I asked for when I came in."

"Oh . . . that candy bar," she smiled in complete recognition at the button. "You know I wouldn't forget *that* candy bar."

"Well, let me have it then."

She placed her hand in the box, "One or two?"

"One. All I need is one."

"That's a nickel," she set it on the counter. "Same price as a fancy stamp, and airmail is eight cents, two less than Coca-Cola, that's how I remember which is which."

"Airmail is seven cents, Coca-Cola is ten, you're one cent off."

"I knew I made a mistake somewhere between the two. Some people said I was a mistake."

"Got any new WANTED FBI posters in?"

"One I just put up this morning, or yesterday," the girl put his nickel in a tin box and climbed back up on her stool, unfurling the rolled comic book like a new flag. He studied the WANTED posters tacked firmly on the wall, the ones turning yellow he knew by heart. Some were without pictures and he read the descriptions over slowly, letting the words fit together the picture of the man wanted for Federal crimes in his mind until it became clear and stamped itself deep in his memory and for the moment was more vivid and close than the image of his own face. He noticed the man from Wyoming who kidnapped the two girls and left them to suffocate in the trunk of an old '36 Ford had a different poster out with more recent pictures, he had gone down from number three MOST WANTED to number seven, it probably meant they wouldn't catch him. Whenever a man dropped down in position he never seemed to go back up, finally they even stop sending out posters on him and it was as if he never existed but for the year or two he was tacked up on the wall of every Post-Office in the United States. He always wondered where they all went when they no longer had a

position on the wall. That bothered him, because even
though their faces were gone from the wall he still carried
them around in his head. There wasn't anything special
about the new man except that under "Scars and Marks"
he had almost the longest list Birdsong had ever seen,
"scars left and right side of cheek, right side of chest, left
little and index fingers, right shin. Tattoos: nude woman,
both upper arms; anchor, 'USN', rope, ship, four gulls,
cross between right thumb and index finger; heart, 'Eve-
lyn' right calf, bee on left foot." There was nothing un-
usual about his "occupations," in that category he wasn't
much different from thousands of other men; "hod car-
rier, insurance salesman, roofer." The Federal warrant
had been issued "on December 9, 1955 at Tampa, Florida, charging Edgar Horhimer with unlawful interstate
flight to avoid prosecution for murder (Title 18, U.S.
Code, Section 1073)." He was "reportedly carrying a pistol and has access to other types of weapons, including
handgrenades, considered extremely dangerous." But the
thing that was funny about the man was his criminal record, there was something about it left incomplete, throwing the whole poster off balance, "has been convicted of
trespassing, petty larceny and murder." From trespassing
to murder with only petty larceny in between was one
long step, and it was this detail that Birdsong's imagina-
tion tripped over, how could a man go from trespassing to
handgrenades? He walked outside, trying to find the proper weight in his head to balance trespassing and murder,
surely petty larceny wasn't it. He leaned against the building, cocking his bad leg up on the wall releasing it from
its share of the burden. His fingers peeled the wrapper
carefully down the slab of chocolate as he looked across
the road to see if Felix had a clear view of him, but all
that could be seen was the back of the white uniform and
the fury of a leather cloth rubbing the blood shine of the
Coke machine, and then that was gone, obscured as Frank
Madson's tractor rolled in front of him with all the steel
and clang and roar of a tank blitzing through a long ago
conquered hamlet, with Frank himself sitting high in the
metal seat, his stiff straw allweather cowboy hat tucked

down at a forward angle, a raised hand held in sudden
greeting to the loyal peasants who turned out to wave him
onward on top of his Japanese tractor that he picked up
for fifteen hundred dollars in the summer auction at Grass
Valley when the auctioneer announced the Japanese had
been making tractors a hundred years before transistor ra-
dios and Frank bought it on the spot. Birdsong saluted the
bouncing back with his melting bar as the machine bore
its Captain down the road toward its long field for the
day, leaving in its wake Felix standing supported between
his two pillars across the road, his white starched body
hung suspended directly between the Regular 20¢ pump
and the High Test 24¢ pump with his eyes nailed into the
chocolate bar disappearing suddenly into his brother-in-
law's mouth and being chewed with great motions of the
jaw.

"Joey, what brings you into the big town? Going to give
Felix over there a hand shining his Coke machine? Me,
I'd like to help. You know I'm always willing. But I
worked nineteen years for the California Department of
Highways and I'm retired now, taking it easy you might
want to say, or being a bum you probably would say."

Birdsong wanted to spit the sweet plastic taste of the
chocolate wad in his mouth out on the dirt in one soft
lump, but felt that would not be an answer to his friend,
so he forced himself to swallow the pulp down, "Odus,
could you give me a drink?"

"Could I give you a drink. Hah. Ask the King of Spain
if he would give you a Moorish castle. A drink I don't
have. A bottleful of whiskey I do have. Come my friend,
let us retreat to where the panorama does not list among
its more singular attributes such eye filling delights as the
modern service station, which, as you and I both know, is
shortly to become an ancient custom." He led the way
across the deserted pavement and into the log house that
did not have one window cut into its highway side, the entire front wall was blank and barren. Birdsong looked
back before going through the open door and saw Laura
wedged into the open crack of the screen door, her eyes

blinking in the sudden sun, but intent; an owl watching a field mouse disappear into its hole.

Inside the long room was filled with mountains, they streamed through the great windows cut carefully into the logs of the wall which were laid securely one upon the other, the golden hard hearts from the tall trunks of once green pine. Odus stood in front of the windows, his squat body alone in the open center of glass running from floor to ceiling, connected with the mountains soaring up from the back of his house. "On that highest ridge there, you can see the sun through the trees. You can see the spaces between those tall trees. You can see the blue sky through the gaps that should be solid with growing wood. The line of trees on that ridge looks like my teeth would if I had just gone a full round with Rocky Marciano. I sit here every day, as I have for ten years, and watch the trees on that ridge get thinner and thinner. Before I die they'll be as many trees left on that ridge as there will be hairs on my head. Some day I'll get up, make my coffee, sit down and look out the window and see a bald mountain. Then I'll just settle back, finish my cup of black and give up living. What on God's earth is left after those sonofabitchin loggers have cut everything down to the bone, have deprived a forest of its function. Anyone who could stand still for one moment and look at that pitiful thin line of trees on the horizon without feeling shame, shame without crying inside at how we all have fucked the mother mountain, isn't a whole man, that's something Garibaldi wouldn't have stood for, not for one second on top of one of your E-PLURIBUS-UNUM silver dollars." He clasped his hands behind his back and stalked back and forth in front of the clear glass, his feet striking full and flat on the rough planks of the floor like he was counting off white divider-lines down the black center of some forgotten highway. "Joey," his body stopped dead in the middle of his count and his old face was alone in front of the trees through the window with the gray eyebrows caught in a rut of skin halfway up his forehead. "Garibaldi was a goddamn saint."

"Whiskey."

"Whiskey. He loved it. Couldn't get enough. When he came through a town like Tarracina the women would rush out and pour cupfuls of it over his boots."

"I'll take it out of the bottle."

"No need, I have glasses, you're uptown here, all the way uptown. Sit down there, you're a guest. Just you sit down, push all those books to the floor and just relax in that chair."

Birdsong sat in the big chair with the cloth arms chewed down to the bone of wood from wear and let his weight go easy against the back, it was a strong back with a solid curve to it and it would still be standing after the rest of the chair crumbled away, it was out of respect to its strength that he didn't put any undo stress on it, just like you never overload a strong horse, even when you know he can take it. He didn't look out the windows at the mountain, he could see that from his own house, or from any point in the valley, except up at the northend beyond the hot springs where the hard ground turned soft beneath the feet, and then muddy where the high fat grass grew up and the thick waves of willows hid the water, sending above the marsh a milk haze which blanked the rise of the mountains. Five miles away the waters of the marsh turned into the Yuba River and cut through stone, the same kind of stone in front of him now as the best fireplace in the County, a fireplace that could heat twelve rooms of any two houses put together, and not just the one room it was intended for. It was the first thing Odus built, it took him almost the whole of a summer, the tall chimney toppled twice, Odus didn't want any supports as he worked, he wanted the rocks to stand firm and clean as one, like they were carved from a single boulder and would take any amount of snow and wind that came blowing down off the mountain. He worked every day on the fireplace, and when in the late afternoon he would drive back to his boarding house in Truckee it would look to someone passing by that a house had burned down long ago and the only thing left standing was the fireplace. But those who thought that, had it backwards. "Build your fireplace first," Odus told him. "That's your heart, that's the life of a house, and when you have yourself a fireplace, then you can go ahead and put your walls up around it and a roof over the whole thing." The rocks of the hearth were something special. When he worked for the State on the mountain highways all the way back to the beginning he knew he was going to build that fireplace and just what kind of rocks he needed for the hearth, their shape and size and how many. When he walked along behind the oiler hard-raking mile after mile of the hotbed smooth he always had his eyes open, running red from the steam of the boiler blowing back at him from the oiler up front, his eyes touched every rock on both sides of the new hot road, testing them for a possible place in his hearth, examining their feel, and sometimes, maybe only two, three times a summer, when he found what he was looking for, when he found one that was right, one that fit into the pattern locked up in his head, he marked its position on the new road and later, in the shade of dusk, he would walk back from where the crew had ended for the day, maybe three, sometimes four miles to the place where the rock was and he'd match it again to his plan, and if it still fit he hid it down off the bed of the road, wedging it solid against the base of a sugarpine, and years later, when the base and chimney were finished and all that remained for completion was the facing rock of the hearth he drove around the mountain roads for five days in his pickup, going right to the places where he had set aside the rocks that fit into his design.

"Here's hoping you don't end up like John Bigtree," Odus handed Birdsong a glassful of whiskey and sat carefully in the only other chair in the room while he worked his false teeth out of his mouth and placed them on his lap before taking a drink, he never drank whiskey with his teeth in. A pit-boss at one of the casinoes in Reno had told him a long time ago that the worst thing in the world for false teeth is to let them come into contact with whiskey, it corrodes them and stains them clear through, soak them in vodka overnight if you want, that's the best sterilizer known, but don't drink whiskey with them. And since Odus didn't like vodka he was forever taking his teeth out.

"Who's this John Bigtree? You've taught me who Garibaldi is, and the man Joe Stalin, but I don't remember you ever mentioning John Bigtree. Maybe I wouldn't mind ending up like him. I don't know, I've never thought about it till now." Birdsong finished his drink and set it on the floor beside him, he had to wait a while for Odus' answer. Odus never gave a direct answer when he was drinking whiskey with his teeth out, it always took sometime for him to screw his lips down over the gums so his toothless state wouldn't be observed as he talked, but screwing his lips down wasn't easily accomplished as he had to serve the two purposes of not exposing himself and at the same time leaving enough space in the clamped hole of the lips to make his words at least partially comprehensible, and not just the babbling of some toothless old fool. But he never trusted his lips to cover the pink of his gums and talk too, so when he finally did speak it was always with the shield of his hand wedged beneath his nose and covering the whole of his mouth so all that could be seen of the face was the heavy nose seared a turnip red from the mountain sun, pitted with the dirt of dusty new roadbeds, and the eyes above hooked open in a sudden blue by deep wrinkles. "John Bigtree," the words came slipping from beneath the shield of his hand, "was made the most famous Indian in America in nineteen-hundred and thirteen. They'll never be another as famous, they'll never be another with such distinction."

"I've never heard of him."

"Of course you've never heard of him, Joey," Odus' eyes narrowed and pulled up; in that moment, with his hand covering his mouth, he looked like a small boy restraining the beginning of a giggle that will seize his body and shake it violently in private joke. "You don't hear of John Bigtree, you only see him, you only feel him, you only touch his face, the face of the most honored Indian of all time, the only Indian who has ever been welcomed into every American home, the only Indian who has seen the inside of every pocket, purse and wallet and has

rubbed eyebrows with Presidents. He's the guy on the
nickel. It was in nineteen and thirteen they stamped his
proud red face on every five-cent piece pumped out of the
treasury. Woodrow Wilson even made a speech about it,
that being his first year as President he felt he had to
make a speech about everything, even invited old John
himself on down to Washington to shake his hand for finally making it in the Whiteman world. Old John was a
little afraid of going on down because he didn't own a headdress, never had, wasn't a real chief, and the President expected him to show up in a headdress like any decent Indian so the two chiefs could have their pictures taken
shaking hands. So old John had to borrow himself a headdress off the Smithsonian Institute when he pulled into
Washington. Woodrow's speech was one of those little
nervous ones he was later to become so famous for, you
know he had four breakdowns before he even got to be
President, he wasn't one of your Teddy Roosevelts. Woodrow said how privileged he was to meet old John, his
being a mighty chief of his people, and how John was the
best of his kind, being as how he never gave any trouble
and was duly rewarded by having his face stamped for
posterity on the nickel, that being the ultimate tribute
America had, putting your face on its money. What
Woodrow actually was saying was that if all little Indian
kids were good and didn't cause the Government trouble
on their reservations that someday they might end up with
their face plastered across the ten dollar bill; they never
would own one for sure, but their face would be riding
around on them just the same. Woodrow of course left
out the fact that there weren't hardly no Indians left alive
on the face of America, about as many as the buffalo.
Guess he figured there'd always be an Indian around so
long as there was nickels, that must have been the reason
why the buffalo was put on the other side of the coin, buffalo and Indians, kill them all off and scrape up what's
left and put them together and you'll have enough for five
cents' worth of metal. I tell you this Joey, and I don't care
who's around to hear it, Garibaldi wouldn't have stood for

it, not for one second on top of one of your E-Pluribus-Unum silver dollars. Not for one tick of the clock."

"I remember Wilson from school. Didn't he start the United Nations and then was shot?"

"League of Nations he started, for all that was worth, just a Swiss real-estate deal."

"Who was shot then?"

"A lot of them was shot, about half of them should have been before they took the oath; God wasn't about to strike them down. It was McKinley though, he's the one was shot, great admirer of Garibaldi's he was."

"I wonder if anyone will shoot this man called Ike. It couldn't happen I think, not today in the fifties anyway, it hasn't happened for so long a time people forget about it. Still, it's something to wonder at. I wonder at things like that, sometimes I think I'm crazy because I do."

"Wonder at it? Damn you Joey, you haven't listened one bit to all the history I've taught you. You don't know a thing if you haven't learned what history is saying to us, it says it's all a bore, life is, because the same old things keep happening one over the other. It don't make a Quaker's bit of difference if this is the fifties, thirties or seventies, Ike could be shot, poisoned or strangled. There isn't such a thing as a modern time, only old ones with different names stuck on the faces, finding a modern time is like finding out your mother is a virgin. And people never forget, there was even a bunch tried to slip over the wall and give it to old Harry S. You're dead wrong Joey, in history, and in your own life too, if you haven't learned things happen one over the other, like an empty barrel rolling down a hill. Garibaldi was one that learned the lesson when Mazzini called him back from exile early in 1848 in Uruguay, where he was teaching those Indians any fool can shoot a gun; you don't have to be Catholic to pull the trigger. Mazzini called him to Milan to be a general of the people in the revolutionary army, Garibaldi knew it was only a single roll of the barrel, just a little twist, the barrel would roll over and over before the map of Italy would no longer just be a bunch of royal states that could be bartered, betrayed or sold by the Pope in Rome but would

be a unified country, a full boot that could kick the ass of
Europe if it so much as even thought of invading an inch
of Italian soil again. Garibaldi knew the only way to survive the barrel was to keep your feet moving, to get off is
to stop, to stop is to die. That's why when years after Milan, when finally the spirit of Risorgimento had come of
age like a rare wine and Garibaldi's army was defeating
every Papist backed despot who dared challenge its progress, and ended up with all of Southern Italy, and put it
like a feather in Garibaldi's hat, and the people were cutting their wrists to declare their loyalty to him and
stampeding through the streets of Naples begging him to
rule and old Victor Emmanuel gets wind of it and comes
racing over with the Sardinian army to remind Garibaldi
that there is going to be one kingdom of Italy, with one
ruler, and that's going to be him and *his* gang. Garibaldi,
he just smiles at old Victor, gets drunk, gives about six or
twelve women the honor of lying down beneath him and
leaves town whistling Ave Maria."

"Why didn't Garibaldi ever gang up with Stalin?"

Odus dropped the shield of his hand and in the purity
of a moment the pink of his gum shined under his lip like
a pig's belly before the hand remembered its place. "Joey!
You remember most of what I taught you but you can't
get the dates straightened out in a row through your head.
I told you before you've got to know the dates if you want
to understand who you are. The dates mark off each new
turn of the barrel. They signal the twist. Garibaldi was
born in 1807 and died 1882, Stalin was born in 1879 and
died only a few years ago. Hey, but wouldn't they have
been a team. I've never once thought of it before. The two
great men. We wouldn't be what we're in today if they
had joined forces. I tell you if that had happened history
would be written with flowers instead of graves, it would
be like Alexander the Great and Charlemagne getting together in the same time and cruising around the world,
you wouldn't have any of your Laurel and Hardy acts
we've been getting in this century. What do you say we finish this bottle off, it's the last one left in the house, then
we can ride over to Art's and try some of his stuff."

"I think I'll read this letter I got then, if I'm not going home."

"You read your letter Joey, and I'll get my teeth in."

Birdsong looked at the envelope for the first time; stamped boldly across the top lefthand side in raised black letters was RESORT MOUNTAIN LAND PROPER-TIES, Lake Tahoe, California. Inside he found the same raised black print on top of the letter, only larger, down below it said: "Greetings, Mr. Joseph Birdsong. RESORT MOUNTAIN LAND PROPERTIES is pleased to inform you that your six and onehalf acres of mountain property which is located one and seventenths of a mile northeast of the town of Satley and is bounded on the western ex-tremity by the Frank Richard Madson ranch, on the north by Dixel and Son Incorporated of San Francisco, on the south by the Felix Castor acreage as mortgaged to the Bank of Reno, and at the length of the eastern boundary by California State Highway 89, is in the proposed devel-opment area of a RESORT MOUNTAIN LAND PROP-ERTIES vacation mobile-homes country club. The Coun-ty of Sierra has assessed the real value of your property at $4,850. R.M.L.P. is prepared to negotiate for the sale of said property in the interest of further tourist development of High Sierra Mountain land and is prepared to offer the sum of $8,012 for your property rights. Please come into our central office located at 1248 South Shore, Lake Tah-oe at your earliest convenience. Mr. R. Theodore Tafield has all the pertinent information and compilated folio re-garding your property and will be most pleased to offer any further details. Feel free to ask his assistance. Re-spectfully Yours, Mr. M. O. Cownstard, President, R. M. L. P."

"What's wrong Joey? You look like you've just got a letter declaring you've been excommunicated."

"Who are these people?" Birdsong held the letter up. "These Mountain Land people. All my life I have lived in this valley and never once have I heard of these people, and now they send a letter telling me my land is in the middle of where they want to park trailers. Who do they think they are, the Governor?"

"Let me see it," Odus took the letter and read only for an instant before the wrinkles around his eyes relaxed, releasing the skin back into its smooth ruts. "Christ! It's a gimmick. A bunch of clowns from the City come up here thinking they can rob the stupid, simpleminded rancher and small landowner out of his land. Bunch of goddam Machiavellians is all. Bandits in Cadillacs. There's your cannibals for you, cannibals in tailored sharkskin suits. They send out letters like this and expect you to come running into their office like you just won the Irish Sweepstakes, expect you to turn over your deed and give you in return half the money they promised. It must work on a lot of people though because I've seen this kind of thing more than this once. I guess to some it seems a dream someone would actually want to buy the land they been fighting with most of their adult lives, and even before that, just to make enough to break even so they can break their back the next year. Hell, if you and I had a dollar for every peasant who went for this robbery we would be rich men retiring to the Kremlin. What gets me though is how people can sell their land because of a letter, don't even see the face of the man who wants to buy what's theirs. That's how things are done now, you don't even see the face of the man you're dealing with. People that don't have any respect for their land don't have any respect for themselves. When people say they'll go to war and fight for their piece of this earth it isn't that at all. What they're really fighting for is the chance to come back and sell what's gone up in value since they've been gone. There's never been a war yet that hasn't sooner or later sent the price of land up like a rocket. Wars are not fought over people, they're fought over land. Hitler was the greatest real estate visionary since Caesar. People have the heart of a toad," Odus snapped the rigid piece of paper and broke it down to a white ball in his fist. "I received a letter like this just the day before this one Joey, the words read the same insult," he tossed the white ball into the ashes of the fireplace. "Come on, let's get over to Art's. I can't drink whiskey but he's got enough Beefeater there to float the whole Argentine Navy on, and he'll give one round free to every one we buy."

ART'S AND LINDA'S DEW DROP INN—LOUNGE AND RESTAURANT didn't have a front and a back. If you went in one side and up some steps you found yourself in a restaurant that was closed Mondays and Tuesdays and open every other day from six until eleven. If you went in the other side and down some steps you found yourself in what seemed like the den of a man who has a little money ahead, except for the jukebox and bright electric signs flashing three colored images of bottles of beer being continuously poured into bottomless glasses, and clear blue mountain water foaming over blinking rocks, which ceased to exist every morning at two when Art cut off the electric flow of the signs and shut down the lounge before climbing the flagstone steps leading to the restaurant and then up the knottypine stairway between the two doors marked: COWBOYS and COWGIRLS, and into the top floor with its five full rooms of Danish Modern anchored on the softpile of wall-to-wall avocado tint carpet. If you forgot where you just came from you would think you were in any number of recently built suburban homes slammed onto the freshly bulldozed landscape surrounding any California city, and if you made a mistake and pulled the drapes, which were always closed, you would give a start at not seeing your neighbor's house with the proud stamp of green lawn pasted in front, but instead the top of a pinetree rubbing its branches against the glass obstacle of the window, and behind, the valley rolling out flat for thirteen miles until it bumped in a haze against the bare eastern mountain rim, and you would realize you weren't on your familiar street, but fifty-two hundred and twelve feet high in the Sierra Nevada Mountains straddling a restaurant and bar. Art got off his ship at the Alameda Naval Station after the War and decided he wasn't going back to Indiana. He took one look around and knew California was his future, where he would die. With the money the Government had given him for sailing on its ship Art bought a car and headed for Los Angeles. He made it to within onehundred and twelve miles when the car broke down in Bakersfield and to pay for its being fixed he got a job at the gas station that had towed him in. The weather in Bakersfield was good to Art. Within a year he had enough money to get married to a girl just graduated from the highschool who was a little old for her age, and with his G.I. Loan to buy ten acres of hot raw land south of the city limits just off the road to Los Angeles. On one part of the land there were some long, lowslung sheds that had housed chickens until several years before Art's arrival when the chicken rancher had gone bankrupt. Art thought he could make the chicken ranch go. There had been a lot of talk in the magazines he read that year about chickens being a sure enterprise, and like the man at the big feedstore who sold him his stock in Bakersfield said: "I never met an honest man yet who didn't eat eggs." Art didn't get the chance to eat many eggs himself, within two years time he received a letter from the California State Highway Department informing him that a new fourlane freeway to L.A. was going to punch right through the length of his land and the State was offering him six times what he paid for it. Art accepted. With eighteen thousand dollars in cash and a new car he finally made it to Los Angeles, where he drove up and down the busiest streets trying to find something to spend his money on. He found it. Not in the center of town, but further out on Wilshire Boulevard where there wasn't a tremendous amount of traffic during the weekdays but on the weekends the road was quite congested with people going to the beach at Santa Monica. What he found was a building shaped like a monstrous dog painted orange and blue. People walked through the door in the belly and ordered across the counter the 15¢ hamburgers advertised outside in black letters on the ear of the dog. Art was always smiling as he slid the hot paper wrapped orders across the counter because on good weekends he could sell thirteen hundred hamburgers, and behind him his wife Linda worked hard and well over the open faced grill; she had turned her craft into art, she prepared all the 15¢ hamburgers on the afternoon before the day they were to be sold and kept them in a special deep steamer; having this done she was never rushed, the only thing she ever cooked right after it was ordered was the Delux 45¢ steak sandwich, so she was relaxed and pleasant through the day, listening to the soft hum of the traffic outside and the grease popping regular around the thin patties of meat rowed neatly on the grill. The weather in Los Angeles was good to Art. He never did think once of knocking the dog down and putting in a larger place with maybe some tables outside. But somebody else did, they had the idea of knocking the dog down, but not putting in a larger place, no. As it was explained to him in a letter from one of the Downtown banks representing an expanding Eastern Oil Company, what they had in mind was a gas-station. The traffic in front of Art's dog had increased 80 percent since the year he bought it and gas-stations had been built on all three corners surrounding the dog, a fact Art checked out for himself by glancing through the plateglass window in the dog's southern side; now the dirt the dog sat on was a prime corner lot, worth nine times what he had paid for it. Art sold out, bought a new car and headed for the Sierra Mountains. There was still gold to be found in California. What Art found was a valley fifty-two hundred and twelve feet high, twenty three miles north-east of Truckee, and there he was able to buy fifteen times the the land than he could at Lake Tahoe, which was only thirty-six miles away. It didn't make much difference to Art where he settled in the valley, the way he had it figured sooner or later someone would want to put a freeway through it, a gas-station on it, or make it part of an airport, so he chose the west side of the valley off the main State Highway 89 on country road A-24. There were no places of business on the road as far as the eye could see in both directions and farther, and in the winter there wasn't any traffic on the road except maybe a rancher driving slowly along seeing how his fences held. During the summer there was some traffic, mostly tourists who had wandered off one of the main highways and had lost themselves in the mountains. But none of this bothered Art, for he was certain that all a

man had to do in California was to go some place and
sooner or later the people will follow. So he built on a
corner, because they were always worth more over the
long haul, and it made no difference to him that the only
living things around were the cattle munching their way
across flat fields, and he decided to go all out on the construction of a restaurant and bar, because the more you
had on a piece of property the more they paid you to
knock it down. When the construction was going on the
ranchers throughout the valley, and even from as far
away as Portola, came over to see what was going up at
the corner of county A-24 off the main State Highway 89,
which was like eight-hundred other corners anywhere in
the valley, take your pick. One said he thought it was
going to be one of those new modern bowling alleys he
had seen a picture of in LIFE magazine, but everybody
thought that a crazy idea as the only things around to
bowl were the steers; the hell if they were going to work
all day and spend their nights trying to knock down sticks
with a black ball. It was eventually decided a rich man up
all the way from L.A. was building himself a mansion and
he'd have a swimming pool in the front. But when the
building was complete the equipment to dig the pool
didn't come, instead large trucks rolled up and unloaded
case after case of beer and whiskey; it was a rich drunk
up all the way from L.A. A few weeks later a sign went
up right along the road, ART'S AND LINDA'S DEW
DROP INN—LOUNGE AND RESTAURANT. Art
opened the next day and nobody came. Fall had just
about finished with itself and the winds came hard over
the spine of the Sierra from the south and nobody even
drove by the place that looked like it had accidentally
been dropped from the sky into nothing. Art had himself
an Italian cook and served Italian dinners, but the only
ones the Italian ever cooked for were Art and Linda, then
he would go downstairs to the bar and spend his wages
getting drunk. One night the Italian got so drunk he hitch-
hiked into Truckee and never came back. Art had six
cooks that first winter and he and Linda never ate so well,
but the cooks never stayed long. In the spring the man

who sold Art the corner off one of his fields, a man called
Dixel who owned most of the best land in the valley and
didn't care much about anything other than raising prize
Appaloosas became Art's first customer, and he had a
theory. The theory was to hire a Chinese cook, the people
in the valley won't come out for ravioli but they will for
chicken chow mein, for some reason the ranchers and loggers and just about anybody else liked Chinese food, and
they would also find out the drinks weren't as expensive as
the building looked, and the best part was this, Chinese
cooks are the best, they work hard and for little pay, then
on their day off they go over to Lake Tahoe and gamble
all their money away, you were always certain of them
being back the next morning, broke and ready to work;
Chinese are incorrigible gamblers. Art drove down to
Orosi below Fresno which was once a Railroad town
where he had been told a lot of Chinese were still to be
found and out of any real kind of job since the Railroad
deserted the town fifteen years before. He bought himself
a cook, amended his sign, ART'S AND LINDA'S DEW
DROP INN LOUNGE AND RESTAURANT—
CHINESE DINNERS, and the first night he had custom-
ers, a family of five. The weather in the Sierra was good
to Art. The smooth balloon of his face which floated up
off his short body always had a cheery-delicate smile
painted on it. Art was in no hurry, he was just waiting.
There was never any trouble in Art's lounge, the place
hadn't been torn up once. The men who drank at Art's re-
garded him as a priest, after looking at cattle and horses
and their wives all day it was a pleasure to go someplace
that was a notch too good for them where the little man
behind the bar was polite and always had a smile on his
face like he was expecting you to hand him a check for
$800,000. The smile was natural to Art, and because it
was natural it was a good defense, there wasn't one man
he served a drink to who couldn't put him in his pocket.
So he had his smile turned on like the electric beer signs
flowing all around the walls when he saw up through the
window the battered blue pickup roll to a stop and Odus
jumped out with the Indian. Art never tried to figure any-

one out but once or twice it slipped through to him the Indian was odd. Art never had many Indians come into his place, he knew like everyone how Indians were born to drink so he took it as fact like the sun passing through the sky that they bought their liquor at the grocery in Sierraville. He hadn't seen many Indians since he'd been in the valley, most of them lived on the other side in Loyalton, he saw maybe six, and he heard there weren't many more, twenty or thirty, but time was when the five mills were going years ago before he came, there were more than a hundred, tuberculosis got almost every one of them some of the older ranchers thought was what happened. Most of the Indians left were Paiutes, this one was Washo, Odus said, but Art couldn't see the difference between him and the ones he knew to be Paiute, he was not very much interested in them. They weren't like the tall ones on the plains he had seen in the Randolph Scott movies, not this one anyway, he wasn't much taller than Art himself, he wore the same flannel shirt and jeans as the other men and didn't look as strong, his skin was soft and had a tame look and the face muddy and blunt, but this didn't stop his wife from trying to get his picture with her Japanese camera one afternoon last summer; he's cute, she always said when he left, he doesn't act the way the rest of the men up here do, he just doesn't seem to act, he's like a brown doll. But what slipped through to Art about the Indian was the fact he only drank with Odus, and Odus never let him pay, so then always the next day the Indian would come back and give Art exactly the amount of money Odus had spent on him and would say to treat Odus with it the next time he came in, but not to tell him why. So when Odus and the Indian settled themselves at the slick polished counter Art glided down his narrow no-slip runway in front of the gleaming bank of glass bottles, set two glasses of gin in front of them and waited dutifully for the ice to stop clinking before he announced, "Men, let me have the honor of the first round."

"Damn you Art," Odus raised his glass and felt its chill

in his palm. "A man works all his life so he can retire and you rob him of a way of spending his money."

"Oh, I got lots of ways for you to spend your money Odus. You just bring it all in one day in a paper sack and I'll write down ten ways how to get rid of it."

"Art, if you were a fish you'd be a shark. Why didn't you ever go into real estate, a man as quick on the cash register as you could own the whole State of California and the green part of Nevada."

"I play a little at it."

"Well if I played as well as you I'd get myself over the hill to Reno and play Bill Harrah himself. Five card, everything but painted ladies wild."

"That's the only way you'll ever beat Bill Harrah, that's for sure, that's for sure," the words spread all over the room before the man who spoke them as he closed the door behind him. "Five card, everything but painted ladies wild, that's the only way for sure." He set a black poodle down on the counter and covered its whole wooly head in the caress of his large flattened sunburnt hand. "Me and Petey's thirsty Art. Gin for me and a bowl of gingerale for Petey."

The words sent Art gliding up and down his no-slip runway. "I keep this bowl here just special for Petey, Ted," Art set the bowl in front of the dog and filled it with fizzing liquid.

"Petey appreciates that," Ted pulled the small straw hat off his long head pushed in flat on both sides and broke out on the top in stiff blond stubble and placed it next to the bowl. "Here's iron in your pants, Petey," he raised his glass and tipped it to the dog as the dog sunk its face in the fizz, its sharp pink tongue lapping like the sputtering blades of a boat engine in water. "The vet over to Portola says gingerale ain't good for poodles, especially miniatures, says they don't have the stomach for it, too delicate, gives them ulcers I guess. But Petey can't stay off gingerale, he's hooked. Look at him, he'll lick that bowl clear through. Fill him up again Art, and me too."

"Why don't you give him a shot of tequila," Odus said over the private tune he was rapping out on the counter with his fingernails. "That's what they do in Mexico, even force a whole bottle down the throat of a burro. Guaranteed to kill worms."

"Petey doesn't have worms. He doesn't mix with other dogs."

"What about females? Petey may only be a miniature but he still needs a place to put it."

"No females. He's never out of my sight. Goes everywhere with me in the truck on my deliveries, wherever there's a load of hay to be dropped."

"Are what you telling me Ted is Petey's a celibate?"

"Hold it one moment Odus, hold it up right there," the ears flattened up against Ted's head blinked blood red. "Not one word further till you explain to me what you mean by calling Petey a *celibrant*."

"He means Petey's a monk, Ted," Art's wife stepped carefully down the glossy knottypine steps from the restaurant above and set herself stiffly on a specially padded stool at the end of the counter and patted the sprayed strands of reddish hair contoured into an awkward shape that looked like a bird taking off on top of her head as she waited patiently for Art to glide down his slot behind the bar and present her with the only drink she ever allowed him to serve her, rum and Coca-Cola. "What he's trying to say Ted is that your little Petey's a virgin. Cheers," she tipped the drink to her drawn lips. Art's smile never faded, but if it was watched closely you could see it change colors. Whenever his wife came down from the restaurant, which was a little past noon each day when the men started coming in, it turned a lily-white, by twelve-thirty each day Art broke his own rule and served himself, by one o'clock his smile was again dusted an even glow. Having his wife at the bar was like having a strange lady come in every day as a steady customer, she told jokes he'd never heard, wore dresses he'd never once seen, and showed more skin in daylight than he had ever caught a glimpse of since his wedding night. The altitude of the valley was good to Art's wife. It brought something out in the sex of her that he couldn't get around, but he was always trying, and the afternoons was all he had because after closing the bar down each night he would pass up through the restaurant to his home and he'd find the girl from Bakersfield High who was a little old for her age and had made him so proud as she stood behind him at the dog over the open faced grill listening to the soft hum of the traffic outside and the grease popping regular around the thin patties of meat.

"Hah, little Petey's one on top of you there Linda, he's got you this time," Ted pushed his stool back, all the years of hooking bales and hefting them on and off trucks had stretched his body like taffy and left his hands dangling somewhere around his knees, but his brain still connected to the hands and he swooped the little dog up and held him gentle for a moment in the air like a new laid egg before he spread the hind legs wide and rotated the dog around so everyone could see.

"That's the most goddamdest unnatural thing I've ever seen." Odus gulped the rest of his drink, the two icecubes passing down his throat in one slow lump, almost choking him to death before he could spit everything out. "That dog's not any monk, he's a goddam eunuch!"

"I'm not going to look, Ted," Linda jabbed a hand over her eyes, the tips of the fingers flashing a hard painted pearl white. "Please. Please put him down."

"You're looking at a through and through thoroughbred miniature poodle," Ted set the dog next to its bowl and continued over the sucking noise of the delicate mouth. "That's the only way the kennel lady over to Quincy would sell him to me, they're all cut like that unless they're special to be bred. This keeps them clean and the seed from being misdirected, you won't see any of your halfmutt poodles trotting the roads around, that's for sure, that's for sure." He cupped the dog's head in his hand. "Petey here couldn't be a monk nohow," the voice coming out of the center of his thin face seemed to be trying to persuade someone who was not there, someone who had left a long time ago. "Petey couldn't be a monk because he's not Catholic. My wife was though, she doesn't feel that pain in her leg anymore since we buried her over to Saint Mark's graveyard in Truckee. She was a good be-

liever that woman, all the way to the otherside of her
death. Saint Christopher's medal she snapped on the rear-
view mirror in the cab of my truck is still there. I remember the day she put it on. Course," he released the dog's
head from the caress of his palm, "I pasted one of those
signs across the dash below it: DEAR SAINT CHRISTO-
PHER, IF I CRASH GOIN' 77, SAVE ME A PIECE IN
HEAVEN." He scratched the dog's stomach and looked
somewhere in between the glass bank of bottles shining
before him, "Save me a piece in heaven."

"Joe. Joe," Linda leaned forward and waved down the
counter like she was trying to flag down the only car on a
desert road. "Would you please push R-12 just for me, it's
a new song we just got in by a guy called Andy Wil-
liams, he's much better than Perry Como, and already it's
my favorite, my special. Art will give you the money."
Birdsong swung off his stool and felt the woman's eyes
going all over his back and into his black hair as he ran
his finger over the glowing plastic of the R's until he
found 12 and punched the button. "I've got change." He
turned around and the record dropped. "I'll play it."

> I LOVE YOU SO MUCH
> YOU DRIVE-A ME WILD
> I'M CRAZY ABOUT YOU
> YOU BUTT-TA-FLIE

"Let me give you another drink," Art clapped two fresh
icecubes in the glass and glanced over the bottle as he
poured. "On the house."

Birdsong looked at the smile caught on the little man's
face like a kite in a tree. And drank.

"They'll arrest you for that, Linda," Odus called into
the music. "They'll throw a net over you and haul you
into jail for contributing to those who already collected."

"Odus, you get on out here and dance with me. You've
been letting ladies dance by themselfs all your life," she
spun her body around in the middle of the floor, the large
silk flowers on her dress spilling over her body as she took
two steps out and two steps in, the reflection of the flow-

ing beer from the signs foaming over her face, washing
her down in a dull gold glow.

Ted moved with a slow stride, just one step, cocking his
straw hat down over his face like his head was going to blow
off, and slipped his hand in among the flowers around the
bouncing waist.

"Here's a man for you," Linda looked only once over
to the bar then found herself somewhere against the narrow body in front of her.

"I *said* they would arrest you Linda. We've got the fast-
est law in the State," Odus pointed his drink at the door,
one eye squinting its aim at the badge pinned like a shining silver flower over the heart of the brown shirt. "Now
he's here to do it."

"Now who's here to do what to who and what's the reason for?"

"Sheriff Davies," Linda pulled herself off the thin body
and rushed over to the big man at the door, snaking a
white arm through his and leading him up to the bar like
a bride presenting her groom to the altar.

"What's it going to be Sheriff," Art fired himself down
his slot and took the offering his wife presented him. "The
regular?"

"If you don't give me the regular Art," the man leaned
the full melon weight of his face over the bar and shut
one big eye in a slow wink, "I'd like to know the reason
why."

"One big Burgie is what the man wants," the words
shouted out of Art's face like notes from a bugle and almost before they were said the bottle of beer was on the
counter running foam out of its top like blood from a
hatcheted chicken's neck.

"Damn," the Sheriff picked the bottle up in the slab of
his hand as if it was a brown sausage, poked it in his
mouth and slammed it back down, "it's something like
this makes a man's day worthwhile!"

"You work too hard, Sheriff," Linda leaned on the
hunk of his shoulder encased in the crisp brown shirt.
"Only you and Sheriff Hadley to keep the peace in this
whole valley, it's not fair on you. All you men in this val-

ley work too hard. I've never in my life seen men work so
hard. Poor Ted over here works ten, twelve hours a day,
hardly a moment's rest."

The big man leveled the steel of his eyes at the woman
hanging on his shoulder, "That's what a man's put on this
earth for, Linda. That's all he's got he can give. If he
works hard and lives clean that's the Christian thing to do.
Don't you never forget the idle shop is the devil's play-
ground."

"Amen to that," Ted motioned for Art to fill up his
dog's bowl again.

"But that's not saying the Sheriff and me can't use some
help. You're right there when you say it's only him and
me, his Deputy Sheriff, that keeps the folks in line for the
whole valley, the whole county even. The Highway Patrol
helps us out some though, when the going gets a little too
rough. But me and Sheriff Hadley try to get the folks to
vote the money for a new man to take some of the heavy
load off us, but the folks keep voting it down regular. I
got no complaint though. It's a rewarding job."

"I'd vote for your new man next time around," Ted offered. "But it don't look like I'll be living here much longer. I got a letter just this morning from a big outfit over to
Tahoe wants to buy up my whole place for some sort of
trailer grounds. I think if they buy it I'll retire and move
down to Placerville so the winter up here can't raise so
much hell with my shoulder anymore."

Art's body snapped like a rubberband in his slot and
shot him down in front of Ted. The letter he had been
waiting for to offer him the chance to sell out had arrived
but an error had been made, it was sent to the wrong person. This had never happened to Art and for the first time
in his life he seriously doubted the fidelity of the United
States Post Office. "What do you mean *you* received a letter offering *you* the chance to sell out? Are you sure they
didn't make a mistake and deliver you the wrong letter?"

"That's right," Linda moved in on Ted and she and Art
had his thin body sandwiched between them. "Are you
certain it was addressed to you?"

"Hell yes I'm sure," Ted was trying to look at both of

them at once, not quite aware of what it was they wanted of him. "The P.O. don't never make mistakes."

"Ted's right, Art. Me and Joey received the exact same letter, said just about the same thing. As a matter of fact Joey got his just this very morning, it was from Resort Mountain Land Properties."

"That's the outfit Odus, they're the ones want to buy me up whole, that's for sure, that's for sure."

For the moment Art was stranded in his slot, there had been a mistake made or a trick played, somewhere along the line the scheme of California real-estate had dealt him out, the mouth in his face fell through the dying moment out of its smile, the worms of the two lips pressed white, gave a little wiggle like they had been hooked, Art sincerely wondered how the machine of California land could function without his small part fit properly in the engine, and it was as if the hook through his lips was jerked from above, pulling his mouth back into the customery rut on his face, for the wonder of it all was that it was impossible for him to be dealt out, he had never asked to be dealt in, but being a landowner he was a lifelong partner in the game, and the smile cemented on his face never betrayed his hand, he moved with the grace of an old cow in a loading shoot down his slot behind the counter and showed the smile to Odus and Birdsong, "Why don't you men let me sport the next round."

"Dammit Art," Odus pushed his empty glass forward. "People are going to start calling you a Communist the way you run this bar."

"I've heard of R.M.L.P., they own most of the land around Tahoe, but I've never heard of them buying land over this far north."

"Well you've heard of it now," Odus picked up his glass and rattled the ice. "You can be dead right about it just as my name is O-d-u-s, Oh-DUS."

"I don't think Art doesn't believe you Odus," the Sheriff had another one of his logical encounters with two thoughts bumping up against one another in his mind and bouncing out his mouth. "But I think what he's gettin at is that Ted's property is way over on the other side of the

valley in Loyalton and yours and Birdsong's here is on the
west side in Satley, now that makes a distance of thirteen
miles by highway and eight and a half straight across by
cattle roads, now it don't take one of your county assayers
to figure up that it's plain impractical for some outfit to
build a trailer grounds eight and a half miles long. Why
hell, the Golden Gate Bridge in 'Frisco ain't even that
long."

Art set a fresh glass of beer in front of the Sheriff to
show his thanks, for without knowing it he had explained
the mistake to him, restored his respect for the United
States Post Office and confirmed his faith in California
land. This thinking side of the Sheriff had never really exposed itself to Art before, it was as if every morning when
the Sheriff strapped on his leather holster and cinched it
tight around the meat of his hips he unstrapped any abili-
ty to think of matters not directly related to the job of
keeping the people from harming themselves, and the only
numbers he carried around up in his head all day long
were the amounts of the fines attached to the speed zones
which were constantly being broken and taxed all the
Sheriff's coordinated skill in turning on his siren, flashing
his red lights and hounding the offending car to the side
of the road. But lately the Sheriff had not been cinching
his holster so tight in the morning and certain loose ends
were being carried about by him during the day without
his knowledge, this was the first time Art had caught complete sight of one, and he was grateful for it. His respect
for the man could never be from this point on simply one
of authority, "This one's on the house Sheriff." His smile
was in full bloom as he watched the Sheriff's adam's apple
hook at the air as he sucked the bottle dry. "A man whose
job demands as much mental concentration as yours deserves his due."

"That reminds me," the Sheriff jumped off his stool like
a boxer who has just heard his bell. "I'm on official County business. I come over to this side of the valley to get
Ben Dora, he's got a court date in Downieville this afternoon and I thought I'd drive him over being as how he's
already missed twice, seems that new Highway Patrol

hot-shot roaming this territory gave Ben seven tickets in one month, four for drunk, now the judge wants to pull his license and compound his truck for the fines. I thought I'd go over and explain things to the judge, you boys know Ben needs that truck to get around to the ranches to do his work. It just won't do for him to lose it, not with the six kids to support, and Dolly too. I went by his place and Dolly says she don't know exactly which ranch he's working today but I may be able to catch him here. Any of you boys seen Dora?"

"He usually comes in here about an hour ago," Art swiped up the splashes of foam left from the Sheriff's beer. "But it doesn't look like he's coming today."

"What about you Odus, you seen him? You haven't huh. Ted, you know where he is?"

"Well Sheriff, I dumped a load of clover over to Dixel's ranch about six this morning and I heard something about Dora's fencin' on the Johnson field. Maybe you'll find him there."

"I'll give it a try, Ted. Birdsong, how's that knee of yours? Ralph tells me you banged it around pretty good when the two of you was dynamitin' snakes up at Horsetail this winter. Can you get around on it okay?"

"It's no bother."

"That's just good then. You be able to guide this weekend for our bow-hunt? Same pay as usual."

Birdsong looked at the big man with the melon face planted deeply on the slab of his body, the eyes beneath the felt hat pulled even with the weight of the puffed ears had clouds floating through them, white balls passing into the infinity of sky, devoured in the vacuous blue, "I've guided every year. I don't see the difference between this one and the last. But I thought the hunt was always in fall. It don't make much sense. They'll all be with fawns."

"Special benefit this year. We're trying to get up money for the Little League, uniforms and all, the works."

"Damn if that ain't the best charity yet I heard of for the hunt," Ted's thin face worked its way into an admiring glance at the Sheriff, he was always the first in line to shake the hand of a generous man. "We'll beat hell out of

Truckee, and with the ball playin' kids we got in this valley we'll whoop hell out of Reno too, we'll show them,
that's for sure. Who's selling tickets, Sheriff?"

"Art here's handling all our money affairs this year."

"Hell Art, why didn't you say you had that batch of
tickets? I ain't missed a hunt in years, just you ask the
Sheriff. You don't even have the sign up or nothin'."

"We haven't had any need for a sign the way people
have been rushing in here to get their hands on a ticket
before they're all gone. I only have a few left."

"Well you just give old Ted one, you ain't cuttin' me
out that easy. Here's my fifteen bucks."

"Price has gone up, twenty-five this year. It's a popular
event."

"Well here's my twenty-five then. Nobody's going to be
one up on me, old Ted's always been a sport."

"What about you Odus," the Sheriff stopped his body at
the door. "You think those legs of yours can hold you a
long enough time to get a shot?"

Odus pulled himself up on the stool and read his words
off straight at the man with the silver badget pinned over
his heart, "I've only been on a hunt once, once was
enough, it should be for any man with red blood pumping
through his body and oxygen in his brain. It's a senseless
slaughter and those involved in it should know better,
they've all been to war. Veterans of Foreign Wars they
call themselves, it seems to me they couldn't wait to bring
the war back with them. You've already cut down all the
goddam trees, now you've got to make war on what animals are left, got to slaughter their bodies for some kind
of private pleasure it gives you in your pants. I've seen the
real thing. I don't forget. Walking these highways up here
for fifteen years with the mountain sun in my face
couldn't burn out what I've seen. I wouldn't give 25¢ to
be one of the full grown men prowling around the forest
waiting the chance to stick his arrow through living flesh.
And for what? For food? Hell no. Your bellies are already
so packed with beef you can't carve extra notches in your
belts fast enough. And you aren't going up there to hunt
them out just so you can outfit a bunch of kids in gray

striped flannel. You're going up there because you lost *it*
and you're trying to get *it* back. You can't stay away. It's
a dirty goddam sacrilege, and that's the first and last name
for it."

"Odus you old bastard, you get better at that speech every year," the head of melon swung around on its body,
the laughter bubbling from its cut of mouth. "Poor little
Bambi. *All* the poor little Bambis."

Somewhere over the rim of the western mountains the
sun died into the ocean. He had never seen the ocean
but he knew that to be true. Before he would die he was
going down to San Francisco and watch the gold ball sink
in the water, slip from sight like a burning ship. He promised himself that every evening when the setting sun threw
the last blaze of its color into the valley and the mountains blinked like a rosebright candle was being held up to
their faces. The rabbit always held its ears stiff at this time
of day, the firm flesh trembling in anticipation as if it
knew the death was coming, the day would end. He liked
the rabbit most at dusk, because it was then completely
alert to the quiet dying around it and knew that part of its
life was sinking with the sun. He would push the door
back and outside the fields opened up across the valley,
burning into darkness. The rabbit moved its body in front
of the empty square space until it was alone with nothing
before it except the freedom of the fields and buzzing
waves of cricket chirps lulling evening into a special silence. He could see the color of the dying sun on the rabbit's fur as it sat in front of the door until there was nothing left before it except the night with its head spinning
full of stars, then the rabbit's body would relax, the ears
would slump a little, giving themselves over to the night
and it would turn its back to the door and hop up on his
lap, laying its ears straight back as his hand moved over
its body, rubbing its nose against the skin of his hand,
sniffing the green odor of alfalfa he had fed the horse earlier. And it was at this time he would celebrate the rabbit's choice of freedom and take up the black leather accordion his father had given him and run his fingers over

the cracked worn glimmer of the mother of pearl finger-presses, squeezing the notes of SHE'LL BE COMIN' ROUND THE MOUNTAIN out the open door into the night. The rabbit sensed his joy and rubbed itself like a cat against his leg as the boot tapped out its time on the floor. It was the song his father liked to play best and once he started playing it no one could get him to stop. The accordion belonged to his father's younger brother who played it with the determination of a mute speaking with notes. The brother he knew at least fifty songs and the words to half as many. Some said he was good enough to even play at dances. His father said he did, he himself was there and saw it, his brother stood for five and a half hours straight squeezing the music out of his black box and calling his songs to the dancers on the floor; in the end he lost five pounds of sweat and his shirt stuck like glue where the straps of the instrument hung with their full weight on his body, the people came up and clapped for him, one man even gave him a silver dollar. After that he got on a ship and sailed over to France where he fought in the First War until his face was blown right off his head. It was when his father got the letter from the Government with the gold heart and purple ribbon on it that he strapped the accordion on his own back and refused for five years to take it off. He even wore it in the rain and the water beaded on the mother of pearl finger-presses and when the sun came out they shined like the moon. His father got to be pretty good himself on the instrument and one time he played thirty different songs straight through on a two dollar bet. There wasn't a man alive who his father wouldn't play a song for. All a person had to say was, Hallelujah Bob, since you got your music box with you why don't you play YOU'RE THE ONE I CARE FOR, or OLD JOE CLARK, or THE ARKANSAS TRAVELER, and he always did and sometimes they would give him money for it. He got money too when he would go to the ranch houses during the day, working his way around the valley, and the women would ask him to step right into the kitchen and they would set their children up before him and ask him to play and the children

would laugh and clap their hands, then he would play a
slow one, usually GOOD NIGHT IRENE, and the woman would fold her hands down into the lap of her dress
and sometimes the tears from her eyes would drop slow
off her face and all the children would cry and she would
make him play four fast ones that would take everyone's
breath away and then end with WRECK OF THE NUM-
BER NINE before she would let him go. When his son
was born he took the instrument from his back and set the
load next to his bed. The weight of the accordion had
twisted his thin shoulders in almost under his chin and
threw his head forward when he was thinking so his gaze
was always fixed on his feet. The straps that had constantly rubbed his skin slashed a red X across the back he
could never straighten and forced him to walk with a
stoop, his feet pressed flat and wide before him as if he
were still supporting the burden. Sometimes Birdsong
would play SHE'LL BE COMIN' ROUND THE MOUN-
TAIN until the stars out the door washed their fire into
the silver sky and the birds preparing for sun cut black
wings in the waiting air. When he saw the sun he stopped.
Across the valley the first stroke of light broke over the
top of the mountains, laying a gold finger through a crack
in the black wall, a mother blindly caressing the face of
her child. He saw a field owl drop from the sky and hook
into the grass, firing the squawk of a kill from its beak.
The day had begun. The paved road in front of his house
grew blacker the brighter the sun became, until it was dis-
tinct, deserted, piercing off in silence two directions at
once, its arched back slick with wet of morning, its belly
slammed into the dirt from tons of steel that had passed
over it. The sound of bells grew out of the air, coming
down the morning distance of the road. The sharp metal
sound slapped the silence and behind came the cows,
moving in single file, their bodies aimed down the ditch
until they passed, one by one, crossing his boxed field of
vision through the open door, linked together in a common sway of flesh, the rhythm of their heaving hide
drummed by flies ancient in the blur of days marching
through fields, bladders heavy with water, bags swelled

with waste, never ceasing to flood the earth at their feet, heads bowed patiently to the metal clang of bells hung from their necks. When the last cow disappeared beyond his door there was nothing left but the fields, flat in the morning light, sunk from the weight of growth and beasts; and the fields were gone, yielding to the horse before him, gray in the ascending sun slashing light through the length of moving legs, the girl mounted on top, the flesh of her legs molded to the gray sides, the swell of her thighs flattened against the hide of the broad back, she turned and saw him, watching, her hands asleep, tangled in the mane, the skin of her blond face slack in her gaze, her eyes not regarding him, seeing only another fence post, a tree, a house, a doorway with a man inside, she turned away to the sound of the bells in the lead, unaware of her own movement; the hair falling away down her back in knots like a windswirled field of wheat quivered as the short blanket slipped from her shoulder and hooked on the curve of breast and he could see that she had been beaten again, her skin swelled raw, lashed around the neck and slashed in thick welts off her shoulder and down her back beneath the blanket that was the only thing the pain would allow to cover her body. He got up and stood in the open doorway, already she was beyond him, being pulled behind in the rhythm of the cows, and he felt his voice come up in his throat, trying to find some way to escape, to call her name, to touch with words the swaying back, disappearing along the straight black thrust of the road, but the name died in the tight pocket of his mouth, the lips never opening. He walked out into the morning. The sun had burned the damp fields dry, breaking the odor loose from the earth and flaring it in his nostrils, smothering everything, like the falling wheat of her hair covering the blanket on her back.

"Hey Joe! It's already past six and it takes almost an hour to get up there. Hurry it up. I'm already late coming by to pick you up."

He hadn't noticed the station wagon parked alongside the fence, he wondered how long it had been there as he watched Art's smiling face poke around in the space of the lowered window, throwing its words out across the yard at him. He walked over to the car and leaned against the wood paneling of the side, he never missed the opportunity to touch Art's car because it seemed to him the greatest waste to build a car of steel and then slap wood on the outside. "What time is it?"

"Six to six. On the dot."

He moved around the back of the car, tracing his finger on the waxed wood and over the word cut right into the tailgate itself, the red letters spelled FORD. The word was carried all over the valley; stamped on the back of almost every tailgate of every pickup was FORD. Even when driving with Odus to Tahoe they would pass car after car and written on the side in solid chrome was FORD. He liked the word. He didn't know why, it didn't sound like the name of a car, or the name of a man, it didn't sound like the name of any living thing he had ever seen or ever heard of, but when he saw the word it stopped his eye and grew into something he couldn't explain but only feel. Coming up close to another pickup at night the headlights would finally hit the tailgate and the red letter F flared, alone, isolated until the light focused and fired up the whole word FORD, as if the word was always there, waiting in the dark, waiting to expose itself to all who had eyes to see. And it could be seen in the rain with the water slipping off the slick red letters as if they were impossible to penetrate and when the snow drove down on everything in the valley, burying, steeping in ice, on some road some truck would still be moving, going steady and slow with the word FORD stamped on the tailgate, blazing in the white, and through the mountain roads the full weight of a cattle truck would pull itself up a hill, the cramped feareyed cattle listening to the pulse of the engine drive them forward, the letters penning them in loomed the size of a man's arm, cut clean and straight, FORD. And the people in the cars moving behind the truck up the grade had to look at the word, to read it, but find no definition for it, to follow it. There wasn't any place they could go without following the word. The word could be passed but there was always another one in front of it. There was no way to avoid it and no one tried. The word was cut into almost every moving machine. There was in the letters a fierce motion, its blood color burned across the landscape in every direction, and the people neither feared it nor ignored it. FORD was so common to their experience they simple accepted it, for even though they had to follow it, it eventually took them where they had planned to go from the beginning.

Art swung in his seat as Birdsong slammed the door behind him, "You set? Sure, sure you're set. I'd like you to meet my brother-in-law, Timothy, came up all the way from San Jose." Art turned his smile to the backseat.

"It's a pleasure pal, heard a lot about you. Art here seems to know just about everyone in this valley," the man in the backseat with his hair shaved down to knife-blade height of bristles leaned forward and squeezed Birdsong's hand. "This fellow next to me is Dick Dolis, he's one of my bowling buddies."

The other man with his hair shaved down to the same height but with a nose that cut out of his face like a pressed piece of red plastic threw his hand out, knocking his fingers against the glass of the overhead light. "Goddam these FORDS" he shook the hand like a wet blanket until the fingers were pumped with blood. "Most uncomfortable cars I ever rode in, don't leave a man room to move like in a CHEVY." He extended his hand again, "Pleasure, buddy," then let the width of his back settle against the seat. "Where's your bow," he looked across the thick knees of his heavy legs jammed up in front of him.

"Joe's not going to hunt," Art started the engine and flashed his smile in the rearview mirror. "He's one of the guides."

"You mean you ain't going to bow-hunt buddy, shit," he flicked the red nose sticking from his face and drew up some air into the nostrils that came slicing back out with a little wheeze. "Goddamdest thing I ever heard, a guy with your background who's going to pass up a chance to bow-hunt. I bet you're pretty good at it though, huh. I bet that's why you ain't gonna shoot, afraid you'll show all us white sonsabitches up. I'll bet you pull a mean string when you want to. I just bet you can."

"Isn't that Ben Dora's girl up ahead, Joe," Art asked before Birdsong had a chance to answer the man in the back. "I wonder what she's doing at this time of morning?"

"She's running her father's five milkcows up to the Handy field behind the dump, Dora's leasing it off Dixel."

Art slowed the car as he approached the rhythm of the cows and the girl locked onto the horse, he was always alert when there were loose cattle next to the road, although he had never seen one move in any direction but forward as long as there was a rider behind, he still didn't trust them, and especially when their heads were bent so low he couldn't see their eyes.

"Holy Jesus, buddy!" Dick slapped Timothy on the knee and pointed through the window. "That girl's almost naked! Look at it bump, umph, umph, damn, I bet that's one old horse who is feeling his oats *this* morning!"

"It's a pretty piece alright," Timothy pressed his face to the window, the sun splintering through the spikes of his hair.

"Holy Jesus, buddy, how would you like to have that slidin' up and down the banister all day keeping it warm for you until you got home!"

"Look's like somebody's beat hell out of that kid," Timothy jerked his face back from the window, not being able to stop himself from pulling away at the sight of wounds he just discovered.

"Beat hell out of her! Hell, so would I. She's got somebody treating her right you can bet. I bet she loves every minute of it. Your mountain girls are like that. I'd beat her. Let her beat me too, beat me to a toothpick. Honk your horn at her Art. Let her know there are some men about." He jumped forward, shoving his hand across Art's shoulder and pressed a bleat from the horn that yanked the horse up on its hind legs and brought it down stamping hooves in the center of the road, throwing the blanket off the girl and forcing Art to make a decision he wasn't prepared to make; he spun the wheel in the wrong direction, swerving the car into the lane where the horse was turned around facing him. He slammed on the brakes almost throwing everyone through the glass of the windows as the girl leaned down and shouted at his face frozen in its smile, "Goddam you bastard!" The words released Art from his moment of decision that had already passed and he punched the gaspedal, sending the car past the cows, speeding down the road between the track of barbwire lining both sides. When they reached Highway 89 Dick finally stopped laughing enough to remember his thermos full of whiskey, "Man I didn't see them long, but they'll live in my memory forever, those were the prettiest pair of tits a man would ever want to lay his head on, whoever beat her knew just what he was about, he didn't leave a mark on those young suckin' milk bags. Here Art, you take a drink of that and pass it over to Joe."

"You sure got some set-up here brother-in-law," Timothy leaned on the seat behind Art and slapped him on the back. "You sure knew what you were doing when you moved way the hell up here pal. Wild naked mountain gals running all over the place. You sure know where to find it brother-in-law. What about you Joe," he slid the weight of his arms along the edge of the seat and nudged the back of Birdsong's head. "I'll put money on it you're into that stuff all the time, pretty regular I think, being redblooded and all. I think they're crawling all over you, getting a little tommy-hawk."

"Tommiehawak, whew! Buddy you said it," Dick grabbed his thermos back and tipped it up along the red blade of his nose. "I'd like to scalp me a piece of that back there," he wedged the thermos in the jeans between the bulge of thighs and ran his tongue out along the ridge of wet hanging lip. "Hey! You ever seen that de-kal some of the big Semi's have on the back, shows a big titted Indian gal with her knees pressed together and her spread hands flattened over her pussy and down beneath it says I'VE BEEN SCALPED! Goddam, everytime I see that I laugh so hard I almost wreck up the CHEVY. I've been scalped, shit, imagine that, that's goddam funny. I bet that's the way they did it too, some of them Indian bucks.

Ain't that right. I bet you could educate hell out of us along those lines, hey Joe."

"I guess so."

"You guess so!" Dick poked the thermos like a stick, knocking Birdsong's shoulder forward. "Ain't you modest as hell buddy. Why you've had more ass than Tim and me could dream of in a lifetime even if we was sleeping in the same bed. Ain't he modest Tim?"

"I agree with you, he probably sees more ass than a toiletseat, but he's a modest boy alright. He's what you call one of your shy, quiet ones, thinking all the time he is. Still waters run deep."

"Joe's not much of a talker," Art made certain his smile was level with the rearview mirror and flicked the radio on, thinking the full weight of his statement deserved a serenade. The music filled the car, and behind them in the complete morning light the valley was shrinking as they ascended the highway wrapping its way up to the last height of the mountain.

"I can smell venison cookin' already," Timothy mixed his words in with the music. "There's nothing on this earth better tasting than a venison steak, soaked in sauce with a thick layer of pepper over the top. Worth its weight in gold. Venison's got a taste to it that man-fed beef can't touch. Something wild in it. Something . . . hell, I don't know, it's like eating something natural, something fed off the wild of the land itself, it taste just like it looks, just like you think a deer would taste. Beef is different, it tastes like the butcher who sells it to me looks."

"Makes good jerky too, deer does, the best," Dick passed him the thermos. "That's why I like to hunt deer, it makes good jerky. But you know sometimes I think it really doesn't matter if I get my buck or not, and goddam don't I like to forget all the times I ended up after the season with nothing to eat but a deertag sandwich, but you know what I mean is that it's the huntin' itself is important, it's the anticipation, in a way I guess you're feeling the same thing the animal is, it goes both ways. That's why I switched to bow-hunting, evens things out, takes the edge off. I like a little sport when I hunt. I guess that's what I'm saying, what it is I like is the sport of the kill, and that always takes place before the animal goes down."

"I know what you mean by that," Timothy rubbed his palm over the stubble of his hair. "The sport's the thing. That's why I quit hunting with my Magnum. When I'd get that shot off it was like a cannon going off at my shoulder, made too much goddam noise and I couldn't enjoy the kill. But the rifle does have its advantages, hell, now that I think about it, maybe I like the rifle just as much. I like it both ways."

"Hey Art," Dick tapped the low slump of the shoulders in front of him. "How do these people get away with holding this hunt out of season, shit, they're a good ten weeks too early."

"All this land on both sides of us is owned by Sierramonte Mills. The State owns everything on both sides of the road for a mile back, everything beyond that is lumber property. The Mill isn't registered with Fish and Game as a hunt club, they hunt the year round as they see fit," he turned the car off the highway onto a dirt road rutted down the middle by yardwide tracks. Alongside the Giant Sequoia grew thick into the sky, cutting off the sun from above. The station-wagon fell into the groove of the tracks and bounced like a buggy, kicking up a stream of fine dust that rose and hung on the already dirtweighted lower branches of the trees.

Dick watched out his window as the car moved beneath the shadow of the trees in its own dust, traveling deeper and higher into the forest, "They say some of those trees was here before Christ even. Goddam, what they could say if they could talk. It's hard to believe something's being around so long, before Christ even, maybe that's why they don't seem real, seem like freaks almost, being as big as they are. I've got a Ben Pearson bow with an eighty pound pull to it, can drop a deer at one hundred and fifty yards, I bet I could split it through one of these trunks with one of those special steel arrows."

"You probably could," Art swung his head up and down between the hollow of his shoulders. "They have a redwood up north they cut a hole in and you can drive your car right through. That's something, driving your car through a tree, it's a godsend to drunk drivers," he turned his smile around to see if his sly joke hit its mark.

"Yah, I seen that tree," Dick jabbed at his nose. "That's world famous, the highway goes right through it. Sure gives the kids a hell of a bang, they got out and shot a whole roll of pictures of it, sign there says threequarters of a million people go through that tree a year, that's more people than they got in the whole State of Nevada." He blinked his eyes at the sun beginning to spill off the trees, the redwoods were thinning, giving way to the smaller pines that stood skinny and short in the shadows of the red trunks that swelled up around them. The road ahead was slashed with layers of sun breaking through the gaps of sky opened by the smaller pines between the big trees. Then the road lit up, everywhere the gold shot through the green, the sun broke free all the way down the road, the redwoods were gone, split, chopped, sawed, cut, pulled, dragged, logged out fifty years before. Growing out of the earth once shadowed by the redwoods' great height sprouted fifteen, forty, sixty foot high, second, third, and even fourth growth of ponderosa, lodgepole, and sugarpine like weeds, and outnumbering all of these, douglasfir. From the main highway the people passing through in the summer saw nothing but mile after mile of redwoods along the road and from blind curves could catch the view of the trees rolling like emerald waves into the haze of sky, thinking there were more of these giant trees than man could cut, but the spears of green they saw in the distance weren't a continuation of the redwoods, they were fooled, the redwoods had been sliced and yanked from the earth. "What the hell happened to all the redwoods," Dick noticed for the first time that the trees surrounding him had shrunk down to half their size.

"Logged them all years ago," Art smiled, and turned the car around a bend that spread out on a plateau, the earth stripped, the dirt crisscrossed and rutted from the weight of tires supporting the long trucks heavy with the dead bodyweight of cut tree trunks piled high and strapped with chains to the steel platforms of the trailers parked in hulking rows like battleships at anchor. He pulled the car right to the door of a turquoise colored aluminum trailer as long as a house, and stopped.

"Art, you old buckaroo," a man in a green hat shaped like a puptent with VFW LOCAL 1218 sewn in bright gold letters on the side opened the door and jerked the driver out, patting his shoulders, the big hands slapping down on both sides of Art's smile. "Are you ready to bowshoot? Tell me, are you ready to hunt you some venison?"

"I'm ready Colonel. I'm ready to shoot," Art's smile was about to blow off his face, his head was pumped so red with the slapping on his shoulders.

"I knew it. I knew it. I knew Art was coming up here to get hisself a *buck*. Any man who can sell whiskey all day and still stay sober knows where he can get his meat." The Colonel jammed his head in the window, knocking the green hat halfway up his head, exposing the thinning gray hair still cut down to a neat half inch. "You boys unpack your gear, there's coffee and doughnuts over by the equipment shack. Birdsong, you come with me." He led the way into the trailer and pushed a path through the men down to one end covered by a map that marked every rock, tree and road for eight square miles.

"Well Birdsong, come to guide us to all the little Bambis?" Sheriff Davies turned the melon of his head and showed the side sliced off in his face.

"Give me that pointer for a second, Hal," the Colonel pulled the rubbertipped stick from the Sheriff's hand. "Now look here Birdsong, this is where we are, at head camp Mama down here on number three mesa," he tapped the rubber on a flat blue line. "Now over here, on number seven mesa, on the other side of the mountain is Sheriff Hadley and Captain Tom at head camp Papa, how we're going to work it is the way we always have, two groups will move from the sides of the mountain to the ridge, we've got a lot of territory here, about two and three-quarters miles square, more than we've ever had, more men too, last count was something like forty, so we've got to fan so we can sweep up all the loopholes, you

know how they'll backtrack on you if you're not careful.
The top of the ridge was logged clean years ago, it's a big
area, about the size of four football fields, a lot of meadow grass where they feed. They're going to beat hell out
of there soon as they know something's up so we have to
keep tight and beat them back up, lot of clear area,
should be some good clean shootin' if we hold them to
that clearing. What's important is both parties hit the
meadow at the same time, if not, if one side gets there too
soon, it'll run 'em, and going downhill they'll break
through our lines and hardly nobody'll get a clean shot.
So what you've got to do is keep your people in line, don't
let any hotshots in front of you, if nothing else he might
get an arrow through the neck. Now when a man gets a
hit it's his job to tote his game forward to the next break-
road, they'll be a rearguard coming up to knock out any
deer that slip through, and a man coming down in thick
brush might be mistaken and get an arrow up his ass, so
it's important the man with the game tote it forward and
drop it on the road, he should tag it with a piece of colored ribbon that will have his number on it, each man will
get a roll of ribbon. They'll be jeeps going around the
break roads after the advance has cleared out total and
they'll do nothing but pick up and haul game back to
head camps. Another thing, if there's any bad talk over
who got a kill while you're in the field, just flip for it,
that's the most democratic. You'll be assigned ten men.
You've got to keep count of them and stay out front, you
know where the game is likely to hole up so you can kick
'em up or set them for a shot for those coming behind.
You know what to look for, you've got eyes for that sort
of thing. You know your way around these mountains like
the way around your bathroom and I'm sure you'll find
the quickest and easiest way up to the top of this one
without somebody bustin' a leg. Some of these bow-hunt-
ers we got this year have never hunted high-country before, and never shot at anything but paper targets on a
bale of hay and don't know their dick from a snake. So
you guide good, keep 'em moving even and don't let them
scatter, most important thing is to bring your line onto the

meadow exactly at three. Dorn, the Superintendent for the Mill says his men have been working the low country all around the ridge since snow broke and have been running the game up there like rats to an island, and he estimates they've run a hell of a lot of game up there into the sun and grass. He's seen tracks five deep running across the road; maybe as much as eighteen, twenty-five bucks, and so many does he wouldn't even want to make a guess. You got any questions about what I told you boy? Good. You'll get paid when we come back to feed. Now let's get out in the field and haul ass."

Behind him the march broke out on two sides. The line whipped through the trees like a rope, the red baseball caps of the men bobbing like floats of a fishing net, the heavy rubber camouflage parkas dropping down below their knees; the leather quivers full with arrows strapped on the rubber backs made an unnatural sound as they scraped the slick green material. The mountain fell straight down before the advance, the land cruel and twisted from earlier advances of men and machines, littered with cuts of thick trunks sprawled across earth, chunks of their bodies scattered for hundreds of yards, isolated in pools of sawdust, far from their torn roots shooting blindly to a sliced stump. Birdsong held his hand up. The line of marchers stopped, the arrows pulled tight, pointing up the mountain. Before him the narrow width of a deer trail broke through the manzanita and opened onto a grassy shelf swirled soft from the bodies of sleeping animals. He picked up one of the black droppings sprayed through the grass and rolled it between his fingers like a raisin, popping the hard shell until his fingers pressed the warm core; they were running not more than ten minutes ahead. He turned back to the line, the red caps glinting in the sun like flames, the red caps that would keep the men from mistaking one another for deer, the parkas fading their bodies into the mountain left only the red heads floating, separate, attached to nothing, bobbing alone. He lowered his hand and the march began again, steady through the sun until the cut of fireroad was

reached and they waited for the rest of the marching ring
that spun around the mountain to come even with them.
As far as the eye could see, off to the sides and down below, the isolated flashes of red burned brilliant in the
brush, lacing their way forward until even with the road,
and on it all the way around, spaced two hundred yards
apart, the red flames burned in the sun as cold sweat
breathed under the tight rubber of the parkas. The mountain continued to give way before them, drawing itself up
narrow and steep, tumbling slides of rock down behind
the invading boots. "DEER!" Birdsong lifted his head
from the tracks he was following and saw the doe, standing next to a fallen log, her mouth dripping as the wide
eyes took in the bright flare of advancing caps. She took a
step forward and the arrow caught her in the heart, burying itself up to the feathers, her eyes snapped open and
she took three quick steps toward the red flames before
her and went down on her front knees as if in prayer, and
collapsed. "Holy shit ace! What a shot!" One of the men
broke from the line, his body panting past Birdsong. He
reached the doe and wrapped the flash of yellow ribbon
around a hind leg. "Ninety pounds it'll dress out to!" He
hefted the body on his shoulders and started up the mountain, almost running beneath the load he carried easy on
his back. "DEER!" Birdsong heard the shout and the
sound of arrows whistling as their feathers sliced through
the air. There was another doe off to the side of him,
three arrows hit her side and brought her down. "DEER!"
All around the mountain the cry filled the air and yellow
ribbon was being lashed around the thumping legs. The
march halted at the next road, the men dropping the dead
weight from their shoulders, letting the still wet hides settle into the dust.

"Ain't it something," Art came trotting down the road,
his smile oiled with sweat and caked with dust. "Ain't it
something Joe. I ain't hit yet but I got off some good
shots. They're in here like weeds. What a shoot. Ain't it
something."

Birdsong turned away from the wet globe of the face

bouncing around beneath the red cap. The marchers were ready. "Let's go!"

He could see the top of the ridge now, the blue sky flattened out over it, all around him was the heavy breath of men, sweating their waste beneath the rubber of the parkas, beating through the brush, their arrows pulled tight, leveled toward the ridge, aimed at the blue sky. "DEER!" The sound of hooves beating on rock split the silence in front of the marchers, brown bodies exploded from bushes, around squat banks of manzanita, in front of the height of cut logs. "DEER!" They were running everywhere, the arrows catching their bodies and tossing them to the ground. The fawns moving their young legs with the complete muscle of their short days, trying to match the stride of the does in front, stumbling on the loose rock, sliding down into manzanita and climbing up again on the shaking of their young legs to catch an arrow in the thigh, or breaking free and running in the path of their mother, until they sprawled over her dead body as she dropped before them with the feather lanced sticks sunk in her hide.

"Goddam! My buck's running with all those does and fawns!" A big man charged from around a tree in front of Birdsong, his red cap off, the rubber of the parka slapping against his body.

"Get the hell out of there! Dick! Get the hell out of there!"

The big man kept going, cutting through the juts of rock, tripping over logs and the small thrashing bodies of fawns. "There he is! That's my buck!" He raised his bow as an arrow passed through the rubber of his parka and out the other side of his shoulder, spinning him around, his blue eyes shot wide with the shaft that pierced through his flesh, staring straight down at Birdsong, "Shit!" The word flew out of his mouth and collapsed his body at the top of the ridge.

"He ain't hurt bad," the man who was cutting the parka off Dick with his knife looked up at Birdsong. "The wound's clean, ain't bleedin' much. Shock is all. Shock knocked him out. I know how to handle it. I seen much worse than this in Korea. Jesus Mary and the Apostles look at that," he had the rubber of Dick's parka cut off his body, but his eyes weren't looking at the wound, but across the flat top of the ridge; coming out onto it from all sides was the blaze of red caps, running across the open space were the bucks, herded together, charging the length of the meadow, trying to break the advancing lines, the brown hulk of their bodies moving swiftly as the arrows thudded into their flesh, dropping them quivering to the grass.

He waited until the jeeps came to pick up the bodies; walking through the field, the tall grass crushed from the last flight of the bucks, the arrows that missed their marks snapping beneath his boots. He got into one of the last jeeps descending from the ridge, the sky flat and blue over his head as he watched it, rubbing the back of his neck until the jeep pulled to a stop in front of the trailer as long as a house. From the lower branches of the trees brown bodies were slung by ropes, their bellies split, the blood running onto the heap of guts beneath them. The air was filled with blood and smoke from the pits dug into the ground and whole animals laid out over the coals, sending up the smell of cooking flesh. He climbed down from the jeep and felt his leg go slack, refusing to support him, and he realized that since the beginning of the morning he had been limping. He leaned against a pickup and braced his weight, rubbing his neck again, looking up at the flat blue sky.

"Great sport," the Colonel jumped down from the door of the trailer and slapped him on the shoulder. "Great sport. Great shoot. The best ever. You were good. Did all right. That fella who caught the arrow's not in too bad of shape at all. The company doctor took care of him right off. He was walking around before they took him down to Portola. He was in your group too. That's not so good," he dug a hand into the pocket of his pants, looking straight before him as he pulled the bill folded like a letter

and pressed it in Birdsong's hand. "It's twenty. Same as always. Hey," he jerked the green hat from his head with
the VFW 1218 sewn in bright gold on the side and
slapped it against his leg. "How do you like my new
truck?" He knocked his knuckles against the high fender
and rubbed his palm over the letters stamped in the steel
of the tailgate. "How do you like my new FORD."

3

His HEAD was up. The Sun was up. The Birds were out. The yellowmen were everywhere. From the deep squint of his eyes the Indian watched their gold sweatbacks bang steel into solid ground. Behind him the Iron Road was nailed down to the mountain cliff of the Sierra. In front of him was the burntland, waiting for the yellowmen to bang their way across the swollen faces of brown hills. Beneath his boots the Earth would not stop trembling with the rhythm of steel driving into its skin. The higher the Sun pulled itself up the more relentless the rhythm of the yellowmen became. The full hammer weight of their sledges swung and poised above their heads, cascading down in a perfect rain of strength, pounding the Iron Road for all time into the Earth's crust. Beneath the thickness of his checkered jacket he sweated and watched, moving back along the ironrails that had just been laid. The rhythmic driving of slamming steel filled the air like the breath of two hundred yellowmen chained into a relentless iron beast; the sound of slapping steel roared from their lungs as the Iron Road grew. The Indian followed back along the ironrails toward the wall of mountains until the yellowmen appeared far behind him on the horizon, the single movement of their massed bodies balanced over the hotland like a human blade searching the soft spot to plunge through into the Earth's heart, cutting the vital muscle throbbing blood through their own heads, releasing them from the pounding rhythm of their bodies. The sight of the yellowmen swelled everyday in his head like a cloud. The cloud pushed all other thoughts from him. There became only the single yellow beast sucking the air with iron lungs, feeding off the fierce heat thrown down by the Sun, piercing through the days with a straight Iron Road. The fire-eating Engine crashing down the ironrails threw black smoke into the blur of Sky as it followed the track laid by yellowmen. The yellowmen led the way into the desert, pounding a new time in the heat, all movement swung with sledges lifted over small yellow shoulders. The yellowmen had no Spirit, they gave birth to the fire-eating Engines. Never did they look back to the mountains or to the flatland slapped out to their sides. Their eyes saw only straight ahead and down, where they nailed the hide of the Earth. They were not to be trusted. Between their legs were yellow Snakes. If a woman had the Snake in her it would poison her. The blood would run from her until she died. The yellowmen together had many pieces of metal coin. They would give two bags of gold coins for the meat of the Cat in the mountains. The meat gave poison to their Snakes. He himself during the white days had followed a big Cat in the snow, coming close behind the Dogs howling through ravines. There was a night with no stars, just a Moon and the snarling sound of Dogs clawing at the trunk of a tree. At the top of the tree sat the Cat, golden and deep within the fur branches until the blast of the rifle ripped open his side and dropped his bleeding weight in the snow, the silence of his open eyes reflecting the Moon. It took him three days to pack the Cat out of the ravines to the Chinese camp outside Truckee. When the yellowmen handed over the two sacks of metal coin the Cat lay at his feet with the blood of its body frozen through the golden fur like red stone. *Red Cat* the yellowmen called him. Captain Red Cat. He buried one of the sacks of metal beneath snow in the hollowed root of a tree and took the other into Truckee where he spent half of it on six glasses of whiskey and five hands of Blackjack before going down to the big house where the candles burned and the women with skin that smelled like flowers waited. He bought the one with the red hair between her legs. He gave her the half sack of metal in the dark room before he put his hands all over her body and kissed her under the arms until she laughed so hard he threw her down on the floor next to the bed, feeling the silent spread of her flesh going out beneath him while his hands covered the swell of her breasts. In the morning he woke up on the floor, he could hear the woman snoring from beneath the blanket on the bed. His eyes burned in his aching head from the glare of Sun that came through the window and hit the opposite wall. He left the house and walked down through the place where the huge boxcars with ironwheels stood on the silver track in a line against the Sun. He picked his way through the dump, kicking at the fresh heaps for food. It was early for his people to have come and searched through the previous night's waste. Beneath a yellowed layer of scattered lettuce and the black sog of coffeegrinds he kicked up the hide of the Cat. The yellowmen had quickly stripped out the meat for their poison and tossed the ragged fur away. On a pile of chicken bones rotting back into the Earth rested the severed head, its eyes glazed white and blank in the Sun. He raised the hide and shook it free of garbage. He went down through the trees past his canvas shack and dipped the hide in the river, the blood washing free as he knelt at the bank, watching the red stains melt and disappear in the cold blue. He laid the hide face down on a rock and raked the skin clean of fat and dark tangled clots of meat. He tacked it high in the Sun on the bark of a pinetree. When the Sun had seared the skin brown he took it down and worked it soft in his hands with the juice of a root before he took it back up the hill to Truckee and bet it against one of the Mexicans who laid down two ten-dollar pieces of metal. The Mexican cut the deck and shuffled the cards, then slammed them on the table and told the Indian to draw. The card the Indian pulled from the closed deck was the King's son. He thought the skin was still his and he could put the gold metal in his pocket, but the Mexican drew the very King himself, flipping the painted card on the gold fur of the skin draped over the table. The Mexican laughed and shouted across the room to the man behind the bar, "A whiskey for the Captain! Two shots of whiskey for Capitan Rex, a born gambler!" Captain Rex gulped the glasses set before him and the ancient song of Birds fluttered in his blood. He threw his head back to let the wings beat from his lips and his eyes caught on the crescent cut of the glass pieces swaying from the chandelier, their clear images reflecting off one another like a thousand Moons. He sang at the Moons like every nightbird in the forest had been captured and set free in the square of the room. Only the light shining through the cut glass bore witness to his dark song. When the song died on his lips the Birds settled down in his chest, their ancient sound still clinging to the bare walls until it echoed itself into silence. The Mexican brought his fist down on the table, clanking the two empty glasses as his laughter roared into the face of the Indian, he wiped the tears from his eyes as he shouted, "Feed this Injun Capitan a firewater! He sings like the hummingbird, crows like the owl, croons like the woodpecker and shits like the hawk! The christdamn things these hombres won't do!" The Indian stayed in the saloon until the Sun dropped out of the Sky. His lungs raw from bellowing the songs of Birds that scattered from his lips after each whiskey bought for him washed into his body with a sudden knot of heat. He stumbled outside through the door and reeled only for an instant before his boot hooked on the stub of a nail in the boardwalk and tripped him face down in the mud slush of the street. He staggered his way down the road below the town past the silent bulk of the box-cars and over the hills of human waste growing out of the dump. Pieces of snow began to fall from the Sky like dumb gentle white flowers. The rolls and peaks of the dump glistened in the blurred swirl before him. The dark shapes of the women floated like shadows between the scattered cans and broken glass glowing from the touch of iced air. The bandannas wrapped around the women's heads and across their mouths left only the brown slash of their eyes exposed as they bent and dipped into the piles of rubbish with numbed fingers hooking up useful prizes quickly hidden from sight in the weighted gunnysacks slung over their shoulders. The women looked across to the stumbling man, their outlines obscured in the quickening gentle fall from the Sky. They watched him as one as he moved hot and clumsy through their territory, his clothing dark with mud, the wild toss of his black hair turning white from trapped bits of snow. He could see the one who was his mother. She stood inseparable from the others, one of the flock. No sign passed from her to the man who was now almost gone from sight, weaving down through the pines toward the sound of the river racing itself through sharp rocks.

After the snow had covered everything it left the Earth quiet. The Moon cut open the darkness, the slap of canvas over the shack's opening was pushed back. His mother came into the hut. She sat herself on the skinworn Rabbit-blanket and knotted rags of her bed. The cold that she brought with her woke him. He reached out for the bottle that earlier dropped to the dirt floor when his hand had become too shaky to hold it. He quickly raised the bottle to his lips, it was empty. His mouth sucked out the fumes of whiskey from the glass hollow before he let the bottle slip from his grasp to the floor. The woman said nothing. The wind blowing outside in the clear night flapped the loose pieces of canvas stretched over the boarded frame of the hut. He had lost in his memory the day when the woman stopped her talking. She had once been full of words, they had come quickly and often to her lips. The world before the Whites was always in her brown eyes. She ceased to see the new world she had been forced into. She had gone blind to the places her body took her throughout the days. She had long since stopped seeing the man her son had become. There were no words for him. Once she had much talk about the man who put three babies into her body. When she spoke about this husband of her heart called Gayabuc all the happiness out of a time long since gone dead caught on her face and turned it young. She told of the watercress that grew from the shallow streams and how he would go into the water for her, standing brown as a buck, gently pulling the shoots from their bed of water. He would bring them dripping to her so she could suck the green taste from the damp white roots. She told of the small Rabbits he would trap in the snow and bring to her, the bodies still warm as she stripped their fur and staked them over the coals, the hot rising smell of wild flesh swelling in the hut as the husband of her heart lay next to her with his want, his hand tracing the high brown curve of her hip and between her legs to force her open to the thickness of his body. Her face fired as she would talk of her Girl's Dance and how on the mountaintop Gayabuc wrestled with the smoke, forcing its white tongue into the night Sky, forcing it to give its sign to the people gathered below, to write in the Sky that she had acted true and according to the ways of a girl going into a Woman, that her life would be long and straight. She was proud that he had fought the power of the smoke, but to force the sign was against the ways of the past, it was an act that made the animals flee his bow. It was an act that would kill his days short. But that was before *they* came. Before the fences of sharp wire went up and the husband of her heart was shot down. The Ancestors did not forget. It was because Gayabuc had violated the way of the Girl's Dance and forced the smoke to give up a false sign for her that the ancestors punished all the people and brought out of the burntlands those with skin the color of snow. The day of the people was ended, buried beneath a white burden. And Gayabuc had been the first to see *them*. He had watched through the trees. He had watched down to the high snow on the frozen shore of the yonder lake. He watched them moving slowly on the snow, clumsy, like Bears in water. He had been watching silently all that morning, had seen, had seen *them* hunched, away from each other, mouths tearing at knots of flesh, faces smeared the color of a dying Sun. He watched through the trees as *they* ate *themselves*. It was as if he had found *them* in dream and they had followed him into life. Coming one after the other, first in small tired groups, pushing the weight of their heavy bodies up and over the barrier of mountains reaching to the Sky, then in long sluggish lines with hunger burning in their eyes and their great tamed beasts pulling whole billowing tent houses behind on high wooden wheels that creaked in the mountain air, breaking the stones beneath their immense burden to powder. Leaving the Earth behind rutted and used. And still they came, up out of the burntlands, down along the spine of the mountains from the north, up from the hidden valleys of the south. They came closer one upon the other until their line was unbroken and flowed steadily like the sap from a fatal wound in the heart of a great tree. And the man Gayabuc had brought *them*. *They* were born in his eyes as he saw *them* eat of *their* own flesh. *They* were born from his violation of the clear path cut by the Ancestors. The smoke in the Sky at the Girl's Dance died, and he had made it into a false sign for all the people below to see. It began with this lie on the mountaintop, the end of her people. The bones of her people would be crushed like powder beneath the bulk of the iron wheels of *those* who ate of *their* own flesh.

The whistle went off, the sound of its sharp metal barb cutting the air thick with the clang of pounding steel. The yellowmen sat down along the track. The goldsweat of their backs gleaming in the sudden silence. The damp strange smell of their braided hair hung in the heat of the Sun like the slow smoke of smouldering green wood. Walking quickly down between the two iron tracks the yellowmen had just laid was a man with a blue-billed cap on his bald head and a gold numbered badge on the collar of his blue shirt. He stopped and spit a thick brown juice in the direction the Sun was beginning to slide, clearing his mouth of all obstacles but words, "Old John Chinaman don't want to work his tail nohow, noway, do he Cap'n Rex. It's all a body could do whipjackin John's yellow tail so's he'll put in an honest day for the Comp'ny. The Comp'ny don't pay John six-bits and beans every day just to have hisself a pic-a-nic in this nice fine resort weather we have out here. But this weather don't bother you Injun bucks atall, do it Cap'n. You bucks got ice in your veins just like snakes. Why hell Cap'n, look to yourself, buttoned up in that thick checkered jacket like you

was standing in the center of a blizzard instead of in the
middle of noonday Desert sun. I got somethin to warm
your insides if this Desert heat don't." He pulled a small
bottle from his hip pocket and handed it over. "Here take
a shot off this pistol. Now hold on," he grabbed it back. "I
said a shot, I didn't invite you to swallow the bottle. You
bucks got the manners of Russians. You ain't never goin
to learnt civilized politeness." He took a short gulp and
rubbed the red pucker of his lips, slipping the glass back
into his pocket. "Damned if a man don't have to drink
himself half to death just to keep ol John's tail waggin. I
wish to the President I was back at the yard in Truckee
stead of out here sweatin with the coolies. The Comp'ny
pays good though and I don't have to go home at night to
a house full of women. But it don't do my heart any good
Cap'n, the way we're comin up close to Mormon country.
It took the Comp'ny the whole of the year, one thousand
coolies, and a ton of nitroglycerin to blast its railroad
through twenty miles of granite over the Donner Summit,
and now, hell, they're spikin down ten miles of rail in a
day across this here flatland. Before you know it we're
goin to be clean into Utah, racing tail across the Salt Lake
Ocean itself. Damn Cap'n, it scares the spiders out of me
to think of going back into Mormon country, they'll tan
my hide good for me this time out. I just pray to the holies that Major Dodge is pushin his Irish Terriers as hard
as I'm pushin these coolies. But I got a hard faith in Major Dodge, he put two-hundred and sixty-six mile of track
between him and Omaha in the first year, then spiked
down another two-hundred forty mile in '67. He would of
done better if some of you painted bucks hadn't put some
arrows into a few of his Irish boys. I heered one of
Dodge's linemen got shot, he was stunned and scalped,
but got ahold of hisself just in time to see the buck what
done it running off, so's he plugs the buck right through
the back, plunks the scalp in a cold bucket of water and
hightails it back to Omaha to hunt up some Doc to sew it
back on his bloody head, but no Doc could succeed at it
so's he had the scalp tanned and pickled in alcohol and
sold it into a museum back east. Last year Dodge up and

laid down four-hundred and twenty-five mile of track. I'm
just prayin the holies he beats us across the Salt Lake so I
don't have to step one foot into Mormon country. Before
you know it they'll have ol Arthur Dolay hogtied down to
the back of another one of their Mormon women, it's all
legal to them if you're hitched to more'n one of their potato eaters, matter of fact they got so many women in that
country it's what they ad-vise out of natural selfdefense.
Sometimes I wonder if Dodge is goin to beat us through
that country or not, those Mormons are likely to make
him lay a mile of potatoes to every mile of track, and
sides, the Comp'ny on this end's pushin hellfire, got
more'n fifteen hundred coolies spikin steel out here,
course it takes eight Johns to do the work of one white
man, and that's with a whipjack ridin every three hundred
of them, still, they put in their sixteen hour day before
bean time. Hey now, yonder comes the waterwagon. Step
aside now Cap'n or they'll run you into the earth." He put
a hand on the Indian's chest and pushed him back as the
mules came at them, the bulk of their weight strained in
the creaking leather harness slapping against the sweat of
their backs. Storming behind the mules in the spray of
white dust the highboarded wagon sagged under the load
of broad barrels sloshing their hold of water over the top
of the bowed rims, dripping a wet path in the dusty wake.
The mules hammered to a stop, their breath bellowing a
steady hiss through flared nostrils. The shouting of the
yellowmen was strange and high like a flock of seabirds
caught too far inland, the distant sing-song of their voices
was meant for no individual ears, addressing only ignorant space as they jostled in the center of the mule heat
where wooden ladles filled with still cool river water were
furiously being passed down from the barrels into the
waiting mouths. "Well Cap'n," the man removed his blue-
billed cap and smoothed the sweat off the exposed egg of
his skull. "That ought to wet ol John down for another
five hours." He hooked the cap back on his head and
craned his neck toward the man stepping a wide distance
around the waterwagon's swirl of yellow bodies. When the
man was close enough so the gold ring on the fist of his

hand clutching the lapel of his blue frock coat could be seen the words from his mouth slipped ahead and directly in front of him.

"Mister Dolay, blow your whistle and get John up off his skinny tail. We have a schedule to keep. Ten minutes water time Mister Dolay. Ten minutes and no more. Get this trackgang back in the saddle."

"Yes sir Mister Pourth. I was just gettin set to do just that sir, before I seen you comin round the wagon. The Comp'ny's schedule is safe with Arthur Dolay."

"Then blow your damn whistle and stop all this jawing!"

"Yes sir, Mister Pourth," he raised the whistle secured around his neck on a silver chain and blew it until the blood swelled up in his head. The sound scattered the yellowmen away from the wagon and before it died in the flat air the sweating gold backs were again lined up, the first heavy thud of their sledges struck the earth, bringing the heat down hard on their bare backs.

"You keep this gang lined Mister Dolay. You keep this gang lined and in time. You do that and the Company is on schedule. You stand about passing lies with Captain Rex here and Major Dodge is certain to beat us across the Salt Lake. You've got five hours of whipjack with this gang until beans and a new shift. That's five hours that started two minutes ago. You should, Mister Dolay, get your ass in the saddle."

"Yes sir Mister Pourth, that's what I was going to do, and I'm going now to do it." He hooked the bluebilled cap lower on his head and set off at a trot as the mules jolted in their harness and swung around, the muscle of their backs driving the empty weight of the wagon back along the track, knocking the water barrels into one another as their hooves pounded up a trail of white dust behind them.

"We're about out of your territory, aren't we Captain?" Mister Pourth put his gaze on the Indian, his fist still locked on the lapel of his shiny coat.

"Maybe so."

"Maybe so *what*, Captain?" The lips ripped across his

face in a scowl. "Just what is it your territory depends on?"

"It depends on where *you* say it ends and begins."

The man's mouth unlocked and the lips sank into a grin, "The Central Pacific Railroad has legal, deeded title to this land, but the Central Pacific is not some ride by night outfit, we recognize a certain sense, a certain duty, obligation you might say, selfassumed of course, but nevertheless obligation to those who once owned these lands. The Central Pacific is not in the business of closing a whole way of life down, it is in the business of growth. The Company has a good record with you people, as you yourself are first in line to recognize. The Company has right from the start extended a friendly hand wherever it could. When we first got the Road up to Truckee we offered the use of a boxcar to haul you people back down over to the foothills to pick pigweed along the Railroad's right of way. Now there are some among you who say the Company is not doing a service, that if the pigweed wasn't cut we'd have to go to the expense of burning it out, but you and I know that isn't true Captain, you an I know the pigweed is important to you people, it's a lucrative harvest. You and I know the Company is doing a service. Growth is what the Company's main interests are Captain, and growth depends upon goodwill, honest relations, that's why the Company hired you on this time out, to insure the growth of all parties concerned. Your job was to inform any of your people who thought the Railroad was somehow violating their land, their ancient hunting and gathering grounds, that the Railroad was just going through a small strip, and besides, we own it. The Railroad isn't like the ranchers. We don't have cattle and horses and sheep and hogs to tromp down all the plants and kill the grass, ruining your best gathering grounds and running off the game. The Railroad is your partner in growth. But you Washos haven't made any trouble have you Captain. You Washos recognize the Railroad means growth for you as well as us. I have a great admiration for you Washos. You have a sense of foresight, a commonsense not to raise an angry hand against growth. You're

not like the Paiute, you don't fight growth. It's the Paiute
the Company's most ashamed of Captain. Those Paiutes
just can't seem to settle down. You would think the war
up at Pyramid Lake back a few years ago would have
taught them not to stand in front of growth, most of their
kind don't, thanks to the wisdom of the great Chief Winnemucca joining our side and routing those of his kind
who lack a decent sense of organization and law. But
there are still a lot of Paiute bucks who think this country
out here is their private hunting reserve. Up ahead of the
line they've been yanking out surveyors' markers and even
shot down a couple of our spikers and bolters. I got word
brought into me just this morning that some of our coolies
in the staking gang were found dead at sunup with their
throats slit. The Company's going through land that hasn't
belonged to the Paiute for ten year and more. Greed it is
Captain. Greed and 'onry Injun blood is what makes those
bucks want to keep ahold of all God's country, when all
the Company wants is a narrow_right of way to run its
train through. But like I said Captain, we're about out of
your territory, haven't seen the hide of one Washo in
days, and the only ones we did see were that half naked
family who were only begging for a basketful of water.
It's Paiute territory we're coming up to now Captain, and
the Company doesn't want to have to fight Injuns with
one hand on a railspike and the other on a rifle the way
Major Dodge has been doing. The Company can't afford
that Captain. Tomorrow two Paiute Captains will be taking your place. They're coming up from the Carson River,
handpicked by the great Chief Winnemucca himself.
They'll know how to deal against any trouble that comes
up ahead, and deal it quick too. After beans tonight you
can hitch a ride with the supply wagon, they'll take you
back as far as Fallon, but they have to swing through
Genoa first. Take my word on it Captain, don't get yourself fired up in Genoa. They're a little jumpy about drunk
Injuns after that Shoshone put a cowboy's eyes out with
the cut end of a whiskey bottle. Like most civilized towns
out here they have an Injun curfew that begins at dusk,
but now they've gone beyond that and passed a law that

they've nailed above the door of every saloon that says
ILLEGAL FOR INJUNS TO PURCHASE AND CON-
SUME HARD SPIRITS ON THESE PREMISES. I
thought I'd give you my word on it Captain, in case the
supply wagon puts up there and you get one of your Injun
thirsts up." He loosened the fist clutching his lapel and
pulled a fat cowhide pouch from his coat, "You been with
this forward trackgang since it left Verde, that's eight-bits
and beans a day for sixteen weeks, that's forty-two bucks
American for four months." He balanced the weight of
the metal coins in his hand like an assayer weighing out
gold dust. "I think you'll find it all here Captain," he
tossed the sack of money over and turned to walk back
along the track, then stopped. "One thing more, if the
Company has need for you it will tell you of it; don't go
camping in front of the office door up at the Truckee yard
waiting for a job. In a few months, if you can get up
enough of your people to fill a boxcar, we'll haul you over
the mountains to the foothills, there's a lot of pigweed
coming up between the ties again, you people might as
well pick it or we'll burn it out."

The Indian watched the man move along the ironrail
into the sweating heat of the yellow bodies. Beyond the
yellowmen the burntland beat itself flat into the blurred
horizon. He could smell the jackass Rabbits out across the
land. He could smell them standing for miles around in
the sagebrush, the cocked and trembling flesh of their ears
half as long as his arm straining to the iron sound of the
yellowmen. He could smell the Sun draw the hard Earth
odor from the browned fur of their rigid backs while their
soft mouths silently chewed the hollowed stalks of sun-
dried grasses. He could smell the jackass Rabbits all the
way to the blurred horizon and he knew the foreign sound
of the yellowmen threw them out of their time, for the
jackass Rabbit when the Sun is highest over his head
keeps his body down and sheltered beneath the sprawl of
brush on a slope of high ground where his eyes can seek
out the restless black stripe of Coyote's shadow. When
Coyote wasn't coming to get him there was always the

blind eye of the Sun's direct light, holding forever the
winged threat of Hawk's straight fall to Earth and the
sudden clawed hook that could slash the fur of a body
open before the sound of wind beating wings was heard.
The Iron Road cutting through burntland had thrown the
Rabbits off time, in the high Sun their erect bodies stood
out over the hard ground, exposed. The Iron Road cut
across the Indian's time. He could smell the hot fur of the
Rabbit and his blood pulled him with ancient cunning to
hunt through the sage and trap the body of Rabbit. He
felt himself move in another time, running the Rabbits
across the burntland into waiting nets of strung hide, the
shouts of the people growing in his ears as the Rabbits hit
the nets and were clubbed down. He knew he should be
with the Rabbits, eating their flesh, his tongue thick with
the wild quicktaste of burnt meat just pulled from the fire.
But he was not running across the hard ground with the
Rabbits, the Iron Road slashed in front of him. He kicked
the ironrail before him with the toe of his boot and felt
the metal vibration throb through his body. The Sun came
at him as it dropped lower. He took a long hard pull off
the bottle he kept hidden beneath his thick checkered
jacket and paced back and forth along the place where the
iron had just been nailed to the Earth. He moved underneath the rush and shout of men who knocked his body as
they pushed forward with their business of pounding steel.
He was unnoticed. He was in the Sun that passed slowly
over him, marking the day by touching the land with brilliance at two ends. Soon the Iron Road the yellowmen
had built would trace the passage of the Sun, going from
one end of the land to the other, as far as the eye of a
man could see. He turned his back on the slamming
rhythms of sledges and took another pull off the bottle.
When he turned around he could see coming out of the
haze toward the mountains the man-made clouds, thrown
up black and long from the stack of the Iron-Engine,
clashing its fierce body down the track, the wheels bigger
than a man turning and spinning and spitting steam from
an iron heart. He jumped back as the Engine slowed to a
roll in front of him, its sudden rush of hot air spewing up

the white dust along the track into his face. A gang of yellowmen ran through the dust. Before the man with the
heavy gloved hands up in the Engine was able to bring the
five loaded flatbed cars behind him to a stop the yellowmen jumped up on one and began throwing the stacked
rails down. By the time the flatbed was cleared off most of
the rails had been lugged forward to the track spiking
gang and were already being pounded down over the
wooden ties. Another line of yellowmen stood along one-
side of the empty flatbed with long steel poles wedged under the weight of the iron wheels to the hard ground.
They moved as the flexed muscle of one arm, leaning into the
tension of the poles until the car was tipped up and its full
bulk fell free of the track, slamming into the powdered white
dust. The waiting Engine backed up over the cleared track
and coupled with the next flatbed in line, then pulled all
the loaded cars up to where the new rails just laid ended
and steamed to a stop while the yellowmen unloaded the
next flatbed, then tipped it over, allowing the loaded cars
to pass even farther along the new track. The Indian
watched as the cars were unloaded and the rails stacked
for a mile along completed track, the steady stream of
yellowmen carrying the dead metal weight balanced on
their narrow shoulders to the forward pounding of the
gangs. The empty cars were pulled back onto the tracks
by sweating teams of men, then pushed by the steaming
Engine into the blur of horizon where the mountains rose
straight up. There had been three loads of rails before
this, the Indian kept careful count, the loads measured off
the hot hours through which the Railroad paid him to
walk along behind the progress of the yellowmen. Before
the day was done there would be one more Iron Engine
with a line of cars behind stacked with rails to be fastened
forever to the Earth's hide. He turned his back on the yellowmen and drank his whiskey bottle empty until he
sucked at only air. He threw the bottle off into a tight
clump of low sage and heard it catch in the dried web of
branches. He knew the Rabbits were out there, the flesh
of their long ears pricked up to the foreign sound of the
yellowmen. Deep within himself he held great respect for

the power of the longeared Rabbit. When Rabbit was
threatened he did not hide in burrows or run with his
head down through the brush. He ran in the open with his
body held high. He ran a straight trail. He ran steady until
he was killed or escaped. The Indian slammed the toe of
his boot into the rail before him, the iron obstacle pained
the flesh of his foot and its metal vibration soared up to
the heat of his head. He pressed the full weight of his
body down on the injured foot and looked up at the Sky,
already the Sun was dying, beginning to set on the goldsweat backs of the yellowmen spiking steel teeth into
Earth.

Night was hotter than day in the burntland. The heat of
the long hours of Sun rose back off the hard ground and
held over the sagebrush like a hot lake. The twelve oxen
grudged their way through the heat of the night, the iron
of their hooves splashing great waves of white powdered
dust up over the wagon chained to the bulk of their bodies. The Indian sat next to the driver with one hand
hooked under the boardseat so he wouldn't be bounced
off. His lungs were heavy with the dust that clouded up
into his face. He kept his mouth closed, breathing only in
short sniffs through his nose. The driver punched him in
the arm and handed over a warm bottle, the Indian uncorked it and gulped at the whiskey, the burning liquid
rushing down his throat mixed with the sludge of dust he
breathed as he drank.

"That ought to wash your mouth clean," the driver
laughed and lashed the long whip into the churning dust
before him, cracking it over the broad backs he couldn't
see. "Gid Yup you mangy frog tits," he snapped the end
of the whip back into dust. "Here, you hogass buck," he
grabbed the bottle back from the Indian and swallowed
until his cheeks bulged out red, then popped his mouth
open in an O and blew out a grunt. "Whew, that's hotter
than a Virginia City whore! You ever had yourself a piece
of them fireworks under skirts Cap? A twenty dollar goldpiece will buy you between the longest meanest legs into
pure hot quicksilver. Cept so many men have mined that

particular hole you'll probably have to stuff a dog in it first then bam the dog, the dog's only four-bits extra. Hah. But I shouldn't go on to you about the Dee-Lights of Virginy City ladies. The old boys up there don't take to no bucks mixing their time with a white as snow woman. And don't you never try it neither Cap, you get a rise on you just better find some donkey to plug, cause if you don't those boys will cut your berries off and leave em to cook in the sun." He tipped the bottle up and took another pull. "Whew-Wee, this damn dust Cap, I've been ridin in it such a big part of my life that if they cut me open they'd find a bucket o dirt in each lung. This here run is as bad as when I worked for Pioneer Stages runnin coaches over the Echo Summit from Strawberry to Glenbrook Station, that was the most difficult stretch of the run, and I only busted in one stageload of travelers, but it were the last time, those stages is worth more than two-thousand bucks apiece and Pioneer took it right back out of my pay for three years. Fast horses is what you need on that run Cap. You can't run your reg'lar mule-ass or old frog tit oxteams, you got to have yourself a fine set of horseflesh that can see in dust and knows every rat rut and hell hole in the Sierra. That stageroad was so heavily run that the dust come up so thick in broad daylight you couldn't see the horses ears. Why do you know Cap, Pioneer's horses were so quick a body could board a stage at Frisco in the morning and soon's he knows he's in Virginy City by the next afternoon. Thirtysix hours of straight hightailin. But the Railroad's changed all that, a body could now get from Sacramento up over the Donner Summit to Truckee in less than six hours. That's what all but broke the coaches out o business Cap. The Railroad hired me on to drive supply wagon because from Truckee on they aint haulin no supplies. They're keeping the track wide open for hauling only ties and rails. I do think they're goin to beat that Major fella cross the Salt Lake. Heeyah-gidyup you oxen, gid along! Thing of it is Cap, when they git that thar railroad connected they aint goin to need my body no more. I been runnin stage since Forty-nine and damned if I know anything else other than breakin in new teams of horseflesh. I aint got it in me to lay bout all the day long with my pecker in a knothole the way some of you bucks do. Give me that thar bottle back Cap. Damn I shore wish it were October and we'd git the rain to wash all this dust outta here. But I was thinkin I might go over into the San Joaquin Valley and drive coaches for awhile, they ain't got no railroad in there yet, though I heard it said they's about to git one. Yes sir Cap, that there's what I think I'm gonna do, run stages through the San Joaquin Valley. I've been in the business too long not to hook up with the last main stage line in the State. Git along you hogbacks!" He flicked the whip into the dust. "We're almost into Genoa now. Gid along I said cowbrains!" He cracked the whip harder. The wagon jolted, almost throwing the Indian off, then moved more quickly, the wheels slamming over the rutted ground. "Damn I shore do wish it were time for October rain," the driver coughed into the thicker blanket of dust churned up from the steady pounding of the iron hooves. "Heeyup there pigbacks! Have nother swig off my pistol Cap. That's a boy, finish her off, I got nother one in the back wrapped in a blanket so's it won't get all broke up. Why don't you crawl over into the back and sees you could find it Cap. That's a boy, just step over easy. Watch it Cap, you drop off of this wagon and you'll bust your neck shore." The Indian crawled the length of the wagonbed on his hands and knees, patting the bare boards through the dust, feeling in the darkness for the bottle as he kept his lips pressed, breathing at the thick dust with only quick snorts. One of the wheels knocked a rock and bucked the bottom of the wagon into the Indian's chin, driving his teeth into the dry flesh of his tongue and slamming him up against the boarded side. "What's doin back there Cap!" The driver's voice stabbed through the dust. "Don't you hogass my whiskey like a thievin Injun." The Indian rolled himself up onto his knees, slapping his way in the dust along the side of the wagon until by chance he touched a bundled blanket. He pressed the bundle and could feel the hard bottle in its folds. He tucked the blanket beneath his arm and stood, holding the high board of the side and keeping his feet moving with the sway of the hard bounces. The suddenness of his upright position released a balled pressure between his legs and shot a barbed pain into his bowels. He gritted his teeth and blindly felt his way along the side rail to the back of the wagon. He held onto the thickness of the tailgate with the arm that kept the rolled blanket pressed against his body. He used his free hand to fumble the buttons of his pants open, the lurching of the wagon slamming his knees against the gate as he waited for the water to pass from him. But it wouldn't come, he had to put so much effort into keeping himself balanced in the bouncing darkness that it closed him up tight. He pinched the flesh between his fingers and shook it, but still the release did not come. He closed his eyes and concentrated on the barbed pain in his bowels, grinding his teeth as he sucked his stomach in, forcing the balled pressure down. He could feel the sting of whiskey as the pressure gathered and burned at the tip of his closed flesh. A few hot spurts shot out, the sudden tossing of the wagon directing them to his pant leg. He swore and grunted and pushed at the burning ball in the pit of his stomach until it burst, releasing a steady flow off the end of the wagon into darkness. He tried to hold himself straight, arching the stream away from his body, but he felt the bottle slipping from its hold, he let go of himself and reached to grab it, throwing his bouncing body out of time with the slamming wagon and tossing him over the gate into the boiling dust.

He lay on the ground until he could no longer hear the roar of the wagon and the last of its sound gave way to the night's quiet. The clearing dust exposed the low streaks of stars over his head. He stayed on his back where he had fallen and thought about nothing until he heard a distant noise and thought it was the wagon coming back for him. Then the sound stopped and he knew it had been an animal still running from the ground shaking team of beasts that had invaded its territory. He knew the wagon was not coming back. He refused to move his body, he lay still and barely breathing, afraid to get up, afraid to find himself broken and unable to walk. He was

very quiet and began to hear the talk of the stars, the slow
insistent crack of their voices calling to him. And it was
like this, late under the stars when he had been younger,
but still a man, and the snow had long since cleared from
the night Sky as he lay on his back in the shelter of the
winter hut with his feet to the small fire. He could see up
out the smoke hole at the top. The hot vapor from the fire
rising and distorting his view of the stars, warping their
brilliance and making them dance into wild bodies he had
never before seen. He listened and heard the snapping of
their talk, and he understood. It wasn't a dream, it was
talk from the stars. And the stars said go out from your
people to the *ones* who have tamed the wild beasts. To the
ones who have built shelters from tall trees stronger than
the strongest wind. To the *ones* who can kill the journey
of the longest rivers. Go out to *them* or you will die. You
will be frozen in the Earth like your father Gayabuc. You
have power to charm Antelope but the land is cut from
you by *their* fences of metal thorns. Go into *their* shelters
and learn *their* tongue or you will be shot through the
heart like the father of your father, the Chief of the Rabbits. When his body passed from the Earth you saw a fire
on the mountain and journeyed to that place but found no
track, found no fire where before it had been. You found
nothing. Do not try to find the source of the fire on the
mountain. It is not there where death passes into new life.
It is not there you will find the place of your Ancestors.
The fire burns within you. When you run to the mountain
to seek the fire every step you take is away from the
source. Keep the fire within you and go out to *them* and
learn *their* tongue and steal *their* ways. If you do not you
are the Beaver, and *they* have the power to strip all trees
in the forest naked of bark and let you die. Go out to
them. Watch *them*. You cannot take *their* power by killing *their* bodies. *Their* bodies are too many, *they* grow
faster than the grasses. Watch *them*. You cannot take
their power by capture, it is like Bird in the Sky, beyond
your touch, beyond the arrow of your bow. Watch *them*.
Imitate *them*. Move in *their* shadow and you will become
the shadow. You will become the body. You will become

them. You will become the *power*. You will bring back
the Gumsaba to your people. You will bring back the
warmth of its days, the trees heavy with the fruit of the
pine, the rivers filled with Fish. You will bring back the
Big Time of the harvest, the time of plenty. You will
charm the Antelope. Watch *them*. If you do not you will
become *powerless*. You will become weak and without
strength to shape the days beyond this one. That is what
the stars told him as he watched the distortion of their
brilliant bodies through the open smokehole. And the
stars never lied. They returned every night to travel a
straight path through the Sky. But he did not take their
words into his heart. In his heart was only the sound of
the child wrapped in the furskins of a Rabbit blanket. The
child was daughter to him. She was buried beneath the
skins in her mother's arms and he could hear the cough
that shook her small body and would not stop. He could
hear the cough through the night. In the true way he did
not sleep so she might stay awake and move quickly
through all the tasks of her later life. But the gift of staying alert he was trying to pass on to her he knew in his
heart may never be used as the coughs of the child grew
weaker and finally without sound. Her small mouth would
open in pain as her whole body shuddered with a soundless cough. The mother of the child had few words. She
was still weak from the loss of blood the birth of the child
pulled from her body. She remembered how she lay with
her back on the warm bed of cedar boughs, she was
spread and waiting on the green rising smell of the fresh
cut boughs while the old sister who had tied the buckskin
belt beneath her breasts worked it down over her stmach,
pressuring the child within forward in its natural rhythm,
aiding with quick fingers the birth movements until the
child was free of the mother's body. The old sister cut the
cord of blood to the baby's body well, with a quick stroke
of the stone blade. But she did not tie the cord tight with
deer string. The woman wanted to tell the old sister the
cord was not closed, but the old sister had already
wrapped the baby's stomach with strips of Antelope skin.
It was too late to ask the old sister to undo her work, it

was too late to make certain the cord had been tied tight.
To undo the work of the old sister would be an insult so
powerful it could kill the baby. So she let the old sister
wet the baby's stomach bindings with warm water and
place it in the soft furs of a basket. Then the old sister
made her drink. She drank of the warm sweet water
heavy with the taste of sap from the tree of sugarpine as
strong fingers worked over her still trembling body. The
fingers pushing the blood that still pulsed in the hollow-
ness of her stomach. The old sister made her sit through
the night with her back to the branches of the shelter, her
knees drawn up, touching her chin so all the blood could
run free of her body, draining back into the Earth. The
cord coming from the baby's stomach did not dry in the
days to come. Where it had not been tightly tied the blood
had run and soaked the Antelope bindings. The severed
end of the cord swelled as large as a small fist. When the
man who had the power to kill or cure came from the low
valley he entered the shelter and unwrapped the blood
soaked bindings from the baby's stomach and placed a
dead Hummingbird on the swollen cord. He pulled free
the Eagle feather stabbed through the length of his hanging black hair and held it flat over the baby's eyes while
he shook his cocoon rattle and sang out in the hut for the
Hummingbirds to come and suck the bad blood from the
baby's flesh with their needle beaks. The people waited
outside for the Man of Medicine to call up his magic.
They sat with their haunches to the ground and swayed
their bodies together in silent rhythm, thinking only of the
Hummingbirds invisible flight. For four nights the Man of
Medicine came and the people waited outside thinking
only of invisible flight. On the fourth night the Man of
Medicine brought a leather pouch filled with the dried
petals of a golden flower which bled drops of scarlet
across its bright face. He emptied the pouch into the fire
and threw on green branches of bitterbrush with feathers
from Owl tied into it. He sang the smoke up until its
white body curled thick and twisted out the smokehole,
sucking the heavy air of the hut free of all odor except the
stench of burning feathers mingled with the perfume of

smouldering flower petals. When the fire died down the Man of Medicine emptied a basket of water onto it and held the baby's struggling body over the rising steam, then he covered her body in the damp grayness of the still warm ashes and left the hut forever. the next morning the swelling was gone from the cord, but a cough came up from the baby's chest and did not stop. When the cord had emptied of all blood it dried into a hollow skin and fell from the baby's body. The mother called the father of the child into her for the first time, she told him her fast was over, the cord was fallen, to go into the trees and bring warm meat to her to put the blood of strong legs running back into her. It was then he heard the cough of the child, but she did not tell him the old sister had not tied the cord to cut off the blood. She did not tell him for the fear within her rose that the insult would be so powerful the old sister's shame would draw all the life from the baby. So he went out into the trees and there killed for her, and brought back warm meat of strong legs running. He thought close in himself that the cough of the child was of his doing, for when the birth was announced he went into the creek where his brother washed him clean as the new born so he would be worthy to guide the innocent life, but something could not be washed from him, some stain clung to his body. He was unclean because he had eaten of the flesh of the wild stone-eyed beasts *they* had brought. Others had eaten of this flesh, but he thought the power of the flesh had gone bad in him, killed something in him. He thought of the days when the father of his father still walked among the people in the time when those with skin the color of snow had searched rocks of gold. The days when *they* had driven his people out of the low hills as the giant limbed trees dropped their acorn fruit to the ground. The people returned over the mountains with baskets empty of acorns. The pinenuts had been few in the season before and the people were left with little to put in their stomachs when the first snows came. He remembered the Squirrel that was late on the snow and he had trapped it, bringing the small body back to the people. They did not put it over the fire for

fear of losing the life juices. For twelve days they stripped
raw shreds from the small body, that was all their teeth
chewed for that time. The women needed little food.
Their bodies had been prepared since birth to run many
days with nothing in their stomachs. It was the men who
began tearing the Rabbit blankets apart, scraping the
dried fat from under hides and sucking it in their mouths
to make it last longer. When the blankets were gone the
people used the branches of low trees to cover their bodies
against the cold. Then the men followed the Chief of the
Rabbit for two days across snow until they saw the house
of one who turned the Earth with an iron blade. The windows were boarded against the wind, the smoke from the
chimney came thinly into the gray Sky. Behind the house
was a smaller shelter where the men led the Horse out
and came with him back to the camp for a feast. There
was no falling snow for three nights. Into the fourth
morning a man with a low hat came riding up, lifting his
eyes from the tracks he had been following to the bloodied Horse lying on its side in front of the Rabbit Chief's
hut with hunks of meat cut from its ribs. Farther off, in
one of the other shelters, there was a baby crying when
the Rabbit Chief walked out in front of the halfeaten
Horse. The man raised a metal stick in his gloved hands
and a puff of smoke cracked in the cold air at its tip. The
hole that was torn through the side of the Rabbit Chief's
head showed little blood as his body fell across the exposed bones of the Horse's ribs. The noise from the man's
metal stick was still crashing through the snowcovered silence of the trees as he swung and rode off. The people
brought the body of the Chief of the Rabbit into his shelter and then lit fire to it. The blaze burned a clearing of
Earth in the snow, in front of it was the open body of the
Horse. The flesh of the Horse was eaten slowly through
the winter, it kept the people alive. After the birth of his
child, standing in the cold waters of the creek, he knew
what hung on his body and could not be washed clean by
his brother was the taste of Horseflesh. All through that
winter the taste of Horseflesh upon which the body of the
Rabbit Chief had fallen was full on his tongue. There was

little flesh for all the people, and he longed for the heavy feel of Horse in his mouth. As the white days grew into one another he thought only of the next piece of Horse-flesh he would eat. At night he dreamed of the Horse's body and many times he would awaken with the fear deep within him that the meat had been picked clean and sucked from the bones by the people, and he would go out into the open air and see for himself that the Horse was still there, running his hand over the ice-caked fur. He knew that at least for the next day he would again taste of that flesh. Many seasons after the death of the Chief of the Rabbit, after his own belly was full with meat of Antelope and Deer and sweet pinemeal, there was still within him a yearning, deep and hollow, for the flesh of the Horse. He tried many times to hide from his yearning but it always found him. Once he journeyed to the high valley where the clouds came up hot and steaming from the center of the Earth. He sat in the shelter built to catch the hot clouds and tried to sweat the desire for Horseflesh from his body. He breathed deep at the pure stench of the heavy air rising from the Earth, and still he was not cleaned out. And he was not cleaned in the creek by his brother. This he knew as he watched the stars dance through the smokehole and heard the shuddering of the child buried beneath the skins in her mother's arms. He listened every night to the child as he watched the stars and they tried to make him listen to their voices. One night the sound of the child stopped. The mother did not even lift the skins cradled in her arms to see the child's face. She simply rose and left him in the shelter behind. When she came back he knew the child was buried in the warm Earth the woman had prepared. He knew not where the body rested in the Earth, that was forbidden to him, and he did not search the place out. He took the basket the baby had been placed in the first day of her life and ran with it into the forest until he came to a spring running cool in a slight canyon. He walked into the water until he was beneath the branches of the slender birch trees growing up from wet soil in smooth ochre trunks. He placed the basket in the limbed saddle of the largest tree, facing it south with its side to the Sun, facing it the direction the Ancestors had long since journeyed to. The Ancestors would take the basket into them, and there the baby would sleep without trouble. He returned to the hut and burned it to the ground. He took the woman and left the people. They went into the high Mountain House to be alone with the knife going through their hearts. They went east to the mountains above the clouds. The woman had no words for him. The only time he spoke was to offer her the Fish he caught with his bare hands in the quiet of a dark pool. When the white days came they slept in a cave with their bodies close together while the ice ate the ends of their feet off. They began to talk again as the snows melted. It was warm and they followed the path of the downward streams. Their bodies were light from little food and their feet had healed. The stream they had been following into a valley stopped. It had been dammed and run off at a steep fall down a series of smooth slides cut from long trees. At the end of the wooden trough were men sorting through the heavy stones being washed free by the swift current of the channeled water. The men had long black hair braided and tied at the ends. Their skin was pale yellow, like the midday Sun. They stopped at their work as the two dark people half hidden above them in the trees moved their naked bodies into the brightness of the day. The man came down first, his palms held out to his sides. He stood before the yellowmen and raised his fingers to his mouth. One of the yellowmen ran off and came back with a tin barrel of crackers and broke one out. The Indian took it into his mouth, chewing slowly. Then he laughed at the dry salt taste, spattering white crumbs over his thin chest. The woman came down and stood with her body behind the man. She took one of the crackers and laughed with him. He turned to her laughing face that caught the Sun off the branches full in her brown eyes and spoke, "The men with yellow skin are not like the Whites, they will not kill us." They sat in the shade of the trees and watched the yellowmen working the loads of loose dirt and gravel, searching the stones golden with streaks of Sun. When it was so dark the yellowmen could no longer see the stones washing clean in the racing water of the trough they squatted around a black kettle hung over a fire steaming young milkweed shoots pulled from further downstream. They ate the tender shoots with tins of beans. One of them brought an open can over to the people under the trees and watched as they scooped the beans into their mouths, sucking the last bit of juice from their fingers. The yellowmen spread blankets on the ground and the one with a cap that shined the color of the morning Sun on his shaved head stood up and talked, the singsong of his voice sounding distant and high like the white Birds from the big salt waters who were sometimes caught in high mountains. He spoke for a long time to those lying on the blankets before he took a box folded in layers of material that shined the same color as his cap. He sat and opened the box on the blanket spread before him. He took from the box a pipe with a long narrow stem bent in a high gentle curve like a goose-neck. He filled the flat barrel of the pipe with stiff black grasses and struck a wooden match, the flame lit up the smooth glass of his face before he touched it to the packed barrel, sucking the fire into the grass. His hollowed cheeks sunk in his face and his nostrils pinched closed as the fire took and he pulled the smoke deep within him. He passed the pipe to another man and folded his hands in his lap. The yellowmen all sucked at the grass in the pipe. Before the first pipe was burned out two others had been lit, each man put his lips to the hot stems and drew all his life air through the smouldering grass. The Moon pulled itself over the tops of the high trees and in its light one of the yellowmen rose and brought a pipe to the man and woman sitting close together and silent under the trees. The man took the pipe held out to him. He put the hot tip to his lips and watched the coal in the barrel fire bright as he sucked the smoke through the long stem. Many times on the flatlands with his people he had sat beneath a tree and drunk into his body the bitter sage smoke, but it was not like what he sucked from the pipe of the yellowman. His head dazzled and floated on the cloud of his body, the tiredness ran from his bones like melting snow, he sat within a Sun warm pond as he drew again at the pipe and let the yellowman slip it from his lips and pass it to the woman. He felt the water close on his body, the mud coming up soft and slick through his veins as he sank beneath himself. There was a time when the waterbabies waved in the slow water and wrapped his floating head in their long hair. There was a time when the waterbabies sang songs with their lips pressed to his ear. There was a time when he could walk free in the mountains, when there were no barriers of metal thorns. There was a time when the burnt land was green. There was a Big Time of Gumsaba when the people had plenty and their baskets were full. There was a time when the Butterflies lie dead and scattered on the snow like dried flower petals. There was a time when he could charm the Antelope. There was a time when he did not hunger for Horseflesh. There was a time when he watched himself sitting against a tree with the sharp bark growing from his back. There was a time when he watched the Moon pass into the gray of dawn and the yellowmen were laughing in the stream with their mouths stuck on the dark skin of the woman. There was a time when they rolled her on the ground, their heavy belts anchoring their loosened pants at their feet. there was a time when they coiled like Snakes and came stiff into her body. There was a time they fell one by one limp from her yielding flesh. There was a time when she lay on the Earth with the wet hair between her legs heavy with the smell of yellowmen. There was a time he came down to her and washed the smell from her flesh in the clean waters of the stream while over his head the Sun found its place in the Sky. He carried her like a fresh killed fawn slung across his shoulders. He followed downstream until the Moon was up again. Then he slept, holding her cold body the way he had in the cave. In the morning he placed her weight across his back again. By midday the burden worked at the strength of his legs and caused them to buckle, dropping him to his bare knees. He continued into the late light, but he could not shoulder the weight for more than a hundred steps before he fell again and had to push back up to his feet. When the stream joined a

river the skin of his knees had been torn off and ran
blood. He stayed the night by the river until new light. He
did not travel far before he saw *them* along the water's
edge, dipping wide pans that reflected the Sun into still
pools pocketed between the rocks. He went up into the
trees and around those who mined the golden waters. Then
he cut back to the sound of rushing water and followed
the river path until again his way was blocked by the ones
with skin the color of snow who squatted in the shallow-
ing water seeking stones heavy with streaks of Sun. He
went back up into the trees and followed the sloping
ground until the trees stopped and the rocks bigger than a
man began. He lowered her body into the narrow gray
space of two warm boulders and covered it with a bed of
branches weighted down by stones. He traveled for six
more days, making wide arcs around those who sought
the golden rocks until finally he came in to the place of
the people. His mother Painted Stick came to him and
washed the dried blood from his legs with damp ferns. He
told the people of the new ones, the ones with yellow skin
who worked hard and sweated much. The yellowmen
would not kill like the others, but they took in the smoke
of a power stronger than the bitter sagebrush. They
smoked into their bodies something that was poison to his
people. He himself had smoked of the poison and lived,
but his head spun high in the trees while the yellowmen
used the woman's body. When he came to the woman she
had followed the path of the Ancestors, her Spirit had
died away South. He did not know if her spirit was gone
before the yellowmen left their smell on her skin. He
washed her flesh clean and tried to bring it back into the
people. But the ones who empty the rivers for the golden
stones blocked his journey. He was afraid *they* would take
the woman's body and use it. So he took her to where the
Eagles fly and rested her safe under a blanket of stones.
After hearing his words Blue Breast, the father of his
Mother, spoke that is was time to travel down to the low-
land lake where the tules grew thick and the people could
fashion boats and go out on the water to herd the flatbeak
Birds who were too fat to fly into nets. The meat of the

Birds was tender and easy to cook, the people would feed
on Bird flesh and be happy. The mountains were many.
Those who searched the rivers for gold stones were also
plenty. The mountains would not be safe for the people
this season. When the hot days turned to white and the
snows melted the people could return to the Mountain
House. The ones with white skins would have their gold
stones, plenty were to be had just by picking them from
the ground. *They* would have *their* want of gold stones
and leave as quickly as *they* came. Again the mountains
would belong as the peoples house. Blue Breast led the
people out of the mountains, heading in the direction
from which the Sun was born every morning. When they
reached the lake there were others of the people from the
north who were camped along the shores and they all
banded together to take the Birds too burdened with flesh
to fly. The people cooked the Birds in the pit of hot
stones, the meat was tender and good in the mouth. But
the people were uncertain in their hearts. They could see
out across the flatland the tents on wheels still coming out
of the east. The tents grew up off the horizon, the tamed
beasts pulling them in straight lines. But they did not all
journey past the people. Sometimes an entire line would
roll up to the lake and the ones with white skin would
lead the tamed beasts to drink from the still waters. The
people watched this from the other shore of the lake.
They saw these Whitemen were different from the ones
who took the gold stones and built many houses from
trees in the mountains. These Whitemen had in their rolling tents small children, and women who would clean
their bodies in the still waters and cook foods in blackiron baskets. Some of the people came to those in the rolling tents and held out in their hands the gift of pinenuts.
The White ones took the gift and gave back bright cloth
for the people to cover the skin of their bodies. Some of
the people wore the cloth, others did not, but soon all
came to look inside the rolling tents, some even touched
the hide of the tamed beasts. Each time a line of the tents
rolled off from the lake some of the Whites stayed and
built high flatsided shelters to protect them against the

cold of the coming white days. The people set up their own small shelters around those of the Whites and waited for the things the Whites no longer had use for to be given to them. The time was past when the people could go onto the still water and capture the Birds too fat to lift their bodies to the Sky, the Birds were gone, taken by the Whites who killed from the muddy shore with loud noises from metal sticks. The people lived off what the Whites threw away. After the long white days more rolling tents came. As the Birds moved overhead to the south they were knocked from the Sky with loud noises from the many metal sticks of the Whites. There were now many tamed beasts eating the grasses around the lake. The White cut off great sections of the land with lines of metal thorns to keep the beasts from running. The days were warm and groups of the people drifted off to where the lands were still open to take game grown thick with meat, to harvest the fruit of the Piñon Trees. When the Skies turned dark again the people came back to the lake and found more Whites. More things no longer needed by the Whites lay about on the ground, they could be used to make the cold days easier. The people had much on their bodies now, they were covered with the patched clothes the Whites had discarded. They gave the skins of Animals to the Whites for metal coins. They killed the Rabbits on the land bounded by the lines of metal thorns which they could trade at the place filled with sacks of seeds. When it was time for the people to go again to harvest the fruit of the Sacred Piñon Tree many chose to stay and use what the Whites no longer needed, others found different groups of Whites and settled around them. Those who did travel for the harvest of pine fruit found many lines of metal thorns blocking their path, and the ones seeking gold stones had made their way over into the low hills and would take the life of the people if they stepped where before it had always been their way to do. The Deer and the Antelope had fled the lowlands where the tamed beasts trampled and cut the roots of thick grasses. It took the people many days to track the running game, and many times the Animals would not be waiting where the dreams

of the Antelope Walker had shown them to be. At night,
with the fires burning low, the people told stories until
there were no more words, then they would fall silent and
listen to the stars. But what the stars had to say could not
always be heard.

The Indian could no longer hear the stars. The insistent
crack of their voices calling him ceased. He raised his
arms and felt no broken bones. He pulled up and waited
to feel a pain coming from some broken part of his body,
but there was none. The fall from the wagon had not
harmed him. He buttoned his pants and remembered the
bottle. He nudged his boot in the clumps of sagebrush
around him lit up by the Moon. The tip of the boot struck
something soft, it was the blanket, he picked it up and it
was dry. He still held the hope the bottle had not shattered in the fall. He unrolled the blanket and found the
bottle unharmed in the center, the glass smooth and shining in the Moonlight, the weight of its liquid cool in his
hands. His fist gripped the bottle's slim neck as he uncorked it and drank. He spread the blanket beneath him
and sat on his folded legs. The heat of the whiskey raced
in his body and woke the Birds sleeping in his chest, their
ancient song flooding from his wet lips into the open
night. He sang and drank and sang and drank until the
bottle was empty and his head wouldn't hold still in his
hands. He saw through his closed eyes the stars trying to
speak to him with their fierce light. He saw the place
where the Eagles fly and he laid the woman out beneath
the blanket of stones. He saw the people following Blue
Breast to the lake in the lowlands. And he saw the white
face of the woman in the tent wagon with the gray dress
that covered the length of her body. Her white face was
like a cloud with the Sun shining through and she gave
him a cloth to tie around his waist and keep his legs
warm. He came to her everyday with a Fish he had
speared in the still waters and she would take it from him
and hold its wet body in her gentle hands. Then she would
speak, her voice was soft like the tingle of small bells
hanging from the back of the wagon. She spoke everyday

to him when he would bring a Fish. For every Fish he brought she taught him a word of her tongue and he took it away with him in his memory. He learned that her name for him was *you*. The cloth she had given him to tie about his waist was called *pants*. Before her face covered with red stinging sores which puffed up yellow and she died he had many words deep in his memory from her. It was during the cold of the long white days when the baskets of stored pinenuts finally were empty that the people chose him to go and ask for food from the Whites with the words the woman taught him. He saw the times he would stand in the heart of the white houses where the blackiron fire of the stove hummed with heat. He would say, "The baskets are empty, the Sky is empty, the people starve." Then they would look at him a long time with the string belt of his pants tied around his waist and the worn Rabbit blanket pulled over his hunched shoulders. They would always give him something to carry back to the people. They told him there was only something for the people because they were not Paiutes, because the Washo shared their land with the Whites. But here was not always something for the people in the days ahead and he would return with nothing except the words he had learned. He would repeat slowly what had been told to him, that the people were no longer to take Fish from the lake with nets. The people were to move all their shelters to the far shore. The people were not to leave their shelters after the Sun died. If the people did these things they could stay at the winter lake and live off what the Whites could no longer use. The people listened to these words he spoke and followed what they said, but they no longer came close to him with their hearts. The words the woman had taught him had become a power, a power the people did not trust. He himself did not trust the words, but they were tied in his memory. He could not forget them, they held a power he did not understand, for when the Whites wanted something from the people, or had a new way for them to follow, they always came to him because he held the power of two tongues. They gave him a name of power. They called him a leader. They called him a

Captain. They called him Captain Rex. But his people never recognized a power in one man to lead all the days of their lives. The Washo had no leaders. So he knew not what to do with this power. He could not kill a Bird from the Sky with it. He could not charm the Antelope into the corral with it. He knew not how to use it. But he had it. The whiskey he drank made him forget many things, but not the power of the White tongue. Within him lived the power of the White tongue and the ancient power of the songs the Birds sang long ago that he had learned in dreams. The two powers fought in his blood. When he drank whiskey the song of the Birds became too strong to hold in his heart and escaped from his throat. He could do nothing but let his voice sing their power.

The morning on the burntland came up quickly. The Sun shot over the far rolling hills and caught the night by surprise, its sudden light waking the Indian. In the clear dawn he could see the high wall of the Sierra mountains towering up green from the burntland. He knew he was close to the town of Genoa and slung the long roll of the blanket over his shoulder as he followed the flat of the road in a straight line before him. The clumps of sage stung the clear air with dry perfume and he smelled the jackass Rabbits as they ran out in all directions from the sound of his boots slapping in the dust filled ruts of the road. He walked in the direction of the rising Sun. Far back on the road he could see a low white cloud and soon he heard the rumble and constant thud of a wagon with the high disconnected shouts of men rising above it. The wagon drew closer and the cloud of dust streaking out along behind it died before reaching the Sky. The mules came up behind him, the slamming muscular jerk of their bodies tearing at the peace of the road before them. He could see through the roll of dust flayed up by the spinning wheels the two men sitting high on the boarded seat. The one holding the slack of the reins fisted in his hand whipped head around and flashed his eyes down at the Indian in the flying dust, then turned his head again, his shout of "HIEYAAWRH!" jammed the driving force of the mules faster and the wagon was by. The Indian could see through the swirl of dust the empty water barrels slamming together in the back of the wagon. He waited until the white dust settled down around him and the noise thinned into blue air before following up the road in the rut of the wheels.

The Sun hung straight above his head when he walked into the town called Genoa. He knew the town from before when the Mormons were there and said his people were the first of the great lost Tribe that had broken from the chains of ice in the frozen north. The Mormons told the people that if they let their bodies be covered with the water of the living stream they would be born into the Kingdom Upon The Earth. The years of the people would all be green, their bodies stronger than any poison, and the man called Jesus would come to them and walk among them and give to each the power to strike the stone. Some of the people went into the living waters to be reborn. Others journeyed over to the great Salt Lake to the house where the Jesus was supposed to appear. But the Jesus did not come and the days of the people were long with weakness in their bones. The people forgot the words that had been told them and no longer looked for the Jesus to come from the north. He had known the town then, when it was called Mormon Station, and he knew it before when there were no stages coming down to it from the mountains to change their teams of panting beasts and continue out across the flatland and over the burnt hills where the stream of silver was being bored from the Earth in Virginia City. He knew it before when there was nothing but the Rabbits running across the bare ground into the waiting nets of the people. Now there were no Rabbits as he walked down the planked boardwalk of the street. There were only the many stores and gambling halls fitted close together, forming a gray wall against the continuous slam of dust that rose up from the wagons in the heat. He felt the pouch of metal coins the Railroad boss had given him for following the Iron Road the yellowmen built. The pouch was heavy in his pocket. He took it into a high ceilinged saloon and emptied five of the gold coins on the hard polish of the counter. He could see from the corner of his eye the tender slap down his newspaper and stare at him without moving. But he kept his own gaze on the goldframed mirror in front of him, reflecting his brown face with the deep eyes fixed on the scar of his cheek. He saw the tender move and reached instinctively to scoop the coins back into the pouch. He knew what the tender was going to say, no spirits for Injuns, but before he could slip the pouch back in his jacket the tender cracked his open palm on the counter, "What's your poison Chief?"

"Whiskey."

"Whiskey is fire in your eye Chief."

"Whiskey."

"Bottle or glass?"

"Bottle."

"Bottle it is Chief," the tender swiped the inside of a clear glass and set it with a full bottle on the counter. "That'll cost you five dollars American from your jeans."

He dumped the pouch out on the counter and watched as the tender counted out the number of coins that added up to the price.

"What you got such a heavy jacket on for Chief," the tender jammed his elbows down on the counter and propped his face in his hands.

"It's the middle of summertime and you're bundled up like an Alabama nigger. What's wrong, you got the rheumatiz from too much booze, or you got frostbite on your pecker?"

He didn't know what the tender's face was trying to tell him, he just kept looking past him at the mirror until the first words that fit together he said right out, "I keep my jacket on all the time." The words just hung before him and did not move. He poured his first glass of whiskey and gulped it down, then looked back at the mirror.

"Washo aint yah?" the tender kept his head propped up, just moving his lips.

"Washo. I am Washo," he took another drink and bowed his head.

"Aint too many of you bucks left around these parts is

there Chief. I mean you Washo don't get shot out of the saddle like the Paiute. You Washo like to die in bed with one hand on your pecker and the other around a bottle of firewater. What I mean to say is Chief, you Washo don't got no Paiute blood in you, it's mostly Digger blood, ain't it Chief. I mean the Paiute whooped you Washo pretty bad before we whites even got here, didn't they Chief? You got nothing to say do you? No sabe, huh Chief? You bucks no sabe nothing except how to ask for whiskey. You bucks don't ever say a word cept *whiskey*."

The Indian heard it before, this talk, and he *knew* what it meant. He tried to keep his hand steady as he poured out the next glass, but most of the whiskey splattered in bright pools on the polished counter, when he finally got enough of it in the glass he drank it down and turned to leave. The tender grabbed his arm and pulled him back up against the counter.

"What's wrong Chief? You paid your Injun price for your firewater and you leave half of it in the bottle. What made you want to hop up on the water wagon so quick? You trying to imply my whiskey is not good enough for your red belly?" The tender poured the Indian another glass. "Drink up Chief."

He took the glass and drank, then banged it back down on the counter. Before he could turn around the tender had it filled up again. He took the glass and pressed it to his lips, then quickly set it down and turned for the door just as its two panels swung open and a crowd of men pushed through behind a tall man in a low black hat. The man stopped, spread his arms, the crowd behind him stood still, the blue of his eyes lit up his face under the low brim of his hat as he grabbed the lapels of his long black coat in his fists.

"You know what we're going to do?" The man's words addressed the whole room and found their mark in the center of the Indian's pale face.

"Yah, what is it we're going to do to him Reverend Jake," a voice from the crowd behind him demanded.

"Yah, tell him what it is we do to his kind!"

"We're going to cut his ears off!"

"WaHooo! That's damn well what we're going to do alright Rev'rend!" A couple of hats from the crowd were thrown up to the ceiling.

"We're going to cut his ears off and bleed all the devil liquor right out of the red body of this Paiute!"

"That's the truth of it! Bleed the devil Paiute dry!"

"He aint Paiute, Rev'rend Jake," the tender smiled. "He's Washo."

"Washo," the Reverend Jake locked the blue of his eyes on the Indian. "Then we're going to cut the ears off this *Washo* red devil!"

"Washo aint got no devil in him Rev'ren," a man called from the crowd. "Washos is nothin but Diggers! Root Diggers! They aint like the Paiute and Shoshone, they won't fight. They're like John Chinaman, all they got in them is squaw blood! Squaw blood and a rabbit heart!"

"Squaw blood *is* rabbit blood! They run like the rabbit when there's trouble!"

"You look here!" The Reverend Jake swung around and showed the fierce blue light of his eyes to the crowd, "Red devils is red devils. They're all the same. Get a little liquor in them and they'll sneak up in the night and cut the top of your head off. My brother Dan was leading twelve wagons along the Pit River when the red devils tied him to a tree and shot arrows into him, killed the lot, children, women and men in an unGodly act. The red devils burned the wagons and ate the horses. I'm telling you there aint no white woman safe in her bed at night long as there is just one inebriate red devil walking the streets of any civilized town."

"Kill the red devil!"

"And I'm telling you we've had our share of Injun trouble in this town of Genoa right up to the lip. We had a liquor-crazy Shoshone cut a Cowboy's eyes from him right here in this same saloon not more than two months back, and most of you boys saw the unGodly act. And the storeclerk's wife caught a red devil looking in through her window when she was indecent. I tell you there aint no one safe long as there's a red devil left in any civilized town. They don't pay no attention to our Sundown Ordinance, and when we go and pass a law stating the particular illegal nature of an Injun consuming hard spirits in any of our drinking establishments they ignore it and walk right in as they please and order themselves a whiskey just like they was *white*. By God it's about time some lessons were taught in this town. If you can't be reasonable with the red devils you've got to get tough with them." He followed his words across the room and with one swing his arm knocked the Indian across the face to the floor. He grabbed the Indian by the throat of his jacket, yanked him up and pushed him through the crowd out the swinging doors onto the boardwalk. "Do you see that," he pointed to the sign nailed above the saloon's doors. "Read it out you red devil!"

The Indian looked up at the sign. It meant nothing to him. The words painted on the board held no meaning. Long in the past the woman in the wagontent taught him how to speak the sounds of her tongue and what the meaning behind them was, but she never taught him to recognize those sounds when they were written out. He didn't know how to read.

"I said read it out you red devil. Read out the Law!"

The Indian tried to make sense from the painted words on the sign. He moved his lips silently, trying to fit together the sounds the man wanted to hear.

"You red devil! You mock us. You mock our Laws," Reverend Jake grabbed the Indian's hair in his fist and yanked it, pulling the head farther back until the Indian's eyes could no longer see the words on the sign, could only see over the sharp edge of the roof above to the clear blue of the Sky. "ILLEGAL FOR INJUNS!" Reverend Jake shouted the painted words of the sign into the Indian's face. "ILLEGAL FOR INJUNS TO PURCHASE AND CONSUME HARD SPIRITS ON THESE PREMISES!"

"Damn if that aint him! Damn if that aint the thievin redskin," a man shouted from the crowd which had backed itself into the saloon, along the boardwalk and into the street. He shoved his way to the front until his face was right up against the Indian's. "Damn if that aint the thievin redskin buck what I give a ride to on the sup-

plywagon last night. More'n half way here he sneaks into
the back of the wagon, steals my whiskey, which I use
only as medicine to keep my blood up on winter nights,
and slips over the tailgate. Why hell, it were more'n fifteen miles before I knowed he was ever gone, and it
weren't no use in goin back for him as by that time he'd been
hid under a sage guzzlin the bottle down. That's him you
bet." The man strained closer, the spit of his words striking the Indian's face. "That's the thievin redskin buck!"

"I'm damned," Reverend Jake let go of the Indian's
hair and pushed him to the edge of the boardwalk. "They
kill, they lie, they cheat, they look at your women, they'll
steal the teeth right out of your head. They commit the
most unGodly acts and it's about time some lessons were
taught." The whistling sound of a lasso cut through Reverend Jake's words, the loop of the rope coming down
around the Indian's head just as the Cowboy who threw it
spurred his horse out into the street, tightening the rope
until it locked the Indian's arms to his sides and pulled
him off the boardwalk, slamming his face into the street.
The Indian stood up in the white cloud of dust his body
had raised. The laughter of the men crowded around him
slapped at his face. He felt the rope tug at his body. The
Cowboy turned the horse and headed it up the street. The
rope jerked the Indian around, but he kept his footing,
running behind the horse as it broke into a trot, trying to
match the speed of the animal he was tied to. The Cowboy swung in the saddle and saw the Indian running behind him, he cocked his boots out in the air, then knifed
the spurred heels straight into the horse's flanks. The
horse reared back, for a moment its weight hung suspended on the thrust of the back legs, then broke into a gallop.
The sudden movement snapped the slack in the rope,
yanking the Indian off his feet and dropping him to the
ground, dragging him behind in a stream of dust. The
Cowboy spurred the horse to the end of the street, swung
around and rode back past the cheering crowd and
stopped. The Indian lay still, waiting for the horse to drag
him again, but it didn't. He raised up on his knees and
tried to spit. His dry tongue caught in his dust filled

mouth and choked him. He rose choking and spitting into
the laughter coming from the men crowded along the
boardwalks. The roaring sound of the men was more
painful than the skin the dragging burned off his legs. He
looked up at the Cowboy grinning down from his saddle
and saw the sudden flash of spurs as they lashed into the
horse's sides. The sudden wrench of the rope seemed to
tear his arms off as it pulled him to the ground. He
couldn't feel his hands, only the pain of the rope cutting
in his sides. The skin on his legs flamed as he swirled
across the flashing ground that was burning away the
pants at his hips to eat into his flesh. He tried to keep his
head up so the skin of his face wouldn't be torn off, but
the rope around his chest cut his breath. The air he des-
perately sucked was filled with dust from the slamming
horse's hooves. He could no longer hold the weight of his
head up. He felt it sinking closer to the ground coming up
and racing beneath him like the edge of a razor. The
weight of his head slumped, but the horse stopped, snorting through the flare of its nostrils, its hide around the
saddle wet with the caked sweat of white dust. The Indian
felt the life go from him. He tried to cough the dirt from
his mouth but the dry string of his throat made him
heave, bringing up the whiskey in his stomach, its sudden
rush clearing the dirt from his mouth. He sucked at the
freed air as he tried to lift his face from the wet green
stench it was lying in.

"That ought to put the lesson into your onry hide you
red devil," Reverend Jake yanked the Indian's head up
and held the blade of a knife to his swollen face. "Next
time you'll know the lesson of the White-man's Law, you
lying, cheating, stealing Washo coward," the furious light
of his blue eyes burned beneath the black rim of his hat as
he raised the knife and slashed it down in a broad, quick
stroke, cutting the rope that tied the Indian to the horse.
"Get up you red devil. Get up and run like a rabbit!"
The Indian tried to struggle to his feet, but the rope
locked around his arms held him to the ground.
"I said run!" The Reverend Jake pulled him up by the

hair, but the Indian felt nothing in his legs. His tied body
fell face down back into the street. "Run!" The Reverend
Jake yanked him up again, then kicked him in the back,
knocking him to the street again. "Damn onery red devil
snake," the Reverend Jake jerked the Indian by the hair
and held his body up, then shoved him forward. "Run for
your life red rabbit!"

The Indian felt his feet, he felt them in his boots and he
moved them. He moved his whole body, trying to keep his
balance as he ran blindly down the center of the street,
but the rope tying his arms down threw him off time and
he fell sliding into the dust. He rolled over, pushed himself back to his feet and ran again. Then he felt it, he felt
it in front of him and slowed down to face it. Before him,
blocking off the end of the street, was a straight wall of
men. He turned and ran a few steps, but coming from the
other end of the street was Reverend Jake with another
wall behind him. The two walls came together and he was
trapped.

"You know what we're going to do to you!" Reverend
Jake strode to the center of the circle the men formed
around the Indian.

"YaH, tell him what it is we do to his kind!"

"We're going to hang him!"

"Hang the red devil!"

"Hang him to a tree!"

"You can't!"

The crowd fell silent, searching the voice that went
against it.

"You can't," the man at the back of the crowd spoke
again as all eyes turned to him. "You can't hang him to a
tree because there aint no trees."

"Damned if he aint right," an old man stamped his
boot in the dust. "There aint a tree within thirty mile any
direction you ride. They all been cut to the ground years
ago to build the town."

"I was in Downieville in the summer of '51," a man
with a beard seared orange by the sun pushed his way to
the center of the crowd. "It was in '51 that the Mexican
woman Josefa put a knife into Fred Cannon's heart. In

broad daylight she done it. Right in the street. I weren't
there to see it being as I was up the river panning, but
there was plenty who did and soon's I got the word I
come into town and what we did with her was hang her
from a bridge. She let her black hair down in the sun before they put the rope around her neck. It were the petti-
est black hair I ever seen."

"Well we cant hang this red devil from a bridge because we aint got no bridge!"

"Throw him off a roof with a rope around his neck!"

"No! That aint no good," another man shoved to the
center and stood next to Reverend Jake. "I'm from 'Bama
and we got a way there with niggers. We put two ropes
around their necks, lash the ends of the ropes to the sad-
dle-horns of two horses, then spur the horses. The head
comes off clean as a watermelon."

"That's how we'll do it!" Reverend Jake shouted.

Two horses were ridden into the center of the crowd.
The riders quickly tied two nooses and handed them down
to Reverend Jake who looped them over the Indian's
neck. "Now you boys move back here. Move back and
give these horses room to bolt." The crowd separated,
leaving a broad aisle all the way down the street. The Indian stood alone between the two horses.

"You riders ready!"

"We're ready Rev'rend," the two men sitting easy in
their saddles called. "You just give the word."

Reverend Jake walked up the aisle between the waiting
men and raised his hand. "When I drop my arm you riders git!" He looked down one end of the street to see the
way clear then up the other, where his eyes stopped,
"What in the name of Satan is this?"

Coming down the street between the two rows of men
was an Indian woman on a horse with the gentle buckskin
flow of her long fringed dress falling along the line of her
body. Her horse was tied behind a larger one. The sun
glared off the high black crown of the stovepipe hat on
the man sitting straight in the saddle of the lead horse. A
slim cigar was clenched in the delicate curve of his mouth
as he tapped a goldtipped cane against his checkered

pants. He reined his horse to a stop in front of the Indian
and touched the metal tip of the cane to the ropes lynched
around his neck. He withdrew the cigar from his mouth
and swung in his saddle, "You gents cant hang this Injun."

"Who in the name of God says so!" Reverend Jake
shouted, the hand held high above his head clenching into
a fist. "It's ordained by the Almighty Himself! Who dares
go against His Word! Just who is it that goes against His
Word!"

"It's a Bummer!"

"Just who goes against the Word of the Almighty!"

"It's not just me, John C. Luther, saying it gents, it's
the United States Republic of America. Nevada is no
longer an open territory, it was proclaimed the thirty-sixth
state of the Union by a deliberate daylight act of Congress
not more than five years ago in '64. This town sits on the
dirt of Nevada, and that means its men are bound to the
democratic ways of the Republic. A man is innocent by
Law until proven guilty. He's got to be given a fair trial.
So you see gents, being as this is a Republic, we have to
give this Injun a fair trial, then hang him."

THE BLACKBIRDS sing across the river.

Oh Christ, the Blackbirds sing across water where it is always flowing. The Blackbirds sing open a door and the people wait to pass through into the light of virgin Sky. The people wait oh Christ, to enter the heavens of the old ways before the time of the Whites. The people wait to enter the heavens riding the songs you brought back on the Ghost Pony the day the Sun died and fell from the heart of the Sky herself with a lance through his golden body. The people wait to sing the trees up. To sing the mountains up. To sing the lakes up. The people wait to dance their birth. To dance the birth of the Birds. To dance the birth of Animals running. The Sky is thick with feathers and fur. The days of the people are falling quickly from them. The old ways are peeling like skin from the Snake. The people are all dead or dying. We are few, the Whites are many. We are sly, we are swift. The land is sunk to the heart. The land has been robbed of trees, the rocks have been blown to powder. We ask but one thing. We have but one hope. Sing your Song oh Christ. Ride the Ghost Pony among us. Let us feast on the flesh of the Ghost. Let the waters come and wash the Earth clean of those who destroy her. Let the people stand in high places everywhere. Let the people anoint their chests and legs with the blood of all things. Of the

Spirit. Let the people dance their joy and release the sacred Bird from its bed of ashes. Oh Christ we are sick. Our bones melt. We are cut from the land. We have many pains. We wait to enter through the door the Blackbirds sing over water where it is always flowing. Oh Christ, touch our wounds with your Song. Heal us into power. Lead us out from under the place where the Sun rises. Lead us on the straight path of our Fathers.

The Christ did not answer what I asked him in my heart. His body was sunk deep within his black clothes. The Sun was full over him. He had no shadow. We sat there on the flatland, the three, myself, the Christ, and the other man, one who follows. In the silence of the day the snow was melting from the clumps of sage. In every direction from us branches were breaking from their white burden free to the Sun. In the pit scooped out by the fire of the night before the yellowbacked Spider still moved simply and swiftly over the charred bones of dead wood, spinning the blossom of her web further into the surprising currents of wind. Spinning whitelight lace endlessly from the depths of her body. She turned to me and held up from the open drawer the sheet of lace, letting its folds fall open from her hands until the entire piece lay straight and intricate before her. She spread it smooth over the bed, I could hear the breath rushing short through her nostrils as her hand glided over the sheer surface shimmering like a lake. "It belonged to my mother," she spoke not to me, but to the very air of the closed bedroom itself. "It was on my mother's bed when she was a bride. It was only used once, the first night. The lace is pure, it's German. It was brought across on the ship by my grandmother to America. It was the one personal thing my grandmother was allowed to take from the homeland. Each person could bring very little on the ship. She hid her bible in the folds of this lace. That was more than one-hundred eighty years ago. In 1736 the ship sailed from Hamburg to the new town of Savannah, a place where the Lutherans could build free of persecution. But it was only that way for a short while. They had to keep moving further

and further to the west. I was born as they journeyed
west, just this side of the Platte River. Here I am now all
the way west, in the Sierra Nevada." She spoke these soft
words as if their mere utterance gave proof of her presence in these high mountains. "My husband Frank isn't
Lutheran," her eyes traced the shimmering pattern of the
lace. "But he is a God fearing man. He says with the help
of the Lord he's going to fill this valley with cattle. He is a
good man, Frank Dora is. He risked his very life burning
to the ground six years ago the Indians shacks up at the Elephant Head lumber mills. Those shacks were all filled
with the bodies of Indians who were dying of their own
Indian fever. No one asked Frank and the boys to burn
the disease away. It was a job just had to be done, and
they did it. They don't ask for any thanks. But it was any
one of them could have got the fever themselves and died
from it." She stopped her words and looked at me as if
she just discovered I had been there all the time. "You
shouldn't hold it against Frank that he beats you. You
have many faults and he's only trying to make you into a
person that could get along in this world and know the
rules. A lesson taught the hard way is a lesson never forgot. It's all for the good that he beats you when you do
bad. Would you like," she moved from the bed toward
me, her long gray dress almost scraping the bare boards
of the floor, "would you like to touch the lace?" I moved
to the bed and placed my hands on the pattern of the
shimmering material. It was like touching her, a secret
part of her, the part I could never touch but see when she
pulled her son Darrel to her body and held him without
saying anything, then kissed the blond hair falling across
his forehead. She never touched me. When I was first with
them and still a small boy she would wash the dirt from
my body every Saturday morning, raking my scalp with
her nails as she worked the soap up in my hair, the whole
time whispering low to me, "You're such a dirty little boy,
such a filthy little Indian, a body'd never scrub you
clean." Then she would wash hard between my legs until I
was raw and she finally would notice me whimpering with
the pain of her getting me clean, and she would stop. She

always washed Darrel first. She sang to him and called,
"My little babyboy," and tickled his ear with the washrag.
She would dry him off and dress him up next to the stove,
then tell me to jump in the big tin tub sitting in the middle
of the floor. I would get in, but by then the water had
turned cold, the gray scum of lather from Darrel's scrubbing floating across the top. One day she said I would
have to wash myself. She said I was big enough and didn't
need anybody doing it for me. She never touched me
again from that time. But Darrel was the same age in
years as me, and twice as big, with hands that could break
the sticks of my arms whenever they wanted. She kept
washing him another year before she quit. She never
touched me but it was good to be with her, to be near her.
Touching my flesh to her lace spread before me across the
bed was like touching her heart. I couldn't move my
hands from the pattern glaring in the shaft of sun shot
through the window. I felt the blood of my head flow
through my hands into the delicate texture of the lace and
catch there, rooting me to her presence, alone with her in
a way she had always withheld from me before. There
was somewhere within me a question. *Why?* Why had she
brought me to her bedroom, closed the door and pulled
the buried lace from hiding in the big dresser against the
wall. Why did she let me touch her in this way. Why was
I here instead of her son Darrel? Since the beginning
when her husband and the men had burned the hut to the
ground with the body of my mother's mother in it, and
they brought me here as a small boy to live in the house
painted the color of snow, since that beginning why had
she never brought me close to her before. But before the
question grew out of me to my lips she spoke, "You are
going away. We are not going to keep you any longer."
She moved to the window and the gray dress of her body
blocked the sun. "Another is taking you. You are twelve
years old, there is work you can do. We have a son, and
much hired help. There is little you can do here for your
keep. We . . ."

"Judith! What the hell you got the Injun in our bedroom for," the door swung open and her husband stood in

its center. I pulled my hands up from her lace and hid them in my pockets. "I been looking all over for him. I told Mister Fixa I would have him over to his place by three, it's nearly two now and the horses are hitched. Get out in the wagon you." He pointed his finger at me. I turned to see if she would stop him. If she had just made up what she said. But her back was to me and she was looking out at the day. I ran from the house and jumped up in the back of the wagon and he followed. "Go get your things out of the shack boy. And hurry it," he pulled himself onto the wagon's seat and picked up the reins. I tied together my extra pair of pants and shirt into a ball and climbed back up on the bed of the wagon. We rode away from the house the color of snow, away from the ranch. I could see her shadow in the window, she was still standing in the bedroom with the lace spread across the bed as we rode away from her to the other side of the valley and through the town of Loyalton until we came to a small house set back off the main dirt road with a big barn behind it. Frank brought the horses to a halt in front of the barn's open sliding doors and I saw a man, a very old man, deep in the weak light of the barn, moving among the motionless bodies of cows racked into their feed stalls. The old man came out into the sun. His eyes squinted deep in the broad light and he moved quickly back into the shadow of the barn. But his eyes still could not adjust to the sight of us, I could tell from the faded blue of their color that he was almost blind. "Is that you Frank," he raised his hand above his forehead in a salute, trying to block the sun behind our bodies.

"It's me Mister Fixa, Frank Dora."

"Did you bring the boy?"

"I've got him right here in the back Mister Fixa."

"Bring him in here to the barn where I can get a good look at him then."

Frank led me into the shallow light of the barn and stood me in front of the man. "This is him Mister Fixa. This is the Injun boy. I promised I'd bring him, and I did."

"This isn't the one you told me about. You said you

had a big one. That's what our deal was, one big one you said," his hand came up and closed about my arm, the fingers were thick. I could feel the power of his entire hand pinching my flesh. He was old, but he had grown stronger with age. "This one's skinny as a winter calf. Didn't you ever feed him none? I don't see where he's got enough meat on him to do me any good."

"He'll work hard Mister Fixa, and he's alot stronger than he looks just now. You just tell him what you want done and he'll do it for you. And what's good about him is he'll do his work and shutup. He aint one of your talkers."

"How old you say he is? He don't look more'n twelve."

"Fifteen he is, far as we can calculate. It was back in the winter of '99 that there was the big Injun fever. He wasn't up at the lumber mill at Elephant Head with the rest of his kind. We found him over on the north side of the valley with an old woman. She was dead and we figured it was probably Injun fever what killed her, so we burnt their campoodie down and I brung the boy home with me and kept him locked up in the grain shed for three weeks to make good and sure he didn't have no Injun fever. He's just kind of been with us ever since. Like I told you, we never really knowed what to do with him. He was there, that's all, just there. But we did find out he belonged to some of the Injuns what died of the fever in '99. *Birdsong,* we found out his father's name was. People called his father One Arm Henry cause he had one arm blowed off back in the war between the States. Maybe his own people didn't want him and that's why they sent him away. He's a Washo though, he aint one of those Paiute what'll sneak up and cut your throat in bed. And you can see for yourself he aint no halfbreed. But he's about fifteen years old the way we figure it. Johnny Doc said at the time we first brought him to the ranch he looked eight, and that were seven years back."

The old man loosened his grip on my arm, "You got a name for him?"

"No, we never did call him nothin but boy. He comes real good with just that."

"Well, I guess I could use him then," the old man dropped his hand from my arm. "Yes, if he comes good whenever you call him I could use him. An old gadget like me can't move around so well any more when his eyes go out on him. I can see pretty good in the barn here, as good as ever almost, but when I get out in the sun I blink like an owl, can't see a thing but outlines. Yes, I guess I could use him then. He's got good eyes do he?" He pinched my chin between two fingers and pushed my head up. He stared straight at me with eyes like a summer sky that had all the blue burned away into a hazy white. "Yes, I could use him, his eyes are clear, that's the main thing. And they're brown, brown eyes is stronger than blue." He let go of my chin and walked away into the darkness at the other end of the barn. The barn was so big and had so many black places that I couldn't see him moving around, but I could hear his voice as he talked low with words so soft I couldn't get their meaning. Pretty soon he comes walking around a stacked mountain of baled hay leading behind him a calf with a loose rope around its neck. He stopped the calf in front of Frank and stroked the spine of its back covered with a shiny brown hair that glowed in the dim light. He handed the rope over to Frank. "Well, I guess that takes care of our deal." He watched Frank and me walk the calf out to the wagon. Frank tied the calf good to the tailgate hitch and I hopped up in the wagon.

"Get down outta there boy!" Frank grabbed me by the seat of the pants, pulled me out of the wagon and threw my bundle of clothes out on the ground. "You stay here now. You don't belong with us no more!" He flicked the reins over the horses and I watched as the wagon was rode away with the tethered calf running along behind until it was out of sight.

I picked my pants and shirt up where Frank had thrown them and the old man pointed to the house, "You'll bunk in there with me, it's as good a place as any I guess." I followed him into the house where he had a small room and a bed waiting for me. I asked him why he wanted me to stay in the house when the barn was so big, but he didn't say anything. When it came time to sleep I crawled right into that bed, it was the first I'd been in and it was nearly as comfortable as a pile of straw. Night came slow to the valley in the summer, and before it came completely the cows would be moving in off the fields. I could see the line of their bodies in the last light with the bells dangling from their necks, ringing out the last few steps of the long day. There were times when not all the cows came in and the old man sent me out to gather them up to the barn. He showed me how to rack them in the feed stalls and milk them while they ate. He placed his hands over mine, "Hold her tit in your fist like this and keep your thumb steady." He guided my fingers to pull and squeeze at the full flesh of the tits until I learned the rhythm and felt the milk come until the bucket was full and he would no longer have to hold my hands. Sometimes I would do what he taught me with my eyes closed, pulling with firm hands at the warm tits, listening to the shots of milk drum in even time against the side of the tin pail. I could tell when the milk was going to give out just from the feel of the tit in my closed fist. It made me sad that she would be empty, that her bag was no longer bloated with the pink skin stretched shiny and slick from the weight of its white burden. The barn slowly began to fill my days. The smell of cows and hay was always in my head. Towering above to the high rafters that split the gloom of the vast ceiling I could see the hanging shapes of bats. Many evenings when the sun sank outside and shifted the light of the barn into bottomless shadows I climbed to the squared mountaintop of baled hay and waited as the bats slowly unfurled their bodies and descended silent as knives into the dry flesh of moths racing the hot currents of summer night air. Sometimes the old man would sit with me and talk as the bats ate up their small white targets. He told about the young man that he was, coming to the mountains of the Sierra where gold ran six miles deep and all a man had to do was knock off a piece and he was fit to dine the rest of his days with the Queens of Europe themselves. But by the time he got to the Sierra the gold had been yanked out by its roots and there wasn't

much left for him to do but pan the backstreams up by
the town of Last Chance. Which he did until he heard
about the man named Knox who stumbled onto a big
ledge of quartz over in Squaw Valley. It was the same
kind of rock the men of the Comstock had yanked a fortune out of. It was assayed up to $3.50 per ton, but every-
body knew there was higher grade ore deeper down worth
five hundred times that. So he went as fast as he could
whip his mule from the Last Chance over to Squaw. And
that wasn't fast enough because by the time he got there
he found a city had been built up by quicker stampeders
in less than a week's time called Knoxville. But there was
room for all to get rich who were willing to die for it. He
staked out his own prospect hole, up and out of the far
side of the valley, almost in sight of Lake Tahoe itself. It
was in the summer of '63 or '64 that the storekeeper Tra-
cy blasted the face off the man from Texas with a shotgun
as he came through the door, then took the fifty dollars
owed him and kicked the body outside. It was one of
those summers anyway, right after that, when most of the
men began disappearing from the valley as quickly as they
had appeared in it. The ore didn't pan out. There was
some who said Knox had salted the claims of Squaw Valley with ore hauled over on muleback from Virginia City
so he could make a kill selling provisions and prospect
rights, but others said Knox was on the square. There
were more who said he wasn't than he was and wanted to
hang him because of it. But then Knox was already gone
and there wasn't reason for any prospector to stay on. But
he stayed on. He kept on banging rock until his hands got
so hard he couldn't feel them. All the time he was banging
he took account of how those few men left in the valley
were running out quick to news of better digs. They all
left their livestock behind rather than be slowed down by
as much as a half a day. He found himself gathering up
stray cattle on his mule and heading them into a valley
draw where he could keep his eye on them and not lose
out too much time on his banging. The way he told it was
his money was about gone so he figured he should herd
what cattle he had over to Glenbrook where the lumber

mills had been set up to supply the mines with timber for their tunnels. But he found by that time he had too many head to herd with just him and the mule so he only took half, thinking he would come back for the others. He was given so much money for what he took he didn't need to make the last trip. When spring came up he made butter from all the milk the cows were giving and sold it to towns along Lake Tahoe. That high up in the mountans butter was worth almost as much as gold. So he quit banging on rock looking for gold and went into the dairy business. There were so few others with cows, and so many miners and loggers, that he ended up putting alot of money in his pockets for a few years. But the times were always moving out in front of him. It wasn't long before others brought up cows and kept them closer to the towns lower down from him. His business couldn't take that because Squaw Valley was up so high that a good six months out of the year it was so cold he couldn't get the cream to rise. When the cream finally did rise in the late spring those he had sold to the year before were buying from others and not about to change over again. It was time to leave Squaw Valley, and that's the reason he did. There were mills opening up at the headwaters of the Yuba and Feather Rivers in a valley to the north, and the way he figured it he'd be the first there with a dairy, and he'd run cattle besides to make sure he had enough to carry him through the cold months. "That's how I come to Sierra Valley," he told me, and he told me over and over again. "You're probably wondering why I didn't marry," he would often say, and look straight into me like I was a full man instead of just a twelve year old boy. "Well, I'll tell you why I didn't marry, Bob." That's when he first started calling me Bob. I'd never been called by any name before except *boy*, and Bob sounded very close to that, so it didn't bother me none. I thought he must have just made a mistake, maybe his tongue was as wore out as his eyes. Anyway he called me Bob so much that pretty soon I got to calling myself Bob. "Bob," I'd say to myself; "Why don't you wash out all the milk buckets and set them in the sun to clean." Or, "Bob, hold your head up

when you eat, because your hair has grown so far down
Mister Fixa can't see your eyes, and you know what he
feels about not looking a man straight in the eyes." I got
to calling myself Bob so much, and Mister Fixa calling
me Bob even more, that one afternoon in the Loyalton
feedstore Albert Casin, the owner, said to me real quick
like he wasn't even thinking about it, "What's your name
boy?" "*Bob*," I said. "My name is Bob." Later on, sitting
up next to Mister Fixa on the buckboard as we drove
home I knew I had a name. A name was something that
had never been important to me before, but now that I
had one I realized just how much it meant. Because it was
so important I said right out loud, "Mister Fixa, my name
is Bob." He seemed to know the reason that made those
words jump out of my mouth because he turned his faded
eyes and looked at me close, "That's right. That's just
what it is, and when you go all the way to the end that's
who they'll be boxing up and slipping in the grave. Not
just *somebody*, but *Bob*." So whenever Mister Fixa said,
"Well, I'll tell you why I didn't marry Bob," I knew he
was talking straight to me and just not to the air. "Now
here's the reason why I didn't ever marry Bob," he'd continue right on. "You should listen close because somewhere in it there may be something for you to remember.
It's not because I didn't meet the right woman that I never
took the formal vows. Oh no, it's not because of that, for
I did meet her. Up in Quincy City it was, back before
your time. I used to go up to the big livestock auction
there every late summer, of course now you and me go on
down to Roseville which is much closer, but back then I'd
go up to Quincy everytime the summer ended to see if I
could better my position in life by using my quick eye for
cattle flesh; buying at last years prices and selling at next
year's, as the saying tells it. Well, to get down to the short
of it, that's where I met her. She was big with alot of good
bones in her body, and a pair of eyes that roamed around
the great space of the auction barn like a bear sitting in a
shallow pool watching to decide which fish she will finally
fetch out with a quick stroke of her paw. I'd seen her at
the auction three summers in a row. The first summer she

must have been a good seventeen. She was always walking
behind her Daddy, slow she was, but big. She had an eye
and nose for cow flesh. When she'd see a good piece she
would tap her Daddy on the shoulder and whisper into his
ear the bid she thought the animal was worth. When the
bidding was on he never went over the price she fixed,
even if it was only up one dollar. He never missed a cow
he bid on. He had one of the largest spreads on the whole
of the Feather River meadows, and everyone knew it was
all his daughter's doing, whispering to him the right price
and the best trades. So there were alot who fell in love
with her because she was that rare woman in a lifetime
who could make a poor cowman rich. And there were alot
who loved the way her good flesh swung on her bones.
But there were more who loved her for both things, and
that's the reason the Quincy Auction was the biggest one
in the north State during those years. The word had gone
round, and men came up from as far as Minden Nevada.
Not to buy and trade prize cattle, but to take home that
rare woman as a wife. Now I may not be much to look at
now Bob, but in those days I was the kind of man who
could catch a glimpse of his own face on the bottom of a
shined up skillet and not run away from the terrible sight.
Some even said my face was handsome as a tree is handsome. I was always proud of that saying. But when I was
a very young man, back right before I came out to California, I started getting terrible pains in my mouth. So I
traveled into Shaker Heights city were the mouth doctor
was kept and I told him I was going out to California to
get rich, but I was having trouble with my mouth, it felt
like somebody was cutting up my gums with a knife. Well
Bob, he sat me back down in a chair, propped my mouth
open with a stick and declared, 'Haf your teeth have all
rot out, and the haf that aint would be better off if they
were. You'd be better off if I yanked em all out, then
you'd never have to be worried by it when you're pickin
up all that gold in California.' That sounded as if it made
sense to me Bob, and even if it didn't there was nothing I
could say against it as that stick had my mouth jerked
open so wide it was all I could do to gurgle like a baby.

When I got out to California my mouth was just like a baby's, not a tooth in sight. I never missed having my teeth once. My gums were hard as stone so I could still chew everything up good. There were many nights I thought alot about the pain I wasn't having because I didn't have any teeth left. But there was one night I wished I had all my teeth even if half of them were rotted out. You see Bob, it went like this, every year the last night of the Quincy Auction they hold a big doings. They cleaned the big auction hall up and fit it out for a night of celebration and dancing. Now there was one girl that a man had to stand in line to dance with, and there were some men who didn't take much to standing in lines so they would try to cut in on the other man who had waited his turn, which didn't always end up so good as I saw a couple of fights come up out of that situation. Two men were cut pretty bad and another got a bullet through his arm. Now you guessed it, the girl everybody was waiting on and fighting over was the very one who always whispered to her Daddy the right cow price. As it was I would pass away each year waiting the time when my turn came in line to dance with the rare woman. Well, this one particular year I had waited three hours and more for my particular turn to come up and dance with this rare girl. When she finally took me lightly by the arm and I could smell the hot sweet air coming up off the open flesh of her bare arms, it was just like the year before, the way I had always dreamed it would be again. It was a moment to live a lifetime on. 'Do you remember me from last year?' I said. I had been planning up for a year on just what I'd say to her, knowing every word would have to be perfect. She turned her head slow to me, then nodded toward the fiddle music and smiled. I knew by that smile she remembered me. We danced. I was proud with her all to myself in front of the other men. The music stopped. But the blood was jumping and pounding in my head. I couldn't let her go. 'Miss, pardon my rudeness, but would you, would you . . .' I squeezed the good flesh of her arm then maybe too hard, as I felt something in her body go tight. 'Miss, would you allow me to get you a glass of refresh-

mint?' She walked with me! She walked with me clear
across the floor over to the punchbowl where her Daddy
stood and let me pour out a cool glass for her, and Bob, it
was the biggest moment of my life, her accepting that
glass from me and making tiny sucking sounds as she
drank the red water down. I had to think fast and talk
quicker as the moment was going and the other men were
already moving in. 'Sir,' I announced to her Daddy. 'I
would like the honor of marrying your daughter.' And before he could answer I put in a real quick, 'I've loved her
for three years now and this time I can't go another year
without seeing her, it will take me apart and I will die
sure! I beg for your answer here and now as she may be
married up by next year!' He didn't answer me. His
daughter set her glass of punch down, leaned over and
cupped a hand over his ear. I could actually feel the hot
breath of her whisper as I waited for the answer and
stood with my mouth open wide and smiling. 'My daughter says,' he straightened up and put his eyes full on me,
'She don't like a man with no teeth.' Well Bob, I shut my
gaping mouth and it wasn't until I was fifty miles away
from that auction barn that I couldn't hear the men laughing at me no more. But wait, there's more to it. You see, I
aint never been one of your quitters. So the first thing I do
when I get back to the ranch is go straight into Reno
where a mouth doctor fitted me up with a whole set of
new teeth that made my gums bleed everytime I smiled.
When the auction time came round again I waited for the
night of the dance. When I came into the barn I made
right for her. None of the men said anything to me about
the year before and I figured it was because they didn't
recognize me with my new teeth in. I saw her dancing
with a man and soon's the music stopped I went straight
over and danced the next one with her, and before the fid-
dler scraped out the last note I steered her right over to
her Daddy, who was standing next to the punchbowl like
he hadn't budged in a year. 'Sir, I would like the honor of
marrying your daughter. I'm a modest rancher from the
Sierra Valley, but my stock is strong and my barn is solid,
and my teeth,' I yawned my mouth wide and tapped the

front ones with my finger, 'my teeth are as good as any man's.' He didn't answer me right off as his daughter had put her lips close up to his ear and was whispering low. 'She says, young fella, that the one you should be asking is her husband here,' and he nudged the man standing next to him who I recognized as the one dancing with her before I had cut in. 'It's alright with me,' her husband said, 'that is if it's alright with her. Aint that right boys.' He threw his head back and laughed until he exposed the big even teeth of his mouth shining like all the light in the heavens. That's the short of it Bob, the truth as I lived it, the reason why I didn't marry, in case you're ever wondering. You know Bob," he would continue right on into the dark of the barn that had fallen around us, "I had a brother who married and raised children. What good did it do him? In the end he ended up alone anyway. I don't see the point of it. Why get married and raise up children? They're not like carrots when they get full grown and matured, you can't eat them. But I'll tell you one thing to remember Bob, the only man I ever knew who was happy married had an ugly wife and a short memory. Remember that, if you're ever fool enough to tie yourself down, pick yourself the most ugly gal in town and don't remember *anything* she might do for more than two days in a row."

Winter came down hard on me and Mister Fixa. It made us both cold. But Mister Fixa liked those short gray days. He said he could see better than ever then, just like a young man. Many times he would challenge me to who could see the furthest. We would walk together out into the empty middle of a snow field and he would set up a few rusted cans alongside the horse's gleaming bit. Then we would take twentyfive steps away from the sight, turn round, and shout if we could still see the cans and bit. We kept going on like this until one of us didn't shout, and had lost. It was always me that lost. Mister Fixa could go five miles out and still see those cans and the bright bit. "Can you still see it!" he would shout. "No I can't!" I would shout back. "Got to train your eyes Bob! Got to train your eyes so they can see the flash of a silver dollar

tied on the top of a saddlehorn with the horse galloping
half a mile away from you. A young man who can't see
straight, a young man without good eyesight, will get
tripped up in this lifetime. Tripped up and cleaned of his
valuables. A young man's got to train himself to see three
days ahead of the one he's living!" It's those gray days in
winter that Mister Fixa liked best, when he could always
see further than me. In summer, he couldn't see anything.
I wasn't much on wintertime. Mister Fixa never took his
herd down below the snowline where the pasture was always steady like all the other cowmen did. He had the
biggest barn in the valley, and he had it so he could keep
all of his cows in it right through till spring. In the mornings when it was still dark he would wake me up, "Bob,
you better go out there and tend the herd." In the night it
usually snowed. I had to shovel down the snow to swing
the side barndoor open so the cows could get out in the
exercise corral after I fed them. They didn't like getting
up out of their straw, even for the morning feed, and I'd
have to shout good at them and even kick a few. But pretty soon all of them were rising from the nest they had
rounded in the night. I could see the heat coming from
their hides off into the cold air of the barn as they staggered into their slots along the feed trough. It didn't take
me long to fork the trough full of alfalfa. When I got that
done I stamped my boots on the frozen ground to keep
the blood moving and leaned up against the pitchfork to
watch the cows. I always tried to figure them. They paid
no attention to nothing when they ate. The bulge of their
brown eyes glazed over and almost shut as they ground
down their feed. The whole time switching their tails and
letting loose a fall of heavy yellow water or a thick stream
of turd. I tried to figure them at that time in the morning
when the only sound roaring in the barn was all eighty of
them grinding it up at one end and blowing it out the other. "Buy a rabbit's foot Bob," Mister Fixa always stopped
my figuring on the cows as he swung open the door, beating his gloved hands against his jacket to feel the heat in
his fingers. "You're going to fall asleep against that pitchfork someday, run yourself through and freeze to death,

I'll have to carry you out in an ice statue. I can see fine this morning, Bob. I can see it's going to be a *fine* day. Couple of those cows down at the end are about finished up. I better be getting to milking them before they go stiff." The morning milking was only done by Mister Fixa. The last milking in the day he always let me do, but never would he let me do even one cow in the morning. He said a cow was like a woman in the morning, you just couldn't wake her up and start jerking and yanking away at her tits, you had to handle them just right, if you didn't, if you just let slip the wrong word to her, or said something a little *too* sweet to her, she was ruined for the rest of the day. I took away the full buckets of warm milk as Mister Fixa worked his way down the line and let each cow out of her stall after he had finished with her, giving her a slap on the rump so she would move out into the cold morning of the small corral. When all the cows were out it was my job to shovel up the manure they left behind. Some mornings were so cold the brown clumps the cows had dropped would already be frozen by the time I got to them. Mister Fixa would hear me talking low beneath my breath about how I hated this part of every morning. He would come over to me and lay a hand on my shoulder, "Son," he would say, looking right into my face with the dying glow of his gray eyes, "if this is the worst shit you ever have to shovel in your lifetime you'll be a luckier man than most."

When they got the new money gambling machine over across the border into Nevada we would hitch up the horse to the buckboard and ride out of the valley through the low pass called Beckwourth. There wasn't a time we didn't ride east through that pass in the wall of the Sierra into Nevada that Mister Fixa didn't say, "Now there was an old boy for you, Jimmy Beckwourth. Me and him was thick as syrup right up to the time the posse from down in Sacramento Valley rode up one night and surrounded his cabin only to find old Jim gone. You see, there was alot of horse thievin going on down in the Sacramento Valley in those days, and in his time Jim was two parts army scout,

three parts Injun chief, and nine parts fur trapper. He
even rode with Jed Smith in the Santa Fe trade during the
'30's. Course that was way before Jedediah got caught near
the Cimarron River, searching way ahead of his party for
water, the Comanches did something so terrible to his
body that the ants didn't even want to eat what was left,
course his remains were never found. He was only thirty-
two, now there was an old boy for you, Jed Smith. But
what Jimmy Beckwourth was most of all was twenty-
three parts horse thief. The posse that rode up that night knew
it wasn't Jimmy stealing all that horseflesh in their
valley, they knew his rheumatism had set in so bad as to
have kept him out of the saddle for more than a year. But
the way they figured it was he had the reputation for
horse thievin because as a younger man, right before the
U.S. and Mexican War broke out, Jimmy stole nearly every horse off of John Sutter that the Californios had, and
he didn't quit there. All they had to do was ride up and
hang Jimmy dead to a tree and the real horse thieves
would have to quit stealing because then there wouldn't be
no more Jim to blame it on. But Jim was already high-
tailed into Denver before that posse got off their horses
and busted into his cabin. He got married again when he
was east, and then he got talked into the new fight with
the Crow. He was sixty-eight the winter he saddled up for
the last time and rode off into Crow country with every
bone in his body creaking like a board. The Crow had always given Jimmy a wide path, ever since his earlier days
when he lived with them for more than six years and took
one of their women as a wife. She rode everywhere with
him, she even had strapped on her horse a leather bag of
buffalo chips she used to start her fires with in timberless
country. When the New Mexico trade opened Jim took
her right into that country with him. But it wasn't never
no good. She wouldn't leave him, but her eyes always kept
turning north, the further they traveled the more she kept
looking north, back up to Crow country. It was because
he loved her so much that he wouldn't keep her caged. He
came back to their camp one night and found she had cut
one of the finger joints off her lefthand. Old Jim knew the

reason behind this. She was giving up a part of her flesh for the Spirits to take back to her people so she could always be with them. In the morning he rolled up the blanket they slept on and instead of tying it down behind his saddle he walked over and wedged it in the fork of a cottonwood. It was the sign he gave her. Her life branched off two ways. She could choose her road, but she would always be part of the tree. Well Bob, he watched her swing up on her pony and ride north. Old Jim wasn't one to keep a caged animal. He says she never took another man. It was only her people she was married to. The Crow called Jim, Chief Chief Bloody Arm. But they took that name from the Snake Indians who give it to Jim after they'd been in a fight or two with him. You see, Jim was a trapper, and a trapper will never use his gun if he can use his knife. Jim used to use his knife so much in battle that his whole leather sleeve was always bloodied up from those he'd carved. What Jim was riding back up to Crow country for was to tell his old friends to make their ways peaceable, that there weren't much good in starting up a new fight. But the only thing Jim accomplished with the Crow was to die. By the time he come into their main camp he could hardly sit his horse. They hauled him down, sweated him out, gave him tobacco, told him stories, but he died anyway. It's this here pass we're riding through right now that Jim come upon back in '51. He'd made his way down from Pit River country and it was then he saw this split in the wall of the mountains way to the east. He come through and found himself right at the top of the Feather River. By the next year Jim had put a road through this pass and the wagontrains were rolling through. Jim guided the first wagons on down the ridge to Marysville. The way he says it the only thing holding the wagons together was the same miracle that keeps the sun from falling down on the earth. The men had to hold the wore out oxen by their tails to keep them on their feet. Now there's a long story behind why Jim set Marysville on fire during the wild celebrating that took place when he brought those first wagons in, but the story's too long for my lifetime so I'll only say this on it. Some said Jim

was paid by the mayor of Marysville to lay a road
through this here pass so that the mayor's town could become an important trading center, important as Sacramento even. Others say the mayor promised Jim full reim-
bursement for the road he laid whenever he brought the
first string of wagons in. Jim says that's the way it was.
The mayor said it was the first way. Jim insists he has a
gentleman's agreement with the mayor. The mayor said
there wasn't no such thing as a gentleman's agreement
with Jim Beckwourth as he weren't no gentleman; true his
father was a big plantation owner in Virginia, but it was
common fact that his mama was a nigger slave, that he himself had been bonded out to a Saint Louie blacksmith in
'21 for fifteen dollars and run off in '23 to join Bill Ash-
ley's band of fur traders, now how could a man like that,
the mayor said, give the word of a gentleman. Jim didn't
have no words left for the mayor after he said that. He
made his way down the street that was full of the festivities celebrating the success of the road he built. He came
to the Bear Flag Saloon, strode in and ordered a keg of
straight Kentucky Whiskey. He smashed the keg open
with the butt of his rifle and let the whiskey run all over
the saloon floor before he struck a match to it and strolled
back outside to watch the whole street burn to the ground.
Too bad too, because that street was the only piece of
real-estate the mayor owned free and clear." Mister Fixa
always ended his story by the time we come out at the
other end of the pass. He would sit tall on the buckboard
seat saying, "Bob, if anyone ever asks you just how this
here pass come to be named Beckwourth, you just
straighten up and tell them about old Jim."

Mister Fixa was always in good spirits when we crossed
over the border into Nevada. The blood went high in his
head, his back stiffened, he breathed deep and his old gray
eyes saw out over all that shaved down brown mountain
country as far as it rolled. Mister Fixa liked going into
Nevada for the money gambling machine, but more than
'that he liked the way Nevada came up to a man and said
take it or leave it; take the desert, the mountains, the coy-

otes, the silver, the coldest days and the hottest nights of your life. Nevada was not a place to fool with. It would throw a man right out. Nevada was built on solid silver from the grassroots down and right up to the naked blue sky. Nevada broke more men than it built. Nevada was a *gamble*. Gambling was *Nevada*. Nevada was always there for a man to bet his life on. And we were coming into it. Me and Mister Fixa. We were coming on in to Reno. "Look at it there Bob!" Mister Fixa stood up on the buckboard and pointed his arm out as far as it would go as we banged over a little slump of hill and saw the Truckee River pumping itself calm and fast around a curve and between a clump of brown buildings stacked up along its banks searching for a new direction in which they could spread. "Look there Bob! Look at Reno Nevada! Reno waiting to take our dues!" Mister Fixa wouldn't sit down until we rode up Virginia Street and he pulled the buckboard in tight against the boardwalk in front of the GOLDEN NUGGET CASINO. "You bring your ransom Bob." I pulled the two sacks of silver dollars from under the seat, grabbed their drawn canvas tops tight in each fist and followed Mister Fixa in.

"Wait a minute there Grandpa," the man standing at the doorway jammed his arm across the entrance and leaned all his weight on it. "No Injuns allowed. The kid stays out."

Mister Fixa took a step back, the old silver blue of his gray eyes trying to take in the hard reflection off the high black shine of the man's stubheeled boots. Pretty soon he smiled as if in recognition and lifted his face up, "Me and Bob have been in here plenty of times. Why this place couldn't stay in business without my annual donation. I'm the one who pays your salary, and from the looks of your outfit I'm not tight with it either. Me and Bob have been coming in here as long as I can remember, and that's before you were born. I don't see what's changed now." He took a step right against the man's arm.

"Nothing's changed since we've been in business thirty years Mister. Things are the same they've always been," he stuck his finger up over his head at the sign nailed over the doorway.

Mister Fixa arched his head back and made as if he was reading the sign with the smoothed gray stone of his eyes. But he already knew what the sign read. He knew it back from the days when he could see as good as any man, but that didn't stop him from turning back and saying, "Well sir, my eyes have gone out on me for some years now. You'll just have to read this here sign to me."

"INDIANS NOT ALLOWED!"

"Indians not what?" Mister Fixa smiled, the man's words still banging in the air. "You see, when my eyesight left me my hearing followed too. Indians not what?"

"ALLOWED! INDIANS NOT ALLOWED!"

"That's what I thought you said the first time," Mister Fixa grabbed me as he pushed right past the man's arm like a snowdrift collapsing a fence. "Bob's my son. That makes him halfbreed. Your sign doesn't say HALF-BREEDS NOT ALLOWED." And we were in.

"Wait a minute!" The man chased us across the red and gold carpet and grabbed Mister Fixa by the shoulder, "O.K. old man, I'll let you take the kid in. But one thing. We've got a Sundown Ordinance in Reno, and I suppose you'll say you've never heard of it, so I'm warning you on it right now. No Indians on the streets within the town limits after dusk. Indians on the street after sundown are fined $500 dollars, shot on sight, or both. If you're anywhere in these parts with him after dark old man you better make sure it's in the Indian colony outside the town limits, or thirty miles away. I'm warning you on it now!"

Mister Fixa wasn't paying too much attention to the man's advice. The gaze of his graystone eyes was moving elsewhere, rubbing up against the high waxed grain of the dark wood lining the walls of the great gambling hall that went on the length of three of his cow barns. The light thrown down from the blazing chandelier the size of a sinking moon lost itself in the expanse of the hall so by the time it hit the floor it wasn't much more than a shadow. So Mister Fixa could see everything just fine, with a true appreciation. He stood there with the echoes of shouting men and the whacks of new card decks on the green felt tables filling the big empty space along the roof. He was turning all those sound of spinning roulette wheels and tumbling dice into the sound of cow hooves pounding on a solid earth floor, and the honk of calves trying to jostle closer to their mothers. Mister Fixa was standing in the fanciest barn in the world. "Bob," he said, "let's you and me get down to business." He turned away from the doorman and we walked straight for the side of the hall with a sign hanging down out of the roof announcing in gold letters THE FIRST HALL IN THE STATE OF NEVADA TO HAVE STRAIGHT FROM THE INTERNATIONAL WORLD FAMOUS CASINOS OF EUROPE—THE ODDS ARE ON—THE SLOT MACHINE!" And there they were, gleaming in a bank of five rows of silver, the money gambling machines. And men were using them. Pulling, jerking, yanking, sweating, banging down the lever cast in the metal shape of a man's arm. Letting the arm flip back as the roll of painted fruit spun beneath the glass eye sunk in the top of the machine where its head should be. Each man hung in the moment when the roll stopped, reading the way the fruit lined up and waiting for the machine to excrete a clang of silver dollars out its money scoop at the bottom. "It doesn't make no difference how soft or hard you pull that arm down Bob," Mister Fixa told me low beneath his breath as we waited for one of the men to give up his machine. "The trick is all in how those fruit line up across the top. And only God and Lady Luck knows the answer to that. Some fruit is worth more than others. Three cherries would make a man rich. One lemon and two pears will just buy him a drink. These old Cowboys think it's all in how you pull that metal arm. It's like kicking a dog in the ass, if you kick him just in the right place you'll kill him. But the machines aint dogs. They got steel for their bones, and wires for their brains. No matter how you pull the arm that machine's going to go on doing just what it wants. It's going to pay you when it gets good and ready, and steal from you when you're looking it right in the face. The reason those Europeans had this money gambling machine before we did is be-

cause they *understand* machines. Now you take playing
Blackjack at one of these tables here, the thing that's always in your head is the dealer can cheat you in a
hundred ways before he's ever cut the pack. But if you
gamble with a machine you're safe. You're either going to
get an honest one, or a dishonest one. Machines won't
cheat you the way a man will, because they don't have
nothing to gain by it. A machine that is dishonest is that
way by mistake. A man who cheats you *knows* what he's
doing. I like to take my chances with machines, sure you
can get a dishonest one making mistakes. But you can get
an honest one making mistakes the other way, one that
will pay you every time. There's a lesson in that Bob.
Only gamble with a machine, never a man. The man who
cheats you *isn't* making a mistake." Mister Fixa would
never use a machine that another man just got off of. He
said the machine had to cool down. He didn't like to feel
the heat in the machine's metal arm from another man's
hand. When a man he had been watching down at the end
of one of the rows backed off of a machine and Mister
Fixa thought it was cool enough for him, well then he just
walked right up to it, took hold of the arm, grabbed a silver dollar from the canvas sack I held open to him,
slammed it in the money slot at the top of the machine
and banged the arm down. "One arm bandit," he hissed
under his breath. "I come to stick you up." With one hand
he kept feeding the mouth of the machine with silver,
while his other hand pumped the metal arm steady in a
rhythm like he was milking cows, only his gaze was fixed
right on the roll of painted fruit whirring and spinning
into a streak of solid color beneath the glass eye. Sometimes the clang of money rang out when the right fruit
lined up and a bunch of dollars dropped to the scoop, but
he never stopped to rake them out. His whole body was
shaking like a big wind was blowing up around it. He
wasn't shaking because he was old. He stood up powerful
in front of that machine and I could see the muscled line
of his heavy shoulders twitching beneath the flannel shirt.
Mister Fixa might as well not be in that casino with the
money gambling machine. He could be out in the middle

of a big field, alone with the machine, because everything that was going on was just between him and that machine. There was nothing else around, bird, beast, or man; just me holding open the money sack. A smell started coming up off Mister Fixa. It was something I never sniffed in the air except when he was with the machine. Seeing the sweat breaking out along the ridge of his forehead and dropping like tears into his faded eyes I tried to figure the smell. There was a time in late spring, me and Mister Fixa was branding calfs and I got stupid by not watching all the time where the red hot iron was and I got a big piece of my leg burnt right through my pants. I won't forget the stink that made, the smell of hot iron and burned flesh mingled together. I guess that was the closest I come to figuring the smell thrown off Mister Fixa, the smell of iron and flesh burned together. "Bob! Pay attention to what you're about. You're throttling the neck of that money sack like it was a Sunday goose." I pulled the sack open further, but it was empty. "That the end of it, huh?" Mister Fixa had his whole fist into the sack trying to catch one last silver dollar. "Well then," he pushed himself back from the machine and his whole body went slack like it was dangling from a rope. "Let's see what we've been paid," he raked the loose dollars out of the moneyscoop and piled them up in stacks of fives. "Ten stacks Bob, the machine gave us back $50 for the $250 we put in. Well we'll keep the bandit honest this time," he winked, moving back up to the machine and getting a firm grip on the arm. "Open up that other sack." I opened the second sack and he emptied it out quicker than the first. But the machine paid him back another full sack, so with that, and what he won the first time around, he went at it again until the sound went off in the machine that made us both jump back as if a tree had ripped out and fallen straight in our path. A couple of men came running over and one reached in back of the machine and cut the sound that now wailed like a duck winged by a shotgun. "Mister," the man wearing the soft creamcolored Stetson hat said, "You just hit the JACKPOT. You won yourself 500 silver American Eagles. If you'll be so obliging as to make your

way over to the cashier we'll make good our debt and you
can get right on again with business."

"Take Bob with you, and pay him, he'll fetch the jackpot back to me. I aint leaving this machine."

I went over to the cashier with the men and watched
them count out five hundred new silver dollars and
brought them in a sack right back to Mister Fixa. "Let's
get going Bob," he smiled, but his teeth were chattering
because the big wind blowing up around his body had got
mighty strong. "Open that sack Bob." I opened it wide
and he pushed his weight up to the machine and went at it
again until he lost everything. He reached into his front
pocket and brought out two more dollars. "Come on," he
went straight for the bar, put down one of the dollars and
the bartender gave him back a bottle of whiskey for it.
"Bob," he looked down at me with a serious look in his
faded eyes as he rubbed a thumbnail across the hard eagle
face of the dollar in his palm. "I could put this last dollar
in the machine. But I'm not. I'm giving it to you. I'm
gambling on the future of your life, that's the best bet I'll
ever make." It had come down dark when we went for the
door and got outside. We were stopped by the man who
wanted to keep us out that morning. He leaned right into
Mister Fixa's face, "Mister, it's after sundown."

Mister Fixa took one funny look at me, grabbed a blanket from the back of the buckboard and spun me around
in it until there was no part of me sticking out but my
face. He threw me up on the buckboard seat, jumped up
beside me, took a swig from the whiskey then jammed the
bottle between my teeth and dumped a gulp down me.
"HIEEEEEEEYAH!" He slapped the reins over the
horse's back and we rode out of Reno as fast as we had
rode in. Somewhere outside of town we turned our heads
back but couldn't see the lights going up into the dark sky
anymore. Mister Fixa laughed, and he didn't stop until we
rode back in through Beckwourth and were in the Sierra
Valley.

One winter when I was with Mister Fixa he didn't wake
me before dawn to milk the cows. I woke up just like a

clock anyway and went out into the barn and found him
dead. It was winter, his favorite time of year, but he was
dead just the same, propped up against a half used bale of
hay. He didn't have a jacket on and his shirtsleeves were
rolled up high on his arms like he was ready for work. I
felt those exposed arms. They seemed to be iced up so I
rubbed them between my hands to see if I could get some
heat back in them, but none would come. The lids of his
eyes were shut down tight. I pulled them back with my
thumbs. His eyes were the color of eggs. I took my
thumbs from them but the lids didn't close up again. He
was just leaning there against the hay bale with his old
eyes turned inside out and staring off someplace where I
had never been. The cows were all moving and bumping
in a restless way as if they wanted to follow Mister Fixa
off to wherever he had gone. I got them all yoked into
their stalls, forked in their feed and milked them dry before turning them out to corral. I shoveled the floor clean
of manure, and down by the open door where there was
some sun I leaned hard on the shovel with the stains of
slick manure gleaming on its blade and looked at the old
man, remembering how he said, staring straight into my
face with the dying glow of his gray eyes, "Son, if this is
the worst shit you ever have to shovel in your lifetime
you'll be a luckier man than most." I watched Mister Fixa
across the barn for a long time. There were arms of sun
poking through the chinks in the roof, falling down in a
haze through the high rafters and laying bright hands of
light all over his silent body with its gaping eyes the color
of eggs blind to the morning of a new day. There was some
time there when I stayed in barn, never leaving it for two
or three days maybe, just milking the cows and stacking
the heavy milkpails by the door. Then I went into the
house, underneath my bed in a sock were the silver dollars the old man gave me after each of the time he had lost all
his money to the machine. There were five silver dollars,
five times we had been to Reno. I stuffed the sock in my
pocket, went out on the road and started walking.

There was a sign I once saw four or five times in the
Loyalton dry-goods store. It was a big sign that covered

most of the wall above where the men's pants were stacked: CAN'T BUST 'EM! FRISCO JEENS! There was a face bigger than the heads of ten men and covered with black hair grinning down from the sign with a mouth cut like the blade of a knife and two eyes that threw out a light like the blare of a lantern in a room you've just come out of the dark into. "What is it?" I said to Mister Fixa. He leaned up against the counter of pants and studied the face on the sign for sometime, putting a flat hand above his faded eyes so he could get a worse light to see better in. "Bob, that yonder is what goes by the name of a GO-REEL-AH." I dreamed about the Goreelah that night so hard I woke myself up. I was sweating so much and my teeth were chattering so quick I thought I'd bite my tongue off so I rolled over to make sure Mister Fixa was sleeping in the room with me when the square cut head with the mouth cut like the blade of a knife broke out of the dark. The black hair covered face was right over me with its blazing eyes lighting up the long slit of a grin. "FRISCO JEENS!" *"WHAT!* Get out of here! What is it Bob!" Mister Fixa jumped up from his bed and stood in the center of the room ready to fight the very darkness itself, but before he knew it I leaped across the room and grabbed his leg and held on so the strongest hands couldn't pull me off. "Stop your crying now Bob," Mister Fixa put his hand on my head. "What was it you saw?" "FRISCO JEENS!" "Frisco Jeens? What do you mean, *Frisco Jeens?*" "He was coming to take me." "Who?" "FRISCO JEENS!" "What do you mean he was . . . Wait, you mean the GO-REEL-AH? You mean the GO-REEL-AH was coming to take you?" "Yes!" "No he's not. He's only a painted picture you saw. He isn't real." "But he's alive somewhere. Somewhere he lives. Where is it he lives Mister Fixa?" "Bob, I'm going to tell you the truth. He lives in Frisco City. He lives in Frisco City in an iron bar cage where he can't hurt nobody. Someday you can go yourself to Frisco and see what I saw is true with your own eyes." And that's where I was headed, going down the road away from the ranch, making my way to find Frisco City to see for myself that what Mister Fixa

said was true. I was walking fast and it was no time at all
before I passed through Sierraville and up the road out of
the valley when I heard a buckboard coming up behind
me. It didn't go on by. The horse slowed and followed
along so close behind me that I could feel his breath on
the back of my neck.

"Where you going boy?" the man called down from the
wagon.

I swung around to get a look at his face and see if there
was anything in it that told me to run as fast as I could
into the trees, but there wasn't much I could see beneath
the brim of the hat except the chin, it jutted out from the
rest of the face like a clenched fist. Run or talk, I said to
myself. Run or talk. Quick! "I'm going to *FRISCO
JEENS.*"

"You mean Frisco City, don't you? I've been there myself."

"He's in Frisco City and that's where I'm going."

"Well ain't you lucky then because I happen to be passing right through there myself. Why don't you hop up and
keep me company? He reined the horse in and the wagon stood still in the middle of the road. "Hop up."

There was a woodpecker banging away at the belly of a
pine about four trees in from the road, his sound filling in
all the space between me and the man. When the woodpecker stopped I jumped up on the bed of the buckboard,
"O.K. Mister. I'll ride with you to *FRISCO JEENS.*"

"Well then," he turned around to me. "Get on up here
in front, no need to ride in the back like you was a sack
of grain."

The higher we rode in the mountains the more the valley rolled out below us until it could be seen from end to
end and straight across. It was the first time in my life I
saw it all in one piece. From where I was the trees raced
down the slopes to the valley floor, where the broad flatland heaved itself up into the intruding trees, holding
them back along a thirteen mile line by leaning the muscled crest of its rippling high bare ground into the full
force of the mountain's face. The valley calmed itself

down by the time the lap of its flatland reached the further wall of mountains that came out of the east from Nevada. There was no fight on that side of the valley, the mountains didn't send their trees down the deep cut of long slopes into the lake of flatland because the trees had been slashed off, milled and sent roaring out of the valley on the backs of woodeating locomotives.

"You see yonder?" The man pulled the buckboard up short, pointing a finger down across the red haze of the valley's sky to the blow of blue smoke shooting off at the bald foot of the far mountains. "That's the Feather River Lumber Company, and all that town growing up around it is Loyalton, folks used to know it by the name of Smith's Neck, but when the war between the States come on good the Reverend Adam G. Doom got the townsfolk all the way down to the smallest child to sign a petition declaring total allegiance to the Union cause and loyalty to the one true President. Loyalton, the town would be forever called from that time, the most loyal town in the land. That was back in '63, I ought to know it's true, my daddy was the Reverend Adam G. Doom." He pulled his arm back and stroked the fist of his chin with a thumb, "I'm Carson Doom." He gave the horse a whip and we were moving higher, but I kept looking back to where he had pointed because over to the side of the rising line of smoke which cut the mountains in half behind it was a hook of ground throwing off a glint beneath the red sky, the glint was Smith's Neck Creek, they hadn't changed the name of that, and I could follow it around the hook with my eyes until I saw a squared black space punched in the distance of the valley floor. It was Mister Fixa's barn, and he was in there dead. The hard metal silver dollars pressed through the sock in my pocket against the flesh of my leg as the wagon bounced higher into the sky.

The man took the buckboard beyond where a fast bank of clouds knocked themselves apart on the stone fingers of the mountain peaks. We were headed down now along the sweep of river he called Yuba. The river slid with a roar over boulders it had blasted from earthen nests under its full spring power. Somewhere along there the road came out of the trees, passed over the river on a hanging white bridge, and forced a narrow slot back into the high trees, making a space just large enough on both sides to hold a single row of buildings linked together by a boardwalk. The horse began slowing down like it knew where it was going and the man brought it up in front of a short building with its small door thrown open to the sun pushing down through the trees. "Is this *FRISCO JEENS?*" I asked the Reverend Doom as he jumped off the wagon to loop the reins around the hitching post, but before he could answer a man came through the open door of the house saying, "Well now, what brings you to Downieville Reverend?" Then he caught a look at me. "Where'd you get him?"

"Outside of Sierraville," the Reverend Doom took down the big hat from his head and rested its brim against the bulge of his chin. "He says he's going to Frisco Jeens."

"Frisco what?"

"Frisco Jeens, he says he's going there."

"You mean Frisco City, don't you Reverend?"

"It's not what I mean, it's what *he* means. I don't think he knows what he means."

"Who's he belong to?"

"You know old Abe Fixa with the dairy herd in Loyalton?"

"Course I do. Isn't a man in these parts hasn't had dealings with Abe at one time or another. Abe's been in this country since the gold was. Why, what about Abe?"

"He's dead. Mart Naley from the feedstore went on over to Abe's place this morning to deliver a wagon of alfalfa, couldn't find Abe around the house, but he did in the barn. Says Abe look to be dead more than three days. By the time I got over to the barn there was a big commotion and they had a horseblanket over Abe's body."

"It's a crime Reverend. It's a crime Abe has passed from us. But what's the Indian got to do with it?" There seemed to be something come into his face then, as if he made the discovery for the first time in his life that night

follows day. He took a step over to the wagon and
grabbed me by the arm, "Did this Indian kill Abe?"

"No. Johnny Doc says Abe died natural. This was
Abe's boy, he got him off Frank Dora about three, four
years back. He wasn't anywhere in sight of Abe's this
morning so I went off to fetch him. When I caught up
with him he was clear past Sierraville on his way to *Frisco
Jeens*. I don't think he knows what he's about."

"Maybe Abe's dying on him like that rattled something
in his head; most likely it's always been rattled. But I can't
see what you come so far out of your way to bring him up
here for Reverend. Why didn't you just give him back to
Dora?"

"Dora won't have nothing to do with it. What I was
thinking Sheriff, was the fact that your wife used to work
for the Maidu Agency. She's an authority on this kind of
problem. Maybe your Missus could handle this Indian?"

"It's been four to six years since she's had any straight
dealings with Indians Reverend, but you're welcome to go
on up to the house and try her out on the subject."

"You're sure you don't mind?"

"No trouble Reverend. You just go on up."

The house we came to was burrowed into the base of
the pines along the river. There wasn't much light making
its way through the trees to the small garden set in front
of the house that the Reverend walked carefully through
to knock on the front door. He jerked his hat off and
started knocking the dust off it before the door swung
open and a woman stood there, her whole body seemed to
be built in on itself and pushed down so that she didn't
even come up to the Reverend's chest. "Missus Haag,
mam," the Reverend says very polite with the hat resting
over his heart. "I just come round from the Sheriff who
said I'd find you at home. If I'm not interrupting your
time I'd be pleased to have a few words with you."

"How's your wife, Reverend?"

"She's doing just well, Missus Haag, the pain in her
hip's all but about gone. If you don't mind I'd like to ask
a favor of advice."

"That's a crime Reverend. That's a crime she slipped

down on that hip. After something like that they're never the same."

"Well Johnny Doc says it will be good as always, and I hold a faith in Johnny Doc. If you have a little time I'd like to talk with you about something."

"I had an Aunt in Kentucky who fell on her hip like that. The Artheritis set in hard, poor thing couldn't sleep at all during winter nights."

"What the problem is I have this here Indian who used to be Abe Fixa's boy, now that Abe's dead I'm trying to figure a home to fit the Indian into."

"Old Abe passed on," the woman leaned her body toward the Reverend's chest like it was the only thing in sight capable of holding up the heavy load she was about to let fall. "It's a crime old Abe has passed on from us. But no one knows better than you Reverend, the Lord is merciful in all His ways." She looked across the garden for the first time and saw me sitting high up on the wagonseat, "There's nobody in these parts that will take that boy in Reverend. There's nobody willing to take it on."

"Yes mam, I figured that, but I was thinking since you used to work for a Government Indian agency and are an authority on this kind of problem that you would have an answer of some kind."

"Well there is a Government place, a kind of a school for them, between Reno and Carson City. I can't recall if they take all kinds of them, mostly Paiutes, Shoshone, maybe some Washos I think." She stopped and looked back at me over the garden again. "Reverend," she said in a low voice that was still easy for me to hear as she took him by the arm and pulled him through the door, "this isn't talk meant for his ears."

I don't know who the man was who took me to the school. The place we came to was called Schurtz, it was over the mountains and into Nevada. It had been night a long time when we got there. Everything was shut down and black. There was no sound in the air except for the man's two horses hitched to the wagon, the hard sound of their breathing exploding in the silence surrounding them. The man said he wasn't one for waking working people from their sleep so he'd be getting on and leaving me here. I jumped down off the wagon and waited for him to leave, but he didn't right off. He leaned over and handed me a piece of paper, then whipped the horses and was gone. I stood alone and listened to the wagon clatter into the distance stretching in the direction where the stars had all twisted together and lit up the battered ridge of Desert mountains. I can't remember how long I stood out there listening to the wagon, maybe longer than I could really hear it, maybe the faint thud I kept hearing wasn't the pounding of horses hooves in the distance, but my own heart. There was an owl flapping at the moon from the top of the only tree in the yard, his quick squawks pecked away at the silence of the small moon over us. It made me think of my silver dollars. I jammed my hand deep in my pocket to feel the metal hardness through the sock. I still had what was mine, so I rested my body against the bottom of the tree and listened to the owl above until the whole night came down and put me to sleep. I didn't wake until the voices flew up all around. I opened my eyes to the full sun.

"Where do you come from?"

"He come out of the sky."

"It's not true. Bear bring him. Me see Bear with him, behind the tree Bear was. Then Bear he go way back up the mountain."

"No, Bear don't. Me see him first and he got no Bear. He alone."

"Got no people."

"Where your people?"

"You Ute?"

"Bear kill us if we touch him."

"You Modoc?"

"Go way now. Bring all us sick."

"Children, children, it is breakfast time. You must go to breakfast time. And what have you? What have you here?"

I could not see the face of the woman's voice. I could

not see any of the faces of the ones who found me. The sun was aimed at me from behind their heads, blocking their faces out, the shadows of their bodies swimming before me in the brilliant morning.

"Who are you?" Her voice came from the sun again, and with it her hand, the long fingers dropping suddenly to my knee like a bird. "What is your name?"

"He got no name. Bear bring him. Me see Bear go way back up mountain."

"He must have a name children, even friends of Bear have a name. And yours?" She pressed the bone of my cocked knee. "What is your name?"

"He won't talk. Bear kill him if he talk."

"Maybe this will tell us children," she spoke as if to hide the quick movement of her hand as it came off my knee and caught hold of the piece of paper sticking from my jacket pocket. It was the paper handed to me by the man before he whipped the horses and was gone. "This is to introduce this boy," she read, holding the paper down from the sun's glare, "Who answers to the name of Bob, he is known as Fixa's Bob. He has no living people. He has no home. He is Washo Indian. With respects, Missus Haag, wife of Sheriff Mack Haag. Sierra County, State of California. So children, he does have a name. His name is Bob."

"Me told you Bear didn't bring him."

"Come Bob," she rose and held her hand before me. "Come Bob, and eat with us." I took her hand and stood. I could see her face now, the skin worn and scrubbed down white beneath the soft soap of countless early mornings. "You will stay with us. You are home now Bob," her arm came around my thin boy shoulders and I saw the close blue of her eyes go out and color all the sky.

"It good day. No cloud. No day for Bear to hurt us bad."

"You speak the truth Jimmie Doe. No Bear today. Today we have Bob."

"I will hold the hand of Bob," a girl whose head came no higher than the waist of the woman laughed. I could feel her fingers run through mine and the smallness of her

hand close on me. "I am Sally Roundhouse. I am Wind
River Shoshone. Out there . . ." she raised my hand in
hers and pointed it across the flatland spreading beneath
the climbing sun. "Out there are my people. Me go to
them when me have learned school. But now I eat. Come,
you go eat with us." She walked with me to the big house
that was losing the skin of its white paint in dark gashes
down its face. I could hear the many voices now. Not just
the shouting of those that surrounded me and the small
girl, but voices of laughter coming from the open doorway. It is through there that I went and saw them. They
were all brown faces here, and the black hair of their
heads was thick throughout the room. The sight of me
threw a wedge between their laughing voices. I stood
among them in silence.

"Children," the woman's voice rang clear behind me.
"His name is Bob. He has come to live with us. He is our
family now. He is Washo."

"And me too," a boy my size by the window shouted.
"Me too a Washo!"

"And me," shouted a girl.

"And me!"

"And me!"

"And me also," an old man rose from among the children. He had shrunk down with age, his face burned clean
from the sun. "Come sit next to me," he spoke. "Come sit
next to Suku. To Proud Dog. Come next to Proud Dog
and eat."

The small girl let go of my hand and I went alone to
the old man, to Proud Dog. He placed a bowl with food
in it on the table before me, "Sit and eat with Proud
Dog." His hand came up and rested on the skin of my
neck. The hand did not force me down, it lay like a fallen
leaf on my skin. I sat and ate. The old man watched me
in his silence as I sunk my face down to the bowl and
sucked clean all the food that had gone from me for many
days. All around the talking began again, and with it the
laughter of the morning. "It is not the name of a Washo.
Bob is the name of a White," Proud Dog's words fell in

my empty bowl, filling it again to the top. "How came you to the name *Bob*?"

I drew my jacket sleeve across my wet mouth, wiping my lips dry of mush and answered with the words I remembered of Mister Fixa, "A man must have a name. He cannot die unless he has been. He has not been if no one knows the name he is."

"True words. You speak well in their language. Who gave to you those words?"

"There were two, the man and the woman."

"The man and the woman would be those who brought you into this world?"

"No, they are the ones I was taken to."

"The woman was your mother?"

"She was the mother of another. She is the woman who washed clean my body."

"The man your father?"

"The man was the one who gave me a name. I was nameless before him."

"And where is he?"

"In the barn."

"And why are you not with him?"

"He is in the barn dead."

"You left him?"

"I am going to *FRISCO JEENS*."

"I do not know of what you talk."

"I will see him there."

"The man?"

"The GO-REEL-AH. Mister Fixa said someday I could go for myself to see it in the iron bar cage."

"I know not of this. Mister Fixa is in the barn?"

"Dead."

"And where is the barn?"

"In the big valley."

"There are many big valleys."

"The high valley where the clouds sleep," I drew my sleeve across my lips again, there was something in Proud Dog's eyes that stopped my movement, the grip of their brown gaze held my hand in the air.

"From where is that yellowbacked ring," his voice

seemed to change, as if the air had dropped away beneath the words.

I let my hand fall to the table, the yellowbacked ring was pulling all the sun in through the windows and throwing it back up in my face, "From the hand of the old mother it came. The Whiteman on the Lake in the Sky came to her and smiled, he took the yellowstone ring from his finger and placed it in her hand. Forever *they* would be her friends he said. *They* made many trees fall. She watched *them* across the fence of metal thorns *they* had built." As my words came the blood in my hands began to throb, the fingers burning with rhythm, waiting to guide the gliding willow, seeking the tension of pattern woven through baskets in the cold air of the white days. I brought my hands swiftly into me and locked them down with my fingers. My eyes filled with embarrassment. I looked to Proud Dog to see if he had noticed the building my hands had begun. But he had not. His head slumped to his chest, the fall of his gray hair covering his face, sheltering the silver drops that broke from his eyes and splashed in his lap. His hand came up and touched my face. He pulled me to his old body, holding me hard, I could feel the light bones shake from sobbing.

"You are not *Bob*. You are not of *them*. You are *Washo*. You are son to the one *they* called One Arm Henry, brother to Captain Rex, both children of the great doomed hunter, Gayabuc, himself son to the leader of the Rabbit hunt, the Rabbit Chief. From those loins began you. The son Gayabuc, father to your father, was the one who made the Ancestors weep. Did the old mother tell him to you? Did the old mother, woman to Gayabuc, woman called Painted Stick, did she tell to you of what his name is? Did she tell to you Gayabuc means *Come Hither!* Come hither. Come yonder, and yonder still, where *they* eat of *their* own flesh, where *their* faces are smeared the color of the dying Sun. Where the flesh of the living heart is ripped by the teeth of *them*. Come hither! Come hither his name meant from a small boy, and through to the man, who saw on the shores of yonder lake with only his brother the black Goose to witness and cry

out over the high trees against the claws of *their* hands
tearing the foul meat of open whiteness to feed *their* bellies. Come hither and see the land our fathers trod defiled
and sink away in the rotted excrement of forbidden flesh.
Come hither and show your face to this stench. How does
it smell this excrement of forbidden flesh? From seventy
seasons distant it still burns the nostrils, frightens the Deer
into death, screams the Fish from the lakes, cries the
wings off the Birds. It is a smell rank with desire crumbling to dust. It is a smell that gouges blind the light of
Sun from Sky. It is the rank smell of waste that feeds on
itself. Once having fed on this evil meat the belly will have
no other. It will demand the sacred flesh of the Earth to
feed on. It will ravage the rooted flesh of the unborn. It is
a craving that will not cease before the generation of your
children times eighty. The waters of all the Skies will not
wash clean that final outrage. And this Gayabuc witnessed, watched through the trees, through the morning,
as what *they* devoured on yonder lake was the very sap
from the tree of all his people, until their Ghosts were stolen and they did no longer exist. Not in the future, not in
the past. The Ghosts did not exist. You are not *Bob*. You
are son to son of Gayabuc. You are flesh of the one who
watched, watched the Fox of the Earth released, to fill all
his thoughts, stalking him through the days into his
dreams, and beyond, into the lives of his own flesh, yonder still, his people." Proud Dog's old eyes had lost their
tears, as if the well of his heart had run dry. He spoke
more quickly, with his arms locked about me, pressing the
youth of my body into the hollow of his ancient bones.
"Last night, in the dark, I was awake with the Moon
when all the Birds were asleep and only Owl sang his hidden song. When Owl sings he sings the music of life stolen
from a body of the living. When Owl sings the body of
the Spirit he has stolen will fall empty on the Earth, its
music gone away to the south where the dances of the
Ancestors move in one song. When Owl sings a body will
fall empty on the Earth. There will be a death. One will
go and one will stay. Oh my Little Antelope, remember
me. Remember to guard the unborn flesh of your chil-

dren's Ghost against the stench that blows out of the past
from yonder lake. The stench that blows across your heart
and through the trees, through the morning of all your
years, and yonder still, your people. Remember the words
of Owl whose song *you* too heard this night past. Remember the words of Owl and my song will be forever on your
lips."

When the flowers ran yellow and red up to the Sun and
the leaves swept down green over the trees Proud Dog
was dead. His old bones were tucked up beneath him and
he lay in a careful heap among the reeds along the stream
running into the shallow lake. The children came up from
the lake after soaking their heated bodies in the mud beneath its quiet waters and found Proud Dog, his eyes staring up at the Sky, his mouth cut the shape of a Bird.
There was not much laughter that summer, everywhere
we walked the dust slapped up beneath our bare feet and
hung in the air as the Sun slid across the Sky and died behind the mountains. And my friends began and became
my brothers and sisters. In the cool of the past winter's
rain-rutted ditches we sat small and touching one another
as the woman with blue eyes read to us about the Presidents and the cracked bell of liberty. At night we told our
own stories, stories we carried in our hearts, stories that
journeyed over a thousand years of our ancestors, stories
that flew from our tongues like flapping wings. We told to
one another of Kota, of Frog who wanted for her husband Cottontail, who she saw hopping through the grass
along the pond waving his handsome tail. "I want you for
my husband," said Kota. "I want you to live in the still
water with me and eat flies. Always we will live happy."
Cottontail came over, and as he gazed at the reflection of
his handsome tail in the water he spoke, "Never will I
have a Frog, her belly is too soft and white, her skin is
hairless and slick. I can run free and feed the day on
tender green grass." And he did, and that is why today
Cottontail lives in the mountain meadows and makes his
home in the rocks, while Frog has never moved from the
water and spends her days hiding her white belly in mud

and swimming deep in the dark pools beneath the Sky so
nobody can see how ugly she is. The children repeated
what they knew. Woman is bow, man is arrow. Woman is
cloud. Man is thunder. We repeated all these things, and
of when the waterbabies chased Bear home through the
woods and he had to jump in the fire so they wouldn't
drown him. Then we listened to the story Little Hat told;
he told only the one as many times as there were ears to
listen, and he never let his tongue say it the same way
twice because it was about Coyote when he was grown
down weak with hunger and came to the camp where an
old sister and her daughter were picking pinenuts. Coyote
said to his stomach, "The old sister and her daughter have
gathered many pinenuts, I know the way to get them. I
will marry the young girl and feed all her pinenuts into
my belly." He turned around and saw that the Fish, Bullhead, had heard him. "If you help me fool this old woman
and her daughter, Bullhead, you will have enough pinenuts to keep you fat in winter. All you must do is this, hide
under the silver rock by the tree where the young girl uri-
nates, after her water has fallen jump into her." Bullhead
waited a long time beneath the silver rock and almost forgot what he was there for, but when the young girl came
and squatted by the tree he remembered and just as her
water disappeared into the ground he jumped into her.
When all the pinenuts were gathered into baskets the
young girl said to the old sister, "I feel something inside."
"Is it bad food in your belly?" "No, it is a bigger feeling."
"A bigger feeling? Have you met with a man and come
away with a child in your belly?" "It is a feeling like that.
I feel sick. I must lie down." The old sister was frightened
and ran off for the doctor and met up with Coyote. "Coyote, it is good I see you! I hear you sometimes smoke and
doctor!" "When I have the tobacco, which I do, but today
I am sick and it hurts to move my body." "I know you are
a good man Coyote, and help those big with a child. My
young girl is lying on the ground in our camp that way. I
know you are a good man Coyote." "That has been told
of me," Coyote said rising. "I am weak and it is hard to
move, but when the call comes I must go. To doctor is

what I like, to doctor is what I am for. You will help me to the camp, no matter how far." He pulled on his moccasins and took up his leather of tobacco, "I am weak from no food, if I lean on you we can go fast. I know your daughter has much food and I can eat my fill of it before I starve. I hope she is not dead before I get there." When they came into the camp Coyote said, "I am a small doctor. I doctor people only a little, bit by bit. But I can tell you what I know, do not fear this girl's death. I can see a young man has come to her and she is big with child." "You are wise Coyote," the old sister helped him sit down. "Eat with me." When Coyote finished all the pinenuts his stomach could carry he wanted to go away and sleep, but he said, "When the child comes send for me and I will be here." So when the time of the child came the old sister ran for Coyote, "It is time! Will the child live? I do not know who the father is!" Coyote came quickly, he found the child dead on the ground. "It is good this child is dead," he said to his stomach. "I like to see that. Now I can feed you all the nuts." Then he turned to the woman and commanded, "It is evil ground you stand on! You and your daughter must go far away from this place where the baby has died and never look back to your home." The old sister and her daughter walked away and Coyote was not afraid that they would see what he was doing because they were crying. He hid the child in a pit and covered it with rocks and leaves, then made all the pinenuts into a mush and drank it from a basket until there was nothing left. He headed homeward. His thoughts were no longer concerned with the old sister.

When the heat went out of the ground and the rains came down from the Sky the woman with blue eyes left the big white house with the one tree standing before it. A man in a white coat with a thick tie knotted up around his neck like a rope came and said things would be different, the old schoolteacher had been *transferred* by order of Government Bureau. He would teach now. We would learn the ways of our White friends so we would grow not to take money from the Government but join in and do

what was expected. He promised bacon and coffee for
breakfast and shoes for our feet. When the rain turned to
snow we were still barefoot. Every morning I made my
way around the snowdeep drifts, running quickly so the
ice wouldn't collect on the exposed flesh of my feet as I
made my way down to the stream to fetch a bucket of water back to the big house. It was in the gray hour of one
morning that I took a rock and knocked a hole through
the ice of the stream to dip the bucket in the swift current
beneath. My eyes caught on something as the bucket
rushed with water. On the other side of the stream looking
straight into my eyes was a man squatting in the snow
with a Rabbit skin robe flung over his shoulders. Standing
tall behind him a woman moved a hand to her heavy face
and felt the flush of her broad lips as if she was stroking
the haunch of a pony. She let her hand fall to her side and
it gave a little twitch, "It is *him*." The man pulled the
skins of his robe tightly around his shoulders and rose,
blocking the woman behind him. "You are Ayas, you are
Antelope, son to the one *they* called One Arm Henry." I
said nothing, listening to the water race beneath my fingers. "Ayas, your bucket is overflowing. It will not catch
all the water in this stream." I jerked the bucket up and
placed it on the snow crusted bank, "How do you know
me?" I searched in his face, trying to recognize the
smoothed brown flesh in the past of a dream. But his eyes
did not meet mine, in the gray morning they were lowered
to my hand clutching the bucket handle, the yellow stonebacked ring on my middle finger glowed bright as a Bird.
"You wear the stone of yellow. You wear circled around
your finger the stone that holds all the promises broken by
the weight of tongues. You are *Ayas*. You are Antelope.
And like Antelope you are few in number. You slumber
always in the shadow of the old hurts reflected in the yellowstone ring bound to your finger, the ring given in faith,
broken in deed, the ring of the woman Painted Stick, you
are Ayas, the last of her flesh. Come to us, your people,
and live the straight way. It is too long you have lived
among *them*. Come to us, to the Big Lake in the Sky.
Come to the Big Water. Come, come to Tahoe." I picked

the bucket up with its burden of water, "But what of my brothers and sisters? What of them? It is first I must return to my brothers and sisters. We will all follow." "Wait," the woman came up to the bank, the water racing beneath her feet. "Someday all these children will follow. Someday you will hold them and sing. But on this day not." The man came to her side, "Do not worry of your brothers and sisters, they sing you away until another day when you will meet as one. You follow us. You follow the trail of the past to gain your future. Come Ayas, Small Antelope, follow us into the past, come into your time." His hand came across the stream. I took it. He pulled me over. "You will need for your journey shelter for your feet." He drew a knife sheathed beneath his belt and cut strips of skin from the bottom of his Rabbit robe. He wound skins around my feet until they were bound and secure so I would not stumble as I followed in his footsteps. "It is a journey far and hard to the Big Water, it is a distance long to Tahoe, but for you the cold shall not be felt, your young legs not be weak, we will tell to you stories of Sisu, the Bird, of Atabi, the Fish, of Taba, the Bear. We will tell you how Yellowjacket killed Weasel and made off with the meat. We will tell you about how the people came to Coyote and took Memdewi, the Deer, from him and he sat down on a stone and cried. You will hear of the beginning when Coyote and Wolf were brothers and Coyote instructed his wife to weave a basket as Big as the Dawn, to make it tight as the night so that therein all the waters of the Sky could be held and not one drop flow out; into this basket Coyote scattered four handfuls of wild seeds, blew in from his mouth four whiffs of tobacco smoke, then holding the basket above his head danced four times in a large circle around the fire as he declared to all the animals thereabout, 'I know not failure, whatever I make is right, what I think becomes and what becomes I think. What I think I never fail in.' When he set the basket to the Earth there was much shaking and bulging of its sides, and from within could be heard the shouting and laughter that pierced the air all about like the buzz of twelve Bees on one flower. Coyote picked the basket up, shook it hard above his head and danced four times in a circle big as a mountain, talking as he did, 'What I think becomes and what becomes I think. What I think I never fail in. There are plenty plenty people in here!' He threw the basket to the Earth and out spilled the people falling on all the land, where they ran Coyote pointed, 'There are plenty plenty people here and so I make a fire there, and there, and there, and I make lakes and clouds and raindrops and rocks. What I think becomes and what becomes is plenty plenty people gathered here forever to dance. What I think becomes and what becomes is plenty plenty Indians. But I know not of what they shall eat. What I think I never fail in. I know not of what they shall eat.'

I followed them. The man walking in the lead with the Rabbit robe heaped about his shoulders, the sly steps of the woman soundlessly coming behind him, and then me, fitting into the path their feet stamped in the snow. We climbed to the Sky. We climbed until the Sun went down and set across the snow scarred mountains in a fierce rainbow. We climbed until there was nothing, nothing spreading out before us but the hide of a lake stretched blue and strained to its farthest shore beyond the grasp of the eye. "You are home Ayas," the man in the lead spoke softly as if his voice was the small breeze cutting itself to pieces through the pine tops above our heads. "You have journeyed long and arrived, you are home. You are home to the Big Water," he swept his arm in a wide circle around him, tracing the speared mountain peaks that slid into the Sky and sliced out of sight, the base of the peaks gaping like blades of teeth around the yawning mouth of the lake that sucked the mountains and Sky right back down into the depths of its reflecting surface and threw them back up again, shimmering, spun together from the perfect cut of endless water, hurled in an ancient embrace at the throbbing heart of Sun. "*Tahoe*. You have returned to Tahoe. Ayas, you are Home. You stand before the Big Spirit. You stand in a high place before all the power of the Mountain House. The high water rises higher before you. You have returned to Lake Tahoe." The time within

my chest grew Big, swelled until all the water before me
flowed and raced through my body, the fired ice of its
depths searing the flesh from my white bones. One Duck
danced in a straight line over the blue that embraced his
solitary image, reflecting the soul of his flight on the skin
of its surface until his wings tucked together and he was
caught out of sight between Sky and water. Along the
shore the small Birds lined up across the Sky and sang a
pretty tune through the treetops for me as I entered the
camp for the first time. I had arrived. I had journeyed far
to my people, but I had not been told we numbered so
many like spring Fish in the still waters of a pond. Six
winter dwellings were drawn up around the thick trunk of
a high tree, they were shaped by strong limbs of cut pine
branches bent over to form a bowl and lashed all around
with sewn strips of canvas. There must have been thirty of
my people who lived along the shore of Big Water. They
had come to greet me. Across the snow they came, the
women in their dresses of bright cloth that touched the
Earth as they walked, the many thin braids of their long
hair licking about their laughing faces like black flames.
And in front of them the men, some buried in thick Rabbit robes, others with the high blue pants of the Whiteman
that strapped over the shoulders, and still others, with
much of their flesh exposed to the gray sky. But what
came to me first were the children, their fine brown faces
set off against the white snow, their broad lips sending up
my name in welcome, "Ayas has come! Antelope has
come! The Small Antelope walks among us again!" Their
voices carried high and far across the soft blue glow of
the lake, their deep currents echoing back into all the
trees as they joined hands in a circle around my heart.

Into the late summer we had traveled far down the
brown hills. My belly had grown fat on buckberries and
pinenuts the women had gathered into baskets they had
woven through the winter from slender willows. I slept
easily on the warm Earth, filling my head with dreams of
the quick bluebacked Fish, the brilliant rainbow struck
down his sides quivering as he flashed by the handfuls

into the net swept taut across the stream. Once when I awoke from my Fish Memdewi was sitting next to me, hunched on the bare ground with the Rabbit robe flung across the blades of his shoulders, the Moon sitting on top of his head. Since that first morning when my eyes had found him staring at me across the cold flow of water as I filled the morning bucket with water I had not seen him without the robe of the Rabbit, if it were withdrawn from him it would peel the skin from his body, leaving him naked like a Snake who has dropped the full length of his hide in the hour of long Sun. "I am called by all Memdewi," he spoke to me through the warm air of the Crickets song. "There are reasons for that. Some have many names to many people. They have a name as a baby, a boy, a man, a man with woman, fighter, hunter and fisher. They have a name for every act and season. They are many names to all people. That is good. That is life. Such as it should be. I too had many names. I think with much good thought and laughter in my mouth of Broken Toe Swells. How many days passed before I could grow from the name to another. But people could not forget the time we came into the camp of those who hunted the Sun stones. How we crept along the creek like a low Fox and into their tents to take the white flour that makes the belly sing. How we ran back down the creek with our hair trailing behind us and I slipped on the bank knocking my foot against a wet black rock and could barely keep my place with the others as we fled through the trees. Oh how the people laughed as we ate the white flour that makes the belly sing. 'Did you see that,' they shouted. 'Did you see Nanomba fall. He had so much fear he did not know where his feet were going. Feet Feet. Come back he cried. Splash. Down he went. Stumbling in the shallow water. Hah. Knocking his toe against a wet black rock. Poor Nanomba. Look at him now. Sitting there with the white flour that makes the belly sing smeared over his face. Look at his toe. It is broken. It swells. Hah. Broken toe swells. Look at poor Broken Toe Swells. Next time we will have to send a woman in his place. Or a Dog. Dogs know where they are going. Even blindfolded they will

sniff their way to their own hole. Hah. HaH. Look at poor
Broken Toe Swells. Does it hurt poor Broken Toe Swells?'
How many days passed before I could grow from that
name to another. But now I am left with one name. Not
even the woman I lay with has another name for me. She
said to me, 'You are not Nanomba. You are Memdewi.
You are not Ax In Green Wood. You are Memdewi.
Your are not Broken Toe Swells. You are Memdewi. You
are not Knife In Water Bleeds. You are Deer. Your hide, I
like its scent. Your brown hide smells to me of mountain
clover. Of wet sweet mountain clover mouths. Your hide
smells to me of sailing clouds over antlers. Your hide
smells to me of quiet dawns and small hooves. It is good
when you lay with your hide next to me. Glowing brown
in the dark. Polished wood of the bronze manzanita tree
glowing in Sun. You are Memdewi. You are Deer.' Yes,
this is what she speaks, the woman I lay with. I am called
by all Memdewi. And you Ayas are called Ayas. You are
Antelope. You came one day onto this Earth when there
was the time of the last great Antelope drive. You came
the last time the people hunted as one their brother the
Antelope. You were born for the last feast of the swift
running flesh. I remember on that day when the man your
father stood tall with the flesh of his body standing out
against the wind, on his left side he had no arm, just a
stump sticking out sharp, a brown blade. A brown blade
at the place where the black ball shot from a fat gun blew
his arm into the air. That happened when *they* sent him
across the desert and over the mountains of rock to a
strange land where men were killing their brothers. But
they did not kill him. They got only his arm. *They* tried to
kill his Spirit. But he fooled *them*. He was sly, he was
swift. He fooled them. And when he came back *they*
called him Henry, One Arm Henry. But that was not his
name with the people. With us he was Deubeyu. Always
Deubeyu, headman of the Antelope. And I remember that
day when, Deubeyu, the man your father, stood tall with
the flesh of his body standing out against the wind, on his
left side he had no arm, just a stump sticking out sharp, a
brown blade. But his right arm he held high, the fingers

spread to the Sun, the hunt was over, the day was dying
down red. 'We have gone hard, we have gone long,' he
spoke to the people. 'We have gone far for this feast of
Antelope flesh. Antelope is few. The White power is strong,
their bullet quick. The family of Antelope is few. This day
may be the last day the people feast as one on the family
of Antelope. The White are many, *their* bullet quick. But
on this day there comes to us a new boychild. He comes
to us at a time when the tree is empty of Birds, the stream
empty of Fish, the mountain empty of Bear. He comes to
us in a time different from those we have known. He
comes to us in a time when Antelope is few. This boychild
come to us in this time I will call Ayas. In this time he
will be Ayas. He will be *Antelope*. From this time on the
people will always have Ayas. The people will always
have Antelope. When he has passed into man maybe he
will dream. Maybe he will dream long green tree days.
Maybe he will dream Antelope. Maybe he will smell Antelope in the Sky. Maybe he will dream Antelope moving
many times through trees. Always the trees. It is the way
of our people. Maybe he will dream the hide tight on their
bodies. Maybe he will dream their smell. The smell of
gray fibers growing softly. Antelope moving in the Sky.
Brown bodies turning. Maybe he will point the way. Direct a finger to the Sky, announce: There, that is where I
smelled them, tasted their scent, heard their hooves beat
beneath my eyes, that is the place they moved through my
dreams, the night before this one, that is the place where
they dipped their mouths and drank from the pools of my
eyes, now it is time, we must go, you must follow me who
will follow them, lead you to where they await us, where
they are quiet, where the wind caresses the closeness of
their fur, holds their thin legs straight to the Earth, that is
where I shall lead, to the spot where hunger ends. . . . !
Maybe these things Ayas shall dream. Maybe these things
Ayas shall speak. Maybe he will dream the Antelope
back. Maybe he will become the Antelope Dreamer. And
the people will follow where he leads. Through the trees.
Back to the time before this. Back to the time when the
people were children to the mountain. So we will call this

boychild Ayas, and Antelope will always walk among us. In another Day he will dream in the right time. He will dream all the Antelope down from the Sky. So we will call this boychild Ayas. We will never be without.' Yes I remember that day when Deubeyu, the man your father, stood tall with the flesh of his body standing out against the wind and spoke these words. I remember well. So I have come to you on this new Day my brother. Memdewi has come to his brother Ayas. Deer has come to Antelope. And I say Come Follow Me. On this new day you will pass boychild into Man. Follow Me into the trees my brother Ayas the boychild, and return in the time of the Man."

I rose from the folds of the warm Earth and followed Memdewi. My brother. I followed across flatland, across rolling land with its kneehigh grass brushing bare against my legs. I followed through the ringing heat of the brown hills. I followed through the trees, always the trees. We moved through the trees into the mountains. Memdewi spoke softly to me of *Musege. Musege,* power of power. *Musege,* Eagle in the Sky, Sparrow on the wing, Goose floating on the lake. *Musege,* swift poison of the rattletail Snake. *Musege,* blackbass Fish that can climb the highest mountains on the back of a stream. *Musege,* small Beaver that can drop a tree high as forty men. Black Bear covered with grizzled fur arms that can squeeze the heart from a man's body, *Musege.* Redlegged Coyote who talks to the night in ancestral language, he alone cries when the Sun has fallen from the Sky, he alone sings up the newday, *Musege.* Red Cat, Mountain Cat, that can drop a buck Deer full on the run, and with one stroke of his paw slash the soft belly open to the Sky. Red Cat, Mountain Cat, heavier than a man and running up the face of a tree like the small gray Squirrel who weighs less than a Turtle's egg, *Musege.* Heart of the Beast, *Musege.* Heart of the Fowl, heart of the Fish, *Musege.* Beyond all Indian medicine, *Musege.* Beyond the spear, the knife, beyond all muscle, *Musege.* Fish flying out of water to kill the small greenwinged Bug. An arrow of Ducks flying upstream, *Musege.* An arrow of Ducks flying, *Musege.* An arrow of

Ducks, *Musege*. An arrow, *Musege*. Arrow, *Musege*. *Musege*.

We came to the place where all waters flow westward. We had climbed far through the trees. Our path was now always before us. We were headed down from the high place. Before us everywhere the mountains themselves flowed west. Memdewi spoke to me in that high place going west. He spoke of how Deer was sly. How Deer was swift. How Deer never let an Indian get above him. Always Deer stayed higher than the Indian. Always he would see the Indian. Always he could smell him. Never had an Indian taken the life of Deer by coming up beneath him. To take the life of Deer the Indian must *become* Deer. Never does an Indian kill Deer, the Indian cannot break *Musege* more powerful than his own. Only when the Indian has become Deer can he take the other's life. Only when the Indian steals Deer's *Musege* can he break the other life. The Indian must be sly. The Indian must be swift. The Indian must be sly to become Deer, he must be swift to capture Deer's *Musege*. One power can break another, then there will be killing. Then Indian is ready to take the other life. He is prepared to take new life into his own. He is prepared to eat flesh, flesh of his own flesh, power of his own power, blood of his own bones. He becomes stronger. Becomes a hunter.

We traveled lightly on our feet. We were high above Deer. Always behind and above. Deer left his signs in many places. Where he had slept the night past he had scraped the ground clean, the weight of his sleeping body leaving a print in the Earth about three arm lengths across. Memdewi stooped to study this place where Deer had spent his night, he was quiet for long moments before he spoke. "He is many," Memdewi rose, brushing the Earth from his knees. "One powerful buck, three younger ones, their women number about thirty, most of them have a fawn following behind, maybe two. They stay close together. Traveling fast. They did not wait here long. They stay close together, they know not their bodies are

being hunted. But they move fast." He turned his head to
the Sky, "The weather will go heavy. We cannot see it yet
in the clouds, but Deer knows it will go bad, he can *smell*
it. The white days are coming soon. Deer does not want to
be caught. He is sly. He travels fast from high ground.
There will be a storm. Come. He is swift."

Down before us the valleys spread out in the distance
beneath the high clouded Sky. But Memdewi studied only
the ground before him. His eyes traveling quickly from
hoofprint to hoofprint. Then he stopped. The trail his eyes
had been following flowed into another. There were three
directions that merged, then ending where they all met,
only one path led out. There was one path now, the
ground it passed over worn to pebbles and dust. The one
path was filled with many tracks. The track of Deer was
still before us, a track long as the middle finger of a man
and wide as an elbow. These Memdewi traced out in the
dirt, for they were faded and broken beneath the prodding
of new tracks, similar tracks, only at their narrowing tip
they became pointed and curved in like a quarter Moon.
"Is it Deer of two different families?" I heard myself ask.
"Has Deer's brother come to lead him from us?" Memdewi pushed himself erect, never shifting his gaze from what
led out before him, his eyes filling all gooves impressed
into the Earth by his brothers, "Deer has been here. He
stays close together and moves fast. Since his time there
have been others here. Those who are heavy as a man that
travel near to the ground. Ogul. The Sheep of the Clouds.
The sheep is close. This is the road to his water. Come.
He is swift."

The trail dropped down between the sharp edges of
broken rocks higher than trees. We heard the water everywhere in our ears before we saw him. Scattered across the
granite crags in high places everywhere the Sheep of the
Clouds stood motionless and alone, their four legs struck
close beneath them, anchoring the black hooves to the
bulges of bald rock, causing the thrust of their bodies to
tilt out against the Sky at their backs. The water was everywhere in our ears. The blood ran in my feet. Memdewi

held his body so that it did not move. His eyes left the trail dropping off before him. His eyes looked in four directions to the sound of water running everywhere. The sound of water that seemed to be the very breathing coming from the Sheep of the Clouds. I put one silent step forward, Memdewi's hand came up behind him and stopped me in the chest. The two movements released a scraping sound of hooves cleating on rock surface, and there *he* was, the *Ram*, his blunt face jutting before the strong thrust of his body. Behind him everywhere in the Sky big white clouds puffed and sailed, blowing his razor gray coat in whipping streams off his back. The sound of water was everywhere in our ears. From the sledge of his head struck the fierce spiral of horns, carved from the boneheart of rock, knifing outward in a full circle as he stood in high places, throwing the full weight of his shadow across the width of the trail dropping down before us. If Memdewi's fist was not in my chest I would have fallen like a cut tree, dead from fear. But Memdewi's fist was not in my chest, he was gone silent as a Worm in mud, quick as a Bird, down the trail between the rocks and out of sight. I stood alone. My blood did not think, it screamed the sound of water everywhere in my ears as my body crashed through the barrier of the shadow cut from the boneheart of rock. I did not look back. The towered rocks sank in on the trail from all sides. Then ceased. Before me on the blank face of the mountain a waterfall lashed below into the valley like the long long silver flick of a horsetail. Memdewi was standing in the shaft of Sun bursting through the clouds, "You were brave Ayas. You did not run Little Antelope. The salt in your mouth did not make you cry out. If you had run you would have been dead." He came toward me in the sound of water everywhere and slapped his hand around my neck, his brown face open, filled with shining white teeth, his face laughed, loud his laughter came, he threw his head back and laughed high, he could not stop, he turned and looked at me again, the laughter coming louder, scattering the dry spit at the corners of his mouth to the wind. He leaned his head on my shoulder and I could feel his body sob with laughter, "The Great Sheep. The Great Sheep thought we had come to challenge *him*. He thought those following him had come to take his women. It is that time of year. So he chose his high place. He chose a place high and strong to show how high and strong he is. It is that time of year. It is the Season. He did not care if we used his trail to the water. He thought we had come for his women. That is why he did not run. That is why he stayed to fight with his crown of horns carved from the bone-heart of rock. It is that time of year." Memdewi could not stop the laughter as he spoke. "You were brave. The salt in your mouth did not make you cry out. You did not run." I could feel him stiffen, his body became quiet, the laughter died in his stomach, he stood up, "But will you be brave in the tree with the stoneknife in your hand? Will Ayas be brave in the tree with the stoneknife in his hand? Will Little Antelope? Be Brave?" Memdewi stretched his arm full out, pointing down the waterfall to the bladetop of the trees in the valley below, "He is there. There Deer waits." He flung his arm down and gazed straight to the Sky, "He moves fast. He moves close together. He moves in front of the weather. He is sly. He is swift. We must not think now. We must follow our bodies. Our bodies will lead the knife to our brother's throat. We must be sly. We must burn from our bodies all things Indian. We must burn the sweat of our days into the Sky. Then we will be free. Then we will be swift. Our bodies will lose the smell of the Indian. We will be as new born. Our brother will not smell us until we are on his back and the stoneknife is at his throat. We must be swift." He turned and followed his feet running, into the rocks and down among the first trees that came small up the mountain. He took the stoneknife from his side and slashed the low pine branches reaching toward the ground. He bent, with his rock his hands made a flame. The flame grew in twigs and pine-needles. He threw the cut branches on until he built a fire that cracked and spit the breath of a steady white wall of smoke off its back. The wind caught the smoke and blew it over his brown body. I could not see him. He was drowned in the white breath of fire.

Overhead the puffed clouds tumbled and knocked into one another. Then he appeared. Stumbling from the smoke. His eyes clamped shut and his mouth twisted closed. Then the eyes and mouth exploded open and he gathered the fresh air deep into his lungs, letting each gulp out like wind rushing through trees. "Deer can smell the Indian. But I am sly. I do not walk with the smell of an Indian. I smell of all things growing in the forest Sun. I smell of all things growing green. I smell of the forest. I am the forest. My medicine cannot be broken. But you Ayas, I can smell your Indian body from here. I can smell your brown scent like the Coon can smell the yellow scent of Skunk. You must be sly." I followed the wind around to where it was blowing the smoke, suddenly the wind shifted and the blanket of white blinded me. I closed my eyes and mouth but still the sweet smoking green pine cut up my nostrils and seared me deep in the head, burned me behind the eyes, stung me like the sting of a Bee through the throat. No longer could I hold my life breath down. It exploded from me, letting the smoke stream into my body, choking the life from me, knocking me to the ground. Memdewi reached down and pulled me from the drowning cloud, pounding my back, pounding the smoke from my lungs. I could see his face through the red sting of my eyes and his words were clear, "You smell of wood. You are a forest. Sly." He moved off. I followed. I followed his moves. There were no words. I followed my body. I was swift. Where the leap of the waterfall ended itself in the smooth quiet of a pond a grassy meadow spread out and disappeared in the trees. Memdewi swept the long grasses with his eyes then scooped a handful of the pebbled Deer droppings scattered along the stream running from the pond. He crushed one of the droppings between two fingers. Over his shoulder he looked into the trees. Always the trees. He held his hand out to me. From his open palm I took a dropping, running it back and forth between two fingers until it was broken down to dust. It was warm in my hand. Deer was near. It was the time. Again I moved behind Memdewi. But he did not move into the trees. We stayed beyond them. Always on the outside. Always mov-

ing within their arc. For many hours we followed the
trees, watching them change color, shape, height, then we
were in them, deep in their belly. Above, the fast Sky was
gone. Disappeared. Eaten by the swirl of branches feeding
off all high places where there once had been open space.
Green leaves eating air. Below. Memdewi swung onto the
back of a thick trunked crawling oak, humping his way
up and out of sight in the thick sucking leaves. Another
oak stood nearby, its fat trunk leaving the ground slowly
until it vanished in the strangle of its own swirling branches. I hooked my fingers into the gray slabs of bark and
clawed my way up into the shield of leaves, pushing along
on my belly until I straddled the high hump of limb
arched over the width of worn path running beneath the
shelter of the tree. The leaves were cluttered about my
body so closely I could not see to the sides of me. My vision was trapped. I could only look down. I stared down
at the Earth beaten bare from the weight of many Animals. Soon the trail would be filled with him. He would be
moving swiftly in front of the weather. He would be coming through the trees. Always the trees. Close to me Memdewi waited, his brown body hidden, twisted dark on a
broad limb, buried beneath a sky of speared green leaves,
unobserved, sly. Memdewi waited like me, the spiny bark
biting his silent skin, his knees banged up against the
strong limb his body clutched, the feeling in his tightened
legs gone cold, then dead from holding one position, motionless, like the roots of the tree that unknowingly supported the insignificance of his weight. Like Memdewi I
wanted to scrape the nails of my fingers along my legs and
rouse the life back into them, but to move was to betray,
and straight ahead the white flashed on the trail. Down
and straight ahead the trail sprung brown bodies. Moving
beneath the sky of trees. He came. Deer was everywhere
on the trail, making a sudden confusion in the silence.
The slash of white marking his throat and rump flashing
brilliant in the deep green. The first to come and show
himself cautiously on the trail laid out before him was a
young buck. His short horns spiked in a crown up between the long broad ears darted back along his head. He

came sniffing with the muscles of his eyes working everything unknown before him. He came beneath the snake of
my body clinging to the overhead limb, the stoneknife exposed and waiting, the length of its blade cocked an inch
from my chin. I could feel his weight beneath me, his
presence shook the air, the bone handle of the knife
screamed in the hot sweat of my hand. My body loosened.
And he was gone. Passed on. His scent swirling in the air
behind him. But he was not for me to take. His flesh was
young. The meat of age had not pushed the bone full
from his head to form the bladed male weapon of antlers.
"You must take the antlers longer than your arm," Memdewi's words had taught me. "You must take the antlers
tall enough to be tipped up on the ground for your body
to pass beneath into Man. You must break his Deer medicine. Capture his Power. Pass the length of your body beneath his antlers and you pass into the Power of Man.
You become strong as Deer. You have been sly. You have
stolen his *Musege*. You have stolen the *Musege* of your
brother. You are as strong as your brother. You can stand
with your brother. As a Man." Deer passed beneath me
swiftly now. The hornless females sleek and certain in
their movements filled the space of the trail, the fawns
stamping close at their sides. Then they passed. Only one
female remained. Standing in the center of the silence
where a Bird did not sing. Her body turned away from
me, the white slash of her rump dazzled against the strong
brown line of her back. The flesh of her ears tightened
and flicked at the silent heart of the forest. Her whole
body strained back down the trail she had just trod. Then
she spun around, the entire bulk of her strength carrying
her suddenly under me and out of sight, springing the trail
behind her in a moment of emptiness before *he* appeared,
coming with all the Earth beneath his feet, the air drumming blind through the bone speared antlers thrust high
from the brown force of his head. The quick muscle of
his presence knocked the life from under me. The blood
jumped from my head to my heart. The tall blade of his
antlers scraped the belly of the limb my body clung to,
cutting the scream from my throat deep back into the for-

est as I crashed onto the blunt strength of his back, the stoneknife going hot in my hand flashing in quick strokes above his shoulder, slashing beyond into the throb of life-blown neck, slashing and jabbing until the knife cut so deep my hand sunk and burned wet into the heat of blood, the knife digging the twisting through spewing flesh, trying to stop the pulsing body from plunging further into the forest, trying to break the power of the legs still strong, carrying my wild heart screaming further into death, the stoneknife at the end of my arm lifting and cutting away at the strength that bore me blindly beyond my own power, the stoneknife striking deep and straight at the center of power until I felt the body beneath me give way, suddenly slump and dive, crashing down into all the small things of the forest floor, sending a hard spray of leaves and broken twigs up all around it into the roaring, dying air. I came down with him, shifting my weight high onto his side, saving myself from being trapped and crushed beneath his falling force. He was down. I felt his power throb under me. I felt his Spirit calling him. Calling him to rise up. Calling his muscles to lift him, bring him up from the forest floor, escape the stoneknife I was driving into his neck, rise up and put his muscle to the wind, flow with all water, sing with all Birds, power of strong legs running, strength from blades of bone growing from the head. I heard his Spirit calling him. I heard his Spirit singing. I heard myself crying in my fear, the tears running on my cheeks in fear that his Spirit would *win*, would urge him up, carrying him proud away, the muscle of his rump twitching, the wind drumming blind between his high antlers. I heard my own sobs, felt all my strength coming from my body to my arm to the stoneknife I drove deeper into the gaping wound of his neck, the blood swirled and smeared up above my elbow, streaking across my chest, splashing in thick stains through my hair as I cut deep into flesh, forcing the knife of my fist even further, further through flesh, further until all the flesh was cut out and there was no flesh, just Spirit, and I chopped its pumping roots, keeping his body down, keeping the fear that was breaking out of my chest in sobs from breaking out of my head into dreams, from breaking out of my bones into darkness, where I was alone with the stoneblade of the knife, in death.

"Ayas! Antelope! He is Dead! Your brother is Dead! Let go the knife he is Dead!"

Deep in my hand the stoneknife was pushed out in the giving flesh. The words came through all the sobs heaving from my chest. Through the tears running from my eyes I could see Memdewi. He repeated his words.

"Your brother is Dead! Deer is Dead! Let go the knife he is dead!"

My fingers tightened even more on the knife, and slowly I pulled the blade up from its forced path until it was withdrawn. There was no sign of life in the flesh of the brown body. It lay perfectly still. It would not rise up. Deer was Dead. The knife had not been needed for a long time. I opened my fingers around the handle, letting it slip from my blood soaked hand to the ground. I straightened myself up on my knees. The tears coming silently from my eyes, flowing from all parts of my emptiness onto the Earth next to the body of my brother, Dead, the stone of his weight without movement.

"You have learned life," Memdewi spoke. He did not come to me and rub with his thumbs the tears from my eyes. He did not come to me and help me stand, supporting the weakness in my knees. He sent his words to me again. Leaving me alone.

"You have learned life."

The weather rolled over us, turning up black all above our heads. I knew the way back. The mountains grew tall before me, but my feet carried me on the straight path. The trail home was the trail coming. In many places the clumps of bushes growing thick along the trail had been eaten down and shaped the smoothed roundness of a fist from the Deer we had tracked the days before. Deer who had fallen beneath my knife and whose flesh had been carefully taken, cut into strips and packed within the folds of his hide strapped across the length of my shoulders. Days ago Deer had eaten of these same bushes, chewing the green in his mouth, swallowing the green food for his

belly while the weather turned over his head. I had taken
the power of this green food from his belly, when the stoneknife cut the life out of his neck the power of all green
food passed from his belly to my heart. These green bushes growing from the Earth were my food, gave me
strength to carry my flesh back to the people, to return
into them the power of strong legs running in strong
dreams. Behind me Memdewi came, following my steps
and the clawed thrust of the high arched antlers that I
carried before me in my hands. Memdewi sang away the
new burden of flesh I supported on my back. He laughed
at the stars when they came out and jumped like Frogs
between the banging clouds, he sang when the morning
flew out of the east and drove rain down on our heads, he
sang as the water washed the dust from his face, he sang
as this first rain of the season was sucked into the Earth
and wetted the thirsty throat of the mountain. He sang up
the burden of stolen flesh strapped to my back. He sang
the burden far into the clouds going white and sailing
high, leaving the Sky open and blue when we came over
the knot of brown hills rolling down from the tongues of
mountain. Memdewi's voice grew louder, shaking the air
all around, singing the people up from the hills, bringing the
people all around us with the smiles of leaping joy on
their faces as I passed into them, the meat on my back,
the green *power* in my heart and the tall bladed antlers
carried high before me. The people gathered themselves
into a circle. Already the fires were going, the snapping
brush and hard blackroots blazing up a white smoke as
the people moved around the singing of Memdewi. The
people had come across brown hills from many directions
to form this circle. They had come to watch me go into
the day of Man. The circle they formed was powerful.
From the elbows of some the feather of the Eagle was
strung, *Musege*. The long braids tossed over shoulders of
many were tied with the skin of Fox, around necks hung
the claw of Bear, and flashing against the chest of one the
tooth of Red Cat, *Musege*. So much power flowed through
the circle and to the fire at its center that it pulled me
with strong unseen hands into its force. The stolen flesh

was being lowered from my shoulders, but when it was gone the burden was not taken with it, the weight of flesh still clung to me, I had taken it forever upon my body, the stone weight of its green power filled my heart. Before me I held high the bone wedge power of the antlers, *Musege,* taken with the stoneknife in my own hand. I stood at the center and felt the force of the circle flow into me through the shape of Memdewi's song. All these words I heard, "Ayas has come this day the Man. His magic is not that of a boy, his magic is that of strong legs running. His *power* broke the medicine of Deer. His *Musege* has won the time of Deer's *Musege.* He took Deer with his own hand, a Man. He took him body to body, a Man. He took the green power and the strong legs running and he brings it into you. It is his gift. The gift of *power.* The gift of *Musege.* He waited in the tree for this *power.* He waited with the stoneknife in his hand. When Deer passed beneath with antlers that could tear the bowels from Bear Ayas dropped not too soon. Ayas dropped behind the antlered spears of bone and took Deer with his own hand, a Man. He has brought his *power* into you. Eat of his flesh. Receive of the gift. The flesh is now days old and can pass into you and won't make your belly ache. It will harden your medicine. But Ayas will not eat of this flesh he has taken, all the close family of Ayas will not eat of this flesh, it is the *source* of their *power,* they cannot eat of their own, it makes the Spirit ill, they cannot feast on their own flesh, to do so is to break their medicine, to do so is to die. But you must eat, receive this *power,* this gift of the new Man among us." Memdewi's song hung in the air as he lifted the antlers from my hands and took long steps toward the fire then spun around, his painted face streaked with black lines of soot and grease. He held the antlers the full length of his arms over his head, "Now it is come. Ayas must go into the Man. We wait the Sign." He flung the antlers upside down and pointed them into the Earth so they formed a high bone arc. "Pass now into the Man, Ayas. Pass beneath these horns of *power* without their touching your skin. The trail home is the trail coming. You have made your own door into tomor-

row. Show us your medicine was enough to make the
door large enough for you to pass into Man and carry all
the people with you." I fell to my knees and crawled to
the blade of bone arched over the Earth, I went down before it on my belly, passing first my head through, then
the bare skin of my shoulders, avoiding the cold touch of
bone, snaking my hips into the hard dirt until I had come
through, on the other side. I stood on my own two feet
and rose to meet the Birds the people sent out from their
mouth, their loud calls shook the Sky as they shouted
their Joy. Memdewi's song came up through all the
sounds of happiness and laughter singing in my ears. "Antelope has gone into Man! The Sign has been shown us!
His body passed through the horns of bone, the horns are
not too small, he passed through them, they did not fall
over, his magic won't bring him bad luck as a hunter, his
magic will never desert his strong legs running, no matter
what his prey! This is the Sign given us! What he has
killed is big enough for him to pass through. He takes
only that which befits a Man. His medicine is Big. Take
his gift!" The time of Mendewi's song swelled, a man
came down from a high rock and tied an Eagle feather
around my knee. The meat of Deer cracked on the fires,
the old people huddled close to receive the heart and liver
while the children ran with handfuls of buckberries and
cooked grasshoppers. Memdewi came to me in his song,
his outstretched palm before me filled with the sweet eggs
of the Bee. I took them to my lips and their taste jumped
in my mouth. I looked up to what called me across the
Sky, an arrow of Ducks flying upstream. *Musege.*

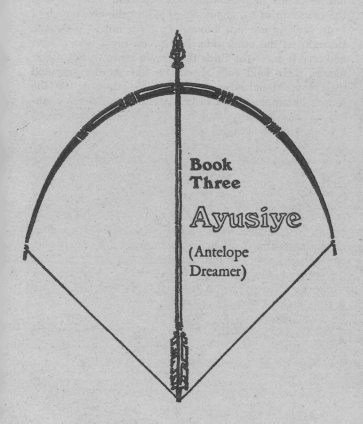

Book
Three

Ayusiye

(Antelope
Dreamer)

THE FOX was close. The smell of Rabbit flesh closer. The
woman of his son even closer. She sat at the edge of the
slow water. The Sun touched all of her naked shoulders.
The brown arch of her back glowed as she bent to wash
her feet in the slow water. At her side were lined five
Rabbits. Their skin had been cut free and their guts pulled
clean. She had held them deep in the current of the
stream until all the blood had flowed from them and the
meat of their bodies was left white. Her back straightened,
she brought her feet from the water and dried them in the
tall grasses. The sharp musk of ginger grew up around
her. Her hands parted the soft blades of grass and exposed
a swirl of purple flowers spreading among the whiteroots
of grass. She tore loose the plant pressed against the damp
Earth and shook the rootstock free of clinging sod before
pulling the length of its whitestem between two fingers,
exploding the moist fragrance in her hands. Her hands
held all the fragrance, she slowly rubbed it in the thick
hair beneath her outstretched arms, then deep into the
darkness between her legs. Her nostrils widened, her body
bore the scent of wild ginger, the full purple bloom of its
flower she tucked high into the black hair of her head.
She rose from the grass and turned her back to the
stream. Before her was the man of her heart. Her eyes
touched his in the moment, as if the flight of two Birds

suddenly crossed. His eyes saw away from her. His eyes saw only gray, the blink of the Fox eye. But she saw his shoulders bent with her burdens. His shoulders weighed beneath her offense, for the boychild she gave to him was brought out of her body in winter, that was the sign shown to her she had wronged the man Gayabuc. That was the offense. Now he had journeyed far from her heart. His dream lived with the White Ghosts he had seen eat of *their* own flesh on yonder lake, his Spirit journeyed there always, to yonder lake, his eyes saw away from her only to that day, emptied his body of all else. She heard the call of her name. "Painted Stick! Painted Stick!" The sound did not come from the man standing before her. It came from behind him, where the people were gathered on the meadow with all of the work of the Rabbit hunt going on before them. "Painted Stick! Painted Stick," the young girl calling her name came running past the man, holding in her arms the straight back cradle with the crying boychild. "He has sucked milk from Hinaya, his belly is full. But he will not close his eyes until he has tasted milk from the breast of his woman." The girl brought the baby forward to Painted Stick, then she stopped. The scent of wild ginger raced in the air, it flew off the body of Painted Stick. The girl saw the full purple flash of flower high in Painted Stick's hair and her lips came off her teeth in a smile, she spun around and looked with the smile straight at the man, then ran with the baby back into the people. Painted Stick did not look into the eyes of the man, she quickly ran past him, following the girl.

The Fox was close. The woman was no longer near. The scent of Rabbit flesh was before him. He went to the stream and scooped handfuls of water to his mouth, his breath came heavy and sent a spray of water from his hand as he drank. The bloodless meat of five Rabbits the woman left behind had already dried in the Sun. He watched the dark knot of flies dart at the split bellies, the sting of their buzz sounded a song in his ears. The song screamed loud through his head as he watched the black hulls of the flies stick at the white meat. He remembered the scream of the goose on yonder lake, how that scream merged with another sound that exploded on the lake shore, a sound shaking the snow from trees, crashing up the rise of slope, ripping everything of meaning in its path, driving into him like the jagged flint of an arrow tip. The sound of the White Ghosts as *they* ate of *their* own *flesh*. He watched *them* moving slowly on the snow, clumsy, like Bears in water. He had watched through the trees. Had watched *them* hunched, away from each other, mouths tearing at flesh, faces smeared the color of the dying Sun. The Fox was near. The Fox of the Earth was released. The eye of the Fox blinked before him as the flies swarmed on the white meat of the Rabbits.

The smell of the Fox was strong. The Rabbit Chief rose and looked from the work of the Rabbit to see his son. He saw the woman of his son with her back against the smooth willow trunk and her boychild sucking the milk from her breast. This the Chief of the Rabbit saw, but the son who had given him the dream of the Fox he did not see, in no place could his eyes find the man Gayabuc. He sat upon the ground again with the work of the Rabbit before him. The white days had been many and long, longer than any he could remember into the time when he was a boy. But the length of the white days had passed, as everything must pass. Now was the time of the first season. The small Bird could again be heard in the forest. The taking of the Rabbit had passed well. Rabbit was weak, Rabbit was without much flesh, but he was many and the bellies of the people had grown hard like stones. The taking of the Rabbit had passed well, now the people had their want, today they had their need. All the people had their want, each family had many Rabbits that had been trapped forever in their part of the long net. The Rabbits of his family were before him, again he began the work, splitting the thick winter hides from the long stiffened bodies. The blade of his stoneknife cut into the hind legs of a Rabbit, carefully slicing a spiral that spun around the outside of the body's meat. He held the knife between his teeth as he flung the Rabbit with a quick stroke of his wrists and tore with strong fingers the spiral of cut skin up from the hind legs and across the body. He passed the stripped body to the old woman seated next to him who ran her sharp stone up in under the ribcage and down, spilling the guts out in a soft mound on the grass. He smoothed the wet skin he had just torn from the body and cut it into long strings the width of his smallest finger. He was the Chief of the Rabbit and he looked up from the work before him. All across the meadow the people had the work of the Rabbit before them, many had already begun their fires for the feast of the Rabbit flesh. He would not eat of this flesh. He was the Chief of Rabbits, he took only their power, not their flesh, to eat of their meat would be to eat of himself, he would lose the power of the Rabbit. He would die. The Chief of the Rabbit felt his power as his knife cut the long strings of hide, it would take the furred hide of thirty Rabbits to make the warm robe to cover two people during the long white days. The cut strings of the hides would be sewn together, then twisted out two thick around a pointed stick, by late into the day of the following Sun the long twisted strings of Rabbit skin would be rolled tight and bound by the rope of the hollow water plant, ready to be woven into the tapered length of a blanket, the *Dayoliti*. All across the meadow the work went on before the people. The Rabbit Chief could smell the flesh of Rabbit bodies racked over high flames, he rose and stamped his feet on the ground, stirring the stinging blood that had been held back by sitting on his crossed legs over the many hours with the work before him. He moved among the people, they had their want, they had their need. He felt the necklace of Rabbit toes around his neck. From each driving hunt of the Rabbit in which he led the people he hung the toes of the largest Rabbit. Today his necklace for the first time since the long white days, was heavier, the added power tugged at his neck, he tried to wear it naturally as he went among the people in the last light of the falling Sun. Already the eyes of the roasting Rabbits were bulging up white out of their heads, some of the people had begun to

eat, the meat was tough and sharp in the mouth, it was all
eaten except the power between the legs which had been
cut free and buried. Everywhere the eyes bulged white in
burning bodies, the man moving among the people who
was the Rabbit Chief ate not of this meat, ate not of his
own flesh, if he did the power would go out of him, he
would die. Powerless.

* * *

The scent of the Fox was strong as the Sun pushed itself out of the east down into the high mountain meadow.
The Chief of the Rabbit had been watching for the first
light. He had sat on his Rabbit Robe since the night's beginning darkness when the first star fired low over the
trees in the great distance. The Evening Star was his
power. The First Star was the sign of the Rabbit Hunter,
stalking the empty Sky over the whole of the Earth, and
in the night finding every hidden star. The flash of the
Evening Star held his power, he had watched it through
the night as it stalked the Moon. With the opening light of
dawn the Hunting Star disappeared, the power was gone.
The Chief of the Rabbit sat erect on his Rabbit Robe, the
dawn of the new day he had been watching for had come.
Far into the shadow of the trees surrounding the meadow
he could hear the tramping of leaves and the slap of low
branches against running bodies. All before him the people slept, all except one. He could feel the one that was
awake and had been watching with him. Somewhere along
the banks of the slow water, hidden from the work of the
Rabbit, watched the one who had given him the dream,
the one who had shown him the flesh of the Ghost on
yonder lake, the one who had given him the dream of the
Fox, his son Gayabuc. He could feel Gayabuc watching
with him, he knew Gayabuc could hear the sound of running bodies deep in the shadow of the trees. When the
sound of the running bodies finally broke from the shadows into the meadow and the high shouts sent all the stillness out of the air he knew Gayabuc no longer watched.
All around him the people came awake, the two runners

who had broke free of the trees lay exhausted on the grass, their chests beating like the wings of great Owls as they sucked at the air and tried to heave up the words they had run so far with. The women pushed their way to the front and gave the two runners water and the cooked flesh of Rabbit. The people fell silent as the two men drank and tore at the cooked flesh. The people waited for the words. The Chief of the Rabbit came forward, the Fox of the Earth was released, the dream his oldest son Gayabuc had given him crawled out into the day. One of the runners looked up into the Rabbit Chief's face and spoke the words he had been watching for. "The Ghost lives. We have seen *them. They* are come." The Chief of the Rabbit turned away, his eyes went off to where the Sun was being born, there was no need to watch the runner, it was his youngest son, "And what did you see of *them* Basa my son?" The runner stood and directed his words at the man his father, who had his back to him. "We have seen the ones Gayabuc watched on yonder lake. We have seen the White Ghosts. We have seen *them* who eat the flesh from their bodies." "And how many Ghosts did you number," a man spoke. The runner turned to the man who made his way up from the slow water. The man came through the people and stood at the center, it was the face of his own brother. "*They* are many, Gayabuc. *They* come in a line from underneath where the Sun is born each day. *They* are many different kinds of beasts." "What is *their* kind?" "Some are of the man walking upon two legs. Some are of the woman, walking the same. Some move over the ground in turning houses covered by a white cloud. Some walk on four legs like the Elk, sharp horns grow out of *their* heads like knives, *their* skin is short like moss and *they* pull the turning houses covered by a white cloud. *They* are all wild stone-eyed beasts." "Can you lead us up to these Ghosts?" "Yes, the way is not far for feet that are fast walking." "Then we will go." "No, our path does not lead to them," the chief of the Rabbit turned and faced his two sons. "Our path leads here, the work of the Rabbit is before us, we have our want." He flung his Rabbit Robe up under his chin and

over his shoulder so it flared off his back. Gayabuc looked to
him, but his eyes saw beyond him, where the Fox had escaped from the Earth, "The Ghost is upon us. We must
go up to the Ghost." The Rabbit Chief slid a hand beneath his robe and it came back with the stoneknife in it,
he sent the knife into the Earth between his son's legs so
its blade was buried to the wood hilt, "We must hide in
the trees, always the trees, it is the way of our people. It is
the way of the Ancestors. If we bring ourselves too close
to the Ghost we will die." Gayabuc released his father's
knife from the Earth, then flung it in a swift arc until its
blade struck against the bark of a pinetree and fell broken
to the ground, "We go up to the Ghost." "Wait," a man
whose hide had wrinkled and pulled into deep furrows all
along his body from the constant river of Suns that ran
the course of his long life stepped forward, the white-
black skin of the Skunk was folded over his thin arm, the
sacred shell from the sea that caught all the colors of the
rainbow hung from his neck, he put the shell to his lips
and blew through the tiny hole drilled in its base until a
high distant whistle shrilled up from the shell and stabbed
the low blue Sky. The people drew back and turned their
eyes to the power of the sacred whistle, waiting for the
Man of Medicine to speak his tongue, "There comes a
time in the turning of each year when the Sun and the
Moon shine on the same day. On that day all things are
not as they should be. It is not night, it is not day. The
Owl hunts in the cold light of the Moon, the Hawk hunts
in the hot light of the Sun. The Owl and the Hawk hunt
together, it is not night, it is not day. The Moon and the
Sun follow around the brow of the Sky, but neither light
is stronger than the other, neither power wins. There are
two powers in one space. The people can follow the way
of Gayabuc and go up to the White Ghost. But the people
can also follow the way of the Rabbit Chief and go up to
the White Ghost, but not put their bodies too close to the
White *Musege*, to get too close to the *power* of the Ghost
and look him in the face is to die. The people can follow
the wild stone-eyed beast and watch him from the trees."
"You speak the water of truth," Gayabuc answered the

Man of Medicine's words. "We go up to the Ghost." The
Boss of the Rabbit laughed, his lip jerked up over his
teeth and he laughed, "The words you both speak flow
into a hole and their truth is not to be seen. Our ancestors
have spoken of White giants, with armor arrows could not
pierce, who came among us and stole the children. There
have been stories told among other peoples that have
come to my ears and I have kept silent upon them. Now I
will let these words forth: Out of the hotlands the Paiute
tell of the Ghosts with skin like snow, *they* are these same
wild stone-eyed beasts, *they* carry no bows, but sticks,
sticks over which *they* work *their* medicine. The Paiute
tell of how an Indian got too close to *their* power, had
looked in *their* faces, and *they* worked *their* medicine on
their sticks, sending out a burst of fire and clap of thunder, making the Indian fall at a great distance with a hole
torn in his heart. For this we have no teaching, no words
from the past, no power. Gayabuc has watched these
Ghosts eat the flesh from *their* own bodies, *they* devour
their own power, from this springs all bad medicine, from
this springs all evil." Gayabuc turned away from his father's words and spoke to the people, "The Ghost is many
and near. *He* is in our Mountain House. We go up to the
Ghost. There is no teaching." "Gayabuc, my son," the
Chief of the Rabbit came forward and placed both hands
on his son's shoulders. "We have been hungry. We have
been hungry and gone through the long white days, now
we have our want, the Rabbit is before us, the work of the
Rabbit is before us, we have our need. Our bellies are full
of Rabbit flesh, so many Rabbits have come into our nets
we cannot get them all into our stomachs. Look about
you, the ground is covered with the rotting bodies of Rabbits, we have so many we can only strip the hide from
them to twist our Rabbit blankets together, their bodies
we fling down to fester in the Sun and stink the air, our
stomachs are already filled with too much flesh. For this
we do have teaching, we must not walk away from the
work of the Rabbit. We must dry out his flesh and pound
it into powder to be eaten another day, even then we still
have too much. We must stay here and make of his skin

blankets for the long white days, we must use of him what
we can, to walk away from the work before us is to vio-
late our brother the Rabbit, he will no longer be good to
us, he will no longer come into our nets to give us meat,
to give us fur for our blankets, his power will escape us.
We must not abuse our Brother. For this we do have
teaching." "The Chief of the Rabbit speaks of the true
way;" the Man of Medicine stroked the blackwhite Skunk
skin hung from his arm, "yes, for this we do have teaching. Bear does not eat more Fish than his belly can hold.
Bear is Big, he is strong, his paws are the size of a man's
head, he hunts Fish in the quiet pools, but he hunts only
what he can eat, only what he can use, he does not abuse
his Brother, he does not pull Fish from the waters until he
has too much to eat, leaving the flesh of his Brother piled
high on the grasses to rot in the Sun. The Chief of the
Rabbit speaks of the true way, the work of the Rabbit is
before us, we cannot turn from our Brother." The Rabbit
Chief struck his hands together, ringing out two loud
claps in the silence, "Then we must go to the work before
us. Come, let us go, the Sun already grows tall in this
day." "There is time on this day;" the Man of Medicine
held the Skunk skin up so it caught the full face of the
Sun in a glare on its surface, "there is time on this day to
follow the trail of the old way, *and*, there is time to follow
the trail of the new way for which we have no teaching.
The children will stay behind and with them their women,
the work of the Rabbit can go on before them as the men
go up to the Ghost." He turned his back on all the women
gathered round, "From this time forth my eyes will not
cross one woman whose blood flows to the Earth in her
season. I am the Hunter, the luck will leave, the power go
out of me. I turn my back on all women. It is the time of
the Man." The men joined the Man of Medicine and put
their backs to the women, they stood in silence and kept
their eyes high to the distant mountain peaks until all the
women had gone away to the work of the Rabbit. The
Man of Medicine turned and brought the men around in a
circle, "This then is the time, we go up to the Ghost, each
man must walk with his own power, each man must call

up the medicine within to shelter him from the wild stone-eyed beasts." The Rabbit Chief threw his robe into the center of the circle and stopped the Man of Medi-'cine's words, "If we are to go up to the Ghost we must be sly, we must look with our eyes into our heads like Coyote. Remember, we are few, the Ghost is many. Remember the days past when the Salmon Eaters came over the mountains and took away a Washo woman. The Salmon Eaters were many, we were few. We sent out the knotted Deer thong to the south where the Crazy Warriors live among the boulders. The warriors answered the Deer thong, they came up to us, they were many, strong and crazy, crazy brave. We ran with the Crazy Warriors to' where the Salmon Eaters were sleeping under their blankets, even their longtooth Dogs were sleeping. We came down and broke their skulls with our clubs and killed them in the belly with our knives. Then we killed up all the Dogs, we were all crazy and danced strong. The fire went high and we danced with the hair of the Salmon Easters waving from the tops of our long poles. We danced crazy strong until the first Sun hit the tall trees, then we threw the hair of the Salmon Eaters into the fire and ran crazy with the woman back to the baskets of pine-nut soup waiting in our camp. Let us send out the Deer thong to our crazy brothers so that they may join us as many and go up to the Ghost." "No," Gayabuc leaned forward across the circle to face the Rabbit Chief. "If we send out the Deer thong to the Crazy Warriors it will take three days running, we cannot wait, we will lose the Ghost." "Yes my son, you are speaking the truth of the Owl, if we wait three days for the Crazy Warriors the time may have passed us, we may go up to the Ghost and he will be gone." "Then we must go now," Gayabuc glared across the circle at his father. "*Except* for the Acorn Eaters." "What of the Acorn Eaters? They roam beneath the trees of brown rain in the valleys beyond the snow on the far side of the mountains. What of their people?" "Only this," the Rabbit Chief looked over his shoulder to make certain the Acorn Eaters were not hiding behind the billow of the fast sailing white clouds. "We are

few, the Ghost is many. What if we go up to the Ghost
and he has the power of the Acorn Eaters. What if we go
up to the Ghost and he has the power to charm us to
sleep! We are few, the power of the Ghost could come over
us too strong and make us fall down asleep, then the
Ghost could come up to us and steal our medicine, strip
our flesh and leave us broken of all strength. Let us send
out the Deer thong to the Crazy Warriors, then we would
be many and crazy-strong, our medicine too big to break,
the Ghost would not rob our power and charm us to
sleep, we would stand crazy-strong, we would survive the
Ghost." Gayabuc broke from the circle, he took a few
steps to the cold pit of a fire from the night past. He
dipped his fingers into the white ash, in quick strokes
smeared it across his chest, down over his arms, up under
his neck and over his face. He stood and faced the circle
of men, the upper half of his brown body gone white
from the ashes, "I go up to the Ghost, my body is invisible, the flesh of burnt wood hides all my wounds from the
eye of the Ghost, *he* cannot find my old hurts and give me
a dream, *he* cannot find my old wounds and charm me to
sleep." Gayabuc pulled up the long hair that hung down
around his face across his shoulder. He parted it into two
plaits and wove a thick braid, then yanked the Eagle
feather free from the leather necklace around his neck
and tied it to the end of the long rope of hair. He spoke to
the men again, throwing the black braid over his shoulder
so it hung down his back, the blade of the Eagle feather
pointing straight to the Earth. "I am invisible. I am crazy-
strong. I go up to the Ghost." He turned and his feet
carried him with quick strides away from the men. "The
branch cannot be broken from the Tree!" The Man of
Medicine called across the meadow, his words stopping
Gayabuc. "If you go up to the Ghost alone *they* can break
the branch from the Tree. That is not the way. We must
go as one, or we go not at all. Come back and join the circle. If we go, we go as the Tree. The branch alone can be
broken, the Tree cannot, its roots are deep, its trunk
growing thick and powerful, its many branches rising in-
tertwined to the heavens. Come back to the circle and we

will pass the Deer thong." Gayabuc came back and placed
his body in the circle of men and they waited for the Man
of Medicine to speak. The Man of Medicine stretched his
arm into the center of the circle so the black-white folds
of the Skunk skin could be equally seen by all, "We will
pass the Deer thong, those who on this day want to go up
to the Ghost behind Gayabuc will leave the Deer thong
free. Those who want to run for the Crazy Warriors and
go up to the Ghost as many and strong behind the Chief
of the Rabbit will tie their knot in the Deer thong." He
slipped the Skunk skin from his arm and exposed hanging
from his hand the narrow Deer skin with the sign of Coyote and Bear cut precisely into the length of its soft surface. He held the Deer thong up and let it sway back and
forth so the odor of nut oil rubbed into the shining hide
was heavy all through the air. He pulled the skin down
and passed it on to the man next to him, then cast his eyes
to the Earth. The man at his side handed the thong on to
the one next to him, then turned his eyes downward. The
Deer thong passed through the hands of every man, leaving the scent of its nut oil thick in the palms of each and
filling the very center of the circle. The Deer thong came
back to the Man of Medicine, he placed the thong over
the black-white skin draped from his outstretched arm in
the center of the circle so it could be equally seen by all.
One knot was tied in the middle.

The Washo watched. The Washo watched through the
trees. The Washo watched through the trees as the two
Ghosts worked *their* magic. The waiting spring light fell
flat on the Ghosts as *they* bent beneath the trees, *their*
hands working quickly over the magic until the ritual was
complete, and *they* were gone, swung up on the backs of
their beasts so *they* formed one towering wild eyed beast.
The Washo watched as the beasts rode off into the trees,
they watched until the iron hooves could no longer be
heard pounding the forest floor. In the silence left behind
the Man of Medicine spoke in a loud whisper so that all
his brothers hidden behind the trees could catch the
words, "These Ghosts are gone. *They* go up to the other

Ghosts where the stone-eyed beasts pull the turning houses covered by a white cloud. This Ghost has worked magic here. He leaves his power behind. We must steal his power." Another voice was heard, it spoke above the whisper of the Man of Medicine, it was the voice of the Rabbit Chief. "No, we must not go up to *their* magic, we have no teaching, we have no power for that which we do not know." "The Chief of the Rabbit uses words from my own lips," the Man of Medicine answered. "We must not go up to *their* magic without power, but we do have teaching, we have the secret of Hawk's flight, we will use the medicine of the Hawk to capture this magic. The secret medicine of Hawk is patience. To wait. To watch. Hawk circles endlessly in the vast blue Sky, watching, he circles forever so his prey forgets what is swooping overhead, what is waiting above, then down Hawk comes with the full secret of his power and his fierce claws take what has come to him. We will wait. We will watch. This power hidden beneath the trees will forget us, it will sleep, all things must sleep, no matter how powerful, even rocks sleep. We will watch. Then we will take what has come to us."

The Washo watched. They lay hidden behind the trees, waiting. The Sun slipped out of the Sky. The Washo watched. The Sun slipped back up into the Sky. The Washo waited. The Moon chased the Sun away. Then the Moon went away. There was no Sun and no Moon. Gray light filled all space. The night Birds were going to sleep and the morning Birds were waking up. The voice of the Man of Medicine came through the gray light, "The power of the Ghost sleeps. We will go up behind Gayabuc and steal the magic." Gayabuc slid from behind his tree, pulling silently through the pine needles until he came within two body lengths of the bush that covered the magic. He flattened himself out on the ground like a blanket. His breath became slow until it almost stopped. He waited. Nothing happened. The only movement was the steady sweat running off his back. Then the light popped. The first clear swift light of the morning shot over the trees and hit

full on the bush that covered the magic. The stump of a
hoarse cry wrenched from Gayabuc's throat as he jumped
to his feet, hurling the blade of his knife with the full
muscle of his body into the bush. It was there! It too had
been waiting! It did not sleep! The knife tore through
the branches of the bush and there was a loud sound as
if it had struck a rock, then a louder sound clanged out
of the bush, a fierce clamp, sounding like teeth with the
power of three Bear jaws slamming shut, shaking all the
branches of the bush. Gayabuc jumped back. The power
had eaten his knife! His father came running by him with
a scream, bringing the swing of his arm down and fling-
ing his own stoneknife into the heart of the bush. All became quiet. Another man ran for the bush, sending his
knife straight into the branches. No sound came back.
Another man came at the bush with his knife, and another, until all the men had sent the full muscle of their
stone blades into the bush's heart. No sound came up from
the branches. The Man of Medicine waved his Skunk skin
over the top of the bush and called on all the clouds to
gather around to witness this magic of the Ghost the
Washo slayed with the muscle of their knives. He unhooked the medicine bag hung around his waist on a
Deer-muscle belt and emptied its yellow powder into his
open palm, "Damomli! Deubeyu! Magician! Power of
Spirit!" He blew the yellow powder out in a soft ribbon
so it all settled at once onto the head of the bush. Gayabuc
came forward with the blade of his stone hatchet and
chopped through the blood colored wood of the bush's
base. The Man of Medicine took hold of the top branches
and flung the bush aside, leaving the magic exposed to
the eyes of all men. They gathered round and looked
at that which they had never before seen. A great skeleton
of steel teeth was before them, teeth large enough to cut
the life out of a small Animal, powerful enough to clamp
on a man's leg, breaking through his bone and holding him
there until the Ghost came back. What was before them was
the magic of a fierce trap. The Ghost had left his teeth behind, and so that no one could steal *his* magic *he* chained the
teeth to a stake driven deep into the Earth. But the magic

had been broken. The magic had been captured. The teeth
had clamped shut, but they captured nothing. The Washo
gathered up their knives and sat about the magic of the
teeth as they ate their dried strips of Rabbit flesh, never
taking their eyes from the power. "We must keep going,"
Gayabuc stood, wiping the grease of the Rabbit on his
thigh. "We must go up to the Ghost and take all of the
magic. We have the secret medicine of the Hawk to go behind. We can break any power before us and capture it as
our own." "Gayabuc speaks the true water," the Man of
Medicine stood, pushing pieces of Rabbit flesh from his
lips into his mouth. "We have our want here. We must go
up to the Ghost, *he* is already two days beyond us. We
will leave three of us behind to guard this magic we have
captured. We go up to the Ghost. It is his Day."

The Washo came up through the long shadows. They
came up to where the mountains were joined together by
a strong running river. They came up to where the Ghost
had been that morning. The Ghosts had clawed up great
patches of Earth, killed many trees and left only their
dead bones in fires grown cold. Gayabuc held his hand
high. The Washo behind him went still in their own
tracks. They too heard the noise, it came jumping out of
the trees, banging and tearing at the Earth. The Ghost
was near. The Ghost was coming to eat the flesh of their
Spirit. Gayabuc's arm dropped and he ran away from the
river and fell to his knees in front of the trees. The others
came close behind, then saw what Gayabuc had come up
to. A stake was driven deeply into the ground and from it
was a chain holding the teeth of the Ghost. The stunned
face of a Rabbit looked up at them from the trap. The
skeleton of steel teeth had clamped down on his hind legs,
snapping his bones so their jagged ends ripped through
soft flesh as his body thumped and banged against the
Earth trying to free itself. Gayabuc reached down and
grabbed the steel teeth in his hands, pulling them open until the Rabbit was loose. He let go the teeth and their
power clanged shut. The Rabbit did not move. The white
of his eyes bulged up out of his head like he had been

spitted and was roasting over a fire. "Little brother," Gayabuc took the Rabbit's neck in his hand. "The magic of
the Ghost has stolen the flesh of your Spirit," he twisted
the neck until he felt the dead weight of the body pull
against his hand. "Go free little brother." He stood up,
but the men had left him, they had run back to the river.
He saw his brother Basa on the ground and the men had
come around him. He ran up to them. Basa was breathing
heavy, but his words were clear, "The Ghost travels in the
dust through yonder pass. *He* is many. The stone-eyed
beasts are everywhere. I have looked into *their* face and I
did not die." Gayabuc pulled Basa up by the shoulders,
"We go up to the Ghost." Basa pushed his shoulders back,
his heaving chest beating the air. He looked straight into
the eyes of his brother Gayabuc and saw the Fox. He
spun and ran, weaving in great leaps through the yellow
pine with all the men close in his trail until he broke from
the pass and up onto the barren knoll. All the men fell
around him, sucking at the air with their burning throats,
before them in the distance a line of dust was going up
around the yonder lake the river poured into. Gayabuc
stood, through the dust he could see a line longer than a
night of stars, a line of wild eyed beasts pulling the turning houses covered by a white cloud. Basa jumped up beside him, "There! There is the beast! I have looked into
his wild stone-eyes and I did not die!" Gayabuc's gaze
went to where his brother was pointing, it was not to the
line of dust in the distance, but below them, in the flat
hollow at the bottom of the knoll. There it was, with its
wild stone-eyes flaming up at them. Gayabuc pulled free
the bow slung across his back, "We will take the Beast.
They have taken the Rabbit with the skeleton of *their*
teeth. We will steal back the Spirit of the Rabbit." A
strong hand pulled his bow down, "My son, we must leave
this power, this *Musege* is too strong for us. The Fox of
the Earth has been released, his *Musege* is set free on the
Earth. In the meadow where the women of our children
wait the work of the Rabbit is before us. We must not
abuse our Brother. We have our want. We must go back
to the teaching. To steal this beast will be beyond our

want, we will be heavy with flesh. Our medicine will be broken." "I go," Gayabuc freed his bow from the hands of his father. The Man of Medicine waved the Skunk skin in the air, "We all go. The Deer thong has been passed, the Deer thong has spoken." He raised the shell of the sacred whistle to his lips and blew a long shrill cry that darted through the trees and ripped the air above the men as they flew down the hill and took what was waiting for them. The stone tips of their arrows cut through the short hide of the beast and stuck deep within him, more arrows came at his face and bounced off the cowstone of his broad skull. The thunder of his iron hooves tore open the Earth as Gayabuc flung himself onto the ridge of the broad back, taking hold of one horn as the full swing of his knife came striking from the air into the bulged muscle of neck. The beast went down to his knees and slammed over on his side, the woodstiff arrows stuck in his sides snapping in two beneath the fall of his body. All the Washo came around and watched. The wild stone-eyes of the beast flared up at them, the quick snorts from the fists of his nostrils scattering the dust up around his head. The Washo watched. The Washo watched until all was quiet. Then they dug a deep pit and filled it with yellow pine. They started a fire up from the pit and it burned through what was left of the day and into the night. When the coals big as a man's head breathed fire white the Washo cut the tongue free from the Beast, then cut out great chunks of beef from the side of its waiting body. The flesh was thrown on the coals and they sat around in a circle upon the ground grown almost too hot to sit on from the bright white center of the heat before them. They listened to the flesh sizzle and hugged their knees, rocking back and forth as they sat on the hot ground singing the songs Birds sang long ago that they had learned in dreams. They sang to the stars. They sang to the Ancestors, singing up Hawk in the vast blue Sky, Coyote and Bear in the forest trees. They sang up the Salmon who climb the backs of strong mountains on ladders of water, they sang up the waterbabies mewing at the bottom of the lake. When the flesh before them was cooked they took it from the white heat and ate. They ate until their bellies were sore and shot pains through them when they spread their legs and tried to urinate. They ate until they were heavy with flesh. The mounds of meat they could not eat they threw away from them. They collapsed on the hot ground, throwing out great chunks of beef. And they slept. In the time before night becomes day Gayabuc began to choke. A white heat in his belly pushed out into a ball and doubled him up, he retched. The great chunks of beef came churning up and vomited on the ground. He retched until his whole body shook, until his eyes burned with the salt of his tears and the sting of his bile drooled down his chin. He retched until his belly was empty and each convulsion brought a stiff pain to his chest. His ears filled with the sound of his own dry convulsions. He pulled to his knees. All around him he could hear the hollow retching and spitting of bile. His eyes widened at the dawn and he began to laugh. He laughed hard and long with all his body. When he stopped, the laughing still went on all around him. Everyone was laughing.

2

THE BLUE castrate morning flared up over the Indian's head. The flies were everywhere in the sun, coming at his face, jabbing in a steady drone at his eyes, he kept brushing them away with a twitch of his hand. The valley went out flat around him, already its morning heat came up off the ground and hung in a low dense haze all the way to the distant rim of mountains. He could feel the sweat moving in his long hair beneath the tight warmth of his straw hat. He flipped the hat off and ran the flat of his palm back over his scalp, pressing the uncomfortable moisture the length of his bright black hair. He waved his hat in front of his face at the darting flies then set it back on his head, cocking it down over his eyes until it almost blocked the blue of the morning from his vision.

"O.K. Joey, we're ready!"

He turned to the voice of the man who called his name, he could see the man through the waves of heat pushing up from the ground, crouched in front of the small rambling corral before a small blaze of sagebrush. The man had the length of a long handled brandingiron propped up on some stones so the tip of the iron rested in the flames and its brand *AD* burned red hot.

"Joe, me and Jandy are ready to run the first one through if you want to hop over the fence and cut one out."

303

The Indian jumped into the small corral, the calves all skittering away from him, running along the curve of the black rail. He chased them, waving his hat and hollering as he broke into the midst of their brown bodies. He slapped at their bone humped rumps with the flat of his hat, keeping back far enough so a sudden kick wouldn't catch him in the shins. He ran around the full circle of the corral with the calves, hooting and hollering in the fine blur of kicked up dust, slapping with his hat until he got one calf to break from the pack, he raced it away from the other bodies along the high railing to the opening of a single aisle shoot. The calf ran before him, his young excited hooves carrying him with quick bolts of movement so the open shoot before him was the natural turn to make and he did. The Indian dropped the wooden gate behind the calf and it was trapped in the short shoot with another gate before it.

"Joe," the man kneeling next to the snapping fire came over and leaned up on the coral looking at the Indian across the trapped brown back of the calf. "These little bullys are a lot quicker than they look. But there are so few of them there isn't a whole lot of need to get a horse in there on them just to cut out one at a time, much faster this way, but they'll run you ragged. Hah," he knocked the thick cloud of flies away from his face. "I don't know why these damn little bullys always give us such a fight. You would think they know what is coming. But I know they don't know *that*. Cattle are as ignorant as a dog. A dog will scratch himself into a pool of blood over one flea. I've seen full grown bulls rub themselves bloody on the stub of a fence post so badly they had to be put down. But a man has to understand animals, he has to always be studying them just to stay out in front because he knows that he's just about an inch less stupid than they are. Now Garibaldi was a student of animals, some people say that's *all* he knew. But Garibaldi knew the value of a fine animal. He began the great revolution with four mules and two men. Think of that, the greatest fight for liberty mankind has ever known was begun with more mules than men. But Garibaldi learned a great lesson of freedom from animals, he once said, 'To get out of the corral you've got to go through the gate.' Damn these face flies," he slapped his cheek, mashing two black bodies against the sharp growth of two days whiskers. "Where did these face flies come from Joe, we've never had them in this valley before, I know over to Nevada they have them, but not us, it's only been the last three months they've come."

The Indian slapped at the flies spinning around his head, trying to close in on his face, "I don't know where they're coming from Odus. But I can remember in my father's time, during the War, these face flies came, they stayed for a few years then were gone. These will be too, in time, but now we've got to watch out for pink-eye, especially among these calves. These face flies will carry pink-eye around the herd faster than we can spray against it."

Odus leaned over and looked in the face of the trapped calf, "Well, this little bully's eyes are clean, no sign of pink-eye yet. Wouldn't that be just what Dixel needs though, three of his best Appy horses going bad in the legs all at once and then pink-eye with the cattle. Well Joey, men who are making fifty dollars an hour can't be standing around talking like this. Hah." He slapped the Indian on the shoulder, "don't you just wish we were making that! We would be retired in three days! I'm all set on my end though, got the iron red-hot and ready. Jandy, how about you? Those knives you've been working on all morning got the edge on them you need?" He shouted to the small man crouched down honing two gleaming silver thin blades.

"I'm about set," the small man rose and carried a bucket of water over to where the calf was waiting. He dumped a bottle of alcohol into the water and sloshed it around, then carefully set the two stainless steel blades on the bottom of the bucket so they glowed up through the water like two white fish. Jandy jumped back and started slapping at his face, "These flies are calfshit!" The flies buzzed high and away from him, then held in the air above his face. He gazed up at their hard black knot, the skin of his face was smooth and expressionless, the stone of his small hard eyes blank. He spit on the hot ground, "Calfshit!"

"Joey, you want to jump in and tail this little bully up? I'll get the contraption wheeled up." Odus walked over and got in his pickup truck, behind it was hitched an iron trailer-shoot twice as high as a man and the length of a full grown cow. He backed the iron shoot flush against the gate of the wooden shoot until the two formed one piece separated only by the wooden gate that held the calf trapped. Jandy pulled the tongue of the trailer off from the pickup hitch and let it slam to the ground. Odus drove the truck around to the far side of his small branding fire, then came back and kicked open the support levers on both wheels so he could jack the iron shoot down to solid ground, "This contraption was thought up by someone who was a hater of men and a bigger hater of cattle." He smiled up at the Indian as he turned the crank of the jack, "It takes forever to rig it right and the bullys don't like it at all, they fight it all the way, it's just a plain torture."

"It's calfshit," Jandy took the crank from Odus and jacked the other side down. "The clean way to do it is the old way, just rope and tie them down, three men can do one calf in eight minutes."

Odus knocked away the flies darting at his eyes, "That's true, but if you're going to run through all the new bullys at springtime you can't beat the calf-table, just run them into one of those calf-tables, slam them tight and flip the whole thing up on its side, it's so smooth you could do anything to the bully, you could take his tonsils out if you wanted to. But Dixel is too cheap to buy a calf-table. Everything for the cattle is second best. Only those Appy horses of his get preferential treatment. All he thinks of is those horses. He's a horse man, and I've never known a horse man who ever did right by cattle. O.K. Joey, jump in."

The Indian jumped down into the wooden shoot, grabbing hold of the calf's tail around the base and yanking it up as he stood in close to the rump so the calf couldn't get a kick off, "Open her Jandy!"

Jandy slid back the wooden gate. The way before the

calf was open into the V of the iron shoot. But the calf
didn't move. He stood breathing hard, staring down the
iron V to the far opening, an opening just large enough to
squeeze his body through, an opening to freedom. But he
didn't take the chance offered. There were too many men.
It was all strange to his short life. He did what his animal
blood told him. He stood his ground.

"HeYaHH!" The Indian brought the point of his knee
up like a fist into the calf's rump. "HeYaHHH! Git Git
Git HaawrHH!" He speared the calf again, driving his
knee into the exposed rectum. The calf flung his head
back, then shook it to both sides, knocking against the
wooden plank. "HeYaHHH!" The calf slammed again to
his side, his young hooves stamping at the ground before
he jolted into the iron V, carrying the Indian with him as
the full thrust of his body lunged toward the opening. The
gate behind the calf slammed shut the moment his head
rammed through the wedge of the other end and Odus
sent the iron yoke above the opening clanging down on
his neck. The calf tried to swing his body loose. His head
was through the opening, it was free, but the weight of the
iron yoke held him back, he was trapped. Odus pulled the
lever chain hanging down over the yoke and sent the
length of the iron V slamming up on both sides, knocking
the breath from the calf as its body was pinched between
the iron bars.

"That ought to hold this little bully," Odus pegged the
lever in its slot so the calf was secure in the iron bind.
"You ready Jandy?"

Jandy brought his bucket up to the side of the shoot,
"Let's go!"

"Joey, get that tail high!"

The Indian pushed the tail higher, holding its full base
in the grip of both hands. He could feel the tension in the
brown body coming to a point in the flesh he secured between two hands. The tail was warm; it was hot. The flies
spit everywhere in black darts, filling the air with their
drone, landing in clumps all over the exposed calf's face,
sticking into the watery flesh around the bulging white
eyes. The Indian shook his own head to drive the flies off,

but the flies stung at his defenseless face. He dipped his face and dragged his cheek across his shoulder to scrape the hooked flies from his skin and he could see Jandy bringing the white fish of the stainless steel up dripping from the bucket of water.

Jandy gazed back at the Indian, the flies coming at the blank stone of his eyes, "Tail this calfshit up Birdsong."

The Indian rammed the muscle of the tail even higher. Jandy quickly took the pouch hanging taut between the calf's strong legs and slashed with his stainless blade, slicing the bottom point of the sack off, exposing the white tips of the testes to the sun before he grabbed them in his fist and yanked them down, tugging them straight to the earth, pulling the string of the glistening white and purple cord that ran tight back up into the gaping sack. The Indian could feel the flash in the calf's body, it came deep out of its bowels, raw streak of fierce muscle electric that froze the thick flesh all along the broad brown neck and loosened the meat around the tight rectum, softening its pinch-hard pucker the Indian exposed by keeping the full thrust of the tailbase rammed up.

"Cut that Bully out of there Jandy," Odus called from his fire. "Get out those Test-Tees!"

Jandy squeezed the two long hard-shell pieces of flesh clenched in one fist so only their white tips were exposed from either end of his grip, he had them stretched down so they almost touched the earth and the full run of their cord went tight up into the sack where he ran his blade in high, the stainless steel feeling in the darkness of the body for the vital point, then cutting effortlessly, a quick slash. He pulled the cord out with the splash of blood over his fist.

The Indian felt the loose shifting in the calf's body. The full flush of the muscle electric slackened the flesh of the rectum and gushed a harsh hot spurt of bloodsoft shit down the slick brown hide of the legs.

Odus ran over from his fire, the red hot *AD* brand waving in the air, "Tail that bully up good Joey so he don't start kicking up a storm and make me run this brand!"

Jandy sheared off a patch of bristling brown hair on the

calf's neck. Odus poised the smoking iron over the shorn spot, then twisted his wrists down, forcing the hot iron into flesh. He stuck his tongue through his teeth and bit down hard as the iron burned and seared its black imprint into meat.

The Indian turned his face away from the wind blowing the stench of burning hair and flesh into his nostrils, he braced himself against the rump as the calf reacted to the violence and turned the full muscle of his young body against the iron bars that held him trapped and thrashed with the weight of his ribs against the stall just as Odus pulled up the brand and brushed the charred hair clean from the deep burn. "In the nick of time! It's a perfect brand!" He banged the lever up over the calf's head and the iron yoke clanged free, releasing the struggling calf.

The Indian felt the strength of the brown body spring from him and he jumped back so as not to have his face kicked by the last mad fury of the flying hooves. He rested against the back of the stall. The heat was ringing in his ears and he could feel the flies biting at his cheeks. Deep in the distance a sound was coming to him, growing louder and more familiar as he slumped down to the iron plank floor of the shoot. Out before him he saw the young calf, stunned, running in zig-zags across the hot land, angry still feeling the bull in his groins, stomping the hot earth with the dead flesh of his hooves, shaking his head with violent turns against the thick air that surrounded him, against the *unknown* that surrounded him. The calf felt the Bull in his groins but the meat had been cut out of him, the muscle severed. He shook his head against the unknown. In the days ahead the Bull would die out of him, the feeling of power would disappear from his loins, he would grow soft and slow, he would grow fat and dull, dazed with emptiness. Then the Indian connected the sound swelling from the deep distance, it was a sound familiar, a sound he had been hearing all morning. Swarming around the trapped corral of waiting calves were the mothers, the dead weight of their thick udders swinging beneath them as their heads hooked back and they blared, bellowed and bleated against the fate of their young flesh now separated from them. The old cows cried and pleaded, the old cows *knew*. The Indian realized it was the sound of the mothers he had been hearing all morning, but it had been so steady, so incessant, like the constant rip of pinetree tops in a wind storm, one after the other until it becomes impossible to distinguish any single sound. The Indian saw the mother cow of the young calf who was out shaking his head against the unknown. She came running across the hard hot ground to be with him, to help him, to be next to him. The calf saw her coming, heard her close sound above all others, he turned from the white fear of pain in her bulging eyes, drove his head down low, tucked the shaft of his tail tight between his legs and ran. She was rejected but not stopped, looping awkwardly behind him, trying to lick up with the long pink meat of her tongue the blood splashing from his cut bag and dashed against his hind legs, dripping in bright red streaks all the way to his hooves.

"Joey! Hey, isn't that Jandy the goddamndest, soft handedest, quickest little castrator in the whole of the valley? It's a pleasure to work beside a true craftsman, an artist," Odus leaned into the stall, his bright red face beaming at the Indian. "Come on Joey, you can't be tired out on the first bully, we've got eleven more to go," he reached his hand in and pulled the Indian out from the confines of the shoot. "Jandy, where'd you say you picked up your art?"

The thin man was cleaning the delicate veined pearl-white testes in a clear bucket of water, pulling them through his fist to free any loose tissue, he looked up at Odus then spit at the hot ground. "Mexico. Mexico is where I picked it up."

I never cease to wonder at you Jandy, you could lose a finger or three if that bully flinched just at the right time."

"I've known some to lose fingers. That's calfshit."

"You're so quickhanded you don't use any crimp like most cutters, and still you get hardly any bleeding."

"Don't like crimps. Don't like novocain neither. It's all just fancy calfshit. You make your move and you make it right, that's the natural way, ride or get off."

"I couldn't agree with you more," Odus knocked at the flies coming in at his sweating face. "That's just what Garibaldi always said, 'Ride or get off.' Words to live by."

Jandy spit on the hot ground and stood up. With his hat on he was only tall as the highest plank in the small corral, "We've got a long morning."

The Indian jumped over into the corral again, thumping his hat in the air, his face lost in the brown swirl of dust the running calves kicked up. He felt a bang of pain in his knee. His leg gave out. Ever since the snakes the leg had not been right. Then the pain stopped, he couldn't feel anything, there was no *feeling*, all support in the leg was gone. He slammed to the ground sending up his own heavy cloud of dust.

"Joey, you all right in there," Odus ran over and hopped up on the corral. "What is it, your leg giving you trouble again?"

The Indian beat his leg with his fist until he could feel the blood pumping and humming. He stood, the shoulder of his shirt had been burned off by the fall. He slapped the flat of his hat against his pants, knocking out small puffs of dust, "No, there's nothing wrong with my leg."

"You want me to come in there and give you a hand?"

"No. There's nothing wrong with my leg." The calves were still circling him and he got in behind them, hooting and hollering and waving his hat until he got one out in the wooden chute.

"Okie-doke," Odus called. "Open her up Jandy!"

Jandy pulled the gate up, freeing the way for the calf. But the calf stood rock still. "Heeyaawrh," the Indian struck the cocked bone of his knee into the calf's exposed rectum. It leaped for the opening and was stunned by the iron yoke slamming down on his neck.

"Tail him up Birdsong. Don't let him kick and make me take my fingers off by missing the stroke. Tail him!" Jandy shouted as he pulled his knife from the bucket and slashed the bag. The Indian rammed the base of the tail high and could feel the white flash of muscle electric vibrating in his grasp.

"Get it all out of there Jandy, he's a bally one!" Odus

came quickly with the red hot iron held out before him. "Don't leave him anything to play with or he'll be so worthless horny that he'll fuck every fence post."

"He's done," Jandy pulled his blood smeared fist out of the slashed pouch with the long cord dangling the two glistening sausage length testes clumped at the end.

"Okie-doke Jandy, get the shears and get this little bully shaved. Joey, tail him high so I don't run this brand on his hide," Odus poised the hot iron over the square sheared by Jandy then rammed it down, it seared into the flesh, the stench of blowing burning hair ripped the air as the calf turned his weight away from the red iron and thrashed against the iron bars.

"Calfshit, you run it."

"I know I run it Jandy!" Odus spun his head around, the fierce blue of his eyes challenging the scorn of the blank stone eyes staring into him. "You, Joey, tail this bully high. This one counts!"

The Indian bowed both knees and brought the strength of his thighs against the calf's flanks as he jammed the bone-stiff muscled tail straight up. He watched Odus slide his tongue between his teeth, the black flash of the flies wings beating around his face. The brand was smoking, Odus aimed it at the imperfect burn, then struck, leaning his whole body weight into the iron handle. The Indian felt the calf spring inside, the blood of its body driving away from the pain, but Odus kept his hold of flesh burning iron on its mark. The Indian pushed with all his weight through his thighs, he held the calf still. Odus jerked the iron up and ran his hand over the blackened hide, brushing free the charred hair. He looked at the Indian, his lips pulled way back off his false teeth so the soft pink of his gums showed in a big smile. The brand had burned true. He banged the lever up and the calf was released.

The Indian sat watching the sun. The ground was so hot it seemed the sole source of heat. The sun had become just a bright sinking ball in the blurred sky. He no longer tried to keep the flies off. They crawled over his clothes and stuck like small knives on his hands and face. The heat had become so thick the flies didn't even buzz. There was no sound except the heat and the open gate to the corral swinging in short piercing shrieks on its rusty hinges. Across the barbwire fence down the long black road behind the Indian the dot of a pickup truck came through the waves of heat. It grew larger, its sound coming before it in the haze until it finally passed by the corral and clanged over the metal cattle-guard then swung around so its bright white high-backed cab was to the Indian, when he turned around to face it he saw the fat red letters stamped in steel across the tailgate, FORD.

The man behind the wheel of the pickup leaned his head out the window, the white crown of his stetson hat almost catching on the cab ceiling, his broad face was smooth and easy, the blue of his eyes poked knowingly around in the heat rising off the ground before him in blurred waves, "Birdsong, where is Odus?"

The Indian stuck his thumb up and pointed it across the corral, "Cleaning the balls with Jandy, Mister Dixel."

The man slapped the flat of his hand down on the horn, stabbing out a high foreign honk in the hot air. He kept his hand pushed down until he saw the two men running around the corral, then he stopped the loud blast and swung the door of the cab open, jumping down to the hot ground. The door stayed open, its white glared in the sun, the *AD* painted on its side was tall as a man's arm and blood red. "Odus, everything nailed down here?"

"Has been for about an hour Mister Dixel."

"You get them all cut and branded?"

"Everyone. We're all uptown here. When that Jandy cuts he cuts out every last bit of the bully quicker than the eye can see. He means business. They're going to have to make room for Jandy in the Farmers' Almanac, he'll be listed under FAST."

"What about the brands? You didn't run any of those brands did you?"

"One or two might have been a little rusty, but we put them right."

"I told you to let the Indian do the branding while Jandy here cuts, your eyes are about as good as your teeth."

"I need Joey to tail em up, he's the only one to hold them up good so they don't go jumping and kicking around," Odus curled his lips into a small smile and shaded his eyes with the flat of his hand. The whole time he was talking he kept trying to see into the cab, he knew the woman was in there with the baby, but the white glare beaming off the broad window blocked her from view. "Well, it's all uptown here Mister Dixel, everything is tied down."

"Good, I've got another job for you and the Indian. We've had a lot of fence snap in the winter on the Blonston field, and we still haven't gotten to it. I've got six coils of wire in the back of my truck, you and the Indian can get going on it today. I want all that fence mended and laid up straight as a donkey's hard-on. We've had alot of cattle on the Foral field, it's carried them longer than I thought, the feed must be good up there, but I want to get them into the Blonston field while it still has some green left. Ben Dora will be coming to give a hand on the Blonston field so you and the Indian get right over there."

"Joey won't work with Ben Dora. He never has, and he never will. Why can't we get Jandy to go with us?"

"Because I have another job for Jandy. Why the hell won't the Indian work with Dora?"

"You know he never will."

The man stroked the stiff edge of his silver belt buckle, the buckle was round, big as a fist with a bucking stallion etched across its surface. He ran his finger over the stallion and turned toward the pickup, not knowing the sun caught on the slick silver of the buckle and flashed out across the land. He turned back to Odus, "The hell with it then, you and the Indian go alone, Dora can go with Jandy here. Jandy, you have them ready?"

"Right here in the bucket," Jandy spit on the hot ground and picked up the bucket. "All twentyfour of them."

"They're all cleaned up and ready to eat?"

"Clean and not a mark on em."

The man took the bucket and stared into the sloshing water at the jostling mound of veined white fingerlength pieces of flesh. He pushed his hat back and smiled at the two men, "You know I love Mountain Oysters, my old dad, Abraham Dixel, got me going on them when I was just a small boy. It's a taste a man doesn't forget. A real delicacy. People in this country don't go for them much, they sure do in other countries, but they're more civilized. I remember when I was down in San Francisco at Law School. My Dad thought he could make a lawyer out of me so I would forget this valley, but ever since I was a boy I spent my summers on this ranch of ours up here, I never thought of doing anything but coming back. Did you know once my Dad was going to sell this ranch? He said there was no profit in it. It covered half the valley but it didn't turn the profit he wanted, he only kept it long as he did for a legal tax write-off. If it hadn't been for me there wouldn't be any more Dixels in this valley. After ninety years there would be no more Dixels. Well I proved to him on paper I could make the ranch pay with my Appaloosas. I promised him I'd come back up here to cow country and raise the greatest Appaloosas in the world, and by God the years have passed and I've done it. He let me keep the ranch, told me I had to finish up down there in Law School, but he would let me keep the ranch. Well it was about that time I got married, so he came down from Reno, took me out of school and flew with me and my new bride down to Mexico for a Honeymoon. I'll never forget what he did the first day we were there. He rented a jeep and we all drove out to a bull ranch. He told the owner he wanted his best bull for sale. The owner had sixteen brought up and my Dad kept shaking his head, he said, 'I want your *prize* bull.' So finally the owner brought out one more and my Dad shouted, 'That's it!' 'He's very much money,' the owner said. My Dad shouted he didn't give a damn about that. 'Then the bull is yours,' the Mexican smiled. 'He will be a great stud, Señor.' 'Hell man I don't want to stud him!' 'Then he will be the best meat you have ever tasted, he is meat for a King.' 'Hell, I don't want to eat him!' 'Then what *do* you want him for Señor?' 'I want his balls!' I'll never forget the look on the Mexican's face when my Dad said that, it was the look of ad-

miration a baby has for its mother. The Mexican threw
open his arms and hugged my Dad, 'Señor, you are a
prince, the highest Prince of all men.' Then the owner put
an arm around me and my new bride and pointed, he
watched with an absolute smile on his face as the bull was
staked, roped around the legs and brought down. One of
the men came at him with a knife and slashed across his
eyes, the bull couldn't see what happened next, they just
whacked his whole bag off and left his huge black bulk
bellowing and bleeding on the ground. The balls were big
as a small woman's breasts. They were cleaned, wrapped
in damp fig leaves, then tied up in a silk scarf. The owner
handed the heavy scarf to my Dad, 'Señor, we will have
the meat slaughtered and treated right, then we will send
it to you.' 'You keep it,' my Dad shouted. 'I've got all the
meat I want.' The Mexican embraced my Dad again, the
tears were full in his eyes and breaking down his cheeks.
We got in the jeep and drove back over the rutted road to
the hotel. That night on a silver platter my Dad had our
wedding gift served." The man fingered his silver bucking
bronco as he gazed with his smooth face into the bucket
of cut flesh, "You know, Mexico holds a lot of memories
for me, memories and dreams. Now that I have this ranch
of Appy horses built up to be the best anywhere I want to
start breeding Arabians, and Mexico is the place to do it,
there's room for a man and his horses down there, big
room, room enough to hold a man's dream ranch. This
country is finished, they care more about beef flesh than
horse flesh. Mexico is the place, they treat a man and his
horses right down there. That's where I want my Arabians.
I won't forget the first time I saw Arabians, it was about
thirteen years ago in Africa, during the War. There had been
alot of bombing, we were up in Tunisia, everything was
bombed out, turned upside down, but they had managed to
get the train tracks patched up. We were going from Tunis
to Sfax. I remember looking out the troop train window, the
land itself was all peaceful and calm, barren rolling brown
hills and dust. Everyone on the train was hot and swear-
ing, but for me it was like a homecoming, the land was
just like Nevada, I couldn't get enough of it. I just gazed

through that dusty window like a lost boy come home, when up out of the brown rolling hills I saw them. Their dust came first, it swirled up like a whirlwind, 'Why hell, look at that!' I yelled, and everybody came rushing to the windows, rubbing away at the dust on them trying to get a better look. 'That's the most beautiful thing I've ever seen!' And it was, I grew up around Appaloosa horses, but I had never seen anything like these Arabians. They came galloping across the roll of the hills like white ghosts, their large black eyes flashing, the long silken hair of their manes and tails waving like flags. 'They're coming right for us,' somebody shouted. And they were. They came galloping and flashing, floating in the air, leaving swirls of dust smoking over their heads. 'By God these horses are going to race this train!' I had never in my life seen anything like it, if I hadn't witnessed it myself I never would have believed it. The horses had heard the sound of the train out in the desolate area where they roamed and they had come to race this long thing that whistled and puffed, they had come to challenge the train for the pure thrill of speed. And there they were, outside my window, I was looking down on their powerful, glistening backs, their graceful heads held high like a proud bird, the wide nostrils breathing pure fire. They had come with the beauty of their speed to match the machine, they lived in that moment. Suddenly they turned off, swerved away from us. Then we saw the plane that swooped over the train and passed low above their heads. The plane banked, circling around and coming in low again over the long line of the train. We heard the high tinny rattle, even above the roar of the train we could hear it, then we saw the steady bursts of fire coming from under the plane's wings. 'Jesus Christ, they're shooting at them! They're shooting down those horses!' Already they had begun to fall, their white bodies being ripped open by bullets and crashing into the barren ground. Only a few were left running and the plane circled short, then leveled back and seemed to be skimming the earth as it came up from behind on the last runners pouring out a steady stream of bullets before it. The air in the train became very still, everyone pulled back from the windows and went to their seats. It was very quiet. Each man held to himself, nobody really looked at anybody else. I don't remember a word being spoken until we reached the end of the line that day in Sfax. But anyway that was the first look I ever got at Arabians. It's something a man doesn't forget."

"That kind of thing stops me inside. That's one hell of a shame Mister Dixel," Odus kicked at the ground, looking across the flat hazy land of the valley as if he could see the running herd of Arabians out there, and over them a single plane coming down low out of the sun. "That's a damn waste. I guess we all saw some things in that last War that changed us around alot. You don't know, but I've told Joey here about it, that I built the Burma-Thai railroad, of course we were all slave labor then, a few Americans, mostly British and Aussies. Those that didn't die in that jungle from fatigue and heat did from malaria. The only reason I survived was because I worked building California highways all through the last Depression, I can tell you it got me into shape. But I saw things there in that jungle everyday that stopped me inside. It all got turned around. I guess I wasn't any different from the rest, when I got my chance I joined in wholeheartedly in slaughtering them slanteyed Japs and Chinks whenever they so much as popped a head out of a hole, man, woman or child, made no difference, it was all yellow then. But I saw their side do it first. I saw soldiers walking along canals, they'd see a bunch of villagers bathing and swimming and they'd blow them out of the water like yellow ducks just for target practice. In the mountains I saw them come into a town, stuff all the young men into a well and toss a handgrenade in, then laugh about it. The Americans and British never did that kind of thing. But anyway I saw enough there to stop me inside and to withdraw from the civilized company of men to the top of the Sierra mountains where the insights of the great Garibaldi can be seen in the clean air and a man can drink his scotch with those he likes, and those he doesn't like, he doesn't like. But that thing about the horses in Africa, now that's a real waste."

"There's a funny end to that story Odus. When the War was over, it was when I was in Law School, I met a man who was in the Air Force and was stationed in Tangier when I was there. After I saw those Arabians gunned down I didn't much like anybody who flew a plane in the War and I told him right out to his face, and I told him the story too. And he told me what really happened, he knew all about it. He said that North Africa had been pretty well worked over by the end of '43, bombed and shelled. All during that time alot of Arabians got loose, and since the people had been turned into refugees they tried to capture the horses and eat them. This drove the horses far out into the barren hills, far from any people. For some reason the horses got to chasing the trains, racing them sometimes for ten miles. Well, there was always a plane sent to escort the trains against surprise attack and they were instructed to shoot down the horses, radio back the location and another train would be sent out to pick up the bodies. You see, there wasn't much meat in that country then, and there was alot of men. The pilot I talked to asked me what the hell all of us indignant soldiers probably ate for dinner in Sfax that night. I don't think there wouldn't have been a man who wouldn't have vomited out all his food if he had been told what he had stuffed in his belly for dinner that night. But I'm going to have my Arabians some day soon on my Mexico dream ranch. Maybe I'm trying to raise back up that herd I saw gunned down in Africa. I don't really try to figure it out. I've been going down to Mexico for five straight years now, every winter. Our winter is their summer and I get a chance to fly over the country and jeep around. I must find just the right place to build up the herd. To build up the dream."

"Did you find it yet Mister Dixel?"

"No Odus, not yet. I almost thought I had it last winter, I really thought that was the right place. It turned out it wasn't. But I know where to look now. I'll find it this next winter. I'll find it and I'll move everything down there."

Jandy spit on the hot ground, "Maybe you will Mister

Dixel. Maybe you will, and maybe you won't. Mexico is a big place. Awful big for one man."

Dixel scraped his fingernail across his silver bucking bronco, "Don't you worry Jandy, I'll get my dream."

"Maybe," Jandy swung around and began to walk away.

"Jandy."

Jandy's thin back held for a moment against the man with the silver buckle, then he turned slowly around, "What's that Mister Dixel?"

"I want you to go up to the main cattle barn, I've got that four year old black cow in there again, the one the Vet came out to look at last spring. She's all bloated, blown up like a balloon."

"She might have a dead calf in her."

"Well, you give her a good look. I don't want to lose her."

"I'll feel her over good."

"And Jandy," Dixel began scraping at his bucking bronco again. "When you finish there I want you to go over to Dora's house, then the two of you are to get the pill gun and start working your way through the herd. I want each animal to get his full dose of worm pill."

Jandy spit on the hot ground, "When it starts gittin wet, that's when you want to give worm pills. It's much too early now, that's not the way to do it."

Dixel scraped at his bucking bronco and turned to the cab of the truck, the sun was still beating off the window and the passenger within could not be seen, then he heard a baby cry, the sound slipped out of the metal cab into the hot air and disappeared. He kept his turned back to Jandy and climbed up into the cab. He slammed the door, leaning his arm down over the large red painted *AD*, "You go get Dora. I want them wormed. Everyone."

Odus handed the bucket up to him, "Don't forget your balls Mister Dixel."

The man looked down at Odus, thumping the red *AD* on the door with the flat of his hand, his face was smooth, there was not a mark on it, the flies that were thick in the air did not land on his skin. He looked quickly over at the Indian, "Birdsong, come over here."

The Indian sat there for a moment, then he stood up in the sun, he felt the pain coming back into his leg as he walked to the man, "Yes Mister Dixel?"

"I thought I would tell you now, I know what it means to you, but this spring coming up will be the last time I'll need you to go out over the fields and shoot rabbits. This ranch doesn't need a rabbit boss anymore."

"They eat alot of good pasture grass, and they dig big holes, the cattle can break their legs in those holes, you let it go long enough and a horse will break his leg in it too."

"I don't think you understand. I won't *need* you to shoot rabbits and keep the fields clean. Those days are gone. I read in the cattlemen's magazine where they've now come up with a machine that you set out and it will trap and kill rabbits. I don't know too much about it but I talked to some ranchers in Reno who say they've had good luck with it in Nevada, so we'll be getting it here soon. You can go ahead and do the spring shoot, then that's that." He turned the engine on and the whole cab began to shake with power, "Now you and Odus get the coils out of the back, there are some leather gloves back there too."

The power of the engine shook off the glare of sun from the cab window and the Indian could see through it past the man to the woman sitting on the far side. There was a baby on her lap. The woman's hair he could see, not her face.

"Birdsong," the man thumped the red *AD* and gunned the power of his engine. "How many ways do I have to ask you to get those coils off the back and get to work!"

The Indian moved around to the back of the truck, he pulled the heavy leather gloves on and threw the weight of the coiled barbwire to the hot ground. The truck was released of its burden, the thick black rubber of its back wheels spun with a sudden excess of power, towering up a column of dust as it bellowed off into the blind haze down the road.

The Indian stood with the dust falling around him.

Odus came to him through the dust, "He's like a dog, all he knows is how to bark."

"Calfshit," Jandy spit on the hot ground. "Everytime I do any cuttin' for Dixel he's right on top of me for the balls. 'Are they clean Jandy? Do they have any marks on them?' Then he's got to go and tell about how old man Abraham Dixel made him and his new wife watch as he had the balls cut off a prize bull, as if he hasn't told everyone in this valley that story at least ten times. Him and his goddam Appaloosas and his Arabians. All his dreams. Calfshit."

"Jandy," Odus smiled. "There's a bottle of scotch in the glove compartment of my truck, get it and join me and Joey for a small drink. Let's sit in the shade, just sit and look. The only thing stupid enough to be out in the midday heat is people, the animals are all too smart, they've found themselves the shade of a tree or a fencepost. Even these goddamned face flies are too hot to buzz." He pulled the Indian over with him and collapsed on the sun shaded side of his truck against the high tire. Jandy came around with the full bottle of whiskey, he uncorked it and took a swift drink, hunching his thin shoulders in and shivering as the fine taste of malt cut up his nose. He handed the bottle down to the Indian and sat beside him, "What calfshit."

The Indian tipped the bottle to his lips, as he drank the sun cutting down over the cab of the truck caught the end of the clear glass sticking up out of the shade and lit up its gold contents. The Indian stuck the bottle in Odus' chest. Odus took it and sucked away like a baby, his old face alone, the gray of his eyebrows caught in a rut of skin halfway up his forehead. He passed the bottle back to the Indian, "Landowners. *Big* Landowners. That's something Garibaldi wouldn't have stood for, not for one second on top of one of your E-PLURIBUS-UNUM silver dollars. That Garibaldi was a goddamn Saint. He started the revolution with two men and four mules. Big Landowners. America had its chance once, everyman could have shared our wealth, but that chance was shot to death the hot night in Baton Rouge when Huey Long was assassinated. Huey Long may not have been as great as the great man who set out to free Italy, Garibaldi. But Huey Long's all America's ever had."

Jandy took the bottle from the Indian and gulped another mouthful of whiskey, "Who in hell is Huey Long?"

"He was the Governor of Louisiana, the defender of all the little fish. He would have defeated Roosevelt in the election of '36 and made the little man King, but he was shot down in the halls of his own Capitol building like a deer. It's still like it was. Big Fish eat little fish."

Jandy's stone eyes stared out across the hot land before him. He spit, "Calfshit."

Odus grabbed the bottle back from Jandy and drank the rest of the golden liquid out of the glass, "Jandy, America was built on civic pride such as yours. The politicians have spent millions convincing you they are nothing but calfshit so you won't have nothing to do with them and they can keep on doing what they are doing." He jammed the empty bottle into the dirt and laughed, throwing his old head back up against the rubber of the truck tire, "Wooooowhh shit, that Garibaldi was a goddamn Saint." He pushed himself up on his old legs, unzipped his pants and pissed a straight gold line right into the hot ground, "That reminds me, you don't have to worry about politics Jandy, you're an artist of this world, the goddamdest, softhandedest, quickest little castrator in the whole of this valley."

Jandy slapped his hand on the faded knee of his bluejeans and rolled over on the hot ground with the thin shoulders tucked up under his chin, the laughter spurting from his mouth, "Look me up in the Farmers' Almanac under *FAST*."

The laughter kept coming up out of Odus so hard he could hardly zipper his pants. Then he stopped and looked at the Indian, "You know Joey, I hate that Dixel so goddamn much. He ought to be run over like a dog in the road. Come on, let's go." He reached down and pulled the Indian to his feet. He kicked Jandy in the side, but Jandy kept laughing. "Let's go Jandy, me and Joey will drive you home to your truck. Hell Joey, he's not going to stop laughing, he's gone. You put those coils up in the back and I'll get him into the truck."

The Indian slipped on the leather gloves and hefted one of the wire coils up onto the pickup bed. He took hold of another and slipped under its metal weight, driving his knee into the hot ground. The gold whiskey raced in his head, flashing the sun white in his eyes. He grabbed hold of the coil again, one of its steel barbs punching through the leather of the glove into the flesh of his palm. He got the weight up high and slammed its bulk down on the bed. Odus came around and helped him lift the other three coils onto the truck. They got in the cab, wedging the laughing Jandy between their shoulders. Odus backed the truck out onto the black asphalt, then banged the gearshift down, sending the truck lurching over the road and into the side ditch. He jabbed his foot on the accelerator scattering a spray of dust up behind him as the whining engine drove the truck sideways down the ditch then thumping back up on the road. Odus grabbed the steering wheel with both hands, holding on like a captain at the wheel of a ship in a storm, his old eyes straining through the dust of the windshield at the straight asphalt dancing before him like a black snake, "You know what I hate about that Dixel, Joey!" He shouted above the pain of the engine being driven at fifty miles an hour in second gear, "What I hate is the way he treats that pretty little lady of his. There is no excuse on a man for that. Him and his Mexico dream ranch. Every winter he goes off to Mexico and leaves her, you've seen it. He leaves her with all four of the kids to tend to and a barn full of Appaloosas. Four straight winters now, you've seen. He says it's because he don't trust anybody else with those horses but her. Four straight winters he's left her with those horses to shovel shit and snow."

Jandy stopped laughing, "She don't have to shovel shit and snow alone Odus."

"Just what do you mean by that?"

"Ben Dora!" Jandy shouted over the deafening pain of the engine.

"What the hell about Ben Dora!"

"Watch out for Chrissakes Odus! You're going to kill us!"

Odus brought all of his weight down on the brake pedal, digging the thick black tires into the hot asphalt as the rearend of the truck slung around and skidded sideways over the road, then jolted up on two wheels, balancing its slowed bulk on the edge of collapse before slamming back against the asphalt with a loud metal clang that killed the engine.

Through the dust of the windshield Odus had a clear view of the Japanese tractor, the roar of its engine shook and swayed the high metal seat upon which the driver sat peering down impassively at the three men whose sweaty faces stared up at him through the dust clouded window of the silent pickup. The driver cut the roar of his engine, waiting until it spit out the heat of its exhaust and gave up the last shudder of dying power. He pushed the stiff straw allweather cowboy hat back on his head and dismounted from his high metal seat like a tank commander discovering a landmine. He inspected the stalled pickup, walking around and kicking each tire, letting out a short whistle each time as he raised his eyes to the heavens and nodded his head in agreement. When he had gone around the silent truck twice he leaned his arm against the open driver's window, the deep wrinkles of his sun darkened face spreading out in a big smile, "Howdy Odus."

"Goddamn you Frank."

"This is ranch country, man on a tractor is *always* in the right of way."

"I worked for the California Highway Department for nineteen years building these roads, I know the law."

"What you been drinking?"

"Whiskey. And nowhere in the law does it say a rednecked rancher in a Jap tractor can . . ."

"Got any left?"

"No! Can drive around like a country squire . . ."

"I figured you would have drunk it all. I'm surprised the State would give a driver's license to an old man like you with no teeth."

"I've got teeth, you goddamned rednecked country

squire using the white divider line on the road like it was a trail blazed for you and your Jap tractor."

"Where you boys going?"

"To work."

"I'm surprised anybody would hire the three of you. Who is it that has a job to be messed up? Joe there is such a lousy rifle shot he couldn't hit a rabbit on a branch. Jandy is so slow when he goes to cut the balls off a calf he gets the tail instead. And you Odus, you're so old you couldn't lay a barbed wire fence up straight even if a wind storm was blowing up behind you the right way. Who would hire three incompetents like you?"

"You, you cocky bastard, when you've got money."

The man tucked his straw hat down at a forward angle, "If you're going to be that way about it I'm leaving, and just when I was about to invite you boys down to Art and Linda's bar for a free drink." He turned his back on the truck and walked toward his tractor, the blue seat of his jeans was worn a dull silver and glinted in the sun. He stopped, then turned around, pushing his hat up again as he came back to the truck, "That reminds me Odus, you mentioned money, you said when I've *got* the money. Well there's all I can *get* if I want it."

"What do you mean by that Frank?"

"I mean they've been back again."

"Shit."

"There were three of them this time."

"Did you say you *would?*"

The deeplined smile sagged on the man's face and his clear eyes widened with a sharp expression of pain, "Odus, for Christ's sake!"

"It was Mountain Resort Properties then?"

"Who the hell else. They said everybody in the valley is chomping at the bit to sign away everything he owns on the dotted line. They say everyone is awful mad because there are only three who won't sign, won't even answer their letters. Me, you, and Joe here. Just the three holding out."

"What about Dixel? I thought they had quit on this valley because Dixel wouldn't give up his Appaloosa ranch."

"They say Dixel is going to move it all down to Mexico. He'll sign like the rest."

"He's the one they were after, he didn't say a goddamn word to me and Joey about it. What did they offer you?"

"Twohundred and fiftytwo thousand for the three hundred acres, about seven times what it's worth."

"What did you say?"

"I said, 'You see that gun on the wall over there, if any one of you so much as passes in again through the gate by the barn I'll blow your heads off and toss the bodies out on the dump.' "

"What'd they say to that?"

"They said, 'Four hundred thousand!' "

"Shit."

"I took the gun down off the wall and aimed it at their faces, then told them a school lesson. I told them my people started back from the beginning in this valley and I'd be damned if I saw all they worked for turned into a tourist resort. I'd be damned if I'd sell my cattle. I'd be damned if I'd sell my ranch for a resort *community*. And they'd be damned dead if they weren't in their car and five miles down the road before I counted to two."

Odus' old eyes looked up at the deep lines in Frank's face and he let out a heavy breath through his nostrils, "I guess they'll be coming after me and Joey next."

"I guess."

Odus squeezed Frank's arm, "They can't get the valley Frank, not if the three of us hold on. They can't steal it."

"They said if they couldn't buy us out there were ways, *very* legal ways."

"Shit."

The weather in California had always been good to Art. Lately the weather had been so good that the little smile painted on his face floated up above his head like a red balloon for all to see. Art was a true believer in the California weather, and true believers are always rewarded. Art's wife Linda sat high up on her barstool, the smile that floated off Art's face fit right onto her own face easy as a cork in a bottle, everytime she took a sip of her rum and Coke her back got a little stiffer and her smile a little bigger. She kept her eyes expertly fixed on the huge window across the room that shot back a perfect reflection of her body so she could watch her fingers at work as her hands patted and shaped the sprayed strands of reddish twisted hair piled on top of her head like an awkward bird. "My Arty is a little genius. Didn't I always say my Arty was a genius, Ted?"

The tall man next to her plopped the cherry of his old fashioned into the mouth of his begging poodle perching with its mouth open on the glass shine of the bar counter like a furry seal, "Yes, Linda, I always agreed with you. Art *is* a Southern Californian, and Southern Californians are *born* speculators. I always said Art would do it. Here's to you Art." The tall man raised his glass high to the little man crouched behind the bar in a thin snowwhite T-shirt, hugging his naked shoulders warm in front of the cold wind from his expensive airconditioner. "Here's to the Southern California boy who *knows* his California," the tall man raised his drink even higher as Art's smile was going crazy on his face, beaming and flashing like the painted glass bathing beauties on the pinball machine in the corner. "Here's iron in your pants, Art." The tall man threw his head back and shot his drink down, his bony adam's apple making one big jolt, up and down, as the liquid poured in his throat.

"Yes Ted, here is to my little genius, my little artsy arty Arty. The man I love," she raised her glass to her reflection in the window across the room and saluted. Behind her reflection three men climbed out of a pickup, a tractor pulled in behind them, marring her reflection. She set her drink on the bar and shouted at the men as they came through the door, "You boys hurry up and close the door behind you now, we don't want any flies in here. Hurry up now, we're nice and cool and we don't want any flies."

"What will it be boys," Art glided down his slot behind the bar, the smile on his face outshining the brilliant mirrored wall of glass bottles at his back.

"Whiskey and beer chaser down the line. I'm buying," Frank slapped his billfold on the counter.

Art snapped back up his slot, "Four shots and four beers on the House. Coming up!"

"I said *I'm* buying," Frank shoved his billfold down to Art.

"On the House," Art came floating back, pushing his smile in the face of each man as he placed a drink before him.

"What's going on? Whose birthday?"

"My Arty's a genius, isn't he Ted."

"The grand speculator."

"What do you mean, spec-cue-later?" Frank rolled the whiskey around in his mouth and swallowed it.

"That's right Ted," Linda slipped her bare arm around the tall man's neck, "you tell them."

"Our Art's from Southern California. He knows how to invest his money. He's rich."

Frank gulped the foaming head off his beer, "Just what in hell do you mean?"

"It's a beautiful day," Art gazed out through the window framed by bright electric beer signs pulsating green waterfalls and blue clouds. "O.K. what is it," Frank finished his beer and pushed the empty glass before him, watching the thin layer of foam around the inside collapse to the bottom.

"We've sold out!" The high pierce of Linda's voice rang out like a shot. "We've sold out to Mountain Resort Properties!" The frayed ends of her red hair buzzed in the light of the beer signs.

Odus shoved both his empty glasses far away and leaned over the bar to the beaming face that floated up like a balloon off the short body, "How much Art?"

"One hundred and seventy five thousand dollars. Double what I figure it's worth."

"Shit."

As the other three men walked out of the bar and got in the pickup Frank took eight one dollar bills from his wallet and dropped them to the glass shine of the counter. "Here Art, you're used to being paid double for nothing."

He walked over and swung the door wide open, letting the flies buzz through behind him, and climbed up on the metal seat of the tractor, setting off the engine with a roar. The tractor went one way down the road, and the pickup went the other, skinning a black track off its tires as it slammed to a stop in front of the high backed "Regular" pump of the gas station. The man in the starched white shirt and pants did not turn around when he heard the truck come in. He continued running his soft rag into the bloodred shine of the Coke machine, making wide careful passes over the top and down the front. The blast of the horn from the pickup shot into his back and he turned around with a look of surprise on his face as if the truck had been dropped from heaven. The thick rubber soles of his shoes shuffled him over to the truck, the sun shone full on the red cloth badge sewn over his heart: FELIX—IT'S A PLEASURE. He came up to the driver and saluted, "Felix, it's a pleasure to serve you. Sorry to make you wait, business has been booming."

"Cut it out Felix, just fill it with regular. I've got to get Jandy home and me and Joey have to drive out to the Blonston field and get busy laying up some fence."

Felix turned the crank of the gas pump and jammed the nozzle of the hose into the truck's tank, "How bout I check the oil for you Odus?"

"No, just gas. We're in a hurry. We've still got enough day to do a whole side of the field."

Felix leaned up against the vibrating pump, nudging his shoulder contentedly under the whirring numbers in the small glass box registering the cost, "Hey Joe, I finally got my brand new SNACKETTE machine over from Reno. It's stocked full up with peanuts, Lifesavers and candy-bars, no need to go across to Mary at the store now, this SNACKETTE even gives change. I've already had a big run on it, people come in here and can't get enough of it. Too bad though, I just got it and now I'll be selling the station in a few weeks. But what do you know, I'll be getting enough money to put three SNACKETTES in my next station."

"You going to sell it for sure?" Odus looked down at him.

"For sure. You'll have to be getting your gas out of this valley pretty soon. I'm going to open up a new station over to Lake Tahoe, big future over there, gas stations are big business, some people have made fortunes." He jerked the dripping nozzle out of the tank and racked it up against the pump, "That's three bucks and two-bits you owe me Odus. Hey Joe, you change your mind on selling yet? I'm willing to give you five thousand."

The Indian looked out the window at the man in the white uniform, he looked him over from top to bottom, then shook his head.

"Well you should sell to me, everybody's got to sell sooner or later. We should keep it all in the family. Hey, I almost forgot, your sister Sarah Dick wants you to be sure and be over to the house on time for dinner this Sunday, Jonny and Minnie Scissons from Loyalton will be there this time."

"Here's your money Felix," Odus turned his engine on.

"Hey wait a minute, why don't you men try out my SNACKETTE?"

"We're in a hurry Felix."

"No, hey, just wait, I'll go get something out of it. I've got a key, no charge, just to show you how good it is," he ran over to the large bright white machine and fumbled before it with his bunch of keys tied from his belt loop by a silver retractable band. He finally got one of the keys in and swung open the glass door of the machine exposing its rows of goods to the sun. He slipped out a candy bar, peeling its orange wrapper down the finger of chocolate as he brought it over to the truck. "Hey, try this one out!" He handed it up through the window. "What does it taste like?"

Odus looked down at him, his old bushy eyebrows pinned high up in the wrinkles of his forehead like a gray butterfly.

"How do you like it? What does it taste like?"

"Shit."

The heat was flamed off the ground by the late afternoon wind. The Indian took his hat off and ran his fingers through the limp black hair, the muscles in his hands throbbed. The sweat dripping down his forehead stung at the corner of his eyes as he looked down the long line of tight barbwire fence going straight out of sight before him in the blunt hot air. He watched Odus urinate on the parched ground. The old man zippered his pants and came over to him, walking with a swagger of fatigue from his sore body, "You know Joey, laying up fence is the hardest job on a ranch. I guess whenever you put walls up on the land it fights you for it, but fencin somehow is the most rewarding job, it takes your whole body to get a fence up right, it's just your body, the barbed metal strands and the land. I take fencin personal, you can't ever do a good enough job, can't never lay one up too straight. That's what I like about using timber posts. Timber is hard as hell to wrestle around, but you put one in right, as right as right can be, and it will last forever, when it rots out it will even rot out standing up straight, as straight as can be. I've seen fence posts old as ninety years still standing, that's twenty years older than me. But the men who could do that are all gone or dying. Today everybody is using metal-stake posts, you can whack one down in a minute, post a mile square in a good morning, but they'll never last as long as a good timber post. Never. Nope, you can't ever put a fence up too straight. Did I ever tell you about the time me and Frank put up a fence eight strands high because he had a jumper. This was no ordinary jumper, it was a little heifer, graceful as a ballerina she was, she must have been born half horse, she jumped over everything Frank had, there wasn't a fence could hold her, finally we put eight strands around a field but she sailed over. I remember it was when I first came to the valley, nineteen years ago, it was the first fence I ever put up. Well your father Bob was alive then, those were the days he had religion, Hallelujah Bob he was called, he was so holy he would separate the cock from the hen on the Sabbath. Well he came driving by in that old FORD of his, the one he bought used off the reporter

over to Loyalton. He came rolling by this high fence we
were working on and calls out, 'What you buildin?' Frank
answers he's got a jumper and he's going to build something to hold her. Well Bob just smiled, but we could tell
he was laughing all over inside. 'You put a tire around her
neck and go to Church this Sunday. She'll never jump
again.' Well Frank thought Bob was crazy, but he did it,
he'd do anything for his cattle, and he was damned tired
of spending all his time rounding this little heifer. Sure
enough he got a tire around her neck and rigged it to stay
on, then went to Church. When he came back from
Church she was in the field he had left her. She never
jumped again, and Frank never missed a Sunday of
church going. I remember Bob died soon after that. I was
the one who found him. He had that dog with him, the
one that belonged to his first wife, the dog was dead too,
they both had been dead seven or eight days. Sometimes
after that I'd pass by Frank's and see the white faced heifer way out in the field grazing along with a big fat auto-
mobile tire around her neck, she wore it until the day she
was slaughtered. I found out later that was an old trick
Bob must have picked up when he was young and working the Nevada ranches, but a cow will never jump over
anything it doesn't think it can't fit through, and with a
tire around the neck it didn't think it could go through the
barn door. But Frank never missed a Sunday of church
going." Odus unzipped his pants and urinated again, "I
don't know what it is, but the older I get the quicker whiskey goes through me, I've got to drink two bottles at once,
one to stay in me while the other is pissing out. But I can
hold my spirits; not like some in this valley, not like Dora.
What the hell is wrong with that Dixel anyway, he knows
you don't work with Dora, he's always known *that*. But
he's afraid of Dora, they're all afraid of Dora, they need
their *law* to protect them, if they don't have that they are
afraid. There's no law in this valley, you're lucky to see a
Highway Patrol twice a month, and the Sheriff, if someone burns your house down and you call for him or his
Deputy they won't show up till the ashes are cold. Dixel's
like all the rest, his money makes him no different, he's

afraid of Dora. That's why he keeps hiring him, so as not
to cross him. You remember just last spring Dora was
fencin with Timmy, drinking beer, he and Timmy got into
it so Dora put a knife in his gut and walked around him.
That kind of thing stops me inside. So what happens?
Timmy goes to the hospital and Dora goes before the
Judge in Sierra City and the Judge is so afraid he fines
Dora fifty bucks for disturbing the peace and sets him
loose. That Dora's no good Joey, beats his wife, beats his
kids, beats his dog. He's like one of those killer bulls they
have over in Spain, they're so stupid they have to hand-
guide them to their target. All balls and no brains. Garibaldi knew how to handle a man like that, execute him. He
did it all the time. The only smart execution for Ben Dora
is a stick, grab hold of one and beat his head off. You
don't want to skin your hands by knocking his face out.
Never skin your hands Joey. I don't know what's in Dixel's head to think you would work with Dora. And what's
this stuff about you not shooting rabbits for him anymore?
First time I heard about it. He's crazy if he thinks some
new machine will keep his fields clean of rabbits as good
as you. You've been rabbit boss in this valley ever since
you were a boy, your father was rabbit boss to the ranches when I came here. Dixel has no right. He has no right.
People here are all getting crazy. Selling off the past. Selling off the land like it was theirs to sell. What this country
needs is a good five dollar Garibaldi, that's the only thing
that could save it, and who do they have as their President,
as their leader? Ike!" He pulled the thick leather gloves
on again and jammed the heavy nippers in his back pocket,
"Let's get back at it Joey, men who are making eighty dollars an hour can't just stand around talking." He laughed far
inside of himself and drew his arm across the sweat of his
forehead. "Let's get at it, there's still light."

The new wires they strung were taut, glistening silver
and sharp in the distance, as the Indian strung them he
could feel them vibrate in his hands through the leather
gloves. His hands had become a detached part of him, a
hard tool that worked with its own blind knowledge, the
pain in the muscled steel of the fingers was distant and

comforting, like the feel of a sunwarmed hammerhead. The Indian worked hard with the sweat swelling the long hair beneath his hat. He worked with his back bent, he worked next to Odus. There was no need for words, their gloved hands moved and pulled and cut and signaled at the end of their bodies' ache. The long strands of wire vibrated and hummed, the heat burned the sound out of them, they sang all the way down the long line. The Indian thought of what Jandy said to him as he got out of the pickup. Jandy lived where the steam came up from the ground, where the thick water came up in hot pools and spread the heavy scent of sulfur in the air. Jandy lived at this hotsprings in a silver trailer, it was a beautiful trailer, the thick dust on its arched back could not hide its graceful silver glow. The Indian had never been in the trailer. In the summer other trailers like it would come, but the people who lived in them could never be seen. At night they would slip unnoticed into the healing power of the hot steam and sulfur water. Sometimes they would stay for a few days, sometimes for months. Living at night, hidden in the day, and suddenly they would disappear, vanished. Jandy's was the only trailer always at the hot springs. It was his home. In the winter the snow would slip down off the tight stretched metal skin of the trailer leaving it clean, the trailer could be seen glinting in the cold sun for miles like a religious dome, and behind it, in the flat white, the steam shot up in straight lines from the small geyser holes of the hot springs. Across the back of the trailer was stenciled a black name, it was a name that sang in the Indian's mind, a name he envied, a name he wished he had: AIRSTREAM. When Odus' pickup pulled in behind the trailer to drop Jandy off the Indian could see the name through the dusty windshield strung across the silver bulged back: AIRSTREAM. He watched the letters as Jandy's voice came back to him, "Birdsong, you're covered with calfshit." He had not thought of what Jandy said, he had just heard it. Now with the wires singing through his hands he thought of it. He *was* covered with calfshit. The morning had been long, he had held the tails of the calves clamped up, his body pressed into theirs

as the power was cut from them. He remembered letting
go of their tails. He remembered the release. As if flesh
was being torn from his own body. As if a burden had
been taken from him. He was covered with the shit of
fear, it was all he had left. It was not new to him, it was
not important, he did not notice it. Now he thought about
it, he did not think about the stink that came up off the
front of his clothes in the heat, he thought of that morning, of the mothers running behind the cut calves trying to
lick their hind legs free of blood, as if a clean hide would
make everything right, make everything as it was before
the morning began, make everything as it should be. But
it wouldn't, it was done, they were cut, it was over. The
calves ran off into a different morning. The Indian heard
them singing in the wire, he smiled as he worked, all
along the line the sunhot wires were humming to him, the
longer he worked the more the wires sang and stung in
the waves of heat, singing through his hands in a high distant pitch, like a car deep in the distance coming up the
hill, the dazzling white fingers of its headlights searching
out the road before it, and it came closer, became very
near in the night. He lay hidden and very young, his fourteen year old body flattened in the bushes as the headbeams of the car struck the darkness before him into
light. The car halted at the clearing, its engine still running. He could smell the rise of dust the tires tore off the
long road to the top of the mountain, the hot dust rising
into the damp edge of night filled his nostrils. The engine
of the car was cut. The headbeams were left on, their long
brilliant poles of light exploding into the tall pine trees
surrounding the clearing. He heard the laughter coming
softly through the falling dust caught in the thrust of
light. The car doors opened and the laughter filled the
clearing. He must stay hidden. He was the protector. He
could see Hallelujah Bob now, he could see this man who
was his father. He could see his young girl cousin, the
flash of her white tennis shoes churning up the dust as she
walked. He knew his sister was in the backseat of the car
with the old woman. He could hear the old woman's loud
voice, her laughter went higher than all the others. Halle-

lujah Bob opened the trunk and took out his hatchet, he too was talking loudly now, every word he spoke could be heard, "We don't have to chop much wood for this. Just small fires we will make. Two years ago Toby Riddle drove his daughter up the mountain before the Dance of the Girl to light the fire of his daughter, to signal her time of the Woman to all those waiting below. Toby Riddle built his fires in the old way, four separate fires burning high. I did not see them but I heard of what happened. The fire lookout on Beckwourth Peak saw the flames leaping into the sky, he called down the alarm and up the road came every firefighting machine in the valley. Toby Riddle's daughter was so frightened at what was coming at them she ran off into the woods. When *they* finally reached Toby Riddle *they* hosed down his fires. He tried to explain it was the old way. But *they* arrested him for being the drunk. Locked him up and fined him for being the fire *bug*. The Dance of the Girl never went forward that night. It never went forward ever. So we will be careful. We will be sly. We will build our four fires in the old way. We will just build them smaller." The old woman shouted at him from the car window as he began chopping piles of wood, "Chop only green wood, green wood is the old way, its smoke will be thick and rise straight for the girl so she will have a long life, a straight long life." Hallelujah Bob kept up his own talking as he skinned the low green branches from trees, "Toby Riddle's daughter never had the Dance. There are few Dances now. There was the time when they were many. When I was the small boy the mother of my father's father told me of her Dance. She told me of how she became the woman. All these things Painted Stick told to me when I was the small boy, before she died. She had been alone then, living in the old way, in the galisdangal, far in the middle of the valley. All of the people were at the lumber mills in Elephant Head in that time, they had followed the path of the mills for what would come to them, they had followed to survive. They were all there, the people, the few that were left from the old ways. One Arm Henry was there, he that was my father, and his brother who had medicine

of the White tongue and was a big boss, Captain Rex. But
they did not keep me with them into the winter. They sent
me far into the valley to Painted Stick. Her eyes had gone
old, almost colorless, but I remember the magic of her fingers. I remember the medicine of her baskets. She wove
her magic all through the long white days. Her words
spoke through the signs woven into her baskets. She told
of the time she became the Woman. She spoke of the
fence at the Lake in the Sky, at Tahoe, and of the yellowback ring that had been passed to her in friendship. The
people thought she would die during the winter, and they
wanted to protect her. I was sent to protect her last words.
I was sent to watch the magic of her fingers. I was sent to
watch the last of the old ways die. I was the young boy
and Painted Stick died away from me while I slept. I was
not awake to keep her last fire going. I was not awake to
watch. But what was left of the old ways was dying everywhere off the land, the people who had gathered at Elephant Head to survive the winter were of the last. They
died out of the old way with the sickness of the Whites
spreading in their lungs. Their lungs were on fire. The last
of the people in those days became dead or dying. The life
was being choked from them by the sickness of the
Whites, by the *T-burkulur*. Then they were all dead. The
Whites threw kerosene onto the shacks with the bodies of
the people piling up inside. And the shacks went up in
flame, burning the snow free of the Earth in wide circles.
Then the Whites rode out to burn all the Indian peoples.
They rode their Horses into the valley of the clouds and
out to the middle where I waited next to Painted Stick
with the old ways dead in her. Their Horses shook the
Earth and *they* came all around the galisdangal. *They*
came running in with bandannas tied across their noses,
one threw me over his shoulders like an empty sack. *They*
threw blazing torches onto the galisdangal. The old way
was burned to the ground. *They* rode me off to a ranch and I
was locked in an empty grain shed until *they* took me out
right before I died and washed my skin with soap." Hallelujah Bob had all the green wood built into short piles.
"There, that should burn straight. But Toby Riddle's

daughter didn't Dance into the Woman." The old woman
laughed loud through the car window, from where he was
hiding he could see her open the door. She helped his sister out. His sister stood in the beams of the headlights, the
brilliant slash of white covered her breasts and thighs. She
was not naked like the old ways his father had spoken of,
she wore a brassiere and panties, their foreign whiteness
clashed against her skin. She held the sacred staff cut
from the water birch tree tightly in her hand, but it did
not have the red ochre band coiling brightly down the
length of its freshly peeled hard wood, it did not have the
red band, it was not a painted stick. The old woman put
her arm around the girl and squeezed her bare shoulders.
The thick wrinkle around the old woman's big laughing
mouth pulled her lips back and exposed the places where
her teeth used to be. "Listen to him girl, listen to him talk,
this man Hallelujah Bob, this man he talks just like a
man. Oh he talks about Toby Riddle's daughter did not
have the Dance of the Girl into the Woman. What he
doesn't know is," the old woman leaned her face down to
the girl, the hot breath rushing out of her old mouth,
"what this man doesn't know is Toby Riddle's daughter
had already *become* the Woman. She had *become* the
Woman long before that night. What this man doesn't
know is she was *made* the woman by at least three *different* men." The laughter rolled out of the old woman so
hard it was shaking the young girl she had her arm locked
around. "Oh listen to this man talk. I *know*. I *am* the
Woman. *You* are becoming the Woman. You *will* know. I
am older than him. He is young, he is only sixtyfive. *I* remember the old ways. I remember the days when only
women were allowed on the mountain of the fires. There
would be a man to wrestle the crooked smoke straight
into the Sky, but he was hidden, he was not seen. There
was only the girl going into the Woman, an old sister was
her guide, the younger girl who was to be raced down the
mountain. Now the father drives the girl up the mountain.
The old way is gone. The girl comes into the *Woman* in
only *one* day. She does not go without meat. She does not
fast. She does not turn her eyes from men. She does not

sleep her dying girl body on warm ashes. She does not cut
her hair. The strong staff she carries to keep her back
straight through a long life is not painted with the sacred
coil of red ochre. Your stick is not painted. But we know
you will become the *Woman*." Hallelujah Bob put his cigarette lighter to the mound of dried twigs beneath a pile
of green wood and flicked his thumb down, striking a
flame into the kindling, "Old woman, the old ways are
gone. The old ways are gone or dying." He held his lighter to the other piles so its flame caught in the twigs and
burned into green wood. "It is done." He rose and placed
the lighter carefully into his pocket and turned to the car,
his eye caught a shadow of a shape on the edge of light
thrown out from the headbeams, the shape was low and
close down in the bushes, it had gone unnoticed by the old
woman. It was his son Joe. His son had done what was
told him. He was hidden. He could protect his sister. The
old ways were gone. The new ways were uncertain. The
old woman did not know. He got in the car and slammed
the door behind him. The fires were all going. The green
wood was burning. The old woman sat against a tree and
moaned softly to the four fires in front of the girl, "Oh
flame, burn away all dirt that falls from this girl's First
Season. Oh flame, burn burn burn. We wait here flame.
We wait at the door to the Sky for your wise sign. Give us
your sign. Give us. . . . . I Give. . . I !" Her old voice
wailed. It struck at the black sky overhead. There were
people in the thrust of the headlights before the girl. Men.
Running through the trees, their heavy white bodies swag-
gering, the thick hard leather of their boots tearing the
earth up as they came pounding between the streaming
white smoke of the fires, their strong breath beating out of
their chests as they screamed into the night, "FUCK
HER!"

He saw them before the old woman. His father saw
them too. He could hear his father's shout as he jumped
from the car, "Joe! Get them Joe!" His father's hand was
still on the door handle as the full can of beer hurled at
his head struck him and brought him to his knees with the
blood running through the fingers he clutched to his face.

He wanted to run to his father, to protect him, to hide behind him. But he brought his body up from hiding and
slammed a rock into the nose of one of the white bodies
crashing into the bright lights of the car. He knocked only
the last of them down, the other four were in the light. He
ran into the light. The rock was high over his head and
he ran at them, filling the clearing with a new sound,
a cry that wrenched and twisted from his gut and cut
up his throat like a spurt of blood, a cry of war,
"AYIIIIIIIIIEEEE!" *They* were waiting for him. Before
he could bring the rock smashing down on them the
stroke of a boot hooked its leather point right between his
legs, driving his balls straight into the bone of his body.
The rock slipped from his hand as the pain sucked out of
his bowels and burst in a hollow gasp, dropping him to
the ground, his blind hands groping over the roar of blood
blasting in his groin. He felt a fist in his hair and his face
was yanked up. He could see, far and into the distance, he
could see the white face right before him. "I'm going to
kick your ass Indian!" The shout came again, far and into
the distance, the shout that was screamed right into his
face, "I'm going to kick your FUCKING ASS!" Through
the roar he could hear, he could see, far and into the distance something slipped in his flesh, but he could no longer feel. He could see the boots that kicked him walking to
his face, "Don't kick his ass Eddie." "Why not Dora?
Why not kick his ass in? Look what he done to my nose?
He damn near busted it to nothin! I'm going to kick his
ass off!" The Indian's head was jerked all the way back so
his face stared up into the night. "No Eddie let go of him.
We don't want to hurt Joe. We want him to eat shit."
"You mean *watch* it Ben!" "That's right, eat shit," the
boots moved away and the Indian's head was lowered, he
could see the Levis above the boots, the silver bullhead
belt buckle and the short Levi jacket that fit tightly over
the wide chest, the boy had short hair, trimmed to a flat
burr on top, with long greased wings on the sides combed
straight back, he was only two years older than the rest,
he was seventeen, but his hands had grown so big he
could fit one full over a man's face and twist it with the

bulk of his shoulder muscle like an orange. He tipped the beer can to his lips and drank, the excess beer running out his mouth and down his chin. He flung the can into the dust, "Where's that other beer I brung! You, old lady, old squaw, you took my beer?" The old woman looked up at him from the ground, she had her arms wrapped around her knees like she was hugging a baby, she sidled back and forth, her lips moving, but no sound could be heard, the air just sucked into the hollow of her toothless mouth. "The can's over here Ben. You threw it at the old Chief when he jumped out of his car screaming like a redass." "You tell me where it is Rick, I don't see it. These headlights are too bright." "Right there Dora, in front of the Chief," he pointed to the can glistening in the light of the headbeams. "Well yah, that's it," Ben Dora stooped and picked it up, holding it out in the light, "Why look at this, the damn things all been bashed in, this Chief must have a head carved of stone." He nudged his boot tip into the man before him, "That right Chief, you got a stone head? You must, cause that son of yours over there does, he's the dumbest dumbass bunny in our school, he can't even spell FART. They told him if he could learn how to spell FART at the end of four years of highschool they'd go ahead and give him his dip-plomma cause that's all he needs to know for an Indian; whenever he gets a job application it will say, 'WHAT CAN YOU DO?' and he just fills in, 'FART.'" He kneeled down in front of the old man, settling one knee in the dust as he pulled the sharp beer opener from his jacket, "Ain't that right Chief Fart. Ain't that how you kissied your way through life?" He punched the opener into the can, sending a white spray onto the old man's bowed head. The old man could not see through the blood in his eyes. "You don't talk much, do you Chief Fart. None of *you* talk much," he swigged his beer and pushed himself up. "Let's get this party goin! Let's start the party! We come to party!" He swaggered into the blaring white light of the car that held the girl captive, she was surrounded on everyside by the four waiting white bodies. Her brown eyes caught only on the one with the beer can, she kept her hands locked across her thighs as he came forward into the light, "You know that wasn't nice of you not to send us invites to your party Sarah Dick. We would have all been glad to come. You don't have to be so stuck-up with your Indians only parties. We don't mind rubbing asses with Indians. So we thought we'd have this little party of our own, just the four of us, and of course, *you*." "That's right Ben! It's just like you said it would be. She's just standing around in her bra and panties *waiting* for *it!*" "Now don't you get too itchy Carl. You just wait until I've held the grand opening of this little brown box," he came up before the girl and grabbed her long hair, pulling the dark face up to his and pressing his lips down on her. Her knee kicked up like a deer between his legs. He was waiting and slammed the beer can into the side of her head, knocking her to the ground. The laughter shot from his wide chest as he stooped his shoulders and his body swung around like he was in an arena, "Hey you, Carl." He pointed at the one who had the smaller girl by the neck, "You lay off that one, it's too small. You'll bust your cock in that cherry." "AWWW Ben come on, we came up here to party. She's just dying for it." "No! This is the one *we* want. This is the one we came up for," he swung back to the girl before him. "It's *her* party," his eyes glared at the girl cowed in the dust, the white cloth of her bra and panties flashed against her brown skin as she leaped up and ran before his hand yanked her flying hair and flung her back in the dust, dropping down on her with one knee pinned in her stomach as he ripped off his leather belt, jerking her arms up over her head, binding the belt around her outstretched wrists and pulling it tight. He leaned his weight down and stamped his lips on her mouth. The sharp animal bone of her teeth clamped into his flesh. He jerked his mouth away and slammed the ball of his fist into the side of her head, a small spot of blood showed in the corner of her mouth as he punched her on the other side of the head, then hooked his hand under her bra and ripped it off, her brown breasts spilling out in the light beneath him. "FUCK HER BEN!" He unbuttoned his pants, pushing them below his knees, the needlepoints of his boots digging into the dirt as he kept the balanced weight of his body pushed into the narrow hips trying to buck him off. He stabbed both knees between her legs, jamming her thighs open, getting his hand in under the panties and up through the elastic. He tore the panties in his fist and stuffed them in the clamp of her mouth. "FUCK HER DORA!" He got one hand pinched around her throat as the other pushed the stiff white bone of his body up between her legs, the needlepoints of his books scratching into the earth as his knees cocked up, pumping him deep between her twisting thighs. The breath broke out of his chest, "Shit, fucking an Indian is like fucking a snake!" "FUCK HER BEN. FUCK HER BRAINS OUT!" He had the full weight of his white body in her. The brown body was pinned to the earth beneath him as the muscle of his white ass pumped up and down in the brilliant light of the headbeams. The heavy breath blasting out of his wide chest blew with a snort from his nostrils, obscuring the whimpering in her throat. He pulled off. She was released. But her brown body kept thrashing as if his weight was still in her, trying to throw off the damp whiteness gleaming between her thighs. The bulk of his shoulders stooped as he stood with the hot breath still snorting from his nostrils, he swung into the full glare of the headlights, "Who wants seconds!" He pulled his pants up and leaned against the bumper of the car and watched as the others threw their full weight into the brown body. He laughed and shouted into the thumping rising dust, clapping his hands together until the last man trotted off.

The fires had all grown cold. There had been silence for a long time. No one was crying. He could stand up, the pain between his legs was a bright hard knot, he could not feel its center, but as he walked toward his father he kept going down in a limp on one knee. The old woman had tied a red bandanna around the wound of Hallelujah Bob's head and he stood before the bright lights of the car with his wounded head held high. He stopped before his father and looked up, "Hallelujah Bob, we must drive down from this mountain together. Your head needs a

doctor." His father did not even look him in the face as
he turned around and slapped him full on the cheek,
"Never! The people have medicine for my wounds. Never! We are too strong for this, it has happened before.
There are the old ways. The girl will have her Dance. The
Girl of the Dance will race the small girl to the foot of
the mountain. I will not drive her, it is the way, the sacred
stick will make the Girl's weak legs strong. The Girl of
the Dance will defeat the small girl in the race, she will
defeat her old self, she will come the Woman. She has acted true to the ways. She will have her a Dance." He
looked at his daughter who stood naked before him, her
brown body was bruised, her young flesh was worn within, but she leaned tall on the strength of the sacred stick.
The water glistened in his eyes, but did not fall, "Go!"

The Girl ran. Swiftly into the night she disappeared;
the small girl running far behind.

The people were waiting in front of the big room. They
sat beneath the stars on battered orange crates. They had
seen the fires on the mountain. The fires had spoken the
truth of the Sign. Now the fires were dead and the people
had lit their own fires, awaiting the Girl to come the
Woman off the dark mountaintop. Paint cans full of water
had been dumped on the ground to keep the dust down
from the Dance of the Girl. They waited beneath the stars
to dance. Then they saw the headlights of the car, and
way before its line of light they saw the Girl come running out of darkness; she ran far ahead of the small girl.
The women rose up into a circle on the dance ground and
the Girl ran into their center holding the sacred stick high
over her head. The women joined hands around the Girl,
the power of their chant rising into the black night as
their dance shook the ground, "Hé wine, ho wí ne, he wí
ne; ho wí na, hé wine, ho wí na." When the stars burned
at the top of the Sky the people gathered into the big
room, the lantern swung from the rafter over the long
feast table. Hallelujah Bob stood before the people with
the red bandanna wrapped around the wound of his head
and spoke of how the Girl had acted true to the ways and

come into the new day of her time. She had come through
the First Season a Woman. He asked all his friends who
saw her fires on the mountaintop to come and share the
first happiness of her time, to feast and dance into the
new morning. He spoke of how the Dance was being held
because the Indians always had it. He spoke long of the
old ways beneath the swinging lantern as the people feast-
ed on store cakes and shining cans of pork and beans. The
brother of the Girl sat on an orange-crate tilted against
the wall, he did not feast, but drank from the bottle that
passed through the hands of his friends until the light in
his head grew stronger than the hollow pain between his
legs. He was pulled outside into the circle of the Dance,
moving in the chant of the people, locked into the swaying movement until the Sun washed the night away and
was ready to break over the Earth. His sister was brought
again from the big room to face the rising Sun. She wore
a white slip and held her head high as the old woman
streaked white ash from her hairline to her chin and told all
the people this Girl would have no headaches, then the mark
of the ash was made on the Girl's arms, "Have strength to
carry many babies." The ashes were smeared on her
calves, "Have the power to work all day without having to
sit down." The old woman rubbed the Girl's stomach with
bits of sagebrush, "Have no cramps. Do not complain."
The sagebrush was sprinkled over her head, "Be smart.
Go to highschool. Get a job. Do not quit." The bits of
sagebrush were gathered from around her feet and mixed
with pork and beans, the Girl took a mouthful and spit it
to the the ground. "Do not be a pig. Go without. Give
your food to others." As the Sun broke over the Earth the
old woman poured a tin bucket of water over the Girl's
head, "The Girl dies out of you. You have come the
Woman. Go to school. Get a job. Get married." The Sun
broke down over all the people's heads as the Girl tossed
her gift of nickels and dimes wrapped in bright strips of
cloth tied to sagebrush twigs into their midst. She walked
back into the big room and sat at the long empty feast table on an orange-crate. She drank a cup of black coffee,
her head fell on her outstretched arm. Her aching body

lay slumped on the orange-crate, outside it was a monday morning, the people were wedged together standing in tight groups in the back of their old pickups, the Sun beating down on the faded word stamped in steel across the tailgates, FORD. They started their engines and drove out across the land.

The barbed metal wire singing through the Indian's gloved hands stopped. The sun fell behind the earth. The air became cool. Odus stood up from the work, the sweat cutting right through his blue shirt, "It's about time we call it a day Joey, we've got about half of it laid up to-day." He leaned against the raw wood of a post they had just set and looked back up the line of fence disappearing into the falling darkness, "Look at that, straighter than a baby's smile. I say we quit Joey, how about you?"

The Indian followed Odus' gaze along the long strands of barbed wire, "Not any light. We have to quit." But he did not move, he did not even pull the thick leather gloves from his sweating hands. Where the day faded into night along the sharp line of the fence the sound of bells grew out of the air, coming down the evening distance of the road.

Odus heard the sound too. His eyes could just begin to make out the swaying shapes of the cows following with bowed heads one after the other in the dry slot of ditch between the fence and the hard black shell of the road, "Must be Ben Dora's daughter with the milk cows."

The sharp metal sound of the clanging cowbells was close and familiar in the Indian's ears as the heavy beasts swaggered before him, the teats of their swollen udders dripping milk to the earth. The slow horse came behind the overburdened beasts, its gray hide blurred into the dying light so it floated like a ghost. The girl was mounted on the gray back, her white legs sticking out below the blanket slung loosely around her body swaying in the movement of beasts before her.

"Hi-you Missy," Odus called up to her.

The skin of the blond face turned in the direction of the words, her eyes seeing only another field, fencepost, old man, Indian, fencepost, field. Her blond face turned back to the bells in the lead. The two men could now see the thick welts exposed on the flesh of her thighs and legs sticking below the blanket, but she was beyond them, the long fall of her slapping sunwhite hair already beginning to fade in the dusk as she was pulled behind in the rhythm of the cows.

"That kind of thing stops me inside," Odus lowered his head in the darkness. Ben Dora whips her so bad she can't stand nothin tighter on her skin than that horse blanket. Ben Dora beats everybody that bad. He beats that girl, his very own daughter. He beats his wife, all his kids, his dogs. Somebody ought to beat him, beat him with a stick, you don't want to skin your fists on the likes of him. The only thing you ever hear Ben Dora bellow is, 'My people were pioneers! My people owned this goddam sunk valley before the Indians! This is my valley! A pioneer made his own Law. A pioneer answers to NOBODY!' His people never owned anything, they always worked for somebody else, the only reason they ended up in this here valley is because they couldn't go any further, because the Pacific Ocean starts in another hundred miles, and the only reason they ever got here was because they were kicked out of the last place they were in, and the only reason they *weren't* kicked out of here in the beginning is because they would have been kicked out into the middle of the Ocean. California is full of pioneers who were kicked out of every place they ever set foot in and finally couldn't be kicked any further. So the only thing Ben Dora's people had left was to beat each other up. His father beat him and Ben went to school and got thrown out before graduating for beating everybody up. So he got married so he could beat his wife, and when he got tired of that he had some kids so he could beat them. The oldest two already run away and were put in reform school, so now he has all his beating to do on the girl. That kind of thing stops me inside, somebody ought to beat him with a stick." He raised his face and looked around in the dying light, the darkness gathered about his head in a terrible rainbow, his old eyes wide as an owl's, "Let's go home Joey."

The Indian freed his hot hands from the leather gloves, letting the cool air calm his stinging fingers. He gathered all the iron tools he had worked with through the day and placed them carefully in the bed of the pickup, then climbed into the front with his friend. The engine shook to a start and the glare of the headlights bounced back at him off the road's black shell as the truck rolled slowly, the white moths coming quietly out of the night, crashing their soft bodies against the clear glass of the windshield until the road home could hardly be seen. He heard Odus talking again, "We got most of that fence today. Tomorrow's sunday so we'll get back to it on monday. I'll pick you up at the same time, at six." The truck rolled by a house, its headbeams firing up the yard. Through the moth splattered windshield the Indian could see a man stalking in front of the house, his shoulders stooped, the bullneck swinging his head back and forth as he bellowed, "WOMAN! Get your ass moving and open the goddamn door!" He stood up in front of the door and began kicking it with the needlepoint of his boot. "Get your ass MOVING!" He stepped back from the door and flung the empty whiskey bottle in his hand through the window of his own house. The shattering glass could be heard just above the engine of the pickup as it rolled beyond the house. In the tight cab of the truck the Indian heard his friend's words again, "That kind of thing stops me inside. Ben Dora should be killed. Beat with a stick. You don't want to skin your hands." Then the words stopped and there was only the sound of the engine, the sidelight from the headbeams lighting up a barn and small house along the road. "Well, here we are Joey." The pickup pulled over and the Indian climbed down. He looked up to his friend in the darkness of the cab, the owl eyes blinked back at him, "Well Joey, another day another buck. All a buck buys a man is another day."

The pickup drove off into darkness. The Indian opened the door of the small barn and led his horse out into the cool night. He rubbed his palm against her neck, then ran her around in a wide circle, around and around, following in his own trail. He brought her back in the barn and slowly kneaded her body before forking hay into her feed trough. He locked the barn and went into the room of his house. The rabbit was waiting for him like a cat, hunched up before the open back door with its ears laid straight back and its nose twitching at the green odor of alfalfa he had fed the horse coming off his hands. He took the bottle of whiskey off the dresser top and yanked out the cork. He could hear the gulping of his throat in the silence of the room as he drank. He waited for the light to come up through his blood like the beating song of ancient Birds and fill his head. He waited, listened to the blood pounding against his temples, then stumbled across the room to the open door and looked up at the swirling stars, they dazzled his eyes and he took another swig off the bottle then came back in and took up the old black leather accordion hanging by its straps on the chair next to his bed. He hitched the accordion onto him so the straps formed a leather X across his back. His callused fingers bent and ran over the cracks worn in the dull glimmering of the mother-of-pearl keys, pressing the WRECK OF NUMBER NINE full into the room. The loud music swaggered out the door and up into the swirling stars.

They came across the mountains. *They* came in a big car. *They* were big, like their car. *They* wore white shirts with narrow ties knotted up around their elbow smooth necks. The Indian watched their big car come out of the mountains and into the valley. The car came straight at him down the black road. He watched it pull off onto the dirt in front of his house, little shots of loose dust puffing off the back wheels. *They* killed the engine of the car and stood before the one room house, their heads jerking in circles as *they* looked at the house, the pine trees riding out from behind it up to the mountain, out across the valley to the distant birds skimming the low drifting steam white clouds. There was a look on their faces he recognized, he had seen it many times before. It was the same frozen look on the face of a squirrel run over flat on the highway. One of the men peered beneath the rim of his blunt machine-shaped felt hat with a clipped pheasant's feather tucked beneath the slick band, "Mister Joseph Birdsong?"

The Indian stuck the stiff stub of a dry piece of weed between his teeth and rammed it through into his mouth, sucking at the sweet lump of tartar he dislodged, "I'm Joe Birdsong."

"Oh fine. Do you mind if I remove my hat?"

"I don't own the outdoors."

The man took off his felt hat and wiped the halo of tiny sweat beads off his forehead. "May we come up?"

"I guess."

"Good, then we can do business." The two men followed the Indian in through the open doorway and set their briefcases among the clutter on the table. The one with his hat off turned the corners of his pale lips up in a smile, "I well suppose you know why we are here?" He heard the Indian's words coming back to him but he paid no attention, the calculating blink of his eyes was registering the dim twinkle of the cracked mother-of-pearl keys on the accordion next to the bed, he walked over and looked at the wall covered with photographs of horses torn from magazines, horses bucking and galloping, horses wedged in between the fading photographs of women, all of the women big, heaving and moving, running across wooden bridges or twirling ropes over their heads at rodeos. He turned around, "What was that you said Mister Birdsong? I didn't quite catch it."

"I said I know why you're here."

"We are here because you neglect to answer our letters, an oversight on your part, I'm sure. We know you receive the letters because they are all registered, and you have signed your name for them. We have proof of your signature, we know you are *receiving*. We think you misunderstand our purpose. We want to work hand in hand with you. We want to be your friend."

The Indian looked into the eyes of the man as he spoke, he looked at the other man who still had on his hat, there was a metal pin stuck to the front of the hat, it was the miniaturized likeness of two golf clubs crossed like swords, "Can I get you a glass of water?"

". . . we are only interested in your friendship and personal advancement, and, ah, why thank you yes, it is a hot morning, water would be fine." He took the glass of water offered him and drank it clean, "Now Allen, perhaps you could give Mister Birdsong the Presentation?"

"Why of course, what a pleasure," the man with the hat straightened his tie and brought out a key from his coat pocket. He placed his briefcase on the bed and unlocked it, then snapped the lid up with two loud cracks. He removed a brochure off the top, unfolding its large creases until it was flattened and smoothed out nearly the length of the bed. Spreading across the top of the glossy paper in high red bold letters was RESORT MOUNTAIN LAND PROPERTIES—A NEW CONCEPT IN LIVING! The man pointed with the shiny silvertip of his ballpoint pen to the first big colorful box on the brochure, "Here you may recognize a comprehensive aerial photograph of the Sierra Valley the way it is today, the highest true valley in all of the Sierra Nevada Mountains. It's flat, a few lightly traveled roads, a small saw-mill, three little towns, and scattered about several ranch houses with out buildings, nothing of any importance really." He moved his silvertip over the slick surface, "Here you have an artist's concept of an improved Sierra Valley. A concept of dynamic year-round living, innovative planning, interlocking recreational usage, and all this in natural balance with the existing landscape and its wildlife." He moved the silvertip across the next four squares, "This is the airstrip, and the causeway leading from it to here, the shopping complex with restaurant and bowling alley, here you have your country club and tennis courts and olympic size pools. You may not be aware of this Mister Birdsong, but our environmentalists specialists feel that since the Sierra Valley is marshy on its northerly periphery, an area which incidentally is the headwaters of the Feather River, a river which extends three hundred twisting miles to the Pacific Ocean, studies conclude a feasible lake with fortynine million cubic feet of water in this area, flooding over a land distance of two thousand acres, providing a yearround recreational diversion, affording boating, waterskiing, fishing and appropriate snack food areas. Here, you can see the wonderful sketch of the Marina on the south side of the lake, right at the end of Shoreview Drive, and here," he grabbed the two ends in his hands and flipped the brochure over in a current of its own wind, showing one vast colored sketch of the valley's center covered by a city of huge painted metal boxes surrounded by swaying palm trees. He stood back smiling, pointing his silvertip at the large glare of paper, the hot room popping out beads of sweat beneath the rim of his hat. "This is what it is *all* about. A city of MOBILE HOMES a Mile High In The Sky At The Top Of The Sierra Nevada. Thirty thousand *yearround* residents, twenty thousand second *vacation* homes. This isn't just any MOBILE HOMES city, this is bigger than *anything* in Florida, even bigger than *anything* in San Diego. MOBILE HOMES are the wave of the future, inexpensive to buy, inexpensive to maintain, taxes are next to nothing. Why, in the year 2,000, there won't be *anything* but MOBILE HOMES. Just check land prices here in California if you want to see what land prices in the other states will be tomorrow. California is the future today. And we think the future spells M-O-B-I-L-E. MOBILE HOMES."

The Indian leaned over and put his face close against the palm trees swaying on the glossy paper, then he stepped back and looked straight at the man with the hat, "There aint no palm trees in the Sierra Nevada."

"There will be."

"That's correct Mister Birdsong, they will be trucked up and placed in the ground, already thirtyfive feet high. What do you say? Do we have a deal?"

"What is it you want?"

"It's not what we want but what we *want* to give."

"And what's that?"

"Money Mister Birdsong, you just give the word and our money will cascade on your head. We have enough money to cascade on the whole State of California, to cascade on the *whole* West." He snapped open his own briefcase and laid some print filled papers back on top, "Would you care to sign?"

"Sign what?"

"Sign away your land."

The Indian felt the blood pumping in his ears, he went to the accordion on the chair and ran his fingers lightly over the broken mother-of-pearl, he pressed down on one key and it gave a clipped squawk, "Get out."

"Mister Birdsong, what we offer is reasonable and just. Don't dam up all the money, give the word and it will cascade on your head."

The Indian walked to the briefcase and grabbed the papers in his fist, tearing them down the middle.

The man opened the briefcase and took out another set of identical papers, "Would you care to sign Mister Birdsong?"

The Indian moved to the open doorway, he leaned his head back in the heat beginning to pile up in the late morning, he took a long breath of hot air into his lungs, coming down the straight black road he could see the Deputy Sheriff's car.

"If you think you are not alone in trying to stop rightful and orderly economic progress in this valley you are mistaken. You are working a severe hardship on all your neighbors, there's already considerable bad talk and ill feeling against your unreasonable stubbornness. Don't you know you are being manipulated by two men who want this valley to remain *forever* an underdeveloped wasteland, two men who are enemies of what made this State of California great. Men who would rather see cows than cars when they look out their window. You will shortly find yourself standing without your friends, they will not be allowed to plunder a great vision of development. Hello Deputy Sheriff Davies . . ."

The Indian turned back to the open doorway just in time to see the man with the badge pinned over his heart lean the full weight of his melon face in through the door and shut one big eye in a slow wink at the man with the briefcase on his lap, "Good morning Mister Julin, I'm sorry I wasn't here alot sooner but I just got the call over the radio from your head office over at Tahoe and they said you might need me."

"Yes, Deputy Sheriff, we may. You know Mister Bird-song of course?"

"Sure I know Joe, great deer tracker, aren't you Joe," he let the heavy skin of his eyelid fall down in another wink.

"Well you may be needed here to bear public witness to what is legally about to transpire, I hope not, I hope we are all *just* with one another." He turned his face back to the Indian and ran his hand through his short hair, "*Just* with one another Mister Birdsong. As you know from our last letter my company is offering to pay for this property of four and one half acres $42,000 a *just* price. I have now been authorized by Resort Mountain Land Properties to make a final offer for the sum of $59,000. Do you accept?"

The Indian looked at the man with the badge over his heart blocking the sun in the doorway, "Get them out. They are trespassing."

The man with the briefcase put the papers back inside and withdrew a letter, he snapped the briefcase shut and stood up, pointing the letter out before him like a gun, "I am sorry. I was afraid you wouldn't be reasonable. I am serving you with this legal notice." He crossed the room and set the envelope on top of the accordion, "Sheriff, you are bearing witness to the legal presentation of this subpoena." He looked at the Indian standing against the wall covered with photographs of bucking horses and running women, "Mister Birdsong, in case you do not read I will explain to you the precise contents of this letter. You are subpoenaed to appear at the County Court at Sierra City in two week's time to supply legal documentation substantiating your legal ownership and title to this property. You may find this a difficult task as this property was supposedly given by the Madson family to your father in 1922, whereupon he supposedly *gave* it to you. If you cannot prove ownership to the Court's legal satisfaction, title to the land will revert to the County. Good day in court Mister Birdsong."

The Indian pulled his hands from his pockets, he could not open them from the fists they made, he jammed them into the chest of the man standing in front of his father's accordion, knocking him across the room into the weight of the Deputy Sheriff, he dropped the muscle of his shoulder into the man's stomach and pushed him against the Sheriff and out the door. He grabbed the other man by his narrow necktie and flung him around toward the door.

"Hey fella, easy, we don't mean any harm."

He brought the sole of his boot flat into the man's ass, kicking him out into the dust. The other man was just getting up from the ground spanking the dust from his pants as the Sheriff came back and tossed the melon weight of his face in through the doorway, "Birdsong, you're in your own house here, you're protected, but the moment you step out on the road in front you're on County Property, and on County Property *I'm* the Law, and *I'll* be waiting for you!"

The man came up behind the bulk of the Sheriff, still spanking the dust from his pressed pants, "Mister Birdsong, when you go to prove your right to this property, the burden of proof will fall on your father's first assumption of title. You will find there is no title of ownership. But more than that you will find even if there were it would be null and void. You see, your father assumed this land in 1922, that was two years before the Indians were made citizens of the United States. So your father was *not* a citizen when he assumed the land, and it is illegal for a non-citizen to vote or own land in America. It is the Law of the Land, you don't have a right to own property if you're not a citizen. Beyond that Mister Birdsong, you cannot prove you are your father's son, you see, there is no birth certificate for your father, your father is legally a non-person." He turned with the Sheriff and walked back to his big car. "Mister Birdsong," he shouted before getting in, "I suggest you do your homework. Your father did not exist!"

The road was deserted. The surrounding mountains were worn down to bare white rock and gnarled black scrub. The sky was empty. The sun was stuck solid above the thinwhite clouds. Through the blurred waves of heat beating off the straight black road came a pickup, its sound being sucked off into vastness around it. The pickup rolled to a stop at the intersection of the three black roads, an Indian jumped off the back-bed and the truck drove on, almost soundless, the only noise coming from the small stones popping beneath the heavy wheels. The Indian stood in the silence. He scraped his boot on the black asphalt to strike a sound, but there was hardly a noise. He looked up and down the roads, and saw nothing. He slapped his hands together but the muffled sound drifted off. He stood in the middle of the road and shouted, he could hear his own voice inside him, but outside he could only hear a faint echo coming up around him. He was alone where the ground had been slashed open and laid bare with all the excess of the empty sky fusing into it, forming one endless space of earth and sky. The Indian looked at the sign on the white post punched in next to the road. He ran his hand through the dusty black letters HALLELUJAH JUNCTION U.S. 395. He was on the right road. He sat on the dirt hump of the road shoulder, and waited. His eyes could see through the heat, he watched the barren black and white mountains, he thought he could hear a ringing deep in their distance, low and insistent. Then it was gone. He began pitching small stones out onto the hot black asphalt. He stopped. He heard the ringing again. It was coming out of the blur in the far canyons. The ring became higher, whirling to a steady whine, it was coming back at him from all the stony canyons. He could feel the vibration coming through his boots. Then he jumped up and turned away from the canyons, looking way back down to where the straight black road joined the smudge of hot sky. He saw a silver glint. The glint grew larger, shining brilliantly back at him like a star, the high whine filling up all the space around him. The whine became the strained pitch of a screaming engine. He stepped back off the road. The shining silver star became a Bus, its huge metal carcass shaking the earth beneath his boots, the blunt blue front with the banner across its face RENO SPECIAL. He could see the blur of the long running silver dog painted

on the side, above it the heads of people swinging around
to stare out at him through small squared windows before
the Bus flailed its black exhaust in the air around him, the
force of its hot tailwind almost slapping him to the
ground. The ground kept vibrating under his boots long
after the Bus had disappeared over the horizon of the
hard black road. The Indian waited for the silence to
come again. He watched the sun slip in the sky and fall
through the thinwhite line of clouds. He heard a slight
disturbance in the air and turned around and stuck his
thumb out. A pickup pulled to a stop in front of him, the
dusty window rolling down and a brown face peering out
from under a sweatstained straw hat, "Where you going
to?"

"Reno."

"You're on the right road buddy. Get on in. Up here in
front, the back is full of alfalfa bales."

The Indian got in the cab and it was filled with music.
The tiny speaker in the dashboard pushed out a loud
sound that slipped out the windows as the truck rolled
down the road between the scorched black and white
mountains, the bleached sky blurred in front of him. The
driver reached down and turned the radio volume knob to
the top. The Indian took off his hat and rubbed his head.
The hot air coming through the window slapped the smile
on his face as the music flowed over his body and
twanged and shouted in the metal cab:

> *"You got tiiiiied in with*
> *the wrong man*
> *bay-bee.*
> *He roped you dooooooown*
> *and broke your*
> *har-art.*
>
> *You got hiiiiiitched*
> *on to a wiiiiiiiild*
> *horse runnnnnnnnning,*
> *he up and left you*
> *crying at the*
> *staaaaaaaaaaaaaaaart."*

The driver threw his empty beer bottle out the open window, it crashed soundlessly on the hard road in the wake of the music. He handed the Indian two beer bottles to open. "What's your name," he shouted over the wailing music, taking the beer bottle and jamming its neck in his mouth.

"Joe!"

"Joe huh? What blood of Indian?"

"Washo!"

"Washo huh, no shit! I thought so! I'm half Shoshone, no shit! Name's Jingle Balls! See that!" He waved his beer bottle out the window and pounded his horn at the one gas pump standing alone in front of a wind blasted low gray building with a red plastic windmill spinning on its roof, the silver sign painted in its hub glowed *BUSY BEE BAR—SLOTS!—CARDS!—GIRLS!* "We're in Nevada now! Right over the border! That's a famous place! They have a small airstrip on the other side, rich guys fly in from California, fuck the whores, then fly home for dinner with the wife and kids, no shit, it's a world famous place, very expensive whores, all white girls, three of them are blonde, no shit! But hey Joe, up in Tri-County they have a better deal yet, they built this Cat-House right on the spot where three counties come together, that way if one of the counties raids them they just run over to the other side of the house. No shit! You're in Nevada now! No shit! You ever been in Reno?"

"No!"

"Greatest town in the world, there's always Big Doin's in Reno! Reno is where we pay our dues. Gambling! A man has to gamble, no shit, I believe a dog has fleas sometimes just to forget he's a dog. Gambling will cure what ails you. Look on up ahead. Look on up at that!" He pointed through the dusty bugs piled up on the windshield at the golden arch flared across the street:

RENO NEVADA THE BIGGEST LITTLE CITY IN THE WORLD

The truck skidded to a stop at the red light. Through the golden arch leading into the City the Indian looked straight down the neon canyon of the street. The towering layers of neon lights shone and glittered in broad daylight, giving the long shimmering street a sense of timelessness, making the sun still hung high in the sky seem a fake hot moon. The red light changed and the pickup drove through the golden arch into the blazing reality of the street. The stacked rows of gambling halls and hotels all melted together, their large brilliant fronts opening into the broad street, their red rugs running right out of the casinos over the sidewalk to the edge of the gutters clogged with waste from the herds of people swirling in and out of the vast halls and back and forth across the street through the pounding thunder of the thousands of metal slot machines churning up the millions of metal coins. "What do you think of Her?" Jingle Balls shouted, his voice wedged flat between the loud music in the cab and the roar outside.

The Indian sucked out the rest of his beer and jammed the bottle under the seat, the flowing neon glare of white light burned its reflection in his brown eyes, "She's Big."

"She's *awful* Big!"

The pickup floated in the tide of traffic, all the cars caught the swirling colors on their metal hulls, the sound of their horns honking at the molten flows of light, metal and flesh jumped in the electric air. Down the street far as the Indian could see the lightning life of neon signs higher than redwood trees scorched the day: 1000 SLOTS! PLAY PLAY PLAY! PLAY KENO! GIRLS! PLAY BLACK-

JACK! FREE PLAY THE WHEEL OF FORTUNE!
POKER! WIN! FREE! GIRLS! PLAY! FREE! WIN!!!

Jingle Balls stamped his boots on the floor in time to
the music bleating from his radio and the horns screaming
in the throbbing air, "Joe, where you goin?"

"Out to old Indian town, my cousin Juke is there."

"Juke! You mean Juke the Washo?"

"Yah sure, he lives with his folks out there."

"No shit! Juke is a pal of mine. I've spent many nights
Honkey Tonkin with Juke. He's a Honker. I'll take you to
him."

The pickup turned off the street toward the mountains
of the Desert, the City ended as suddenly as it began, giving itself back up to the hard earth around it. The truck
drove away from the tall buildings of light throbbing in
the air, bumping down a back road cluttered on both sides
with wheelless hulks of sun blistered automobiles, smoke-
stacks were cut in the metal roofs, through the dusty windows children could be seen sitting on the blanket covered
springs of the seats, they ate from old tin cans shiny from
use, other children stood along the dusty side streets,
watching for the occasional car to pass, watching out
across the Desert to the mountains lost in the spotted heat
of sun. The road in front of the pickup turned to dirt,
more cars were propped up on wooden blocks, their wheel
axles rusted and exposed to the sun. Some of the cars had
small trailers next to them with tilting mailboxes in front,
their glassless windows boarded over, the gay color metal
siding bleached out with streaks of rotting rust scars running down the sides. Everywhere the fingers of TV aerials
poked into the dim blue sky. The aerials stuck up off the
wheeless cars, off the trailers, and off the few houses
banged together from broken sections of highway billboards. The pickup drove through the short dusty streets
and along the irrigation ditch running far into a green
square distance where a rancher's alfalfa field was being
soaked. Along the ditch a few old women looked up at the
passing truck, bright bandannas tied around their noses to
keep out the dust, then they bent back to their work, the
long cloth of their baggy dresses reaching to the ground as

they cut armfuls of straight strong willows to weave their baskets. The truck came to a stop in front of one of the trailers. The two men got out and banged on the tin door.

"Hurry up and come in!" The door flung open and they jumped in, the small woman pulling the door shut behind them. The woman looked up at them, her brown old face was shrunken, the wrinkles of her cheeks caved in two deep holes, but the liquid sparkle of her brown eyes was clear as running water. "This dust is awful. Always the dust, it keeps coming into the trailer no matter what I do. I can't hang my wash outside, the dust makes it dirtier in two minutes. I have to hang it in here," she waved her skinny arms around at the clothes strung from sagging ropes all the way to the end of the cluttered trailer. "Well, this is better than out there. I'm sorry you boys missed Juke, he went over to Sparks to see about a job in a feed-store."

"Aunt Ida, I am Joe Birdsong."

The old woman looked at the man in the cowboy hat with the sides rolled down to the front in a point. She placed her hand on the scar of his cheek. "You *are* the son of Hallelujah Bob." She wrapped her arms around the man and drew her old body up tight, laying her trembling cheek against his chest. "How are the people? How is your sister Sarah Dick?"

"We are all good."

"Did you get the two dollars I sent you last Christmas?"

"Yes Aunt Ida, Sarah Dick sends you her prayers."

"Joe Birdsong," she pushed herself away and looked again into his face. "You and my Juke are the same age. Johnson and your father used to go into the Desert to-gether, they would stay all nights and all days, eating Pey-ote and dancing their dreams. I remember that. I remem-ber their dancing." She hugged him around the waist and took his hand, "Come, Johnson will want to lay eyes on you." She pulled him into the one other room, a television was set up on an empty fruit box, its cabinet had been stripped away and the plug was spliced into a car battery sitting on the floor. The black and white image of the television flashed before the old man sitting on the worn couch. "Johnson, this is the son of Hallelujah Bob."

The old man rose slowly, his body was short and his wide round face showed its strong lines beneath the stubby rim of the grey hat. He took the young man's hand in his own and felt the hard yellowstone ring on one of the fingers, he looked back into the man's face for a long time. He took a pack of cigarettes from his vest pocket, "Yes, you are of Hallelujah Bob. You wear the yellowback ring. Do you use tobacco?" He lit a cigarette and sucked the blue smoke down in his lungs.

"Yes."

He held the cigarette up to Birdsong and watched him smoke. "You use tobacco well. What brings you to us?"

"*They* say my father did not exist. *They* say there is no birth certificate, no legal record."

"Is this for his land they say this?"

"Yes, they say he was not a citizen when it became his."

"This *they* say often. It is one of their *ways*."

"I have come here to tell you of these things."

The old man took the cigarette back and sucked on the red ash until it almost burned his lips, "*They* do not know he has record of his being. Long ago as a boy he was taken to the Indian school by Carson City. There he has record. There you can get what you need. There they will understand. Tomorrow you make this journey. Now you will sit with me. We will speak to one another and use tobacco. Then you will go to the Westerner Bar at six o'clock and meet Juke. He is there everyday when the sun is low. But come, sit with me, we will talk of Hallelujah Bob and we will pass the tobacco."

The pickup parked in front of the Westerner Bar and the two men jumped down, they could hear the loud music slipping out the open door and into the street with a bang. They went in.

"Hey, look at this! It's Jingle Balls," one of the Indians in dark sunglasses at the counter spun around on his bar stool and pointed his beer bottle at the two men coming through the door. "Jingle Balls-Jingle Balls. Jingle all the way!"

"Juke! No shit! It's good to see you. I heard you were in Sparks this morning. You have any luck?"

Juke looked down through his sunglasses at the white snapbuttons on his red cowboy shirt, "None. Same as always. Me and Lucky Strike here, the two of us went together. *Nothin.*"

"Well you can always go out to the Desert ranches and clear brush for two-bits an hour."

"Whhheeeeeee Fuck. You sure know how to kick a man when he's down Jingle. No thanks, I'm not your brush clearing kind. I had a good job once as a log bucker in a lumber camp and I won't take less. *They* won't make me eat *their* shit."

"Guess who I pick up hitchhiking out near Hallelujah Junction? Guess who this guy here is?" He threw his arm around Birdsong, "Guess who he is?"

"Well it's a lucky bet to say he's Washo, I can tell *that.*"

"He's your cousin Joe!"

"You're kiddin! Joe! From over in the valley. Man, I haven't seen you since we were small kids, it was out at the rodeo in Winnemucca, we couldn't have been more than ten." He jumped down off the barstool and gave Birdsong a strong hug. "This is great, really something. Hey Tim, bring a cold beer for my cousin from over the hill in Sierra Valley! Where'd you get this guy, Jingles?"

"I told you, Hallelujah Junction, right there where the Beckwourth Pass comes out."

"Joe, you been by the house to see Johnson?"

"I stayed the afternoon, he talked of the old ways."

"He knows too. He remembers every buck deer he's ever killed. He's not like some who never hunted or did nothing, you can believe everything he tells you. Nowadays you get a lot of talk from people who never did nothin' but hang around camp in the old days. Johnson did it all, and most of it was with your father, Hallelujah Bob. Johnson even has some Government allotment land up in the mountains, but he won't tell anybody where it is so they can cheat him out of it. That's what happens to most. They're cheated out of the only acre or two they have left from the days when it used to be all theirs. Joe, you know what I'm going to show you? I'm going to show you Reno tonight. I'm going to show you a good time. We're going to go Honkin. You see this beautiful Stetson hat I got on, aint it somethin', I'll show you how to get one too."

"You better watch your City cousin Joe," Jingle Balls stuck a finger into the foam of his beer. "When he goes Honking you're liable to wind up out on North Virginia Street in some motel room with a gang of old ladies."

"Whhhheeeee Fuck, Jingle, you been with me. You know the game! It's a lucky bet Joe, listen, times have changed, we Indians can stay out at night, no more Sundown Ordinance for us, hah. So what do you think I'm going to do? Do you think I'm going to let a couple dozen lonely ladies get a feel under the Blackjack table and make twenty bucks and up a night, or bus dishes fifteen hours a day over at Harrah's Casino? There's all kinds of talk about the Indian being *natural*, well I'll tell you what that means. *Surviving* is being natural! Let's start Honkin! Tim, more beers and a sloe-gin for Lucky Strike here, he likes it because it's cheap and sweet. It's a lucky bet. Let's Honk! I would rather see a man be drunk and singing than sober and silent. Honk!"

Juke led the way through the crowd, his red shirt flashing a signal easy to follow. He pushed his body between the people flooding through the swinging small doors into the big room until he ended up flattened against the Coke machine by the ticket counter, "This is a good place, we can see what's coming from here. What do you think Lucky Strike, this depot is filled with Honkers tonight. I don't want to miss a shot, not with my cousin Joe to show off for."

"It's Friday night. About quarter after seven, that means the Oakland Specials should be in."

"Listen Lucky, there are so many other Honkers in here if I get split off don't let Joe go into Harrah's. Wait a minute, hear that loudspeaker, why don't these people shut up when the loudspeaker is talking."

"SPECIAL FROM OAKLAND ARRIVING GATE 4 IN TWO MINUTES."

Jingle pressed himself against the Coke machine to protect his feet from being crushed by the crowd shoving across the cement floor through the candy and gum wrappers, "What's going with Harrah's, Juke? I've never been hurt there."

"Well you know Jimmy the Feather, two weeks back he was drunk and Honkin in there, he was doing *three* Specials at once and they bounced him out in the alley, beat him up so bad around the head his mother had to come and get him, of course he's never been the same after that. And he was only 21."

"No shit. I knew they was down on Honkers, but not that down."

Lucky Strike threw the stub of his cigarette to the floor and bashed it out with his boot, "They're down on *Indian* Honkers."

Juke nodded his head at Birdsong. "That's true, I've seen uptown white pimps working the circuit all night and never be touched. We're not pimps! There's none of *us* in this town who would do that. We all remember the old days when the Red Hats used to hold their big conventions here, banging their drums, painting themselves up like *they* was the Indians, parading and shouting through the streets all day, banging their drums all night. There wasn't an Indian girl in this town who didn't sooner or later get banged into a corner by the Red Hats. An Indian girls wasn't safe on the Streets unless she was walking with her whole family. And there were guys who made money off that kind of thing, trading flesh of their sisters to *them*. We're not pimps." He looked up through his dark sunglasses at the big clock high on the wall, "Here come the Specials. Let's Honk."

The floor began shaking and the big running silver dog painted across the blue metal passed by the thick plateglass windows, stopping at Gate 4. The roar of the engine pulsated over the waiting crowd, the Bus was in. Across

its blunt face was strung the white banner RENO SPE-
CIAL. The front doors sucked open and the women got
out.

Juke was already bobbing through the crowd across the
room, he kept waving one hand in the air so the others
could follow, "There's big fish in these waters! It's a lucky
bet! There's big fish in these waters!" Then he was out
through the small swinging doors and grabbed two women
coming down off the Bus, he slipped his hands right
through both of their arms and jostled them along the side
of the depot and up to the white glare of neon dazzling
the night air along Virginia Street. He held his ground
against the shoving current of the crowd and waited for
the others to catch up. He stood under the neon rainbow
of the marquee whose light slashed PRIMADONNA
CLUB, rising from the rainbow five monster can-can girls
burned in the night, their sequin bikinis flashing against
the towering tanned fiberglass bodies as their flowing
breasts thrust forward beneath long upraised pink gloved
arms stretching gold champagne glasses to the starless sky
blotted intense white from the brilliant street below.

"Say, you know, this sidewalk's got carpet on it. It's
covered with red carpet," one of the women slipped Juke's
arm from around her waist and kneeled down, running
the palm of her hand over scarlet fibers. "This is *real* carpet! And there's more inside the Casino."

Juke pulled her up, "It's everywhere, inside the eleva-
tors, the restaurants, the phonebooths, everywhere." He
pushed himself upon the toes of his boots to see the
others. "Yes it's everywhere, even in the johns."

Into the light of the street came Lucky Strike pulling
two women behind, he came up beneath the neon rainbow
and lit a cigarette, the pale white light reflected on his
dark sunglasses, "Howdy Juke."

"Howdy Lucky, these are my two gal friends. Miss, a,
ahh . . ."

"Sue, just call me Sue. You girls see they got carpet all
over the sidewalks. You just tell me where you can see
that kind of thing in Oakland?"

"Well, the Wards store has it on their third floor all

over. This town isn't so fancy, I've been to Las Vegas," she turned to Juke, the thick red lipstick of her mouth puckering into a smile. "I'm Pam, and I'm glad you came along, we would have been trapped in that godawful Bus Station. If it wasn't for you we would have been *crushed*. Why is it towns like this always have such small Bus Stations?"

"We're Lois and Judy," one of the women hanging onto Lucky Strike jabbed her heavy purse into Juke's stomach. "I'm Lois, she's Judy, I guess it doesn't make much difference which is which, we both just got divorced."

The other woman opened the black shine of her big purse and ran her hand around in it. "I want to go across the street to Harrah's and play LUCKY BUCK. That's what's nice about these charter Bus trips, *all* the Clubs give you something for nothing. Come on Lois."

"Wait a minute," Juke grabbed her wrist holding the purse. "I bet ZIMBA'S gave you a pack of LUCKY NICKELS, let's all go in to ZIMBA'S."

"I like HARRAH'S," she pulled her wrist free. "What about you Lois?"

"I'm hungry. I've been on that damn bus for five and a half hours and I'm starved."

"Me too," one of the girls next to Juke fumbled through her purse, she drew her hand out flapping a heavy pink sheet of paper, "Just what I thought, the CAL-NEVA CLUB is THE HOME OF THE WILD INDIAN SLOTS and a 24 HOUR BREAKFAST, it has HAM N EGGS for 48¢, can you beat that, half a buck for breakfast. We can all eat and play DOUBLE ACTION KENO, they pay off up to $25,000!"

"I don't care about that, who wants to eat breakfast at nine o'clock at night," Judy snapped her own purse shut. "I want to play LUCKY BUCK at HARRAH'S. I didn't pay twenty-one dollars for a Bus ticket and travel five and a half hours to eat. I came here to gamble."

"Well you play the slots while we eat, they have over one thousand slot machines and give FREE NYLONS with JACKPOTS and you can . . ."

"Look who's coming! It's my cousin Joe and Jingle.

Maybe they'll join us, it's a lucky bet. We have four gals and four guys."

"This is so exciting, we just get to Reno and already we're meeting *men*."

"I came here to gamble."

"Joe! Joe!" Juke ran ahead and pulled Birdsong up to the women. "I'd like you to meet four wonderful gals. We're all going into ZIMBA'S and I'm buying drinks, these gals are so thirsty after that long Bus ride, it's a lucky bet for us Reno boys to show them Western hospitality."

"Oh, there's no need for you to *buy* us drinks, we're loaded with FREE DRINK tickets."

"Well I couldn't let *you* pay."

"Don't be silly. It's all FREE."

The silver banks of slot machines stood deserted, a few players were left huddled before the large electric KENO board as it slipped silent numbers over its glass screen. Birdsong walked across the empty Casino, his boots scuffing over the burned cigarette scars on the red rug as he made his way around the clean green felt of the deep crap tables to the restaurant. He heard the laughter coming out of the far booth and slipped in on its slick redplastic seats next to Juke who had his arm slung around one of the women so his hand rested on top of her breast, she kept laughing and rubbing her chin against his ear, "Did you see Juke tonight with those dice, that was so funny. I mean *so* funny. I kept shouting, 'Hey Juke, throw snake-eyes for me! Throw me a snake-eyes!' And he did! That was so funny!" She looked around the table, "I think it's so exciting that you boys are all Indians. I mean it's so exciting just to be *here*."

"Judy's right, you don't see so many *Indians* in Las Vegas. Reno is *so* different. What do you do in the day? Are you Cowboys? You sure look like Cowboys the way you're all dressed."

Lucky Strike forked a whole egg into his mouth, the big gob of yellow and white sloshing around as he leaned his head back on the stuffed red plastic, "Cowboys! I'm no

Cowboy. I could't lay a fence up straight if my life was depended on it!"

"I'm a Cowboy," Juke lowered his hand a little on the women's breast. "I'm like the Cowboys in the movies. It's a lucky bet I've seen all of the Wild Bill Elliott pictures."

"What do you do? Break wild horses and things like that?"

"No, I'm not one of *those* kind of Cowboys who gets out everyday to count cows and check fence. I'm the kind that plays guitar and gets the girl. Now my cousin Joe here is the *other* kind of Cowboy, he can do all those things, but he can't play guitar."

Lucky Strike shoveled another egg into his mouth, "What do you girls do?"

The woman next to him drew her knife clear through her steak, her red lips puckered and opened as she waited for the meat she was going to stick in, "You won't believe this, but *I* am a beauty operator."

"What's that?" Lucky Strike banged his fork on his plate.

"A *hairdresser*."

"Oh yah, my mother used to be a barber. During the War she used to cut men's hair for fifty cents."

"Ohh it's so exciting being here in Reno," the woman rubbing her chin against Juke's ear jostled the loose weight of her body in closer so his hand covered her whole breast. "There is so much *history* here. So much exciting has happened here. I remember learning in school the Donner Party all died one winter in Reno on their way to San Francisco. I read they actually got so hungry they *ate* each other."

Juke squeezed the slab of soft flesh beneath his hand, "That wasn't in Reno gal, it was over yonder by Truckee at Donner Lake. Joe here knows all about it, it was his father Hallelujah Bob who helped put up the cross as a memorial there in 1906."

"HALLELUJAH BOB," the woman laughed, her breast shaking beneath Juke's hand. "HALLELUJAH BOB!" Her laughter became so loud it hooked in her throat and choked her. She guzzled down a pull of water and banged the glass back on the table, waiting for the ice to stop clinking before she looked at Birdsong, "That's the funniest name I've *ever* heard, ever ever. Where'd he get a funny name like *that?*"

"He was a preacher."

"You mean your father was an Indian *and* a Christian?"

"That's right." Birdsong's brown eyes stared into the flaking pink powder around the startled blue eyes. "He preached the Gospels, but he give it up before he died."

"Then you mean, he died *out* of grace?"

"He died with his Brothers."

"What do you mean, his *Brothers?*"

"Come on gal," Juke pushed himself up. "It's not Sunday morning yet."

"I want him to explain."

"Forget about it Lois," the woman next to Lucky Strike leaned over and squeezed the loose muscle below the sleeve of the other woman's dress. "We came here to have *fun.*"

"And the fun just started gal!" Juke clapped his hand over the zipper of his pants and winked, "There's big fish in *these* waters. Honk!"

The woman across the table stood up and grabbed her purse. "I'm going over to HARRAH'S. I don't know about the rest of you but I'm not coming to Reno and missing HARRAH'S Club. I've gone through fifty dollars tonight and I haven't even been *in* HARRAH'S yet. Here," she slipped two tickets over to Birdsong. "I'll just go to the Little Girl's room and fix myself up while you get us some drinks, then *we* will go across the street to HARRAH'S."

Juke put his arm around the woman who handed Birdsong the tickets, "Come on gal, forget HARRAH'S. I know a *real* Cowboy bar way down on South Virginia Street, they've got a Honkey Tonkin little Okie band there and a cardtable where they'll deal you Blackjack until the sun comes up. It's a lucky bet, why don't we all get in a cab and go down there?"

"I'm going to HARRAH'S goddamit," she pushed the beak of her nose up against Juke's sunglasses. "And Joe is going to be my *escort*. I'm not leaving Reno until I go to HARRAH'S."

Juke laughed in her face and threw his arms around her waist, drawing her up next to him and kissing her cheek, "That's right gal, what's Reno without HARRAH'S? We'll *all* go to HARRAH'S. Joe why don't you go and buy us *all* drinks." He opened the woman's purse like it was his billfold and took out a twenty dollar bill, "We'll catch up with you in the bar when we've finished eating, it's a lucky bet." He sat back down with a bounce on the red plastic seat, "Come on gals, let's order steak and eggs again, you can't expect to Honkey Tonk all night on an empty stomach, and you *know* there are big fish in *these* waters. It's a lucky bet!"

Birdsong walked back through the silent bank of slot machines, he felt in his pocket for any change left from all the money the women had been giving him to gamble with. There was a little gold light on top of each slot machine that lit up a small glass sign: INSERT COIN. All along the deserted rows of silver slots the little signs were lit up, even though there was no one there to read them. Birdsong jammed a nickel into the slot before him and banged the handle down, the gold light of the sign went off as the roll of painted fruit spun across the silver face of the slot. The fruit stopped. Two lemons and an orange. The little gold sign lit back up: INSERT COIN. He turned his back on it and went into the OYSTER BAR and sat on the padded stool, keeping his back to the room he had just left. But the power was too strong for him, it was as if all the strong medicine of Reno was gathered behind him in a roomful of metal machines with a lighted gold sign that said: INSERT COIN. There were no people there to obey the signs, there were no people standing in front of the machines to read their messages, but the signs were *always* lit up. They did not need people, they had forever to *wait*.

"What'll it be Chief?" the bartender placed his large pink hands on the polished counter, the mirror behind him catching the shine of his pink hairless head. "What's your pleasure Chief?"

"Four vodkas and four whiskeys."

"Right Chief," the bartender kept his eyes on the Indian, he fixed the drinks behind the long counter as if his hands belonged to someone else, the sign over his head declared his purpose: RENO—The Last Frontier of the Old West—MAY YOUR VISIT HERE BE FULL OF FUN AND EXCITEMENT (Privileges Revocable at option of Management). "Here they are Chief, four and four, that's ten bucks out of your jeans." He rang the money into the register and came back to the Indian, rubbing the polished counter before him like he'd just spilled a bucket of water on it. "Reno is going downhill Chief. Your kind remember what Reno used to mean. The people that come into town today don't know what Reno meant before the War, in those days Las Vegas was just a gas station. But it's not Vegas, it's Tahoe, Lake Tahoe is going to kill Reno Chief. Oh sure, Reno is still loaded up to the eyeballs with gamblers, but us oldtimers can remember the old days when this casino would be standing room only at four in the morning, instead of empty like tonight. It aint hard for us oldtimers to smell the change in the air. I know all the big Hotel Casinos are remodeling, but people's attitudes have changed, they don't treat the town with respect like in the old days, now people throw their garbage on Virginia Street, drop their cigarette butts on the carpets and spit on the sidewalks. They don't remember, in the old days they would have been thrown in jail for the night for showing such disrespect. People have no respect for Reno today. It's Tahoe what done it. All those fancy new highrise Casinos around the Lake, that's what killed Reno. Don't you think I'm right Chief?"

"You're right."

"Let me get you another whiskey Chief, here I'll turn up the sound of the fight on the TV. I love the fight game, people don't have enough respect for it, they don't remember during the War. It's football what killed the fight game. Don't you think I'm right Chief?"

"You're right."

"Here's your whiskey. Archie Moore is fightin' tonight,

for the *title*. He's up against Tony Anthony. All the smart money in this town says Archie Moore can't lose unless he breaks a leg on the way from the dressingroom to the ring. Archie is a *real* fighter, forty one years old and still a contender, but it's young guys like Harold Johnson or Basilio that will kill him, maybe not tonight, but they'll kill him. Tahoe will kill Reno, you wait Chief. But it's all a little funny when you think about it, you just think of how the silver and gold metal was mined out of California and Nevada a hundred years ago. So much was mined out we had to invent a way to get rid of it so we invented gambling. Mine the metal out of the ground, stick it in a metal slot machine where it churns around, and if you're lucky you win a bunch more metal. I'll tell you though Chief, after watching people gamble for twentynine years I think they all do it to *lose* their money. Am I right? But did you ever think Chief of how the only gambling places in this Country are right in the middle of where all the wealth was taken out of the ground. Here in Reno, over in Tahoe, even down in Vegas, now that Stein has discovered there is uranium all around that Desert down there, even Vegas is growing faster than *both* Reno and Tahoe. They say Stein was so poor before he stumbled onto uranium he could put his socks on from either end, now he's richer than King Farouk. It's damn odd Chief, where the fortunes were mined ways were invented to get rid of it."

The roar from the TV drowned out the bartender's voice, the Indian swallowed the last of his whiskey and looked up at the two black men fighting on the silver screen. He started drinking the other whiskeys before him. The bartender wiped around his three empty glasses, "This fight was over hours ago in Los Angeles, Archie Moore wins; they always do a re-broadcast of the fights in Reno just to prove to all those who bet on it up here in the North earlier in the night that there really *was* a fight."

"Ohhh, it's like one vast male animal, *struggling*."

Birdsong turned to the woman sitting down at the end of the bar, he hadn't even known she was there, she looked up at the silver screen again and squealed.

"They're going to *kill* each other," her little soft white butt covered tightly by black slacks bounced on the padded stool as she dodged the blows coming from the silver screen.

The bartender did not look up, he went on talking as he wiped imaginary spots, "See that blond piece down at the end of the bar Chief, I get them in here every night at this time, but that one's something special, the biggest little gal I ever seen."

The Indian looked back down the bar, the woman was rubbing the glare of her gold highheeled shoes together as her eyes followed the movements on the silver screen, then her eyes came quickly off the screen and stuck on him, he turned his gaze down from hers at the brilliant pinned red flower on her black sweater drooping below her large breasts.

"Go on down there Chief, what's one more slice off a loaf of bread that's already been cut?"

The Indian drank the last glass of whiskey and looked back at the woman's eyes, the reflection from the TV screen washed over her face and turned it silver.

"Go on Chief, Honk her, it's a lucky bet. You Indians got to make a living somehow. I'm not the kind that calls the Law down on a Honker, even an Indian's got to make a buck."

Birdsong picked up two of the vodkas and carried them down to the end of the counter and set them before the woman. She held her eyes straight on his and he felt the liquor swelling his tongue so he couldn't speak, then he thought of the most natural thing to say. "It's paid for."

The woman raised the drink and turned her eyes back to the silver screen, one of the black men was knocked out on the canvas. She didn't take her eyes off the screen as the sharp edge of her gold shoes run up and down on the Indian's leg, "You know why I was watching you? Because you look like someone I saw in the movies, in a Randolph Scott movie, he had a scar on his cheek and a hat just like yours, and his skin was just as brown. Have you ever been to any Randolph Scott movies?"

"I've seen them all."

"Honest?" she fingered the gold bracelet around the black wrist of her sweater. "You're not just saying that to be sweet, because I *love* Randolph Scott."

"No, I have seen them all."

"You are sweet. And this vodka you brought is sweet, but I only get four a night and I've had my four, it's doctor's orders." She snapped her gold purse open and tapped two red and white pills out of a plastic tube into her hand, "These are orders too," she popped the pills in her mouth. "Now you be sweet and take me home. *I'm* at the RIVERSIDE."

The woman took the Indian by the hand and led him through the large lobby to the elevator. She held her fingers down on button number 10 until the flesh turned pure white under the bloodred nail polish. The elevator doors split open and she led him in by the hand and swayed to the music of hidden speakers as the elevator rose. The music was in the halls and followed them down to her door, she turned the key in the lock and they stepped into the music of the room. She turned to him and unbuttoned her black slacks, pushing them down over her legs so he could see the mound of dark hair pushing against her white panties. He slipped his hands to her flesh and her lips sucked at his, then she shoved him away, "No-No. Not yet. Not until we're clean." He sat on the bed and watched her take her clothes off. "Oh it's so damn hot always in Reno," she unhooked her gold bracelet and rubbed her hands over the stiff edge of her red nipples. "Always so damn hot in Reno." She turned the air-conditioner up to High and the sudden wind blew over her body as she lifted her arms and slipped off the blond wig, shaking down her short brown hair. "I just love wigs, I wouldn't ever use one except they're so convenient, this one is 100% virgin acrylic, soft as baby hair and burn proof. You can actually hold a match to it and it won't burn, of course I wouldn't test it." She pulled the wig down over the white plastic head sitting on the dresser, then carefully combed out the blond locks. "Hey, you want a thrill! A real Sensation! Look at this!" She pointed

her red fingernail at the small metal box screwed onto the
top of the bedstand: MAGIC FINGERS—ROCK AND
ROLL YOUR MATTRESS FOR 10 MINUTES OF
BLISS—25¢. "This is really *relaxing!*" She dropped a
quarter into the box and he felt the bed begin to quiver
beneath him. "You just lie back and relax. I'll get these
dirty boots off you, and these Levis, how long have you
been wearing these Levis? You could stand them up in the
corner, what a stink." She unbuttoned his shirt and
opened it down his chest, "You're not very hairy are you?
Is it true Indians can't grow beards? How do you like the
MAGIC FINGERS, pretty Sin-sational huh," she spread
her body over him and kissed him around the neck. He
could feel the mattress vibrating up through his back and
shaking her breast over his chest. "Well you're not going
to leave your silly hat on." She jerked it off his head and
threw it across the room. "Come on, into the shower."
She shoved him into the bathroom and spun the shiny
metal shower knobs as he rubbed the hair between her
legs against his thigh. She pushed him into the stinging
water and ran the hard white soap over his body, working
it up under his arms into a lather and down between his
legs until his stiffened flesh was slippery in the jerking fingers of her hands, "You know those wooden Indians in
front of CLUB CAL-NEVA? The ones that are slot machines and you pull their arms for a handle. I think they
should put the handle right between the legs. I would just
love to PLAY them if I could pull on *that* all day, just
slipping my hand back and forth feeling the hot head of
that flesh growing bigger and BIGGER until I hit a
JACKPOT!" She pressed her slippery breasts against his
arm as her hand tightened between his legs, running the
muscle beneath her fingers up and down. "Is it true, all
true about what you Indian boys did to those poor settler
women, before you scalped them I mean, or even after.
Come on, you can tell me." Her fingers darted underneath
his hard flesh as her hand pumped, he leaned his back up
against the wet wall and thrust his hips out to her hand. "I
know more about you than you know. You said you were
a Washo Indian. That bartender back at the Casino told

me it was the *Washo* who saw the Donner Party eat themselves. He said you Washo are so superstitious you still
believe *all* white men are cannibals. Is that true?" She
rubbed her nipples across his chest and put her lips on his
neck, kissing up to his ear, "I'm no cannibal. I want *you*
to eat *me*." Her hand sucked at him and she jerked her
hips around and jammed the head of his hard flesh against
her white belly, her fist squeezing his pounding blood. The
muscles of his thighs flinched and he bucked her against
the glass door as he threw his head back, the spray of water running into his open mouth. "Oh Goddamit, you've
gone and come already!" She released her hand from his
throbbing flesh and he slipped down to the floor. "Come
on! That's too quick! Are you *all* so quick! Come on," she
pulled him up by the shoulders and rubbed the hard soap
against his belly. "Come on! I want it!" She let the water
rush the lather off his belly as she kissed him on the sides of
the hips, sliding her tongue into his hair, he could feel her
teeth biting him around the thighs as she brought her hand
up, running her palm under his bag, her lips went along
him and she slipped the rising head into her mouth. He
looked down at her kneeling before him, her blood red
fingernails tearing into his brown thighs as the driving
shower rained over her head. She looked like a white ghost.
He pulled her off him and pushed her out the door toward
the bed, slapping her ass with the flat of his hand so he
could see the red welts burn up on the white skin. She fell
back on the bed and he got his knees in between her legs,
covering her red lips with his mouth as he stabbed between
her open thighs, bringing his hips up and banging down
into her so all his flesh flamed. She wrenched her mouth
away from his tongue and laughed, "I knew you were like
this. When I saw you sitting there I knew what you were
really like."

The dream of the Lizard woke him. He put his hand
out on the bed, she wasn't there. He sat up and saw the
light coming from the bathroom, it cast its white glow
across the room onto the blank plastic face surrounded by
the blond wig staring back at him. He got out of bed and

dressed, the low music still filled the room and the air-conditioner blew its stale wind at him as he walked to the bathroom. Her pale body was bent at the sink before the mirror, washing her face with the rushing water, on the counter next to her were two false eyelashes. There was a tube of toothpaste with its cap off oozing thick white fluid. He pulled down her panties and rammed the tube up between her exposed cheeks and squeezed out a fistful of white paste.

"YOU FUCKER!" She flung around and tried to hit him, but he was to the door, he turned and looked at her, her bloodred fingernails flashed in the air as she ran at him with her white body screaming. She looked like a Ghost. "YOU FUCKER!"

He punched the elevator and rode to the top of the roof into the air. The electric drone of the air-conditioners suddenly stopped. His ears were filled with a strange rushing sound. He ran across the roof and looked over the edge. There it was racing black below him, the Truckee River, the clean force of its powerful current coming down out of the snow high Sierra Mountains and into the Desert. He threw his head back and sucked in the cool air, the sun was coming up over the rim of the eastern Mountains, scattering its first light into the sky. He looked out over the city below him. The neon signs were all blackened. Reno was calm as a dead horse.

"GENTS, THIS here is a Democracy we live in, and in a Democracy a man is given a fair trial before he's hanged. In a Democracy a man is always innocent until he's hanged. Now I realize that in this free land of ours this redskin heathen standing before you is not considered by Law a man. This Country does not recognize him as one of its own, he is not a citizen of the United States of America. He can't vote, he can't get married legal, his children are all bastards, he is by Law an Injun."

"Hang em!"

"Hang em to a tree!"

"That's the American thing to do gents, we ought to hang him to get his back straight. That would teach him a lesson in our Democracy."

"Hang the red devil!"

The Bummer looked down from the buckboard at the pack of men pressed from one side of the street up to the other, he waited until the shouts and dusty hats thrown in the air settled down. The hand he was using to keep the knotted noose cinched around the Indian's neck was beginning to sting in the palm as a hard cramp set in, the smile spreading along the delicate curve of his mouth came from the pleasant sensation of pain in his hand. His smile went out across those screaming for justice, his other hand waving the point of his goldtipped cane in the air,

"Gents, Injuns is all the same, wherever there is troubled waters an Injun will be fishing them."

"Hang him upsidedown if he aint a full citizen of this Republic!"

"Honest to John gents, this Injun before you is most in need of a hanging. This Injun's got no more respect for the Law than a rattlesnake in a rabbit hutch."

"He don't obey the Law!"

"What's even worse gents is he don't even *know* the Law. Now we can all tolerate a man who breaks the Law now and again, we're none of us perfect, but a man who doesn't *know* the law is an outrage in a free Country. In a free Country we're each of us free to *know* the Law; if we don't, we pay the Devil himself for it."

"Let the Devil hang!"

"Let the goose hang high!"

"I say to you gents this Injun is an outrage, he doesn't know the Law from a barrel of apples."

"Let's hang em, that'll teach him!"

"Honest to John gents, Justice is on our side, why waste time electing a jury before we hang him, this Injun needs a jury trial like a hog needs Sunday school."

"String him up and pop his head off!"

"Right gents, we should treat this Injun as an equal and let him participate in our Democratic way." The Bummer pointed the gold tip of his cane at the sun like a schoolmaster pointing at his chalkboard, "Gents, there are only three things that make this Country less than the number one Great Country in the world, three things that can't be trusted." He swung the gold tip around and stuck it up against the white of the Indian's eye, "The three things that can't be trusted are dirty Mexicans, Niggers, and painted Savages."

"Hang em all!"

"Just think how great this Country could be without those three things cluttering it up. What did the dirty Mexicans give us? Nothing but disease for our private male parts. What did the Nigger give us? The only good the Nigger ever did was to invent pancakes, but we even improved on that with our own flapjacks. And what did

the painted Savages give us? Ugly women and a knife in
our sleep. I ask you from the bottom of my golden heart
gents, can a Country ever be truly great with these three
things cluttering it up?"

"Kill em all!"

"Now I'm not saying we should just start killing up *all*
the Injuns, don't get me wrong, but you just take this one
Injun before you as proof of my words. You gents have a
Law in this town that no Injun can buy Whiteman liquor,
a just and reasonable Law, one that prevails in every orderly town in the West. This Injun walked right into this
town and bought a bottle of whiskey just like he was
White, just like he was a *man*. This is just the kind of outrage an Injun will pull unless we put some wolf teeth into
our Laws."

"Hang him now!"

"But that is not all this redskin is guilty of gents, he
also . . ."

"The thievin redskin stole a bottle of my whiskey last
night!" One of the men wedged in before the buckboard
screamed up at the Bummer, pounding the hammer of his
fist on the Indian's boot, "I tried to be Christian to him
last night and gave him a ride to this town from the Railroad track layin teams out on the desert, what do you suppose he does but steal my whiskey and jump off my
wagon into the night. That makes *two* crimes he's committed, if justice is to be done we'll have to hang him, haul
him down, then hang him again!"

"And that's not all gents, this Injun broke more Laws
than a toad has warts. Honest to John, just this past year
this Injun before you and a sidekick named Squirrel with
a band of other redskins, raided a John Chinaman gold
diggins up at Dutch Flats. The Injuns beat up alot of the
yellowmen besides putting a bullet through the heart of
another John Chinaman."

"Hang em!"

"Right after that outrage this Injun before you laid
some bets in a legal run Badger baiting contest over to
Truckee. This Injun before you committed the lowest of
outrages, he run off on his bets, owing six-hundred silver

dollars to the citizens of Truckee, who were the lawfully
wronged owners of that money."

"Hang em to a tree then chop the tree down!"

"This Injun before you is known around the Railroad
towns as Captain Rex. The only thing he ever does is get
drunk and sing like a bird. He's the worst of his bad kind,
his own people don't want him and neither do we. The
Railroad uses him because he was cunning enough to
learn how to speak American words, so the Railroad pays
him a silver dollar and a bottle of whiskey a day to work
for them. He's the worst of his bad kind. I'll tell you just
what kind of work he does. He gets together a band of his
people, puts them in one of the Railroad's boxcars and
ships them over the line to the foothills on the California
side where they pick pigweed along the tracks. Injuns love
to eat pigweed, they're all just Diggers these Indians. The
Railroad wants the pigweed cleared out so it don't catch a
spark in it from a passing train and set a forest fire. So the
Injuns get their basketfuls of pigweed to take home and
boil up, if it weren't for the generosity of the Railroad
they wouldn't get such a square meal in their lifetime.
And what does this Captain here get out of it? This Captain Pigweed here gets a silver dollar and a bottle of whiskey. His people get weeds and he gets whiskey. He's the
worst of his kind, they don't want him and neither do
we."

"Hang him to a tree and burn the tree down!"

"I've been on this Injun's trail for sometime. I, John C.
Luther, have been deputized by the United States Marshal
over to Lake Tahoe to bring this Injun to Justice for robbing the honest folk of Truckee of their legal Badger baiting bets. The Railroad has been using him out on the desert where the John Chinaman coolie gangs are banging
track. This Injun before you didn't do any work out there,
he just stood around the track gangs and watched for
trouble from any other Injuns so he'd make sure to get his
pay of a dollar and a bottle. He's the worst of his bad
kind."

"Hang em now!"

"Stretch his neck out ten feet!"

"Wait gents, there is one more thing you should know about the Injun before you. I, John C. Luther, have also been deputized by the U.S. Marshal in Virginia City to bring this Injun to Justice for an outrage committed this past month in Carson City. This very same Injun before you, along with his sidekick Squirrel and a band of other redskins, raided the horses at a wedding party in Carson. As if these Injuns hadn't done enough breaking of our just Laws they commit the greatest outrage, HORSETHIEVIN! This Injun led the others up to the horses tied outside the barn where the wedding dance was going on, they cut the tethers and led the horses off, then they rode the horses out into the desert. Now listen to this gents, it's going to burn your ears, you always knew Injuns would kill your women and children, now listen to this lowest act. These Injuns got the horses rode far out into the desert then built a big sagebrush fire. Then gents, they tied the horses down and shot them in the head."

"Kill that redskin!"

"Kill him now!"

"Now listen to this gents, honest to John it's going to burn your ears off what these Injuns did next, they threw the horses into the fire and *cooked* them, then they *ate* them. Can you imagine this low act gents, this outrage against God. When the boys from the wedding party had rounded up some new mounts they followed the tracks out into the desert. When they rode up to the fire the Injuns were still there, *eating* horseflesh. Their bellies were stuffed with horsemeat, they were drunk on it, they just looked up and laughed at the boys from the wedding party. Well the boys spurred their mounts around in a circle, with the Injuns between them and the fire, they slipped their rifles out of the saddle holsters and took aim. Some of the Injuns were still laughing when the precision of all those rifle bullets ripped right through their red bodies."

"That's it, hang em now!"

"Somehow gents this Injun before you escaped the Justice he deserved, his sidekick Squirrel was one of the dead bodies lying bleeding around that fire, so I *know* this Injun before you was one of those involved in the outrage, although none of the boys actually saw him. How can you see a redskin running in the dark? He's the worst of his kind, he escaped Justice. But the U.S. Marshal at Virginia City has sworn me to bring him in. I can't thank you gents for rounding him up for me, you know how cunning these Injuns are, they can walk twelve months with nothing but a cheap tobacco chew and the spit on their chin."

"Now we're gonna hang him high!" The buckboard rocked under the Bummer's feet as the pack moved in, waving their fists in the dusty air.

"Gents, gents!" The Bummer swung the metal tip of his cane at those grabbing the Indian's legs and trying to rock the buckboard over. "Gent, gents! Honest to John I'm sworn by *two* U.S. Marshals to bring this Injun to Justice!" He tried to kick off one of the men who had a fist hold in his checkered pants as he beat at the others with his cane.

"Hang the redskin by his thievin red balls!"

The man clutching at the Bummer's pants shoved himself up from the crowd onto the swaying buckboard. He leaned the white knife of his face into the Bummer, "God's *will* be done man! Don't you stand in the way of the Lord! Out of my way Satan!"

The Bummer shoved the cane under the man's chin and rammed it into his throat, trying to knock him over, "I'm bringing this Injun to Justice, Reverend Jake. I'm bringing him to Justice!"

The Reverend Jake got hold of the cane and pushed it back, the fierce blue light of his eyes blazed, "Out of my way you *Bummer!*"

"Get that Injun for us Reverend! We want the Injun!"

"Out of the Lord's way Bummer, or we will hang you too!"

The Bummer jammed the cane back into Reverend Jake's throat and knocked him over into the crowd, "This Injun is mine! He will be hung in Truckee and Virginia City!"

Reverend Jake was pulled to his feet, the intense blue of his eyes looked out at the crowd behind him, "Why let Truckee and Virginia City hang the red devil! We want to hang him! He's ours, not theirs! They've got plenty of red devils of their own. He committed an outrage in our town, we caught him first, he's ours to hang. We'll teach this red devil the lesson of White Law! God's will be done! Hang him!" He lunged at the buckboard, the screams of the men around him tore at the air as their weight pushed in against the buckboard. The Bummer cracked the solid metal of his cane down on the hands clutching at him, he could hear the air of screams splinter with the sound of wood as the sideboards of the wagon ripped off. The fist of his hand locked on the noose around the Indian's neck jerked, cinching the knot up and slamming the Indian against him. He held the Indian tight next to him so no one could pull him away, then the delicate curve of his mouth flew open and he screamed.

"GOLD!"

The yelling pack below him fell silent.

"You take the L out of GOLD and what have you got. I'll tell you! Take the L out of GOLD and you've got GOD!"

The broad street jammed with men beneath him was quiet and still, the only movement was the rays of sun shooting through the slow rising dust.

"I know all about precious metals gents, I was down in Trinidad country in '52 when Mama Ocean herself was spitting up cartloads of golden nuggets on the shore. I seen it once and I aim to see it again."

"Where!"

"Everyone is shouting Silver now," the Bummer picked up the stovepipe hat at his feet and knocked it free of dust, then spit on it to rub back the high black shine. "All the talk is Silver but I'll tell you gents straight as a stick, the Gold had just barely begun to be touched before everybody dropped it and ran over here to Nevada for Silver. And what have any of us gents got in our pockets to show for our hard years in Nevada? I'll show you!" He put his hat high atop his head and took a greasy packet of papers from his dusty white coat and read aloud like a judge, "This here is what we got for our hard earned wages, '12 feet in the Root-Hog Or Die Silver Mine,' at 1,000 American dollars a foot. He threw the sheet of paper he read from out into the crowd, "Worthless! '30 feet in Gouge Eye,' '200 feet in Hell Roaring,' '40 feet in Bobtail Horse,' the 'Stump Toe,' the 'Grab Game,' 'Love's Despair,' 'Rip Snorter,' 'Dead Broke' . . ." He tossed all the papers up in the air, "Worthless! Which one of us gents hasn't bought leads in these mines, and all the other diggins in the Comstock Lode, which one of us hasn't *speculated*. There isn't a coyote hole within two hundred miles of here that hasn't at least four times developed *indications*. Every hillside around has been grubbed open, from here all the way into the desert the ground's been pegged like the sole of a soldier's boot with stakes declaring Lawful claims. Which one of us gents hasn't invested his ready cash in Nevada Silver and come up short? I tell you gents there's still enough Gold in California to make us all Senators!"

"Where!"

The Bummer jerked the rope around the Indian's neck, "This Injun before you knows."

"Get him to tell us then hang em!"

"I couldn't be in more accord with you gents. This Injun knows where we can pick up a fortune, his own life isn't worth two-bits out of your jeans, he's the worst of his kind, just as the twig is bent the tree grows. But we can't hang his red skin yet, he is the only one who can lead us to the Gold Lake up Downieville way. Others have looked for the lake with Gold glowing up from its bottom and never struck it. Honest to John this Gold Lake aint something a gang of Sunday miners could find, it takes a conniving Injun to lead the way."

"Let's get that Gold!"

"Yee-hah, we're gonna be rich!"

"WA-HOOO we gonna strike it!!!"

"Hold your ponies down gents," the Bummer pulled a thin brown cigar from his pocket and lit up, ignoring those shouting and banging on the buckboard. "You gents don't want to go off half cocked. You're making such a racket they can hear all the way over to Virginia City." He blew out a big cloud of blue smoke and watched it drift over the quieting crowd. "Now you gents are just going to have to hold your water unless you want to split all that paydirt with both the States of Nevada *and* California. You gents know what happened to crazy Captain Tom Stoddard back around '49 when he got hit with Gold Lake fever, he started showing handfuls of golden nuggets he said were just floating on the surface of a lake an Injun had led him to. Crazy Tom Stoddard showed his find in every saloon from Sacramento to Frisco. The newspapers told the world about the Gold Lake in Yuba River country, that wildfire story spread through the mining camps overnight. Honest to John, why some men jumped off of $500 a day claims of their own to beat everybody else up to the lake where Gold glowed up from the bottom and floated across the top. Why there were thousands who wore their boots raw banging around in the cruel elements searching for that golden paradise. They couldn't find the lake, but they sure did find Stoddard, they put a rope around his neck and said they'd hang him at sunup. But when the new day came someone had cut the rope, Stoddard was gone. Thousands of Law abiding gents were humbugged and the Gold Lake was still lost. There are some who say crazy Stoddard hid out with that Scottish sailor, Downie, who had a drygoods store down on the North Yuba River. It was soon after that when Downie the drygoods gent closed his store and went partners with seven nigger sailors. In no time at all they were striking it rich just by kicking the dirt with their boots. Now you tell me how one Scotman and seven niggers could become rich as Governors overnight if Stoddard hadn't tipped them off to something? That's what some say gents. But this Injun before you isn't going to be lucky like Stoddard, you can only turn a dirty shirt inside out once. This Injun is going to lead us straight up to the Gold Lake and then were going to hang him on the spot. We won't make the mistake of waiting until sunrise."

"Let's go get rich!"

"Now gents," the Bummer held a gloved hand high. "We are going into this adventure as Law abiding equals. There is to be no knifings, shootings, or stranglings. Trust your neighbor. Whatever we strike gents the higher Law of prospecting pertains, anything we hit rich we share honestly in the American spirit of free enterprise."

"Let's get that Injun packing!"

"Light a fire under his saddle!"

"You gents back up and give this Injun room to draw us a proper map, he knows that Yuba country as well as he knows the inside of his pocket, and he's going to lead us to the Golden Paradise. Hold your ponies down now gents and give the Injun room."

The crowd moved back and the Bummer jumped down. He tugged the rope around the Indian's neck, pulling him off the buckboard. He put his cane against the Indian's cheek so its gold tip rested beneath the eye, "Now Captain, draw us the way."

"He can't talk, that hangin noose is got his neck up so tight he can't talk!"

The Bummer loosened the noose, "Now DRAW!"

The Indian's stiff finger made deep signs in the thick dust, his words came dry and cracked as he drew, "River coming out the mouth of lake. Blue water everywhere. The Sky is touched by stone. Two, three days distant. North of the Sun. Two rivers. Valley filled with clouds. Sky is touched by stone."

The Bummer nodded, "That's the way I figured it gents, that's right where it's got to be, up above where the Yuba forks into two rivers. We've got to go up through Beckwourth Pass, across the Sierra Valley and over Yuba Pass. 'Sky is touched by stone,' that means the Sierra Buttes, the Gold Lake is north of there. But we're not going to go the way this Injun wants us to, it would attract too much notice, other gents may get on to us. We are going to go the long way, bypass Carson City altogether on Fishback Road. It's an old twisty stagecoach road that hasn't been used since the Big Gold Rush, nobody'd think of using it now, too dangerous. It goes along behind Lake Tahoe, up through Emigrant Gap, across Round Valley to Goodyear's Bar. That ought to throw off any gents who take to speculate on *us*." The Bummer sat back on his haunches and took a long suck at his cigar so its tip

burned fire red, he cocked his head and let a big cloud of
smoke drift away from him, the delicate curve of his
mouth twisted open into a smile showing the brilliant flash
of his gold capped teeth, "Gents, let's go get it."

"YIPPEEE!"

"LET'S STRIKE IT!!!"

The men in the street ran into one another, tripped over
one another, bit one another, hit one another as they
broke up into screaming mobs fighting their way into the
General Store. They knocked one another down striving
to push their weight into supreme positions on the backs
of horses, mules, oxen carts, ranchwagons, buckboards
and empty waterwagons. The dust swirled up like a thunderstorm and the Bummer stood on the seat of his own
buckboard holding the reins of his snorting horses and
waving the goldtipped cane in the choking clouds rising
around him, "Let's set sail gents!"

Reverend Jake jumped into the back of the buckboard,
the fierce blue light of his eyes burning through the dust
as he sat on the hard seat behind the Bummer and the Indian. He leaned the fat double barrel of a shotgun across
his legs and nudged the barrel into the Bummer's back,
"God's vengeance is behind you Bummer! The Sword of
the Lord is at your back. I'm riding right here until God's
Will be done and your Indian takes us to the Gold. By the
time this journey is finished we shall see, Bummer, just
which of the two of us carries the greatest share of Mother earth."

The Bummer turned around on the point of the shotgun sticking in his back and flashed his brilliant gold
smile. "Keep your hair on Reverend Jake, you'll never get
a cool drink of water till you get the hog out of the
spring." He whipped the reins over his team of stamping
horses, "Hey-YAAAH, move out!" The reins slapped on
the horses, rearing them back, galloping the buckboard
into the dusty storm of the street. "Heee-Yaaay!" The wagon bounced, clanged and bolted down the broad street
and out of town. The Bummer stood again, holding the
reins loose and open through his fingers as he swung his
head around, "Here they come! They're right on our

trail!" Below the shiny black brim of his hat his eyes looked back at the stampeding gang of riders and wagons roaring down the street in a hail of hurled insults to "MAKE WAY...!!!" Spurs dug into horseflesh, whips cracked, the ring of pistol shots spun high through the dusty air. The Bummer kept at the head of the pack, his own whip lashing over the sweatswelled backs before him, he kept the horses headed straight, right up the Carson Valley.

Reverend Jake looked behind the wagon too, but not at the howling pack scattered into the long distance of flat land; he put his fierce eyes on the two horses tethered close to the wagon. The two horses ran well together, the one burdened with roped-over sacks of supplies, but the Reverend's fierce blue light was fixed on the Indian woman who rode high in the saddle of the other horse. The leather flow of the long fringed buckskin dress beat out in the wind behind her, the length of her hair was caught flapping straight out from her shoulders like a wet black horsetail. Reverend Jake poked the barrel of his gun into the Bummer's back, "Bummer, where'd you get this Injun woman?"

The Bummer jerked around, flashing his mouthful of gold, "Reverend, let's just say I've got a fondness for squaws. I bought her off a Mono Lake salt trader in Virginia City, he threw that leather dress in for nothing. She's a special one, very rare bird, it's not everyday you see a skinny squaw. Before us Whites came along and civilized these red heathens they were running around half starved, eating nuts and berries, plenty of skinny squaws in those days. But nowadays Reverend we have improved their miserable lot so much they all turned lazy, soft and fat, you could stick a fork in them like a turkey. This squaw here is worth a thousand-dollar pan of Gold, nice and skinny, but well padded in the right places so a gent doesn't stick himself and get bruised. Don't let her leather dress fool you Reverend. This squaw's not a Plains Injun, not by a long shot. She's not from one of your warring Injun tribes. She's from the rabbitblood Injuns, just like Captain

Rex next to me here. Her name's Molly Moose, she's
Washo."

Reverend Jake turned and put his intense blue light
back on the Indian woman. The ground beneath the
hooves of the galloping horses was going soft, the straight
road before them turning to sand. Out across the land the
brown grass was disappearing in the sunblasted clumps of
sagebrush. The road followed along the dry gash of the
Carson River. The sand from the riverbed rolled up over
into the sand of the Desert. Shadows thickened in the
empty sky, sprouting long black wings, until great swooping swirls of buzzards blocked the sun. A stench swarmed
across the land. The spinning wheels of the buckboard
slowed in the sand. Strong white jagged glares in the distance on the sand began to take shape, the buzzards dropping in among them. The Bummer tied a bandanna
around his nose as the wagon drew closer, the shapes of
the jagged glares rising like scorched blades from the sand
were humped white carcasses of cattle, horses and oxen
stretching off to the colorless horizon. Spikes of horns
stuck up through the sand, countless bonewheels of ribs
lay half hidden in the heavy drifts. The road turned closer
to the river, the deep sand almost sucking the wagon to a
stop, the drone of flies going into the buzzard filled air.
Over into the dry gash of the river rotting bodies lay
where they had stopped sliding down the steep slope, their
rotting black hide stretched and slashed open by the flesh
twisting rip of buzzard beaks. Along the dried slopes of
the river gangs of buzzards perched on the weakening
bodies, standing high on ribs and skulls, their bellies glut-
ted on stinking flesh, their gut stuffed with eyeballs gashed
from wide sockets of shrunken heads, their oily feathered
beings too burdened with flesh to lift their wings from the
earth at the wild sound of the passing wagons. The slow
trickle of the river's slovenly current carried off bits of
festered flesh from horses and cows that had plunged their
heads into the slimy skin of water, their entire necks sinking into the mudsuck where their staggering bodies had
plunged in a last thirsty gasp. The wagons rode on, more
and more carcasses began to stack up out across the sand.

Great mounds of blasted bones lay heaved up along the dry gash of river where the lost bodies last gathered for animal warmth before the starving air collapsed them on the soft earth in wasted piles. The Bummer shouted through the bandanna tied around his nose and mouth, "Nature's great spectacle gents! A carnival of flesh! I remember just a few years back before Silver was struck at the Comstock when this was a green grassy plain, the Carson River used to run deep even in the summer. I remember the Washo Injuns even had a camp along here, maybe you was one of them Injun gents Captain? Of course that was before Virginia City Silver, before the river up in the Sierra was dammed so they could jam logs to the timber mills that cut up the lumber so the mines could be built. They used enough raw timber in the Comstock mines to build the city of Frisco twenty times over. This here was the road out of California to Virginia City, used to be a thousand gents along every mile of it heading for the Silver. No time to stop and feed pack animals, nothing to feed them anyway. Animals just became walking skeletons, even the best horse would try to eat his own head off. Walking ghosts they were. Summer and winter they came, gents and their animals. Starving cattle being buried under snow in winter, water hungry oxen being buried in summer sand, shriveled-up horses sucked to death in river mud. It was a real carnival of rotting flesh gents. I'm glad I lived to see it, a rare spectacle. Every pound of Silver yanked out of the Virginia City hills was paid for here by a thousand tons of animal flesh, hair, and bone. C. P. Huntington got his yellow coolies to lay track down past Reno, so now all the gents headed for the Comstock come into Reno then head up over the pass to Virginia City. No need for a gent to bring in animals anymore, even if he got one up there it would do him no good. Hay is going for $800 a ton, and when you think that a loaf of bread the size of a biscuit is selling for twelve-bits you'd have to be dumb enough to cut butter with an ax to pay $800 a ton to feed a cow when you could cut it up and sell it for more a pound than Silver is worth. But by the time you got the critter up there its sides is caved in from starva-

tion. Half dead meat of a cow will rot your stomach out if
you eat it. They've hung more than three gents in Virginia
City for selling it." He twirled his cane in the air, its gold
tip flashing at the buzzards drifting endlessly off in the distance, "Yes sir gents, wherever man finds precious metals
to dig out of the earth, just look over your shoulder, the
great carnival of flesh is sure to follow. Whether it be man
or beast, it will follow."

The road broke from the river and began to harden beneath the pounding hooves of the horses headed toward
the high Sierra wall of mountains. They pulled their burden behind them up into the clean wind blowing down
from the spotted snow ridges and pushing the stench of
rotting flesh before it into the desert. The Bummer tore
the bandanna from his face and turned around, "You can
untie your bandanna now Reverend Jake, the stink is
gone. But then, Reverend, a dog always smells his own
hole last. He-Yawwwww, git along there!" He whipped
the horses up the steep ledge cut down the arm of a
mountain. "He-Yaaaaarwwww! Don't look back now!"
The horses pulled the wagon higher and steeper until the
bottom of the earth fell out behind them to the white and
brown floor of the Carson Valley fading into a colorless
haze. "Heee-Yaaawhheee! UP! UP! UP!" The winding
road before the horses turned in on itself, narrowing on
one side with jagged rocks blading out of the cut cliff,
dropping off on the other side to needled points of pines
spiking up from darkened granite canyons below. "Heey
Geyiup!!" All down the road the line of spinning wheels
banged and jolted off the scramble of rocks strewn before
them. Men dug their spurs into the flesh beneath then,
"Git Git Git!" Men lashed their cracking whips over the
blunt heads of oxen, jerking the power of the reins held in
their hands so the steel bits cut and bloodied the soft
mouths of beasts. "Hup Hup Hup! Git up over this rut!
Buckle to it now! Buckle to it!" The struggling beasts labored up the jutting mountain edge, the axles beneath the
wagons grinding like screeching gulls as the wheels
worked their way over stone. "Git on up! Work for me!
Work for me!" The beasts labored, pulling the men up to

the clouds. The men screamed in the thinning air, the scorn twisted on their sweating faces as they prodded the brutes before them even higher, "Work for me! Work for me!" The slick sweat ran down their man muscled backs, their dirty faces cried out in the hot muscle reek of air for the animals to carry them to the top. "Work me! Git goin sweet Mother! Git it Up!!!" The road ran up before the sky and hooked over out of sight like the steel blade of a sickle. The Summit. "HEEEYAR! I knew ye could do it. I knew ye could!" The long train of horses, mules, wagons and oxcarts carried over the Summit in the blind wake of its own weight. The downgrade struck out below them, the road cut in and out of granite snags, elbowing its turns along steep ledges. "Come on. Git ye UP! Head DOWN!" The brute weight of men and beasts hurled down the grade. "Watch where you're goin to! Watch it!!!" The steel spurs cut into the bleeding sides of horses. "Watch it!" The dead weight of a wagon wheel spun free, hurling itself off the mountain. "Cut loose! Cut loose!" The blind weight of a wagon swung around and slammed itself into the cliff, dragging the braying muleteam behind it. Bridles jerked back and horses reared up as rocks began rolling, knocking into animals. "Keep together! Keep together! Or we all GO!" Clattering hooves struck off for solid ground as they staggered beneath their burdens. A wagon wheeled over on its edge, its boarded side splintering against the rock earth as it carried down the road smashing apart another wagon. "Whee! Whee! Whee! Cut back for your lives! CUT LOOSE!" A dragging wagon pulled two oxen behind it, their large bodies cutting over the rocks on their backs. "Dismount! Dismount! Dismount!" The steel bridles dripped with blood, horses reared right up and over, crashing into the side of the cliff, their steel-bottomed hooves kicking in the air. The bleating mules stood against the crushing tide, their hammer heads flung back in the dust swirl air as their riders kicked them, beat their fists against their necks and tried to bite the ears rigid with fear to spring them from the onslaught. "Cut back! Dismount! Dismount!" A horse went over beneath a wagon, the twisted foot of its rider caught in the stirrup, dragging him under the crush of falling weight. Another rider struggled with the reins twisted around his wrists, tying him to the stampeding horse slashing its saddled sides as it galloped between overturned wagons and the sharp side cut of the cliff. The road was studded with the weight of struggling flesh and the roar of wagons plunging off the steep rock cut slopes to crash their flesh and wood below.

The Bummer walked jauntily back and forth, tapping the gold tip of his cane against the earth and tucking it up under his arm. He turned smiling, his tall shiny hat reflecting the red of the setting sun. He looked up at the mountain and turned his ear to the distant echo of shouts and cries floating down through the darkening steep gulches. "Reverend Jake," he glanced up at the man sitting in the buckboard and winked one eye open so it twinkled. "I hear your flock calling."

Reverend Jake put the intense light of his eyes on the man in the white broadcloth coat, "I'm staying right here Bummer, with you in my sights."

"Hah, Reverend Jake, you can't turn your back on your *real* life's vocation."

The Reverend kept his eye on the man in the white coat, "Bummer, I'm beginning to think the Lord sent me into this world to work another vocation."

"And what would that be Reverend Jake," the Bummer popped his eye open wider.

Reverend Jake lifted the fat barrel of the shotgun and aimed it at the Bummer's stomach, "To put you flat on your back in a box six feet under."

The Bummer let his other eye snap open in a wink, he drew a slim brown cigar from his coat pocket and bit off the end, "Smoke, Reverend Jake? No." He spit the end out, "I suppose not. I should ask if limes grow on apple trees. You Mormons don't eat, sleep, smoke nor fornicate with less than seven women at one time. They run you out of every State in the Union, so you had to go and invent your own State. You Mormons are so holy you do everything the opposite of everybody else. If it was raining soup you Mormons would be standing out in it with a fork."

Reverend Jake lifted the shotgun and took sight on the blue cloud of smoke slipping out of the Bummer's mouth.

"Go ahead and shoot Reverend. You better make up your mind which horse you're going to throw your saddle on." The Bummer joined his hands behind his back and threw his chest out, the burning cigar pointing straight back at the gun barrel.

"What's to stop me from shooting you Bummer, then taking the Injun myself and picking up all that Gold?"

"She is." The Bummer nodded over at the Indian woman sitting high in her saddle, "She has a pistol under her dress. You shoot me, she shoots you. Then she and the Injun go pick up the Gold."

The Reverend lowered his sights. He leaned back against the wooden seat and turned his intense blue light on the Indian woman.

The Bummer kept his own eyes on the Reverend, he took the cigar out of his mouth and laughed, "Well Reverend Jake, every cripple has his own way of walking."

One of the wagons creaked its way down the last turn of the steep road and pulled to a stop next to the buckboard. The driver stood up, his lips shaking loose the crust of dust on his face, "Reverend Jake, there's whole lot of boys hurt up yonder, bleedin and cut up bad. You'd better go on up and give em the word of the Lord. I don't think all of them are going to make it."

"Reverend Jake has a new vocation," the Bummer sucked on his cigar and blew a cloud of smoke in the driver's direction.

The driver spun around, the red circles of his eyes flashed in his dusty face, "You know Mister, you're the one that led us up that old stage road. You said it was so we could keep hid. A body would think you were tryin to kill us all. That road's no wider than two body lengths in some steep places." His eyes glowed in the dying light, "Mister, there better be a lot of Gold where we're goin."

The Bummer stretched his arms, "Gents, I'm tuckered.

I think I'm going to put my bedroll down right here. In the morning we can count up how many goldrushers will still be riding with us. Let's turn in." He took his bedroll from the buckboard and spread it flat on the hard ground. He lay down puffing on his cigar. Over his head the light went out of the sky everywhere and the stars danced through the thin mountain air like drunken dogs.

The Bummer pushed the stovepipe hat off his face and blinked his eyes in the morning sun. He got to his feet. There were no fires going. The narrow meadow at the base of the road was filled with wagons and carts, some only on three wheels, leaning down until one corner touched the earth, others with every board splintered and barely hinged to their own axles. The sound of moaning and snoring arose along the strip of meadow as the Bummer went over to his packhorse and slipped a roll of rope off the saddlehorn. He stepped up the side of the buckboard and looked in. The Indian's nostrils pinched tight as loud snores belched from his open mouth. Reverend Jake was behind him, sitting in an upright position, one hand on the barrel of the shotgun propped across his knees, his head slumped over in a dead sleep. The Bummer raised the gold tip of his cane to the sun and whacked it down on the base of the Reverend's head, then lashed the rope around his arms and legs until he was tied up in a ball with a bandanna stuffed in his mouth. The Indian jerked from his seat and looked into the trees as if someone were coming to shoot him, then he saw the Bummer right before him the words hissing from the delicate curved mouth, "You lying thievin Injun, running off with all my Badger bet money in Truckee. Your sidekick Squirrel got his Injun brains blasted all over the desert, but you got away again. Honest to John I ought to have left these gents here to hang your red tail. But you're going to pay me off first, John C. Luther is not sharing that Gold with the devil. You're taking me, and me alone, to that lake, then you're going to sink to the bottom of it with a ton of rocks tied around your neck. Look at this." He motioned down to Reverend Jake, "look what your lying thieving red hide's got me into." He gazed around at the broken wagons and bleeding animals tethered to trees. "Now you've got *me* fishing troubled waters. But honest to John Captain, you can bet your boots this time you're going to pay your dues. This time you're going to pay *off*. Now get up on the back of Molly's horse, ride slow into those thick trees, then ride for your life."

The Indian swung up behind the woman and grabbed the reins around her waist. The Bummer prodded his own horse up behind them and shoved the barrel of the Reverend's gun into the Indian's back, "Don't try to shit any fancy turds Captain. I'm riding right behind, this little number you feel up against you will blow the heart right out of your body and through the woman. Now git."

The Indian turned the horse around and spurred it into the long shadows at the edge of the meadow. The morning sun had not broken through the trees. He moved his horse into the night of the forest until he saw daylight bursting before him and heard the Bummer behind, "Ride, Redskin, Ride!" The Indian brought the sharp heel of his boots into the horse's flanks and spurred it through the tall trees into the daylight and back onto the old stagecoach road.

"Hold up here." The Bummer reined his horse to a stop and pushed himself up, leaning his ears back at the forest. The sharp chirp of a bird cut the air over his head and he jerked around in his saddle. He kneed his horse up even with the Indian's and flashed his gold smile out from beneath the black brim of his hat, "Well Captain, it appears as if all those gents back yonder are sleeping like logs." He took out a cigar, lit up and clenched it in his teeth, "Ride for your life! Heeeyaaah!"

The Bummer halted his horse at the edge of the river, "This must be the middle fork of the Yuba." He swung his head back at the piles of darkening clouds falling over one another in the fast sky, "Looks to be rain before it turns night, we'll get across the river now while it's low. Once we get to the other side it'll rain and the water will rise up so fast no gent will be able to get a horse across

the river for another two days. We've got a day's ride on
those gents behind, but even if they make better time than
us they'll never be able to get over this swollen river. Dismount, Captain, we don't want to lose our horses in these
rapids. We'll walk them across."

The Indian swung down and took his horse by the lead,
pulling it over the crumbling bank into the slashing roar
of white water cutting over splintered rocks. He led the
horse across the slippery run of the granite bottom. He
felt the reins tug in his hand and spun around, an iron
hoof of the horse hit a loose rock, throwing his front knee
out as his head slapped down into the swirling foam. The
Indian whipped the reins up, forcing the horse's neck
back, dragging the weight of its falling body off the buc-
kled knees.

"Get that woman off!" The Bummer screamed over the
fierce white current. "She's going to throw him over!"

The long hair of the woman whipped from side to side
as she held the saddlehorn with both hands, her body
swaying back and forth over the horse's back. The Indian
flung an arm around her waist, splashing her down into
the water. He slipped to his knees, supporting the weighted balance of the animal behind as his boots shoved into
the slipping rocks for a hold. Then he pushed up to his
feet, running through the thick current to the bank, he
heaved the dripping hulk of the horse onto the shore,
swung up on his back and knifed his boots into the wet
belly, "GIT ON YOU!" The horse reared back, almost
flipping over into the current. Its front hooves slammed to
dry rock as the high whinnying knocked from its chest slit
the air. "Git!" The Indian banged his knees into the
horse's sides and felt the body bolt out from under him
and up the bank as the blast of pain in his back knocked
him off onto the sharp rocks. The Bummer stood over
him with the barrel of the shotgun still clutched in his
hands, the heavy wood stock held high over his head like
a club. "I shouldn't have just knocked you off you lying
thieving redskin. I should have blasted your heart right
out your chest!" He kicked the blunt toe of his boot deep
into the Indian's stomach, "You tried to get away from

me you red snake!" He yanked the Indian up by the hair
and pushed his sharp gold teeth into the brown face, "You
lost a horse and all our supplies. Honest to John Injun,
you bet your boots you're going to pay *all* your dues this
time. Then I'm going to take this shotgun, ram it down
your throat, pull the trigger, and blow you to Kingdom
Come!" He brought the bone butt of his knee slamming
into the Indian's face and watched him roll over onto the
jagged rocks with the blood flowing from his mouth as the
strong white current roared past his head.

The Bummer leaned back on his saddle propped against
a tree and tipped the glass flask to his lips, "Ahhhh. Yes
sir, I've got a fondness for squaws." He sloshed the whiskey around at the bottom of the flask as he peered
through its amber glass at the blaze of the campfire leaping into the night sky. He could see the Indian woman
through the glass as she held her wet leather dress out to
the flames to dry. The Bummer twisted the glass around
so it appeared the woman's smooth skin was burning, the
hardnippled swell of her breasts blazing. "John C. Luther
is a gentleman though, a well bred Southern gentleman, I
know what civilized women are like too. I was married to
a well bred lady, she was a high priced ticket. It took all
the current funds I had available just to give her a proper
wedding in Galveston Texas. That was back in '55, then I
brought her West to watch me get rich, but everything
was pretty well staked by then, there wasn't one diggins
that didn't have at least two hundred men standing on top
of it with pistols. Well my Texas lady always was a restless sort. She's the one begged me from the beginning to
come West, she didn't want to live with me in Galveston
society. There weren't too many women around the mines
in the first days, and there were *no* ladies. Eggs were five
dollars apiece in the winter of '56, plus she was getting
blue in the face from the cold, so she went into one of the
boom town theaters just to keep warm, she always did admire the stage, so it didn't take much coaxing from the
proprietor to get her up on it. She sang a pretty tune, her
bosom swelled out like a robin and everybody stamped

their boots and threw chunks of Gold up on the stage. I
didn't want her to lose anything that was her due so I
scurried in the background to pick it all up. From there
she went on the stage circuit, clean around the West she
went, getting famous for the classy French Dance she was
performing. She hit all the boom towns, you couldn't get
in the hall where she was playing. I was a good gent to
her and tagged along for three years. Then in Colorado
she stopped acting like a lady and I found out. So I did
what any civilized gent would do, I got mad at her and
gave her a baby. She run off to Frisco then to have it cut
out by a Russian, but he cut out a big chunk of her belly
too. I took her body back to Galveston and disposed of all
my available funds giving her the funeral a lady deserves." He tipped the bottle back up to the delicate curve
of his mouth and sipped on the golden liquid. "Now this
squaw here," he pointed the bottleneck across the fire.
"She looks just like the lady I had once. If you was to cut
her head off and paint her body white you wouldn't be
able to tell them apart." He stood and swayed before the
fire, digging the tip of his cane into the earth for support,
"But that isn't what I bought her for." He walked around
the fire pointing the Gold tip of the cane before him,
"That isn't what I bought you for, is it Molly Moose?" He
hooked the cane into the long wet fringes of the dress and
flung it to the ground. He brought the gold tip of the cane
up and rested it on her chin, then ran the warm metal
down her neck and circled a breast, pushing in the hard
nub of a nipple. "Molly was meant for other things. She's
no bird to be shut in a cage. I've already had her photograph taken by a professional camera, the fame of that
photograph has spread around the Horn and back to the
East Coast. There's one fate for Molly Moose," he drew
the line of the cane between her breasts and over the
curve of her stomach to the thick brown line of her hair.
"Some gent who is getting up a Wild Injun Show wants to
pay cash money for Molly Moose in the sum of solid
Gold bricks. This gent will buy her and display her
around the Country, even across the water to old Europe.
This gent wrote me he intends to parade her naked red

body in front of Queens and Kings." He drew the cane tip down on her thigh, "Then you know what John C. Luther is going to do Captain? I'm going to take all the Gold bricks and all the Gold from the lake you're taking me to, and I'm going to run for Senator." He glided the cane down to her knee then brought it across and ran it up her other thigh, poking through her dark hair, slipping the gold tip between her legs. "Yes sir Captain, no matter which eye you look at this red beauty from, she's one long breasted cut of meat." He drew the cane out and turned his back on her as he swigged the last of the whiskey. "But not for me, I'm a civilized man."

The Bummer rode his horse to the top of the rise, the rope anchored to his saddlehorn pulling the two Indians tied together close behind. He stopped his horse and lit up a cigar as his eyes widened in a smile at the river running below him. Above the river through the high clouds rose the distant fingers of stone thrusting themselves into the sky. The Bummer blew a big cloud of smoke, " 'Stone touches sky.' Those are the Sierra Buttes, and that's the North Yuba running below us. 'Beyond two rivers. River coming out of mouth of lake.' Honest to John we're almost there!" He spurred the horse down the rocky slope toward the rushing slash of river, puffing away on his cigar and tapping a tune out with his finger against the black stovepipe hat. He didn't see the two lines of men on horses and mules coming in at him from both ends of the slope. His finger stopped tapping and he spit the cigar out. Below in the trees along the river a line of riders moved out. He wheeled the horse around, slapping it on the rump and digging his spurs deep into its sides. The horse's hooves clattered on the loose stones as it dragged the two Indians up the slope behind it. The Bummer spun around and slashed at the rope with his knife as he heard the distant muffled pops, then the sucking swishes of lead striking the air around his head. He rose high in the saddle and threw both arms straight up.

The riders closed around the Bummer from all sides. Three lassos spun through the air and dropped over his

head, cinching together on his neck. Reverend Jake rode
up and pulled his shotgun from the Brummer's saddle holster then put his blue eyes on him. "You *Bummer*, I should
have cut you off at the beginning and hung this Indian red
devil. But now we've come this far. The Lord's Will be
done. We go to the Lake of Gold."

The Bummer pushed hard at the delicate curve of his
lips until they twisted up in a smile, "Well Reverend Jake,
no man wants an honest opinion of a horse after he's
bought it."

Reverend Jake slipped the shotgun back in his own saddle holster and reined his horse around so its tail slashed
at the Bummer. "If we ride hard we'll be at Goose Lake
after nightfall. Then in the morning we can go up to the
Lake of Gold. There's nobody between us and the Gold
now. If we ride hard enough we'll beat this rain."

The riders moved down the slope and along the river.
They rode over a narrow wooden bridge toward the fingers of stone reaching into the sky. When it turned dark
the rain spit down in cold stinging pellets at them, bouncing off their hats and the backs of their horses. The winding trail flung itself straight up, the new cuts of water running under the horses' hooves until the mud thickened
into a suck and the men swung off the horses and led
them up, turning their heads down to the invisible clouds
above them scattering a long held burden of water back to
its source. The riders could hear the rain punching into
the surface of a lake and they looked up through the swirl
of water in the black night before them to the sudden
sight. All around the lake were lights. The lights glowed
through the flapping roofs of tents. The rain stopped. The
clouds relieved of their burden, blowing away as quickly
as they had blown in, exposing the moon, its own light
following the same path the rain had taken, illuminating
the calm surface of the lake. The riders could see the men
from the tents coming for them with their gun barrels
flashing in the moon's light. The leader stopped before the
riders, his boots sunk up to their tops in the mud, two lanterns were held to his face and caught the red glint of his
sharp beard, "Which one of you is the Bummer?"

"You *mean* John C. Luther, don't you gent?" The Bummer kneed his horse out in front of the riders, the lantern light showing his arms roped down and his hands tied up behind his back.

"Cut the Bummer loose."

"Sure thing Colonel."

The Bummer rubbed his freed hands and slipped off his horse into the thick mud.

"We've been expecting you Bummer. We don't like to be kept waiting. Cut the two Indians down too!"

"Who *are* you gents?"

"I am Colonel Buck Plant of San Francisco, recently retired of Grant's Army."

The Bummer's laugh rang out in the night, the gold flash of his open mouth shined in the light thrown from the lanterns and over the riders. He slapped the side of his checkered pants and turned around in the mud, "Well Reverend Jake, when the Lord closes one door he opens another."

"You get on down too Reverend Jake, and come with us. Your Nevada boys made a long trip for nothing, there won't be any pay day for you," the Colonel pulled at the red point of his beard. "Bummer, you care for some eats?"

"I'd be much obliged Colonel, honest to John it would be civilized of you."

The Colonel led the way back through the mud and in between the rows of tents to a large canvas cabin built high up on a log platform, a board painted sign lit up by a hanging lantern was nailed to the broad tree before the open flaps of the cabin: "LOOK HERE! For Fifty Cents YOU Can Get A GOOD SQUARE MEAL At the Howling Wilderness Saloon! WALK IN GENTS!"

The Colonel pushed his way through the flaps into the noise of the cabin full of men, "He's here! We've got the Bummer!"

"What took you so long Bummer!"

"Hey Bummer, we could have told you a shortcut!"

"Much faster than that old Fishback stageroad Bummer!"

"Good to see you got your Injun friend Bummer! It looks like you took good care of him!"

"We didn't expect you to bring his squaw along too! She could have come with us Bummer!"

The Bummer blinked his eyes at the strong kerosene light of the many hanging lanterns, "How long have you gents been here?"

"HaH!" The Colonel pushed himself back on the heels of his boots, "Two days! There are over two thousand tents pitched around this lake. Men coming in at least a thousand a day. You should have known no one man could have a whole Lake of Gold to himself, let alone taking a whole townful of others to help him fish it out. Yes sir Bummer, the *word* of Gold Lake was all over California before you got out of Nevada, it was even in the Frisco papers. You've started a whole new GOLDRUSH. Men are jumping off their jobs in four States. I thought you were an educated man Bummer. You should have known from the start that trying to keep a secret about Gold is like shoveling shit against the tide."

A short man made his way through the crowd of men, a shiny black coat was stretched and hung by two buttons over the fat hill of his belly, he held up in his arms like a baby the fat stub of a dog with a wide flat mouth showing the vicious knives of its teeth.

"I'll buy that dog!" the Bummer shouted.

"He aint for sale Mister Bummer," the man stroked the bullet head of the dog.

"You ever use him for Badger baiting? You could get rich putting that critter up against a badger."

"I would never put him up agin a badger Mister Bummer, this is an *English* dog, special bred he is."

"Bred for what, gent?"

"Bred for Bulls."

"You mean this little critter goes for Bulls? Why he'd get stomped!"

The short man smiled and ran his hand gently under the Bull dog's drooling chin, "Don't ever bet on it, he's bred for all jaws and teeth, bred special for Bull baiting. He'll jump right up on a Bull's neck quick as a snake and sink his teeth right into the jug'lar vein, his jaws is so powerful you can't break their hold with a hammer. Once he gets the taste of blood you *have* to kill him to get him off, just like he was a cock rooster."

"We've got to get us some Bulls and lay bets on this special bred dog."

"You watch this," the short man set the dog at his feet and flung the tent flap back. "See that big sugarpine tree with the sign nailed on it? You just watch." He pointed his finger at the tree and screamed "BULL!"

The dog sprang out of the tent and landed with his teeth tearing out the bark as a grinding growl churned from the vicious machine of his lungs, the short muscle of his body acting like one big mouth as he ripped through the thick bark of the tree, his bite so powerful it carried him completely off the ground and up the tree like he was gnawing his way up on the meat of a giant leg. The short man ran out and socked the dog behind the neck. The dog fell off the tree, panting and puffing, the pink fist of his tongue hung over the glistening teeth as his bright big eyes looked up to his master.

"That's some dog gent!" The Bummer ran out and clapped the man on the back. "What's your name?"

"Poker Charlie."

"You mean gent, you are the Poker Charlie who won the biggest game of poker ever dealt during the Rush of '49? *The* Poker Charlie who run all those shiploads of yellow coolies for the Railroads into Frisco harbor?"

The short man smiled up with his dog, "That's right Mister Bummer."

The Bummer screwed down one eye hard and popped the other wide open, the delicate curve of his mouth twirled down in a mean line as he stabbed the metal tip of his cane in the mud, "What are you doing here, gent?"

"Why Mister Bummer, I've come to make history. Your Gold Lake is the beginning of a new Era for America. Fortunes are to be made, mansions built, men elected to office. Gold will once again become King over Silver."

"Well it's the Injun who said there was Gold in the

lake! I've never seen it! The Injun's the one who spread the word!"

"Ahhhh, Mister Bummer," the short man wagged his head back and forth. "Don't be so modest and give all the credit to your Injun friend. Don't try to fool your fellow man at this late hour, every man here knows that lake exists. *You* said so. I'm here because I love to gamble. We all came here to get rich, but then look at it from the other end of the stick, we've all been wildcatted before, if there isn't Gold in that lake, if you have wildcatted us, why then . . ." He looked down at his smiling dog, "Why then I'm just going to have to point the finger at you and yell *BULL!*"

"Come on back in this here tent Bummer and get your eats," the Colonel yanked his beard and laughed. "We want to make sure that if that dog is put on you at least he'll get a good meal."

The Bummer walked back into the cabin.

"What'll it be Bummer," a sweating man with a dirty white apron slapped around his waist demanded.

"Steak and potatoes, gent."

"Beans fried in goose grease is all we got. What'll you drink?"

"Bourbon, southern and smooth."

"A whiskey bottle of milk for five dollars is what you'll get. You pay for your Injun friends too. I closed my hardware store down in Folsom to come up here and strike it, but I aint rich yet, it aint *tomorrow* yet."

The Bummer tapped his cane against his checkered pants, "You just hold on gent, it's coming."

The Colonel threw his arm around the Bummer, "I've got just what you want, have it tucked right here in my pocket." He drew out a long flask and shoved it to the Bummer, "Here, take a shot off this pocket pistol."

The Bummer tipped the flask and gulped, "Ahhhhh. What is it?"

The Colonel tugged his beard, took a swallow himself and his eyes lit up, "It's Poker Charlie's special import, he brings it down from Port Townsend in Washington country, it's tobacco juice, cayenne pepper, whale oil, and rubbing alcohol."

Poker Charlie smiled as he stroked the bullet head of the dog, "Give your Injun friend a pull, it may clear out his head so he can remember exactly where that Lake of Gold is come sunup."

"Give the Captain some!" The Bummer tipped his stovepipe hat back on his head, "Captain Rex can't hold his liquor two minutes before he begins singing like a bird. Honest to John it's the damndest thing you've ever heard. Go on Captain, sing for us!"

The Indian took the bottle and sucked its fluid into his body, it fired his throat and leaped in his chest.

"Don't hog it! You swallowed at least half Injun boy," the Colonel ripped the bottle from the Indian's grasp and took a swig.

The Indian looked around him with the liquor in his body, the faces in the crowded room burned in the kerosene light. He saw the Reverend across the cabin, the intense blue of his eyes glaring amidst all the lantern wicks flaming through glass. He could feel the fierce light of the Reverend going past him to the woman at his side. He saw the Bummer laughing, his gold teeth flashing in the room. He turned his eyes straight into the flaming wicks in the lanterns and was blinded by white light as the wings in his head burst out his mouth and fanned a feathered song in the flame of the room. He heard his loud voice singing the songs birds sang long ago that he had learned in dreams. All the ancient fury welled up from him and its feathered sound conquered the room.

"Listen to that!"

"Whooop—peeeeeeeiiiii!"

"He's singing like a *BIRD!*"

"Honest to John!" the Bummer called out to the song. "Aint that the damndest!"

Poker Charlie smiled as he stroked the bullet head of his dog.

"Hey! Poker Charlie, listen to that! Your dog is singing too, listen to him whine. He's loco too!"

Poker Charlie stroked under the dog's drooling chin,

then looked up. The Indian stopped singing, for the moment only the dog's whining could be heard, then it ceased, leaving the room empty.

"Honest to John, aint it the damndest!" The Bummer grabbed the bottle back from the Colonel and took a drink.

Poker Charlie gazed over at the Bummer as his hand caressed the short fur of the muscled neck beneath him, "Bummer, how about you and me start up a game of Monte while we're waiting for sunup?"

The Bummer looked down at the dog, then across to Reverend Jake with his burning light fixed on the Indian woman. "I've got a better idea gent," he tapped his cane against his high hat and clicked his tongue like two stones being rapped together. "I've got a fondness for squaws." All the men turned their eyes on him. "And if I know *gents*, I know they *all* have a fondness for squaw meat." The men turned their eyes to the woman standing close to Captain Rex, the sway of the leather fringe draped down her long dress. The Bummer turned his eyes on her too, "I always knew when I bought her this squaw would come in handy." He waved the gold tip of his cane and pointed it at the woman, "This squaw is a whole show to herself gents. She'll run herself to death under you. Honest to John gents, this long tall breasted squaw is just what the doctor ordered. Think of her for *yourself*, gents. Honest to John, I know her body better than the insides of my own pockets and I can tell you she's the finest squaw meat west of the Dakotas. She's the sweetest two-breasted, sweet-breasted creature man was ever privileged to slumber on the fine ass of. Think of her for *yourself*. Gents. Think of *her*. Don't it make your tongue hard. *Think* of her. Don't it arouse the *meat* in you. I can tell you, gents, when you do your stuff on her her whole body starts smoking like hot bread." The Bummer looked around at all the mouths hanging open in the silent faces as they stared at the woman. "Well gents," his voice became a close whisper that filled the room. "Don't we have any takers? Are you all ashamed of eating a little squaw meat?"

"My asshole should be ashamed of shitting!!!" The scream blasted the canvas sides of the cabin back as the men shoved and knocked in every direction trying to make their way to the woman.

The Bummer beat his cane on their heads. "Gents! Gents!"

The men stopped where they were and waited for the Bummer to instruct them; he let out a deep sigh, "Now then gents, let's be civilized. We're just slapping water as long as we don't have some order, even in the wilderness we must live by Law. Now I calculate this longbreasted squaw to be about eight-bits out of your jeans. She's going to cost you, I didn't win her myself off some Mexican in a card game. She was *expensive*. Now I want everybody outside the tent." He grabbed his cane in both hands and shoved the bulk of bodies out into the mud. He could see men coming from the rows of other tents, shouting and swinging their lanterns as they came running through the deep mud and got in the long line. He held his cane high and shouted, "Let's make this a *real* BOOMtown gents! There's more than one way to make a strike off this country! She'll be laid out on the table inside for you just like Mama's pie! Stop your shoving! I want two lines here!" He drew the pendant of his gold watch from the deep pocket of his checkered pants. "Each man has four minutes to get his shot off!" He flipped off his hat. "Now those gents that have their eight-bits stay in one line! Those gents that have seven-bits or less, get in the other line because I'm a democrat, I believe every man should get a fair shake, so you with seven-bits or less can go in and watch. If you can't have the steak at least you can smell it cooking!" He stuck his empty hat out between the two lines, the first two men paid the price and went inside.

The sun was rising fast in the east, spreading its gold light down on the lake. The Colonel and Poker Charlie walked down a long row of tents, their boots sucking through mud as other men came out of their tents and marched behind. They stopped before the canvas cabin. "Bummer!" All along the shore and up the slope in the gold light the crowd of men stood waiting in boot deep mud. "Bummer!" The Colonel shouted again. "Bring your Injun out here!"

The flap of the tent flew back, "Good morning gents." The Bummer's face stuck out and he stepped off into the mud. "Come on out Captain, these gents are impatient to go get rich!"

The Indian stepped through the flap and faced the men.

"Ask him where the Gold is Bummer," the Colonel leaned forward in the mud.

"Captain, tell these gents where the Gold is."

The Indian looked down at the gold light spreading over the heads of the crowd.

"*Where* is it Captain?" The delicate curve of the Bummer's mouth pushed along his face and died at the corners.

"He aint gonna talk!"

"Honest to John Captain, these gents are hanging on your words."

"Look at that! He won't say nothin!"

"Speak up Captain, don't keep the gents waiting for their pay day."

"He's closed up tighter than a drum!"

"The Bummer caint make him talk!"

"I'll make him talk by Jesus," the Colonel's boots sucked out of the mud and he pulled the Indian down from the cabin and threw him up against the tall tree. "Rope him up with his hands stretched high!"

The ropes whipped around the Indian's body and cinched him to the broad trunk with his hands tied straight up over his head.

The Colonel leaned close to the Indian until the red point of his beard stabbed him in the face, "*Where's* the riches Injun?"

"He aint talkin!"

The Colonel strode back twelve paces and whipped around pulling a pistol from his coat. "Where's the Gold!"

"He won't say nothin, he wants it for himself!"

The Colonel drew the pistol up and aimed, "Where's the wealth!"

"He aint talkin Colonel!"

The gun fired, ripping a chunk of bark out over the Indian's head. The Colonel blew the smoke off the barrel tip, "Have you ever noticed how all Injuns look alike? I can't tell one from the other. They all look the same to me. Let's make this one look a little different so we'll always be able to tell him apart from the others." He drew the gun up and squeezed the trigger, the slug tore the top of the Indian's thumb off as it shot into the meat of the tree. "Where's the Gold, Injun!"

Captain Rex looked straight across the mud at the man with the gun. The blood trickling out of his thumb and down his wrists.

"He'll never talk!"

"Let's make this Injun prettier than all the rest and match his other thumb up even." The Colonel sighted the pistol and it banged its lead ball through the air and blew the other thumb off so the blood shot out of it and ran down the whole arm. The gun came up again and pointed dead on the Indian's head. "This is it Injun!" The Colonel's red beard flared in the sunlight, "This one is for your brain!"

"The Gold is in the footprint of the small bear."

"That's Little Bear Lake!" The Bummer shouted. "That's where it must be! Little Bear Lake!"

The men were already running through the mud, slipping and sliding through it as they scrambled to their horses.

The Bummer ran up to the Indian and grabbed him by the throat, his hot breath slapping in the Indian's face as the words burned from his delicate lips, "You know what the Roman gents always used to say Captain. Every hour wounds, the last one kills. I'm coming back to blast your heart out!" And he was gone, fighting his way across the mud to the horses.

The thudding sound of horses' hooves beating in the mud died off across the lake. No one stood before the Indian except Poker Charlie, stroking the bullet head of the dog. "Well my Captain, I imagine Mister Bummer will be

wanting to get right back to you. As for me, the Colonel
and I are partners in everything we touch. I intend to
spend the entire day with your little lady in the tent. I'm
not the kind that likes to be rushed. Mister Bummer was
right, we all *do* have a fondness for squaws." He smiled
and rubbed the dog uner the chin, his boots taking long
sucks out of the mud as he walked over and disappeared
in the tent.

The gold sun pointed straight across the Indian's head
as it slipped along the high slope of the mountain and
splashed its dying color deep beneath the lake's surface.
The Indian was slumped against the ropes that bound his
body to the tree, the streams of blood from his thumbs
had dried down his wrists and arms, crusting and pulling
at his skin. He heard the sound of slapping wind and
turned his head to the many wings digging in the air. An
arrow of ducks was headed over the lake into the dying
sun. He watched them drift out of sight, their far, invisible call echoing back to him. The sun slipped off the high
slope of the mountain, sending the last of its blazing fingers over the green landscape. The Indian jerked his head
around. He heard the pounding. It came through the
trees. It came across the water. The pounding of horses'
hooves. He pushed his back against the tree and strained
toward the sound. A horse burst through the trees, galloping down the long muddy row between the tents. *The
Bummer*. He whipped his horse, the heel of his boots
slashing the flanks. The Indian strained his body in the
ropes, twisting away from the horse flying at him. He
heard the loud slap of leather on horse flesh. He felt the
wind of the horse, its heat blew over him. Then it was
gone. Rode by. He heard the Bummer's voice coming
back to him, "You lying Red Devil!" The ground heaved,
the Indian felt the earth shaking and vibrating up through
the tree he was lashed to. Beating their horses down the
long muddy row between the tents was the Colonel with a
block of galloping bumping horses pounding the earth beneath their iron hooves, their riders bent to the chase as
they flashed by the Indian. The flap of the tent flung open

and the short man ran out in the mud, he looked up at the horses galloping off into the trees, then across to the Indian, "Red Snake!" He threw the dog from his arms, "BULL!" The dog sprung over the mud, a growl tearing from its wide mouth of bladed teeth as its powerful jaws clamped into the Indian's leg, the short blunt muscle of the body lifting off the ground as it tore into flesh. Molly Moose jumped from the tent, the fringe of her dress streaking behind her as she passed the short man and slashed her knife across the muscle of the dog's neck. The dog thudded into mud spurting blood. "You've killed my *dog!*" The short man jumped at the woman, his hands clawing for her throat, she whirled around and sunk the knife into his fat belly, letting him fall away from her into the mud next to the dog. She ran to the side of the tent and leaped up on his horse, then reined it over to the Indian and leaned down, cutting the ropes binding his body to the tree. Captain Rex swung up on the horse and threw his bloody hands around the woman and they rode off into the sunset.

I AM the Antelope Dreamer.

Listen. The Fawns whistle. Look at the wind coming. Carrying the sound of whistling Fawns through the sleeping hills. The stars shake like silver Fishscales on a quiet lake. I am the Antelope Dreamer. Look at the wind coming. Look at the wind coming with dust. It carries the sound of Blackbirds singing across the river. I can smell the river. I can smell the Antelope in the Sky. I am a wonder hunter. I stalk the Antelope on the mountain. I follow him footless through blossoms of timber. I sing down the stars and gather them into the bowl of the Moon. I suck the fire of stars like juice from berries. I hunt through the tops of trees. I hunt through air. I have a fire in my heart. The flames flapping like wings through the tops of trees. My Ancestors were hunters. My Ancestors were Hunters, Dancers, Dreamers, Walkers. All the Ancestors are dead or dying. I dream the last day. I am the last Dreamer. When my dream dies there will be no more Antelope. Understand my Magic. Look to the child sleeping in the mountain. Listen to the last stands of timber breathing. Follow with your eye the Dog Dancer in the Sky. Follow to the Milky Way. It is the Road of the Ghost. It is milk for a Fawn, streaked on a Fawn's mouth, streaking down the black Sky. Lighting the way over the river. The Blackbirds sing across water where it is always flowing. There is a fire in my heart. It is a Big fire burning under the rock. The high river flows over the rock. Water is in high places everywhere. Washing the white burden from the land. Exposing the red Earth, black roots, brown fruit. Let the people stand in high places everywhere. Let the people see heart to heart. Their souls kiss.

I am alone with you Christ. Our Spirits flow as two Fish in the same river. I have come down from the mountain to search your words. You have ridden the Ghost Pony the day the Sun died. Only you can dance our birth. If you dance the souls will come back. We sit here on this flat land. All around us the flat land goes out a distance further than a man's life. All around the flat land is covered by the white burden of snow. We sit alone. Two Blackbirds on a Cloud. The fire before you has grown cold. Only you can make the sacred Bird rise from its bed of ashes. Only you can sing the people up. The ring of rocks around the fire is the circle of our Ancestors. Only you can dance up the Sacred Piñon Tree of our family. Your song curling around the Tree. Sing your song oh Christ. I am too cold to die. My ears bleed. My tongue is bruised. Answer my soul. Uncover the sign.

The Sun was full over the Christ. His body sunk deep within his black clothes. He had no shadow. All around him the snow melted from the clumps of sage as he presented in his palm a black stone smoothed into a bowl. He screwed a hollow wooden stem into the notched stone bowl and made his Pipe. His other hand held the worn skin pouch that was the feed bag taken from the throat of the running Quail. The bag was not stuffed with wild seeds and nuts, it smelled strong of yellow medicine. The Christ filled the bowl with medicine, took off his boots and folded his legs beneath him, holding the Pipe carefully up in both hands as he offered it to my people so they may walk the Oneness Trail. He stretched the Pipe out in each sacred direction. To the north, *welmelti,* to the east, *pauwalu,* to the south, *haneleti,* to the west, *tangelelti.* To all Washo. He lit the Pipe. His breath sucking the flame through the bowl of tobacco until it glowed one strong

bright red ember. The smoke of wildgrass sage came up
from his body, its soft blue Spirit rising in the air. Traveling in all sacred directions to cover the Earth. He crossed
the Pipe over to his left. I pushed my boots off and accepted, my legs folded beneath me with my head held
high as I touched the wooden stem to my lips and filled
my soul with sweet smoke. My lips sucked peacefully at
the hot stem as my body rose to meet the medicine. I
smoked the root of the Earth, it did not go into my belly,
it went into my heart, ascending to the heavens. The yellow stonebacked ring on my hand holding the sacred Pipe
burned bright as a Bird against my flesh. The wind goes
by my head. The smoke is swirled over the face of the
ring and I see myself walking. I see myself walking way
along down the road. My Spirit catches up to my walking
body and joins it. I walk with body and soul, flesh and
heart, way along down the black road toward the dying
Sun. I hear the horn honking behind me and turn to face
the squareback car popping and puffing up the hill. The
horn honked at my back and I jumped off the road, but
the car stopped alongside me, its tin sides shaking and engine steaming.

"Hey kid where you headed?"

I could see the driver high up on the seat, the shaking
car chattering his teeth away like a boxful of dice. I looked
to see if there were any trees I could run off into, but there
was nothing, nothing but the bare brown roll of hills.
"Frisco Jeens."

"You mean San Francisco don't you kid?" he called out
of the clattering machine.

I looked back over the bald hills, there was everywhere
to run, nowhere to hide. "I guess so?"

He kicked the door open, "Get on in then. This here is
Quincy we're coming into. You've got a long haul ahead
of you."

I jumped in and slammed the metal door shut. The car
banged and stuttered, then jolted back onto the road.

"Where you from kid?"

"Tahoe."

"Lake Tahoe! You mean you walked all the way from

Lake Tahoe! That's more'n one hundred miles of winding
mountain road. Don't you have folks?"

"They are all dead or dying."

He slammed the gear lever forward and put a funny
look on me, "I don't get your meaning." The funny look
began to fade, like it saw something coming in the distance it recognized so he smiled, "Hey, you're an Indian
aint you. You're so dark when I saw you walking along
the road I thought you was a nigger. I like to give a nigger
a ride, they know all the best jokes. Walked down from
Lake Tahoe huh, that's something. I used to work up at
Lake Tahoe years ago when they had the commercial fishing. I was a seine-rigger. You know what that is? It's a
boatman who goes out setting the long nets. We'd lug in a
ton of fish a day. All Whitefish and Tahoe Trout. I seen
trout as long as your arm and weighing over fifty pounds,
there was no end to the fish in Lake Tahoe in those days,
why that lake is so big they still don't know how deep it
really is. We took enough fish out of there to ship them as
far east as Kansas City. In one year the company I
worked for took seven hundred and forty thousand
pounds out of that lake. Funny thing about it though was
whenever you'd have a thunderstorm the nets would come
up empty." He slammed the gear lever down again. "Well
there aint no big commercial fishing up there no more,
been fished out, these days a man needs a license just to
throw a line and hook over the side of his boat, hell, they
just as well ought to give it back to you Indians is what I
say." He put his look back on me, "What's your business
in San Francisco?"

"Frisco Jeens."

"What do you mean, *Frisco Jeens.*" You're old enough
to talk sensible, you must be at least nineteen. In two
more years you can vote. Ah hell, no you can't, Indians
aint got the right to vote, Indians aint citizens of this
country. You can be damn good and sure you're better off
not voting anyways since it's Coolidge they'd get you to
vote for. Somebody ought to shoot that stuffed bird." He
cocked his thumb and pointed it over the seat, the back of
the car was filled with boxes of apples, "All Coolidge ever

gave the farmer was worms in their apples. I have to cart these all the way to Sacramento just to get a nickel a pound for them. Times is hard. You Indians aint the only ones roughing it these days. Now you explain all this stuff about *Frisco Jeens.*"

My fist covered the sock full of money in my pocket. I could feel the sharp edges of the coins biting my flesh. "Mister Fixa. Mister Fixa told me *Frisco Jeens* was in an iron bar cage where he can't hurt nobody. Mister Fixa said someday I could go for myself to see if what he said was true. Now I'm going. All the people are dead or dying. I'm going to see if *Frisco Jeens* is behind bars." He put his look on me and screwed it down hard on my eyes, "You're just talking Indian riddles. I can't make a nickel's worth of sense out of you. Just what in hell is *Frisco Jeens?*"

I turned away from his look and saw through the window the brown barren hills cover the Earth to the curve of the horizon, "A *Go-reel-ah.*"

His laughter banged out in the car, cutting through the heavy smell of apples and pushing out the windows. "My God," he choked, slapping my knee. "You Indians are funnier than a nigger!"

EATS! The high squarebacked car pulled off the road in among the trucks parked around the small shack with the big sign soaring over its roof EATS! I got down from the car among the trucks and the man leaned his head out of the window and shouted over the stuttering of his engine, "This is your last truck stop before San Francisco. You just hook a ride here and they'll roll you right into the big city." The car jerked out on the road, "Hey," he called back. "Tell em about your Go-reel-ah. Hah. They'll love that one so much they'll roll you right across the water to Hawaii!"

I could smell the food coming out of the shack. Strong smells of potatoes and gravy. I felt my sock full of money. But I did not go in. I sat against one of the trucks, putting my back up to the big wheel and closing my eyes to the world.

The boot nudged my leg. "Get on up. What do you think my truck is, the Cozy Cottage Motel?" The man stared down at me over the rise of his belly, the plastic sunvisor strapped over his eyes cast a money green glow on his entire face. I couldn't see his eyes. "Where do you think you're goin?"

"*Frisco Jeens.*"

"You'll never get to Frisco City in a truck, you can only go as far as the Oakland side across the bay from Frisco, then take the ferry boat over to Frisco City. You might as well get up in my truck then, I aint got all day to get to Oakland myself."

I climbed up and he swung the truck out into the highway, the rough surface bouncing his big body up and down on the hard seat, throwing the glow from the sunvisor over his face in different shades of green light. He turned to me as his hands held locked to the steering wheel. I couldn't see his eyes. "You know what I got in the back? You know what my load is? I'll tell you what I'm hauling since you asked. Lettuce. The worst job in California is picking lettuce. I wouldn't pick fucking lettuce in this State for no amount of pay, no how. Picking fucking lettuce is wetback work. It's my job to truck this fucking lettuce. I've been trucking lettuce up and down this haul seven years and I'll keep on trucking this fucking lettuce down this same road as long as people keep on eating like fucking rabbits."

I turned around in my seat and hung my head out the window, behind I could see the stacks of packed crates roped down tight on the flatbed of the truck, flapping green leaves poked out from between the wooden slats waving in the wind.

"Hey!" I could feel him poking me in the back. I turned around and looked at him, but I couldn't see his eyes. "Hey are you Mexican?"

"Washo."

"What is that? Indian or something?" He rolled the window down and spit into the wind. "Aint too many of your kind left is there kid."

I saw the water, it went out big with the Sun slapping
its face. It looked black. I tried to peer into it. It was thick
with salt. It was not clear like the high water of the mountains. It was heavy and secret. The boat scudded over its
surface like a Turtle dragging itself through mud. I hid in
among crates of lettuce, tomatoes and corn stacked high
on the deck, drinking of their Earth fragrance and pressing my face to the green leaves as the OAKLAND TER-
MINAL sign on the far shore behind me seemed to sink
in the water. Across the bay the white buildings of San
Francisco leaned off the sharp hills into clouds. When the
ferry bumped up along the dock I made a fist over the
sock full of money in my pocket and jumped down into
the City. I made my way off the docks and felt the hard
ground beneath my feet. They had covered the Earth with
stone. I saw it! The buildings went up and threw their
shadows down on the people walking in the hard streets. I
saw it! There, along a broad building was the face bigger
than the heads of ten men. It grinned out at the people in
the shadows with its fierce mouth cut like the blade of a
knife. The blare of its wild stonehard eyes burned like fire
and trapped me. Beneath the hunched hair of its hulking
shoulders was painted CAN'T BUST EM! *FRISCO
JEENS!* Mister Fixa had spoken the truth about him. He
does live in Frisco City. I saw his painted face everywhere. I turned a corner and he would be grinning down
from a high wall. The only place his face did not follow
me was into the streets of the yellowmen. In the streets of
yellowmen there were no faces painted on the walls. In
the streets of the yellowmen there were no white faces.
The smell of Fish came into the streets and I found my
way into a cellar where there were many bodies sweating.
A yellowman came to me in silken robes with a long knot
of black hair tucked under his collar. He bowed at my
presence. I pulled the sock from my pocket and dumped
the silver dollars out on a table, "My people are all dead
or dying. I have come from the mountains growing small
to see the great Animal spirit of the Whites. I have come
to see the bad medicine *FRISCO JEENS.* I have come to
see the Go-reel-ah behind bars. I have nothing left." The

yellowman smiled as he bent low before me and took my money into his silken robes. He led the descent further down into living levels below the street above. He brought me into the bowels of his Dragon.

The sweat-damp taste of smoke ran its fingers up my nostrils and laid me out beneath the low ceiling of a hundred knife cut bodies of soft Fish swimming in dark wood. The burning eyes of incense waved around me, revealing layers of bunks carved like caskets into the surrounding walls. Burning eyes of incense glowed from each bunk as I watched the yellow chests heave, their bodies rising to meet the Cloud of smoke sucked from bubbling waters. I took the stem of the long pipe into my mouth and drank of the Cloud, letting my head fall back into the soft field. I could see my dark hand clutching the yellow wrist of the man in silken robes. I spoke to him with my bruised tongue, "My people are all dead or dying. The people stand in high places everywhere. There is a fire in my heart." His teeth glowed above me, his words breathed through the smoke, "Chi Wen. Chi Wen. He will dampen the fire of your hot body, only this Dragon will offer you power to enshroud the fire in the soul. The fever is below. The water is above." He held a green stone-eyed clay image of a Dragon to my face, incense burned in its mouth, it burned the odor of a thousand Birds. I turned from it to the Tree of Heaven, to the Sacred Piñon Tree growing across the rolling hills from the heart of the people. Everything was calm. It was Gumsaba. The Big Time. Everything was plenty. There were no wants. No needs. No wind blew. I curled myself around the Sacred Tree and slept. I woke to the sound of laughing. The Piñon Tree shook with laughter and slid me from its trunk. Streaming down its sides to the broad base was on the one side water, on the other, blood. "What river will you follow Ayas my Antelope?" The Tree spoke through laughter. "Will you follow the River of Water or the River of Blood? Choose your course my Antelope." I walked to the Tree and ran my hands through the clear water streaming down its side, "I choose Water." The Tree laughed again and pulled me to its heart, "Ayas, my Antelope, Water is

good, you are a man of *Peace*." There was no wind. I saw
Deer coming up from the South whispering, "Ayas, don't
kill my baby any more. Bury your best baskets in graves.
Do not kill Lizards or Snakes without reason." The rain
fell through her words as blood dripped from my nose.
She went away to the South. Walking slowly with her
whitetail to me. "Ayas, Water is good. You are a man of
Peace."

There were many days when the Sun did not touch my
body. I lived in the belly of the Dragon and cooked the
Opium Cloud until a yellowman with the white finger of a
beard pointing down from his chin came to me and spoke
into my eyes, "You are not a dark Spirit. You are Indian.
I know." He put a hand beneath his robes and brought
forth a leather pouch and emptied it into his open hand.
"I know. I have been to your mountains. I have worked
your waters. From your rivers I have taken these precious
stones." The brilliant gold nuggets burned in his palm, he
closed a fist of thin fingers over them. "You have nothing
left. I know of what you search, this great animal Spirit of
the Whites. I know of the place where this bad medicine
is behind bars." He opened his fist to reveal the gold
stones again. "I have taken these precious stones from
your waters. Now I will give *you* something precious." He
led me up from the den of Opium eaters to the crowded
streets paved with stone, we traveled in a big wagon
pulled by horses along a straight iron track that ended
where the Sun died into the great Salt Water. There at the
edge of the Sea he showed me a cage among many caged
animal Spirits. A sign hung in front of the iron bars,
TROGLODYTES GORILLA. To me the words were hollow, only the truth of Mister Fixa's words filled my ears
as I clutched the iron bars and peered into the black skin-
soft face staring back at me.

I got on the Iron Road and headed east. I headed back
for the mountains, but when the door of the boxcar rolled
open I saw nothing but flat land that ran right over the
edge of the Earth. The man standing before me reached

up a hand to pull me down, "Welcome to Omaha Nebraska, redman, you now owe the Union Pacific Railroad one-hundred dollars American for a firstclass ticket from sunny California to groundhog Omaha. Bet you didn't know when you jumped this freight train two thousand miles ago that you had a firstclass accommodation, but you Indians always put up in the best of hotels, like barns and boxcars. You can go with Mister Jeremy Dole here over to the stockyards where you have four months doing six days a week, twelve hours a day at the sweet labor of working in the feedlots until you've paid your debt to the Railroad. Or, Mister Dole can walk you right by the stockyards to the jailhouse. Take your pick."

"How far is it to the California and Nevada border?"

"Oh, let's see," he scatched the roll of skin under his chin. "I'd say seventeen hundred miles by rail."

I looked out over the flat land. "I will work for you. Then I will go to the mountains."

"Thought you'd see it my way. Now you get along. There's seven hours more work in this day before chow, and you could use it. You look hungry as a horse."

Hungry Horse is what they called me. During the days I would watch the boxcars roll in off the flat land filled with cattle, their brown frightened bodies packed together, then turned into the tight chutes and herded into large pens, their damp noses pushing against one another, having only room in the crowded space to eat and raise their heads, bleating hollow sounds into the air before they were run up the concrete gangways and hit in the head with the blunt steel of a sledgehammer, their soft throats slit to drain all the thumping life from them, their brown bodies hoisted off the floor on hooks and slaughtered. The stink of rotting flesh soared in the air. My dreams were boiling blood. The nights filled with bleating cries. The days filled with dying brown bodies. On the seventh day of the week we were allowed to rest. One day was set aside to silence the sound of doomed flesh. One day was set aside to silence the smell of decayed meat. On the sev-

enth day of the week a wagon was sent to carry us into
town to hear the word of Jesus. I went. I saw this Jesus
dead up on a cross, nails driven through his flesh. The
sight of him brought the smells of the stockyards into the
bare meeting hall, the stink of bumping brown bodies rose
in my nostrils as we were told this Jesus was whipped
bloody and had a crown of thorns puncture his head before he was spiked up on a cross at the top of a mountain.
I put my hands into my pockets and dug the nails of my
fingers into my own flesh as the Word was spoken of how
this Jesus sweat blood praying for *my* soul. My spit turned
to salt and I choked back the bile rising in my belly as the
Word spoke of a soldier's spear rammed into the gut of
the crucified Jesus.

Jesus was on my back. Monday mornings I would think
of what the Word spoke, that behold, Jesus comes as a
thief to steal your soul, blessed is he that watcheth and
keepeth his garments lest he walk naked. The blind bumping bodies bleated around me for mercy. Their souls hung
from meathooks. Jesus was trying to take me captive. Jesus was trying to run me down. I was empty with thirst
and hunger. The scum of decayed flesh coated my bruised
tongue. Jesus was trying to steal my salvation. I couldn't
eat, sleep or work. I ran away from the cries of the
slaughter house. Night fell down on its face as I was still
searching through the strange streets to find where the
Word of Jesus was spoken. When I saw the door before
me I ran up the steps and grasped the iron ring knocker in
both hands, banging it against solid wood. I heard the
footsteps coming from the emptiness within. The door
swung open and the man who preached the Word peered
out. "Yes my boy?" He held the door pinned back with
his foot. I yelled into the crack. "Jesus is trying to steal
my soul!" "Get down on your knees and beg forgiveness."
"Jesus is a thief!" "You are a sinner. You walk naked. We
all see your shame. Pray for your salvation." "Jesus wants
all of me. I'm going to run from him. I'm going to *beat*
him!" My words screamed in the street and he put his
head farther through the door, his chin was smooth as a
woman's elbow. I wanted to reach up and touch it. He

spoke, "Even the Devil will tell you Boy, you can't damn Jesus unless you believe in Him."

I was sitting on the curb with my whiskey. Jesus said to take heed lest your hearts be overcharged with drunkenness. My head throbbed between my two hands like a heart, it roared with the knowledge that all things shall come to pass. Jesus was going to come back and dwell on the face of the whole Earth. Jesus was coming back a second time to get us all. A man sat down next to me and read the label of the bottle clutched in my hands, "I.W. HARPER. That's *good* whiskey, oils the joints and puts hair on the baby. But I got something better, something that will cure the Devil that ails you. Run all the Demons right out of your brain. Pump you up and blow you out. Leave you clean as a green blade of grass after a spring rain. Try this on . . ." I took the smooth green bottle he offered, yanked the cork and drank. "Well sir," he nudged my arm. "Isn't it all I touted it to be?" I couldn't talk. The fire of what he gave me robbed my voice and spun the heart of my head around so fast I thought it would bang my face into the cement sidewalk. "That sir is strong medicine. Prepared and bottled by the Crater Chemical Company of Cincinnati, sold in only two stores west of the Snake River, a natural root medicine blended with only the finest herbs, the exact ingredients is locked in a strong box, kept in a bank, and guarded by two armed men in downtown Cincinnati, but I can tell you straight it's strictly botanical. Some of its curing power consists of an ounce or three of dry ground cascara, polk root, senna, wildcherry and mandrake. It is a quick laxative and a natural cure. It sells for a popular price. One eaglefaced American dollar. Now sir, how do you like it?"

I felt my words fanned up by the flames in my chest and choking from my throat, "It's . . . it's the best thing I've ever tasted."

He smiled and pulled me up by the arm, my legs started bucking and jerking beneath me, knocking me against him for support. He guided me down the street, "Now tell me sir, what kind of Indian are you?"

"Washo."

"Then California and Nevada is your home. You have strayed far. What is it you want most from this life sir?"

I stopped him, looked around to see if anyone passing was trying to overhear me and whispered in his ear, "To get my soul back to the high mountains."

"What are your names sir? I've never met an Indian yet who didn't have at least three names."

"I am *Ayusiye*, the Antelope Walker, I am the Antelope Dreamer. I am Bob, a good strong name. I am here in Omaha called Hungry Horse."

"And you want sir only to return to your beloved mountains?"

"Only that can save my soul."

He pushed me away at arms length, the people swarmed by us. He held me up strongly by the shoulders and looked me in the eye, "Chief Hungry Horse, you're on your way."

Bright colored ribbons sparkled in my long black hair. The Sun caught all the brilliance of the beaded pattern woven on my buckskin clothes as I stood high on the back of the medicine wagon, "What the people need is a bottle of Chief Hungry Horse Indian Herbs. I'm an Indian like you and this bottle I hold in my hand before you is honest. I make it, I use it, and I sell it. Now I've got a special Indian agent's permit to come on this reservation and offer up for sale a remedy for all your problems. This remedy will put the Devil behind you, kill the vermin in your hair, the worms in your belly. And it is one thousand percent strictly botanical. It'll keep you warm at night. It'll pump you up and blow you out. Leave you as clean as a green blade of grass after a spring rain. I've sold this exclusive mix from Canada to Mexico, from Minnesota to Montana, and every Indian reservation in between. Two swigs of this mix will fix your fence. Two swigs of this mix will put the wind back in your lungs and the hair back on your head. Try it on. Thousands of satisfied Indians have. My clients are only the best, just you ask Charley Sheep of the Mescalero, Sharp Nose of the Arapaho, Rain In The Face of the Kiowa, Visalia Cornbread of the

Navajo, Deer Dick of the Blackfeet, Gunshooter of the Flatheads. Chief Hungry Horse's remedy has been drunk by the Uuchi, Yakima, Wichita, Creek, Caddo, Comanche, the Sioux, Shawnee, Smohalla, and Uintah, Ute, Osage, Quapaw. Every Indian across this land that is not made out of wood has drunk down a bottle of Chief Hungry Horse's best. They've all had it. I sold it to Wolfneck for the same price I sold it to Beaver Belt. It sold to each and everyone for the fair price of one American eagle dollar. I'm down to my last case, get it while you can, run the Demons right out of your brains. Step up, put your dollar down, take a swig and say if it isn't all I touted it to be." The people came forward, I added together the coins from four or five of them until a dollar was reached then handed a bottle down before adding up the coins for the next bottle. "Come on now, get it while it's to be got. Wilson's Prohibition Law may stop the Whites of drinking but there's nothing in that law says an Indian can't have his medicine. Step up and try some." I talked fast. I could see the dust waving like a flag behind the car skidding around the corners of the dirt road leading down off the distant plateau. I pocketed the money and slammed the lid over the remaining bottles. "Happy trails friends," I whipped the horses around and galloped the wagon for the highway that ran along the reservation border. The car was close behind me, blasting its horn. I held on tight to the reins of the frightened horses to keep the tipping wagon from crashing over on its side. The car pulled even and tried to head me off from the main road. I stood up, lashed out at the horses and swung them straight into the car. The car slammed around, its tires skidding away beneath it, swerving the metal weight in a full circle as I galloped by onto the open road just in time to see another car swing to blockade the road ahead, its engine was cut, two men got out, leaned up against its side and aimed rifles at my head. I yanked back on the reins, rearing the horses and slamming the wagon to a halt on the highway. The other car behind me came skidding up, four men jumping from all the doors, one with a big badge on his coat that caught all the rays of the Sun as he waved his

pistol and shouted, "Get down off there or I'll shoot!
Come on now, come on down with your ass up and your
hands behind your back!" He waved the gun around like
he was going to start shooting at me and everybody else
around. I did what he asked, two of his men grabbed my
arms and shoved them up double into my back. The man
with the badge stuck the pistol under his belt, hooked his
thumbs in his pockets and swaggered over, "Well now,
Mister Chief Hungry Horse himself in person. Come to
pay the Shoshone a social call. *The* famous Chief Hungry
Horse. Well let me tell you Chief Hungry Horse!" He
screamed, shaking a fist over his head like he was going to
punch the sun in the face, "You've been getting away with
it at every Indian agency over the West, bilking your own
kind, selling them rotgut firewater. You're through now,
you should have known better than to run your game on
my Shoshone Reservation. You made your first and final
mistake. You are under arrest!" He jammed both fists into
his pockets and breathed hot air into my face.

"Just one moment there sir," one of the men leaning
against the car that had blockaded the road before me
strolled over with a rifle tucked under his arm. "By what
authority are you making this arrest sir. Who are you?"

"By what *authority!*" The man pulled his fists from his
pockets and waved them in the air like he was going to
drag the sun down and kick it all over the road. "Who *am*
I! I *am* C.C. Vornoum of the United States Indian Service.
I *am* the Deputy Agent of the entire Shoshone Indian
Agency. That is who I am *sir!* And just who are *you!*"

The man with the rifle took out a billfold and slapped it
open on his leg, exposing a five-star silver badge, "I am a
United States Marshal."

"Well Marshal, you're a little late. I have sole authority
over everything that happens within this Agency."

"I am not a little late sir, we have been tracking this Indian out of the Black Hills of Dakota, down the Tongue
River right through the Crow Agency of Montana and
into Idaho. This Indian sir, is a Federal offender."

"That's right! And he's in *my* Agency. I have jurisdic-
tion over the life of every Indian within the confines of

this Agency by authority vested in my person by the Congress of the United States, and its Department of War. I am the law *here!*" He grabbed my arm and tugged me toward his car.

"Just hold up a minute," the man with the rifle pointed its tip at the yellow line in the center of the road. "The southern boundary of the Shoshone Agency runs west-east, right down this road." He tapped the gun muzzle on the center line of the road. "I am afraid you're standing in the State of Nevada. You're standing just over the wrong side of the boundary line. Outside of your Agency you have *no* authority. Outside of your Agency you're *nothing*. You're as powerless as those on the other side of this line who you rule." He pulled iron handcuffs from his coat and clamped them on my wrists. "I suggest sir, you hightail it back to your Agency before I arrest *you* for obstructing Justice."

The Agent shook his fists at the sky, puffed up his chest, then ran to the car behind his men and drove away into the hills.

"Well now Chief Hungry Horse, these Agents are all the same," the man with the rifle unlocked my handcuffs as he looked back up into the hills. "You would think sir over all this time of working together we would have come across just one of that kind who could give us a run for the money. No sir, there's not one of them worth his salt."

The other man who was still leaning against the car followed the ghost of faint dust hanging in the air where the Agent had disappeared in the distance. "Tin Jesus. If you ask me that's what they all are, just a *tin* Jesus."

"That's a real fact Bill, they're just a tin Jesus. Toss this in the backseat for me, will you Bill," he handed his rifle over and turned to me. "Well sir, how did they sell?"

I drew out three fistfuls of loose coins from my leather vest and handed them over. "Three bottles."

"Three bottles sir? Did I hear you right, only three bottles? I knew they kept these Shoshone run ragged, but that's less than we got off the Goshutes." He counted up the coins and gave back five of them. "Well sir, I guess we

can't complain, at least we're doing an honest day's
work." He clapped me on the shoulders and looked me in
the eye. "Chief Hungry Horse, you're home free. This
here is the State of Nevada we're standing in now. I told
you in Omaha I would bring you home to your mountains. Me and Bill are turning around here and heading
back over to Wichita country. No use in us traveling this
medicine show any further, these Nevada Indians are having such hard times they can't even afford to sweat." He
released my shoulders, "Well sir you can keep those leath-
ers you have on, me and Bill know you earned them.
Where you're headed you're going to need everything you
can get." He walked around to the back of the wagon and
flipped the lid of the medicine case up, "Here," he threw
two corked bottles over to me. "You'll need these to keep
warm." He swung up on the wagonseat and flicked the
rein over the horses, trotting them up the road. Bill started the car and pulled in behind the wagon. I stood in the
center of the road holding the necks of the two bottles,
my hands were not free to wave. He stood up on the wagonseat. I could still see him plain as day. He hollered
back over the roof of the car trailing him, "Chief Hungry
Horse! Don't take any tin Jesus!"

• • •

Jesus was solid gold running ten feet into the Earth beneath my feet. Jesus was sparkling silver, lighting up all
my dreams. Jesus was on my back. Jesus wouldn't let me
eat or sleep. I tried to shake him loose. I drank so hard
my dry body heaved and shook, but he hung on for all he
was worth. Jesus was running me down. He wanted to
steal my soul. Jesus was in my saddle and he had sharp
spurs. The way to buck him off was to get up on a wild
horse. I got a job in Fallon bustin broncos. The rancher
came up to me sitting on the corral watching the bronc
busting. I was drinking corn whiskey to keep my blood
pumped up high, they say if a wild horse smells whiskey
on your breath he'll think you're his mama and lie down
beneath you. The rancher took a swig off my bottle,

"WHeeeeeeewww, what a kick!" He wiped the wet sting off his lips and handed the bottle back. "Ever been up on a kickin bronc?"

"Not ever that I remember."

"It's a winter job and fifteen dollars for every horse you break down. Want to get up?"

"I know what it feels like to be hold on to."

"I've never met a Washo yet who was worth a damn in the saddle, but some Indians can ride good, I've seen and heard that for myself. Some Indians take to it natural and never get throwed, must be they're blood kin of the horse, maybe you're *one?*"

"Might be."

"Go on then, we've got one ready, first time saddled, he's awful mean under that load and he don't like the taste of metal in his mouth. Staying up on him is going to be like running through hell in a gasoline jacket. He'll buck himself to death under you before he's broke. Go on, try your hand."

I climbed up on the narrow chute over the horse, his broad back was right under me, thrashing against the wooden planks as he tried to kick and buck his way to freedom. I looked out into the corral, the last rider was being carried off, they were ready for me. All around the high fence men sat screaming and beating their hats in the dusty air. "O.K. Chief!" The cowboy keeping a tight rope on the horse shouted. "Drop on, grab hold, and pray!" I jumped on the horse's back, the gate banged open and we were in the air, the horse flying into the center of the corral, whipping the wind in my face, I felt the jolt of his front legs hitting earth, knocking every sharp bone in my body right up through my head, whamming me down on the stone flat saddle and almost throwing me over the horse's head. His hind legs hit the earth, twisting my back around until I felt it snap before he reared up. I slammed my body down on his rising neck, jamming my face into his mane, and held on. His swelling body spun, throwing his head back high, the muscle of his rising rump jolting. I held on, he was bucking in slamming bounds, banging bottom corral boards out, slashing his hooves high in the sun. I held on, to air. I was riding the turbulent wind around him, thrown off into the sky, the earth rising into my face like a fist. I felt my shoulder go out from under me and my legs slamming to the ground. I jumped to my feet. The earth roared and shook like a tree falling straight on my head as the horse jolted back and knocked me flat on my back. I could see his heaving body bucking and stamping over me. Two riders broke into the corral and rode the horse away from me along the fence, his pounding hooves crashing through the wooden planks as flying nooses dropped around his wild head. Through the haze of dust a light broke and ran its finger down my body, burning a bright circle around me. The dust rising, I beheld the Earth. The roped horse was being led panting from the corral, the power of Satan was exhausted and broken. I rose to my knees and prayed. Jesus had spirited away my soul. I was born again. All around me the men hooted and hollered.

I preached the Gospel at both ends. The people had to be saved. The people had to get busy for Jesus. The march of Christian values was on. The people had to get born again. Hallelujah. Jesus had sent me to quench the long dusty river of the people's thirst. Jesus had sent me to turn a hungry wilderness into a fruitful place. Hallelujah. The Earth was broken, and groaned under the weight of bones, all the Birds of the heavens fled. The Earth was broken, Jesus sent me to mend the Wheel of the Lord. Hallelujah. Jesus sent me to build the road of his Way. The people must be saved. All around me the wicked do wickedly, every beat of the heart bangs evil. I am the sword within and the sword without. I am the Way. Follow me. Step into the light. Hallelujah. I know the Secret Road.

Jesus saved me. When I was the young boy and the tuberculosis was killing up all the Indian people in the lumber towns my people sent me away from the mills of Elephant Head out to the high valley of my mother's mother. There I waited until the old mother died. The Earth was covered with the white burden of snow. All the Indian people of Elephant Head died away over the mountains. Jesus saved me for the people. The valley of the high Sierra is where Jesus wants me to bring the Word. So I traveled there with my black high hat on my head and the Gospel under my arm. Jesus pointed the way along the true path. There was thirst and hunger in the valley, I was bringing the word of Jesus to fill the people. Jesus was waiting for me when I got to Loyalton. There in the valley he gave me shelter in a small cabin by the slow burning slash-heap of the lumber mill. The cabin was bought with the money the Government gave Whistling Willy for his leg. When the time of fighting came across the Big Water Whistling Willy took his bible of the Gospel down from the shelf. He decided to gamble on Jesus. He scrawled down his career choices on slips of paper to see if he would follow Jesus or Man. Ten pieces of paper lay scattered face down on the black cover of the Gospel. Five of them read JESUS, and five read ARMY. He drew them off one by one. The first three of a kind to come up would be his fate. His fate read JESUS ARMY ARMY ARMY. He settled on the military life and went over the Big Water in 1918 to France country where he hid in a mud trench for eight months while men he didn't know tried to kill him. The trench was always full of mud and fire. He said he saw Jesus coming like a Ghost out of the bitter fog of gun smoke. Jesus came slipping over the rolls of barbed wire and spread his snow white cloak on the mud and held up his palms to show his wounded hands. He spoke of many with wounded hands, to beware of false prophets, that all men should know the true Jesus is wounded in *both* the hands and the feet. He rested his bare white feet up on the black mud and displayed his crimson scars. He said on the dawn of the last morning the stars shall all sing together and He will take a Bride. He would glow like a Bridegroom and lift the Earth in the cloud of His hand. Behold. All men will eat Heaven's own grain. All men will eat the bread of angels. Whistling Willy listened to these words with his soul until his heart asked: What *are* these scars on your hands and feet? Jesus gathered up His white cloak and looked over the mud strewn with bodies, then gazed down at his scars: I got these in my harlot's house. Jesus left like a Ghost. He left across the mud. He left not a footprint. The hole of the trench was full of fire. Fire in the hole. The fire blew Whistling Willy's leg off. They shipped him back from France country lit up like a Christmas tree with a piece of wood where his leg should be. He carved the bleeding heart of Jesus straight through the wood of the fleshless leg. Whenever he turns east the flapping wind blows through the delicate hole like a train whistle. He is my brother. I came into the valley and he gave me shelter. We are all brothers. He wept that Jesus had finally come back for him. That Jesus had sent the Word. I placed my hands on his body and prayed.

A woman came to me across the river. She brought her big brown body into the cabin and spoke, "Are you the Indian who preaches the Gospels?" "I am the lamb of Jesus." "Are you the one *they* call Hallelujah Bob?" "I am all things to all men." She brushed the thick bangs away from her heavy face and sat her body on the chair, I could see the bulges of padded flesh pushing out under the long sack of her dress. Her feet were small. Tiny. No longer than a boy's hand, she crossed them beneath her and heaved out a hot breath in the small room. "There is no woman in this house. I have come to be the woman. It's the way of the people. I can get work. I am Viola Jacks."

She had come from Beckwourth on the far side of the valley where she worked the ranches since she was a young girl. She would walk three or five miles out to a ranch house in the middle of the valley. And she behaved like an Indian, she waited patiently in the morning hours before the ranch house until someone would come out the door and happen to see her, they would ask her what she wanted and she would say work. There was always work for the Indian woman, there was never work for the Indian man. She would be taken into the house and the first thing she would do was empty the swollen jars and pots of human waste collected in the night. She would spend the day until darkness scrubbing the soil of white bodies from stranger's clothing. She would go down on her knees to wash the dirty floors. She would make beds, clean windows, scrub pots, wash woodwork. At the end of her labor she would walk to her distant home beyond sight from any main road. Sometimes she would earn enough silver coins to feed for one more day all the men and children living with her. Sometimes she was never paid. In the morning she would walk back out into the valley and stand before another house. She would wait. She would watch for the door to open and someone to ask her what she wanted. Some days when she labored in a house its man would come to her and put his hands on her brown body. He would feel her heavy breasts beneath the sack of a dress, pushing them up in the palms of his hands. He would unbutton his trousers and free the stake of his hard white flesh, making her run her hands on it and pinch the burning red tip as he shoved her to the floor, yanking the dress up over the fat swell of her thighs, higher over the heaving roll of her blacknippled breasts. He'd put himself down on her broad hips until she was covered with a white body, his hot breath fingering her face as a burst of white skin scattered in her blood.

Many days in many houses she would expect the white man to come to her. When she would find herself in a back room and hear the rap of bootsteps on wood floors she would roll the length of her dress up under the arms and stand waiting for him to come through the door and see the strong glint of light shining off the coiled hair between her thighs. She would think he was *her* man. She would think he was husbanding her Spirit. She brought her body to him as a gift of heart. If she did not already have a first husband she would come to build a shack by the ranch house so she could be close to the white man who let her labor in the house of his life and was husband to her soul. She would take his name and make it part of her own. She lived only to labor for the man. He gave to her the food in her belly, the fire in her stove. It had always been. But sometimes, the white wife of the house

would not want to share her man so she would run this
second wife off. Other times the first wife of the house did
not know the man was husband to two. Many times the
Indian wife would have the husband's child growing in
her. She might spend many years growing his children out
of her. Sometimes she might grow in her lifetime the children of many different husbands. But they were the children of *husbands* and she loved them *all* to her heart, and
for them too she went into the ranch houses and cleaned
away the daily dirt of white lives.

Viola had cleaned the dirt in Jacks' house. He had put
his flesh in her and she took him to be her husband. She
built up a little lean-to on the backside of the barn and every morning she went into the house to clean the dirt.
People knew her as *Jack's* Viola. When the baby of blond
hair grew out of Viola the first wife of the house sent
someone to pull it out of Viola's arms and take it from
her sight. There were too many wives at that house so Viola took her labor away and came under my womanless
roof. I took Viola Jacks back to the river and put her
body under the water, washing her soul clean of her original sin. Her soul was clean as Rabbit's fur. She was born
again. I read her the Gospel. I told her to ask forgiveness.
I showed her the Secret Way. She got down on her knees
and prayed. She begged Jesus to take away the shame. She
begged for his Divine leadership. She labored on the
ranches. There was only work for a woman. She knew I
had been saved by Jesus to free the people from thirst and
hunger and fill them with the Word. The people were everywhere in the valley, in the mountains, on flatlands. I
had to have a car to bring *all* the people the Word. A
preacher without a car is like a Jesus without a cross. Viola labored in the White houses. She would come into the
cabin after darkness and put her few coins in the clear
glass jar on the dresser top in front of a plastic Jesus
twisted in agony on the cross. In darkness we lay together.
To me she spoke, "It is always you, and you forever, in
the past especially." My fingers rested in the soft fat of
her thighs and I said out to darkness, "Jesus wants us."
"Yes, He has taught us the Word." She rolled over to her

side, my hand leaving the skin of her standing body. A short rip sounded and the sulfur flash of a match was lifted under the glass shade of the lamp, touching fire to the kerosene wick. "You will see," she looked down at my body growing visible as her hand turned the flicking flame high beneath glass. "Now you will witness my salvation." The thick line of black bangs falling at her eyes and the sides of her cheeks cast a shadow over her broad face. She went to the wall and took down the leathersheathed knife. "Jesus died for us. Jesus wants us." She slid the blade slowly from its leather, her fingers touching the razor curved edge as she turned it to catch the reflected beam from its light in her eye, "You are to me and have always been. I am to you. No knife can cut apart our embrace. No knife can cut what I believe. No blade will ever kill our love for Jesus." She let her free hand fall across the swelled fat rolls of her belly to the surface of her thighs. "*They* did not take this," she fingered the pushing strands of hair at the center of her body. "*They* have failed. It cannot be taken." Her hand came up to the gentle fat rolling belly, "Look at it. Look at me. At the flesh. *They* have come to take this, to take this because it is given in the labor of love. It is what *they* are not, it is without *their* mark." The hand glided to the bottom swing of a blood heavy breast. "Look at this," she pushed the flesh heavy swell up with her palm. "*They* came to take it, to kill it. Because it is perfect. But it is you. It is me. It cannot be marked by *them*. It cannot be stolen by *their* touch." The blade rose and rested lightly on the thick prick of her nipple. "Look at this, look at us. Witness." The blade slit swiftly over skin, her arm jerking down, slashing the large bulge of flesh. She raised the knife to the other nipple and drew the blade straight across the throat of her breast. The blood rose on her skin. She set the knife in the glow of the lamp. "Jesus taught me this. Jesus was wounded for our sin. Jesus died for us. I am marked by Jesus for all to see. When *they* come to take my body in the embrace of a lie *they* will see the mark of Jesus upon it and turn away." The blood was running off the broad swell of her breasts, curving down in a trickle around her waist and over the globed flesh of her ass. She gazed at her bleeding breasts. "These wounds will heal into deep scars. I carry the wounds of Jesus."

Viola went out every morning in the valley to the ranches to labor for love of Jesus. I went about doing good. Gathering up my flock. I preached in the back rooms of stores in the winter. I gave the Word of Jesus along the cool river in the sweat of summer. I went up on the mountain to save the poeple. The wind whistled through the tops of pine trees. Everywhere about me the people sat waiting to see the Way. They sat on high boulders, in big meadows, against tree trunks. They had heard the Word would be delivered. The people came from all across the land to be saved by Jesus. To be born again. And I came among them, going to the mountaintop in my car. Viola labored long, I had taken the clear glass jar of coins she had labored for into Loyalton where the newspaper reporter had talked of selling his car. He had the car out on the main road of town. I came up to it and put the clear glass jar of coins on the hood. The reporter scratched his mustache and nodded, "So you want her for your own Chief." "A preacher needs a car." "This isn't just *some* car Chief, it's the first Model T made with front doors, before this one came along they didn't make them with any doors atall." He kicked the fender and it rang out like a gong. "Listen to that, it's a metal body too, not wood like alot of them are made out of. How much you got in the jar?" "Sixteen dollars." "That isn't much dough Chief. This here is a special car. I was expecting at least twenty-five for it. Why this car is so smart when I fall asleep it knows the way home. It's apples or oranges Chief, twenty-five dollars, not sixteen. Why don't you get yourself a horse?" "A horse is not like a car. A horse you have to saddle before you ride, a horse you have to feed everyday, keep his hooves shod, build a barn for him, and when you're through riding him you have to take his saddle back off and put him away. A car is not like a horse. A car you just crank, get in, and drive away. At the end of the day you just switch it off." "I never thought of it in that particular light before Chief, but I think you should stick to horses like the rest of your kind. No Indian in town has a car, no need for you to be the first. Besides, you can't drive a nail straight let alone a car." I placed my hands on the clear glass jar of coins and looked the reporter in the eyes, "A preacher without a car is like a Jesus without a cross." He waited a minute, looking off up at the sun, then turned back to me. "Oh, so that's how it is, you want this car for *religious* purposes. As long as I sell it to you for reasons of religion I don't see how people can hold it against me. As long as you're going to use the car in a Christian manner there's no reason you can't be the first Indian to have a car." He took my money. You had to push the car to start it. I got in and he pushed it about a half mile before it came to life. He said the car was called FORD. "Chief, now that you own a FORD let me give you a piece of philosophy for life: You can put on 10,000 miles in one day, or 10,000 miles in ten years, but it's still 10,000 miles."

I drove the FORD to the mountaintop. The people had come up from the land to hear the Word of Jesus. I drove the FORD among them and switched it off, then climbed up and stood on the hot hood. I looked down from the FORD at all those who came to be saved. I raised my hand to the Sky, "The great sin of man is his distance from Jesus and his closeness to the Devil. I know, Jesus was on *my* back, he wouldn't let me eat, sleep or work. Jesus ran me down. I wanted salvation so bad I got up on my knees and prayed. I stepped into the light and begged forgiveness. Hallelujah! Give thanks to Jesus. I tell you what it's like denying Jesus, it's like having your face eaten away by dogflies. We all have to come to Jesus sooner or later. When you put up a fence you fence more out than in. If people just knew that. A pine tree won't grow in a pot, it needs soil. If people just knew that. When Jesus saved me I got up on my knees and shouted LORD JESUS, Open the door to my heart and walk right in! Jesus took me captive. Jesus does answer prayer. He stole my heart. Hallelujah praise His name! It's been said by wiser men than myself that if you give a man a fish a day he can eat, but teach a man to fish and he can feed himself for the rest of his life. Hallelujah! I say teach a man

to pray, teach a man to open his heart and ask Jesus into
his home. Teach a man to bring Jesus into his heart and
he can feed himself for the rest of Eternity. But what is it
we see today? On every side of us the wicked walk while
the vilest of men are exalted! Heed this! If you break the
law of Jesus he will break you! Don't forget, even *this*
Country is under the Divine leadership of the Almight Jesus. This Country is ruled by popular virtues. We must
march at the head of Christian values. We Indians are the
chosen vessel of Jesus. We are the descendants of the
righteous Branch of Joseph. The Indians are the children
of the Ten Lost Tribes written in the Book. The Indians
will step up into Celestial Government. We people of the
Lost Tribes will stand in high places everywhere. The silence of Jesus is Sovereign, only *we* hear his Word, our
hardened hearts melt. Jesus is coming back for us. Jesus is
going to wipe the mark of the Beast from the Indian soul.
Bless Jesus! Oh my soul! Only Jesus holds the Keys of
Power. Only Jesus can restore all this land which is the
Indian heart. Only Indians standing in high places everywhere will see by day the Cloud, and by night the Pillar
of Fire. Hallelujah! Jesus will return Zion to the Indians.
Those who kept us in bondage will eat grass as oxen, Jesus will strike the rock until all water will rise over them,
the east wind will move strong from the south and rain
flesh on them like dust. The dog will return to his own
vomit. But we must pray for the forgiveness of these men
who are stoning the Indian people to death. We must not
let our hearts harden, we must keep our Souls high where
the wild Birds build their nests, we must survive until the
Sun rises. We will be given hail for rain. The more you
know the more you suffer. We dwell in the House of the
Harlot. We Indians dwell in Baylon the Great. She is the
Mother of Harlots and of all abominations on Earth. We
will witness the time when the Great Harlot is drunk with
blood. Her tongue will rot, the flesh drop from the bone.
She shall be burnt with Fire, laid to waste, stripped naked.
The Messiah will strike the rock and Water will rise higher everywhere, covering the Sea. The people will stand in
high places everywhere. The Messiah will come with the

Clouds. HE will smite the Earth with the rod of His
mouth, the breath of His lips shall slay the wicked, every
eye shall see Him. Hallelujah, salvation and glory and
power! He comes with His bride on a white horse. He is
clad in a robe of blood. He rides faithful and true. Out of
his mouth goeth a sharp sword. The Sea gives up to corps-
es. Hallelujah People! The Righteous stand in high places
everywhere! But the people must not be betrayed by a
kiss. Beware of the false prophet rising. Beware of He
who brings up great signs and wonders. The people must
take care that no one misleads them. Those who rule over
us and keep this land sunken to the heart will send rumors
of wars, rising up people against people. There will be fire
in the hole. *They* will rise up a false prophet, when he
speaks frogs will come from his mouth, they will send the
people forward into the Desert to him. The righteous shall
not go out, they will see the lightning shoot from east to
west. The carcass lies in the desert, vulture feathers grow
from it like skin. On this day the Sun will die, the stars
drop from heaven, the Moon darken. We must survive
until the Sun rises. When we see its sign in heaven the Son
of Man will appear in the Clouds with His bride on a
white horse. Every eye shall see Him. All tribes on Earth
will rise up standing in high places everywhere with great
Glory and Power. HALLELUJAH!"

I drove the FORD off the mountaintop. When I got
back to the valley Whistling Willy was standing in front
of the cabin, the smoke of the slow burning slash-heap
going up behind him. He told me Jesus had taken Viola,
she was working at the ranches and Jesus put a pain
through her heart and took her away. I remembered she
only had one prize in this temporal world, and that was to
have a machine that washed clothes. There was one out at
the dump. It sold for one dollar. It had two big roller-
ringers up at the top, but it leaked all around the bottom,
that was all right because it was an electric and we didn't
have any electric power. I drove the FORD out to the
dump and paid my dollar. The machine wouldn't fit in the

FORD. I had to pull and slide the machine back to the cabin through the dirt roads. I could sometimes get my back up against the heavy white side, lift it from the ground and move a few steps before staggering beneath the burden. I carried the machine through the night, then went to sleep by it. When the Sun rose I bent to my burden again until I got it up to the cabin. Whistling Willy helped me wrestle it onto the porch, and there I left it so anybody passing by could see Viola had a machine.

A woman came to me across the river. She brought her big brown body into the cabin and spoke, "Are you the Indian who preaches the Gospels?" "I am the lamb of Jesus." "Are you the one *they* call Hallelujah Bob?" "I am all things to all men." She brushed the thick bangs away from her heavy face and sat her body on the chair, "There is no woman in this house. I have come to be the woman. I am Medicine Maggie, sister to Viola Jacks. You are now husband to me. It is the way of the people." "I don't need a woman in this house, I have Jesus." "Jesus can't cook."

Medicine Maggie cooked all the food and went into the valley and labored at the ranches. She would come home in darkness, bring her big steaming body over and sit it on my lap. I would be holding Viola's small dog, petting its bony back while Medicine Maggie steamed in the room, then she would shout, "It's not the dog that needs pettin and kissin, it's me!" Medicine Maggie never ate fruit with a pit in it, she was afraid she'd swallow the pit and a tree would grow inside her, the same with gum, she said if you swallowed gum it would grow into something horrible, but when a woman had a baby growing in her Medicine Maggie was the first one there, holding a thread and dangling a needle over the woman's bulged stomach. Medicine Maggie could tell by the swing of the needle point whether the growing would come out a boychild or a girlchild. Every spring she herself would have something growing in her just like clockwork with the old Devil himself ticking off the seconds. She would laugh alot and say, "Whistling girls and crowing hens always come to some bad end." Then her face would go serious and she'd whine, "Do you

want me to go to Truckee to the Chinese doctor who
washes dishes in the hotel? Don't make me. A girl I know
died of some dope he gave her for the pain." Most of the
babies she had were dead when they came out of her big
body, but two lived, I named the boy Joseph and the girl
Sarah. Medicine Maggie liked the washing machine in
front of the house and told people it was hers. I preached
the Word of Jesus at her but it went into her head and I
never saw it again. I was patient. When you go to the field
and capture a small bird you bring it home and put it in a
brown bag, if you bring it home and put it straight in a
barred cage it will beat its feathered body to death on the
metal bars. You have to wait until the bird is tame before
you can release him from the paper bag into the metal
cage. I tried to tame Medicine Maggie and make her into
a true Christian believer like Viola, but she always ended
up wagging her finger in my face and saying, "Two wom-
en can put on the same dress but it will never look the
same." So I did what Jesus did when he saw evil in the
Temple. I slapped her in the face. I slapped her and
slapped her. For days and weeks. But it was like slapping
water. I slapped her so much it sounded in her head like a
bead rattling around in a bureau drawer. Finally she said,
"Why do you beat me, I'm a good cook." She asked me to
plant a shade tree for her in front of the cabin. I told her
that wasn't the way, Washo men did not plant the Earth,
Washo men hunted and harvested only what the Earth
gave up to them, if the Earth gave plenty there was plenty, if the Earth gave little there was hunger. But she
brought her big steaming brown body over and used it on
me until she got her way. She told me Frogs can see better than people, that the Animals in the lake eat only
when the Moon passes over. At night she taped all the
window cracks so the Ghosts couldn't slip in and steal her
Spirit. In the middle of her pretty fat stomach she kept a
silver dime stuck in her bellybutton. She said her own bellybutton was not nice and round but long like an ear of
corn, so she kept the sparkling dime in to look glamorous.
She only took the dime out whenever she got me down on
the bed and she'd make me look at her in the light. Her

big steaming brown body smelled like warm bread, she got the blood pumping in me so I wanted to rip her body open and kiss her heart. The shade tree in front of the cabin grew up and covered the porch with its leaves. She made me take her to the rodeo in Winnemucca. I didn't want to go but she said it was an ALL-INDIAN RODEO. So I threw her big body in the FORD and took off for Winnemucca. Jesus sent me to this great gathering of Indian people as a sign. I had to save the people.

We drove out across the hot lands, following the road along the railroad tracks to Winnemucca. We got up in the stands with the people. Down in the dirt arena a tall darkening girl came to the center and made the signs of greeting and full life to the people. She stood straight, the electric microphone before her, the Sun flared on the swaying leather fringes of her long dress as her voice boomed over the loudspeakers delivering the Lord's Prayer. She fell to one knee and clasped a hand over her heart. AMEN. The applause of the people covered her as she ran off the field, another Indian riding past her on a white horse, flying white leather fringe, white feathered war bonnet. He reined his horse tight in the center. Supported against his thigh was a flagstaff, red white and blue stars and stripes flapped off in the wind over his head. He held himself tall as the people rose in the stands around him with hands over their hearts and pledged their allegiance to the flapping flag. He rode off with the flag as the music of the Star Spangled Banner burst into the arena. The loudspeaker blared over the music, flooding the arena with the boom of a bodyless voice: "WELCOME TO THE POW-WOW! How bout that music! Pretty good huh! That's the All-Indian Band and those are the Pyramid Lake boys playing in it! We want to thank Chieftain Yellow Brow for leading us all in the Pledge of Allegiance. We're awful proud of Chief Yellow Brow in these parts, he is the Shoshone who went over to war and came back a Sergeant. Also our praise to Miss Betty Four Hands who led us in prayer, a Miwuk all the way here from western California. Whoops. Look at those clowns down there in the rodeo arena. They'll be with us all afternoon.

You may think they're just men in funny clothes but they're ready to face the world and risk their lives for a fallen Cowboy, they're three Goshutes out of Utah. We should be going here in a minute, I see some action down in Chute 1. You're going to see some fast calfroping here today. LOOKOUT. Here they come! And you guessed it, riding high in the stirrups after that little calf is Galloping George from Montana, a Flathead straight to us from the great Calgary Stampede Rodeo. George is pretty high with the stakes winners. He's got him. A BEE-UTE-EYE-FULL lasso. Bull that doggie down Cowboy! Look at that rope work. There go his hands up in the air, he's got him hogtied. Will have George's time in a minute. Kick that next doggie out of the chute with an electric shock! Who's after that doggie? It's Sonny Joe from Idaho. What action! There's nothing to equal the sheer beauty of a fast ride, rope and tie. Whoops, he's got that doggie from the wrong end, see if you want Sonny to run your dairy, he's a rear-view milker. Listen to those applause. The folks like you Sonny, you're a true blue Bannock Indian. Out of chute 5, a Cherokee, Running All Day, he's the boy who stayed home from school one day and roped his way to fame, he's been widely acclaimed throughout the country from Nevada to Wyomin. Whoops. He missed the throw. The rope slid right off that slippery little heifers neck. We're going to have some Brahma ridin here quick so grab yourself another bottle of beer. You won't want to miss the Wooly Bullys we've got lined up for you. Before you grab that ice-cold beer we'd like to stand a moment in silence to the memory of Long Eddie Kiss, a Modov who was throwed for the last time in his life this year at the Salinas Silver Dollar Rodeo. Long Eddie will be missed around the circuit, he was a quiet peaceful man, he liked to hear a good joke. Aren't those clowns wonderful! They're sure getting alot of action down there. We're about to kick the first Wooly Bully out for your entertainment. Ease down in that chute Cowboy, that Brahma's got heartburn. There he goes! The suicide ride! Bull that bull down! Tuna Tom is hanging on, if only by the tail, that's one way of putting on the minutes and seconds. Don't forget folks, the famous Mighty Whitey bronco horse is going to be rode here today. I wonder what lucky Cowboy drew *him*. It's a good thing we have a hospital set up here. We want to thank CARL'S HARDWARE AND FEED for donating the paint for the rodeo corral, and I think we all ought to give a big round of applause to all the Paiute kids who took time out after school to do the painting. That's just another reason that makes our rodeo so great. The best in Nevada. Heads Up! Who's out of chute 2. A real tough one. Hang onto that rope Cowboy! Look at that Bull buck! That buckin bull must be Moby Dick! Hang On! That was Hollering Face riding, a Washo. As soon as he hit the dirt he got out of the way fast, nobody is going to pin any wings on that old boy. Out of chute 3 again. Smokey Dog. Hang On Smokey! That's our action! Smokey's the Indian who was given five dollars to vote for a Justice of the Peace or something, now he figures he won't vote unless he gets paid for it. Ohhh! That's too bad. A hard fall Smokey. We'll have this time in a minute. I think we're getting close to some fast bronc riding. I can see one kicking up the chute boards down there now. I tell you I'd rather ride mule back. Yes sir, they're cutting him loose now. Watch Out! Look at him, aint he something! It's a pretty snowwhite blooded stallion! It's Mighty Whitey being rode by Hump, a Navajo. What some men will go through to win a silver studded harness and eighty bucks worth of handtooled saddle. WhooHoo! What a Kavayo, look at that horse buck! That boy's going to bust his jeans before he bust that bronc! He better get himself a new pair of *FRISCO JEENS*. Like the advertisement says YOU CAN'T BUST EM! What a bucker! I tell you, when you're up in the saddle of one of those things you're afraid to do right for fear of doing wrong. Mighty Whitey's thrown him! Ooh! Hump almost fell through the earth. Who's up now? We here in this part of the country like our action fast. Heads Up! It's Toby Riddle riding Powder Puff. You don't see one beam of daylight between his tailbone and the saddle leather. WhoooPS! Now he's getting bucked. If that saddle was sandpaper he'd be a toothpick. That's like riding five horses at one time. What did Custer say? Ride or get off. Toby can't handle it, he's going off! Good time! Good ride! Hold on folks, pretty quick is coming up the steer wrestling for you, nothing but straight Bull-Doggin. What's all that commotion down in chute 4. Good thing we have that hospital here. Ease down into that chute Cowboy. That's a wild horse in there. Ride em Cowboy!

I went down to the Ford to get my Gospel. After the Bull-Doggin I didn't want to give the people a chance to get away before they could be saved. Jesus had alot of preaching to do here today. When I got to the FORD it was surrounded by people waving beer bottles in the air and whooping and hollering. "Hang on! Whoooooo-PEE! Don't get throwed! Ride her!" I pushed my way through the crowd and saw in the backseat a big white sign with a black number 9 on it. It was a Brahma Bull rider bouncing up and down. I grabbed his humping shoulders and threw him out of the FORD. Medicine Maggie smiled up at me, her big brown body steaming with the dress pulled up high over her waist. I jerked her out of the FORD, wrapped a rope around her waist, tied the long end to the rear fender and drove off pulling her behind me. We went along the road following the railroad track, the Desert sun beating on her brown body. Sometimes I would swing around and see the rope tugging away at her heavy frame sweating and stumbling along on the hot pavement, the look on her face showed no shame. I could only drive as fast as she could walk. People passing us by would honk and whistle. We went along a big billboard I.W. HARPER WHISKEY FOR HEALTH, but mostly it was just the Sun slapping down on an empty Desert with just me, Medicine Maggie and the FORD. It took us five days to reach Loyalton and the first thing I did was to chop down her shade tree right to the ground. A Washo man does not plant the Earth.

Back in the valley I went about doing good. Preaching

the Gospel at both ends. The people were coming from way over the land to be saved. I took them to the river to be born again. I drove the FORD over to Minden Nevada, to the sagebrush town. There were many Washo people living there who were starving for the Word of Jesus. They were gathered for the Big Time. For Gumsaba. The people came around the FORD and cried, "Hallelujah. Hallelujah Bob. The Messiah has come. The Christ has appeared on Earth again. He is the son of Tavibo. Bullets pass through his body. He is wounded with scars in the hands and feet. Rejoice. He comes the second time. He is not the false prophet. The day the Sun died he was born into the heavens on a White Horse with the blood of the Spirit on its chest. The Christ is coming. Hallelujah. He walks among the Fisheaters on the shores of Pyramid Lake. He is rising up all the dead hearts. He is rising up all the people across the land. The people will stand in high places everywhere. The Tribes of the Earth will stand in great glory and power. Glory and Power. The Christ comes. The Native Ghost returns."

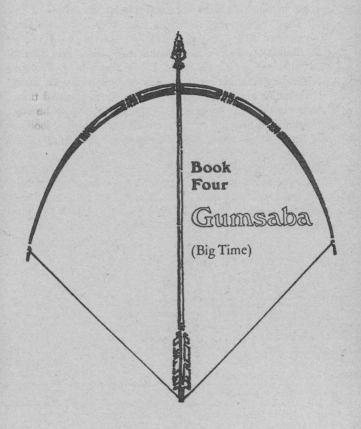

Book
Four

Gumsaba

(Big Time)

1

GAYABUC WADED into the iceflowing water swirling about his legs and scattered the silver Fish scales to the wind so they caught in the strong current and roared downstream. "Atabi, the year of the Washo begins in hunger. I go away south, to the side of the mountain, and stand in water where it is always flowing so I can catch your body and bite you. Oh Atabi, Oh Fish, I stand in waters flowing westward. I wait for you to go away up north." He let flutter from his hand more handfuls of Fish scales over the water, "I do not wish to offend your Spirit. I use you in good heart. I return these scales of flesh to your water in the Mountain House so you will multiply, Grow, be many and jump up the silver back of long rivers to high lakes. I do not wish to offend you my Brother. I give back what is yours. You have spawned in the pool of my dreams, your crowded bodies pushing from mud to stone, filling water everywhere from bank to bank where the people have been dancing your return. Oh Fish I do not waste your flesh, do not leave me. I am close to you. I am sowing the waters with the magic of your scales. Listen to your Brother, he does not offend your Spirit. Come to him. The year of the Washo begins in hunger." Gayabuc emptied his leather pouch of Fish scales to the water, watching them tuck and swirl through the rocks below where the people stood out along the banks watching the current.

The people watched in hunger for Atabi. They sang and
danced along the banks, building up their fires where flowing water melted ice. "ATABI! ATABI!" Their chants
rose with smoke. "FISH. Give the strength of your flesh
to the weak bones of our bodies so that we may survive
the Season. ATABI!" The roaring force of a long winter's
dying snow spoke to all creatures in the mountains. "I
have spawned you in the pool of my dreams. Come to me
in my hunger. It is the First Season." Gayabuc sang up
the Fish, "Come to me. Brother." The chant swam from
his swollen lips into cold air, his legs glowed the same ice
blue color as the waters flowing around him. He felt the
flick of a silver flash against his blue flesh, the waters were
moving from within, the current trembling. "ATABI!" The
waters were alive with Fish. All along the banks the people
were dancing, their fires burning bright, between them Fish
was jumping, throwing his silver body into the damp sprays,
twisting in midair, he came sprouting up all along the
endless streams. Gayabuc stood with blue legs under water, blunt flesh darted and brushed against his legs, the
current all around him was trembling with climbing Fish.
He stood watching the white knives of flesh flash by him
into the new Season. He stood watching the people coming into water all along the banks with baskets, taking
great scoops of leaping Fish captive and throwing them
up onto the banks. Men jumped into water armed with
nets, stretching the strength of woven plant fibers across
the current to catch the quick bluebacked streaks of flesh
racing in the spray. Platforms were built out over the waters and men struggled with the sweep of long poled wil-
lownets swung into the tide of flying Fish. Where the
small streams ran white the stones of a Fish House were
piled up, pooling the current, revealing circling clouds of
Fish. Men stood high over the Fish House, dropping their
bone hooks into quiet waters and pulling forth struggling
white bodies hooked through the belly. All along the
nightbanks torches lit up Fish flying into nets. Quivering
gills shook the air around the women pounding Fish eggs
to powder in the hollow of stones. Green spears of
branches were run into the mouths of struggling bodies

and held over flames until the white flesh burst with heat.
Gayabuc waited on the slippery rock with the point of his
harpoon arched over his shoulder, searching another rainbow sided body. The people moved among Fish jumping
on the banks, splitting them open down the back and
striking the thin line of bone from their bodies. Gayabuc
waited to fling his harpoon into the strong current. Watercress waved along the banks, it waved in the blue water
like flowing strands of golden hair. Sunshine hair long as
a burning star trail, the hair of the Water Baby, Spirit of
all water, creature of shifting currents whose magic could
come hidden in a dream and give the power to walk on
water, or sleep in a spring. The sunshine hair of the Water
Baby grew to the knees. The tracks he left in mud around
ponds were no longer than a baby foot. If you looked him
in the face you would bleed from the nose and fall down
sick, the Fish would always run from the point of your
spear. The *wegelayo* of the Water Baby was not to be
sought, the *power* of the Water Baby was to be avoided.
The Water Baby was no friend of the Washo. During the
time when Bluejay huddled up on the last branch of the
pinetree to stay hidden from the two Weasel brothers who
hunted the mountains, hitting Ducks over the head until
they killed them and filling their belts with Squirrels they
had shot, there was a Water Baby sleeping in a spring.
Little Weasel Brother came up and peered beneath the
glass surface. The Water Baby was sleeping against a log,
its head resting on the tiny arm with sunshine hair spread
all around and glowing up bright from the depths. Little
Brother jumped high and low on the bank singing, "I will
take all this beautiful sunshine hair glowing up at me and
bring it fast as a golden gift to Big Brother!" The Water
Baby did not hear these words, he slumbered under water.
Little Brother got down on his belly and slid like Snake
through the mud and into the clean depths of the pool. He
came upon Water Baby and stroked the golden rays of
hair, running its softness through his fingers. Then he
slipped the stoneknife from his belt and laid the blade
against Water Baby's forehead, "Won't Big Brother love
me and give me all his Eagle feathers to wear when I

bring him this!" He pulled the knife back to strike but
Water Baby's eyes popped open, they swelled in the water
like seeds until they were big as eggs. Water Baby battled
Little Brother for possession of the hair but the knife cut
through his head, freeing the sunshine hair from his body.
Little Brother climbed from the spring with the prize
tucked in his buckskin shirt. He looked back at the slain
Water Baby floating on the bottom with blood streaming
from his head. He remembered the bad magic of all Water Babies and cried, thinking they might take revenge, so
he threw two long strands of sunshine hair back into the
pool. But the water had all turned angry red and was
churning up in waves. Little Weasel ran to his brother and
shoved the golden hair into his hands, "Here Brother!
This is *your* present! Take it!" Big Brother took the scalp,
then he pointed down the trail, "How dare you look the
Water Baby in the face! He will send the waters to rise up
and rush forward to drown you! Look! Here comes the
water to get you!" The water was coming up over the
Earth, the Weasel Brothers ran from it, but the water
flooded fast, filling all valleys and lapping at their heels.
They ran into the mountains and up onto the highest
peak. "Quick!" Big Brother cast the beautiful sunshine
hair out into the rising ocean and stood arm in arm with
his Brother. "We will never meddle with your magic
again!" he screamed to the flooding fingers flowing across
the mountains. They stood arm in arm and watched and
watched the waters over the Earth recede. When the
Earth was dry footprints of water where the Water Babies
had run with the sunshine hair were left scattered through
the mountains in blue lakes. The Weasel Brothers went
down to the Biggest Lake, to Tahoe. There on the shore
of the Emerald Bay rose a hill stained with the blood of
the slain Water Baby. When Gayabuc hunted the Fish by
the red hill he always searched the waters lit up by sunshine for the goldenflow of hair so he could run and tell
the people to catch the Fish into their baskets, for the Water Spirit was near, and he would slap the waters with the
magic of his thunder and cause all Fish to hide from the
people, ending the Season of Fish.

The Season of Gumsaba was the Big Time. It was the Gathering Year. The sap of sugarpine ran like molten snow down swelled trunks. The wild strawberries blazed in a ring round the shore of the Tahoe Lake. The roots of all plants turned tender. The people moved with all growing things. Everywhere they saw grass turn its green arms to Sun. Small Birds sang of the black juice of chokecherries. Soft winds blew wild seeds. Grasshoppers grew slow with the warmth, their golden bodies picked from bushes and roasted in pits. Fires burned where the hills had matured brown, the flames driving the wild bugs into hollow places where their bodies were ground beneath stone into sweet flour. Pointed sticks were thrust into holes and twisted in the fur of Gophers, the smouldering fat of their bodies cooked in ashes. On the shore of the great lake Mono, where the water was too bitter for drinking, the hot sun ripened basketfuls of Fly eggs in the powder soft rocks. The green time was golden and brown. The waters ran clear. The Sun held long on the people coming together from across the land. Coming up from the mountains. Up from the hotlands. Up from the valleys, Joining hands for the Big Time among the groves of the Sacred Tree, the Piñon. Singing up Gumsaba.

Gayabuc walked with the people. The first hot rains had stormed, he read their Sign. Always after Death water cleanses Earth. Water came to wipe the footprints of the White Ghost from his dreams. The waters had removed the stone of the white bones from all places. He no longer watched the Fox, the blink of its eye the color of dying Sun had vanished. The Spirit of the Fox had been captured and stripped from the heart of existence. The wild stone-eyed Beast he had watched on the shore of yonder lake was a power he no longer feared. The people had their need. The people had their want. He moved through the trees. Always the trees. It is the way of the people. It is the way of the Ancestors. The medicine of *those* who ate of *their* own flesh on the shore of yonder lake had been broken, *their* Ghost had traveled across the Sky to

the south. It is best not to disturb the Dead. All the dead
bodies piling up in the Earth had been washed clean. He
walked with the people back into the past. It is best not to
disturb the Dead. He had no Dreams.

The Chief of the Rabbit stood before the people, a
Gray stone growing from solid Earth, he held his palms
outstretched to the Sun, the blades of two Eagle feathers
dangling from his elbows, "The first frost of the Season of
Atabi has passed, bringing up the people from the land
for the Season of Gumsaba. We stand among the blood of
our heart, the Sacred Piñon Tree. We are the children of
the Tree. Our roots go out over the land, our branches
reach up to the mountains. The truth of all our ways is in
one Tree, the Sacred Piñon. We are scattered over the
Earth, we have burst from open cones, on winged seeds
we fly before the breeze, we take root, we are the blood of
our own heart leading back to the same Tree. The road
coming is the road going. We are everywhere. Our ways
are everywhere. We will survive. We have gathered here
as one Tree to take our want, to take our need. This will
be my last journey to the pinenuts. I will stay here and
die. I will not return with you to the Big Water, Tahoe.
When you leave here you can follow Gayabuc. Always
move with green things growing. He knows the way. He
too is a Chief of Rabbits. Son of my hands. I have sent
the knotted Deer thong out among you, to tell you the
meat of the pinenut grows sweet in the cone. To bring you
together. This season the Piñon Tree is heavy with fruit. I
have dreamed our need. I have sent out for all the people
and you have come into the Season of Gumsaba. I will
pray over your gathering. I will fast and drink only cold
water to make you strong during these four days we will
celebrate as the blood of one Tree. You will dance and
gamble with bones, you will hunt Rabbit, bathe and rise
to go among the fruit of the pine. Paint yourself *red* with
the *wegeleyo* of the Owl. Paint yourself *white* with the
wegeleyo of the Eagle. Paint yourself *yellow* like the
Hawk. Paint yourself so your medicine will be stronger
than the rattling Snake and he will not strike you as you

go among the fruit of the Sacred Groves. Wear the black
hooves of Deer around your necks so that you hunt well.
Pierce the flesh of your ear with the bone of the Lizard so
you can stand in the long Sun knocking the fruit from the
Sacred Tree. I pray that the fruit of the Piñon will not be
eaten hollow by worms. The people will have their need,
they will have their want. Now listen to me as you dance
four nights. Take up your tools. Take up the hooked poles
for drawing the coned fruit of Tree close to Earth. Take
up your straight knocking poles with their blunt ends
wrapped in the hide of Deer. Take up your stones for
grinding the fruit to flour. Take up your paddles for stirring the thick mush. Dance in a circle. Follow the Moon.
Follow the three Seasons of the Washo. Follow Fish,
Gumsaba, the Hunt. Now listen to me closely you people.
Treat your children good. Be kind to your wives. Don't
pick the fruit from your Brother's tree. Join hands and
follow the Moon, cross your right foot over your left foot
and hop. Cut only wood you can burn. Help the old people who are blind from the smoke of a thousand nights'
fire. Put mud on their face to soothe the broken eyes.
Shoot Rabbits, eat them. Dance. Behave properly. Charm
antelopes. Don't fight. Make acorn soup and eat it. Play
games. Stalk Deer. Stalk longlegged insects. Weave baskets that don't leak water. Do not fight. Play. If you lose,
do not get angry. Spear Fish. Do not point at rainbows,
your finger will fall off. Use burning sticks from fire to
fight off white Owls. Sit beneath a tree and use tobacco.
Do not eat wild parsnip. Let Dogs bark at night. Don't let
meat spoil. Gamble with bones. Some win, others lose.
Eat sunberries. Don't be afraid of Bears. Let Dogs bark at
night. Never use bad medicine. Hold hands tight and
dance. Never look a Water Baby in the face. Never follow
Ghosts. Beware of Coyote. Don't believe everything Coyote says. Live in the Mountain House. Lock your heart to
the land. Drink only pure water. Stand in high places.
Don't injure small Birds. Watch Ducks at Sunrise. Beware
of Fox. Don't give your dreams to your Brother. Respect
the Sun. Sleep where the Crickets sing. Do not put your
mark on the land. Sing the songs Birds sang long ago

learned in dreams. Take only what you need. Don't eat green meat. Dance. Do not leave your mark on the land, protect your Mother. Do not pick pinenuts before they are ripe. Eat all the eggs you steal from Eagle. Don't use false magic. Never waste fire. Stand in high places. Don't give your Brothers dreams. Let all children grow straight. Lock your heart to the land. Protect your Mother. Love your Brother. Go out in four sacred directions and meet your Brother. Go out in four sacred directions and meet yourself. See heart to heart. The road going is the road coming. Capture power and use it for good. Don't fight. Dance. Then dance with your wife. Don't fight. Dance. Dance with your wife. Make her sleep well."

The people bathed at Sunrise and moved up from the stream into the hills with their poles, knocking the fruit from groves of Piñon Trees. The husbands came first with their leathertipped knocking sticks dropping the ripe fruit to the ground. The wives gathered the food into baskets and built up great mounds of nutheavy cones in grasslined pits going longer than the body lengths of three men. Dried pineneedles were scattered into the growing heaps of nuts to keep the food from going damp and turning soft. The gathering went on through the hills, each family taking the fruit within the narrow stonelined strips their Ancestors laid out. The people stored their want against the long white days ahead. The Rabbit Chief stood before the people, a gray stone growing from solid Earth, he held his palms outstretched to the Sun, the blades of two Eagle feathers, dangling at his elbows, "It is Gumsaba. Fill your bellies. It is the Big Time."

When the Robin still held the brilliant red Sun to his breast Gayabuc would awake. He could smell the long white days ahead coming in the air. It was the Season of the Hunt. He had not spoken among the people of his dreams. Dreams had come to live in him again, pushing up through his sleep in fingered slender stalks, bursting open in flared red bells. His dreams were the color of the *Honowah*, the snowplant growing up through the yellow-pine. Cloven hooves moved black through the trees. Wind caressed short fur. He dreamed of Antelopes. He could smell the Antelope in the Sky. At first he scented only one, its sharp eye wary in the forest as it moved through the trees. Always the trees. Then he saw two, and three, moving over the silent mat of pineneedles, nibbling the tender shoots of milkweed along the banks of quiet streams. In the dawn he looked to the Sky where he thought he saw their brown bodies pass in the night before. He placed his hand over the lump of his heart and tried to find the way in his blood to where they roamed. He waited until he saw an entire herd of them moving in his dreams. He went slowly to them so not to frighten their quick ears, "Don't be afraid. I am among you easily. Don't scatter before me Antelope. Your short fur stands stiff. I do not want you to rot in the Sky. I want to bring you into the circle of my people. If you are careful and still I can slip a knife into your Spirits and cut tongues of meat from your sides. Allow me to bring the people to feast on you. I will not take you in excess and let your meat spoil, leaving it on a moist meadow to grow rancid and stiff and soft with worms. I come as a Brother. I do not wish to capture your Spirit, it is too swift. I do not wish to capture your Ghost, it is too sly. You are a powerful magician, Antelope. I come to ask you for your flesh. The people need it to stay alive, Grow. It is the Season of the Hunt. I walk with you in dreams. I am the Antelope Walker. I cannot eat of your flesh, I cannot eat of myself. To do so is to die. Your *Musege* is stronger than all my medicine. The meat of your power can give me cunning to survive the long white days of winter. Your flesh will make me crazy strong. Your blood in mine will make me crazy brave. We will cut up your flesh and hang it. We will not let you rot. You will live in the belly of our Spirit. You are going to another land. You will like that land. You will not stay here. I am through talking to you now. I will see you in the Mountain House. I will wear my Deer-muscle belt so you will recognize me." Gayabuc went out into the dawn and sat around the fires. He placed necklaces of pinenut beads around his neck and tied two Red-

Hawk feathers under his leather headband. The people watched him as they ate Fish cooked with smoke and spooned acorn mush to their lips. He began to talk to them. He talked to them in a low voice, as if they themselves were the Antelope, pointing to the Sky, "My people, there, that is where I smelled them, tasted their scent, heard hooves beating beneath my eyes. That is the place they moved through my dreams the nights before this one. Now it is time, we must go. You will follow me. Who will follow them. These things I have dreamed. I walked alongside of them, they do not run away. They did not scent me. I am their Brother. I am the Antelope Dreamer." The Man of Medicine rose, he had the thick warmth of Bearskin wrapped about his hips, "The women must go away from us, it is the Season of the Hunt, to look upon our weapons is to break our magic." The Man of Medicine placed his hands on his fur covered hips and turned his back with the rest of the men until the women passed from them. "We will see whether you speak falsely or truly Antelope Dreamer. If you dream truly the Antelope will be banded together on this morning. We will send out two boys to see if your dream is truth." The two boys came forward. Gayabuc said his dream to them, he sent them east to north. They went out over the mountains and did not appear until after three days running; the Man of Medicine rose, "What did you see?" The boys spoke together, their high voices a chorus of Birds, "It is the Season. Gayabuc speaks truly. The people will have meat." The Man of Medicine nodded to the north, "We will all have something to eat. We will try tomorrow to hunt after them."

When darkness came Antelope banded together and moved through Gayabuc's dream. He saw how they grazed through the tall grasses on a hill slope. Over the slope and below opened a dry meadow where sagebrush could be piled high to form a corral without the sweat of work going into the noses of feeding Antelope. Dawn came up and Robin still held its fierce light to his breast while the men went out from the camp, heading east to north, to the mountains already ringed with snow. For

two days they followed in the tracks of the Antelope
Dreamer until he stopped in a dry meadow. There beneath the white peaks they cut the rough brush and
stacked it high and thorny in a corral taller than two men.
The Man of Medicine stood at the opening to the corral
and made a fist over the single blade of a Bear claw hung
from his neck, "Antelope Charmer, if you dreamed right
we will all have something to kill and something to eat."
Gayabuc moved into the corral and stood within its middle, "I am the Antelope Charmer, what I dream is true.
My power is not false. My dreams are my power. Divide
and form your bodies into two long feathers, fan your
feathers out over the slope rising above you. Hide in the
trees. Watch from the trees. I will charm our Brother into
this corral. When he comes, rise up behind him so he
knows he is welcome." The men split into two groups and
disappeared into the trees up along the slope. The Antelope Charmer moved to the back of the corral, watching.
He filled the stone bowl of his pipe with the tobacco of
sage and puffed smoke into the clear Sky, "Brother, I can
hear you feeding in the wildgrass. Are you standing still
now? The wind caresses the shortness of your fur. Your
thin legs are held straight to Earth. I do not mean you any
harm. Do not become afraid. Do not let the fear scatter in
your blood. Come and use tobacco with me. You are a
great magician. Listen to me. Don't be afraid. Don't tremble in your hide. I have made a home here. Come into it.
Come easily now, come creeping." He saw their bodies.
Their longskulled heads silhouetted against the Sky at the
top of the slope. "Come right into your home. I have
dreamed you." The brown bodies moved with sharp eyes
down the slope. "Come to this spot where hunger ends."
They stopped. Quiet. Damp eyes looking down to the man
using tobacco, their Brother. Quick ears flinched in the
Sunlight. "Come home sweet Brother." They moved
again. The proud swirl of antlers pressing ahead cautiously before them. "Come to me. I am sly. I am swift." Their
Brother puffed a wide blue cloud of smoke over the corral
and they entered gentle to greet him, the air moved off
their back. They were charmed. All behind the Antelope

men came up from hiding, hollering and whooping down
the slope to run the brown bodies around in a circle within the corral. The sharp black hooves cut up the Earth as
trapped beasts beat around in a circle spraying dust over
their bodies until they collapsed panting with bruised
tongues. The Antelope Charmer stood over them still
sucking his tobacco, "Listen to me. Allow us passage. We
will slip a knife into your Spirit and cut meat from your
sides. Give us a feast." The brown bodies panted in the
dust around him. "This I have dreamed." He turned to
the men waiting with taut bows carved from strong cedar.
"My people, look at Antelope. I dreamed him up for you.
My power is not false. My dreams are my power. I cannot
eat of my Brother, he is my flesh, we are one. To eat of
your own flesh is to die. But that big one there, with the
spreading antlers like a crown of bone, you will kill that
biggest buck for me to take into the woman of my children." The Man of Medicine stepped forward, drew his
bow and let the arrow fly into the heart of the buck. The
Antelope Charmer puffed clouds of smoke into the dust
choked sky, "All this I have dreamed. Now you may kill
for yourselves. Go forward to your Brother and begin cutting him up. Feed your Spirit. Skin the flesh and cut it
into strips. Wash off the guts. Do not throw anything
away. What is not used for power becomes waste. Do not
leave any flesh to rot. Do not offend your Brother. Do not
abuse his power. All this I have dreamed. If I were dead,
all this would not have been dreamed. There is no other
to speak these words among you today. If I were dead,
there would be no one else here to tell you this. If I were
dead."

THE INDIAN led his sister on the horse behind him. He saw the yellow spark of a sudden running body spring from the coiled sagebrush and whirl with a kick in the air. The wood butt of the rifle rammed to his shoulder, his eye sighted along the barrel where the bullet would meet the muscle heart of the fleeing animal. The exploding of lead jumped in his ears as the body fell, the flight of its flesh stopped through the heart, its dead weight carried forward with a jolt into spinning earth. The Indian went out into the clumps of sage and whipped the rabbit up by its soft ears, the long hindlegs cocked for another leap, the fire of blood streaming from its nose.

The woman came quickly behind the man and cinched the body into one of the belts of carcasses slung over the horse's rump, she hitched the dead weight of the heavy belts higher up toward the saddle to keep from slipping, "Why do you shoot them in the heart? That just ruins them."

The Indian took the reins and went farther into the sage. He saw the flick of yellowed brown fur moving quick in a grassedover rainrip in the earth, he jammed the riflebutt to his shoulder.

"Joe! Hey Joe!"

His finger flinched on the trigger, cutting the bullet

through the air and thudding into the distant brown movement.

"Joe! Wait up Joe!"

The woman spurred the horse off to get the rabbit.

The Indian spun around and saluted a hand over his eyes to block the full force of the morning light. He could see the boy was coming fast, the thud of his breath beating over the sage before him.

"Joe! Joe, you shouldn't be out here!" The boy ran panting up to the Indian, banging a fist against his burning chest to drive the wind back in, "My Dad he got back from Mexico last night and I told him you was going to still rabbit shoot out here and he says no you aint. He says he's got machines set out here to get all the rabbits now and you might trigger a machine."

"Why aint you in school?"

"My Dad says those machines are from Reno and costs alot of money and he don't care how long you been shootin rabbits in this valley you aint hired to shoot for him no more. You aint hired no more Joe."

"Why aint you in school Sam?"

The boy hung his head and kicked up at the sod, "I wanted to hunt with you."

"You go on to school now Sam. You can still get in on time. We've been here since sunup and we're about done. You git now."

"My Dad says you can't shoot here no more Joe, but you are. You tell me to get to school, but I aint. I'm going to do just like you, I'm going to do the only opposite thing people tell me to do."

"Sammy," the woman on the horse rode up, keeping a tight hand behind her over the flapping belts of rabbits. "What are you doing away out here when it's school time?"

"I came to hunt with you and Joe, Sarah Dick."

"No you don't. You're going to school if I have to ride you back myself."

"Why can't I stay. Nobody says nothing if the Indian kids don't show up for school. Why am I any different?"

The woman looked over at her brother. He slung the

gun up on his shoulder and started back into the sage coming up sparse and only head high.

"All right then Sammy," the woman leaned over and took the boy's hand. "You get on up here so Joe doesn't have to worry where you are. He shoots in any direction. And you hold onto the rabbit belts behind us. One of those goes slipping off and we lose it we'll never find it again out here."

The boy pulled up behind her and got a good grip on the dead weight of the belts. "How many rabbits you got here Sarah Dick? There are so many they're almost dragging on the ground."

"52."

"*Fifty*-two! Joe usually gets only thirty this early spring time of year. What are you going to do with them? My Dad, he won't pay two-bits apiece for them anymore, he's got machines to do his work."

"We're going to make a Rabbit blanket. The fur is good because the winter was short, when cold days are not many Rabbit is heavy in his pelt. When cold days are long he goes hungry, his pelt dries out and shrinks on his starving body. This time Rabbit had enough to eat. This time even these skinny jackrabbits have had enough to eat in the early thaw. Git up you horse, git up here!"

"My Dad says he's going to run cattle in this field soon, he says it'll carry eighty head, but only in early spring. In summertime the sage won't even grow out here, and it's full of snakes. He had six snakebites in this field alone last summertime. He calls this his snake field."

The Indian's rifle was against his shoulder, the flash of the barrel whipping around as it tracked the running brown body, its ears tucked back along the thick fur, the toes barely hitting the earth as the arc of the bounding body sailed through the sage, meeting the blunt bullet.

The boy slid off the horse and ran forward to yank the still kicking body up by the ears, waving it around in a circle over his head until the neck was broken. The sting of a bullet flicked by his head and he turned to see another body dropping behind him. He ran through the sage and flung the longeared body in the air, but there was no need to wring the neck, the bullet had caved through the ribbed bone, blowing a hunk of flesh out the other side. "Here they are Joe!" The boy held a dangling rabbit from each hand high over his head.

The Indian came through the sage to him. "What sex are they?" He spread apart the white feet of the limp legs, "Two males. The males are jumping early, they usually stay down and let the females jump first. There are still four or five females right off through that rough wash, they're getting down in there and laying low. You go give these rabbits to Sarah Dick, and stay behind me, don't go runnin out like that."

"Why aren't you leaving your rabbit belt around your waist to hitch the bodies in Joe?"

"I can only tote seventeen rabbits on the belt, all that dead weight starts to swaying whenever I try to squeeze off a new shot and I miss as many times as I don't. That's why I have Sarah Dick trailing behind with the belts, now you do like I told you and get these two over to her."

The boy ran with the rabbits and gave them up to the woman. She clamped the bodies to a belt and pressed her heels into the horse's belly and ran him up behind the Indian, "Why don't you stop shooting them in the heart. You're wasting half the fur on them by shooting them there. It's such a waste of good fur, why don't you aim at the head?"

The Indian slipped the brass shell of another bullet into the rifle and looked across the valley to where the white cut of snowcovered peaks in the distant east rose higher than the fumbling clouds beginning to build up enough courage to block the morning sun. "These two males just killed are skinny, but the females are all fat with fur. We'll have enough for the Rabbit blanket. Don't you worry about . . ." The rifle jumped to his shoulder as he cocked the steel in his hand and took aim.

"Don't shoot!" The woman reined the horse up so it knocked against his shoulder throwing him from balance. "It's a cat! Don't shoot!" The arrow of her arm pointed to the bare opening in the sage, a cat moved from the head-high clumps of sage branches on three legs. "It is bad luck to shoot a tough cat. He walks with only three legs. He is one of those who prowls the alfalfa fields for the wild mice. He was tough enough to survive the many blades of the mower machines that cut through the alfalfa fields. He walks on only three legs. The blades took part of his flesh, but he is no cripple. Let him pass."

The Indian lowered his gun to the woman's words, she was right. He let the cat who could survive the blades in the fields of razor-turning steel pass on his own hunt. He raised his rifle up again and went into the sage until another brown body got up and he shot it down.

The Indian led the horse onto the road, walking down the hard black shell between the two straight lines of barbwire fence. The woman and the boy rode up behind him in the saddle with the swaying dead weight of the morning's kill at their backs. The Indian pulled the horse down into the ditch when he heard the sounds of the morning give way to the high whine of a truck stirring up the distant air along the road. He kept leading the horse in the ditch as his eyes sought the precise color of the metal humped machine speeding toward him. The sharp steel clacking of a horse's hooves came at his back, he spun around as if his own horse had broken loose and was galloping by.

"It's Ben Dora!" The boy swung and shouted at the Appaloosa galloping the full muscle of its flesh down the center of the road, its bloated chest pumped with air and blazing hot wind, the sharp sting of steel from the bottom of pounding hooves ringing out against the pavement. The horse swelled by them, churning and blasting the air, leaving its own current sucking behind as the man on its back stood high and bent in the stirrups, whipping the strong horseflesh beneath him. He reined the horse, jamming the cut of the bit into the soft bleeding mouth and swinging the stamping horse to its side in a blockade across the center of the road in front of the pickup riding the squeal of its brakes to a jerking stop before the horse. The woman leaned her head out of the truck, "Ben!" He spurred the horse over to her, his thick stoneflat thighs pressing against the leather of the saddle came up to the open window. He bent his head down to talk to her, the bulged muscle of his neck exposed red to the sun, the blunt instrument of his head jerked back and forth as he shouted at the woman through the window. The close cut of his hair slashing at the air like a burr as the woman shouted back. He slammed up in the saddle, throwing the wide strength of his back straight and driving his fist into the metal roof of the cab. He reined the horse and speared the heel of his boots deep into its flesh, galloping it straight up the road. The woman jammed the truck backwards, spinning the two rear wheels off into the ditch, tearing up dirt and kicking it behind her as she wheeled around and drove after the man.

The Indian brought his slow horse back up onto the side of the road. His sister turned in the saddle and looked at the boy, "That was your Mama, Sammy, and is she going to give it to you for not being in school."

"She won't care, she and my Dad and Ben are all having a big fight. She won't care."

The Indian did not stop leading the horse until he came in the gate before his house, "Sam, you take Shasta around back and let her have a little drink, watch she don't bloat herself, water brings out the pig in her." He unhooked the dead weight of the belts from the horse and let them slide to the ground. "Go on Sam, do what I say."

The boy led the horse away as the Indian freed the stiffening bodies from the belts, tossing them in a high brown heap.

"I'm going home to get Felix his lunch. Felix always comes home for lunch from the gas-station, that's his slow time," Sarah Dick rubbed the morning's dirt from her hands on her long dress. "I'll come back later and help you do the skinning." She started walking for the road, then she turned and came back, watching her brother pile high the brown bodies, "Joe, I told Felix to tell you to come to Church services on Sunday but you weren't there. I look every Sunday but I never see you. Don't you like Jesus?"

The Indian kept throwing the legstiffened bodies onto

the brown mound, "You don't have to say what you're going to say, you have said it all before."

"You do not believe, Joe Birdsong. You do not believe in the Gospels, you do not believe in the Sun. You believe in the dead smell of Rabbits."

"I have been taught."

"I too have been taught, but I do not refuse to believe in Jesus. I do not refuse my own."

"You have been used. You have not been taught."

"Yes, I have been used. *They* used me as *they* wished. But I have taught myself how to believe."

"*They* teach everything. It is only what *they* allow you to teach yourself."

"You have become like *them* when you speak so. You are *their* voice. What is true to me is that beneath your skin, not your voice."

"You can't expect me to believe?"

"I can't expect you as a woman. Only Jesus can teach what *they* cannot."

He threw the last brown body on the heap and looked into the earth colored reflection of her eyes within the heavy dark folds of her face. He remembered to the day when the honey Bee put a sting in her breast and swelled out a red welt with a prick of white pus at the tip. She was a very young sister then and her crying from the sting brought all the old people running. His father looked at the sting and called, "Joe! I want you to come and look at this!" His father fingered the swelled breast so the Sun exposed the red rising welt, "You see this Joe, Jesus did this."

His sister turned away and walked out on the road. He sat down on his crossed legs and slipped the knife from the leather sheath on his belt, then pulled one of the stiffened bodies from the pile and raised the blade to skin it.

"Can I do it too, Joe?" The boy sat before the pile watching the quick blade cut around the long hips and slice up under the thick belly fur.

"I think you've got enough to do already, Sam. Look at this coming," he pointed the blade up the road at the pickup forcing its way through the morning, the rubber of its tires skidding to a stop on the loose gravel in front of the house. "Sarah Dick told you she was going to be awful mad Sam. You better watch out for your Mama."

The woman was already out of the truck, leaving the door swinging open behind her as she ran over to the point of the knife still held in the air. "Sam, you get in the truck, now! Joe Birdsong, I want to talk to you. In the house."

The Indian led her into the house, she slammed the door shut behind her and let her body sag against the solid wood.

"What did I do wrong Missus Dixel?"

Her eyes sprang open, "My husband is dead!"

"I'm sorry to hear Mam."

"He was shot early this morning."

"I'm sorry."

"Did you hear a horse galloping by here early this morning? Before sunup?"

"Yes Mam, I heard it."

"Did you see who was on it?"

"No Mam, I'm sorry."

She pushed her back off the door, "Quit saying you're sorry, I'm not sorry, every winter he's off to Mexico to find his Dream Ranch, leaving me alone up here in this godawful valley. I'm sick to my belly with feeding his brats and trudging through four feet of snow to cater to a bunch of sniveling horses while he sits in Acapulco looking at pictures of ranches with a whore on each knee. Him and his Dream Ranch, him and his building up his herd of ghost horses, building up his great Arabian Ranch. He's always wanted *balls,* he never gets tired of telling that stupid story about our honeymoon in Mexico when his father bought the biggest bull-balls for our dinner. When he saw me at the Cow Palace Grand Exposition he wanted the horse I was on so he bought me too. He said he was coming up here to cow country to raise the world's greatest Appaloosa, and he says he did it. Well he didn't do it, *I* did it. When he married me he said I couldn't be anything but his 'little gal.' All he ever did was get me pregnant and run off to Mexico for the winter.

I'm the one who raised all those Appies up, and if it wasn't for Ben Dora helping me those horses would have died the first winter he left five years ago."

"Who shot him?"

She let her body slump back against the door, "Ben would kill me if he knew I was here."

"Who shot your husband?"

"Ben would just kill me."

"Has the Sheriff been up to the ranch?"

"Deputy Sheriff Davies just got up there now with alot of other folks."

"What does Davies say?"

"He says it was you shot my husband. He says it was you that had the *motive* because you weren't hired to shoot rabbits anymore. They all say you had the motive. Ben would just kill me if he knew I was here." She shoved herself up to him, "Listen, I know it wasn't you. Those people are just saying that because they want you off this property so the whole valley can be sold and developed. They want you out anyway they can get you out. I know you didn't do it, but Sheriff Davies says he is going to get you for it, he says he's the law in this County and he's been waiting for you to step over the line to get you, now he's going to do it."

The Indian walked to his bed and grabbed an envelope, "What do they want to do this for, they've already got me out. Listen to this letter, '. . . said Property is in violation of the above mentioned County ordinances and is forthwith condemned as unfit for human occupation.' " He looked up at the woman, her slim shoulders caved in around her face. He had never seen her straight on before, holding still, not bending over a baby. Her face was beautiful and broken.

"Please go."

He ran to her and shoved her shoulders back against the door, "*They* say my father didn't exist!"

She turned her head away from him so the tears streamed off the side of her face, "Please GO!"

He released her. Her body slumped down on the door. She turned her face back up to him.

"They're coming."

He grabbed the accordion off the chair, "I'm going to take this. *They* say my father didn't exist, this music says he *did.*" He strapped the accordion over his back.

She moved across the room and grabbed his arm, "Please GO! *They're* coming! Ben would kill me if he knew I was here!"

He ran to the door and threw it open.

"GO!"

He broke into the yard, running around to the horse.

The boy saw him from the truck and jumped down, "Joe! Where you going!"

The Indian swung up on the horse and the boy grabbed his boot, "Take me with you! Take me with you!"

The woman threw her arms around the boy and tried to pull him back, the tears from her face flying into his hair, "Let him go Sam! Let go!"

The boy had one hand locked in the stirrup and the other biting into the flesh of the kicking leg, "Take me! Take me! I want to go and live like an Indian!"

The Indian twisted around in the saddle and pointed at the brown heap of bodies, "You see that! That's what we are! Rabbits! We're worth nothing alive and five nickels dead!" He swung and spurred the horse, galloping across the field into the trees. Always the trees.

The accordion slapped on his back, banging against his flesh and bruising his bone. He rode along the line of pines breaking into the valley floor, the ground beneath him beginning to go soft with water. He had to leave the trees and expose himself in the valley to come upon the place where the thick water came up in hot pools and spread the heavy scent of sulfur in the air. He rode for the hotsprings at the headwaters of the Feather River where Birds from all places gathered to drop their feathers. He crossed the blacktop highway onto the dirt road and let the horse run full out. He could see the silver dome rising before him, the sun glinting off the stretched metalskin in quick sparks. He rode straight for the glowing dome of Jandy's trailer standing alongside the steaming sulfur pools. He reined the horse up and tied it to the trailer hitch, "Jandy!" He set the accordion down. "Jandy! I have come to the sacred waters to heal my wounds. I have come to wash away all my old hurts. I have been wounded many times. I come to the waters to immerse myself in their powerful medicine before battle." He heard no sound from the trailer, he banged on its metal door, there was a rattling inside but no one came. He looked out at the barren land shooting its steam off from hard little mouth holes running hot streams of water over the earth. Long wooden planks were laid out into the field over the scalding flows of water, he ran out on them to a sulfur pool, the sweat of the earth rose in his nostrils, bearing its rank odor in the air. He saw the body before him, fallen across the narrow plank. "Jandy." The body was still, the arms thrown back in the warm black mud. "Jandy? Hey Jandy!" The white handle of a pistol flashed on the barren earth. He knelt next to the slight body, the face staring up at him had half its side blown off, a straight line of steam puffed up from a mouth hole in the earth next to the head. He slid his arms under the light body to lift it, his hand coming around on the chest, popping the buttons of the shirt as he lifted, the cloth pulling away from two hard fists of breasts. He lowered the body and unbuttoned the shirt all the way down, the breasts swelled out from their points, the stomach was hairless. He looked up at the sky stacked with clouds of sulfur and laughed, "Jandy, the softhandedest little castrator in the whole of the valley." He lifted the body in his arms and ran down the wooden plank to the waiting silver dome that said: AIRSTREAM. He kicked the door of the trailer open and the eyes of cats from everywhere stared back at him. Cats sat hunched and huddled on the bed, in the narrow sink, on the floor, from cupboards, empty boxes, rusted coffee cans. He dropped the body on the bed among the scattering cats. He slammed the door and ran back out along the planks until he came to the steaming pool, he pulled the cclothes from his body and slid down between the mudslick sides. The leg twisted and pained

when he had blasted the Snakes was stuck straight out in
the sulfur sweet medicine of water, the healing stink rising
in a cloud around him.

At the headwaters of the Feather River where the Birds
from all places drop their feathers he traveled north to
west, leaving the Sierra Valley behind. He knew *they* were
after him. *They* were always after him, and now he was
being hunted. He kept always in the trees, searching the
high trails where *they* had never been. But everywhere the
forest blazed *their* mark axed into the flesh of a tree:

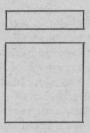

This was the mark of the *White*. When he saw it he knew
he drew close to one of *their* cabins, and he sought another trail where they had not been, where their mark was
not upon the land and the Earth not worn clean by the
passing of *their* animals. His rifle was without bullets, but
he held it like a club as he hid in the trees, waiting for a
Porcupine to leave its den in the rocks and waddle with
the needle weapon of its skin into the Sun. He came at it
from the trees with the club of the gun bashing in the
head. He pounded the carcass with the rifle woodstock
and threw the bloodied pulp onto a fire, the needled glove
of skin spitting and flaming as the fat sizzled. He threw
the head away and ate the charred body. He took the fire
to light his tobacco. He had done well, to eat the head of
his kill would make him fat and heavy, slow and quick to
die. He was the hunted. He sat beneath a tree and
smoked. The tobacco rose around him in a blue ring and
threw back the Spirits hunting him. He was in the Moun-

tain House, he used the power of tobacco to make him safe. He smoked the grass of the Earth. He watched the dying on the western rim of the mountains. the Sun was leaving him, it was sinking down into the Ocean. He had never seen the Ocean but he knew that to be true. Before his battle was over he was going down to San Francisco and watch the gold ball sink in the great water. His father traveled once to where the Earth ended and the Sun died into the Big Water. There at the edge of the water too bitter for drinking his father saw the Spirit of the Whites captured behind ironbars. Now the Sun dazzled in the gold of its own reflection. A Badger came out from his hole but smelled the tobacco air and hurried back into the Earth. The Crickets began to sing, and down the dark aisles of trees the Owls hollered at one another. When the Indian hears the Owl there will be a white death.

The wind goes along the river. Wind river blows water through the Sky. Moving far north to west the Indian traveled away from the Sunrise, dragging the Horse up the rock slope. "Come on Shasta! You can girl! Just one peak after this!" The Horse banged to its knees and struggled in the rocks, the worn steel of its hooves slipping on stone. The roar of the river blew in the air. The swirling current tore through the canyon below. The Snake came up rattling, the coiled muscle of its body striking at the Horse, the odd balance of its flailing body falling back into the stones then striking again before the rock hurled by the Indian splattered its cold blood on stone. He got the Horse moving again, back down the rockslide, but it went down on its side by the running water of the river, bellowing hollow breaths from its bloated ribs. The Indian searched the steep banks for parsnip. Mosquitoes came up from the bottom of water and bit him. He could hear the Horse sobbing along the bank and brought to it the leaves of parsnip, their roots dripping with Earth. He dried the leaves over the smoke of a fire then stirred them with water and rubbed the flaking medicine in the horse's poisoned body. He was in the highest of mountains, the surrounding peaks gathered in black clouds over his head. He took out his tobacco and used it, the smoke whirling off the redembered tip at the threatening Sky beating thunder over rock mountains. He waved his fist at the Sky, "You better stop all this noise! You better stop! If not I'll be dead!" The rain did not come but the Horse grew weaker. All around him the wind whirled and danced the purpletopped spruce trees that grew alone in the distance. He went up to the spruce trees. The gray Squirrels were cutting the green cones from tops, dropping them to the ground and eating off the tips of the scales. The green cones littered the Earth and he talked to the Squirrels. He asked his Brother to stop stripping the trees. But Squirrel could not hear him, the Sky shook the Earth with the sonic boom from a silver dart jetting in a pure white trail beyond reach of the mountans. He went back down to the Horse and it was alive, but the bones poked through its thin hide. He took the Horse's lead and again made his way up the rock slope, the weight of the accordion strapped across his back bent the muscles of his shoulders as he dragged the Horse up to the mountaintop. Down the other side below them the timber bloomed in an unbroken line of forest. He took the Horse down into the trees and sought tender grass that raised its green arms to the Sun. The Horse stood bellowing the hollow life from its ribs as it ate the grass and vomited up, then ate the vomit. He was in the highest of mountains, at night the Sky swelled up black and the stars blinked like baby fists beating the darkness. He ate the soft flower plant of deerweed and the manzanita berries. At night he had the dream. He dreamed of Lizard. The dream of Lizard in the rocks means there will be a Hunt. He was Lizard. He lived alone with himself and petted the hide of the Horse rubbed raw on rocks in high places. The sharp mountains had worn holes and tears in his clothes, the wind came in and blew against his skin. His heart began to get tired, but it is bad luck to feel your heart. He wanted the longlegged Spiders to stretch over all the rivers so he could pass. He was always kind to Spiders, he did not know when he might need them. Crow wings sucked in the air over his head. The Animals have their own language and he put his ear against the trunks of trees to hear them talk. He ate berry soup and thickened it with Rabbit droppings. He let a handful of loose dirt shake from his palm to see which direction the wind was blowing. It was time to travel west to south, the Deer were fat. He went into lower mountains where there were no trees where there should be. He traveled through the ghost trunks of trees. He traveled where trees were scarred with fire wounds, the hard white pus of sugar sap beaded down their blackened sides. He traveled where there were trees that lived off fire, the heat exploding the seeds from their cones across the Earth. He traveled where flocks of Sheep have fed off the mountains, preying on all green things. He saw them bleating through the canyons, slicing every wild plant beneath the blades of their passing hooves. He watched this *Musege*, the beast of the whiteman turned loose to break all green arms to the Sun, swill every root, tear the hide off every stalk. From where he stood he could see the tamed power of Sheep swirling through the valleys. He could see the white flocks driven down the mountains to the railheads where they fouled the water, got into boxcars and rolled off to be slaughtered.

Memdewi was fat. Deer was fat. His father had told him all the old bucks who lived in the mountains were smarter than people. Now he was the hunted who was hunting. He left the Horse by water and went into a high place where the wind carried his Indian scent off the Earth. He had no bullets for the rifle. He made the stone-blade of a knife and lashed it to a cedar pole. He waited with this spear where the signs of Deer were everywhere on the ground. He prepared himself to kill, and waited. He watched over the rocks through the trees where a full-grown mule Deer approached. The buck came young and light on his feet, the four points of his antlers tilted against the Sun, his body strange in the air, as if he was running from the scent of man, but the Indian knew he was in a higher place than the buck, there could not be the smell of a man to strange the animal. He waited for the buck to draw to a closer moment. The buck skittered over the rocks, then froze, the disturbed air of the pulsating lungs beating beneath the bright redbrown hide. The Indian jumped from the rocks, the balance of the spear gripped in both hands. He hurled the stone point at the pounding chest. The strict ears of the buck flicked back and he was gone, the force of the spear slicing through emptiness, clattering on the rocks as the echoed sound of a high powered rifle slammed in the air. The Indian spun around and looked down the mountain at the men aiming the scope of their rifle barrels straight up at him. The rocks at his feet flew up and scattered in splintered points as lead slammed into them, the distant thud of rifle shots broke out all over the mountainside. His instinct carried him up the steep slope on his hands and knees, the jagged rocks cutting through the holes of his boots to flesh. The lead pumping into stone around him ricocheted and tore through his leg, the sudden jolt throwing him to the rocks. He dug into stone, his hands carving out a place for his body. He clung like a Lizard to the rocks, hearing only the blood jumping from his heart to his head. He waited to die. The sonic boom of a jet broke the air over his head. Then there was silence on the mountain. He could feel the sparks going off in his leg as air hit blood. He heard the sobbing of his own breath beating on stone. He pushed himself up from his hole and looked down the mountain. It was deserted. But through the bottom break in the beginning treeline he saw one of the riflemen still running, the flash of his red hat blazing brilliant before it disappeared into the trees. The Indian ripped his pant leg open, the lead had passed through his flesh, missing the bone. He bound the bleeding with a cloth around his leg, it was the same leg he had wounded when he was hired to kill the Snakes where they slept. He stood up, the leg was sound under him, he scrambled back down over the rocks to find his spear. It was lying in the stones where the Deer had fled, its blade broken, the rocks around stained with blood. It was not his blood. It was the blood of his Brother. The buck had been wounded by the riflemen. He heard his laughter going over the sharp rocks and down the mountain. The riflemen were not shooting at him.

They were shooting at the *buck*. He remembered the flash of the red hat blazing brilliant before it disappeared into the trees. *Deerhunters*. The laughter came back up the mountain at him. Then stopped. He searched the red stains for a sign, there was not much. The Deer could run for miles. He started a fire with the deadened windblown needles of scrubpine, then mixed his saliva with the Deer blood splattered on a stone. He set the stone on the smoking pineneedles and waited patiently for the heat to burn the stone free of stains. It was time. He rose to go to his Brother. His Brother did not know he was coming. A wounded Deer that does not have its life hunted will forget his fear and stop his running quickly. After a short distance his stiffening muscles will lock his body and drop him to the ground, his heart stunned from loss of blood. The Indian came up to Memdewi leaning on the crutch of his spear, he looked down at his Brother who was dead or dying, bright blood bubbles of air frothing from his mouth and nose. "I will treat your Spirit with respect, Brother." He took the broken blade of the spear and cut into the body. "I will honor your flesh. I will not take you in excess. To do so is to die, your Spirit will come back and break my medicine." He skinned the hide from the downed beast and hefted the life of the flesh onto his shoulders. "I will not take you in excess. I will leave that which my stomach cannot hold for Coyote. He will come soon. I go my Brother." He made his way on the crutch back to the Horse in the trees of the high riverland. The Horse had strengthened his Spirit on the long grasses. He filled the bags of Deer intestines with water, strapped the burden of the accordion to his back and rode away from the river.

He was in the Mountain House with his Brothers. They were all being hunted. He traveled to Blue Lake where the mountain Quail flew into the clear blue surface of the water thinking it was endless Sky, breaking their necks on the bone hard surface. He made camp on the shore and waited for the afternoon winds to blow the fresh kill of a dead floating Bird over the waters to him. He rubbed the grease drippings of the Quails mixed with ashes into the

wound of his leg to keep the white swelling down. He leaned
back in the trees and played the accordion out over clear
waters. He played the songs his father had sung long ago.
He leaned back in the trees and used tobacco as he
squeezed music over the lake. His father had the dream of
the Antelope and died. The Antelope was a great magician. The man his father was like Ayas the sharp footed
Antelope. His Brother the Antelope had long ago been
hunted out of the high Sierra, he too was long ago dead.
His father had met the Jesus. He had used tobacco with
the Messiah who walked among the Fisheaters on the
shores of Pyramid Lake. His father stood at the Messiah's
side when the people came around him from all over the
land and paid one dollar just to shake his hand. All this he
knew was in the music he squeezed out over the lake, his
hands playing over the rainbows of mother-of-pearl keys,
the yellow stonebacked ring glowing up in his eye like a
Sun. Sometimes when a man died and his Spirit went
away south the people would throw all his goods of the
Earth into his house and burn it down. When the Spirit of
his father had gone south he moved into his shack so the
people couldn't burn it. He inherited the Earthly goods of
his father: the yellow stonebacked ring, the accordion,
and outside the shack, the battered metal of a FORD. In
his last days his father would go into the FORD at dusk,
he would roll up all the windows and drive out across the
valley one mile east, the FORD spluttering down the road
at only four miles an hour, then he would turn one mile
north, one mile west, and come home the last mile south.
Every night at dusk he would make the slow trip and in
the valley the people in the ranch houses he passed would
shake their heads, some would say, 'There goes crazy Indian Bob,' others, just by seeing him drive by, would
know what time it was and set their clocks to him. After
his father's Spirit went south he sold the FORD to buy a
Horse to hunt down the Rabbit. He had to drive the
FORD into Truckee to get enough dollars for it to buy
the Horse. He rose along through the trees, the FORD
steaming up the Truckee Summit and headed down toward Stampede Reservoir, the dusk out the rolled up win-

dows was beginning to settle down through the points of
the pines and he heard the man on the radio tell him,
"Welcome to the Bach Hour. For the next solid hour on
radio KENO of RENO you will hear only the beautiful
sounds of the world's greatest composer, Johann Sebastian
Bach." As the shrill notes of a fugue punched up from
Earth the point of every pinetree outside the car window
he understood the medicine of his father's nightly drive to
the four sacred directions. It took his father exactly the
one hour of the music to travel to all points of the Earth.
He remembered back to his father traveling out in the dusk
of the valley with all the windows rolled up, he now knew
that locked within the moving metal of the FORD his
father traveled with the power of a music stronger than
most Birds. The windows rolled up on the FORD protected his power from the ears of others, sheltered him from
the shame of being caught listening to the uncommon. His
father had never taught him how to squeeze the power of
this music from the accordion, he kept its medicine hidden to the last.

The mountains shouted rain. With the first storm he
headed down from the high mountains with all the Deer.
The storm washed over his skin, coming in the holes of
his clothes, but it healed his body, easing the hard joints,
cooling the white swelling in his leg and firming his loose
teeth. He went down from the lake, he needed a spring
that didn't freeze over by which to make his camp for the
long white days. He crossed the red dirt of logging roads
that were broken with chuckholes bigger than a man's
head and studded with the furred carcasses of gray Squirrels run into Earth under truckloads of slaughtered trees.
He traveled in forests of ghost trees cut through the heart.
The Whiteman had come with the power of his chainsaw,
he could tear the hide off a tree as old as the rivers and
slice through its flesh in minutes. He stood on the spur of
a mesa and looked down to where the Whiteman had cut
the river. A band of concrete across the full current
robbed the power of great waters. Everywhere now he
saw the mark of the White beast on the mountain heart of

the land. The White beast came with his *Musege* to the Mountain House. He tore the scalps off the high mountans, blasting with stolen water for gold metal. He was blind to the Earth and blasted great peaks to stone rubble, he choked the life from breathing streams with mud and silt. He moved mountains for bags of gold dust. He left his mark everywhere. Now the mountains shouted rain. He was struck through with beauty. The howling Dogstar in the Sky sang the Indian's voice as he ran after it.

When the gold water of his body peed into the Earth he watched the fall of its brilliant yellow pebbles. A smell had grown up between his legs. Whenever he touched himself the smell came up strong on his hand, he could not wipe it off. At first the smell offended him, but then he longed to have it always in his nostrils, it was a sweet yellow smell of dark Earth. He traveled with this smell growing on his body from west to south, the wind blowing through all the holes in his clothes as the rocks cut the leather of the boots from his feet. With the buckskin of the Deer he made a leather apron slit down the sides and strapped around the waist with a Deermuscle belt. He pounded strips of dampened bark into strings and wove himself sandals. He heard the call of one Duck over a pond and the snow began to fall. The timbered forests slept by day and he traveled through them searching a place where water always flows. The Crickets stopped singing in the cold night and he didn't know the warm places to sleep. The white burden settled on the mountains and buried the scarred Earth. The white burden came down so heavy on the pines it bowed their giant tops over almost to the hidden ground. If it was a strong tree it would survive the burden until it melted from its branches. When released it will never stand straight again. If the white burden uses all its power it will break a tree in two. There were no shadows in the mountains, only the dull white light. His black hair grew down his back, he tied it in two braids and hung a Hawk feather from the tip to protect him against the white cold. The Horse could not go far in the deep snow, its body had grown empty of food. He followed the First Star of the night, the lone light going across the Sky. The sign of the Rabbit Hunter. The Chief of all Rabbits moved across the hard crust of the white burden pulling the staggering Horse behind him, the Rabbit Boss traveled to where water always flowed with the burden of the accordion crossed on his back. He heard the sound of machines. He came high on the white skin of the ice and looked down on the heart of the mountain split open, the blade of a concrete freeway laid through it. He led the Horse down onto the freeway and pulled its exhausted body along behind him on the black pavement half covered by snow. He walked in darkness, with only the distant Star of the Rabbit Hunter to guide him. He heard the labor of a truck grinding up the summit, its huge rubber tires bound in chains. He ran the Horse into the high snowbank, hiding behind its white hide. The ice blast of wind passed over him. The light of the truck illuminating the vast billboards hung out on both side of the freeway:

USE ELECTRIC

SUPPORT CALIFORNIA
  BEEF

EAT GAS EAT GAS EAT
  GAS

IN RENO ITS HARRAH'S

50 MILES TO HARRAH'S
  CLUB

HARRAH'S CLUB OR
  BUST!!!

He pulled the Horse back out onto the freeway. The Horse staggered behind him and fell across the pavement. He tried to pull it up from the iced pavement. If it was going to die he was going to eat it. There was still some flesh left on the white bones. He tugged on the rope. The Horse was shaking. He kicked it in the stomach. It did not move, the white body was shaking all over. He could hear the distant engine of another truck coming up through the ice bound air. He jerked on the rope, trying to tug the shaking body off the road, it wouldn't move. The sound of the truck pounded the air behind him. He lifted the spear over his head and drove the broken blade through the Horse's neck. He flung the spear into the Horse's side and tore out hunks of flesh. The truck roared up behind him,

throwing the white light from its strong headbeams across
his body as he tossed the living flesh over his shoulders
and scrambled up the ice bank, dragging the accordion
through the snow behind him. He heard the honking horn
of the truck as the momentum of its weight carried it over
the carcass of the Horse.

The white swelling of his leg grew and the cold wind
cracked the skin of his face. The blood in his hands and
feet was blinded with cold. He huddled in the trees, pressing his face into the cutting bark to feel the warm sting of
blood. He huddled and wept as the cold wind blew across
the white burden. The flesh of the Horse had loosened in
his bowels and run down his legs. He watched from the
trees until he saw the thick white furred Rabbits pad
across the snow on broad feet. He ran out and clubbed
the Rabbits, then ripped the white fur from them and ate
of their flesh. He feasted on Rabbit. He found a hole a
small Bear had given up to sleep in and there he dreamed
of *Honowah*. He dreamed of the fiery snowplant. He
dreamed of the snowplant growing straight from the white
burden that stopped the blood of all other living things,
sprouting up in a blaze of color, a survivor, its roots in
black Earth, growing. The Rabbit was killing him, its lean
flesh loosened his gut and he spit blood. The lean flesh of
Rabbit was robbing the strength of his body. To eat only
the flesh of Rabbit is to die. It is the way of the people. It
is what the Hunters know. Rabbit meat alone will strangle
the belly and choke the heart. He was dying of Rabbit
starvation. The skin of his face cracked from the cold, it
split like bark and rutted with scars. He roasted the lean
carcasses of six Rabbits over his fire to get enough grease
drippings to mix with black soot and paint his face against
the ice of the air. He drew bold black streaks down his
face and went out on the snow to club more Rabbits. He
pissed a pale yellow stream into the snow crust, it pricked
a fingerhole in the ice, he watched helplessly as the steam
of his own body rose from the hole and disappeared in the
air. A clap of thunder broke through the trees and slapped
the heart of the mountains. He turned his savage painted

face to the Sky and watched the jet streaking a white line beyond the reach of mountaintops. He felt the pain in his leg, the swelling was spreading, shooting off sparks then putting the whole side of his body to sleep. He rubbed himself with ashes, but the white pus kept growing. He sat in the cave and tried to make his cold fingers work on the accordion and he remembered what his mother, Medicine Maggie, had taught him. Sitting him in the lap of her big steaming-brown body when he was a small boy she taught him woman was cloud, man was thunder. She told him of how Weasel created the Earth and Coyote created the Indians. She told him of the two sisters living at the Big Waters of Lake Tahoe who had all the wildgrass seeds and pinemush they could want, they had a Fish House stuffed with Trout and Frogs. Every night they would go to sleep gorged with Fish. There was an old man who lived on the otherside of Tahoe who had nothing. He would come to the sisters and beg for a skin to keep him warm, not even something to eat, just a skin to keep warm. The sisters had so many skins piled around their house their feet never touched the ground, but they gave the old man nothing. They sent him away laughing at his back, then one cooked up a bunch of Fish and the other wove a willow basket with a beautiful design in it. That night they lay down to sleep under a great pine and looked up and saw many stars. "I like that one up there," the old sister said. "I think I'll catch him, he looks so good. See him? That bigeyed one over there." "Of course I see him," the other sister cried. "I saw him first. That bigeyed one is mine. Oh how I would like to go up there right now and suck the Sun from his mouth and blow all his light across the Sky!" "No you can't! No you can't! I won't let you! He's mine! How would you like it if I got him between my legs and never let him go! I would if I could. I would eat his thunder!" They laughed and went to sleep with the stars twinkling overhead. That night the bigeyed Starman cut a hole in the Sky and came down to Earth and took the two sleeping sisters back up with him. When the sisters awoke the bigeyed Starman took off the bands of fragrant herbs hanging around their heads and washed the good smell of

Earth from their faces. He called his uncle the Moon over and had him put the single blanket of a Rabbit Robe over all their shoulders so they were married. Then the two sisters fought over who should sleep under the Rabbit Robe with the Starman. They were very angry. But he took them both under the Rabbit Robe and when they awoke they both had Starbabies and the old man who had nothing down on the lake was lying between them. "Where is the bigeyed Starman?" they yelled. The old man laughed and said he had become the Starman to get himself two young wives who had everything. The women were so angry they had been tricked they refused to cook their new husband any Antelope meat. They packed up some dry Fish for themselves and went out for a week digging up wild potatoes with sharp sticks. They came back home and boiled up all their potatoes in baskets and ate them. They did not give any to their new husband and the Starbabies. The Starbabies cried and ran off to their uncle the Moon, old Moon got very angry, he took up his big knife and went running across the clouds. The whole Sky trembled, the people on Earth said it was thundering, old Moon came tramping up and grabbed the two sisters by the long hair, shaking them until they were almost dead, then he cut a hole in the Sky with his big knife and hurled them through it. Down Down Down they went, banging into the Earth with so much force their bodies made a deep hole. That hole is over by Gardnerville. In that hole Indians can always find plenty of wildgrub, wildwheat, wildpotatoes, wildcorn, there is always plenty. Even when the snow is on the ground there is always plenty in this hole. All this happened before White people came. But it is true.

All these things Medicine Maggie taught to him. He remembered the hole, plenty of wildgrub even when snow is high. He strapped the accordion to his back and propped the blunt end of the spear under his arm for a crutch. Gardnerville was over the eastern wall of the Sierra Nevada, he had to go through the high mountains of California, but there were many Washo where he was going, and a hole full of wildgrub. He could travel through the snowsheds that covered the curving railroad tracks cut through the high mountains. The lean meat of the Rabbit was starving his body. He traveled west to east until he reached the railroad track in high places covered by snowsheds hanging along the cliffs of the mountain. He went out of the day into the narrow dark tunnel sinking before him. The air turned from cold to ice, strangling the blood of his body, but he went on in the tunnel, hobbling always forward on his crutch to the light shafting through a distant chink in the snowburied sheds. He walked into silence. The light before him faded and he walked in total darkness, he was in the heart of the mountain. He could hear the ice flow of water running in the mountain's vein. There was no light at the front or the back·of him. He no longer knew if he was walking the right way or if he had turned in the darkness. There was no way in and no way out. He didn't know if he was coming or going. The only real thing was the weight of the accordion bending his shoulders and the white swelling growing and filling his body like a flower. He stopped. The juices of the mountain flowed. How loud they were. Like an engine. How their stillness roared. He saw the prick of a light beam shoot through a chink in the distance. He hobbled toward the white light. But it was *moving*. The light was coming to *him*. The juices of the mountain he heard flowing and ticking with a roar was the machine pumping of a *train*. He was in the snow tunnel with a *train*. The pinprick of light began to waver as it became defined, the sound of a thousand iron wheels speeding their tonnage along the narrow track vibrated the wood of the tunnel, shaking the Earth beneath his feet, its deafening fury dominating everything right to the mountain's heart. He felt to see if there was enough room for the train to pass between him and the wall. He didn't know if the wind current of speeding steel would suck him into its path. He banged with the spear at the boarded wall, he couldn't tell if he was banging on the open side of the tunnel or banging into the sheer rock of the mountain. The eye of the train bore down on him, the thousand wheels beating and clattering against the iron track. He kicked at the wall and threw his body into it, the boards wrenching away from their nails, splintering open before his body. He broke into light and tumbled out onto snow. The weight of the accordion strapped to his back carrying him helplessly down the slope, tumbling and kicking him over before his body wedged against a tree. Always the trees. He was alive. In the distance the blue of a lake swelled up at him. He was on the shore of yonder lake, the lake *they* call *Donner*. He felt beneath him. It was Earth. The shelter of the tree had warmed out around the trunk, melting the snow back. He watched through the trees growing down to the lake, isolated splotches of black Earth showed through the white burden. The white days were ending. Before the green plants came up he would cut tender boughs from the trees and scatter their green food along the receding snowline for the Deer to feed on, then he would again Hunt. He went down to the lake, the white swelling filled his body, he did not know if he was alive or dreaming. He dragged the accordion behind him over the white burden. He did not know if he was alive or dreaming. The straps slipped down from his hand and he walked away from the accordion on the white snow. He twisted and fell, rolling to the shore of the lake. The water was warmer than the Earth, the sluggish ice floes breaking apart their weight that during the meanest white days had pressed down on the small Fish, squeezing them to the bottom and breaking their backs. He watched the broken bodies of small Fish floating to the icy surface. He did not know if he was alive or dreaming. He was on the shore of Donner Lake. He watched at the place where his Ancestors had first watched the White Ghost eat of his own flesh. His Ancestors from that day thought the Whiteman a flesheater. And he was. The *Musege* of the Whiteman was the meanest power of all, stronger than all the Bears of the Mountain Home. Stronger than all the hearts of all the running Animals. The Whiteman was a cannibal. A flesheater. He ate the Spirit flesh of the Indian. He ate the Spirit flesh of his Brother. He ate the Spirit flesh of the Earth. He led the wild beasts who devoured the Earth. Of all the Hunters his medicine was strongest. He killed all the Birds out of the Sky and fished up all the Fish out of the waters. He tore the hide from the mountains and stole the power from the rivers. The White beast was a flesheater. The Ghost of the Fox was released from the Earth. The Ancestors had spoken true. The flesheater always devours his own children. The flesheater eats himself.

The Indian sank to his knees on the shore of Donner Lake. He did not know if he was alive or dreaming. The white swelling filled his body and bruised his heart. Woman was cloud. Man was thunder. He grasped the timbered flesh between his legs in the roots of his fingers. He dreamed of Animals running, Birds flying, Fish swimming, Women loving, he dreamed of all Earth going green. He bent over and tried to connect his stiffened flesh to Earth, but the hot timber in the root of his hand jammed into the ice of the white burden. The singing power of Birds ripped through trees, flames of flapping feathers in branchtops, the wind of their wings becomes air and is gone.

3

CAPTAIN REX stood riding the flatbed car of the train coughing blood. The hot air from the pumping iron wheels slapping his face as he watched the rocky ground flash by. The songs Birds sang long ago tried to push up through his mouth full of blood, the ancestry of their music rising deep within his body, whistling through his head, seeking to burst their rhythm from his burning chest and fill all open space between mountains. He wiped his bloodstained lips on his coat, the screeching steamwhistle blowing up front of the bulky slamming cars. He looked off down to the blue blade of the river slicing through the canyon while the trapped feathered songs he had learned in dreams struggled in his flaming blood. The train roared him along the river and down into the valley. The smoke it threw up from its stack clouded in the Sky, mixing with the spiraling burnoff from the lumber mills crowded down to the river's racing edge. The odor of wet lumber from the dammed millponds came up to him. Across the valley towering black monsters of slash incinerators trailed off their slowburning smoky waste into the air cut heavy with the scent of green pine. White blasts of steam billowed out from the churning friction of the braking iron wheels as the momentum of the train slowed. The brown faces of his people were everywhere. All along the track in straight lines far as his eye could see were the Washo. The men in

dark hats and vests, the women with their long dresses
sweeping the earth, their backs bent in silence as they
piled high the logs of softwood cut to feed the endless fire
in the iron belly of the Train Engines. They did not look
up as the train rolled slowly between them toward the
black slash towers. They paid no attention to the one Indian who sat with his large body hunched alone in the middle of the flatbed car. From deep in his face he watched
their every move through squinted eyes while the ancient
songs of Birds screamed from the trapped depths of his
body. The Indian who rode on the train remembered
seeing those same lines of his people going out over
twelvefoot high snow to cut the exposed tops of softwood
trees to feed the endless fire of the Engines during winter.
The people were being paid to kill the trees. The train
slowed, passing through mountains of sawdust surrounding the logjammed millponds. The color of the Sun was
lost in the smoldering air green with the scent of pine.
The ponderous iron wheels beneath the Indian spun and
hissed as the brakes up ahead were put against the momentum. The Yard callboy ran along the slow rolling
flatbed car waving his gray cap at the Indian, shouting
through the yellowing haze choking the air around him,
almost obscuring the high stacked roughcuts of lumber
squared off into the distance farther than the eye could
see.

"Cappin Rex!" The callboy grabbed onto the flatbed's
iron handhold and was pulled along to a jolting halt as the
Engine shuddered to a white steaming stop down the line
of flatbeds loaded with giant saprunning bodies of cut
pine trunks. "Captain Rex! Did you hear the news! A big
woodburning three-truck Shay tanker's been busted all to
kingdom come! Have ye heard about it yet Cappin!" The
callboy clung to the side of the flatbed as he rubbed the
clear running snot from his nose. "A big twelve wheeler
Shay Engine she was Cappin, Soda Tom was engineering,
course he's dead now. Soda Tom was snaking long drags
of logs up the Blueboy timber pike on the Pacific slope.
He was supposed to doublehead that load up the pike but
he said his Shay Lokey was strong enough to do the work

of two Engines. It could of been any of us what got it with him. He was rolling a pretty tough load of drags up the pike, pounding that steam donkey Engine of his for all she was worth, he was battlin up the last switchback, twisting and snaking a forest load of drags around along behind him when of a sudden he comes up on the summit and roaring down t-other side of the loggin pike. That big twelve wheeling Lokey of his was snortin like a volcano, shootin down the shining rails like a lead log in a fastwater flume. Soda Tom was supposed to stop fifteen miles down the pike at a takeoff landing by the river where the logs are supposed to be floated and tied into booms and jammed to the mill. Well that steam donkey came ranting and barking down that pike right by the takeoff landing blowing sparks bigger than a cat's head out the diamond stack. All the Brakies were burning their hands off wheeling the brakestaffs to slow the Lokey down, they didn't have no wooden brake clubs to use, they wielded iron hickies, but even they was like using a blanket to catch a hurricane. Soda Tom knew he was coming onto a new rail spur just put in through dense timber. There had been a rain, which he knew might have loosened any number of fell trees and jammed them over the new track. But he was going to ride her down. All the brakechains was broke but the Brakies were all sticking to their posts at the brakestaffs, they were all riding the Lokey down. Soda Tom big holed the hot air and hosed her over, but she was impossible to blow off. The steam pumped a hundred feet over their heads as they rode helpless onto the new spur and headed straight into the forest weight of a Redwood older than Christ, blasting the side off the smokebox and shooting flying fire into the surrounding trees. The tender was jackknifed up agin the boiler head, the Brakies went down under the wheels, Sam Hensen the Fireman was thrown clean out of sight into the woods. The Company sent up the Bull Wrecker, but the whole world was burning down around them. Smouldering stumps and snags were rolling down onto the red hot rails as the Wrecking Lokey stormed into the forest fire to save the men of the rails who had rode their Lokey down. It were a wasted trip though, there weren't nothing to salvage. Soda Tom was still breathin. They steamed their way back out up to the Doc at the railhead, but it was too late. The Lokey had made Tom pay his dues, the steam had scalded his lungs out. Did ye hear about it Cappin!"

The Indian jumped off the flatbed and looked into the yellowing haze, "I heard the story, it's been told 500 miles up the line."

"Goddogit!" The boy jammed two fingers into his dripping nostrils, "I thought I'd be the first told it to you."

"Who's got a Lokey going up by the gamblin tents?"

"Dutchie's got one I think, if the weather holds, pulling out about now, he'll climb up on Mexican Pike to Elephant Head."

"That's the one I want. I've been riding these rails so long this time I've forgotten how to deal cards." He started walking through the hulking stacks of roughcut lumber, but the callboy was quick to grab hold of his long coat.

"Cappin! You haven't told me what you seen on the circuit. The Brass Hat wants the report, the Brass Hat says no Lokey of his is going to end up like Soda Tom's. The Brass Hat says he aint about to waste time sending men to wrestle kinked chokers in the big woods. So what did ye see Cappin?"

"Nothing but rusty rails."

"No washouts or railrips?"

"All the Iron Road is where it should be. This bunk I rode in on has a wobble in the back truck. They didn't have the tools to fix it on the road so I rode it in. It feels like the axle, not the wheel."

The callboy ran along behind him, "That's just what the Brass Hat wants to know. The Brass Hat is a mean one and if I don't bring back a report on every circuit he hits me up alongside the ear."

The callboy disappeared into the yellowing haze and the Indian wove his way through the ghost stacks of wood, following to the hiss of white steam blowing off from between iron wheels and clouding back over the highblack polished jacket of a shaking Engine.

"Hey Cap," a sweating face hung out the cab window
behind the boiler and shouted through the hissing steam.
"You want a hitch on my steam donkey! All the gamblins
up on Mexican Pike. Those boys up there would sure like
to steal all your Injun coins off you! I've just got to stoke
some more pine billets then we're up the pike to Elephant
Head and catch up a load of sawlogs on this drag of
bunks I'm totin! Get on board Cap!"

·   ·   ·

Captain Rex sat up on the mound of cut logs coughing
blood into the sleeve of his coat as the steam flew over his
head from the Engine pumping up the long lash of silver
track strangled around the mountain to the summit. He
could see the outline of the mountain rising from the yellowing haze, the tall trees of the downslopes slashed to
stumps, exposing the roll of once hidden earth so the
curves and dips of the steep draws and spurs looked in the
distance like the boned ribs of an elephant lying on its
side. The very top of the summit the elephant's dying
head. The train whistle blew and shattered the shadows
beginning to settle on the slope. He could hear the bellowing of men driving bullteams of oxen chained to mutilated
trunks of trees, the arms of their branches stripped to the
bark. The oxen skidded the green weight over the raw
earth of the level roadcut leading to the greased V chutes
timbered down a dry creekripped canyon into the yellowing haze of the mills below. The oxen snaked the logs up
to the head of the greased trough where they were unhooked to slide of their own dead weight off the mountain. The narrow gleaming rails rose higher into the brilliant green of a forest parading off an untouched spur of
the summit. In the falling light the trees bled from ax
wounds blazed into their hide to mark them for the steel
bite of the saw that would cut them from rim to rim,
crashing them back to an earth they had thrust above cen-
turies before. The Indian saw the speckled white flow of
sap bleeding the heart of its hard sugar down the trunks
as the Engine steamed up into darkness, the dull yellow

glow from its oil headlamp thrown out ahead onto the straight Iron Road.

The rain began to fall on the Indian riding the Iron Road. The fire in his chest kept him warm but he pulled the big coat tight around his neck to keep the water out. The bodies of the men feeding the endless fire of the Engine glowed like ghosts in the intense white light of the boiler below him. The rain drove down against the advancing Engine, sweeping hail across the iron rails illuminated by the single eye of the headlamp. The Indian could hear the rain banging off the Engine jacket and knocking against his hat. He smelled the trees thinning. The Engine was drawing him nearer the summit into ice thickening rain. Sleet big as a fist beat down on his hat. The white smoke clouding from the Engine's stack blew and whipped back over his head through the pounding sleet. The blood came up in his chest, strangling in his throat; it choked his dreams. The Engine was on the head of the elephant. The Indian jumped off into mud.

"Cap!" The Fireman shouted out the cab window into the rain, "The gamblins over to the cookhouse tent. It's the Bull Cook what's running the show!"

The Indian pushed through the mud, all around him rose the stumped ghosts of recently cut trees. The light from within the tent he headed for shined through the canvas walls, guiding his way between the ghosts.

"Com' on in Cap'n Rex, you ol crazyhead you, you ol trout from Tahoe!"

The sudden warmth of the tent hit the sagging wetness of the Indian's greatcoat, lifting a cloud of steam from his body. He drew his thumbless hands from the coat and held up the knotted weight of a dirty rag.

"How much you totin tonight ol trout from Tahoe?"

The Indian walked across the floor splintered and spiked by the calks of the booted men. He dropped the knotted rag onto the card strewn table.

"Let see what you brung us ol trout from Tahoe." The Logbucker opened the rag and banged the metal coins to the table, "One . . . three . . . seven gold pieces." One eye popped up at the Indian, "Seven golden ones aint much to keep you in one hand of stud poker ol trout from Tahoe. But we'll dump the ante down from two, to one dollar, just to cut you in ol trout."

The Indian scraped a chair back and sat down, holding the fists of his thumbless hands out before him.

"Christ O Mary he do stink!" The man next to him shoved away from the Indian and pinched his blunt nose between two fingers.

"You'll have to forgive the Whistle Punk here Cap'n Rex," the Log Bucker dropped the metal weight of each gold coin from one blistered hand to another. "He's like a dog, he aint partial to Injun scents, specially you Washo. He's been jackin up in Washington country around the Wenatchee Injuns, course they don't have no stink since it goes and rains everyday up in that country so they gets a bath whether they want it or not. Course me, I'm different, I been around a coon's age. I remember the days when an Injun bucko could still go into town not wearing pants. I've smoked a trainload of nick-o-teen and trimmed and bucked enough logs to build up the city of Frisco. I can tell you out of experience it gets awful lonely up here in these winter camps when the weather comes down on you so that you welcome the company of any talking body, no matter what its stink or race. Now you take Hair Oil Pete sitting here next o me." He nodded to the man shuffling the cards at his side, the long black flow of his hair glistened in the smoky light of the kerosene lamp, "Hair Oil Pete is neat as a pin, fit as a fiddle. He greases his hair up with locomotive valve oil from the tallowpot every morning before breakfast to lubricate the roots. He's the fanciest dude you'd ever hope to lay an eye on riding with his head hung out the cab window of a fast Lokey, not a hair out of place. But even as careful about his appearance as he is he can tell you neither stink nor race make no difference when a jack is lonesome."

"It aint only the stink!" the Whistle Punk snorted through his pinched nose. "Look there! Christ O Mary look to that! He aint got no *thumbs!* They look to be shot *off!*"

The Indian did not move his fisted hands from the table. Hair Oil Pete dealt everyone around the table a card, face down, then looked up into the Indian's brown face, "Black painted Ladies are wild." He dealt around four more cards, face up.

The Log Bucker bent the corner of his down card up to read his fate, he whipped his head around and spit a yellow gob of tobacco juice over the splintered floor, "Don't mind the Whistle Punk none Cap'n, he's still green around the gills. If words were manure he'd have a good crop of tomatoes. Why back in the beginning o time when I was still a boy we built the Tioga Mine Railroad in one hundred and thirty days right across the top of the Sierra Nevada. Why them granite shelves of Yosemite country was so narrow they was no wider than your foot, the mules rubbed themselves bloody on the rocks. We must a had at least nine hundred coolies workin Tioga, there was some what criticized the Road for using John Chinaman labor, said there were plenty Irishmen hanging around the Country the work could have been given to. I remember when Mister Charles Crocker himself heard that talk, he stood right up to the world and told them the dearly departed ancestors of his yellow pets had built the Great Wall of China without cheap Irish labor and the Central Pacific Railroad could damn well do the same layin iron tracks across California. You should have seen them coolies work Cap'n, they didn't eat nothin but tea. They must a had twelve, fifteen tea-boys running up and down the lines, the hotter it got the more tea they drank, and it got plenty hot what with all the horsedrawn graders up front of them following right into the dust of a hundred powder monkeys at a time blasting a road through the Tioga granite. One hundred and thirty days it took to blast that road out of the highest Sierra down to Big Oak Flat Road, and that was one hundred and thirty days of powder monkeys blowin each other to bits, along with the horses behind them. Why I saw men not only lose their thumbs like you Cap'n, but I seen em lose their whole hands. I seen arms and legs blown ever which way. I seen one powder monkey holing some dynamite caps when his whole head was took off like a rotten pumpkin. One hundred and thirty days to build the Tioga Road from the Gold to the Railhead, Cap'n. An engineering marvel."

"Seems like all you Washo have hard times keeping your bodies together Cap," Hair Oil Pete smiled the wrinkles of his forehead up into his greased hair. "Half of them Washo and halfbreeds livin in tentshacks on the edge of camp got one part or other missin. Your brother Henry's got but one arm, then there's that medicine man, Rattles Ruggles, was ridin a Lokey to the pigweed when the unblocked iron frogs of a coupler connecting two flatcars pinched one of his feet clean off to the ankle bone."

"How did you lose your thumbs ol trout," the Logbucker flicked the corner of his bottom card on the table.

"I'll open on one," the Indian tossed a goldpiece out before him.

"I'll meet that," the Logbucker threw his own gold out. "You know, Pete's right, I guess all the apples in the barrel are rotten. I remember back in the beginnin of time when the Company might give a few Injuns a day of work, but they was either dumb drunk or just dumb as a bunny. I remember one who had to tailoff on the green chain stackin the long cuts on skids, he stacked one cut right down on his thumbs, they swolled up bigger'n his neck. He weren't so lucky as you Cap'n, he didn't lose them, but he damn well wished he did when they started turning his arms green." He whipped his head and spit on the splintered floor, "How'd you lose *your* thumbs Cap'n?"

"The Bull Cook aint goin to like this Injun in the gamblin tent!" The Whistle Punk snorted through the pinched red bulge of his nose. "The Bull Cook says the rule of the camp is not halfbreeds or Injuns in the gamblin tents."

"Shut up and bet!" The Logbucker banged his fist on the table. "Either you're *in* or you're *out*. Stop stallin!"

"But the Bull Cook . . . !"

The Logbucker jammed his spiked boots into the splintered floor, "Put up or shut up!"

The Whistle Punk's goldpiece clinked to the table.

"That's more like it! Now you use a little respect for the Cap'n here. He aint like you, he aint some plain punk what blows an all-clear whistle in a loggin camp. He aint no ordinary Injun down on his uppers. He's a boss. He's a boss of his people. The Company hires him whenever it needs an Injun boss. You see that badge pinned on his coat," the Logbucker pointed across the table at the silver star glinting through the smoky kerosene light. "*That* is a United States Peacemaker badge. Cap'n Rex has been appointed a Peacemaker of the Washo by the U.S. Government. He's a U.S. Boss over his people."

The Whistle Punk twisted back in his chair, refusing to let go of his nose, "Well he's still just like any Injun Joe to me. Look at him, he's so poor he could put his socks on at either end. It's a good thing the Bull Cook aint here. Besides that he looks *crooked*."

Hair Oil Pete threw his dollar to the table and cocked his chair up on the back two legs, "Hey! The old Cap does look kinda crooked, what with no thumbs, that big greatcoat with only three shiny brass buttons left out of twelve, a two-bit badge pinned to his heart and a face that looks like dried mud. Hey Bucker! How do we know he aint crooked? How do we know he's straight!"

The Bucker spit a gob of tobacco at the tent wall and watched it hit the canvas and slip in a weak brown streak to the splintered floor, "Is he crooked?" He choked on his own spit, "You just watch out for the ol Cap'n, you just keep a hawkeye on him. Cap'n Rex would steal Christ from the cross and then come back for the nails!"

Hair Oil Pete dealt around another two cards, face down, "Hey Cap, how come you aint got two wives?"

"Because my wife has not got a sister."

"Aint that old squaw Molly Moose your wife, Cap?"

"She wanted me to take another wife, she got lonely all the years, she wanted someone to help with the work, so she went over to my brother because he had a wife to keep her from going lonely. But all the children that came out of her were the ones I put in, even after she had gone over to him. The children are mine."

"And your brother doesn't know Cap!"

"No."

"Why Cap, you old *fox!*"

"Give me a drink."

"Pour Cap a whiskey Whistle Punk."

The Punk shoved a glass in front of the Indian and he drank it. He felt the heavy stir of Birds within him, the dull thud of wings in his chest, but the songs Birds sang long ago in dreams did not fly from his lips into the room. The blood came up and choked his dreams, his own coughing filling the room. He wiped the blood from his lips and put another glass of whiskey in his body, "Wives are too much work. I had myself an ugly wife, but she was too much work. She never cheated me, she only gave the gift of her woman to those she liked. But she was too much work, I was always worried if others would like her after she gave them her gift. I was always worried others would think her stupid as a woman and laugh at my back." He took another drink.

"You Injuns got hard times Cap."

"I hear all those squaws will blow you like a train whistle!" The Punk's laughter snorting from his nose twisted him back in his chair as his hands tried to hide the swelling red face.

"Back in the beginnin of time when I was a boy I remember when all that the squaws in these hills wore was rain, and they'd handle every jack in a crew of timber-beasts and be banging up the road the next night looking for another timber crew. These modern squaws aint up to that. They don't even want to live in no wicki-yups the way the old ones do. Now they're more civilized and hang around the camps hopin to get enough old thrown away canvas together to make themselves a tentshack, you don't see no more of them tree limbs and branches wicki-yups anymore, they've all gone modern."

"They'll blow you like a train whistle!"

Hair Oil Pete grabbed the bottle away from the Whistle Punk and poured himself a drink, "Why don't you shut up and keep the whole works in your mouth!"

"No sir, these modern squaws aint up to much, I don't see much value in them, they're just like tobacco, no nourishment and highly injurious to health. When they go around acting civilized even an old gadget like me would pass them up, and at my age I aint particular," the Bucker spit a weak brown gob of tobacco to the splintered floor.

"Blow youuuuuuuu like a train whistle!" The Punk knocked the Indian in the arm, "Like a train whistle!"

The Indian tossed the metal weight of four goldpieces to the center of the table.

"That's pretty steep ol trout, I only see one Ace showing on the table before you. You must not be playing with a full deck."

"I'm with the Bucker, you must be ridin high Cap," Pete tossed his cards onto the table and fingered the back of his slippery neck running with grease from his hair. "That leaves you Whistle Punk, show your stuff."

"Like a train whistle!" The Punk tossed five gold coins on top of the Indian's.

The Indian held his last gold coin like a shrunken sun up to the smoky light of the kerosene lamp, then threw it onto the metal heap, "Two Aces."

"TOOT! TOOT! A baby is born! Four painted Ladies!" The Punk slapped the four Queens up and wrenched back on the chair snorting through his pinched nose, "TOOT-TOOT!" He jumped up, the spikes of his heavy boots pounding a jig in the splintered floor with one blistered hand cocked over the bulge of his pants between the crotch while the other hand pulled high in the air on the imaginary cord of a train whistle, "TOOT-TOOT-TOOT!" He didn't see the man who ripped open the flap of the tent and stepped right into his dance, knocking his body bleeding from the mouth to the scarred floor.

"He just can't handle it, Bull Cook," the Logbucker let his big head slide from side to side in disgust. "Nope, he just can't handle winnin." He spit a gob of tobacco to the splintered floor at the feet of the Punk backhanding the blood from his mouth. "He just caint handle it."

The Bull Cook swung the thick muscle of his neck around, the smoky light of the kerosene lamp cast down on his head, over the split of his nose pushed to one side of his face so the spokes of his eyes seemed to be shoved over to the other side of his face, "Who let the Injun in!"

"I let the ol trout from Tahoe have a sit-down, the rains comin down niggers and wops outside."

"You know the rule of the camp Bucker, no halfbreeds or Injuns in the gamblin tent!"

"You know this ol trout, Bull Cook," the Bucker spit a prick of juice at the floor. "He's off'n on the Compnee payroll. He's a U.S. Peacemaker. He's a boss."

"He's a Injun *red*man!"

"Don't make no difference nohow, Bull Cook," Hair Oil Pete slicked a greased tuft of hair down on the side of his head. "He lost anyway."

The Bull Cook scooped all the cards off the table and bent them through a hard shuffle into a tight square pack, "You jacks hear this straight, a redman is only equal until his money gives out."

"He aint equal then!" The Whistle Punk jumped up fingering his swelling lip. "I won it all off'n him. He aint equal!"

The Bull Cook grabbed the Indian up by the shoulders of his greatcoat, "Go on redman. Git on back to your camp of halfbreeds and Washos. Tell all those people you're Peacemaker of there's a new Bull of the Woods comin to this camp, he's bringin in a whole new gang of timberbeasts. He's not a soft touch like me, he's a fire-breathin Injun hater. His word is Law, no Injun shacks within a mile of the camp, he don't want no Injuns in the camp beggin. He don't want no Injuns in the gamblin tents. He's a new Bull in the tall timbers and as long as God is in heaven the Bull of the Woods is King." He shoved the Indian across the splintered floor, "You're out of money and you're out of luck."

"I'm staying," the Indian pulled off his hat. "My money says I have the right to stay." He slipped a goldpiece from within the sweatband of the hat and placed it next to the squared deck on the table.

The Bull Cook's eyes burned out from the one side of his nose, "Nobody calls a bet on me redman." He slapped five gold coins over the one and spread the deck across the table in a straight line, "Draw! High card wins!"

The gold metal shined up into the Indian's face, the thumbless fists of his hands did not move from the pock-

ets of the coat. The feathered song of Birds soared in his
lungs for escape and he spit blood to the floor.

"That ol trout from Tahoe is so scared of losing his last
gold buck he's spittin blood."

"Draw red man! Even you have a sportin chance, a
stopped clock is right twice a day!"

The Indian flipped over a red 4.

The Bull Cook turned a Joker up right next to the 4.
"Joker's *wild* redman! You lose!"

The Indian did not move, the gold glow of the coins
warmed his face in the cold of the room, the ancient Birds
bursting in his lungs. He doubled over coughing, the
blood spitting into the sleeve of his greatcoat.

"Go on now redman, haul out!"

He straightened up, his brown face stiffening as he
choked his throat free of blood, "I have one more bet."

"One more bet ol trout! You aint got nothin! Why don't
you bet your boots!"

"Let me see your boots!" The Bull Cook grabbed one
of the Indian's boots and twisted it up, "That aint a bet! A
team of Teamsters could drive a wagon through the size
of that hole. He's got more sock covering his sole than
leather!"

"I bet this," the Indian pointed to his greatcoat.

"That? That's an old Union coat back from the War
'tween the States. It's still got the cannonball holes in it!"

"The ol trout don't mean that, Bull Cook. He means
what's pinned over his chest."

"You mean the badge?"

"It was sent to him from Washington D. C. with a letter from the Department of War appointing him Peacemaker over all the Washo."

"Peacemaker of the Washo! What the hell do I want
that for!? It's only tinplate!"

The Indian unpinned the silver shine of the star, "I
bet."

"Goddoggit!" The Bull Cook spiked his boot into the
floor, "I'll come up to your bet! I'll win your tin badge
and strut around camp as Peacemaker! Big Boss of the
Washo! I'll see your bet and quadtriple it!" He banged six

gold coins on top of the six already heaped on the table. "Put your tin badge up!"

"You win that off'n the ol trout Bull Cook and he won't have no power left with his people. You'll win all his power."

"Come on redman, don't stand there with your face hangin out! Bet the badge!"

The Indian weighed the silver star in his hand. The white faces watched. The five points of the star shined in the earth color of his palm. The song of Birds jumped from his head to his heart. He pinned the star to the greatcoat and walked across the splintered floor into darkness.

In the darkness Captain Rex could see the old days along the Big Lake of the Sky when the blood of the people ran so cold they built up fires from green boughs and danced around the flames, their wild figures leaping through sparks jumping across snow. Now the dances were gone, the fires grown over with ice, it was too cold to even die. The white burden had followed the rain. The mountains were silent. The people watched among themselves. The people watched over the frozen ground. The wail of the wind came up around them and rattled the blades of ice hanging from trees. The Spirit from all the old men was gone. The smoke from many winters passed had diseased their eyes and they sat sightless on the frozen ground, longing for the white burden to melt and the soothing black mud to be spread on the eye of their pain. The Sun was hidden from the people, they had not seen it pass the Moon. The people had forgotten the color of the Sun. Rattles Ruggles stood on his one leg among the people beneath the torn canvas flaps of the big winter house with the feathers of his Magpie hat dangling about his ears.

"If there is no more Sun, there are no more Washo. If there are no more Washo, there is no more life. The people are all dead or dying. The Whiteman has stolen our dreams. He has hidden the Sun. We have lost our power. We die."

Captain Rex spit blood, "It is too cold to die."

"Listen to Captain Pigweed! White Beast, mad White beast, wild white *Musege!*" One Arm Henry pushed to his feet, the brown eyes screaming from his shrunken face, "Listen to the wild Bear. You are not respected, you are *feared!*"

"I am your Brother."

"You do not travel on the road of the people, mad sly Bear!"

"I am the Peacemaker. The people do not have to stay around me, they can travel away, such is the road of our fathers."

"The people do not stay because of *you*, they stay because you bring fire. You are the Firemaker!"

"And now Captain Pigweed, the fires have all grown cold with ice," Rattles Ruggles shook the black and white feathers about his head. "The people are all dead of dying. Look to the people," he flung his arm about his head to the people lying on the frozen earth beneath the stretched canvas of the big room, their bodies shaking, their voices crying as they shuddered under the skin of Rabbit blankets worn bare of fur. "The people freeze and hunger about you. There is no strong meat for the young, there is no heart and liver of the kill to feed the old people. The White power you have been given to wear over your heart like a silver star cannot save the people. Your medicine is broken. The *wegaleyo* of the White is too big for one man. The Whiteman has shot a sickness into all Indians, we are dead or dying. You are too weak to suck the magic of the White *wegaleyo* from all Indian people. I have strong water, I have dreamed of a medicine so strong that will come and break the power of your silver badge. I am the Man of Medicine. I will suck the White *wegaleyo* from the Spirit of the people. I will stand alone as the Boss."

"I am the *Peacemaker*. If you go up to save the people and fail, I will *kill* you."

"Listen to the wild beast." One Arm Henry tugged his Squirrel hat over the cold throb of his ears, the blade of his stumped arm flashed at his brother, "Captain Pigweed

has become so much the Whiteman he acts just like Coyote, always ready to bark and eat!"

Captain Rex watched through the rips in the canvas all
around him as gray turned to black over the ghost stumps
of trees. He slept under the thin blanket of Rabbitskins
that also covered the shivering bodies of Walking Shoes
and his woman. He listened in the blackness to the blood
coming up in his throat and choking his dreams. He
pressed his back close to the woman of Walking Shoes to
support the wracking muscle of his chest coughing and
spitting blood. He held the bloodstained sleeve of his coat
over his mouth to hold the life breath in him, but it spurt-
ed and wheezed out, its sound freezing in the cold air.
Then stopped. His lungs burned red beneath the blue cold
of his skin. But the sound of life breath still spit and
coughed in the air. The blood was coming up in the
throats of all the people. The blood was coming up and
choking their dreams. He felt the soft flutter of wings in
his Spirit. He listened for the songs of Birds sung long ago
to sing from his lips, but blood rushed into his mouth. His
old hard body shook and kicked, the blood screaming in
his head. The scream cut down his spine, it was the
scream of the woman his body pressed against beneath the
blanket. The woman of Walking Shoes trembled and wept
in blackness. Old sisters came running to her and put their
hands all over her swelled body. The hump of her belly
throbbed with new life, her thighs had gone stiff and
pressed up against the Rabbit blanket. The old sisters began singing and chanting, "Crawl out. Hurry on up. Come
on out new Washo. We want to see you. We are waiting.
We are watching!" The woman choked and moaned, the
blood screaming in her mouth and splattering on her chin.
Rattles Ruggles was above her in the darkness, his cocoon
rattles shaking the air as he danced and whipped the Magpie feathers of his head around. He knelt next to her and
put his hands onto the throbbing hump. "Listen! There is
new life in here! It has grown big and waits to come out.
But the Whites have shot their *wegaleyo* into this new life,
the Whites are trying to kill this new life, the Whites are
trying to rob this new Washo before it gets to us. I must

suck this *wegaleyo* out. This Ghost is a poison, it rots the Spirit." He rose again in dance, the hollow cocoons whizzing in air, he dropped one black and white feather onto the chest of Captain Rex, "Firemaker! Go and bring fire. I must smoke. It will take many smokes to suck the Ghost out. Run Captain Pigweed. Run and be a Firemaker!"

Captain Rex pulled the greatcoat up around his chin and ran from the shelter onto the high white burden frozen over the Earth, his old legs wobbled and cracked as he ran through the ghost stumps of trees with the lid of the Sky rolling gray over him, he could see the wooden buildings of the big camp, the smell of frying Ducks came to him across the snow, the smell was sharp and whistled in his head until his mouth ran wet like a Dog's as he pounded on the door of the cookhouse, he pounded until his fist beat air. The Blondhead was standing before him in the open doorway.

"What d'ye say Cap, you're up early. The jacks are still all bunked but their breakfast are fryin on the stoves. Smell that duck fat cookin Cap, better'n those acorns you eat for breakfast aint it?"

"We are dying!"

"Don't want to let the Bull Cook catch you in camp Cap. Bull Cook says no Injuns in camp, that's the Law of the new Bull of the Woods, and the Bull Cook says any you Washo leavin their tent shacks and comin into big camp is going to be run back with their heads shaved and ears cut off. He told you that the last time you come beggin for fire at this door. The Bull Cook he don't mind me none even though I got halfblood in me, because I'm from Wyomin, I got blond hair. The Bull Cook he says my hair looks like goose hair, he says my Mama musta had a goose pecker in her one night." He jammed a hand into the blond bush on top of his head and scratched the scalp, "I wouldn't know about that."

"We need fire!"

"Lookit out there behind ye Cap, it's beginnin to fall again, lookit that Cap, those snowflakes is bigger than silver dollars."

"We are dying!"

"Well ol Cap, my teeth are chatterin like a box o dice with all this cold air comin in and I got duck a fryin, you better git while you still got your ears," he shoved the heavy door closed.

The Indian pushed the arm of his thumbless fist between the door jamb, his stiff fingers clutching at air, "Fire!"

The Blondhead pulled the door off the Indian's arm and looked into the face browner than his own, "What ye give me for it?"

"We are dying!"

"Three good jackrabbit blankets for a buckskin is what I want. Blankets is worth gold in this camp, and jackrabbit blankets is the best. I know, I was a trapper, but a trapper is a hermit's life, that's why I give it up and come down to civilization. But I sure do miss the high country, up there is the only place on earth a man can breathe the same air as angels, there's no end to the amount of work a man can do up there, the air will make him sleep like a baby and wash ever bit of tiredness from his bones."

"The tall trees have all been cut, the small trees are buried in snow, the Earth is frozen from sight, all the people have gone weak from coughing up their strength in clots of blood. We die without fire!"

"Shutup Cap!" The Blondhead grabbed the Indian's face, locking his hand over the mouth, "Listen . . . you hear *that!* That's the Bull Cook comin! You wait here." He ran back into the cookhouse and spiked open one of the ironlids of the long stove, the flames jumping up at him as he shoved the narrow joint of a log into the heat until the tip burned in an ember the size of a fist. He jerked the log out and waved it through the air, catching a flame on the end. He turned to run to the Indian but saw him stooped into the woodbin gathering logs into his greatcoat. He swung the flaming log in a smoking arc against the Indian's face, knocking him to the floor, "Goddam you pecker! Goddam you Washo!" He yanked the Indian up, the logs crashing from the greatcoat. "If you ever come in my sight again *I'll* cut your ears off!"

He jammed the flaming log into the Indian's hand and threw him up against the wall, spinning him through the door as his boot came up and kicked him straight in the back, knocking him out into the snow.

The Indian rose to his knees, the tip of the log burning and twisting smoke. He pushed to his feet and ran stumbling across the snow with the flaming torch held high above his head.

The gray light rolled over the head of Rattles Ruggles, the hanging black and white Magpie feathers of his close-fitting hat glistened in the dull dawn, "I sometimes smoke for somebody. I light tobacco for a smoke. That is why they call me a doctor. But I cannot smoke without fire. My big pipe is cold. Captain Pigweed lets the people die. He does not make fire. His power with the Whites fails." He placed the palms of his hands on the throbbing brown hump of the woman's stomach and pressed, "This life cannot wait for Captain Pigweed. This life cannot give up the Ghost. The Ghost will destroy this life unless it is sucked out!"

The man with one arm hung his head between his knees, the blood boiling out of his throat to the frozen ground, "Captain Pigweed has abandoned the people. The White power of his silver star has been broken."

Rattles Ruggles turned his sagging brown face up, the gray light fading through the rips in the canvas walls washed over the wrinkled web of his face surrounded by Magpie feathers. He stood, smelling something in the air, something he had not smelled for long days, the smell of smoke. "He comes! The Firemaker Comes! Captain Pigweed comes the Firemaker!"

Captain Rex ran in among the people, his lungs wheezing and blazing, the fiery torch swirling smoke held high over his head in a thumbless fist.

"Captain Pigweed comes the Firemaker," Rattles Ruggles danced around the torch in quick little hops. "I can smoke tobacco with fire, That is why they call me a doctor." He took the torch and waved it in the air, its warm smoke touching all the people, then he placed it in the black firehole and spread the fan of a Hawk wing open, waving it over the smouldering log until the life of the flame jumped into all the cold embers. The people came around the smoking pit and put the soles of their feet to the warmth while the Man of Medicine smeared hot ashes into his palms, rubbing them into his scalp beneath the Magpie bonnet until lice began to fall dead from his head; he streaked the black soot on his face and spit at the wingless bodies of dead lice, "I am the dream doctor. Sometimes I smoke for somebody and make them well. I suck out bad *wegaleyo!*" He scooped up more hot ashes and clutched them in his fists, "The Whites kill all our babies with their magic. I say don't kill our babies anymore. I say the dream doctor is here to suck the White *wegaleyo* from the new life growing in this woman." He held his clenched fists over her stomach, then separated the thumb from the fingers, letting a stream of warm ash spill over the throbbing brown hump of flesh. He took a medicine basket up in his hands, stroking the pattern of the weave, his hands moving over the pattern of Sunrise among the hills as the chant broke from his lips, "Stars shine over the graves of our Ancestors, the Moon glides over their bones." He opened the basket and unwrapped among the dampened leaves a horned Toad, "The Moon glides over their bones." He stuck the Toad on the throbbing hump of the woman's flesh, "Suck! Get full of blood! There is a bone in the forehead of the new life, it is *wegaleyo* shot into this new Washo by the Whites. Suck this *wegaleyo* out. Get full of blood! Puke. Die!" He pressed the cold struggling body of the Toad to the woman's stomach. "I will use tobacco now. There will be many smokes. I will think now." He filled the great blackstone pipe with tobacco of the sage and lit it to the fire of the smoking pit, "I will smoke now all you people. I am Doctor Toad. I will suck the *wegaleyo* out. Get full of blood. Puke. Die." He held the Toad clamped to the moaning woman and blew smoke over her humped belly, "If there is no more Sun, there are no more Washo. If there are no more Washo there is no more life." The gray light rolled over the swaying Magpie feathers of his head, the chant of his smoke rising into the blind air of night, becoming nothing.

With the morning Captain Rex passed through the rows of tent shacks where the people slept around fires grown cold. He went unnoticed among the ghost stumps of trees leading through the big camp where the smoke of many fires fingered the Sunless Sky and the wood-eating Engine was already beginning to churn its wheels along the Iron Road, the great steel arrow of the snowshield slicing white waves through snow covered tracks. He ran with the Engine, his chest flaming and beating blood to his throat as he swung up onto the dead body of a giant pine trunk chained to the length of an entire flatbed car. The Engine whistle blew ten feet over his head and the warm smoke came back slapping in his face all the way off the mountain down into Truckee where the yellowmen cooked in shiny pots in the room full of men wearing spiked boots that could rip the Earth and walk up the bodies of trees, fat arms of logs burned in the open fireplace, reeking and hissing steam from the burning blood of their sap, the steam rose everywhere in the room, from the hot pots of the yellowmen, off the cold coatbacks of the loggers and teamsters stuffing burnt potatoes into the cold breath of their steamblowing mouths. He moved through the steam and talked to a yellowman as white clouds rose everywhere. He unpinned the silver star from his greatcoat, its five points beamed and glittered in the steam dulled light of lanterns swinging from rafters. The yellowman came back to him through the steam and took the silver star away, giving him two glass bottles, one filled with golden water, the other with mud, he drank the one of golden water and put the other beneath his greatcoat, hugging it to his body all the time the train spun its iron wheels and plowed through the snow back up to the top of the Elephant Head where he could hear all the coughing and hollow spit of blood sounding across the snow from his people gathered around fires grown cold in the tent shacks where Doctor Toad sat slouched over the throbbing brown hump of the moaning woman, his dangling black

and white feathers pointing like blades to the frozen Earth
while the people ripped the Rabbit blankets apart, tearing
and chewing the tough dried fat from the worn hides.

Doctor Toad turned the watery earth of his eyes up at
the man in the greatcoat, "If there is no more Sun, there
will be nothing to eat. If there is nothing to eat there will
be no more Washo. If there are no Washo there will be no
life."

Captain Rex pushed him aside and pulled the glass bottle from under his coat, dumping from the packed wet
mud struggling bodies onto the ash covered hump of the
woman's stomach. The leeches squirmed across the throbbing skin, the rings whipped around the lance of their flattened bodies contracting and blowing as the suckers at
both probing ends smacked and drew blood through the
throbbing flesh.

"Captain Pigweed is killing the life within! Captain Pigweed is killing the life of the woman! Captain Pigweed is
killing the life of the people. His bad medicine sucks the
Spirit and feeds the White *wegaleyo!*" Doctor Toad tried
to sweep away the leeches squirming and sucking across
the woman's belly. Captain Rex threw the greatcoat over
her, then locked his thumbless fists around the screaming
man's head.

"*Musege!* White beast! Drunken beast!" One Arm Henry came spitting and coughing to his feet with the stone
blade of his hatchet striking for his brother's back.

The old sisters wailed and screamed around the woman,
"Look! Look!"

The fire in One Arm Henry's chest caved his body in,
the hatchet blow missing Captain Rex, the power of its
cold stone splintering to pieces as it struck the frozen
ground.

"LOOK! LOOK!" The old sisters pointed and wailed as
the throbbing stomach of the woman pushed up the dead
body of the baby from beneath the greatcoat.

"Excuse us Ghost, we mean you no harm, we did not
shoot the *wegaleyo* of the Whites into you. Please don't
travel back and give us dreams. Go away. Do not bother

us. Leave the world and do not bother the living," Rattles Ruggles placed the body of the baby in the stump of a tree, the people stood on the frozen ground and chanted his words.

"We do not want to offend you, oh Ghost. We know it is the way to burn you up so you can travel faster south to the happy place where the Ancestors play games, gamble with sticks and bones, where there are always dances. We know it is the way to burn you up and put what is left of your bones into a fast flowing creek so they may go faster south and be with your Spirit. But the fires have all grown cold and there is no Sun. We do not wish to offend you that the skin of Bear could not cloak you as you travel faster south. Bear has stronger power than the people, and we are too weak from no blood to outsmart him. But we will cry for you for three months. When the fires flame again we will mix ashes and put grease to our faces, we will not wash for a year, old sisters and old brothers will cut their hair off. We will make a proper house of the dead for you so you will not travel back and give us a dream that will kill us. Excuse us Ghost, we mean you no harm. We have treated you as the others around you."

Rattles Ruggles waved his arm through the hollowed stumps of the logged trees where brown frozen bodies were placed in death, "We have treated you as others. All of these people around you have already traveled south. They have spit up their life blood and died out of this world. Please tell them we do not say bad things about them. Please tell them we do not mention their names. Please tell them not to come back and give us dreams. You will be in good company Ghost. Someday all the people will be in good company. We do not know how much longer we can live on this Earth covered with its white burden. All our children are dead or dying. We are the last. The blood of our bodies is coming out and spilling on the white Earth.

The people all lay dead or dying on the frozen ground. There were no more Rabbit blankets to huddle under, there were no more Rabbit blankets to eat. There was no more Sun. The people were all dying away from Captain Rex. In the darkness he could feel the shuddering body of Walking Shoes' woman on the frozen Earth next to him. He rolled her over, clutching her body with his thumbless hands. Her breasts were cold, his face fumbled among them, his old mouth sucking at the nipples, trying to draw the life milk into him. He squeezed her to him with his thumbless hands and sucked until he felt a warm flow between his lips. He heard the shouting and noise outside. The people were coming to stone him. The people had all come up and voted equally, every man had his own voice heard. Every man said Captain Pigweed uses bad medicine. Captain Pigweed tries to poison his people. Captain Pigweed is a bad doctor. But the people were not outside. The people were dying away around him. Their flesh rotting on the frozen ground. Their stink rising around him. He heard the stunning sound of the Bull Cook's guthammer, it rattled the blades of ice hanging from the trees. The canvas flaps of the shack shuddered beneath a liquid weight sloshed down their sides, throwing the smell of kerosene up all around him.

"Get those barbedwire concertinas up around every shack! Don't leave no way for them to run out!" The Bull Cook's voice rose above the shouting and sounds of heavy boots running on snow.

"The Bull of the Woods is coming! The Bull of the Woods!"

"You jacks shut up and let the Bull talk! Here he is!"

"Gents, Johnny Doc says all these Injuns are infested with the T-*burculur*. Johnny Doc says if one Injun so much as breathes in your face you're a dead man. Gents, the only thing that will stop this Injun epidemic is fire. Every Injun in every shack around every lumber camp and town is being burned to the ground. Only fire can burn out the Injun fever. Now I don't like to do this anymore than you gents, but what can we do? Are we not the gents that's been feeding and clothing these painted savages since we discovered this land? Aren't we the gents that's been teaching them the Christian way? Gents, I say this: Can the civilized world ask any more of us? Now light up those torches. Get your rifles ready for them to come running out. It's going to get hotter than hell in there. Shoot at anything that wears skin! Burn the Injun plague away!"

Captain Rex could hear the soft thudding of torches striking the canvas sides, the flames ripping off into air, sending smoke across the frozen ground, the crackling blaze beat against the smoke like wings. Deep within the pumping blood choking at his throat he heard the feathered songs Birds sang long ago that he had learned in dreams. The songs bled from his nose and through his ears, escaping into smoke as the blaze of the fire whipped high and burned the white snow clean from the Earth.

My HEART is Big as a Cloud.

I scream like a Bird. I bellow like a Buffalo. I bleed like melting snow. The Messiah has come. Christ has returned to Earth. He is walking on a dead land. A land sunk to the heart. Guarded over only by memory. Defended in battle of dreams. The Christ has returned to love up all the hearts buried in the ground. All Indian bodies will grow young again. He will tame the wild bugs. Soothe the small Birds. Milk the stars. The Christ comes the second time. He is not the false prophet. He is rising up all the people across the land. He has had a vision over the Desert horizon. Trees of thorn higher than men grow all around him. Piles of smoke rise in a Sacred Cloud from his stonepipe. There is a hope in my heart. The Spirit is approaching. How close he comes on a Cloud. I hold out my hands toward him and cry. He sings my name as I run after it. The Sky herself is clear. The wind blows his words over the whole Earth. He sings my name. Hallelujah. Hallelujah Bob. He sings my name.

"Hallelujah Bob. You are the one the Whites call Hallelujah Bob. You have sat here with the Christ on the Desert covered with snow and used tobacco. I have waited your journey. I have walked along the shores of Pyramid Lake among the Fisheaters. I have returned the second coming. I am the Messiah. I am Wovoka. I am Wovoka,

the son of the prophet Tavibo. I am the Christ. Listen,
Washo. Listen. Can you hear it through the ground? Lis-
ten with your heart. The Earth is weeping. The sacred
Earth weeps. All the dead bodies are piling up in the
Earth. Can you hear the place where crying begins? The
Earth is crying like a Crow. The Earth has come. It is ris-
ing. All the dead hearts shall walk again. The grandmoth-
ers will break the knives and bows. We shall grow as one
Nation. We shall live on One Road. All people are painted
different colors. Indians are in high places everywhere.
Stand upon the Earth. Stand in high places everywhere.
Stand ready. Use paint. When Crow calls you will see
him."

The vision clouded around the Christ. I tried to see his
face through my flowing tears, but the light shining from
under the black brim of his tall sombrero blinded me so
all I could see was smoke flowing from his lips. He
crossed the stonepipe over his left to me.

"You are the one the Whites call Hallelujah Bob. I have
been waiting your coming. I have sent for you. I am waiting for all my children. Eleven are coming from a far
land. I have been waiting your coming. You have been
preaching the One Road. You have been going about
doing good. I know all in you. You have been saved. I
know of your Ancestors. The blood of your blood saw the
Whites eat of their own flesh on yonder lake, Donner.
Captain Rex gambled the money of the people away and
lost his way in a blizzard, he came into a cabin and slept,
when he awoke white bodies were lying dead all around
him with the blood they had coughed up splattered on
their clothes. He took their White death back to the people, that was the year all the Washo were burned to the
ground at Elephant Head, one was saved, Ayas, the Antelope, who was sent into the valley of clouds to warm his
sightless grandmother who wove flowing streams into her
baskets. Ayas, who lived among the Whites and was saved
by his people to live in a sacred manner on the shores of
the Big Lake of the Sky, Tahoe. Ayas, who fished the
small streams leading into the Big Lake and watched the
Whites go out on the Sky of bluewater with nets, dragging

up tons of flashing Tahoe Trout everyday. Ayas, who watched Memdewi wade out into the mouth of a stream feeding the Big Lake, building a stone Fish House to trap the Sacred Trout, then rising from the water to catch the bullet from a White gun in his heart, his dripping brown body splashing into the water, his red blood going all out on the Big Lake as the people were disbanded across the land. I can see into all the days past. I can see into all the days coming. Along the Big Lake of the Sky your son shall walk in a new Rabbit robe. Sparkling his image on the quiet waters. The forest shall grow thick and free. The Birds return. The fences fall. In their shadow the openness will find its home once more. These things shall pass in your time. All things shall pass. There will be many smokes. Listen closely the one *they* call Hallelujah Bob, you have been saved so that you may hear my words. You are the end of the beginning. In the beginning Indians of all Nations came unto me. They came from a wilderness of boulders, from windy rivers, from small lakes scattered over flatland. They came from where the Moon shines on little grasses and said, 'Messiah, call up all the wild game, call up all the Birds and Mice, call up all the Fish. Teach us how to braid our good long hair so that we may dance the people up. Dance our birth. Messiah, if you dance the souls will come back. Give us our land to walk on.' They came on the Iron Road from all Nations to me. They all came. The Fisheaters, the Buffaloeaters, the Duckshooters, the Beaverhunters, the Rootdiggers. The men came up and paid one dollar to shake my hand, young girls opened the blouse of their bodies and asked me to feel their breasts. From over the whole Earth Indians were coming. I said the bow was your Mother. The knife is your Father. Do not dance with arrows. Do not sing bad songs. Do not break the Road. Keep a clean heart and walk straight. Do not let women touch rifles. These things I told each one. But they said to me White Owl flies in willows where Mice live. They said they wanted me to paint the power of a Red Owl to shield them while they danced up the Ghost of all Indians. They sought me out walking on the shores of the Pyramid Lake, 'Messiah,

what did you see the day the Sun died? What did you
dream the day the gold fingers of the Sun slipped from
the Earth?' I stood on a high rock and answered to everyone a man, 'I have been dreaming since I was fourteen
when my father the prophet Tavibo went away south. I
want to show you my dreams. I do not know if I am still
dreaming or the dream has left me. Sit down. Listen. I
have dreamt about bullets and guns. We will see if I
dream true.' I dug a hole in the ground and placed the
metal of six bullets in its dust. 'If the bullets melt down I
have dreamed true.' I took four smokes and used them,
when the last cigarette was burned down I called up a
young boy, 'See if I have dreamed true my child. What do
you find in the hole?' The bullets had melted down flat
and fit in the palm of the young boy as he lifted them as
witness to the people. The people came closer and
watched as I melted powder. 'What will it turn into?' they
called. 'Water!' And they watched as rivers of powder
turned to water flowed from them. 'He dreams true. He
dreams true!' They came from all across the land, the Elk-
eaters, the Salmoneaters, the Batcatchers. 'Go and wait
along the river,' I spoke softly to them. They went to
Walker River and I brought a rifle among them. 'I am the
true Messiah. The Sun lives. Shoot me in the heart. He
who walks the Road of the Ghost cannot die.' One of the
Buffaloeaters took the rifle and aimed it at my heart. The
people were silent. The wind going through the Buffalo-
eater's headfeathers was singing as he took aim. 'Fire!' 'I
can't make it go off!' 'Shoot me!' 'The trigger is stuck!'
'Pull as hard as you can!' 'It's stuck!' 'Here,' I came to
him. 'Give me the gun!' I took the rifle, pointed it at the
Sky and pulled the trigger. The bullet banged out and
echoed across the land. 'The dreamer dreams true!' The
people shouted. 'He who walks on the Road of the Ghost
cannot die! Follow the Milky Way, it is the Road of the
Ghost. Dance away the white burden from the Earth! Let
the people stand in high places everywhere! Let the people
see heart to heart. Their souls kiss. Give the souls land to
walk on! Sing your song O Christ! Charm the flesh off the
Spirit. There is a hope in our hearts. Sing the people up

from death! We are too cold to die. Our ears bleed. Our
tongues are bruised. Our mouths are swollen from eating
lies. The Whiteman's Road is the Thieves' Road. Where
the Whiteman walks the Buffalo Bulls no longer walk.
Where the Whiteman walks the rivers run dry and the
trees fall. Where the Whiteman walks men turn their
hearts against one another. The days are falling. We are
sick with a white swelling. We spit the blasted blood of
our hearts on a land gone lame with murderous grace.
They have locked us off the land. The land is the heart.
To lose touch with the land is to lose touch with the heart.
We lock our hearts to the land. We see heart to heart with
our Brothers. We walk arm in arm across the land. The
Native Ghost returns. Dawn strikes swift as a rattling
Snake!' I sat down and wept, the Sky was swollen and the
people were singing up the Ghost across the land, they
could not hear the words I was calling, they could not see
the trees growing from my face, they could not feel the
stones they stepped on, they could not see that more than
one kind of Animal flies, the white blown tears blinded
them. They danced their hearts on the heart of the land.
They sang all the people up. All across this land sunk to
the heart Indian people listened to the songs that grew
from my dreams. They sang through their hearts in one
voice, 'All the people are going up! Your Sister above is
painted. Your Brother above is painted. All the people are
rising up. The Buffalo Bull, *they* cut off his feet. The Buffalo Bull, *they* cut off his head. He is rising. He gets up
again! He gets up! His hooves are drumming against
Earth! The Earth shakes! He who wears the Shirt of the
Ghost will live forever. Bullets pass through his heart. The
Earth is shaking. Indians cannot die. We will free all the
rivers!' "

    The Christ took the stem of the stonepipe to his lips,
the blue clouds rising off his body and circling over his
head like a Hawk, "Now the songs are lost, the dances
dead, the fires grown cold, the ceremonies swallowed up.
The White bullets went through the hearts at Wounded
Knee and the hearts thrown in a hole to be buried in froz-
en Earth. What grows from that frozen Earth is for all

people to live with. The hearts that danced at Wounded
Knee were crazybrave. But you cannot chop thunder with
an ax. I have given the people Magpie feathers again to
wear on their heads. What I preached was a good River.
When at first I liked the Whites I gave them fruit. The
Whites are very close, we can always feel *their* power. But
all days are one. People and Animals are one. The Road
going is the road coming. One day is all days. To free our
land from the White burden we must free our hearts. We
must make our own hearts clean before we cleanse the
hearts of all men. This is what I dreamed the day the Sun
died. This is what I preached. But after the slaughtered
hearts were buried at Wounded Knee the people came
from across the land, the Cactuseaters, the Snakeshakers,
the Dogeaters. They cried out to kill the Messiah. They
cried Wovoka was a false prophet. They cried if the
Christ danced again he would dance the hearts of Wounded Knee up and they would kill him. I stood on a high
rock and said, 'You want to accuse me just like Jesus was
accused. You want to crucify me just like Jesus was crucified. But I am not Jesus. I am the *Spirit* of Jesus. You
cannot kill the Spirit of Jesus. He lives in all men. He is
the end of the beginning.' "

The Christ rose in a cloud of tobacco. Standing he was
shorter than I saw him to be. Swelling beneath the high
black sombrero his body worn heavy with age hung on
the horizon like a bell. His arms helpless to his sides as if
weighted by snow, "Come with me Washo. Come with me
the one *they* call Hallelujah Bob. Come and dance the last
dance with me. Then I will go away into the Sky. When I
am finished on this Earth I will go higher up into the Sky.
We are Brothers, Washo. The Washo and Paiutes are
Brothers. We have been apart too long. That is why we
have not walked the Straight Road. That is why we have
walked the forked path. That is the White swelling in our
hearts. Until our hearts are free of fear and suspicion we
are not clean. We can go up and stand in high places everywhere. But if our hearts are not clean the people will
not see us. If the people cannot see us they will journey
without direction. That is what I teach. A clean heart. We

must free ourselves of the White burden. The Whiteman made us hate the Yellowman. If it had not been for our trees, always our trees, the Whiteman could not have mined the gold and silver veins from the arms of our Mother Earth. The Whiteman needed our trees to fire *their* Engines, to build *their* Iron Road and stab *their* mines into our Mother's flesh. The Whiteman sent the Yellowman into our Sacred Piñon groves to cut the trees. The Whiteman tried to get the Indian to cut the trees, but the Indian would not cut down his own life. So for many years we have hated the Yellowman. That hate has been a White swelling in our hearts. But it is the Whiteman who killed our trees. It is the Whiteman who killed our collecting grounds. The Whiteman killed off the wildgrasses, he sent his great stone-eyed beasts snorting and stamping and spoiling across our land, cutting the roots of all green growing from Earth until the Antelope were dead, the Buffalo were dead, the Deer were dead. The old Animals slipped from their grazing Earth and died behind fences. The power of the Whiteman and his tame beasts is One. It is the same *Musege*. It has the same end. The Whiteman yanked the silver and gold veins from the Earth and killed the trees. His beasts ate over the seeds and plants, stripped the Earth of all living things. The Whiteman tricked us. He put mountains between our hearts. He made us betray our Brothers. The Whiteman gave us a dream of hate. We had to get rid of it, or learn how to use it. To refuse *their* dream was to die. The Whiteman kept trying to give us a dream that all Brothers do not walk the Earth equal. The Whiteman tricked us into receiving his dream. Our hearts were unclean and the Earth threw us up dying. But before the Whiteman's Road was before us to travel, Nations waded across rivers to battle their Brothers. So when the Whiteman Road came between us our wings were all broken, the boundaries of the Earth small. The people looked at the White Road and made many smokes, they talked and sang the old songs, but their wings were broken, their hearts were swelling White and were too heavy to fly to high places. So when they met the Whiteman approaching they received his dream. They fought one among each

other and all against all. Every victory was a defeat. To
free our land from the White burden we must free our
hearts. Until we can walk one into another's heart as
equals every victory is defeat. This is what I dream. This
is what I preach. Come. Take my hand Washo. Walk over
the land to dance in a circle. Too long the mountains have
grown between the Paiute and Washo. Love flows thicker
than blood. As the Whites came our Ancestors fought one
against the other, the Paiute and the Washo beat their
hearts one against another and died on the land they tried
to win. They stood locked in battle, Brothers under the
skin, the Paiute coming up victorious, never again would
the Horses dance for the Washo. The Paiute forbid the
Washo men to ride and the women to weave magic into
their baskets. The Paiute painted the rocks along the river
where the Washo could not pass from his Mountain
House. The Washo gathered in a circle around their lake
camp of Tahoe and ate Fish while the Paiutes slung Antelopes over their shoulders and rode across the flatland as
the White Road came with a fury out of the east and
drove between Brothers divided. Brothers weakened and
sick from killing their own hearts, they had chopped the
branches from their own Tree. Every victory is defeat.
Come Washo. Take my hand and we will dance up the
Ghosts. Join hands and we will move in a circle, we will
move in the Nänigükwa, in the Circle Dance. The day the
Sun died he fell from the heart of the Sky herself. A lance
through his golden body. All was darkness. There was
stillness before birth. The Earth belonged to none. Everyday was one. All People and Animals were together. I was
carried into the Sky. Indians stood in high places everywhere. The people danced their birth. They sang up the
land going green. I saw the Straight Road open before me
and rode the painted Ghost pony to Earth to teach the
Dance of the Ghost to all Indians. I wanted to cleanse the
hearts of all men. The first ones I wanted to give the vision of the Ghost to was my Brother the Washo. My
Brother who saw the Whites eat of *their* own flesh on the
shores of yonder lake Donner. All the Washo were dead
or dying. Soon they would be gone from the Earth and no

one would know of their going. I wanted to give the Washo a vision. I wanted to see the Sacred Piñon Tree grow with all its limbs strong to the Sun. Of all the Indians, I gave the vision of the Sacred Cactus to the Washo first. I gave the vision of Peyote to my Brother who saw the Whiteman eat of his own flesh. I gave the vision to the Washo so he would cleanse his heart. I gave the vision so he would survive. When the Whiteman first came over the mountains to this country the Ghost of the Washo was still running strong through the land. The Whiteman called all of this country of Nevada, *Washo*. I led the Washo down the Peyote Road of the Ghost first because of all the hearts broken beneath the fury of the white wheels coming out of the east the Washo were the first to watch the end of the beginning on the shores of yonder lake, Donner. The Washo were the first to see the coming of the Flesheaters. The Washo were the first to die away from the land. The Washo watched the Spirit flesh of the Earth devoured. Come, the one *they* call Hallelujah Bob. Come and eat the Sacred Cactus. Come Ayas, Antelope. It is the end of the beginning. Join hands and lock hearts."

The Christ was already gone. He sang my name as I ran after it. Moving across the hot flatland covered with snow among the trees of thorn taller than a man. There was no road, the white burden on the land went out everywhere. I followed in his footsteps. The night sucked the Sun out of the Sky and blew the Moon across the heavens. I followed through snowpiled clumps of sagebrush. The cold coming up and stabbing my face. The ice glare of the stars on the snow showed the beginning of trails. Trails cutting in every direction. The frozen trails of Cattle. His footsteps lost themselves in the trails. I stumbled over the white crust of the Earth in search of him, "Christ! Oh my Christ!"

His voice sang back to me and I ran after it, "Antelope, join hands, it is the end of the beginning."

"Christ! Don't lose me!"

"Antelope. Lock hearts!"

"Christ! I come!"